THE FURYCK SAGA

WINTER'S FURY

THE BURNING SEA

NIGHT OF THE SHADOW MOON

HALLOW WOOD

THE RAVEN'S WARNING

VALE OF THE GODS

KINGS OF FATE
A Prequel Novella

THE LORDS OF ALEKKA

EYE OF THE WOLF

MARK OF THE HUNTER

BLOOD OF THE RAVEN

HEART OF THE KING

FURY OF THE QUEEN

WRATH OF THE SUN

FATE OF THE FURYCKS

THE SHADOW ISLE

TOWER OF BLOOD AND FLAME

Sign up to my newsletter, so you don't miss out on new release information!

http://www.aerayne.com/sign-up

THE BURNING SEA

THE FURYCK SAGA: BOOK 2

A.E. RAYNE

For Jack

Osterland

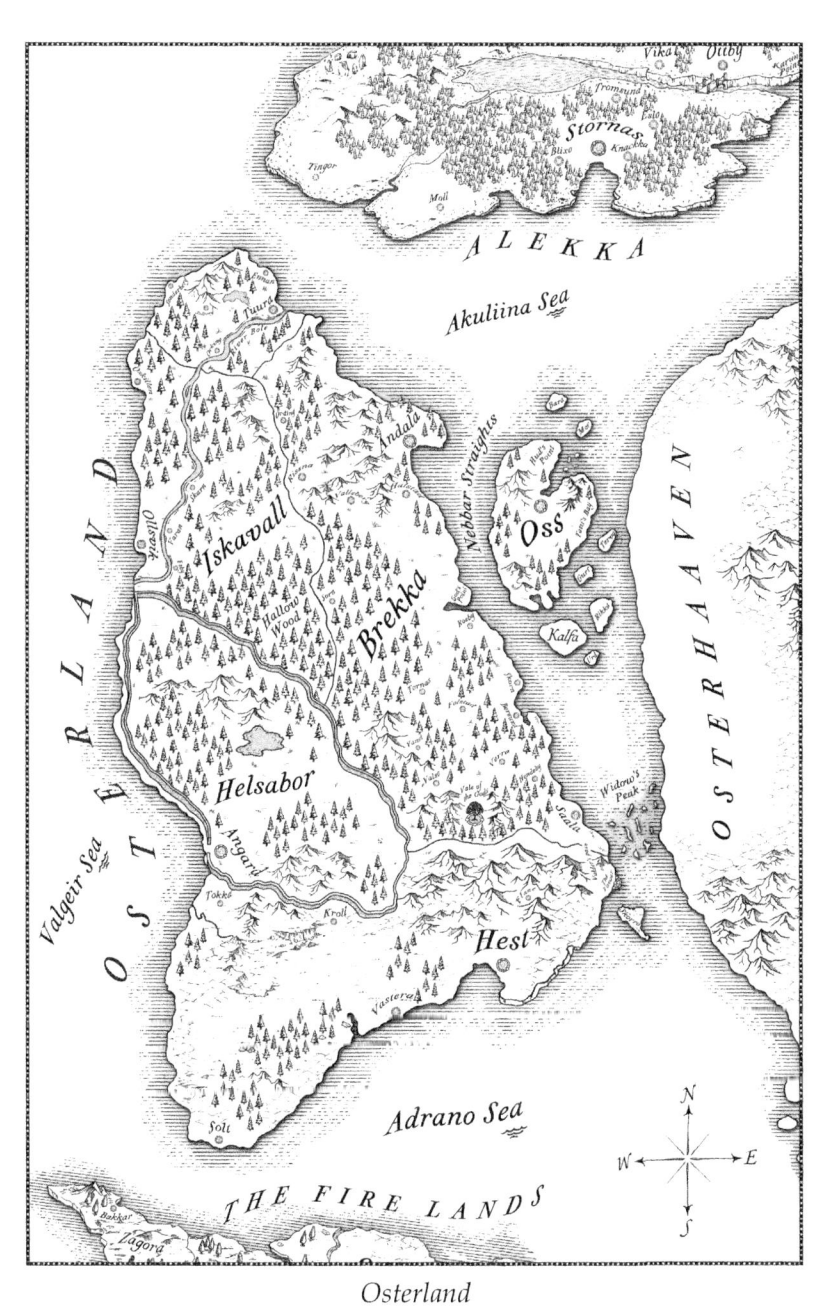

CHARACTERS

THE KINGDOM OF BREKKA
In Andala
Lothar Furyck, King of Brekka
Gisila Furyck, Queen of Brekka
Aleksander Lehr
Edela Saeveld
Osbert Furyck
Axl Furyck
Amma Furyck
Gant Olborn

In Saala
Rexon Boas, Lord of Saala
Demaeya Boas, Lady of Saala

* * *

THE KINGDOM OF HEST
Haaron Dragos, King of Hest
Bayla Dragos, Queen of Hest
Haegen Dragos
Irenna Dragos
Karsten Dragos
Nicolene Dragos
Berard Dragos
Jaeger Dragos
Varna Gallas
Meena Gallas
Egil Asgun

CHARACTERS

THE SLAVE ISLANDS
On the Island of Oss
Jael Furyck
Eadmund Skalleson
Eirik Skalleson, King of The Slave Islands
Eydis Skalleson
Thorgils Svanter
Brynna 'Biddy' Halvor
Fyn Gallas
Runa Gallas
Entorp Bray
Tanja Tulo
Odda Svanter
Torstan Berg
Otto Arnwald
Sevrin Jorri
Beorn Rignor

On the Island of Kalfa
Ivaar Skalleson, Lord of Kalfa
Isaura Skalleson, Lady of Kalfa
Ayla Adea

On the Island of Rikka
Hassi Arvo, Lord of Rikka
Morana Gallas
Evaine Gallas
Morac Gallas

CHARACTERS

On the Island of Tervo
Torborn Sverri, Lord of Tervo

On the Island of Bara
Frits Hallstein, Lord of Bara

On the Island of Gurro
Ador Roall, Lord of Gurro

On the Island of Urd
Ovi Eadlund, Lord of Urd

On the Island of Mord
Viktor Morus, Lord of Mord

PROLOGUE

'And when the Darkness comes,
Furia's daughter will emerge from the shadows,
clasping the Sword of Light...'

'Dara!' her aunt called urgently. 'Stop reading, please! I need to arrive in Tuura while it is still dark, so as not to be seen. And when I return, we have to leave. I must get you to safety.'
'But you have to give the prophecy to Sersha!'
'I will, of course. I sent a note. She will meet me.'
'They need to know what will happen. They need to know how to stop her, how to stop all of it,' Dara muttered anxiously as she rolled the scroll, her nine-year-old hands shaking with fear. 'They have to make the sword!'
It was all she could do.
But would it be enough?

PART ONE

A Crack in the Ice

CHAPTER ONE

'So, that's Aleksander?'

Eadmund turned to his wife, but Jael was already rushing across the glistening black stones towards her grandmother, who was being helped over the side of the Brekkan ship.

'Jael!' Edela's ashen face broke into a smile as she was swept into a bone-crushing hug. 'You're alright!'

Jael stepped back, happy but puzzled. 'Alright?' She shook her head. 'Yes, of course. And so are you, which is even better!' Her face froze as she turned to the figure waiting awkwardly next to Edela.

'Jael.'

That voice. So familiar.

'Aleksander.' Jael swallowed, her eyes flicking nervously towards his face. She could feel the rain misting lightly over them as they stood shivering on the beach. It was early spring, but snow was still lingering on the ground, and the air was frigid. The beach was a hive of activity, though, as the Osslanders hurried to prepare their ships for the upcoming battle with Hest, and Jael was suddenly conscious that the shipbuilders' attention had drifted towards her. 'Let's get you inside, Grandmother,' she said quickly, her deep-green eyes running away from Aleksander's dark, searching ones. 'You look chilled to the bone!'

'Well, it's not everyone I would cross those evil straights for,' Edela shuddered, her wrinkled face mottled with cold. 'And yes, a fire would be welcome. I haven't felt my toes since we left Andala!'

'You go with Jael, Edela,' Aleksander mumbled. 'I'll see to the men and bring your chest.'

'Your chest?' Jael looked surprised. 'You're staying a while, then?'

Edela glanced at Aleksander, who blinked and turned back to the ships. 'If you'll have me, I may,' she croaked. 'Anything to avoid heading out to sea again!'

Jael frowned, her eyes wandering from her shivering grandmother to the Brekkan warriors jumping down onto the sucking foreshore. She wondered why they had come in two ships but resisted the urge to turn around, not wanting to catch Aleksander's eye. She kept her gaze fixed straight ahead as she helped Edela across the slippery stones towards the hill that led up to the fort.

'Eadmund?' Edela blinked up at the powerful-looking man waiting for them, his thick bear-fur cloak billowing in the stiff breeze. She turned and stared at her granddaughter, a smile curling her pale lips. 'The tincture worked, then?'

Jael laughed. 'I suppose it did.' She smiled at her husband, who stared at her with no warmth in his usually cheerful hazel eyes.

'Yes, it worked very well, thank you. And it is good to see you again, Edela,' Eadmund said politely. 'Although I'm not sure I even remember our first meeting.' He took the old woman's hand and slipped it through his arm, leading her up the muddy hill towards the fort.

'Well, I expect you had other things on your mind, like marrying my granddaughter here,' Edela smiled, squeezing Jael's hand, so happy to see her again.

'Or, it could have been the twenty cups of ale I had before you arrived,' Eadmund said wryly.

'Perhaps,' Edela chuckled, shivering as low-lying clouds swallowed the sun. It had been a fair afternoon, but rain was quickly sweeping in. 'It appears that you have come a long way since then.'

'Yes,' Eadmund murmured through tight lips. 'I have. Hopefully, we all have.'

Jael peered at him, hearing the tension in his voice, still battling the urge to turn around and see how Aleksander was faring. Her long dark hair, damp from the rain, clung to her angular cheekbones. Her body was tense and numb from the cold, but she could feel an unfamiliar heat burning her cheeks. Jael wasn't sure how Eadmund was going to cope with having to face Aleksander. Not now. Not when everything had fallen into place for him.

For both of them.

And then there was the matter of her pounding heart and her fluttering stomach.

***

'Edela!' Biddy scrambled out of Eadmund's chair, where she'd been darning socks by the fire, and hurried to help her inside. 'Quick, come and sit down.'

'Grandmother?' Jael peered at Edela's face which was rapidly turning whiter than snow. 'You don't look well at all. Are you feeling alright?'

'Yes, yes, I'm fine,' Edela muttered, collapsing into Eadmund's chair, grateful for the softness of the thick furs that lined it; grateful too for its proximity to a blazing fire.

She couldn't stop shaking.

'What are you doing here?' Biddy wondered as she bent Edela forward and unpinned her wet cloak. She hung it quickly over a stool, wrapped a fur around Edela's shoulders, and started removing her boots. 'Are you alone?'

'No, Aleksander brought me,' Edela murmured, her voice faint now. She glanced towards the door, confused. 'But where has he gone?'

'Aleksander?' Biddy's eyes widened, meeting Jael's.

Jael turned hers to the floor.

Eadmund hovered behind his wife, trying to keep the wriggling puppies from rushing over to investigate their visitor. 'I suppose I'd better go and find him.' Not looking at anyone, he ducked his head and slipped through the door.

Jael hurried to Edela, ignoring Eadmund's abrupt departure and Biddy's furtive looks. Their large house was well insulated and warm, but Jael could see that Edela was shaking. She reached out and touched her head. 'You're not cold at all, Grandmother. You're burning hot!'

Biddy left Edela's damp boots next to the fire and felt her forehead. 'Yes, you're very hot, Edela,' she frowned. 'Let's get you into bed, and I'll go and make something for that fever.'

***

'Do you need some help there?' Thorgils Svanter asked, his head cocked to one side, studying the stranger who was struggling up the hill with an old, wooden sea chest, a long line of Brekkans trailing in his wake. The king had been told about the unfamiliar ships down on his beach, and he'd sent Thorgils to investigate. No one had been expecting visitors this close to their departure for Saala.

'Not with the chest,' Aleksander panted. It was a steep climb up to the fort, and the mud made it slow going. 'But I do need to find my way around inside.' He looked up at the thick stone walls of King Eirik Skalleson's fort.

Jael's new home.

He didn't want to be here.

Thorgils reached out a hand. 'Here, give me a handle, and I'll show you where to go. Are you here to see someone in particular?'

'Jael.'

They both looked up.

'He's here to see Jael,' Eadmund said matter-of-factly, staring at the tall, dark-haired figure before him. 'This is Aleksander Lehr.' Eadmund turned, and, without waiting for either of them, he headed towards the gates. 'I'll show you to the hall. Your men will find food and ale there. Then we can go to the house.'

Thorgils' bright-blue eyes popped out from under his mop of bushy red hair as he hurried to catch up. He peered at Eadmund's unimpressed face, then looked back at Aleksander's wary one. 'Ahhh, Aleksander. We've heard all about you, haven't we, Eadmund? The only man who can beat Jael Furyck in a fight. Well, apart from me, that is!'

'You?' Aleksander blinked. '*You* beat Jael?'

'Well, you needn't look so surprised,' Thorgils huffed. 'It was a fair fight, but she proved no match for my superior skill with a sword.'

'She let you win,' Eadmund grumbled. 'And you know it.'

Thorgils inhaled sharply. 'Well, that would be one version of events, but no matter what anyone might insinuate, Jael has never admitted to it.'

'No, she's far too kind for that,' Eadmund muttered.

'Jael? Kind?' Aleksander snorted. 'In a fight?'

Both men stopped and stared at him, unsettled by his easy familiarity with the woman they both felt some ownership of.

Aleksander didn't know where to look.

'We should go.' Eadmund turned his head up to the darkening sky. 'It's about to piss down.'

Aleksander nodded, lowering his eyes, not wanting another sight of the man who had taken Jael from him. Here he was, near her again, and all he wanted to do was grab her hand, run to the ships and disappear back to Andala. He shut that thought away, though, knowing it was too late now.

Jael was lost to him.

He had known it the moment he saw her.

***

'Edela!' Aleksander dropped his side of the chest to the floor and rushed to the bed. 'What happened?' He looked up at Biddy who was applying a wet cloth to Edela's pale forehead.

'She has a fever,' Jael said quietly, moving out of Biddy's way. 'Didn't you notice?'

'*Me?*' Aleksander looked surprised as he sat down on the bed, grasping Edela's icy hand. He shook his head. 'She was very quiet, but you know how much she hates the sea. I just thought it was that.' His dark eyebrows pinched together in concern. Aleksander had become increasingly close to Edela since Jael had left Andala. She had always been like a grandmother to him, but recently she'd become his closest friend.

'My ears *do* still work, you know,' Edela grumbled, her eyes closed tight. 'And you needn't worry about me. No doubt all that rain and freezing water just gave me a chill.' She coughed, and it rattled deep in her chest. 'I shall be on my feet soon, so don't go and collect wood for my pyre just yet!'

Jael smiled, and her eyes met Aleksander's. She looked away, feeling that annoying heat on her face again. 'Well, try to sleep. You look worn through. We'll leave you with Biddy and come back when you've had a good rest.'

'Alright, alright,' Edela sighed. Her eyes felt so heavy and grainy that she had no desire to open them at all. 'I won't need long, I promise. I have so much to tell you...'

Jael stared curiously at Aleksander.

It was his turn to look away.

'Why don't we go to the hall?' Eadmund suggested. 'I'm sure you could do with a drink after your journey and my father will be getting impatient to speak to you.' He patted Thorgils on the shoulder and headed for the door.

Thorgils remained frozen to the spot. He had seen the looks between Jael and Aleksander, subtle as they may have been, and he was certain that Eadmund had seen them too. He wasn't sure that he wanted to go to the hall with any of them. 'That sounds like a good idea,' he said unconvincingly, inclining his head towards the door.

'Come on,' Jael smiled at Aleksander, who seemed reluctant to leave Edela. 'It will give Biddy a chance to think.'

Biddy looked up from the kitchen table where she was already sorting through her dried herbs, picking out some elderberry flowers and yarrow leaves, ready to make a fever tea. 'Yes, you go,' she murmured distractedly. 'Have something to eat there. Edela looks as though she needs a good rest after such a trying day.'

Aleksander sighed, took one last look at the sleeping patient, and followed Jael to the door. He stopped, turning around. 'It's good to see you again, Biddy.'

Biddy's eyes were bright as she stared at that familiar face. 'And you. Now hurry along, and leave me to my thinking!'

***

Oss' hall was filling quickly as sodden warriors cut short their training sessions in the Pit and hurried inside to dry themselves by a warm fire with a well-earned cup of ale.

Eirik Skalleson twirled the ends of his long white moustache as he watched Eadmund and Thorgils rush through the doors, Thorgils shaking the rain from his bushy hair like a giant red dog.

He frowned, rolling his hands over the well-worn armrests of his wooden throne. 'Your brother's here,' he muttered to Eydis, his thirteen-year-old daughter, who sat alongside him. She was blind, and although her other senses worked better than most, she had stopped being able to smell Eadmund coming since he'd been knocked into shape by Jael over the winter.

He'd never smelled so good.

'And Jael?' Eydis asked, sitting a little taller, shuffling towards the edge of her small wooden chair.

'Yes, and Thorgils, and...'

'And Fyn?' Eydis blushed, but her father was too busy frowning to notice.

'No, someone new. The someone who is hopefully going to explain why two of Lothar Furyck's ships are taking up room on my beach and why all these Brekkans are drinking in my hall!' Eirik eased himself out of his chair with a grimace, making his way towards the stranger who had stopped by the nearest fire to warm his frozen hands.

'Eadmund, Thorgils,' Eirik nodded, taking a cup of ale from his attentive steward, who quickly disappeared back to the kitchen to see how the meal was coming. 'Jael.'

'Hello, Eirik,' Jael said distractedly. 'This is Aleksander Lehr. From Andala. He brought my grandmother to visit me.'

Eirik's wild eyebrows shot up, his sharp blue eyes full of surprise. 'Oh, did he now?' He peered at Aleksander. 'And Lothar lent you *two* ships for that, did he?'

Aleksander stumbled beneath his fiercesome glare. 'I, ahhh, no. He sent you a gift. Well, it's from Edela, really. Lothar wanted it safely delivered so you could start your preparations. Edela wanted to come and see Jael.'

'Preparations?' Jael's focus sharpened. 'For what?'

'Yes, what is this gift you've brought me, besides an old dreamer, who, I must admit, might come in very handy,' Eirik mused, pulling on his beard, his fingers catching in the little silver nuggets braided into its white tip.

Aleksander coughed. The salty sea had dried his throat, and his awkwardness around Jael and her husband had only worsened it. 'I have a note from Lothar which explains it.' He dug into the small leather pouch hanging from his swordbelt, pulling out a damp looking scroll, which he handed to Eirik. 'But in short, Edela has made a weapon for your attack on Skorro.'

'Edela?' Jael looked confused. 'Made a *weapon*?'

Aleksander took the cup of ale Thorgils offered him, supping deeply. 'Mmmm, she found the idea for it in an old Tuuran book. We experimented, she and I, and then took it to Lothar.' He smiled sadly, unsettled by Edela's sudden decline. 'It will help, but you'll need some time to prepare your ships if you're to use it. That's why I'm here. To show you how it works.'

Eadmund frowned, and not for the first time since those ships had arrived in Oss' harbour. 'We're leaving in ten days. Will there be time?'

Aleksander's stomach rumbled loudly, his eyes drifting to the servants who were filling the tightly packed tables with trays of herring, whale, mackerel...

'Aleksander,' Jael muttered, nudging him in the ribs. 'Will there be time?'

'Yes, yes,' he nodded, scratching his short dark beard. 'We'll have to work fast, but yes, there'll be time.'

Eydis snuck her arms around her brother's waist, squeezing him tightly, and Eadmund found his first real smile of the day. 'Hello, Little Thing.'

Eydis didn't speak. She knew there was a stranger present, and she could feel an awkwardness in the group because of it.

'Hello, Eydis,' Jael smiled. 'I've got news for you. My grandmother is here. You remember her from the wedding, don't you?'

Eydis' milky eyes lit up. 'Is she? Really?' She frowned, confused, certain that the person in front of her, who she couldn't see, was not an old Tuuran dreamer.

'Yes, my friend Aleksander brought her here from Andala.'

'Oh.'

Aleksander squirmed. It seemed that no one wanted him here, not even a little blind girl. 'Hello, Eydis,' he said gently. 'Edela has told me all about you. She's looking forward to helping you with your dreams.'

'Is she?' Eydis' heart-shaped face shone as she turned it towards the unfamiliar voice. 'But where is she?'

'She took ill on the journey,' Jael said quietly. 'She's back at the house. Biddy is making something to help her.'

Eadmund could see the worry etched onto his wife's pale face and he momentarily forgot his ornery mood. 'And you know how quickly Biddy can cure a fever. I'm sure Edela will feel better soon,' he said encouragingly, hoping to reassure both Jael and Eydis.

The deep crease between Eirik's eyebrows relaxed slightly. He turned to Aleksander. 'Perhaps we should get something into your growling belly before we speak further? Come up to my table,' he smiled. 'You can sit next to me. I want to hear all about this weapon. Made by an old woman?' Eirik shook his head in disbelief as he led them up to the high table where Thorgils was already waiting. In fact, Thorgils wasn't waiting at all. He had a herring roll in one hand and a dumpling in the other. 'And perhaps when Edela is well she can tell me what she sees for our attack on Skorro?' Eirik said, his eyes twitching as he helped his daughter onto the bench. Eydis was yet to reveal any useful visions about their upcoming battle with Haaron Dragos, and he found himself growing more pessimistic by the day.

Aleksander mumbled to himself as he took a seat on the other side of the king.

'Is there something I should know?' Eirik wondered sharply, grabbing a herring roll before Thorgils emptied the platter. His eyes lit up. 'Something Edela has seen, perhaps?'

Aleksander instinctively looked towards Jael.

Jael seemed just as interested as Eirik, ignoring her plate and the ale she was being offered by a smiling servant.

'Well, yes, she has seen that it will... not be a success. She tried to tell Lothar. Many times. But he didn't want to hear anything she had to say. He threatened her to be quiet. He doesn't want word of her dreams spread around Brekka, or the islands.' Aleksander couldn't ignore the mouth-watering food any longer, and he quickly pulled his eating knife from its scabbard. 'Lothar was relieved when Edela asked to come with me to see Jael,' he said through a mouthful of piping-hot smoked mackerel.

'Oh.' Eirik looked crestfallen. He turned to Jael. 'And have your grandmother's dreams ever been wrong?'

Jael could feel everyone's eyes on her, and she hesitated. It was Edela who had convinced her to leave Aleksander and start this new life on Oss with Eadmund. Edela who had seen how happy they would become. 'No,' she almost whispered. 'No, she hasn't.'

Eirik's shoulders slumped as he worked the deep crease back into the space between his eyebrows. 'Well, that's not what I need to hear, but I suppose it is no more than you've been warning me all winter,' he grunted, lifting his head to survey the filthy warriors elbowing their way to the tables around the hall, knives out, lips wet. His warriors, who had spent the bitter, storm-chased winter training for this battle. His loyal men, who would risk their lives to fight for their king because he had chosen to make an alliance with Lothar Furyck.

Eirik didn't doubt the wisdom of that alliance when he looked at Eadmund, who, despite his miserable face, had finally returned to him and was a warrior once more. But it was Eirik, as king, who was responsible for his men's lives, and he who would have to bear the heavy weight of their deaths.

Eydis squeezed her father's hand, sensing his distress, feeling guilty for her failure to dream of what would come. After Ayla had left, returning to Kalfa with Ivaar, her ability to focus her dreams had slipped away, disappearing almost entirely.

'But perhaps Edela has only seen what will befall the Brekkans?' Jael suggested, trying to cheer Eirik up. 'We might have better luck against Haaron's ships?' She could sense Aleksander's eyes bulging at that. 'Especially with this weapon of hers.' But looking at the downcast faces around her, Jael realised that she was going to have a hard time convincing anyone else of that.

***

Biddy frowned as she laid the wet cloth over Edela's forehead. She was definitely getting hotter. Biddy Halvor had dealt with many fevers in her fifty-four years, and she knew that they were often the first sign of a very bad end, especially in the elderly. And Edela, despite the youthful twinkle in her eyes, was certainly that now.

The door flew open, and Jael rushed in, escaping a heavy downpour, Aleksander close behind her. Jael's two Osterland hound puppies, Ido and Vella, shook themselves awake and hurried to investigate the stranger. Aleksander put his hand down for them to sniff, and they seemed satisfied enough that he wasn't going to cause any trouble.

Biddy raised an eyebrow, noting Eadmund's absence. As much as she was thrilled to see Aleksander, she'd seen the troubled look on Eadmund's face, and she worried about what effect Aleksander's arrival would have on Eadmund's sobriety.

'How is she?' Jael wondered, hanging her sodden cloak over a stool before going to check on her sleeping grandmother.

'Getting worse, so far,' Biddy muttered, removing the cloth from Edela's forehead. It was almost as warm as Edela now. She dipped it into a bucket of water, wringing it out. 'But hopefully, the sleep is helping. I'm sure she just got a bad chill on that ship today. Nothing more.'

Aleksander came to stand beside Jael, his face as anxious as hers. 'I hope so. She seemed well before we left. She couldn't wait to get here.'

Biddy placed the cloth back on Edela's head and stood up. 'Well, knowing Edela, she'll be bustling about in the morning as though nothing happened.' And lifting up the bucket, Biddy wandered through the kitchen, into the back storage room. 'There's stew left in the cauldron if you're still hungry!' she called over her shoulder. 'I didn't have much of an appetite.'

Jael glanced at Aleksander, not hungry at all. She looked down at her grandmother again, trying to remember if she had ever seen her ill, but she couldn't.

'Jael,' Aleksander said softly, touching her arm. 'We can't make Edela better by staring at her. You need to come and warm up. You're shaking.'

Jael followed him to the fire, perching on a stool, quiet and distracted as she removed her wet boots. She looked up suddenly, frowning. 'Why did you really come?'

Aleksander ignored her question, holding his hands to the flames instead. It was a warm house, he thought, but a cold island and the rain had left him shaking too. 'Edela came to keep you safe,' he mumbled, at last, not wanting to lose himself in those eyes again. Those green eyes of Jael's had haunted him for six months. The absence of them had left a hole in his heart, and it was nowhere near repaired yet.

'Safe?' Jael shook her head, confused. 'And you? It must have been hard to convince Lothar to let you go?'

'It was,' he said wryly. 'Naturally. But I needed to come to keep Edela safe. Although, that part hasn't worked very well.'

'Safe from what?'

'It's a long story,' Aleksander said quietly, his voice disappearing under the loud crack and spit of the fire as rain dripped down the smoke hole. 'Best told by Edela. Hopefully soon.'

Jael knew better than most how stubborn Aleksander could be. One quick look at his serious face told her that there was nothing more coming on that subject. She picked up a log and added it to the fire, desperate for more heat. 'How are things in

Andala, then? How is my uncle?'

'Happier than you could imagine now that he's married your mother.'

Jael's head snapped up. 'What? What do you mean, married? *How*?'

'Well, poor Gisila... Lothar gave her no choice apparently. Just told her it was going to happen. He didn't even wait for us to return from Tuura. They were married when Edela and I arrived home.'

Jael blinked, feeling the thud of her heart, loud in her ears. 'Tuura?' She shook her head in disbelief. 'You went to *Tuura*? Why would you do that?' She was horrified. Tuura was nowhere any of them should have gone again.

Not after that night.

Aleksander ducked his head, not wanting the memories of their visit to haunt him anew. 'Well, that's part of the reason we're here.'

'And you won't talk about it until Edela wakes up?'

Aleksander stared at her blankly. He wanted to tell Jael everything, but what he and Edela had uncovered in Tuura was a dark tangle of mystery and threat, and it was Edela's tale to tell. He only hoped that she would be well enough to tell it before they all left for Saala.

Jael sighed, worried and frustrated. 'So my mother is the Queen of Brekka again, you've been to Tuura, and what about Axl?'

'Axl?' Aleksander sat back from the fire, warm at last. 'He's changed. You'd be impressed.'

'Ha!' Jael scoffed. 'He's stopped listening to those stupid boys, then? Stopped dreaming of taking the throne from Lothar?' She wriggled her frozen toes, sticking her wet socks closer to the flames.

'He has, or so he says, at least. He's been training with Gant and me. He's staying at the hall again, in his old bedchamber. You've nothing to worry about there that I can see.'

Jael was surprised. She wondered why her brother had changed. Or what had changed him. 'And you? How are you?'

Aleksander's dark eyes retreated. 'Best we don't talk about that.'

Jael felt incredibly sad. They had known each other their whole lives. Aleksander had been raised in her family after his parents were killed when he was ten-years-old. They had been inseparable; lovers since they were fifteen.

And now?

Now they were here, together again, but so far apart. It felt as though there was a great mountain between them, and as much as she wanted to, Jael couldn't just reach out and touch him. Make him smile again.

'You seem to like it here, though...' Aleksander looked up at her, and his eyes were harder, more challenging now. 'With him.' He glanced at the door, but they were still alone. Biddy had not returned from the back room, obviously keen to give them some privacy.

Jael opened her mouth to speak, but the words refused to come out. She stared at those challenging eyes, remembering their goodbye, when they had promised to be together again. When she had sworn to come back to him.

Six months ago.

And the guilt of all that had happened since then lay heavy on her heart like the weight of a giant anchor, pushing her down to the bottom of a cold, dark sea.

***

'How many is that, then?'

'Three,' Eadmund grumbled irritably. 'I've had three.'

'More than usual for you these days.'

'Well, it's a more than usual day, wouldn't you say?'

Thorgils sighed as he glanced around the barely lit hall. Despite the arrival of two shiploads of Brekkans, it had been a quiet sort of evening, with most conversations taking part in small groups; some around the fires, some in shadowy corners. The Osslanders had kept mostly to themselves, uncomfortable with the idea of forging friendships with those they had grown up determined to destroy.

There had been a thoughtful hush around Oss for weeks as everyone prepared themselves for the battle to come. There was excitement, and the days were filled with earnest preparation and last-minute training, but it was also a time for contemplation. It was no easy thing for a small cluster of islands to take on the mighty Kingdom of Hest, even if they were allied with the power of Brekka now. Their last attack on Skorro had been an ill-conceived disaster. The ships that had come back, had come back light, and it had taken four years to rebuild their fleet. And their confidence.

Thorgils tried to smile as he drained the last mouthful of ale from his cup and wiped a hand over his bushy red beard. 'I wouldn't think about it. Nothing to worry about there.'

Eadmund eyed him morosely. 'No? You're not thinking about Isaura anymore? Wishing you could be with her?'

Thorgils frowned, pulling a small whetstone from his pouch. He picked up his blunt eating knife, which had barely coped with a tender piece of whale, and began scraping it across the stone. He'd done nothing but think about Isaura since she'd been forced to marry Eadmund's brother nearly eight years ago. And he'd thought about her even more since her visit to Oss over the winter. Every day was fresh torture, imagining her with Ivaar, so far away from him. 'It's not the same,' he tried unconvincingly.

'It *is* the same. Exactly the same,' Eadmund said harshly, not wanting to feel the truth of it on his tongue, but there it was. There was no escaping it. He'd seen it in Jael's eyes. 'You and Isaura loved each other since you were children. She was taken away from you and forced to marry someone else. You saw each other again, and nothing had changed between you. You'd be with her in a heartbeat, and she you.' Eadmund pushed away his cup, not wanting to feel even worse. 'How is that any different from Jael and him?'

Thorgils glanced around, but there was no one near their table. He leaned forward, lowering his voice anyway. 'It *is* different,' he insisted hoarsely. 'You have to remember that. It *is* different because I've been alone since Isaura left. There's been no one else for me. No one but my nagging mother. But Jael fell in love with you. And you know it. Everyone can see it. The way she looks at you? The way she is around you?' Thorgils sighed, feeling wistful. 'Jael loves you. She may have loved Aleksander, but now she loves you.' He turned his attention back to his sharpening. 'It's late. Go home to your wife. That's where you need to be. Not here, keeping that cup company.'

Eadmund wanted to believe it was as simple as Thorgils insisted, but the voices whispering in the darkness of his mind warned him that everything had changed and that nothing would ever be the same again.

***

Jael closed her eyes as the door creaked open.

She hadn't been able to fall asleep, worrying about Edela, fighting the urge to get up and check on her, even though she knew that Biddy was there, sleeping near her. And Aleksander. Eadmund hadn't come back from the hall, and that had left her unsettled too, though, in an odd way, Jael had almost been glad of his absence.

Eadmund crept towards the bed with a frown. Jael hadn't left a lamp burning for him, which made it impossible to see. The night sky was submerged beneath heavy rain clouds, so there wasn't even any help from the moon. He reached out a hand and was happy to feel the furry lump that was Vella, lying in her favourite spot, on his corner of the bed. She was much fluffier and softer than her brother, so even Eydis could tell them apart.

Jael didn't stir as Eadmund sat down and yanked off his boots. Leaving his cloak in a heap beside the bed and his trousers on top of it, he slid onto the thickly padded mattress, pulling two layers of furs over himself. His body remained tense, though, and he made no move towards his silent wife.

Sighing loudly, he wriggled down the bed, pushing Vella around with his cold feet until he had slipped them under her warm, little lump.

Eadmund stared into the black abyss of the room. He would speak to Jael in the morning. Before things ran away from them both, he would definitely speak to her.

CHAPTER TWO

'My lord?' Egil poked his head around the heavy wooden door, his face tense.

Jaeger Dragos sat slumped over a small table overflowing with scrolls, books, empty wine jugs, goblets, and dirty plates, his head in his hands. He ignored his servant. It was too early for conversation, and he was too tired and irritable to trust himself with any words just yet.

Egil was not an especially tall man, and he stooped even lower as he pushed cautiously on the door, edging his rotund frame into the dark chamber. Morning was barely breaking, and the only light in the long room was a single spluttering candle on the table; most of its wax having cascaded onto the flagstones during the night.

Egil hesitated, taking a breath deep into his protruding belly. 'My lord?' he tried again. 'Your father, he... ahhh, he wishes to see you in the hall. Your brothers have also been summoned.' He waited anxiously, shivering in the chill of the room, which, he noted, needed a fire set.

Jaeger scratched his closely-cropped blonde hair in annoyance. He lifted his handsome face to reveal a pair of intense amber eyes glowering beneath thick eyebrows. 'What?' he spat.

Egil blanched. His master's mood had been disintegrating for weeks, and it looked as though he had not slept in days, which he knew, would only make things worse. 'Your f-f-f-father,' Egil stammered, his heavy jowls jiggling. 'He wishes to discuss plans for the battle before breakfast is served. He is waiting in the hall.'

Jaeger sighed, and his powerful shoulders dropped. 'Fine,' he growled. 'Tell the old bastard I'll be there soon.'

Egil nodded, edging towards the door. 'Of course, my lord,' he murmured, ducking his balding head before turning and scurrying away.

Jaeger watched his servant flee like a frightened beetle before turning his attention back to the old book that lay open on the table, as it had all night, taunting him.

The book of riddles. The book of indecipherable scrawls.

The Book of Darkness.

But what use was it to him if he couldn't read any of it?

Jaeger screwed up his heavy eyes and slammed it shut. There had to be a way to understand it. Surely there was someone powerful enough to unlock its secrets? There was one person he could ask for help, of course, but he wasn't ready for that.

Not yet.

Not until he had exhausted all possibilities would Jaeger tell Varna what he had found.

***

'Axl!'

Axl Furyck laughed, slipping away from his cousin.

'Axl!' Amma squealed again. 'We have to go! My father will wonder what has happened to me.' She reached for her cloak, which he had stolen away as they dressed, not wanting to leave their secret place just yet.

'Why would he be thinking about *you*?' Axl wondered, admitting defeat and handing back the light-blue cloak, which Amma quickly wrapped around her shoulders. 'All he's thinking about is Hest and Haaron Dragos. I'm not sure he knows anything else exists.'

Amma's large brown eyes flooded with fear. 'Oh, don't talk about it. Please! I'm not sure I can take thinking about it again. Especially after what Edela warned will happen.'

Axl frowned, his messy hair falling over his eyes as it usually did. He brushed it away, turning his determined young face towards Amma. 'Gant thinks Edela is right. I'm sure most people do. But it's not going to stop Lothar. He's desperate to claim Hest, no matter how many of us he kills trying to achieve it.'

They were in a clearing, a private little spot that Axl had found nestled in the forest; a place where they could be alone, together. It had been a few months now since the wedding of his mother to Amma's father, and their relationship had become far more complicated than either had anticipated. Amma was the daughter of the king, and Lothar had plans to marry her to someone who wasn't her cousin.

'You must be careful,' Amma insisted as she finished pinning her cloak and stepped towards Axl, reaching up to tidy his floppy hair. 'You must stay by Gant and Aleksander. Keep out of danger.'

'Amma!' Axl laughed, pinning his own cloak onto his right shoulder. 'It's a war we're going to be waging. Battles, swords, death. I can hardly hide behind Gant, hoping not to die. I wouldn't want to!'

Amma's head dropped. 'But if something happens to you...' she whispered.

Axl lifted her chin with a finger, staring into her worried eyes. 'Nothing will happen to me. Edela has quite happily left to be with Jael. She didn't hug me goodbye as though we'd never see each other again,' he said confidently. 'She didn't look troubled about me at all, so I doubt I'm in any real danger. Unless Osbert is going to try and do away with me in the middle of things!'

Axl laughed, but Amma looked concerned as they walked towards their horses, who were pulling on shoots of wet grass and spring flowers amongst the maze of trees. 'Well, the way he's been looking at you these past few months, I wouldn't be surprised if he tried to. He believes my father favours you now that he's married Gisila.'

'I don't think Lothar is as lovesick for my mother as that!' Axl insisted. He pulled Amma's hood over her long chestnut-brown hair and kissed her quickly before boosting her up onto her horse. 'He won't forget that I'm Ranuf's son and that *I'm* the one who's supposed to be king here.'

'No, of course not,' Amma murmured, settling her cloak over her frozen legs before grabbing the reins. 'But Osbert is desperate to get rid of you, that I do know. Just as he is me. We both have to watch him carefully.'

Axl hoisted himself into his saddle and grinned at her. 'Oh, you don't need to worry about that, I promise. I'm working on my own plans for Osbert.'

***

Jaeger Dragos was a broad-chested, solidly-built mountain of a man. Strong, young, and hungry for power, he was desperate to break free from the suffocating yoke of his father. But he was the youngest of Haaron's four living sons, and even if he were to finally find a way to destroy his controlling father, his two eldest brothers, Haegen and Karsten, were waiting to wear the crown. Jaeger was going to have to do something extraordinary to claim the prize of Hest for himself; the prize, it seemed, that everyone wanted.

King Haaron's right eye twitched as his youngest and most belligerent son sauntered into the hall. There had always been something about the boy that rankled, that had crawled under his skin since Jaeger's birth, twenty-six years ago. Perhaps it was that Jaeger was his wife's favourite. Perhaps too, he could sense the desperation rising from his son when he ran his eyes over the dragon throne.

Haaron Dragos was a sharp-eyed, razor-tongued man, always on edge despite the fact that Hest was easily the wealthiest kingdom in Osterland. Its moderate climate and prime position meant that merchants from the even wealthier Fire Lands would travel across the well-tempered Adrano Sea all year round to trade spices, horn, linens, and slaves in Hest's extensive marketplace.

But despite his thriving marketplace, and his bulging coffers, Haaron had reigned unsated. Power and wealth had been teasing mistresses, and despite his ever-advancing years, which had dulled his enthusiasm for war lately, he was hungry for more. Though, he mused, raising one hand to his heavily pock-marked face, perhaps now there was more wisdom to be found in forging alliances?

'At last!' Haaron growled, rising from his ancient throne. The enormous chair was the centre-piece of his hall. A furious stone dragon rose up from the rear; wings and tail wrapping around the throne; thick legs curling into armrests; feet pressing onto the skulls of a few of the thousands of slaves who had died building Hest's imposing castle for their demanding kings. 'It is kind of you to join us, Jaeger.'

'Father,' Jaeger yawned, ignoring the bite in Haaron's words. He couldn't remember the last time he'd slept through the night. His eyes felt filled with sand, and he was in no mood to endure the barbed tongue of the man who had hounded, bullied, and humiliated him since he was born. Proud and supportive of his eldest sons, Haaron had never had any time for his youngest two.

No wonder they spent all their time plotting against him.

Berard stifled his own yawn as Jaeger approached the table. He felt just as tired as his brother looked. They had both been kept awake by the frustrating Book of Darkness, though Berard was far less keen to learn its secrets than his desperate brother. 'Jaeger,' he smiled. 'Busy sleeping, were we?'

Jaeger ignored him, nodding briefly at Haegen and Karsten.

'We must discuss the annoying problem of Lothar Furyck and his equally annoying little friend, Eirik Skalleson,' Haaron began, stalking towards the long table where his sons waited, mulling over the intricate map carved into its surface.

'If we don't destroy Lothar this time, he'll keep trying,' Karsten grumbled. 'He's not like Ranuf at all. He wants to conquer us!' He shook his head, incredulous that anyone should think such a thing possible. 'He must actually believe he can to try again so quickly.'

'Well, he may think that,' Haaron said evenly. 'But what Lothar Furyck thinks, and what we will give him in return are two quite different things, as he will soon discover.' He smiled so confidently, then, that the folds of leathery skin sagging around his cheeks almost consumed his cold blue eyes.

***

'Aren't you worried, Father?' Osbert asked, looking worried.

'About Edela?' Lothar snorted loudly, his expansive belly jiggling. 'You think the old crone is *that* valuable to me?'

Osbert frowned. He had no love for Edela Saeveld or any of her revolting family, but she had been a king's dreamer since her daughter Gisila had married Ranuf Furyck, over thirty years ago now. And despite what his father might think, Osbert had no recollection of Edela's visions ever being wrong. He scuffed his boots as they walked towards the piers, wondering how to get through to him. 'I think dreamers are always valuable, especially in times of war.'

Again Lothar snorted. 'And what did she have to tell me besides the warning that we would fail? He laughed. 'Those were her exact words... you will fail miserably!' He turned to his only son, and his dark eyes were hard. 'But she is wrong, for I do not plan to fail at all. This time I *will* conquer Hest. I *will* take what Haaron has and make it mine. With the islands behind us now, we'll have the ships and the men to swallow them whole!'

'And what of Eirik if we conquer Hest? What will he want in return?'

'Eirik?' Lothar mused as he skirted a pile of slush melting across the wooden boards of the pier, dripping through to the green water below. 'If Eirik holds up his end of our alliance, then he shall be rewarded, of course. There is more gold in Hest than either of us could hope to spend in our lifetimes.'

'But he expects more than gold, surely? He will want land, power, position. It wasn't so long ago that he was trying to claim *our* land to expand his kingdom.'

Lothar raised an unruly eyebrow as he stopped next to one of the newly launched ships he had come to inspect. It was tied to the pier, rolling lightly in the gentle swell of Andala's protected harbour. 'What Eirik wants will be a matter of discussion *once* we have conquered Haaron and his sons. And that is not something you need concern yourself with now. Not when your attention should be on preparing our men for what lies ahead.'

Osbert blinked. His father's obsession with claiming Hest had clouded his judgement so much that he appeared to see no reason at all. 'Edela said they know we're coming.'

'And?'

'You have no guarantee that Eirik will take Skorro.'

Lothar ran his tongue over his teeth, narrowing his eyes. He had been in a joyous mood after leaving his very naked wife but was now growing irritated by his son's attempt to turn him foul. 'Eirik will do as he's promised, have no fear of that. Have no fear of anything, my son, except my wrath if you fail to lead our army to a successful conquest. For, despite what Edela sees, I see only victory, and if you do not deliver that, you and I shall have to discuss your increasingly fragile position as my heir!'

Osbert's small mouth puckered as Lothar stormed off ahead of him. His father was turning against him, and it was all her doing. Gisila. His stepmother. Axl's mother. The woman who had carefully wound Lothar around her little finger.

And Osbert knew that if he wasn't careful, soon she would convince Lothar to make Axl his heir.

***

'You must keep him safe.'

'I will try, Gisila, of course,' Gant said awkwardly, shuffling his feet, glancing around at the men and women elbowing each other to the front of the busy market stalls; uncomfortable that she had cornered him in such a public place. 'But I can't promise that he'll return unharmed.'

'But you kept Ranuf safe,' Gisila implored, her dark-brown eyes wide with worry. 'All those years you fought by his side. It was your job to keep him alive, and you did.'

Gant let himself smile then. 'Well, I think that was mainly down to Ranuf. He was rather good with a sword if you remember.'

Gisila sighed, staring across the crowded marketplace. Spring had brought an influx of ships from Alekka, loaded high with weapons and furs, their prosperous traders' pockets filling quickly with coins to spend, much to her husband's delight. She cringed, still horrified that she had somehow ended up married to her loathsome brother-in-law. 'And Axl's not, is he?'

Lothar didn't enjoy anyone talking to his new wife, so Gant didn't want to stay long, but Gisila was worried about Axl going off to his first battle. He knew that she needed his reassurance, and he wanted to give it to her, but the words felt rather feeble on his tongue. 'Axl is... getting better,' he tried, the fine lines around his grey eyes crinkling as he smiled. 'He is working hard, focusing, but... he is not Jael.'

Gisila turned towards the door of the small cottage they were standing in front of. 'No, I realise that. And, of course, Ranuf realised it too. But I don't care. Do whatever you have to. Train him all day long until you leave. Anything. Just keep him away from Osbert. Keep him safe and bring him home. To me. Please, Gant.'

'I will. Try. I will try, Gisila.' It was all he could offer her.

Gisila sighed, the tension in her shoulders biting at her as it did every day now. She was desperate. It had been nearly three years since she'd lost Ranuf and with him every piece of security she'd held dear. Her daughter had been married off, she had been forced into Lothar's bed, and now he was about to start a war with Hest again. What they'd once had and who she'd once been felt so far away now that Gisila wondered if she could ever find her way back.

Not if Lothar's arrogant ambition destroyed them all.

***

'Jaeger and Berard will go to Skorro,' Haaron announced, picking up two wooden figures – one red and one yellow – and placing them on the small island, enjoying Jaeger's irritated scowl at that nothing sort of fate. 'That's where Eirik will bring his ships, thinking we'll be too occupied with Lothar's approach through Valder's Pass to notice him coming.' He picked up two more wooden figures – one green, one blue. 'Haegen, you and Karsten will lead your men through the pass to block the Brekkans' assault.'

Haegen looked confused. 'And where will you be, Father?'

Haaron stared at his eldest son, a sharp glint in his eye. He picked up the remaining black figure and placed it on an outlying neck of land. 'I will be here. In the Tower. Watching all of you destroy our enemies.'

All four of his sons shared a look of shock. Their father had been battle-hungry their entire lives. He had led them into every fight, screaming from the front, thirsting for blood and victory. And they had attacked their enemies from behind him.

'But why, Father?' Karsten wondered, shaking the long blonde braid that ran down his back. 'Don't you wish to make Lothar Furyck bleed on your sword?'

'Me?' Haaron laughed. 'Care about that fat slug? No, Lothar is just a poor imitation of his brother. Ranuf was a true Brekkan king. There's no pleasure to be found in his usurper's death. Besides, what point is there in having four able sons if I'm to do all the work myself? And at my age too...' He turned, running an eye over his offspring.

Haegen, being the eldest, was the most sensible; strong, predictable, reliable, as tall as Jaeger but nowhere near as threatening. Karsten had a temper and could be foolish in the grip of it; unpredictable but full of cunning. Berard was a constant disappointment. His other sons were tall, muscular warriors, skilled in swordcraft, blooded in battle. Handsome too. But Berard... his skill was with words, when he wasn't stumbling over them. And as for Jaeger... he was like a roaring bear. Pure aggression. Fury. Strength. But he didn't know his place. And Jaeger's place was as the fourth son of the King of Hest. And there he would remain until his end of days, unless one of his brothers put him down first.

Haaron was determined that Hest would never be his.

'But Father,' Karsten said carefully, 'perhaps it is better that I go to Skorro? Jaeger and Berard will hardly make much of a team. And my expertise in sea warfare is surely needed there?'

'Why? Because you wish to fight Jael Furyck? Take revenge upon her for the eye she took from you?'

Karsten tensed, resisting the urge to reach up and touch his leather eye patch which he'd worn since his last battle with the Brekkans. That bitch had disfigured him with her knife. He'd barely lived. Of course he wanted his revenge. And not just an eye either. There was more of Jael Furyck he'd like to take before he killed her. 'My experience -'

'Your experience?' Haaron laughed. 'Ha! You may be able to fool your wife or your brothers with that honeyed tongue of yours, but I hear your words as they truly are. And no, you'll follow *my* plan. Your revenge is of no concern to me. Perhaps if your brothers fail miserably without my leadership, perhaps you will find Jael Furyck at your door with her knife out, ready to claim your other eye. Although, this time I'm sure she'll be smart enough to take out your heart instead!'

Karsten looked away from his father's cruel eyes.

'There will be no plan here other than *mine*!' Haaron barked. 'Varna has seen what will be. And you will follow my orders if you wish to keep your places here, around *my* table.' He glared at each face in turn. Three of his sons looked down towards the map.

One stared straight into his eyes, unblinking.

Haaron glared at Jaeger, wishing he could run his sword through him. He wasn't old enough to be put aside, overthrown by this arrogant child. His time was not over. Varna had seen how things would go on Skorro.

His sons did not need to know that part.

***

'Axl!' Gant walked over to where Axl had stopped, jiggling anxiously on the spot. 'Your mother's been searching for you all morning.'

Axl frowned, slightly pink around the cheeks. His sneaking around with Amma had him permanently on edge. 'What for?'

'You'd have to ask her,' Gant muttered. 'I suspect she's just worried about you. There's not much time until we leave now.'

'There are too many worrying women around here,' Axl grumbled, fiddling with his scabbard as he stared at Gant. 'Makes me miss Jael. I imagine she can't wait for things to start.'

Gant smiled wistfully; he missed her too. 'Mmmm, your sister will be thinking about nothing else, I'm sure. Although, with Aleksander and Edela there, perhaps there'll be other things on her mind now?'

Axl's eyes darted about. They were standing in front of the harbour gates, and he could see Lothar and Osbert deep in conversation with two of Andala's helmsmen as they inspected the new ships. 'If I die in this battle, what will become of Brekka? With Jael on Oss, and me gone, what hope would there be with Lothar and Osbert here?'

'You sound as pessimistic as your mother!' Gant laughed, following Axl's gaze. 'Yours will be a prized death to seek, there's no doubt of that. You are Ranuf's son, and Haaron hated Ranuf. But if you keep your head and don't go looking for glory, then you'll live to fight again.' He stared at the boy, who was finally starting to turn into a man, although there still wasn't much hair on his face. Gisila was right, he wasn't ready. Not as ready as Gant would have liked him to be, but there was nothing more he could do for Axl except to try and get him thinking about the right goal. He lowered his voice. 'If you truly want to steal that crown back from Lothar's head, you'll need to keep your wits about you and return from this battle in one piece. Imagine what would happen to your mother, or Amma, if you don't?'

Axl swallowed hard and looked away, catching Amma's eyes as she hurried towards the hall. He could still taste the sweet scent of her skin. His feelings for her had surprised him, but in a short amount of time, they had become inseparable. He would do anything he could to keep her from becoming another pawn in Lothar's reckless quest for power.

***

'Oh, Edela. Dear, *old* Edela. You thought you were going to save Jael, didn't you? But who is going to save you? You seem to be in a very bad way. Drifting away. How very sad.'

The voice was cold, hard, menacing. Like the glint of a blade held near a flame, it sparked in the darkness, and Edela felt her heart race, thundering like a galloping horse. It was that voice. The one who came to torment her dreams, to toy with her, to tease and play, to roll back the corners of the shadows just enough, before letting the curtain fall again.

What did it want? What did *she* want?

Whoever she was...

'It's your own fault, Edela. So quick to trust the word of a Tuuran, weren't you? And yet, what truth do those secret keepers ever tell? Really? What do they ever care about but themselves and the sanctity of their precious temple?'

Laughter echoed around the cavernous void. 'And when you die, Edela, what will happen to your beloved Jael? If you're the only one who can save her, then surely she will die. Just as you will die. And soon.'

Edela tried to swallow, but her throat was so dry, so thick that she could barely breathe. She was trapped, unable to move. Her chest felt tight, constricted, as though there was a heavy weight pressing down upon her. She panicked, desperate to move. She had to move. She had to escape.

She had to save Jael.

CHAPTER THREE

Jael had quickly bitten her fingernails down to nothing.

'Here.' Eadmund handed her a bowl of reheated stew.

She shook her head, her pale lips clamped tightly together. She was cold. Hungry. But she had no appetite for anything.

'You should eat,' Biddy scolded gently. 'Edela doesn't need you to starve for her.'

Jael blinked, readying an irritable retort but she had no irritation in her, just fear for her grandmother, who was much the same as last night, if not worse. Edela had woken early and tried to speak, but she'd been so weak that her eyelids had closed before she'd formed any words. Jael sighed, reluctantly turning away from her. 'Alright,' she mumbled, taking the bowl.

Eadmund was surprised by that. He started filling another. 'Would you like one?' he asked Aleksander, who sat by Edela, looking just as anxious as Jael.

'Well, I'd better not say no,' Aleksander said, sharing a small smile with Biddy, who wrung out a wet cloth before placing it on Edela's forehead.

'No, you'd better not,' Biddy grumbled, heading back to the kitchen. 'I don't need to be looking after any more of you right now!'

Eadmund handed the bowl to Aleksander and made one for himself. He shooed away Ido whose wet nose was approaching, ready for his own breakfast, and walked over to the table. He had no appetite either, but he sat down and stuck his wooden spoon into the lumpy chicken stew. 'Are you going riding this morning?'

Jael barely heard him. 'What?'

'Riding? Tig?'

Jael shook her head. 'I don't think so.' She glanced back at Edela. 'Besides, Aleksander's going to show us his surprise this morning, aren't you?'

Aleksander blew on the hot stew. 'Edela's surprise, you mean,' he said sadly, glancing back at her. 'I think you're going to like it.'

There was a knock on the door. Everyone turned towards it except Ido and Vella, who continued to stare intently at the trencher of scraps Biddy held in her hands.

Eadmund got up and opened the door. His little sister stood there, shaking the rain from her raven-like hair, Entorp hunched over awkwardly beside her. 'Eydis! Come in. Entorp, you too.' Eadmund ushered them inside, and the large house suddenly felt full.

Jael frowned, surprised by the visitors, especially Entorp, who did not often venture far from his little house. 'Are you alright, Eydis?'

'Yes,' Eydis said quietly as Eadmund removed her wet cloak. 'We came to try and help Edela. I told Entorp about her illness, and he made a special salve for her. He thinks it will cure her.'

Entorp looked as wildly unkempt as ever, his short orange hair standing on end as he shuffled about next to Biddy, who appeared unconvinced by that notion. 'Has he now?' she muttered, placing the trencher on the floor for the puppies. They attacked it quickly, scattering scraps everywhere. 'Well, come on, then, let me see it.'

Entorp pulled a small jar from beneath his cloak and handed it to Biddy. She uncorked it, and an overwhelmingly vile stink flooded the room.

Jael grimaced. 'That smells almost as bad as the paste you made for my tattoos!' she cringed.

Entorp smiled shyly. 'True, but it healed them quickly, didn't it?'

'And you think this can help Edela?' Jael asked anxiously.

'Oh yes, it can. It will,' he insisted. 'I'm certain of it.'

Aleksander raised an eyebrow at this strange old man with bright orange hair, who muttered as he spoke and looked as though he lived in a forest, with only owls for company.

He hoped he knew what he was doing.

Jael saw doubt flicker across Aleksander's face. 'Entorp is from Tuura,' she said, hoping to give him confidence, but it only made Aleksander scowl.

Entorp dropped his eyes. 'A long time ago now,' he almost whispered.

Biddy sniffed the jar. 'Yarrow, peppermint... ginger...' She sniffed again. 'Something else...'

Entorp nodded. 'A few other things, yes. It's an old recipe, handed down from my great-grandmother.'

Biddy pursed her lips, realising that he wasn't about to reveal any more. 'Well, show me where I should apply it, then, and let's see if it will work.'

Aleksander and Jael moved away to give Entorp and Biddy access to Edela.

'It *will* work, Jael,' Eydis insisted. 'I dreamed about it. Entorp will save her.'

***

'Here's hoping your sister is right,' Eirik said as he walked along the foreshore with Eadmund, his boots half-submerged in the wet sand. The beach was crowded now with his entire fleet. All twelve ships were propped up on wooden frames as the shipbuilders, and their helpers clambered over deck and under hull, preparing them for battle. 'I can't have Lothar thinking that everyone he sends here ends up dead!'

Eadmund smiled. Despite the cold drizzle, it felt good to escape the house for a while, although, he was finding it hard to stop thinking about what might be happening there without him. 'Well, if he sends any more pieces of shit over like that Tiras, I'd be happy for them to end up dead. But Edela?' He shook his head. 'No, that would be a bad thing. Jael is very close to her. She'd be devastated.'

'Mmmm, true,' Eirik murmured, watching a flock of seabirds rise up from the black stones that lay before them, circling off into the distance in an angry cacophony. 'We don't need Jael in a bad way before we leave for Saala, do we?'

'Really? That's all you're thinking about? Conquering Hest?' Eadmund frowned. 'You're becoming as obsessed as Lothar Furyck!'

Eirik laughed, shaking his head. 'No, but I've had a bad feeling about this attack for a while now. And if an experienced dreamer sees that we'll fail, what hope do we have? Although, you wouldn't think that by Lothar's note. He's already planning the victory feast!'

Eadmund was thoughtful as he watched the shipbuilders at work, directing the men who were caulking the hulls, ensuring they were watertight. 'Well, only everyone's better instincts, and the word of an old dreamer stand between Hest and Lothar. Who's to say he's not right?'

'Ahhh, well, perhaps there's some hope,' Eirik smiled wryly. 'But the Hestians are so good. On land. On sea. They're like an army of monsters. Unbeatable.'

'But you thought you could beat them once. You made the alliance with Lothar, agreeing to attack them with him. You must have thought it possible?'

'It was the only way he'd agree to a marriage between you and Jael,' Eirik said, stopping to look up at his son's troubled face. He could see cheekbones now, and only one chin. The past few months had finally seen the return of the Eadmund he remembered; something he'd never thought possible. Because of Jael. But now he had to keep his end of the bargain and attack Hest with Lothar; doom many of his men to their deaths, perhaps even Eadmund and Jael too.

Eadmund smiled sadly as he thought of Jael, forced to come here when being a wife was the last thing she'd wanted. But she had been happy, hadn't she, here with him?

'You're very quiet today,' Eirik noted, inhaling the brisk morning air, tasting the remnants of the recent rain on his tongue. 'Worried about Jael's visitor, perhaps?'

Eadmund blinked, shaking his head dismissively. 'No, no, just thinking about the battle. It's an odd thing to go to war with your wife.'

Eirik laughed. 'True! Especially when she's going to be in charge of you.'

Eadmund's eyes narrowed. 'What do you mean, *in charge*?'

'She didn't tell you?' Eirik looked surprised, a smile playing around his hairy lips. 'I finally removed Otto and put Jael in command. She'll be leading our attack,' he announced happily. 'I look forward to seeing Lothar's face when he finds that out!'

Eadmund scratched his damp coppery beard. He didn't doubt that Jael was the right person for the job, but why hadn't she told him?

'Jael has more experience fighting Haaron and his sons than any of us,' Eirik insisted, seeing the disturbed look on Eadmund's face. 'Besides, you haven't sniffed a battle in years, Otto is entirely useless, and I'm too old to do much better. She was the best choice.'

Eadmund frowned, glancing back up to the fort. 'I'm sure you're right,' he murmured distractedly. 'I only hope the surprise Lothar sent you is going to make her job a lot easier.'

***

'Grrrr!' Jaeger roared, slamming the door behind his brother. 'Skorro? He's sending us to Skorro?' He stormed over to the table, filling a large goblet with wine. '*Skorro?*'

Berard blinked. Jaeger in this sort of mood was impossible to placate. It was better to let him cool down on his own. He glanced nervously at the door.

Jaeger spun around, eyeing his older brother who hunched even lower than usual, uncomfortable under his intense scowl. 'And he's going to sit in the Tower? *Watching* us?'

'You can't blame him,' Berard tried, his practical head outthinking his cautious tongue. 'He wants us to prove ourselves. On our own.'

'Why?' Jaeger spat. 'Why, when he knows that Haegen is his heir? Why worry about the rest of us? What does he care?' He drained his goblet, quickly filling it again, wine slopping over its silver rim.

Berard looked apprehensive, brushing his light-brown curls out of his eyes. 'Well, something could happen to Haegen. Father needs to know who else he can rely upon. Karsten is... impulsive.'

'So why isn't Father sending *him* to Skorro?' Jaeger grumbled, slumping down into a fur-covered chair, his frenzied eyes darting around the chamber. 'Why send us?'

'Well,' Berard said carefully as he perched on a stool. 'For all that you think Skorro will be a nothing sort of battle, things can happen, can't they? Go wrong? Their ships will likely outnumber ours this time. We have to send half our forces to defend the pass.'

'Ha!' Jaeger sneered. 'Have you not heard Varna's dream? She says we'll crush them. That it will be another comfortable victory over Lothar.'

Berard was a small man compared to his three large brothers, and Jaeger, especially, towered over him. But he was wiry, often clever, and for all his nerves and discomfort at being a member of such an aggressive brotherhood, he could hold his own in many a fight. He leaned towards the table, his voice calm and quiet. 'I've heard her say that about the Brekkans who will come through the pass, but what has she said about Skorro and the battle of ships? Nothing. So, no, Brother,' he said, shaking his head, 'I don't believe that it will be an easy victory for us. Skorro, in fact, might be the best way for you to prove yourself to Father.'

Jaeger glanced up, his eyes losing their fire for a moment. He was no longer seeking his father's approval or affection – that time was lost in the past – but the idea that their victory could overshadow Haegen and Karsten's set him to thinking. He poured Berard a goblet of wine, pushing it towards his brother. 'Perhaps,' he considered with a crooked smile, running a hand over his morning stubble. 'It would be no bad thing to send Eirik Skalleson's ships to the bottom of the Adrano for Ran and her sea monsters to pick over. Father would be pleased. For a day at least.' Jaeger's mouth quickly lost any hint of a smile, and he scowled again as his eyes caught sight of the book poking out from under a napkin. He sighed. 'But we're going to need more than one battle victory to change our situation. There must be a way to understand that book. We cannot hope to hold any power in this land until we do.'

Berard's eyes widened as Jaeger removed the napkin and opened the book, a musty odour lifting from its crackling vellum pages. 'Well, we could try Varna?' he suggested carefully.

'Varna's almost dead!' Jaeger scoffed. 'She can barely see, except in her sleep, and even then, who knows how accurate her dreams are these days.'

'But she is high up in The Following,' Berard whispered, suddenly conscious of the sound of his voice as it echoed around the quiet stone chamber. 'She must know someone who can read it, even if she can't?'

'She might, but at what cost?' Jaeger wondered. 'Likely she'd turn it over to them or keep it for herself.'

'But if she sees everything, then why hasn't she seen that you have the book? Why hasn't she told Father?'

Jaeger leaned forward, hands around his goblet, his eyes suddenly sparking with hope. He took a long drink, staring at Berard. 'No, Brother, Varna is not the person to help us now, but her granddaughter might be...'

***

'That's it?' Thorgils looked less than impressed as he picked up a medium-sized clay jar with a solid wooden lid, sealed in place by a thick layer of wax. It might not have been large, but it was heavy. 'We're going to throw jars at them?' He shook his head. 'Not quite what I had in mind.'

Jael rolled her eyes as she shivered next to him. 'Why don't you stop talking for once and let Aleksander show us how it's supposed to work!'

Aleksander had come down to the beach with Jael, Thorgils, Fyn, and Torstan, followed by an eager crowd of Osslanders. Rumours had spread around the fort like smoke about what the vast hoard of mysterious jars sitting in the two Brekkan ships was going to be used for.

Otto grumbled next to Jael, still simmering with discontent over his demotion as head of the fleet. 'Well, I can't see what use they're going to be. We might make a few holes in their ships, but they'll still be afloat by the time we're all dead from the arrows they'll shower over us from the Tower.'

Aleksander smiled at the grumbling old man. He was looking forward to this.

Jael eyed the catapult that Eirik had ordered wheeled down for Aleksander, wondering what he was planning.

'You expect us to mount a catapult on each ship?' Eirik wondered as Aleksander picked up a jar and carefully placed it into the spoon-shaped arm. 'So we can throw *jars* at them?'

'Small ones, yes,' Aleksander said distractedly, looking around for Jael who was holding his bow and arrow. 'You won't need them on every ship, but you will need them on four or five at least. They won't take long to construct at that size.'

The look on Otto's face told everyone just what he thought of that happening in time.

Aleksander nocked an arrow into his bow and walked over to one of the fires the shipbuilders kept burning while they worked on the beach. He'd wrapped a knot of pitch-soaked cloth around the arrowhead, and he dipped it into the flames, watching as it caught alight.

Thorgils' eyes widened as Aleksander strode back to the catapult.

There was little wind, and the flame stayed strong as he nodded to Thorgils. 'Release the tension when you're ready.'

With Thorgils' help, Aleksander had positioned the catapult near the edge of the shore, nestled deeply into the bed of black stones, facing the cliffs on the other side of the harbour. At the foot of those cliffs were flat steps of rock and Aleksander was hoping that the catapult's range was as accurate as Thorgils had suggested.

Thorgils released the rope and hopped away as the arm snapped through the air with a whistle, firing the jar across the mist-touched water, smashing it to pieces on the edge of the rocky shelf. Its viscous, black liquid contents slid across the rocks, into the watery abyss.

Aleksander smiled at Jael, relieved.

Otto snorted at Eirik, unimpressed.

Eadmund frowned at Aleksander, who drew back the bow, his bicep straining his tunic with the effort. Aleksander narrowed his eyes on his target and released the flaming arrow, watching as it arced with whisper-silent speed towards the broken shards.

Suddenly the water exploded into flames. A tall curtain of fire rose up from the rocky outcrop, flooding across the harbour, bursting and sparking with hungry intensity.

And kept on growing.

Aleksander took a step back and turned around to enjoy the blank looks on the faces of the silent Osslanders around him.

'The water is on fire,' Jael stated plainly.

Aleksander grinned, watching her bemused face.

'The water,' she said again. 'The *water* is on fire. And the rocks.'

'Yes, those too.'

Eirik turned to his master shipbuilder, Beorn. 'We need to build catapults on the ships. Now! At least half of them, wouldn't you say?' He aimed his question at Aleksander.

'Well, as many as you can get built in time. I've brought one hundred jars. If you fit catapults to five ships, you could have twenty jars on each ship.'

'What's *in* those jars?' Thorgils wondered, tugging on his beard, not taking his eyes off the burning sea.

'Ahhh, well that would be Tuuran sea-fire. Edela's secret recipe,' Aleksander smiled. 'Her gift to Jael.'

***

'Hello, Meena.'

Jaeger had roused himself into a better mood, spurred on by the thought of Meena Gallas and what she might be able to do to help him.

She was a homely young woman, with wide eyes that bulged nervously, and a habit of tapping her head when she was anxious, as she was now, squirming away from the king's youngest son. 'My lord,' Meena nodded, mumbling into her chest as her fingers worked away at the sides of her head, twisting into her wild red hair which hung about her in a mess of unbound frizzy curls.

'How are you, Meena?' Jaeger smiled, oozing charm all over the nervous little mouse. 'I've not seen much of you of late.'

'No, my lord.' Meena's big, blue eyes rushed around her boots, not daring to meet his. 'My grandmother has kept me in the gardens, collecting herbs for her.'

'Well, that makes sense,' Jaeger said lightly, trying to control his building irritation at her constant tapping. 'It's that time of year, I suppose.'

Meena didn't say anything, but her tapping stopped as she wondered what was coming next. She started shuffling her feet.

'I want you to come to my chamber,' Jaeger murmured, wrapping an arm around Meena's rigid back. 'I need your help, but it's not something we should discuss here.' He looked around the hall, watching as shaven-headed slaves cleared away the morning meal. 'Too many eyes and ears in the castle for that. We need to be alone for what I have in mind.'

Meena looked up in horror, shrinking away from him. Her mouth opened and closed, but no words would come out.

Jaeger smiled, taking that as a yes, and he urged her along with him, his large, muscular arm still curled around her now shaking back.

***

Jael had left everyone down on the beach, surrounding Aleksander, peppering him with questions, doubts, problems. He'd looked pleadingly at her as she'd disappeared across the stones, but she'd left him to it, desperate to see if there had been any improvement in Edela.

Fyn had tagged along.

'I've never seen anything like that!' he said, shaking his head in amazement as he trotted beside her, ignoring, in his youthful confidence, the ever-present danger of the slick stones. 'We'll surely stand a good chance now.'

Jael's confidence had been boosted by the demonstration, and she too felt their chances had improved, but still, between Skorro and the Tower, they would be subjected to a devastating barrage of arrows. 'Perhaps. But we may all be pinned to our own ships before we've had a chance to sink theirs. Besides, Edela doesn't think that Lothar will get through the pass, so inevitably we're doomed.'

Fyn frowned, not liking the sound of being doomed in his first battle. He was only nineteen-years-old and jangling with nervous excitement to finally test himself as a warrior. Training with Jael and Thorgils over the winter had given him a confidence he had not experienced before. He was keen to prove to both of them that he'd been worth their time and effort. 'Well, I shall hope you're wrong, Jael,' he said firmly, turning around to smile at her, but his eyes wandered to a familiar ship rolling its way towards the foreshore, and his cheerful expression fell away. He shuddered.

'What is it?' Jael frowned, following his gaze.

They were climbing the hill to the fort now, which gave them a clear view of the harbour, and Fyn's eyes were sharp enough to recognise the ship and the tall, gaunt man who stood in the bow, gripping the curled neck of the dragon prow.

Morac Gallas.

His father.

***

'You're not a dreamer are you, Meena?' Jaeger purred, circling the small chair he had wedged Meena into near his blazing fire. 'You don't see the future like your grandmother?'

Meena's bulbous eyes flittered about. She didn't know where

to look, nor what Jaeger wanted with her. The flames had heated her quickly, and she could smell the stench of anxiety as it drifted up from her armpits. She started tapping her right foot. 'No, no, my lord, I don't,' she croaked.

'But you know a lot of things about... magic, don't you?' he wondered, leaning in closer. 'I'm sure Varna has taught you many things about spellwork and magic. Maybe even... dark magic?'

Meena frowned, worried by the gleam in his amber eyes, distracted by the strong smell of wine on his breath. Jaeger was a man to fear – everyone in the castle knew that – and what he wanted he usually got, except, of course, where his father was concerned. She nibbled on a fingernail, shaking. 'Magic? No, no, not really, no.' Meena pushed herself up out of the chair, then sat back down again. 'I, I, my grandmother shows me things but, I, I don't perform the magic. I only help her. I am her... assistant.' Meena glanced anxiously at Jaeger, but he didn't appear bothered by that.

Walking over to the table, Jaeger picked up the book. It was not a large book, and certainly not heavy. He laid it over Meena's shaking legs and opened it casually. 'It is very good to hear that you're an assistant,' he smiled, showing off a set of straight white teeth, 'for I happen to be looking for some *assistance* to help me interpret the magic in this book.'

Meena's eyes popped open. She could smell the book. It smelled like Varna's books, and fear gripped her like a vice. 'I, ahhh...'

Jaeger eased his face down towards hers until their noses were almost touching. 'All I need to know is whether you can read any of these spells. That's it. Then you can go.' He kept his voice low and calm.

Meena glanced down at the book, trying to ignore the close proximity of Jaeger's body to hers. She ran her eyes quickly over the page and frowned.

Jaeger almost pounced on her. 'What? What is it?'

Meena started tapping the side of her head. 'It's, it's, it's,' she stumbled, chewing harder on her fingernail. 'It's very old,' she mumbled. 'I have seen something like it before, but I'm not sure where. Perhaps my grandmother –'

'No!' Jaeger barked.

Meena jumped, shivering at the sudden change in his face. His teeth were bared as he glared at her. There was no warmth in his eyes now.

'No, Meena, this is not something you can *ever* tell your grandmother,' Jaeger warned, trying to regain his composure. 'You see, Varna is loyal to my father, and this book... it is a secret that very few people know about. And now, Meena, you are one of those special people. You must keep it a secret too. You must help me solve its puzzles so that I can help our kingdom in the battle with the Brekkans.'

Meena looked confused, doubtful even. 'But my grandmother says that we will defeat them easily.'

'Perhaps this time,' Jaeger said carefully as he reached out to still her shaking leg. Meena flinched. 'But they will come again. Lothar Furyck will never give up trying to take what we have. And my father is old, and my brothers are weak, so I must find another way to help us stop them before we are all lying dead in our beds, covered in blood.' He leaned in closer, staring into those terrified, bulging eyes. She was such an unfortunately ugly woman, he thought to himself. 'And you, Meena... you are going to help me.'

CHAPTER FOUR

'I didn't expect you'd return,' Eirik grumbled, running his fading eyes over his old friend. He was thinner, he thought. Older. Like a stone on the beach, the years were wearing away at him. 'Not after all this time.'

Morac Gallas ducked his head, avoiding those searching eyes he knew so well. He swirled the wine in his cup and sighed. 'I expect you didn't.' He looked up. 'I couldn't leave Evaine. She was in a bad way.'

As curious as Eirik was to find out what that meant, he bit down on any urge to ask questions and simply grunted, leaning forward to poke at the fire that was shrinking between them. Evening had come to claim the day, and his back was aching from the cold. His private chamber, though usually warm, had been aired by his servants, and it had taken far too long to heat the room again. He frowned, unable to decide if he was annoyed at them, or just cross with his friend who had deserted him. 'But now you're back.'

'I am.'

'And for how long shall I be enjoying your company, then?' Eirik muttered. 'I expect you need to rush back to your daughter?'

Morac took a sip of wine. He closed his eyes, appreciating the depth of the velvety liquid as it slid down his throat. His months on the tiny island of Rikka had deprived him of all luxury, and he had missed, with a desperate thirst, the lush, rich flavours of

Eirik's wine. 'Well, that depends on you, I think.'

Eirik frowned.

'Evaine has had the baby,' Morac started, ignoring the irritated look on his king's face. 'He came much earlier than expected, and he has struggled, and she with him. The birth did not go smoothly.'

'And why are you telling me this?' Eirik growled. 'I made it clear that I've no desire to know about that girl and her child.'

Morac took a deep breath, reminded of their last conversation, which had set fire to their friendship. 'You did, that is true. But you are my oldest friend. After all that we've been through... how could you not wish to know that your grandson has been born? The grandson we share.'

'And?' Eirik picked up his cup.

Morac was incredulous. He'd imagined that time would have softened Eirik's stance on Evaine and the baby. '*And*? And, do you not wish to know his name? How he fares?'

'No. As I said to you, that child and his mother are nothing to do with Oss anymore.'

'But...'

'But what?'

'I want to bring them here. To live,' Morac said quietly, watching Eirik's eyes widen, already knowing his answer.

'No.'

Morac shifted to the edge of his sheepskin-covered chair, his knees close to the fire. 'It is not good on Rikka for Evaine, Eirik. She hates it there with Morana. Her cottage is... barely habitable.'

'Then build her a new one. With all the gold and silver you took from me over the years, you should have enough to build a castle!' Eirik snapped.

'Took? I never took anything you didn't give! And I certainly worked hard for everything I have,' Morac snapped back. He stood. 'Well, I can see that time has not healed our wounds. I think it's best I leave.'

Eirik felt caught as he watched his friend turn away. He had

THE BURNING SEA

missed his presence around the fort. Morac knew more about how Oss ran than he did. If it wasn't for that girl... 'Leave Oss? Again? And what about Runa?' Eirik wondered as he stood, grimacing. 'What about the wife you abandoned. Or Fyn?'

Morac froze. He turned back around, his eyes flaring.

'Oh yes, while you were gone, I found out how you had me get rid of the boy. Why? Because you never liked him? Didn't think he was good enough?'

Morac sighed, his long face pale in the dull glow of the fire. 'No. He was never mine.'

'What do you mean?'

Morac's shoulders sagged, his baggy eyes drifting towards the flames. 'Runa and I could never have children. As much as we tried, she never fell pregnant. You remember that?'

'Of course.'

'So, when we went raiding all those years ago, that time when we were gone for months in Alekka, in The Murk... I returned home to find her pregnant,' he almost whispered, the memories surprisingly raw, despite being twenty-years-old. 'What was I to think? It certainly wasn't mine. He was never mine,' Morac frowned. 'Why should I have wanted him around? Why should I have cared for and trained him as though he were *my* son?'

Eirik walked towards his friend. 'And what did Runa say?'

'About the boy?' Morac asked. 'We never spoke of it. She could barely look me in the eye when I returned. There was nothing to say.'

'She wouldn't be the only woman who found another man to warm her bed while her husband was away raiding.'

'No, so I forgave her,' Morac said. 'But him? I spent eighteen years looking at him, wondering whose son he really was. I'd had enough of looking at that boy.'

'So you made him suffer? When he'd done nothing! You had me send him away because you'd grown tired of him?' Eirik shook his head. 'He was nearly killed!'

Morac didn't even blink. 'And?'

'And Jael and Eadmund saved him, and now he's here, with Runa, so you'll have to decide what you plan to do about that, old friend. And quickly.'

***

'But where will you go?' Runa Gallas asked, her eyes brimming with tears.

'Thorgils is trying to sweeten Odda up, so she'll let Fyn move in there,' Jael said. 'If not, he'll stay with me.'

Fyn was frantically throwing his clothes into a pile, desperate to get out of the house before his father arrived.

'Odda Svanter?' Runa looked horrified. 'But what room does she have in that dingy shack of hers?'

'I'm well used to living in a dingy shack, Mother,' Fyn assured her as he handed his tiny pile of clothes to Jael and grabbed his weapons. 'Thanks to *him*!'

Runa looked distraught. The past few months with Fyn had been joyful. No Evaine. And no Morac either. Runa had thought that his absence might hurt more, but she had enjoyed the solitude of the house and the quiet company of her sweet son.

And now, he was leaving.

'It won't be the same as last time,' Jael insisted. 'He'll still be here, in the fort. And he will have my protection and Eirik's. Morac won't be able to touch him.'

Runa ran her hands down the front of her light-grey dress. 'But Eirik is loyal to Morac,' she murmured anxiously. 'He sent Fyn away at Morac's bidding.'

'Only because he didn't know the truth of it,' Jael insisted, following Fyn to the door. 'There's nothing Morac can do to Fyn anymore.'

'Come on, Jael,' Fyn urged. 'We need to go. Please.'

'Fyn!' Jael called as he disappeared through the door. 'At least say goodbye!'

Fyn ducked his tall frame back inside. 'Goodbye, Mother,' he mumbled. 'Don't worry about me, I'll be fine. I will send a note, and we can meet to say goodbye before I leave for Saala.'

Runa opened both her arms and her mouth, but before she could say a word, he was gone.

'He's not the boy he was,' Jael promised her. 'He's almost a man now. You don't have to worry about him.'

Runa looked at her sadly, tears wetting her sagging cheeks. 'When you have children, Jael, you'll understand that you never stop worrying about them. Never stop wanting to keep them safe, no matter how old they get.'

***

'My wife,' Lothar sighed, slipping under the furs beside Gisila. 'My most beautiful wife. How I have missed you today!'

Gisila's stomach lurched, her toes clenching as he clambered towards her, the bed groaning and sighing under Lothar's mountainous weight. She gritted her teeth. Thankfully, she'd doused enough candles to ensure that he wouldn't accidentally catch a glimpse of the distaste upon her face. 'You have?'

'Oh, yes,' Lothar breathed, his warm hand grabbing her thigh as he heaved himself up and over her. 'But you are getting so thin, Gisila,' he frowned. 'You must fatten yourself up while I'm gone, for what will I have to grab hold of if you turn to bone?' He bent down, wet lips kissing her cheek.

Gisila tried not to turn away. She smiled tightly. 'I will try, of course.'

'Mmmm,' Lothar murmured, kissing around her jaw, his tongue trailing over her neck, his hand exploring higher up her thigh. 'Perhaps I need to get a new cook? Someone who can tempt you with their fare? Just as you tempt me with your spellbinding body.' He sighed again. 'Oh, Gisila, I shall miss your sweet, succulent skin.'

Gisila's spirits rose at the reminder that Lothar would be leaving in a few days, but that was quickly tempered by the fact that so would Axl. 'And I, you, of course,' she said mutely as Lothar circled her face.

'And what about Gant?' he asked suddenly, his dark eyes sharpening, focused on hers. 'Will you miss him too?'

Gisila froze as Lothar moved his face to within a breath of hers. 'Gant?' she whispered.

'I've heard reports that you and he were talking today,' he said softly, rubbing one fat finger firmly across her lips.

'Reports?' Gisila frowned beneath his finger, her heart quickening. 'From who? What does that mean? Are you having me followed?'

'Followed? I would not say so, but you are *mine*, Gisila. My wife and my queen. Brekka's queen. What you do, and who you do it with concerns me greatly,' he murmured, kissing delicately around her lips, running his hand over her shivering breasts. 'I take great care of all my possessions. I want to keep them safe. Perfect. Untouched, except by me.'

'Possessions?' Gisila felt too irritated to notice where he was touching her now. 'You wish to keep me in a cage like a gilded bird?'

Lothar smiled as he lowered himself on top of her.

Gisila felt all the air leave her body. She couldn't face that giant weight crushing her again.

'You are *my* gilded bird, Gisila,' Lothar grunted as he lifted his nightshirt, jiggling about, trying to find her underneath his rolls of fat. 'And I won't have anyone else petting you, especially not Gant. Ahhh,' he groaned, finding what he was looking for at last. 'That's what I've been thinking about all day.'

Gisila closed her eyes, cringing, wishing he'd get on with

it. She was tired, tired of Lothar and the heavy weight he was determined to crush her with every night. She prayed that Furia would crush him in battle; destroy every last vile piece of him. Slowly though, so that every moment before his death was a bloody, painful, aching terror as he was dragged away to the Nothing – that empty, bleak hole in the Afterlife, where the most useless pieces of shit that walked the Earth were thrown.

And nobody deserved that fate more than her husband.

'I was asking Gant about Axl,' Gisila whispered as Lothar bent down, grunting as he thrust himself into her. She could barely catch her breath as it was rhythmically squeezed out of her lungs. 'Whether he thought that Axl was ready for the battle? Whether he would stay safe? If anything were to happen to him...' She felt the tears fill her eyes so quickly.

'If anything were to happen to him,' Lothar said breathlessly between clenched teeth, 'you would have me. There is no need to fear, my love, for I promise I shall return to you.' He closed his eyes, shunting his body into hers with a lustful groan. 'There is nothing I wouldn't do to return to you, sweet Gisila.'

***

'Poor Fyn,' Eadmund mumbled between mouthfuls. 'I think I'd rather have stayed and faced Morac than sleep under Odda's roof!'

Eydis didn't say anything as she spooned soup into her mouth, but her cheeks spoke volumes. Even in the dull firelight of the hall, Jael could see the colour that rose quickly on them. It had been that way since Fyn had returned to the fort.

Jael smiled. 'Well, perhaps your father should have him come and live in the hall? There are spare bedchambers here, aren't there?'

Eydis spluttered a spoonful of nettle soup all over her bright red dress.

'Are you alright?' Eadmund wondered, ripping off a piece of bread to soak up the remnants of his soup, half-listening to Thorgils on his other side.

'Yes, yes, fine,' his little sister mumbled, dabbing her dress with a napkin.

'Here, let me help you,' Jael said guiltily, taking the napkin and wiping the splatters of soup from Eydis' dress. She caught Aleksander's eye as he watched her from across the hall and smiled. He'd decided to eat with his men, much to Jael's relief. It gave her a chance to talk to Eadmund, which was something she was beginning to realise she was avoiding. They had barely spoken a word to each other since the arrival of the visitors.

'Thank you, Jael,' Eydis said gratefully, trying to forget Fyn for a moment. 'Is there any change in your grandmother yet?'

'No,' Jael said sadly. 'No, but she's not worse, which is a good sign, Biddy says. Her fever is steady. Perhaps she may even start to improve tomorrow?'

'She will,' Eydis insisted, pushing her bowl away. 'My dream was very strong. I haven't had one like it for a while.'

Eadmund was distracted as Thorgils mumbled on about Odda. He was watching his father and Morac as they stood around the fire with Otto and Sevrin. Judging by the smiles on everyone's faces, Morac was being welcomed back into the fold. But what about Evaine? Had she had the baby? His mind was all over the place. Taking a quick sip of ale, Eadmund left Thorgils to moan to Torstan instead, and turned to his sister, trying to distract himself. 'Father tells me that he's making you stay with Biddy while we're gone.'

Eydis frowned, pouting, looking very much like a thirteen-year-old girl all of a sudden. 'He is. Yes.'

Eadmund laughed. 'You think you should be left here by yourself? In the hall? Alone?'

'No, but I don't see why I can't come with you. At least to

Saala,' she pleaded, and not for the first time. 'I could help.'

'Help?' Eadmund snorted. 'What? Feed and water the horses sort of help?'

'I could help with dreams!'

Eadmund gently wrapped an arm around Eydis' shoulder. 'Yes, I'm sure you could.'

'You won't have a dreamer,' she reminded him. 'What happens if I dream something important? A warning? There would be no one to hear me. To stop it from happening.'

'It?' Jael wondered, trying not to peer at Morac. She despised the miserable-looking man for what he had done to Fyn, and she'd been fighting the urge to confront him all evening.

Eydis dropped her head, her shoulders slumping sadly. 'Father's death. What if it happens in the battle with Haaron?' she sighed. 'It must, mustn't it? And I won't be there. I won't be able to help like I did with you.'

Eadmund and Jael exchanged a rare look, a look of happiness that she had survived Tarak; that Eadmund had saved her, just in time.

Thanks to Eydis.

'Well, perhaps it isn't such a bad idea,' Jael mused.

Eadmund shook his head firmly. 'Edela sees this battle going wrong, Eydis. Whether it's the Brekkans or the Islanders, who knows what will happen. And Saala is too close to the border to have you there. Not if Haaron runs through us.'

'But if Haaron runs through you, then what hope will there be anyway?' Eydis insisted. 'He will come for Andala, and he will come for the islands. So what does it matter if I die at Saala or on Oss? If you are all to die, and I am to die, then I would rather have done something to help, and at least not be left here on my own!'

Jael raised an eyebrow at Eadmund, who still looked unconvinced, but she suddenly had the strongest feeling that Eydis should come.

A dreamer would always come in handy.

***

'You're going to stay here,' Ivaar Skalleson said matter-of-factly as he rolled off Ayla and wandered over to the night bucket to piss. 'I'll have no need for you in Saala.'

Ayla looked relieved as she slipped her nightdress over her head. Ivaar had been spending so many nights in her cottage that it felt as though she couldn't even breathe without him knowing. It would be a relief to have him gone, but a part of her felt as though she should be there, with him. Something was gnawing away at her, and had been for a long time; something she needed to dream on. But with Ivaar suffocating her, Ayla couldn't even think, let alone dream. 'As you wish,' she murmured, rolling over and pulling the furs up to her chin, hoping that he would just leave her be.

But Ivaar rushed back to bed, sliding in beside her. He frowned, thinking of Saala and having to face his father again. And his brother. Not to mention Jael, who was responsible for everything going wrong. His reinstatement as his father's heir had been so close until she turned Eirik to her favour. Hers and Eadmund's. But Ivaar was not prepared to sit back and watch as they stole the throne away from him. His father would not last long, Ayla was certain of that.

Soon it would be time to put his plan in place.

***

Jael felt caught between two pairs of eyes, and neither of them looked especially pleased with her.

Oss was Eadmund's home, and he was comfortable here, but Aleksander was her oldest friend, and she could tell that he wasn't comfortable at all. So, risking Eadmund's wrath, Jael left the high table to join Aleksander by the fire. 'I still can't believe that sea-fire,' she marvelled, her eyes glowing in the flames as she approached. 'How did Edela know how to make it?'

'It was in a book she saw in Tuura,' Aleksander said, happy for her company. It had been torturous to watch her with her husband; odd to feel as though they were strangers now, when he knew her better than anyone. 'I'm not sure the elders knew it was there. Edela said it was hidden away inside some other potion. A dream led her to it. As it often does,' he smiled sadly.

'You really should tell me what happened in Tuura,' Jael whispered, leaning closer to him, blinking at the surprising familiarity of his scent. 'Why you went there? In winter!'

Aleksander sipped his ale. He'd drunk more cups than he could count now, desperate to disappear inside a numb haze. 'It's a spider's web of confusion,' he murmured. 'No point in starting things Edela must finish. Be patient.'

'Ha! Have you forgotten me that quickly?' Jael laughed.

Aleksander found himself relaxing, enjoying her closeness. 'Oh no, I remember all too well how much trouble you are. In fact, it's been quite a relief to have you gone.'

Jael punched his arm, smiling.

'Shall we go?' Eadmund muttered as he came up behind his wife. He was almost a head taller than her – as tall as Aleksander – but whereas Aleksander was lean and angular, Eadmund was thick and bulky; bulk that had been drink-saturated fat for many years, but had slowly refined to muscle during the winter.

Jael's smile dropped at the look on Eadmund's face. She turned to Aleksander. 'Are you ready?'

Aleksander peered hazily around the hall. His men seemed happy enough, mingling more easily with the Osslanders now. It had been a louder, more festive night, which was a good sign. 'Let's go,' he said, at last, glancing at Eadmund whose face looked much like his own must have when Jael was taken from him. But despite any sympathy Aleksander might feel for her husband, he was just as ready to gut him with his knife and take Jael back home to Andala.

Eirik nodded at Eadmund as he disappeared after his wife, then turned, watching Morac bid goodnight to Sevrin and Otto. They'd shared more than a few cups together, and he couldn't deny that it had been pleasant. He'd missed Morac's company and the ease that years of familiarity breeds. But it wasn't the same. It could never be the same after the words they'd thrown at each other like spears. Those wounds had left scars, and those scars hadn't healed.

Morac's smile faded as he turned to face his thoughtful king. He drained his cup, handing it to the nearest servant. 'I should find my way back to Runa now, I think.'

Eirik looked surprised. 'And is she happy to have you back? With Fyn there?'

Morac's mouth hung open while he searched for an answer. 'Well, no, I don't suppose she is. Not after she found out about my part in things.' He stroked his pointed grey beard, his eyes wandering the hall again. He kept expecting to see Fyn and that unpleasant thought had him on edge. 'But she is my wife. We have been through a lot, she and I. It will just take some time.'

Eirik picked at his teeth, feeling weary, needing his bed. 'Well, I wish you luck there. It's been many years since I had a wife, but I do remember how it goes. And generally not well if she's annoyed with you!'

Morac laughed. 'I think you're right there, but I can only try.'

'So you wish to stay on Oss, then?'

Morac squirmed. 'Well, I promised Evaine that I would return for her. Perhaps, as you say, I must build a house on Rikka. Get her out of that crumbling shack. Although...'

Eirik shook his head quickly. 'No, she's not welcome here. I've told you that. I am in no need of another daughter-in-law. I'm more than happy with the one I have. And soon *she* will provide Eadmund with an heir.'

Morac raised a tired eyebrow. 'You don't think she's too busy going to war for that?'

Eirik smiled. 'Perhaps, but there will be time, of course there will. Jael knows the importance of an heir, no matter what she may think of actually having to do it. I have faith in her. She returned Eadmund to me. And soon, their marriage will be complete. Hopefully, before I'm burning on my pyre!'

Morac clamped his teeth together to hide his irritation. Jael Furyck had well and truly clawed her way into Eirik's heart. He had a soft spot for her now, that was obvious, but then again, Eirik had always been weak when it came to women. Except for one, of course.

And now, that would come around to haunt him.

***

The moon was just a sliver amongst the stars – barely enough for most people to see by – but Morana Gallas was not like most people. And she certainly didn't want any light to illuminate her escape from Rikka.

She had been hiding in her cave in the mountains for weeks, ever since she had bid goodbye to her daughter. It had to be that way. For everything to fall into place, they could no longer be together. She had barely felt a pang, though. None of this was about Evaine. She was merely a useful tool.

Like a sharp knife, Evaine would cut the heart out of her mortal enemy.

Jael Furyck.

They all thought that Furia's daughter could stop it.

Save them from what was coming, and soon. But Morana had dreamed of the Book of Darkness.

And she was going to get it.

***

'Are you alright?' Jael murmured, stretching out her cold legs, considering where to place them. They were lying next to each other like two wooden poles, rigid, motionless, neither one touching the other. But as frozen as Jael's feet were, it didn't feel right to claim her husband's warmth.

'Alright?' Eadmund asked blankly into the dark silence of the room as Vella crept closer, sniffing his beard. He pushed her away, down into the crook of his arm. She started licking his hand.

He didn't know what to say.

'There's a lot to think about...' Jael tried.

'Is there?' Eadmund sounded worried.

'I mean, with leaving for Saala and facing Haaron's fleet. The battle. Edela too. And...' she trailed off, unsure whether it was wise to say any more.

'And?'

'Well, it's not easy having Aleksander here, is it? For you,' she said quietly. Bluntly. Wise or not, better not to have the great unsaid thing sitting in the corner of the room, unsaid.

Eadmund frowned, his body tense. 'For me? And you?' he asked, swallowing. 'Is it easy for you?'

Jael's chest tightened. 'No, it's not. It hasn't been long enough.'

'What does that mean?'

'I... we were together for so many years, Aleksander and I. Our mothers were best friends. We grew up with each other, and then, when his parents died, he became part of my family. We were inseparable until I left to marry you...'

'It's *confusing* for you?'

Jael paused. 'No. No. Just difficult... he's my friend. He's always been my friend.'

'But he was more than that,' Eadmund said coldly. 'Why didn't you marry him if you were so close? You loved him.'

Jael listened to the soft snores from Ido, who had curled up on her feet. 'Marriage is ownership,' she said at last. 'I had no desire to be owned, even by someone I loved.'

'And now?' Eadmund asked hesitantly.

'Now?'

'Do you feel owned by me?'

'No,' she admitted. 'But the law says that I'm owned by you. That you can decide my fate.'

Eadmund lay perfectly still, feeling no movement in his body at all, apart from the quickening thud of his worried heart. 'Perhaps, but I hardly think you're about to let *me* decide your fate, are you? Not without a fight, I'm sure.'

Jael frowned, listening to Edela's hacking cough through the wall. Their conversation was heading down a path that led to a long drop off a high cliff. Better to leave it until her tongue wasn't so weary. 'We should get some sleep. There's a lot to do tomorrow. We need to be training the archers all day. They still haven't mastered the houses. And now with the sea-fire... we need to think how we're going to keep it on board safely, and we have to sort out the braziers too...'

'Mmmm,' Eadmund murmured sadly, not caring about the braziers or the sea-fire. 'Sleep well, then.' He rolled over.

It was so strange not to even touch each other, Jael thought as they lay there like islands, separated by a vast, quickly freezing sea. 'Sleep well.'

CHAPTER FIVE

It was an unusually warm day for the beginning of spring and Jaeger could feel beads of sweat bursting along his upper lip as he wandered back towards the castle after an early morning swim in Fool's Cove. Hest had a dry, warm climate but he had not expected to change his quilted tunic for a light linen one this early in the season.

'And where are you scurrying away to?' Bayla smiled, grabbing her son's bulging arm and peering up at his tired face. 'Sneaking away from some poor love-sick girl?' He didn't reply. 'You certainly look as though sleep is not something you've been getting a lot of lately.'

Jaeger stopped under an archway of curling white blossoms and scowled. 'I know you didn't like my wife, Mother, but have some respect. Elissa's ashes are still warm. Not to mention my son's.' He shook off his mother's hand, glaring at her.

Bayla blinked away the spark of irritation that flared at his rudeness. She was used to it, and besides, he was right, she conceded. She *had* never liked the girl. Elissa had been pretty enough to look at but far too silly for her liking. Haaron had made a poor choice there. At least now that she was gone there was a chance to make a much better match for her favourite son. 'You're right,' Bayla murmured. 'I know it is hard for you with such heavy losses to bear. And now, with the Furycks to fight. *Again.*' She resisted the urge to roll her cool blue eyes at the boredom of it all. 'The last thing you need, I'm sure.'

'I'd rather destroy the Furycks than watch Father fawn over Haegen every day.'

'Of course, but what makes you think you can destroy them? Why this time over any other?' Bayla was tired herself. She had barely slept, but it had been worth it. She sighed, smiling at the memory of her new lover. What a pleasure it was to spend time with a young man. She slipped her arm through her moody son's and walked with him towards the castle, deciding to forgo her own swim until after breakfast.

'Well, Varna says we'll be victorious.'

'Ha!' Bayla scoffed. 'Varna always says that. She wants to please your father. But have we ever truly been victorious? Have we taken their land and destroyed their army? Not in my memory!' she insisted. 'We kill their men, burn their halls, but they never fall. They rise and rise again. Continue to keep us out. Continue to deny us what we need. More land. Fertile land. Not like this cumbersome rock we perch upon!' She shook her head, and a loose, golden strand came undone from her softly bound bun. 'Yet, your father keeps going without any real purpose. He really is the most useless king Hest has ever had. His will be a legacy of abject failure.'

Jaeger frowned, glancing quickly around, but the only people he could see were the blacksmith, the armourer, and their helpers, red-faced and furiously rushing to finish the new weapons and armour they would take to Skorro.

'Oh, don't worry about his thick ears hearing my words. I know for certain that your father is down at the piers with Haegen and Karsten.'

'But still...'

'But still, nothing,' Bayla glowered. 'I've been married to that man for thirty-seven torturous years. I remember when he was powerful and ruthless, handsome even... once,' she sighed, her memory taunting her with images of a young couple in love. 'But now? Now I've grown bored of looking at that crumbling face of his. Tired of listening to his voice hiss through his teeth because he's too old and lazy to even open his mouth to speak. That sound! Like an odorous fart leaving a dead body! I would rather throw myself from the Tower than listen to another word hissed through that man's teeth!' Bayla's own teeth were bared as she contemplated her husband with distaste. Haaron. Her king.

She pressed her heavily lined lips together.

'Perhaps *you're* the one who needs more sleep, Mother?' Jaeger suggested, bemused. Their shared contempt for Haaron was something they had always bonded over, but Bayla had grown overconfident in her position lately. A queen was never truly safe. Not one with a tongue as poisonous as Bayla Dragos. Not when there were scores of younger, prettier, and more amenable women waiting to take her place.

Bayla smiled. 'Well, I would say that the opposite is true. There's just so much to do when you're not sleeping, I find. So much more fun to be had!'

Jaeger stopped and turned to his mother. 'You underestimate Father if you think he won't care about what you do with other men. He will not wish to be made a fool of, I can promise you that.'

'Why should either of us care what *he* thinks? When he cares so little for either one of us,' she said dismissively, brushing away a pollinating bee. 'You do realise that he's sending you to Skorro because Varna thinks there'll be trouble there? He hasn't told you that, has he?' She swallowed, suddenly anxious. 'Perhaps he's hoping that you and Berard won't come back?'

Jaeger looked up at the pale stone walls of the castle that Valder Dragos had started construction on centuries before. Each king that followed him had demanded it be grander, more imposing than the last, so it had existed in a permanent state of incompletion, and even now, Jaeger could see the half-finished towers his father had ordered built, protruding from the roof.

Jaeger sighed, certain that Haaron's time would come to an end soon. His father was an old man now, and the gods had surely had their fill of him. Haaron had ultimately proven himself weak, and a disappointment to all the ambitious Dragos kings who had come before him.

But the one who would follow him?

Jaeger smiled. That king would command an army so powerful that they would claim every kingdom in Osterland for Hest.

But first, he had to find a way to unlock the secrets of that mysterious book.

***

'Where's Fyn?' Jael called as Thorgils ambled across the stones towards them, his eyes barely open, straining against the unusually bright morning sun.

'Who?' he mumbled, shielding his face with one hand.

Jael shook her head, turning to Aleksander. 'He's such a giant turd.'

'It's true!' Thorgils grinned, coming to a stop before them. 'Everything about me is giant. *Everything*!' He winked at Aleksander.

Jael rolled her eyes and wandered off, not bothering to wait for either man as she headed towards Eadmund, who was busy running the archers through training drills. 'Did your mother kill Fyn in the night and cook him up for breakfast?' she called over her shoulder.

'Ha! Very possibly. He was like a day-old loaf of bread this morning, lying there snoring, so I left him to the wrath of Odda. I expect we'll soon see him charging down the hill with a flea in his ear!'

'And probably ready to move straight into my house!' Jael turned and smiled at him.

'Who could blame him? With Biddy's cooking and all those extras beds? Perhaps when your visitors leave, I shall join him? Keep you and Eadmund company!' He nodded at Aleksander, who was busy trying not to be annoyed that Jael had found herself so many new friends.

'I've been meaning to ask, what are those?' Aleksander wondered, bemused by the wooden house-like structures that ran down the length of each ship.

'That's our plan to keep Haaron's arrows at bay,' Jael informed him, nodding at Eadmund, who gave her a tight smile back. He had left before she'd woken, without speaking to anyone.

'What?' Aleksander laughed. 'You're going to hide in your little houses until they run out of arrows?'

'Not quite,' Jael said, shaking her head. 'Just watch before you scoff.'

So Aleksander did.

Every house had four hinged flaps in its slanted roof: two on each side. Eadmund called 'nock!', 'draw!', then 'open!', and the flaps were shunted up by men holding long poles inside the house. The flaps hit wooden bracers that ran along the roof and stood up vertically as eight archers popped up along one side, four in each hole, arrows nocked into their bowstrings. On Eadmund's quickly followed shout of 'aim!', they narrowed on their target: a row of hide-wrapped shields set far out on the headland. Eadmund yelled, 'release!' and the arrows whistled through the air, then 'down!' and they ducked into the houses, the pole-men quickly pulling the flaps shut after them as the arrows slammed into the shields.

But Eadmund didn't stop there. His next call of 'nock' came after barely a breath, and he went through the entire drill again and again in quick succession.

'Can you fit everyone in there?' Aleksander mused. 'A whole crew?'

'Well, it's a squeeze, especially around the mast, but yes, they can all fit in,' Jael said confidently. 'Hopefully, there'll be enough room for the catapults in the space between the house and the bow. Beorn seems to think so.'

Aleksander was impressed. 'It's a good idea. With the height they'll have from the Tower, it will be raining arrows as you get closer. It won't matter how many ships you bring with that advantage.'

'Exactly,' Jael agreed. 'It's not perfect, and their arrows will penetrate the houses eventually, but it should lessen the impact. And if I know Haaron, he'll be planning to have most of our crews pinned to the decks before he attacks.'

'He'll be in for a surprise then, won't he?' Aleksander smiled.

'Yes, but perhaps we'll need to build some sort of shelter to help those working the catapults too?' Thorgils frowned. 'We won't be able to launch any jars otherwise.'

'Well, everyone's going to have to grab a hammer then, aren't they? With all this extra building, we're going to be cutting it very fine,' Jael muttered. 'I should go and talk to Beorn. We're in danger of overloading the ships. And we have to keep the jars from exploding before they're launched, especially if they use fire arrows. We don't want to be the ones sinking to the bottom of the Adrano!'

'Ahhh, so much to do when you're in charge, isn't there, Jael?' Thorgils grinned. 'You'd better hop along then, leave the rest of us mortals to our training.'

Aleksander turned to Jael. 'You're in charge? Of what?'

Jael shrugged distractedly as she looked around for Beorn. 'The fleet.'

'Really? All of it?' Aleksander was surprised. 'You certainly seem to have earned Eirik's trust. To put you in charge of his entire fleet?'

'Well, you needn't look so surprised!' Jael sniffed. 'I'm perfectly capable of commanding a few ships.'

Aleksander didn't doubt it, but he smiled at her moodiness. He had missed her. Desperately. It was as if no time had passed at all, and they had slipped back into an easy friendship. But there had been so much more to their relationship than that.

Once.

Aleksander hurried after Jael as she strode off towards Beorn, feeling the aching loss of her heart, which had once belonged solely to him.

***

Fyn stopped to let a mother and her gaggle of bawling children pass. The red-faced woman gave him a frazzled nod of thanks and hurried away. He smiled to himself, feeling sorry for her, then turned towards the gates and came face to face with his father.

'I think it's time you and I had a talk, don't you?'

Fyn felt the air rush from his lungs. He was taller and stronger than he'd been a year ago. His arms and chest had filled out over the winter. A sword hung at his side now; a sword he knew how to use. But at that moment, under the scrutiny of his father's cold grey eyes, he felt all the confidence he had worked so hard to build, disintegrate. He didn't know what to say.

He was a boy again.

Morac frowned, instantly irritated by the drooping, floppy-haired boy who he'd been thrilled to see the back of. He had changed, there was no doubting that, but everything about his stance, his look... everything reminded Morac that Fyn wasn't his, and never would be.

'A talk about what?' Fyn croaked, trying to meet his father's eyes with some courage.

'Well, your mother is... *unhappy* you left,' Morac muttered as he motioned towards a table. Ketil already had a long line waiting for the charred meat that he and his sister served from their fire pit every day, but Morac had no appetite for food. He didn't even have an appetite for this conversation, but he did want to appease

Runa. Despite everything, he loved his wife, and he wanted her to be on his side. He needed to put his family back together, and for that to happen, he had to make peace with her son.

Fyn reluctantly sat down, fingering the cold iron pommel of his sword. He tried to remind himself how different he was from the boy who didn't even know how to hold onto a weapon; he tried to remember that he was about to go to battle, trusted to stand by Jael's side, worthy of the two swords she had given him now. 'I had no choice but to leave,' he muttered. 'After what you did.'

Anger twitched at the corners of Morac's unforgiving eyes. 'What *I* did?' he said slowly, taking a deep breath. 'I did what I believed was the right thing.' He laid his hands on the table, staring at them rather than Fyn. 'I believed what I saw. What was happening.'

Fyn shook his head, both cross at his father's excuse, and uncomfortable with a return to the moment when Morac had discovered Tarak raping him and then convinced Eirik to banish him. For a year. But it was about so much more than that. It was a lifetime of feeling like a useless nothing around a man who had barely glanced at him since he was born. Who had never shown him a look of approval or affection. Who had never invested any time in training him how to be a man. Who had simply dismissed him and ignored him, and, in the end, been disgusted by him.

Fyn swallowed, tasting bile in his mouth. 'You didn't even speak to me to find out what had happened... what he'd been doing to me since I was a boy.'

Morac's eyebrows rose at that. He ignored a twinge of guilt and looked up. 'I did what I thought was the right thing. But it appears that I made a... mistake. So, I'm here to suggest that we bury it in the past, for your mother's sake.' He braved those skittish blue eyes, which were not his eyes at all. 'Her happiness matters to both of us, I'm sure.'

Fyn felt a spark of anger, furious that his mother had to put up with that miserable man again, when she'd been so happy with just the two of them in the house. She had never looked so relaxed and carefree. 'If her happiness mattered to you, why did you send her son away? Why did you leave her for so long?' He stood up, pushing back his shoulders, shaking as he glared down at his father. 'Her happiness matters to *me*. And as long as I have breath in my body, I'll do everything I can to protect her from you. You will never hurt her, or me, again!'

And with one last look filled with as much fury as Fyn could muster, he stormed off, trying to control his shaking knees, his palm sweaty on his sword.

He didn't look back.

***

After spending most of the morning making decisions about how to adapt the ships with Beorn, Jael and Aleksander had hurried back to the house, both too distracted by thoughts of Edela to put their minds to much else. There had been no change, though, and Biddy had shooed them out after a while, insisting that Edela would hardly have a chance to recover if they sat on the bed, peering at her with their miserable faces for the rest of the day.

'That salve reeks! I'm surprised Edela hasn't woken up and insisted on a wash!' Aleksander smiled, hoping to encourage Jael to do the same.

'Mmmm,' Jael murmured distractedly, noticing Fyn and Thorgils training in the drizzle. The morning's clear weather had been quickly gobbled up by gloom and rain. 'Entorp's salve helped my arm heal quickly, I'm sure of it.'

'What happened to your arm?' Aleksander asked, worried, wanting to reach out and touch her. How odd it was, he realised, that he couldn't anymore.

Jael stopped at the railings of the Pit, nodding at Thorgils, who battered Fyn on the side of the head with his wooden sword. She smiled, then turned to Aleksander. 'A mountainous beast broke it,' she said, flexing her right arm. It ached constantly and was stiffer than her left, but she'd been pleased with its progress and was relieved that she'd been able to train as usual for the past few weeks.

Aleksander raised an eyebrow, wanting to ask more, but Jael's eyes weren't inviting any further questions.

'Have you come to join in? Or do you just want to stand there and admire the quality on display?' Thorgils grinned as he came sauntering over to the railings, leaving Fyn to pick himself up out of the mud.

'What? You mean Fyn?' Jael smiled tartly.

Thorgils ignored her entirely. 'How about you then, Aleksander?' he wondered. 'Jael is always telling us how good her old training partner was. How we will never compare to the great Aleksander Lehr!' He rolled his eyes. 'Isn't that right, Fyn?'

Fyn was digging mud out of his ear as he approached, looking a little nervous in the presence of the stern stranger. He smiled shyly at Aleksander through his hair but didn't say a word.

'Well, it's true that not many could beat Jael in Andala,' Aleksander admitted.

'Not many?' Jael snorted.

'Well, Gant could. Your father could.'

'When I was a child, maybe!'

Aleksander sucked in his cheeks. 'Perhaps...'

'But *you* beat her, didn't you?' Thorgils prodded. 'Plenty of times?'

Jael shot Aleksander a look that he happily ignored. 'Not plenty of times,' she insisted.

Aleksander peered at her. 'Have you been away so long that your memories have already faded?'

'A handful of times is not *plenty* of times. Once or twice is not *plenty*!'

'Once or twice?' Aleksander's eyes widened. 'What was in

the salve that old man made you?'

'Well, seems to me that you should resolve this difference of opinion,' Thorgils suggested eagerly. 'Don't you think? Fyn and I need a little rest. We can watch and learn how the Brekkans do it.'

Jael looked less keen. 'I don't imagine Aleksander would enjoy being made a fool of here, in front of all these hairy Osslanders.' She swept her arm around the large, railed enclosure which was almost full of training matches.

Aleksander shrugged. 'No, I've no problem with that. But perhaps your arm is too weak to fight against me? Maybe it's better if you just train with the Osslanders who will give you an easier time?'

Thorgils licked his lips, grinning gleefully at Fyn. He knew Jael well enough now to know that she would not back away from that. And handing Aleksander his sword, he ducked through the railings.

'Oh, and who have you been training with? Axl?' Jael retorted, taking the sword Fyn handed her as he came out to join them. She didn't even look down at it as she eyed Aleksander. There was no smile on her face.

'I have, actually,' Aleksander said coolly. 'And he's getting much better because of it.'

Jael noticed the joy on Thorgils' face. She frowned. As much as she'd missed fighting Aleksander, it was not necessarily the wisest thing to do. Half her mind was on Edela, and the rest was tangled up with thoughts of Eadmund. She was muddled, distracted, and irritable, but she sighed, knowing that there was nothing like fighting to release some tension. 'Well then, perhaps I can teach you a few things to pass on to him?' Jael raised an eyebrow, shrugging off her cloak as Thorgils whooped beside her. 'This is the Pit,' she smiled, slipping through the railings. 'Come and see how we fight here on Oss.'

***

Eadmund hadn't wanted to go back to the house to eat. Aleksander and Jael had quickly become inseparable, and while he couldn't blame her for wanting to show Aleksander around and discuss the upcoming battle, Eadmund was too out of sorts to want to witness any more of their obvious affection for one another.

He'd slept badly, terrorised by dreams of Melaena, his first wife, and the reminder of how she had betrayed him with his brother. He felt such a fool for not seeing her true feelings, and it coloured everything he felt now when he looked at Jael. He was overcome with fear, hiding it behind a wall of simmering anger.

Eadmund sat at one of Ketil's tables, staring at his half-eaten meat-stick, his appetite sinking with his mood.

'Eadmund?'

Eadmund looked up, fighting the urge to grimace. Morac Gallas had never been his favourite person, but after how he'd treated Fyn and abandoned his father, he was even more inclined to shun his company.

'You look very well,' Morac smiled as he sat down opposite Eadmund, not waiting for an invitation. 'Very well, indeed. I hardly recognised you. You must be half the size you were the last time I saw you!'

Eadmund could tell that Morac was trying hard to be nice, which didn't come naturally, and his usually miserable face looked oddly contorted because of it. 'Well, I suppose that's what happens when you do some training and drink a little less,' he said dismissively.

'Yes, your father tells me that your wife has been helping you.'

Morac wasn't wrong, but today that rankled. 'My wife? Yes, she likes to work everyone hard. Including me, it seems.'

'It's good to see you looking so well,' Morac smiled, then leaned in, lowering his voice. 'I shall be sure to tell Evaine. She's been very concerned about you these past few months.'

Guilt tightened Eadmund's throat. He knew he'd used Evaine, and badly. She had wanted so much more than him, and he'd never had enough courage in his heart to break hers. But then, he had been drink-sodden for most of their time together and in no state to think about anything except where his next jug of ale was coming from. 'How is Evaine?' he asked quietly, glancing around. 'Has she had the baby?'

'Oh, yes,' Morac said, beaming with pride. 'Didn't your father tell you?'

Eadmund looked annoyed. 'No.'

'Yes, that is why I've come,' Morac said. 'To talk your father into letting Evaine and your son return.'

'My son?' Eadmund felt strange, his body tingling unexpectedly.

'His name is Sigmund,' Morac smiled. 'He came very early, and he's small, struggling somewhat.' He frowned, looking earnestly into Eadmund's eyes. 'In truth, Evaine has had a terrible time on Rikka with Morana. My sister means well, but she is not... maternal. And her home is not warm. It is barely big enough for her alone. Evaine has been in poor health, pining for her mother, for Oss, and of course, for you.'

Eadmund's guilt grew. 'And what did Eirik say, about her returning with the baby?'

'Well, he refused,' Morac sighed. 'He won't have her here again. He disowns the boy entirely, so I shall have to return to Rikka and see what I can do for Evaine, to help her and Sigmund.'

Sigmund.

It was a name that sounded strange in his head. Not a baby's name. Not really. The thought of him tugged at Eadmund's heart though. His flesh and blood. His own child.

'Evaine gave me something for you,' Morac said, digging inside the small pouch attached to his belt. 'She didn't imagine that Eirik would want her back. She was wiser than me, it seems. She gave me this. For you.' He pulled out a tiny blonde curl tied to a thin leather strap. 'Something for you to keep. A reminder of your son.'

Eadmund didn't know what to think as he reached out and took the strap. The hair was so light. It reminded him of Evaine's. So soft and delicate. He ran his finger over the tiny curl and swallowed.

His son.

CHAPTER SIX

Aleksander handed his cloak and swordbelt to Thorgils and ducked through the railings after Jael. He followed her to the centre of the Pit, past groups of red-faced, grunting men hammering each other with wooden swords. After weeks of near-constant rain, the ground was a chopped-up, sloppy mess.

Aleksander looked down the length of his battered sword. 'Do you train with shields?'

'Sometimes,' Jael said, glancing around. It was not a good surface to fight on, she thought, wistful for the frozen, hard ground of deep winter. She shivered, already missing her thick fur cloak. 'Why? Do you think you'll need one?' Walking up to Aleksander, Jael touched her sword to his.

'No, I don't believe so,' he said, his eyes not leaving hers. 'You?'

'No, I don't plan on defending.' Jael swung her sword back and struck Aleksander on the shoulder.

He barely flinched as he dropped to the right, aiming for her waist. Jael jumped back, missing his blow, skidding through the mud. Her boots were quickly soaked through, but she didn't notice as she danced backwards, making him come after her. Jael tried not to smile, but it felt good to fight him again. It was so instantly familiar. She knew everything he would do, and there was perfect joy in that. The sheer speed of their blows as their blades met and were parried with ease showed how well they knew each other.

Aleksander lunged forward, slashing his sword through the rain. Jael slid back and grinned. 'Forgotten how this goes, old friend? You're supposed to hit *me* with your sword!' She spun around, thrusting out with the tip of hers, jabbing his stomach.

Again, Aleksander didn't even blink. He rolled his tongue around his mouth, ignoring the sting, remembering just how frustrating a creature she could be in this sort of mood. But he knew her. And he knew how to beat her. 'Old friend? Is that what we are now? *Friends*?'

His voice was measured, low, but even so, Jael found her eyes darting to the railings.

'Ha!' Aleksander laughed, charging at her, his sword slapping her ribs. 'Worried what your *new* husband thinks about your *old* friend?'

Jael grimaced, slipping to the side. 'Ahhh, same old friend, always talking too much.' She noticed a slight hint of distraction as Aleksander's eyes wandered to her lips, and she whacked him hard on the knee with her sword, kicking out at his thigh before retreating quickly.

Now, Aleksander did flinch as his leg buckled. He recovered swiftly though and chased her with his sword, slashing sharply from side to side. Jael caught each blow on the edge of her blade, pushing him back as he slid in the mud. Aleksander struggled for any certain footing, fighting off Jael's sword as she steadily gained the upper hand. She'd been training hard, he thought to himself.

But so had he.

Thorgils elbowed Fyn. 'Why don't you hop off and find us some ale? It looks as though they'll put on a good show, and I do like a nice drop of ale with my entertainment!'

Fyn lifted one unimpressed eyebrow at Thorgils before turning back to the fight.

Thorgils shrugged and smiled, his eyes following the fighters as they circled each other with intent.

Aleksander retreated, looking for a way to stall Jael's

momentum, but she followed him, smiling. 'Axl hasn't helped you much, has he?' She skidded to the left, spun and kicked him hard in the stomach. Aleksander fell into the mud with a plop.

A loud roar went up from the crowd. Aleksander kicked out at her in frustration, but Jael skipped away, too quick for his angry boot. Furious now, he scrambled to his feet and stood there, dripping with mud. Gritting his teeth, he threw away his sword.

Jael grinned, throwing hers away too.

'Oh.' Fyn's eyes bulged. 'That will make it interesting.'

'Just a bit!' Thorgils chortled, rubbing his hands together. 'Now we shall really see some fun. If only we had that ale...'

'What's going on?' Eirik wondered, stopping behind Thorgils. 'Why are you all lolling about outside the Pit, when you should be training *inside* it?' His eyes widened as he peered around Fyn. Fyn hurried to step out of the way, and Eirik moved up to the railings, a smile quickly cheering his stern face. He turned to Eadmund who had frozen as soon as he'd seen who was in the Pit. 'Come on, then, come and watch your wife beat another man to a dirty pulp!'

Eadmund looked uncertain until Thorgils seized his arm and pulled him to the railings. 'Come on!' he insisted. 'They're just about to start wrestling. Jael's already had him on his arse. As she does!'

Eadmund stood awkwardly, watching happiness bloom on Jael's red-cheeked face as she approached the mud-covered Aleksander. He felt an odd mix of rage and fear surging through his body.

Jael rushed at Aleksander as if to push him over but instead, she dropped to the ground and snapped her leg around, taking out his legs. Aleksander caught her ankle between his feet as he fell, twisting his legs, and she couldn't get up. He was over her instantly, but Jael drove her feet into his chest, kicking him away. Aleksander rolled and was back up and grabbing for her arms, trying to control her. She smacked him aside, and they grappled furiously, Jael grimacing at the pain in her right forearm as it cracked against his, mud splattering everywhere.

Finally untangling herself, Jael was up, hastily rubbing the mud out of her eyes. Aleksander followed. She turned to face him, thrashing her boot into the side of his arm. It was the soft option, she knew, and her hesitation over it made her slow. Aleksander's reflexes were sharp, and with Jael, well-honed. He grabbed her boot, to the delight of Thorgils and Fyn, who both cheered at the sight of that boot's comeuppance.

Jael gritted her teeth, hopped on her left foot, twisted her body with every bit of strength she had and snapped her left leg up, into the side of Aleksander's head. He fell, still gripping her right boot, and she went with him, her feet around his neck now, her body quickly sliding down towards his muddy face.

Thorgils and Fyn exchanged open-mouthed looks of disbelief as the crowd fell silent, shaking their heads in confusion and surprise.

Aleksander's ears were ringing as Jael leaned her forearm over his throat.

'I think you're done,' she breathed with a smile, cringing at the pain shooting up to her elbow before falling into an exhausted, filthy heap beside him.

Aleksander laughed as he rolled towards her. 'Well, what sort of friend would I be if I humiliated you in front of *your* people?'

Jael growled, punching his arm. 'How kind you are,' she taunted, sitting up, trying to catch her breath.

She froze as her eyes caught Eadmund's.

He barely acknowledged her, before turning to leave.

***

Varna Gallas was older than anyone Haaron knew. She smelled like the piss-soaked swaddling cloth of a small child, and as much as he welcomed their talks, there was nothing worse than sticking her near a fire when the door was closed. He could barely stop himself gagging at her foul odour. But Varna loved to be as close to the fire as possible. Her skin was almost translucent as it sagged around her ancient bones; there was no longer any warmth in it at all. She was far too thin, she knew, but she could do little about it now. She had no real interest in food, or sleep, could only tolerate an occasional cup of wine, and could not abide the company of anyone, apart from Haaron, and her granddaughter. As much as Varna was ready for death – well past ready to be claimed by the old gods – her iron-clad will would not let her be taken until she had ensured Hest's future.

And now, as things stood, Varna knew that Hest was in peril.

Haaron stood, heading away from the fire to pour himself another cup of ale. He needed to take a breath of something that wasn't Varna. 'Are you sure I can't get you a cup?' he wondered, exhaling deeply.

Varna rolled her rheumy eyes and ignored him. She turned her head towards the flames, watching as they wove themselves around each other in a slow dance of heat and mystery. She had been dreaming endlessly of late, though she was far too old for such a heavy load of dreams. If only Meena could help her, but the girl was almost entirely useless. There was no one, no one she could trust; no one Haaron could trust either. She had kept him safe on his throne for twenty-five years, but she could feel the danger he was in growing stronger by the day.

Without her by his side, what hope did he have?

Haaron filled his cup high with ale, inhaling its earthy scent as he walked back to his chair.

'He is growing powerful.'

'Who?'

'The Bear,' Varna growled, her voice as dry as the red dirt of Hest. She scratched at the matted strands of white hair hanging down either side of her face. Once her hair had been as wild and thick as Meena's, but now it was barely there. Much like her. 'He is in my dreams every night.'

Haaron frowned, leaning forward. 'You mean Jaeger?'

Varna ignored him again as she bent lower in her chair, the ache in her back excruciating. She looked up suddenly, her eyes wide. 'He wants to kill you!'

Haaron laughed, the leathery skin of his face folding back like curtains. 'You don't need to be a dreamer to tell me that!'

'He is growing powerful,' she repeated. 'Somehow. But he seeks more. More power. I see him filled with it. Growing stronger and stronger. Swallowed whole!'

Haaron inched towards the edge of his chair, dropping his voice to a whisper, despite the fact that they were alone in his very private chamber. 'And?'

'He will kill Haegen and Karsten. Of that, you can be sure. They stand in his way. As do you. His care is only for himself and his revenge upon you, for favouring them all his life.'

'This is nothing new you are telling me, Varna,' Haaron insisted, relaxing his shoulders as he sipped his ale. 'I should have gotten rid of the boy years ago, before it came to this. Before he became this bear you warn me of.'

'But you didn't. And you don't,' the old woman spat. 'Because of her.'

Haaron didn't acknowledge her judgemental scowl, but he could feel its displeasure as it tried to consume him. 'There are many things I have done, many that I would do differently,' he said slowly. 'But you are right. I don't like the boy. I've never liked him or the way he's looked at me all these years. But, he is Bayla's favourite –'

'And you love her *still*?'

Haaron frowned. 'She is my wife. If I were to kill her favourite son –'

'Yet, she despises you too!'

'If he were to fall in battle...' Haaron braved those scorn-filled eyes. 'She could mourn. We could all mourn. But it would be nothing to do with me. There would be no one for her to curse but the gods themselves.'

'Then we can only hope that things on Skorro become as dire as I fear they may. As I see in my dreams.'

Haaron drained his cup, distracted. He wanted Jaeger gone, there was no doubt about that, but at what cost? What would he have to lose in order to destroy his vengeful son?

***

'How is your grandmother?' Fyn wondered, looking up from his meat-stick.

'Much the same,' Jael sighed as she sat down next to him, motioning for Aleksander to take the empty space next to Thorgils. She had no idea where Eadmund was, and she couldn't decide whether to be worried or annoyed at his childish way of disappearing whenever something uncomfortable occurred. 'Biddy seems pleased by that, though. Perhaps there will be better news soon?'

Aleksander wasn't sure if he had much of an appetite, but the smell of charred meat drifting towards him had his stomach growling. 'Do you want something to eat?' he asked Jael.

'Mmmm, please,' Jael said. They were both covered in dried mud and needed a good bath.

'You haven't noticed your husband lately, have you?' Thorgils wondered slowly as he watched Aleksander take his place in line. 'He doesn't look too pleased with things, if you know what I mean.'

Jael glared at him. '*Things*?'

'Well, you and Aleksander... the fight,' Thorgils spluttered through a mouthful of meat. 'It's not easy for him to watch the way you are with each other. Any man would have a hard time with that.'

Jael blinked. She didn't know what to say. Her eyes drifted towards Aleksander as he stood, chatting to some of his men who had obviously discovered the joy of Ketil's fire pit too. Ketil and his sister were red-faced as they hurried about trying to keep up with the extra demand that two shiploads of Brekkans had created. Aleksander turned around and smiled, his shoulder-length dark hair hanging around his face like a muddy cloak. Jael felt a stab in her heart. 'We're old friends,' she tried.

Thorgils gave her a doubtful look as he finished his mouthful, wiping a greasy hand through his beard, smoothing out his moustache. He leaned over the table towards her. 'If that were so, then I don't think it would be like this, do you?' He sharpened his eyebrows. 'You might need to find your husband and give him a smile or two to see him through.'

Fire coursed up into Jael's mouth. She wanted to be furious with Thorgils for poking his nose into her marriage, but she knew he was right. Taking a deep breath, she decided to ignore both him and her darkening mood. 'And how is Odda?' she asked Fyn, changing the subject.

Fyn's eyes bulged, and he squirmed on the bench. There wasn't much more to say than that.

Jael and Thorgils laughed.

'I think young Fyn is wondering how I turned out to be such a cheerful soul!' Thorgils grinned. 'And probably reconsidering if he could suffer through Morac's miserable company instead.'

Fyn looked horrified. 'No! No, I'm not thinking that. Not ever! Not anymore. I don't have to endure him anymore, do I?'

'No,' Jael said, watching his panic. 'Of course you don't. But as for your mother...'

'My mother needs to find a way to stand up to him,' Fyn said firmly. 'But she won't. She doesn't want him there, but what can she do?' He lost his appetite and pushed his half-finished stick away.

Thorgils eyed the neglected meat.

'Well, she could divorce him, couldn't she?' Jael wondered.

Both Thorgils and Fyn look shocked by that suggestion.

'Why not? He abandoned her. For nearly half a year,' Jael said, smiling at Aleksander as he returned and handed her a piping hot meat-stick of her own. 'Surely that's reason enough?'

Thorgils stole Fyn's abandoned stick, almost inhaling the meat in one breath. 'Mmmm, Runa could ask for a divorce because of that. I remember my father reciting all the ways he could get a divorce from Odda every couple of weeks. I know them by heart!' He belched, then lowered his voice, glancing around. 'But would she?'

Aleksander had no idea what anyone was talking about, but the serious looks on everyone's faces were reason enough to stay out of it, and besides, his food smelled too delicious to waste time on words.

Fyn shook his head sadly. 'I wish she would, but I'm not sure she's brave enough to try.'

'But is Morac even going to stay?' Jael wondered. 'Perhaps he's just visiting?'

'You can only hope,' Thorgils smiled, nudging his morose companion. 'Now, come on, we don't have time for all this gossip,' he muttered, standing up with a groan. 'We need to get back to the Pit. I want Jael to show me how she did that thing with her legs. I'd like to try it on Ivaar when we get to Saala!'

***

They sat apart, barely speaking. Runa didn't want to look at that mean face anymore. She hadn't missed it. Not at all. She had anticipated that she would; that she would feel the loss of her close companion after so many years together.

But she hadn't. Not one bit.

Instead, she had enjoyed the freedom to think and feel

independently; to sit in the silence and appreciate simple pleasures. Alone. Without fear of upsetting anyone, or anyone upsetting her. And with Fyn back, she had been so content. Her once drawn face had rounded, her eyes had brightened, and her spirits had lifted.

And then Morac had returned.

The fire was dying, but neither of them were attending to it, nor asking Respa to either. They just sat there like moss-covered boulders on a hill.

'I shall have to return to Rikka soon, to see about building a house for Evaine and the child.'

Runa looked up. Just the sound of that name pricked the back of her neck. 'Will you not be going to war with Eirik, then?'

Morac stared at her, pleased that she was speaking to him at last. 'Well, no,' he said slowly, 'I had not thought that I would. My position here is no longer what it was,' he admitted. 'Eirik did not request my help.'

'He has Jael. And Eadmund,' Runa said coldly. 'He relies on their advice and guidance now. Thorgils and Sevrin too.'

'Well, who could blame him?' Morac muttered with a hint of irritation. 'A king must seek opinions in order to form his own. That I know well.'

'But not yours. Not anymore.'

'No, I suppose not.'

'Though, if he asks?' Runa mused. 'Would you go?'

'To battle Haaron Dragos?' Morac rubbed his chilled hands together, suddenly aware of the absence of flames in the fire pit. 'If he asks? Yes, I would. Of course. Whether I'm here or on Rikka, Eirik is still my king, and I must answer his call.'

'And if you go back to Rikka?' Runa wondered without meeting her husband's eyes. 'Will you stay there?'

'Eirik will not have Evaine here,' Morac said quietly, considering things. 'So yes, I expect that I would have to stay there. She needs me. They both do.'

Runa glared at Morac, wanting to throw accusations at him,

but then she realised that she honestly didn't care anymore. She didn't feel betrayed or hurt. She was empty of everything now but the desire for him to be gone. 'Well, then, it's best that you return to Evaine as soon as you can, for, as you say, she needs you.'

***

Amma couldn't tell if her father was sleeping, or whether he had just closed his eyes for a moment. He certainly had just eaten an enormous meal, and it was his usual pattern of behaviour to fall into an overstuffed doze.

She crept towards him, her long lilac dress swaying softly across the freshly changed reeds. 'Father?' she whispered, stopping just before his throne.

There was no one around, but Amma knew that she only had a moment before Osbert, Gisila, or even Axl walked in. 'Father?' she tried again.

'What?!' Lothar croaked, his eyes bursting open, his head swinging around in confusion. He tried to focus on his daughter, who stood there, almost crouching before him. 'What is it, my dear?' He looked around. 'Alp!' he barked. 'Alp!'

His servant came rushing towards his bellowing master, bowing immediately. 'My lord?'

'Wine,' Lothar yawned. 'Bring the jug.' He turned his attention back to Amma as Alp scuttled away. 'Now, what can I do for you, Daughter?'

'Ummm, I ahhh, I wanted to talk to you about going to Saala,' Amma mumbled, her words tumbling over one another as they raced to get out of her mouth before she changed her mind.

'What?' Lothar stuck a finger in his ear as if to clear it out. 'What for? You want to be like Jael, now, do you?' he laughed mockingly at her.

Amma looked horrified. 'No, not to fight, Father,' she said, shaking her head. 'Never that. I just... I would like to come. To offer my support... to you. And Osbert, of course,' she lied boldly, dropping her eyes lest her father spot the lies she was weaving.

Lothar was puzzled.

Amma looked up, sensing his hesitation. She raced to take advantage of it. 'Saala is far enough away from where you will fight, so I'll be perfectly safe there in your camp,' she said quickly. 'And I know that one day I will be a wife, and it would be good experience for me to understand the role of a woman in supporting her husband when he goes to battle. Just as Mother did with you all those years ago when we were in Iskavall.' She widened her eyes with as much child-like innocence as she could muster.

Lothar frowned at his youngest daughter. She was blooming, and he could see that soon he would indeed have to find her a husband. There would be many suitors for a princess as easy on the eye as Amma. It certainly would not hurt her to have a taste of a battle camp, he thought to himself. 'But I thought you would keep Gisila company here.'

'Oh.' Amma's hopes sunk.

Lothar stroked his beard, and, picking out a piece of roasted lamb that had fallen into it, he popped it into his mouth. He noted his daughter's disappointed face and an idea sparked. 'But, of course, if Gisila were to come along as well, then you could keep each other company,' he mused. 'And, as you say, Saala is far enough away from where we will attack Haaron, so you'll both be perfectly safe, I'm sure,' he smiled. 'Mmmm, I think that is a good idea you have there, my daughter. I'm sure Gisila will thank you for it!'

Amma squirmed. As pleased as she was to have convinced her father to bring her along, she knew that Gisila would not be thanking her at all.

***

'No.'

His father had a way of making a 'no' impossible to argue against. Something about the set of his mouth, the slant of his sharp blue eyes made his 'no' an immovable object.

Eadmund sighed.

'You really think your wife would enjoy having that girl here again? Parading your mistake around the fort? Dangling him in front of her every day? You'd put Jael through that?'

Eadmund leaned back in his chair, so unsettled by the thought of Evaine and his son that he could barely see straight. 'You think Jael would mind so much?'

Eirik grunted, bending down to remove his boots. 'You tell me, she's your wife!' He looked up, frowning. 'If she were mine, I'd not want to incur her wrath. Especially after seeing what she did today with those legs of hers! I've no idea how she twisted herself around like that. Like a wild cat!'

Eadmund didn't appreciate the reminder.

'Here, tug on this boot for me,' Eirik grumbled, annoyed by the damp leather's reluctance to part with his wet sock. 'Now look,' he said as Eadmund eased the boot off. 'Imagine how you would feel if she brought that man, Aleksander, here to stay. For good. And not only that but say he brought their child with him. By the look on your face these past few days, I can imagine how that would go.'

Eadmund bit down on a fresh burst of irritation at just the mention of that name.

'So how do you think bringing them here would make Jael feel?' Eirik asked. 'What would that do to her position? You'd undermine her. Unsettle her. She would look as miserable as you do right now. Every single day.'

Eadmund wanted his father to be wrong, but he wasn't. He wasn't even sure he was serious about bringing Evaine back. Not for her sake, although he certainly felt guilty for his part in her banishment. But the baby. Sigmund. His son. How could he just abandon him? 'Then I will go there. Visit him.'

'Why?' Eirik looked cross now. 'Why stir a pot full of bees when you don't need to? Are you looking to get stung?'

'He's my son!'

'And?'

'What does *that* mean?' Eadmund asked angrily, relieved to be in Eirik's private chamber and not in front of all the eyes and ears of Oss. 'You don't think I have a responsibility to care for him?'

'No,' Eirik insisted. 'You have a responsibility to Oss. To your wife. He was a mistake. A bastard. His mother's problem. Not yours.'

Eadmund's mouth hung open.

'What? You think that's cruel?' Eirik scoffed. 'You will be king here before long, my son. And kings must be cruel and just, and everything in between. But always, always, kings must put their kingdom first!'

'What has that got to do with my son?'

'You bring that boy back here, with his mother... that girl?' Eirik bent forward, seeking Eadmund's eyes. 'That girl is more trouble than you know. If you bring her here, you'll put this kingdom at risk, I'm certain of it.'

Eadmund stared blankly at his father, puzzled by the ferocity of his argument. But then again, Eirik had always disliked Evaine for some reason. There was no way he would ever accept her child, but Sigmund Skalleson was his grandson.

And that made him part of Oss' future, whether Eirik liked it or not.

***

'She is cooler,' Biddy smiled reassuringly from her stool by the fire. 'I've been rubbing that evil salve over her chest all day. I think it's helping.'

'I can smell it!' Jael grimaced as she sat down on the bed. She touched Edela's hand, sighing. 'It's hard to think about much else. Not while she's like this. Not when she won't even open her eyes.'

'But you must,' Biddy warned her. 'You have a lot of responsibility now. You can't worry about Edela. She wouldn't want you to. She'd want you to focus on the battle, wouldn't she?' Biddy directed this at Aleksander as she ran an anxious hand through her flyaway curls.

'Of course she would,' Aleksander said sadly. 'She hates a fuss.'

'She does, that's true,' Jael murmured as she kissed her grandmother's warm head, leaving the bed to go and sit by the fire. She was cold, her arm was aching, and she hadn't seen Eadmund all afternoon. Groaning, Jael lowered herself into a chair, smiling as Vella came padding over and put her paws on her knee. Jael picked her up, absentmindedly stroking her thick grey coat. Ido sat far away, ignoring her, waiting by the door.

Biddy stood up. 'I think I'll make us all some hot milk before I go to bed. What do you think?'

Aleksander walked over to the fire, smiling. 'Hot milk?' He hadn't enjoyed that bedtime favourite since Biddy and Jael had left Andala. Memories came rushing back of sitting around the fire in their miserable, cold cottage together. 'It's been a long time', he sighed, plonking himself down in Eadmund's chair.

Jael opened her mouth to suggest he move, but Eadmund wasn't there to be offended, so she closed it. There were simply too many things in her head, all competing for her attention. She didn't have the energy to think of Eadmund as well. Not now.

Biddy brought a small cauldron of milk to the fire and hung it from the hook, suspending it over the flames. 'You two watch that. I'm going to check on the chickens. They're making a lot of noise for this time of night.'

Aleksander made to stand up, but Biddy shooed him back down into the chair. 'I can manage a hungry fox or two, don't you worry about that,' she muttered with a twinkle in her eye. 'Just don't let that milk boil over!' And grabbing her cloak from a peg near the door, she headed outside.

'How bad are things?' Jael wondered, turning to Aleksander. 'For Gisila and Axl? Having to live with Lothar?'

Aleksander picked up a log and added it to the fire, eager to heat the milk quickly. 'Not so bad for Axl, I'd say, but your mother? I imagine she spends all her days thinking of ways to kill herself.'

Jael felt a twinge of pity. 'Well, who could blame her with that giant slug writhing all over her every night.'

Aleksander cringed. 'No! Don't make me imagine Lothar naked!'

Jael laughed, screwing up her face. 'Hopefully, he only comes for her in the dark!'

Eadmund pushed open the door, watching Jael and Aleksander giggling like children. He tried not to frown.

He tried not to notice that Aleksander was in his chair.

'Where have you been all day?' Jael wondered irritably, masking her relief that he was back. 'We've already eaten.'

'So have I,' Eadmund mumbled as he took off his cloak, bending down to pat Ido who was wiggling himself sideways with joy. 'I was with my father. We ate together.'

'Oh.'

It was awkward, the silence that crept around them all. The sounds of the house suddenly became louder: Edela's hoarse breathing, the spitting of the fire.

'Well, don't let me interrupt you. I was just heading to bed.'

Jael frowned, annoyed at herself for not having smoothed things over with Eadmund yet; they were becoming more wrinkled by the moment. Tomorrow, she told herself, she would do it tomorrow. He was festering, and she couldn't blame him.

She remembered how it had felt to watch him with Evaine. 'Are you sure you don't want some hot milk first?' she asked in an attempt to make things right.

Eadmund looked wistfully towards the fire, shaking his head. 'No. We have a long day trying to sort the catapults out tomorrow, so I'll get some sleep. Goodnight.' And, barely looking at his wife, and not even acknowledging Aleksander, he turned and disappeared into the bedchamber.

'What did I tell you about that milk!' Biddy exclaimed as she came inside, rushing towards the cauldron. 'One job,' she muttered. 'You only had one job!' And grumbling away to herself, she hurried to unhook the cauldron, taking it to the kitchen to cool the milk down.

Aleksander laughed, glancing at Jael, but she had turned towards the bedchamber, watching as the door closed.

***

Eadmund sat down on the bed as Ido jumped onto the furs, making a little nest for himself, ready for sleep.

He pulled off his boots and sighed.

Nothing felt right.

That was *his* wife out there. In *his* house. With another man. And it would be completely ridiculous of him to rush out and demand Aleksander get up out of his chair and go and stay somewhere else. Not with Edela so ill. Not when he was Jael's oldest friend. Her family.

He yawned, and dropping his head, he pulled off his trousers. The leather strap with his son's hair fell to the floor. Frowning, he picked it up, holding it in his hand, staring at that tiny blonde lock.

So very small. Just like he must be.

His father was right, though. Eadmund had run every option through his mind and come to the same conclusion as Eirik. It would destroy everything he had with Jael to bring Sigmund here. But... how could he just abandon his own flesh and blood?

Eadmund sighed, slipping the leather strap under his pillow. He slid under the furs, confused. He had to put it all out of his mind.

He needed to let his son go.

CHAPTER SEVEN

There was a storm.

It was almost too dark to see, but Eadmund had followed the wailing sound to a door. He was certain it was a door.

'Evaine!' he panicked. 'Evaine!' Eadmund felt around the rough panels of wood, and there it was: a handle. His cold fingers fumbling, he turned it, pushing open the creaking door.

Evaine turned, her tear-filled blue eyes bursting open with surprise. 'Eadmund! Help me, please. Please! He won't move!'

Eadmund hurried to where she was kneeling on the reeds. There was only one lamp in the cottage, its meagre flame blowing about on the whim of the wind as it rushed down the smoke hole and in through the crumbling walls.

There was no fire.

Eadmund dropped to the floor next to Evaine, his breath rushing from his mouth, making great clouds of smoky air. Sigmund lay there on a swaddling cloth.

Blue.

Evaine was screaming. 'Help me, Eadmund! Help me wake him up. Please! He won't open his eyes!'

Eadmund was numb. He wanted to turn away from the horror that was quickly shutting down every part of him. Instead, he reached out a hand, trying to ignore Evaine's screeching or his own best instincts, which knew...

His hand shaking, he touched the baby's icy skin and

shuddered. He pulled his hand away, rocking back on his heels, pain flooding his body.

'Eadmund, please!' Evaine begged, grabbing his sleeve. 'Please, save him! Morana wouldn't help me. She just left us here. Please, Eadmund! Help me! You must help me!'

***

Jael woke with a smile.

She had slept deeply and dreamed freely for the first time in days. Of Eadmund. And Eskild's Cave. Its secret hot-water pool was one of their favourite places to disappear to together. She stretched languidly, ignoring her cold toes, remembering her dream: how they had slipped into the hot water, naked, kissing under the shimmering sky of tiny blue lights.

Jael rolled over, her smile fading, surprised to find that Eadmund wasn't there.

***

'And?' Jaeger frowned.

Meena had stumbled, mumbled, and tapped her way through a rambling explanation that had ended up nowhere he could understand at all. His patience was running away with speed.

'Well, I, I... found this,' Meena stuttered, at last, pulling a crumpled scrap of vellum from her purse.

Jaeger frowned, snatching it from her. 'It looks familiar,' he breathed, his eyes suddenly alert. He rushed to the table and opened the book. Flicking through the ancient pages, he eventually found what he was looking for. 'Do you see it?' he asked impatiently, glaring at her.

Meena leaned over, squinting, uncomfortably close to Jaeger; so close that she could feel the furious heat as it rose from him. She looked from the book to the scrap of vellum, and her eyes bulged. 'It's the same!' she exclaimed. 'The same sort of symbols.'

'It is,' Jaeger marvelled. He turned to her, his eyes alive with hope. 'Where did you get this?'

Meena gulped. 'My grandmother's chest,' she said quietly, her cheeks reddening with the guilt of her crime. 'She had it hidden inside an old book. I just... I remembered seeing something like this. I knew I had.'

'Varna can read this?' Jaeger wondered. 'She uses it?'

'I, I don't know.' Meena shuffled quickly away from him, tapping her head, then her ears. 'She has used the book I found this in many times, but... I have never seen her use this spell.' Her voice was faint, almost disappearing into the loud rain as it battered the windows.

Jaeger felt a surge of urgency grip his body.

He didn't want to wait any longer, suffer his father's disparaging looks anymore, be at his mercy and watch as he groomed Haegen as his look-alike, do-nothing replacement.

It was time for things to change.

It was time for Hest to be his.

**

Gisila spat out her wine.

She had taken to drinking wine with breakfast, wine with lunch and supper, wine before bed. Especially before bed. 'What do you mean, go to Saala?' she spluttered, grabbing the napkin Amma handed her. 'But you are going to war!'

'We are, of course,' Lothar said happily between mouthfuls of warm bread and smoked cheese. 'Did you never accompany Ranuf to battle? I'm sure you must have.'

Gisila shook her head, searching for air, trying to gather her scattered senses. 'No, he never wished me to go.'

'Well, I cannot imagine why,' Lothar mumbled. 'Many men take their women along with them. It makes no sense to leave a woman behind, not when she can offer comfort and succour, as Amma reminded me yesterday when she asked to come along.'

Gisila's head snapped to Amma, who glanced down at her plate, avoiding everyone's eyes as they frantically sought hers.

'Oh, did she now?' Osbert hummed, wondering what his sister was up to. 'So you'll be joining us on the road to Saala, Sister?' he murmured, watching her squirm beneath Gisila's obvious displeasure.

'I shall,' Amma said quietly, her voice heavy with the guilt of Gisila's distress, and the anger she knew she would face from Axl. 'I was so anxious about you all going off to war. I didn't want to be left behind, so far away, when I could do nothing to help.'

Lothar drank from his cup. 'Indeed, we shall all be grateful for your support, and Gisila's too, won't we, Axl?' He nudged his stepson, whose lips were so pursed with fury, they'd almost entirely disappeared.

'Indeed, we shall.' Axl forced the words through his teeth, too cross to even look Amma's way. What was she thinking?

'Although, we shan't be going on the road with you and the men, Osbert,' Lothar smiled at his son, belching violently as he pushed his empty plate away. 'The women will accompany me on *Storm Chaser*. It makes no sense for them to endure six days on horses, or being jolted about in a shit-heap of a wagon. Much more comfort awaits you ladies on board, I can assure you!' he smiled cheerfully.

Gisila wanted to demand more wine, but she did not want to give the impression that she was falling to pieces.

But she was falling to pieces.

The sweet respite of Lothar's coming absence had been all she had clung to for months; the dream of being alone every night without his eager hands pawing at her, thrusting himself into her, crushing the breath from her ever-shrinking frame. Her shoulders drooped as her spirits sank. There was only one hope left: that Lothar would fall in battle. But she had her doubts as to whether he would even put himself into a position where that could occur.

Lothar Furyck was not renowned for his bravery.

Axl didn't bother to finish his eggs. He pushed his plate away and stood. 'If you'll excuse me, Mother, Uncle,' he nodded and made to leave, ignoring Amma and Osbert entirely. 'I must finish packing my saddlebags.' And quickly adjusting his swordbelt, he strode out of the hall before anyone could protest.

***

'You're awake!'

Jael's smile was wide as she hurried to her grandmother's side. Edela was propped up against a wall of pillows, her face drawn and pale, but there was a hint of life about her now. Of hope.

'That I am,' Edela grinned, her voice faint, her body heaving with the effort of speaking.

Biddy and Aleksander were sitting on the bed next to her, their own faces reflecting the relief on Jael's.

'Her fever has gone,' Biddy announced with a smile. 'Completely!'

'Which means that I am cured,' Edela decided.

'Cured but weak,' Biddy insisted. 'Very weak, so you must try not to rush about.'

'Oh, I don't think you'll have to worry about that,' Edela croaked. She wasn't sure she even had enough strength to move an eyebrow, let alone take herself out of bed.

'It's good to have you back!' Jael said happily, kissing her grandmother's head, which felt cool for the first time in days. 'I was so worried.'

'You?' Edela snorted. 'I must have been in a bad way to make you worry!' She glanced behind Jael. 'Where is that husband of yours? Is he still asleep?'

Jael looked around, but there was no Eadmund, just Ido and Vella who were sniffing the kitchen floor, hoping for crumbs. 'No. I imagine he's down on the beach with Thorgils, working on the ships.'

Edela frowned, noticing the tension on Jael's face. 'Now that I am well –'

'You're not well yet, Edela,' Biddy reminded her.

Edela rolled her eyes. 'Forgive me. Now that I am *better*, we can talk about why I'm here. Why we have both come.' She reached out for Jael's hand. 'Aleksander tells me that he hasn't said a word yet.'

'No, he hasn't,' Jael grumbled, glaring at Aleksander. 'Annoyingly.'

Edela smiled. 'I've trained him well, it seems. It's not just *your* temper he has learned to be afraid of!' She yawned, and her shoulders sagged.

'I think it's best that you take your time, Edela,' Biddy advised. 'You need more strength. I shall make a bone broth. It will give you some energy.'

'Mmmm,' Edela sighed, feeling the heaviness of her eyelids as her head sunk more deeply into the pillows. 'I'm far too weary to argue. Perhaps I just need a little sleep to strengthen my tongue?'

'That's a good idea,' Jael said, squeezing Edela's hand. 'It will give me a chance to check on everything down on the beach. It's not long until we leave and I'm supposed to have some idea about what we're going to do once we get to Saala. Now that you're not near death, I can finally turn my mind to it!' She smiled, but it was forced, because, although she was relieved that Edela was better, she couldn't help wondering what had happened to Eadmund.

***

'Eydis!' Fyn cried. 'Are you alright?' He hurried down the hill after her, watching as she pulled herself out of the mud she has just fallen into.

Eydis' small face quickly turned pink. She could feel the heat on her cheeks as she dropped her head to her chest. 'I'm fine,' she muttered crossly. 'I just stumbled.'

'Here, let me help you,' Fyn offered, grabbing hold of her arm.

Eydis, mortified that he was touching her, cringed away from him. 'I, I can manage on my own, thank you,' she huffed. 'I am perfectly able to walk, you know!'

Fyn stepped back, not wanting to make things worse. He felt like a clumsy fool around Eydis; always caught between wanting to be helpful and not knowing how to achieve it. 'I'm sorry,' he tried. 'It's just so muddy with the men going up and down to the ships all day long. You really need your stick to get down the hill safely.' It sounded like a reprimand, and Fyn hadn't meant it to, but he could see from the vexed expression on Eydis' face that she had certainly taken it as that.

'I cannot find my stick,' she said stiffly. 'But I don't need it. I only use it to please my father.' And with that, she took a deep breath and started walking towards the edge of the hill.

'Eydis!' Fyn called out and hurried after her again, this time grabbing her shoulders. 'Here, at least let me point you in the right direction.' He turned her gently towards the beach. 'There you go, that's better.'

His voice sounded so kind that it dampened Eydis' ire. She turned to him, conscious of the thick mud clinging to her ankles.

'I think you're right,' she said boldly. 'Some help down to the beach would be useful. If you wouldn't mind?'

Fyn smiled, suddenly as flustered as Eydis as her eyes sought to focus somewhere near his voice. 'Yes, of course,' he mumbled, slipping her delicate arm through his.

'Well, what's this, then?' Thorgils snickered behind them. 'I wouldn't let the king see you walking hand in hand with his daughter. She's not of marrying age yet, you know. And when she is, I doubt he'd want a nothing weed like you for a son-in-law!'

Fyn blushed, annoyed, and not for the first time because of Thorgils' giant-sized mouth.

Eydis spun around, and Thorgils closed his giant-sized mouth and didn't say another word as he followed them down the hill.

The beach was full of men and ships and noise as the shipbuilders and their crews hurried to erect small catapults and storage boxes for the sea-fire jars on five of Eirik's ships.

Beorn was gesticulating at Jael as they walked carefully across the stones, Eydis still with her arm through Fyn's.

'I don't see how we'll have the time!' Beorn exclaimed with wild eyes, his short, grey curls bouncing about in the brisk wind.

'There's no choice but to find the time!' Jael insisted just as strongly. 'If you need to work under torch-light, we can organise that, Beorn. Whatever you need. The jars cannot roll about, not with fire on board. We can't have any leaks, any accidents. You need to copy what they have on the Brekkan ships, the way the jars are so tightly packed together, unable to move about.' She glanced at Aleksander, the line between her dark eyebrows deepening with every moment.

'Well, perhaps we should go and look at my ships again?' Aleksander suggested calmly to Beorn, sensing that Jael was ready to lose her temper. He looked at her to join them, but she shook her head, seeing that Eydis had come.

'You go,' she said shortly. 'It will be easier without me there, I'm sure.'

Aleksander shrugged and led a muttering Beorn down to the farthest end of the beach where his men were carefully unloading the jars from their ships.

'Eydis,' Jael smiled, trying to shake off the irritation that was sharpening her tongue. 'Are you alright?' She looked down at Eydis' mud-covered cloak. 'Did you fall over?'

Eydis looked embarrassed and said nothing.

Fyn felt sorry for her. 'It's very muddy on the hill after all the rain,' he said quietly.

'Well, best you use your stick, then, don't you think?' Jael said firmly. 'Have you seen Eadmund this morning?' She spun around to Thorgils with barely a breath, her eyes darting about, unsettled by the continued absence of him.

'No.' Thorgils shook his head. 'I thought he'd be here. The archers aren't training, so I assumed he was with you.'

'Jael.' Eydis looked pained as she gripped Fyn's arm to steady herself on the slippery stones. 'That's why I'm here. I had a dream about Eadmund.'

Jael felt her throat tighten. 'About Eadmund? What about Eadmund?'

Eydis took a deep breath, feeling her heart thudding with urgency. 'He's gone! Eadmund's gone to Rikka.'

***

The girl sat alone. Her sleek black hair blew across her beautiful face, tangling in the wind. She didn't notice. Sobs rose up from her chest like waves of heartache heaving through her lithe body. She fell to the ground, screaming into the snow, begging the gods to come and claim her, demanding they tell her why they had done this to her family? Why they had let the Brekkans and the Tuurans do this?

Was there no justice? No one with the power to right this wrong?

He stepped out of the shadows then.

She didn't notice him. He was silent, and her crying had filled the secluded grove of ancient trees with overwhelming pain and noise.

She was lying there, so lost, and yet so desperately mesmerising in her sadness. He had been transfixed by her for a long time. From a distance. She was, after all, the most beautiful girl in Tuura; more beautiful than any goddess. And she was broken, her heart ripped into little pieces. Let down. Abandoned.

He couldn't stand back and watch her suffer anymore. Not her. The one he loved. 'I can help you,' he murmured.

The girl didn't hear him, but she suddenly felt his presence behind her, and she jumped, frightened. The man was dressed in a simple, grey linen tunic, but there was snow, thick on the ground. Where was his cloak?

He was young, handsome, timid, with short dark hair and a kind smile. But his eyes were full of something she had seen before. She looked away, not caring, not wishing to hear what he had to say.

'I can help you,' the man tried again.

'How?' She turned to him, her ice-blue eyes sharp on his. 'Why?'

He came to her, kneeling before her, taking one hand, his eyes never leaving hers. He was gentle. Warm. 'Because I know how. Because I love you.'

She frowned but didn't pull away. He had drawn her into him with those eyes of his. They were hypnotic. 'What can you do to help me when no one else can? When no one else will?'

He looked at her, unblinking. 'I know of a book.'

***

Edela woke, gagging. It was as though something was stuck in her throat, or perhaps it was just that she was so parched after days of sleeping that she could no longer swallow properly.

'Grandmother!' Jael grabbed her hand as Aleksander helped her to sit up. Biddy hurried away to get some water. 'Take a deep breath. You were having a dream.'

Edela blinked, unsettled, confused, her thoughts slowly tumbling back into place. She was on Oss, with Jael. And Aleksander.

Her breath started flowing more steadily now, and she felt her chest loosen as she reached for the cup Biddy held out to her. 'Oh,' Edela sighed. 'Oh...'

'Was it a bad dream?' Aleksander wondered.

Edela frowned, brushing strands of silvery hair out of her eyes. 'Bad?' She stared at him, uncertain. 'No, I wouldn't say so.' She took a long drink of water. 'No, not bad. Perhaps helpful. Another breadcrumb, but I can't quite make sense of it yet.' Edela peered around at the worried faces, unsettled anew. 'What is it?' She noticed Eydis for the first time. 'What has happened?'

'I think it's time to tell Jael everything, Edela,' Aleksander said somberly. 'Eydis has had a dream. I'm afraid we might be too late.'

CHAPTER EIGHT

'But why?' Axl asked for the third time. 'Why put yourself in unnecessary danger? If you don't think I can protect myself from Osbert, what hope do I have against Haaron and his sons?' He paced around anxiously, too irritated to stand still. It wasn't only Jael who'd inherited the Furyck temper.

'You don't know Osbert,' Amma tried. 'He's not normal!' She reached for Axl's hand, trying to calm him down. 'I've seen him watching you. He thinks Gisila is pushing you forward to be my father's heir, to take his place!'

Axl laughed. 'How can he possibly think that? *How*?' His eyes darted amongst the trees, checking for intruders upon this, which was supposed to be their final goodbye. 'But even if that were true, what did you think you were going to do to stop him?'

'Oh, I can stop him,' Amma said with determination. 'He's a bully, but he's also a coward. And I'm not about to let him hurt you.'

Axl looked down at his cousin, at all the fire in her usually gentle eyes, and he burst out laughing. She looked cross as he took her face in his hands. 'I'm not sure I've ever been happier,' he smiled. 'To know that there's someone who thinks I'm worth saving. With her own two hands.' His face was suddenly serious as he leaned in. 'Thank you, my sweet Amma, for wanting to save me.' He kissed her softly.

'What do you mean?' she wondered when he stepped back.

'Your mother, Edela, Jael... they all think you're worth saving. Aleksander, Gant...'

Axl shook his head and walked away from her to where his horse stood. He stroked her long dark mane, reminded of his father. 'I'm not sure that's true,' he murmured. 'Not really. You see, I'm not Jael.' He turned to face Amma. 'Ranuf never saw any value in me. All his attention was on Jael, as though she were his prize possession. He barely even noticed I was there. My mother and grandmother felt sorry for me, and Jael ignored me because I was her little brother. Because of Tuura,' he shuddered. 'And Gant and Aleksander just put up with me, because what else were they to do? I was the son of the king, the heir to the king, but no one knew why!' He looked at her sadly. *'I* don't even know why! When Ranuf had Jael? Why did he choose me?'

Amma could see the pain in his eyes. She didn't know what to say.

'But he made a mistake, didn't he? Because when he died, no one believed in me. No one wanted me to be king. None of his men, not even Gant! They turned their backs on me and went to Lothar. Lothar!' he cried. '*Lothar* over me! And you love me, Amma, but you think you need to come to Saala to protect me from Osbert. Osbert, who is a spineless coward, just like his father. Who will be king over me, just like his father, unless I do something to earn everyone's respect. To show all of them that I'm a Furyck. Ranuf's son. Not just some spare, accidentally made his heir. But that there was a reason behind his choice.' His voice trailed off into the silence of the forest. 'Not just a mistake...'

Amma hurried towards Axl and wrapped her arms around his waist, clinging to his shaking frame. 'I'm sorry.'

He stroked her hair. 'No, I'm sorry,' he sighed, bending his head towards hers. 'I just want a chance to prove myself. I've never had a chance to step away from all their long shadows before.'

Amma looked up at him. 'Well, you have a chance. No one can stop you, not now.' She gripped his hand. 'I believe in you.'

Axl smiled, pulling her closer, his head full of memories of his father and Jael and their shared disappointment in him, barely listening as Amma murmured into his chest. He was too busy thinking of how he would show them all how wrong they had been.

***

'Gone?' Edela's face grew even paler. 'Are you sure?'

'Yes,' Jael murmured, her lips barely moving. 'He was seen leaving early this morning. On a ship. To Rikka.'

'Oh.' Edela's eyes were weary, but as she glanced around at Eydis, Jael, Aleksander, and Biddy, she felt the urgency of the situation. She pulled the bed fur up to her shoulders. 'There is so much to tell you, but don't worry, we are not too late,' she said with a reassuring smile, patting Jael's hand. 'Because you are still here, and so am I.'

'Well, then, why did you go to Tuura of all places?' Jael asked desperately, hating even the feel of that word on her tongue.

'To follow the breadcrumbs,' Edela sighed. 'Of which there were many.' She leaned back against the pillows and told them about her dreams of the beheaded girls, of the taunting voice that came to tease her with threats of darkness. Her visits to the temple.

The book.

The sword.

Jael's mouth fell open. 'My sword was made three hundred years ago?' She shook her head. 'For me? *Me*?'

'More than three hundred years ago. Nearly four hundred. And yes. For you.'

Jael sat back on the bed in shock. 'But why? What am I supposed to do with it?'

'Now that I don't know,' Edela frowned. 'We had to leave Tuura before we had all the answers.' She glanced quickly at Aleksander. Jael didn't need to know about his mother's role in any of it. Not yet. Neither of them were any closer to discovering what part Fianna Lehr had played in that night in Tuura, or what reason she might have had to harm Jael. There was no need to complicate things just yet.

'There is a prophecy,' Aleksander began, sensing Edela's energy fade. 'About you. The elders know of it, but they wouldn't tell Edela what it says or what is supposed to happen. All we can do is assume that something bad is coming. Tuura is turning into a fortress. You wouldn't recognise it. They have an army, soldiers, walls higher than a castle. And they made that sword, for you.'

Jael fingered the round moonstone that sat at the very tip of her sword. *Toothpick*. The sword Edela had given her the day she married Eadmund. 'Is Eadmund in danger?' Jael asked suddenly.

Edela shook her head. 'No, not that I know of.' She coughed, and it rattled her bones. 'No, this is not about Eadmund. You are the one in danger.'

Eydis' eyes were wide as she listened. She hadn't wanted to intrude. She'd wanted to leave with Fyn and Thorgils, but Jael had insisted she stay.

'Danger from what?' Jael wondered.

Edela, tiring fast, blinked at Aleksander, who continued the story. 'From Evaine Gallas. And her mother, Morana.'

Eydis gasped. 'Her mother?'

'She wasn't raised by her, was she?' Edela asked. 'But she is living with her now?'

'Yes,' Eydis said quietly. 'And that is where Eadmund has gone.'

'But why?' Biddy wondered. 'Why did he just leave without a word? That's not like him at all.'

Jael raised an eyebrow in her direction.

'Well, not anymore it's not,' Biddy insisted. 'Not for a long time now. Not since you cured him.'

'The baby,' Eydis said. 'Morac told him about the baby. Evaine has had a little boy. That's what I saw.'

Jael felt as though she was caught in a gathering storm. She couldn't think for all the noise swarming around her head. 'I suppose that's why Morac came.'

'Morac?' Aleksander looked puzzled.

'Morana's brother,' Jael explained. 'Evaine's father, or at least he has raised her as his own. I've no idea who he truly is to her now.' She shook her head. 'But whatever the family connections, why does this Morana want to kill me? It's obvious why Evaine would, but what does her mother want with me?'

'We don't know,' Aleksander admitted with a sigh. 'The prophecy, if we could ever find it, might tell us. It would explain what your purpose is. The purpose of the sword. But without it, all we have are Edela's dreams. And they've not been helpful lately, have they?'

Edela shook her weary head. 'No. I sleep most nights with that evil voice trapping me in dark places. It's as though she's stopping me from getting to my real dreams, the dreams I need to be having. I do not see as much as I used to. Not about what I need to, at least.' She reached out and took Eydis' hand, a twinkle in her eye. 'I think I could use some help from you, Eydis. Together, perhaps we can find our way to more answers. To help Jael. And Eadmund.'

Eydis blinked. She couldn't help, could she? She trembled nervously, then remembered her dream of Eadmund and Evaine. If there was something she could do to stop it happening, she would.

Anything to stop *that* from happening.

***

Gisila clung to her son, her tears flowing like a spring stream. She couldn't stop them. Axl was all she had now. He was just a boy, she thought, ignoring the fact that he towered over her and had filled out recently to look just like every other man he was going into battle with. But he was her boy who had loved her so much; who had always been kind to her when Jael had ignored her in favour of Ranuf. Axl had been all hers. And Gisila had doted on him. Perhaps that had been a mistake? Would he be too soft to do what he needed to survive?

It was hard to watch his mother cry, to feel her chest heaving against him with such pain. But at the same time, Axl wished she had a little more faith that he would survive what was coming; that his death wasn't the foregone conclusion she appeared to think it was. 'I will see you in Saala, Mother,' he reminded her, easing her out of his arms, imagining Gant's impatient eyes boring holes in the back of his head.

It was a dull, grey morning, and the sky was already threatening rain, but as miserable as the day promised to be for their ride, he couldn't have been more excited to begin.

'Yes, of course,' Gisila sniffed, wiping her eyes with a very damp cloth and stepping back. She looked quickly at Gant, who gave her the slightest of nods as he mounted his enormous white horse. 'But we'll not have the chance to say a proper goodbye there. You'll not have time for me then, I'm sure.'

'Mother!' Axl put his hands on her shoulders and bent down to kiss her wet cheek. 'I will be fine. I'm a Furyck. Never forget that. Just look after yourself. Keep safe.' He straightened up, gave her a crooked smile only half-filled with bravado, and swung himself up onto his saddlebag-laden horse. Adjusting himself in the saddle, he turned his horse's head away, following Gant. Axl knew that Amma was there, with Lothar, but they had said their goodbyes, and he did not wish to do so again in public.

Osbert looked away from Gisila's miserable face, back to his father, trying to take in some of what he was saying. Lothar was issuing random, last-minute orders, suddenly frantic to ensure that everything would be perfect for his own arrival in Saala. The bulk of their forces were leaving now. They were taking the heaviest of their weapons, horses, food, servants, and some of their women, who would cook and clean and comfort as required. Lothar would follow in a ship, bringing more weapons and supplies, and Amma and Gisila. It was a much more comfortable way to travel, and quicker too. Their journey would take only two days, whereas the marchers were facing six long days on the road.

Osbert had been annoyed to find out that he wasn't accompanying Lothar on board *Storm Chaser,* but then again, his father had tasked him with leading their men into battle, and it made sense for him to show his endeavour and willingness to lead from the start.

'You will listen to Gant,' Lothar muttered, trying to loosen his stubborn belt, which had tightened considerably after his large breakfast. 'For all your eagerness, you lack real experience. And without me there to guide you, I have instructed Gant to watch over you. So, if he thinks you need a kick back into line, he has my authority to do so. Understood?'

Osbert frowned, cross at the public rebuke; crosser still at the smile that grew on his sister's face as she listened next to him. 'Of course, Father,' he muttered.

'Good!' Lothar exclaimed with a relieved grunt as he finally undid his belt, his bloated guts sagging contentedly over his straining trousers. 'Then you had better hurry up, as everyone appears to be leaving without you!' He gave Osbert a brief nod and turned to Amma, who was suddenly downcast, having just caught a glimpse of Axl's excited face as he followed Gant through the gates. 'Do not worry my dear,' he assured her, squeezing her hand. 'Your brother will be fine. He is a Furyck, and Furycks do not fall in battle!'

Amma forced herself to smile, but her father wasn't even looking. He was already waddling towards Gisila. Amma sighed sadly, fighting the urge to run after Axl and remind him about Osbert. She knew better than anyone that all of Osbert's weaknesses added up to make him a very dangerous enemy indeed.

To both of them.

***

'And over here?' Jael wondered, pointing to the line on the map that marked the cliffs of Osterhaaven, the land her Furyck ancestors had abandoned eight-hundred-and-fifty years ago when a devastating series of volcanic eruptions had rendered it an uninhabitable lump of ash-covered rock. 'How far can we go before we risk the ships?' Jael was trying to keep her mind on the meeting she and Eirik were having with the helmsmen, but it kept wandering back to the things Edela and Aleksander had revealed.

Too many things.

She couldn't get them out of her head as they fought each another, vying for her attention.

'There are deep shelves of rock there,' Villas, a craggy-faced helmsman mumbled, pointing at the map. He looked at Otto, ignoring Jael entirely. 'We need to stay a good distance from the cliffs. At least three to four ship lengths to be safe.'

Jael frowned. She could certainly see a way things might work. In theory. But theories didn't matter much in battle. Still, there was hope now that they had the sea-fire; hope they could survive Haaron's arrows. Of which, there would be many.

'Perhaps we divide the fleet?' Eirik wondered.

'Well, that was my thought before, but now we have the sea-fire –'

'If it works,' Otto interrupted.

There were a few nods and grunts from the grey-and-white heads around him. It appeared that being a helmsman was an older man's game on Oss. Or perhaps it was that the sea weathered you quickly, like the barnacled hull of a fisherman's boat. Whatever the case, there was not much interest amongst the gathered men in what Jael thought about anything, apart from Beorn, who happened to dislike Otto intensely and was happy to support anyone leading his ships into battle who wasn't him.

Jael glared at Otto, ready to unleash her temper upon anyone who pushed just a little too hard. 'You've *seen* that it works,' she said harshly, 'so I'm not sure why you'd say that. We just need to ensure that the jars stay safe, so we don't explode. And Beorn has already found a simple way to do that.'

'And the catapults are easy enough to put together,' Beorn added. 'We've tested *Sea Bear* with everything on board, and there's not much loss of steerage at all. It will be a bit tougher on the arms, but the men have been training for that. We'll be ready.'

'And the final sails?' Jael wondered, remembering that they were still waiting on two sails to be completed. It took months to weave a new sail out of thick, homespun wool, and Beorn had only realised halfway through winter that two of their sails had rotted through.

'Almost done,' Beorn assured her. 'My wife is overseeing the weavers. She thinks they'll be ready later today.'

'That's good to hear,' Eirik smiled. His confidence had risen after Aleksander's demonstration, and despite his own misgivings, he was eager to leave for Saala. 'We'll meet at the beach tomorrow afternoon, then, once the sails have been fitted. Jael and I can go over the ships together.'

Otto rolled his eyes at Villas.

Eirik chose to ignore him. He had more things on his mind than needing to sort out petty squabbles and soothe bruised egos.

The men nodded and left, mumbling to each other from pursed, hairy lips.

'Are you sure you don't want to reinstate Otto?' Jael wondered with a sigh.

'They'll be fine,' Eirik insisted, taking his cup of ale up to his chair. 'When the battle is underway they won't care whose voice is commanding them. Those old fools certainly can't think for themselves anymore! And I wouldn't trust them to either. Especially Otto. Not after last time.' He grimaced as he bent into the soft furs, feeling older by the day.

Jael didn't look convinced as she turned towards him, her face troubled.

'What has happened?' Eirik wondered. 'And where's Eadmund?'

Jael blinked, grasping for an answer that would stop Eirik exploding like a jar of sea-fire, but her mind remained completely blank.

***

As much as Edela needed to sleep, she knew that she'd been sleeping for too long. Perhaps it was too late now, for Eadmund at least. But what about Jael? The elderman had told her that she was the only one who could save Jael.

But how?

She glanced at Eydis, who was sitting beside her, stroking one of the dogs. The grey one. Edela didn't know its name. Aleksander had gone down to the beach to check on his men. Biddy had disappeared to milk the goat. 'You know this girl, Eydis. Much better than I ever will. I'll need you to help me so I can help Jael.'

Eydis raised her head, turning it towards Edela's ragged voice. She sounded tired, Eydis thought. 'But you are a true dreamer, and I'm just a...'

'A what?'

'I've had no training, apart from a little help,' Eydis insisted. 'Entorp... he is a good friend, but he's not a dreamer.'

'Is he not?' Edela mused. She couldn't remember the man who

had brought the stinking salve. He had slipped away and never returned. 'But he is Tuuran. And wise. And useful to both of us, I'm sure. He may also have saved my life. You must take me to him soon so that we can all talk together. We three are Tuuran, and we must protect Jael from whatever those women are planning,' she said quietly. 'I'm certain I won't be able to do it alone.'

***

Jael's eyes bulged like a startled deer. 'Eadmund... is...' She swallowed, staring at Eirik, whose frown was starting to consume his entire face. 'Gone.'

Eirik felt his body tense. 'Gone?' He put his ale to one side, ignoring his sudden desire to drain the whole cup. 'Gone where?'

'Rikka.'

Eirik's eyes narrowed into slits. '*Rikka?*' He shook his head. 'This is Morac's doing!'

'Morac?'

'How else did Eadmund get the idea to go to Rikka?' Eirik was furious; furious that he hadn't just booted Morac straight off the island. That was obviously his reason for coming: to turn Eadmund towards that girl again. He clenched his jaw. 'And did you not try to stop him?' he asked irritably.

Jael stared at her father-in-law, still too shocked to feel a thing. 'He was gone when I woke up.'

Eirik shook his head. 'This is a bad thing, Jael,' he muttered. 'Why did he have to do this now? When we're leaving in a few days! When all our attention must be on the battle with Haaron!' Eirik glanced around, but there were only servants nearby and none who were foolish enough to stop and listen.

'It does not have to be so bad, does it?' Jael tried to convince them both. 'Perhaps he'll just visit and return quickly? Maybe he was just curious about the baby?'

Eirik rolled his eyes and took a long drink. 'Morac wanted me to have her back. That girl. To have her and the boy here so they could get away from the witch, Morana. I refused.'

'Morana?' Jael looked puzzled. 'Why does Evaine want to get away from her? I thought Morana was her mother?'

Eirik spat a mouthful of ale all over his tunic. He lurched out of his chair, seized Jael by the arm and pulled her through the green curtain, towards his private chamber.

Once inside, he closed the door quickly, leading Jael to the inviting fire and the fur-covered chairs that waited there, far away from the ears that would no doubt be pressing against the door before long.

'What do you know of Morana Gallas?' he hissed as they sat down. 'Why do you think she's Evaine's mother?'

'My grandmother told me,' Jael said. 'She had a dream about her. That she meant me harm.'

'Who? Morana?' Eirik frowned. 'Well, she's so broken and twisted that I believe she means everyone harm. And yes, if she thought you were standing in Evaine's way, I imagine she'd do anything to remove you.'

'You know her well, then?'

Eirik sighed, falling back into the past, into memories he no longer wanted any part of. 'We were... lovers for a time. At different times. She was captivating when she was younger. But always strange.' He stared into the flames, uncomfortable with such talk. 'Morana wanted to be my queen, but I married Odila, which incensed her, although we continued to be together because Odila was not... very interested in me. But then I saw Eskild, Eadmund's mother, and from that point on no other woman existed. Of course, you know what happened to Odila after I divorced her.' He glanced at Jael, embarrassed. 'But Morana... she just disappeared into herself. Into her books. Turning herself slowly into a true witch.'

It started raining again, but Jael barely noticed the big drops as they fell down the smoke hole, splashing onto the flames. Her eyes were fixed on Eirik's tense face.

'I didn't care, nor even notice, but she gradually developed a reputation. People began seeking her out when they wanted help to take revenge. Small things. Petty squabbles,' he muttered. 'But she was Morac's sister. We had all grown up together, taken care of each other. I turned a blind eye when people brought their fears to my attention, which I shouldn't have done.'

'Why?'

Eirik leaned forward, his arms resting on his knees, his head heavy in his hands. 'She killed Eskild.'

Jael's eyes widened in shock. 'What?'

'I couldn't prove it. To this very day, I cannot prove it. But I know she did. It was her revenge upon me. And my mistake.'

'But why? How?'

'Eskild asked me to get rid of her. Morana had never been nice to anyone, but she hated Eskild most of all. Eskild endured it, but what she couldn't endure was what Morana was getting very good at doing. Dark things, hurting people. Helping people hurt others with her magic. So, finally, I sent her away,' he said. 'I never wanted to know where she went. Morac took care of it. I would've had her killed if not for him.' He sighed, the regret a deep wound, still fresh. 'A few years later, she sent word to him that she was carrying a child. A child she didn't want. She offered it to him. They had struggled for children, Morac and Runa.' He frowned, remembering what Morac had told him about Fyn's parentage. 'Morac was eager to take the child and raise it as their own. I didn't like the idea. But Morac... I owed him a lot. There were many debts to repay,' Eirik said mutely. 'They left for a few months, and returned with this baby.' He shook his head. 'It was never right, though, her daughter being here. And now look at what has come from it. And somehow, I know, this was Morana's plan all along.'

Jael was caught between wanting to tell Eirik everything that Edela and Aleksander had revealed, and not wanting him to feel worse because of it. She bit her lip. 'But why do you think Morana killed Eskild? If she wasn't on Oss, how did she do it?'

'Eskild fell through the ice.'

Jael blinked, surprised. Surprised too, that she didn't know that already.

'Why was she on the ice?' Eirik asked sadly. 'That is a question I've never been able to answer.' He stared intently at Jael, his eyes tight with pain. 'Eskild had started acting strangely. Having terrible dreams. Seeing things that weren't there.'

The wind whistled mournfully down the smoke hole. Despite the heat from the fire, Jael shivered.

'I was too busy planning an invasion of Brekka. Preoccupied. She was pregnant, you see.' His eyes were misty as he turned them towards his lap. 'I thought that was the reason. We had lost twins the previous winter. A boy and a girl. Eskild had not recovered. She was not right.' He picked at his fingernails, his voice slowly disappearing. 'Someone saw her wandering across the ice. She was far out, so far away from the beach, heading for the spires. They found Eadmund, and then me, and we went after her, but it was too late. She went through the ice. We couldn't save her.' Eirik's voice wobbled as he rubbed his eyes.

'I'm so sorry,' Jael said softly. 'And you think Morana twisted Eskild's mind? Led her out there somehow?'

'I do. I always have. I blamed her in drunken rages, but everyone thought I was going as mad as Eskild had.' He swallowed hard. 'They thought that... that she had killed herself. Just like Odila. They thought that the gods had put a curse upon me when I killed my father.' He shook his head. 'Perhaps they were right, I don't know. But I do know that Morana killed my wife. Somehow. Eskild had been happy with me. The loss of the babies had broken her heart, but she would have recovered, I know she would have. Morana killed her, I'm certain.'

'And now her daughter has Eadmund's child.'

'Yes.'

Jael shook her head. 'But what can we do?'

PART TWO

Unravelling

CHAPTER NINE

'You underestimate him,' Bayla whispered in her husband's ear.

It was not a gentle whisper. Her voice was heavy with threat.

Haaron could hear her distaste for him, thick and unctuous as it coated her bitter tongue. It made him sad. He still loved her, still wanted her, but she was far away from him; had been for years. His shoulders slumped. 'Well, let us both hope that's true, as Skorro will be a test for him. Varna promises me that.'

Bayla ignored him, smiling at Jaeger who stood waiting near his ship, saying goodbye to Haegen, Karsten, and their wives. He looked as displeased as she did; both of them with their forced smiles, their lips pressed tightly together.

So much pretence, of family.

Berard stumbled into view, nervous and awkward in his ill-fitting mail. He had suffered through a sweating sickness over the winter and had lost a lot of weight. The slimmer figure suited him, but his old mail did not.

'Where have you been?' Haaron hissed impatiently. 'It does not impress your men to be late. At least Jaeger was here early to show some sign of leadership!' He frowned at the large sack Berard was lugging over his shoulder. 'And what's in that?'

'My things,' Berard puffed, trying to catch his breath. 'I wasn't sure what to bring. I didn't know how long we'd be away.'

'Well, hopefully, you won't be away long at all,' Bayla said, one eyebrow arched in her husband's direction. 'The Islanders have never given us much trouble, and the Brekkans haven't dared go near Skorro in years. I'm not sure why anyone thinks it will be such an effort this time.'

Berard's sack was cumbersome. He was yet to marry, and his mother had never been interested in mothering – him, at least – so he'd always lacked a woman's touch. A wife or a mother would have known that clothes were important, that he needn't pack his own goblet, and that he should have packed everything into his chest like the rest of the men.

Haaron gave Bayla a knowing look, and she barely concealed a snort of disdain. Berard sighed, thinking it best to leave them to it. His sack was straining his back, and he needed to get it onto the ship. Hefting the sack higher, he struggled down the pier towards his large brothers and their elegant wives.

Nicolene Dragos didn't look up as he approached. She stood beside her husband, Karsten, dressed in a light-blue silk dress, her blonde hair cascading in long, braided loops across her back, her neck draped in Siluran silverwork of the highest quality. But for all her finery and poise, she was a thin, scowling creature, with no warmth in her sharp face at all.

Nicolene clung to Karsten, but her eyes were fixed on Jaeger. Berard didn't blame her. Most women found it impossible not to stare at his brother. Jaeger was the epitome of what he assumed a man was supposed to look like, with his towering height, his broad, thick shoulders, his chiselled jaw and high cheekbones. Those brooding amber eyes. But for all that he looked the part of a warrior and would-be king, Berard wasn't sure that men were supposed to possess as much darkness as Jaeger held inside his soul.

'I thought we'd have to leave without you, Brother!' Jaeger smiled.

He looked even wearier than usual, if that was possible, Berard thought to himself. But happy. No one looked forward to a battle more than Jaeger, except possibly Karsten, especially if Jael Furyck was going to be on the opposing side. 'I was just trying to gather my things, trying to think of what I would need,' Berard mumbled, dropping his sack to the wooden boards of the pier with a clang.

'What did you pack in there, Berard?' Haegen laughed, winking at his petite wife, Irenna, who stood next to him, her dark hair pulled back tightly from her pale face in a twisted bun. 'We need to find him a wife before it's too late!'

Berard reddened from all their attention.

'Oh, leave him alone!' Irenna scolded. 'I'm sure Berard will find a wife when he's ready. Better to wait for the right woman, than settle for the wrong one. She would only make you miserable.' Irenna couldn't help her soft grey-blue eyes from wandering towards Nicolene.

'It may be too late now, Berard,' Karsten warned. 'Perhaps you're about to meet your end on Skorro?'

Jaeger was quickly irritated. 'Or perhaps Berard will fight Jael Furyck and take an eye from her to bring back for you?'

Karsten clenched his jaw, his clear-blue eye snapping to his youngest brother. 'If Berard could even *find* her face with a sword, I'd drop to my knees, for that would truly be a miracle!'

Jaeger stepped forward.

Berard hunched away.

Haegen stepped in. 'Anyone who gets near Jael Furyck is going to be a lucky man indeed. And that man, whoever he is, will need to be quick with his thoughts *and* his sword, for you'll only get one chance with her.' He turned to Karsten. 'I'm sure you'd agree, Brother?'

Karsten instinctively touched his eye-patch, rage tensing his muscles at the thought of what that bitch had done to him. 'It's a sea battle,' he said shortly, 'so you'd best practice your skills with a bow if you want to get anywhere near her.'

Bayla and Haaron had finally stopped bickering long enough to join the rest of the family. Bayla reached up and dragged Jaeger into her arms. 'Take care of yourself. Please. Don't do anything foolish.' She stepped back and stared up at his scowling face.

'Promise me.'

Jaeger glanced around impatiently. He could see his mother's lip quivering, and he was desperate to be gone before she started weeping. 'I will. Of course,' he muttered. 'Berard, hurry up and grab that sack. We're the last ones now.'

'I hardly think they're going to leave without you,' Haaron growled. There was no affection in his eyes as he considered his two youngest sons. His standards were high. He wanted a victory. How they achieved that, and what they sacrificed to deliver it, he would have to endure. Hopefully, Bayla could do the same, and not blame him for the outcome.

Haaron clapped Jaeger on the arm as Bayla hugged Berard. 'Do not underestimate your enemy,' he instructed. 'You're a Dragos. Remember that. Skorro has never been lost to us. It's up to you to ensure that remains the case.'

Jaeger looked down on Haaron with scorn. He didn't care what his father thought, he tried to convince himself. He would defeat the Islanders, then return to the book.

And then he would destroy his father.

***

Jael wasn't listening.

She had filled the last few days with an endless stream of tasks, determined not to give her thoughts any room to wander.

Towards Eadmund.

She'd kept her head down, barely smiling, not meeting anyone's sympathetic eyes.

News of Eadmund's disappearance had raced around the fort like a furious wind, and no one knew quite what to say to her, which was just as well, as she was determined not to dwell on it for even a moment.

'Are you not listening, then?' Thorgils wondered gently. 'Jael?'

They were standing in front of the fort, deciding whether to take the horses for a ride or if the dark clouds in the distance that threatened a storm were worth paying serious attention to.

'What did you say?' Jael muttered, turning away from the wind to face him.

'I said that it doesn't look good. Perhaps we need to get those ships onto the beach?'

'Agreed,' she nodded, turning back around to run her eye over the grim sky.

'And definitely no ride.'

Jael didn't move or say another word.

Thorgils followed her gaze. He squinted. His eyes had never been particularly strong, but there was definitely a ship entering the harbour. 'You think it's him?'

'I do,' Jael said distantly, desperate to disappear back into the fort. 'We should go and greet him.'

Thorgils' body froze, his face contorting with discomfort. 'Are you sure?'

But Jael had already started walking into the stiff wind, down the muddy hill, towards the beach. Her shoulders were tight, her dark hair whipping behind her in messy braids as she stepped onto the stones.

Beorn had already decided that the ships being tested in the harbour needed to come out of the water. And fast. With Aleksander's help, he was organising the men on the beach to bring them in.

Aleksander turned to see Jael and Thorgils making their way towards him. He smiled sadly. Jael had taken Eadmund's sudden disappearance badly. Her lack of words spoke louder to him than anyone else. He could almost feel the pain of her loss as it mingled with his own.

'Here she comes again,' Beorn grumbled, scurrying away.

Aleksander laughed. 'You're getting very unpopular down

here!'

Thorgils shot him a look that was almost as serious as Jael's and Aleksander turned to see what she was staring at.

'Don't worry, we're bringing those ships in now,' he assured her.

Jael didn't reply as she walked past him, across the stones, Thorgils following closely in her wake.

Aleksander spotted the ship as it suddenly appeared from behind another, rolling its way towards the sandy foreshore. He saw Eadmund in the bow, helping to take down the tall, curled dragon prow. Resisting the urge to follow Jael, he stayed back. There was nothing he could do to make this any better for her.

Jael wanted to rush at the ship as Edrun's men jumped down into the cold water and hurried to pull it onto the beach. She wanted to grab Eadmund, scream at him, demand to know what he'd been thinking. Although a small part of her was relieved that he was back, most of her was ready to throw him to the ground and demand answers.

'Dig your toes into the stones, my friend,' Thorgils advised quietly, sensing Jael's whole body preparing to launch itself at her husband. 'Remember what you always tell me. Don't let your heart overwhelm your head. Keep thinking.' He tapped the side of his own head, his eyes fixed firmly on Eadmund as he jumped down onto the sand, then turned back to the ship and lifted out the small, white-cloaked figure of Evaine Gallas.

Eadmund placed Evaine gently on the beach, checked on the baby she was cradling close to her chest beneath a thick wrap of fur, then ushered her forward.

Towards Jael.

Eadmund swallowed. Jael's face was unreadable.

Thorgils' was not.

Eadmund glanced away, concentrating on helping Evaine navigate the slippery stones and the buffeting wind.

They stopped a few paces before Jael and Thorgils.

Jael dug her boots into the stones, trying to stop the poisonous words she was rolling around her mouth from leaving the tip of her tongue. She shivered as the wind wailed around them; the only noise there was now. The beach was silent. Jael could sense everyone watching. She wanted to scream, but instead, she spoke quietly. 'You're back, then?'

Eadmund coughed, braving his wife's eyes. 'Yes.' He tried to smile. 'We are. You remember Evaine?'

Evaine bobbed her head, barely glancing at Jael.

Jael kept her eyes focused on Eadmund. 'Your father doesn't want her here. He told you that.'

Thorgils could feel himself tensing as he stared at the girl who was almost entirely submerged beneath her cloak as it flapped around her.

'I shall speak to him about it,' Eadmund said calmly. 'Evaine couldn't stay on Rikka. The baby... he is not well. And Morana's cottage... it was no place for a child to be raised.'

Jael's expression didn't alter. There wasn't a drop of sympathy in her hard, green eyes, nor a hint of a smile on her face. 'Well then, you'd better take your visitors up to the fort.'

'I can do that,' Thorgils offered quickly, wanting to give Jael and Eadmund a chance to talk away from that vile girl.

Evaine's eyes flared, and she turned towards Eadmund to protest, but he patted her arm. 'You go with Thorgils. He'll take you to your mother. I'll be along to check on you both soon.'

Evaine blinked rapidly, turning her big blue eyes towards her tiny bundle, pulling her son closer to her chest. She nodded reluctantly, allowing Thorgils to lead her away.

Eadmund watched them go.

Jael stared at him, demanding his attention with the sheer strength of her will. She was angry, so angry that she had to bite her teeth together to stop herself from yelling.

Eadmund turned to her at last. He'd been married to Jael Furyck long enough to know that he'd set fire to a great fury inside her; a fire that looked ready to explode. But no matter the consequences, he knew he had done the right thing.

He had saved his son.

***

'Please,' Runa implored as Fyn headed for the door. 'Don't go just yet. Your father won't be back until much later. He's with Eirik in the hall. Hopefully, he'll be there for the rest of the day.'

'I don't want to be here when he returns,' Fyn said firmly. 'I just came to check on you. To make sure you were alright.'

Runa sighed, reaching up to brush his hair out of his eyes. She was reaching further these days. Fyn was still growing, looking more like a man every day, but she was still his mother, and she wasn't ready to lose him again. 'You've no need to worry about me,' she insisted. 'Your father will return to Rikka soon, to have a house built for Evaine. He'll be staying away for some time. Maybe for good. You can come home.'

Fyn's eyebrows rose. His mother obviously hadn't heard about Eadmund's disappearance and what everyone feared would happen next. He didn't want to disappoint her.

'But you shouldn't even be thinking about that,' Runa said sadly. 'With this battle coming... you should make sure you're doing everything you can to prepare. I want you to be safe.'

Fyn sighed. He'd had this conversation with his mother so many times. She still saw him through Morac's eyes. And Morac had always seen a worthless child. Fyn was grateful that Jael had not. He welcomed this battle, desperate for a chance to rewrite the story that Morac had told everyone: that he was a boy not worth bothering over. A foolish, clumsy boy. Never a man.

Fyn wrapped his calloused hands around the leather grip of his sword. 'Mother... I can't promise you anything, except that I'll stay by Jael's side and follow her orders.'

'Well, that is something,' Runa supposed. 'She'll not let

anything happen to you, I'm sure.'

The door flew open suddenly, banging into Fyn. And there, standing in front of a wind-swept Thorgils, was Evaine; a ghostly creature dressed all in white, a wailing child cradled in her arms.

'Hello, Brother,' Evaine smiled coldly. 'Did you miss me?'

***

Jael stood outside the door, not wanting to go into the house. Edela and Biddy were in there, she knew, and she was reluctant to have their conversation inside, in front of them.

She was reluctant to have the conversation at all.

Jael turned towards Eadmund. 'You should go and check on them.'

Eadmund stared at his wife, not going anywhere. He had missed her. As confusing and strange as it had been to see Evaine again, he'd not been able to stop thinking about Jael. 'Not yet. We need to talk.'

Jael glared at him. 'I don't think we do. Not anymore. That talk should have happened *before* you left. To get *her*.'

Eadmund frowned, reaching out to touch Jael's face. She shied away, her eyes not meeting his.

'I didn't leave to get Evaine,' Eadmund insisted quietly, looking around as Askel wandered out of the stables. He nodded at the middle-aged man, waiting for him to leave before continuing. 'I had a dream about my son. He was in danger. I felt it. I dreamed that he was dying. I had to go.'

'Are you a dreamer now?' Jael scoffed, shaking her head. 'And even if you were, why not tell me? Or your father? Or Thorgils?' Jael's tongue was loosening, and she knew it. She needed to walk away, but she also wanted to know why. Desperately. Why? 'You just left, Eadmund. You left me... without a word.'

Eadmund slumped under the force of those accusatory eyes. He felt muddled. Odd. His thoughts were a scattered mess. 'I needed to make sure he was safe. You would've tried to stop me. You and Eirik. You both would have.' His excuse felt weak, falling short of anything that made sense.

'Well, it doesn't matter now, does it?' Jael said quickly. 'He's here. So why not go and be with him? And her. Make sure they settle in.' She turned and gripped the door handle, her hand shaking in fury. 'It's probably best if you sleep somewhere else, don't you think? For now. We leave in two days. There's no time to think about anything but this battle. I'll have Askel take your chest to your old cottage.' Jael opened the door and disappeared inside, pulling it quickly closed behind her.

Eadmund didn't move. Sadness coursed through every part of him as he stared at the door, smelling the familiar aroma of Biddy's stew, watching the smoke curl out of the hole in the roof. He wanted to go inside. It was his house too. But then Eadmund thought of his son and he turned away. He needed to make sure that Sigmund was alright.

He had to speak to his father.

***

Thorgils wasn't sure who looked more shocked, but as neither Runa nor Fyn were speaking, he found himself standing astride a gaping hole that was widening quickly beneath his feet. 'Eadmund has brought Evaine and the child back to stay,' he tried, hating both the sound and implications of those words.

What had Eadmund been thinking?

That didn't prompt any reaction. Runa and Fyn continued to stare at the crying lump Evaine was clutching to her chest.

Evaine sighed, pushing her way inside, past her brother.

'I must get the baby to the fire,' she said breathlessly. 'It was freezing on that ship!'

Runa swallowed, blinking at Fyn, who appeared ready to leave with Thorgils. She looked at him, pleadingly, not wanting to be left alone with that girl. Again.

Thorgils shunted Fyn towards his mother. 'Well, I'll leave you all to it, then.' He ignored the pained look on his friend's face, turning quickly away into a sudden downpour of rain. 'No doubt I'll see you later!' he called over his shoulder.

Fyn gaped after Thorgils as his mother, spurred into action, at last, hurried to shut the rain outside. She turned to her son, her eyes full of trepidation.

'Do you not even wish to meet your grandson, *Mother*?' Evaine asked irritably. 'Or will you be standing by the door all afternoon?'

Fyn shook himself awake. His mind jumped quickly to Jael. Did she know? 'Why are you here?'

Evaine unwrapped her fur-covered bundle and lifted out a blonde-haired baby. A tiny, whimpering child. Her child with Eadmund.

'Why are *you* here?' Evaine threw back at him as she settled down into a chair by the fire. 'I need a pillow!' she ordered, unpinning her dress.

Fyn looked away, sensing what she was about to do.

'Fyn was pardoned by Eirik,' Runa said quietly as she hurried to grab a pillow from one of the beds that ran around the walls of their lavish house. 'I thought Eadmund might have told you that.'

Evaine looked less than impressed, bending her face towards her son, grimacing as his desperate pink lips gripped hold of her swollen pink nipple. 'Eadmund and I had far too many important things to discuss for him to mention *your* return.' She readjusted the baby's head, leaning back into the chair. 'You live here now?'

Fyn shook his head firmly. 'No, I don't. Not at the moment.'

'Well, that's some good news, at least,' Evaine sniffed. 'Sigmund and I will require peace and quiet. It would do him no good at all to have you bumbling about.'

Runa grimaced, not even wanting to look at the child. She glanced at Fyn, her eyes full of sadness. It had all unravelled so quickly: the pleasure of being in the house, just the two of them.

'Eirik does not want you here, Evaine,' Fyn said bravely. He had grown up terrorised by his younger, demanding, highly-strung sister; cowering with his mother as her violent temper dominated the house. But now? Now, she was a threat to Jael. And he would do anything to protect Jael.

Evaine eyed her brother. 'You've grown so tall,' she purred. 'And with a swordbelt too. Almost a man. But not quite,' she smirked, her face twisting now. 'I can see you over there, shaking in your boots. How will that serve you in battle, I wonder?' She looked down at her baby, cringing at the discomfort of his desperate attempt to feed. He pulled away from her, milk spilling from his lips, grizzling in frustration. Evaine scowled. 'Grrrr! He will never suck for long!' She tried to soothe her miserable son. 'You must find me a wet nurse. Somebody to help with the feeding. I am so weak, I can barely manage to keep him quiet at all.' Evaine glared insistently at Runa, who sighed and finally walked towards her.

'Here,' Runa said reluctantly, holding out her arms. 'Give him to me.'

'And what about Eadmund?' Fyn wondered, not about to let his sister ignore him again. 'What are you planning to do about him? He is married to Jael, you know.'

Evaine stood up, re-pinning her dress. 'Jael?' she smiled. 'Yes, he is.' And her smile grew. 'For now.'

She stared into her brother's blinking eyes and Fyn's heart froze.

***

'Eadmund!'

Thorgils hurried after his friend who had stopped just before the hall doors. Rain was teeming down, and neither one of them had any inclination to stand about in it; not when it was this wild and heavy. Thorgils motioned for Eadmund to follow him around the corner to a small shelter where Eirik kept his milking goats, and where his men would often curl up on a stack of hay after a heavy night of drinking.

Eadmund held up a hand. 'Don't start! I know what you think.'

Thorgils was almost too angry to speak. His mouth made all sorts of odd shapes, his eyes rolling around until he finally found words. 'But...' he spluttered. 'What were you thinking? You've humiliated your wife! Completely humiliated her!' He shook his head. 'She's just about to lead us in our biggest battle, and you've made her look a fool! In front of everyone!' The rain was loud, and the disturbed goats were bleating, drowning out much of the fury in his words, but his hands flailed about with such urgency that it was not lost on Eadmund how angry Thorgils truly was.

'I wasn't trying to hurt Jael. Or humiliate her,' Eadmund said calmly.

'Why leave, then? Without telling her? Why bring that girl back here?' Thorgils asked, gobsmacked. 'You have a wife! A wife who saved you. And you didn't even think you owed her an explanation?'

Eadmund sighed, dropping his head. 'You don't understand...'

'What? Understand what?'

'My son –'

'You really think we should all believe that you went there for *him*?' Thorgils scoffed.

'I had to!' Eadmund insisted. 'Morac told me that he was not doing well. Not thriving. That Evaine was not thriving. Then I had a dream that he was dead. I was too late. I couldn't save him!'

Thorgils could see the pain there, the confusion in Eadmund's eyes, but it barely dampened his rage. 'But Jael...'

'She'll understand in time, I know she will. I love Jael, but Sigmund's my son, my responsibility. I can't just close my eyes to the fact that he exists now. I don't want to. He's mine.'

'And Jael?'

'She's my wife. That doesn't change. Ever.'

'You do *know* your wife?' Thorgils asked. 'She's not taken this well.'

'No.'

'And why should she? It wasn't her fault that Aleksander came. She didn't bring him here or ask him to come. He came, you hated it, so you wanted to punish her!'

'No!'

'She had her old lover here, so you went to get yours!'

'No! This is nothing to do with Jael!'

'But it is, don't you see? She had a choice. Ivaar gave her one. Did she ever tell you that? He would have set her free to go back to Aleksander if she'd backed him as Eirik's heir!' Thorgils cried over the rain, which was thundering down now. 'But she didn't. She chose to stay and help you. To bring you back and save you. And she did. She chose to make her home here, with you. And now...'

'Now?'

Thorgils shrugged his broad shoulders. 'Now, I honestly don't know what she'll do.'

CHAPTER TEN

The laughter was not new.

Edela tried to wrench herself away from the harsh, cackling sound, but she was tied, her arms bound tightly on either side of her. Coarse ropes scoured her skin every time she moved. She tried to quell the panic charging through her body. She tried to breathe in a steady rhythm, but it was impossible. Because she was helpless. And something was coming. Edela could feel it. Not see it. Never that. It was always dark, and she was always alone.

Except for that voice.

'Can you *feel* it? Do you know what that is? What that thudding, creeping, terrifying sound is?'

Edela turned her head to the right, searching for light. Somewhere. Anywhere.

She swallowed repeatedly.

'That is the sound of... me.'

Edela frowned. Confused. Listening.

It sounded like footsteps, heavy and ominous.

'I am coming, Edela. I am coming for you,' the voice rasped. 'You think you can stand in my way? *You*? You will need more than a blind girl and an old man to help you. To stop me? You will need an army!'

***

'We need to talk about Eadmund.'

Jael sighed, her shoulders so tight they barely moved. She stared at the pale-blue sky as the sun rose over the harbour, serenely calm before them after a stormy night. 'We're leaving tomorrow.'

'Exactly,' Eirik said quietly. He, like Jael, had been too disturbed by Eadmund's return to sleep much. 'It cannot stay like this. He slept in the hall last night.'

A small part of Jael felt some relief at that. 'You think I should smile and welcome him home?'

Eirik frowned. 'I don't think that at all.' He stared at his motionless daughter-in-law. He'd never seen her look so troubled. 'But Eadmund believes his reasons are sound. He thinks the boy would not have survived there, with that witch.'

'He went against you.'

'He did. And I would happily put both the girl and her child back on Edrun's ship and return them to Rikka today.'

'You can't.'

'I know,' Eirik admitted ruefully. 'It would only make things worse. So, it appears that we are in a bind, you and I.'

'If we choose to be, then I suppose we are.' Jael glanced at Eirik, her eyes grainy and tired. 'We're leaving tomorrow, though. I can't think about any of it. Not Eadmund or her or the boy. We're leaving tomorrow, Eirik.'

The attack on Skorro. It was all that mattered now.

She had to get Eadmund out of her head.

***

Edela took a deep breath and steadied herself against Aleksander's arm.

'I don't think this is a good idea,' Biddy grumbled behind them.

'I'm warmly dressed!' Edela retorted. 'And we won't go far, will we?'

'We definitely won't go far,' Aleksander promised as he led Edela through the door, shooing Ido and Vella out of their path.

Biddy sighed as she watched them go. 'Well, don't be long!' she called anxiously. 'It's very cold this morning!'

They didn't turn around, but Aleksander smiled. 'I've missed that voice,' he chuckled. 'Calling out to me every time I leave. She doesn't change!'

'No,' Edela agreed. 'Which is a good thing, don't you think? Being cared for?' She squeezed his arm, inhaling the many unfamiliar scents of the fort as she looked around. 'So, here we are on Oss. Not exactly where either of us would choose to be, but be here we must. For Jael.'

The line between Aleksander's dark eyebrows deepened. 'Especially now that Evaine's here.'

'Mmmm,' Edela mused. 'She is indeed, so now I must find out all about her. I'm looking forward to that.'

'You are?' Aleksander was surprised. Edela had been so weak since they'd arrived, but he could sense the first signs of strength returning now. It made him smile.

'That voice in my dreams,' Edela croaked, straightening up. 'Whoever she is. She wants to intimidate me, to frighten me. But if she thinks she can do that, she doesn't know me at all.'

Edela froze suddenly, and Aleksander peered at the ground, but there was nothing there. Looking up, he saw a girl walking with Eadmund. Walking towards them.

Edela urged Aleksander onwards.

'Edela,' Eadmund smiled awkwardly as he came to a stop. 'It's good to see you up and about.'

'Thank you,' Edela said. 'I've gotten stronger very quickly, thanks to Biddy and Entorp.'

'I'm glad to hear it,' Eadmund mumbled, avoiding Aleksander's scowling face.

'And you must be Evaine,' Edela said sweetly. 'I've heard much about you.' She stared at the girl, her blue eyes sharp as they took everything in. She was pretty, Edela thought to herself, but her eyes were cold and wintry, like the pale tone of her flawless skin.

Evaine almost jumped to be addressed so. 'You have?'

'Oh, yes,' Edela enthused. 'Many different people have spoken to me about you, and, of course, I have seen you in my dreams, so I'm pleased to meet you at last. I am Edela, Jael's grandmother. I'm a dreamer, from Tuura.'

Evaine was instantly unsettled by Edela's unblinking stare. She looked at Aleksander instead. 'I don't think we've met,' she smiled.

'This is Aleksander,' Eadmund muttered impatiently, desperate to drag Evaine away before she got herself in trouble. 'He brought Edela to Oss.'

'Oh?' Evaine purred. 'I've heard about you.'

Aleksander didn't know what to make of her. It was hard not to be distracted by her undeniable beauty, but it was plainly surface deep. Her eyes were scheming, and her smile forced. He kept expecting to see her face turn into the scorched mask of darkness Edela had seen. Aleksander nodded briefly at her. 'We should be going, Edela. I don't want you to get cold.'

'Of course, we must hurry along. I have many things to do now that I've regained my strength.' She narrowed her eyes at Evaine, glared sternly at Eadmund, and allowed herself to be pulled away by Aleksander.

Evaine's body tensed as they left. Edela was an old woman, she tried to reassure herself, shaking away the memory of those unrelenting eyes.

Just an old woman.

***

'Well, come on then.' Thorgils jabbed her gently with his wooden sword. 'One final practice? Might make you feel better?'

He was worried. She was so quiet.

Jael stared at Thorgils over the railings, with his lop-sided grin and his mischievous eyes. She didn't want to fight him. Not him. 'I don't think so,' she said, her lips barely moving. 'Besides, you've got Fyn there. You keep going.'

'Oh, no, Jael,' Fyn insisted, trotting towards her. 'I've had far too much of Thorgils this morning. I could do with a break!'

Thorgils eyed him crossly. 'You ungrateful turd! Get out then, and let us show you how real warriors train!'

Jael couldn't help but smile as Fyn frowned, taking Thorgils' bait, stepping towards him with a puffed-up chest. 'You two can have your fun without me. I have to go and check on the ships.' She turned to leave and caught sight of Eadmund helping Evaine across the square, his arm around her back. Fire rose up through her limbs until she felt ready to burst. 'Although...' She turned back to the Pit, her eyes sparking. 'Perhaps I might be tempted, if you were to make it more interesting?'

Thorgils saw Eadmund with Evaine and noted the bloodthirsty look in Jael's eyes. He swallowed. 'Interesting... how?'

***

Entorp was uncomfortable.

His house was small and muddled. He had lived alone for years, in a great pile of curiosities. He hoarded, collected, and experimented with herbs, food, stones... objects of every kind. But there was no order; everything was a scattered mess. It suited him well... until he had visitors.

Edela tried not to look around too much, but she was curious about this mysterious healer, who was wild in appearance but gentle in nature. And Tuuran. 'You're not a dreamer, then?' she wondered, trying to focus on his well-worn face, which was flushed pink with obvious discomfort.

Entorp wasn't expecting that. 'No, no, I'm not.' He glanced towards Eydis, who was sitting quietly on a stool next to him. They were all sitting on stools around a bright fire, each with a cup of small ale in their hands. It was not a well-insulated cottage – its wattle and daub walls needed urgent repairing – but the fire helped.

Aleksander adjusted himself on his wobbling stool. It was tiny and unbalanced, but there appeared to be no better option that he could see. 'So, you cured Edela with magic, then?'

Entorp shook his head. 'I don't really practice magic. Not as you would imagine it. But I do know plants and healing and symbols. There's much in there that is magical.'

'And you have wisdom and knowledge,' Edela said slowly. 'Everything we are going to need to keep Jael safe.'

Entorp nodded, nervously scratching his orange-and-white beard. 'Now that Evaine has returned.'

'Indeed,' Edela said. 'She wants Eadmund for herself. For her child. But is that all? I don't imagine so.'

'Do you know of Morana Gallas?' Aleksander asked.

Entorp shivered as though a cold breeze had slipped past his body. 'I've heard of her. People talk. They tell some terrifying tales.'

The fire spat loudly. Eydis jumped.

'Morana wants to remove Jael as well,' Edela said, stroking one of Entorp's white cats as it weaved itself around her legs. 'Because Jael is meant for something. A Tuuran prophecy says so. The elders would not tell me much, but they did warn me that I was the only one who could save her. I'm certain I'll not be able to do it alone.'

Entorp nodded. 'I agree. I saw Evaine this morning, and she is not the same.'

'No?' Aleksander wondered.

'No, she is not,' Eydis muttered, shaking her head. 'I've seen her in my dreams, and she is powerful now.'

'Yes, she is,' Entorp agreed. 'She has knowledge. From Morana.'

Aleksander glanced at Edela, worried.

'And that knowledge will make her a dangerous enemy indeed,' Edela murmured, sipping her ale, desperate to soothe her ragged throat. She was suddenly exhausted, and her back was aching as she stooped over on the uncomfortable stool. Cold too. But more than anything, she needed to know how she was going to keep Jael safe.

***

Jael was finding it hard to catch her breath. That was a good thing. There was no time to think when you had to focus all of your energy on simply breathing.

Fyn skittered to the right, Thorgils to the left, both taunting her to attack.

Fighting her friends had been therapeutic. Her limbs felt lighter, her shoulders looser. She smiled, firming her grip on the swords.

Two swords.

She hadn't done that in a while.

'I really do need to go and see Beorn,' she said loudly, between breaths. 'Time we ended our little game, wouldn't you say?'

'I couldn't agree more, Jael!' Thorgils bellowed, rushing at her, a smile already curling his hairy lips.

He had a plan.

He feinted to the left, throwing out his wooden sword, but at the last moment, Jael saw the twinkle in his eye. She jerked to the left, leaving Thorgils to fall face first into the mud. The Pit erupted with laughter as Jael stalked towards Fyn, her two swords free for just him now. She swung them around in a twirling movement, teasing him, distracting him.

Fyn didn't even blink as Jael approached. He had a shield, and he used it, butting it towards her, his sword tip poking over the rim, ready to attack. Jael leaned back and kicked his shield as hard as she could, following it up with an explosive battering from both swords. Fyn lost his balance, slipping in the mud. He pushed his leg back, but it was too late, and he was down. He tried to scramble to his feet, but Jael was over him in a heartbeat, her swords across his throat.

She rolled away quickly as a mud-covered, red-headed tree came charging to claim his revenge. Jael skirted Thorgils in a flash, rapping the backs of his legs with her swords, kicking him in the back as he tried to stay upright. Thorgils' legs buckled, tangled, and he tumbled on top of Fyn, who had not hurried to get up after his defeat.

Jael burst out laughing at the sight of Thorgils lying on top of poor Fyn in the mud. She wasn't alone. Their fight had captured the attention of most in the Pit, and the men who stood around watching had enjoyed the show, as they often did when Jael was fighting.

'It's a wonder you have any friends, Jael!' Thorgils called after her as she bowed to him and headed out of the Pit towards Aleksander who was leaning over the railings, smiling at her.

Jael sighed, pleased to see him. 'Let's go for a ride.'

***

Morac looked at Eirik, who looked at Eadmund, who squirmed.

It was Evaine who eventually broke the silence. 'Perhaps you would just allow us to stay until you return from the battle, my lord? Just until then,' she said demurely, her eyes on the floor. 'It would give us both a chance to recover our strength. My mother will care for us, her and the servants. And being inside a warm house will help. With real food too.'

Eirik could see it now when he looked at her.

Morana.

Morana's hair had been fair once; as blonde as sun-dappled snow. But, by the time he had banished her, it had turned half black. Black and white and terrifying to look at; much like Morana when he had last seen her. Eirik shook his head. He didn't want to be devoured by any more memories. Let them come to claim him when he was dead.

They were standing in the hall. Eirik didn't care who saw. It was no secret what Eadmund had done, and he was eager for everyone to see just how opposed he was to this... mistake, on Eadmund's part; opposed, but still fair. It would not look good for a king to throw out a girl and her sick baby, especially as the baby in question was his own grandson. And, of course, Evaine knew that, he could see. He could hear it in her words too. She was clever, but young. And age brought with it many gifts. So Eirik could see through Evaine and her carefully moderated voice, and her solemn demeanour; through her sober attire and her submissive posture. She was a manipulative child, he thought to himself. And Eadmund, unfortunately, had not been old enough or wise enough to see through her from the start.

'You may,' Eirik said at last. As Jael had told him, there was no choice. Not now. Not yet. But in time, they would find a way to rid Oss of Evaine, and with her, Morac, and that bastard son of hers. 'But only until we return. By then, as you say, you will have your strength, so you can return to Rikka. And, if Eadmund wishes, he may visit you and the boy from time to time, in the new, warm house that Morac has promised to build for you both.'

Morac nodded. It was more than he had hoped for, considering how furious Eirik had been. He smiled encouragingly at Evaine.

Eadmund was not sure how to feel. Pleased? Relieved?

There would be time, of course, to change Eirik's mind, because now that he had met his son, he couldn't imagine being without him. He would have to find a way to convince both Eirik and Jael that Sigmund's place was on Oss.

Evaine glanced at Eadmund. She could sense him turning towards her now, his loyalty slowly shifting. It was all starting to fall into place, just as Morana had promised.

***

Jael ran her cold hand down Tig's cold face. She'd missed him. There had been so much for her to attend to, so many distractions lately. He wasn't mad, though, which made a change, as he bumped his head gently against hers.

'Are you sure Eadmund won't mind?' Aleksander wondered.

Jael arched a moody eyebrow in his direction.

'Well, alright then!' he laughed, throwing himself up onto Leada's back. She was a large horse, much larger than Sky; pure white, very agreeable. 'I'm looking forward to taking a good look around this place before I leave. There must be some reason you like it here so much. And besides, I don't imagine I'll be back again,' he added quietly.

Jael hoisted herself up into the saddle. She leaned forward to pat Tig's sleek, black coat, gathering the reins into her lap. Something had shifted when she'd dispatched Fyn and Thorgils in the Pit; she'd started to remember who she was. And this ride would surely help blow away any remaining cobwebs before their departure for Saala. 'Well, who knows what will happen? Perhaps only the gods? Or the dreamers? But certainly not us!'

She smiled at Aleksander and nudged Tig ahead of him. 'I'm supposed to be on the beach, but I've a feeling no one would really welcome me down there anyway. We can check on things before nightfall, ready for tomorrow.'

Aleksander lightly tapped his boots against Leada's flanks, clicking his tongue, and she walked slowly after Tig. It had been an odd, strange time, confusing and heartbreaking, but he couldn't imagine having to say goodbye to Jael.

Not again.

They walked the horses down the muddy street that led to the square, straight past Eadmund and Evaine, who emerged from the hall as they passed.

Eadmund sucked in a sharp breath to see Aleksander on his horse, going riding with his wife. He frowned, barely noticing that Evaine had gripped hold of his arm.

Jael noticed Evaine gripping hold of Eadmund's arm, a satisfied smile on her perfectly-formed face. She turned her gaze toward the gates.

You smug little bitch, she thought, clenching her jaw.

You will not defeat me.

CHAPTER ELEVEN

Meena didn't know why she felt compelled to look.

Jaeger had left. Perhaps never to return? No, he would, she was certain. But, even so, what was she trying to achieve, sneaking about, risking the wrath of her grandmother?

Meena shivered as she pictured his face. It was a face she tried to imagine when she lay in bed at night. Her grandmother hated him – the Bear, she called him – but Meena? Meena was fascinated by Jaeger Dragos. Terrified and fascinated all at the same time; filled to overflowing with confusing feelings that awakened her body in ways that were new and unsettling.

She was determined to do whatever she could to help him. To surprise him on his return.

'And?' Varna's voice boomed around the walls of her stone chamber as she creaked open the door.

Meena jumped, her heart stuttering.

'*And?*' Varna asked again, creeping towards her now cowering granddaughter. 'If you help him... what then? Will he care, do you think? Love you even?' She laughed, reaching for Meena's arm, grabbing it between her bony, gnarled fingers, her long yellow nails digging into Meena's skin. 'Love you? Ha! You foolish girl!'

Meena didn't move. Doing so would only make it worse, she knew.

'And what is in my books that intrigues him so? Is he looking for magic to destroy his father? Is that what he will resort to now? With you as his willing helper? His new *assistant*...'

Meena started tapping her foot. It was the least she wanted to do. Her whole body was screaming at her to move, to do something to feel safe again. She fought fiercely against the desire to simply run away.

Varna didn't notice. 'Tell me, girl! Tell me what he wants with my books. What are you looking for?'

Meena shivered. 'It was, it was n-nothing. He didn't ask me. I just... I... I just... thought I could help him.'

'Help him?' Varna snarled, gripping Meena's arm tighter, her rotting teeth grinding together, her putrid breath warm on Meena's face. 'What is he looking for?'

Meena's lips contorted, opening and closing. Confused. She didn't want to betray Jaeger, but her loyalty had always been solely claimed by her grandmother. Until now. She blinked rapidly, unable to control her eyelids. 'Nothing. Nothing. Nothing,' she repeated. 'Nothing, Grandmother, I promise. Nothing.'

Varna frowned, disturbed by the power Jaeger had already exerted over her weak little Meena. She had seen him in her dreams, twisting Meena into a shaking mess, so she was surprised to see how loyal her granddaughter was being to him.

But Meena was a foolish girl, with little sense between her ears.

It would not be hard to find out what she was up to.

***

Edela was tired, Eirik could tell, but he was the king; the king who was leaving in the morning. He had been as patient as he could, but he couldn't put it off any longer. He needed to hear from her. Desperately.

Eirik leaned forward, holding his hands to the flames. 'You're the third dreamer I've tried,' he began, a crooked smile only just moving his bearded lips. 'The oldest, and hopefully, the wisest.' Any hint of a smile quickly faded. 'I'm hoping you can tell me how I'll die. What you see for my end?'

Edela took a deep breath. 'I see some things,' she croaked, clearing her throat, enjoying the comfort of the furs beneath her back; the warmth of the one over her knees. 'Not all that you would wish to hear, I'm sure, but yes, I've seen fleeting visions of your death. I don't know if any of them are truly helpful to you, if, in fact, you wish to prevent it.'

'You don't think I should try?'

Edela studied Eirik Skalleson, noting the desperation in his eyes, the overwhelming desire to know the truth. 'You will be killed,' she said plainly. 'Do not ask me how. But someone will kill you. The gods will not take you gently. You will suffer. I can see that.'

Eirik could not hold back his shock at the starkness of her words. He shivered, despite the warmth of his bear-fur cloak and the heat from the blazing fire. He had not expected her to know anything. Not really. But there it was.

He didn't know what to say.

'But how?' Edela prompted, studying his distressed face. 'I do not know. But you will not expect it. I have seen your face as you die.' She closed her eyes, suddenly weary, grateful for the darkness that greeted her. Inhaling a deep breath, she opened them again, glancing at Eirik. 'You are surprised?'

Eirik blinked. 'Yes, I suppose I am. It is more than I've known before. Not enough, though. Never enough to truly help me, but... something.'

'You must not worry about death,' Edela tried to reassure him. 'You are old enough to have lived all that you wanted to, surely? To have done those things you could only have dreamed of as a slave child? To have made yourself a king!' she exclaimed. 'A father and a husband. A free man. That is something. Perhaps enough?'

Eirik sighed. 'I might have thought so a few days ago. But now?' He looked around the empty house. There had been hope in this house over the winter, and now it was fading quickly. 'Jael saved Eadmund. Jael and that tincture of yours,' he said quietly. 'And with it, my kingdom. But I fear that everything is about to unravel because of that girl and her son.'

Edela was thoughtful. 'It very well may,' she admitted. 'But often unravelling allows us to start again. It does not necessarily mean an end. Sometimes it is the opportunity for a new beginning. If... if we don't let go of the threads.'

'And if I'm gone?' Eirik asked sadly. '*When* I'm gone... what will happen to everyone? To Eydis and Eadmund?'

'You must never worry about Eydis,' Edela insisted. 'She is loved here, I can tell. She will be protected. Entorp watches over her. Eadmund cares for her. Jael, Biddy. And me. I will be here too.'

'You will?'

'Yes,' Edela smiled. 'I wish to stay here with Jael now. She is going to need me.'

'Is she?' Eirik looked worried. 'And Eadmund?'

Edela stared into the flames, wishing she could hide her face from him, just for a moment. She was never very good at masking her true feelings, much like her fiery granddaughter. 'Eadmund...' Edela swallowed, braving Eirik's eyes once more. 'Eadmund is stronger than you think. Stronger than he realises. It might not seem like it sometimes, but I believe you can have faith in Eadmund. I see him in my dreams. He is a good man.'

'But...' Eirik swallowed, 'is he strong enough for what will come?'

'Yes.' Edela was so certain that she didn't hesitate. 'Yes. He is your son. Do not forget that.'

Eirik wanted some wine. A lot of wine. He had grown impatient waiting for their departure, but now it was coming too quickly. 'And the battle with Haaron?'

Edela dropped her eyes immediately, and he knew.

'The sea-fire will help you,' Edela said, sensing his disappointment. 'And Jael. She knows Haaron and his sons better than she would wish to.'

But Eirik didn't hear her. He was lost in the flames, listening for the sound of the gods as they hurried to claim him; to take him away from all that he loved. Once he would have welcomed it: as a child, when he was nothing; when he was older, and his heart was raw with pain after Eskild had died, and then Rada.

But now?

Now, he needed to stay alive to keep everyone safe. To keep his kingdom whole.

He wasn't ready.

***

They stopped by Ver's Waterfall, named for the God of Nature. It had become Jael's favourite place to ride to since the Thaw. She was mesmerised by the violent fury of the water as it crashed and pounded the rocky shelf below.

'This is a surprise!' Aleksander called over the thunderous noise.

Jael smiled. The tips of her fingers were completely numb in her gloves, as they had been since her arrival on Oss, but the ride had finally cleared her scattered mind, and she felt calmer than she had in days. 'You should see it when it's frozen!'

Aleksander was pleased to see her coming back, talking again. It was a start.

He nudged Leada closer to Tig, stroking her smooth white coat.

'Do you have a new horse?' Jael wondered, turning Tig away from the edge of the falls.

Aleksander looked sad, remembering his horse, Ren, who had died just before Jael left Andala. 'I do,' he said, following Jael as she walked Tig over to a thick patch of white clover. 'Sky.'

'Sky?' Jael mused. 'A mare?'

'She is,' he smiled. 'Sweet and kind, just like you.'

'Ha!' Jael laughed. 'I don't think so.'

'Well, some might not agree, but I do,' Aleksander said seriously. 'I know you better than anyone.' His eyes sought hers, and he was pleased that they didn't run away.

'I've missed you,' Jael almost whispered.

'I know. I've missed you too.'

Jael looked away, hanging her head. 'I never meant for this to happen.'

'This?' Aleksander frowned. 'You mean loving Eadmund?'

This time Jael's eyes did run away.

Aleksander grabbed her hand, smiling at how cold it felt beneath her woollen glove. 'It's alright, I don't blame you. It's alright.' He felt ready to cry because he didn't know if he meant it, but when he looked into those eyes, Aleksander knew that he loved her as much as he did the day she left.

He just wanted her to be happy.

However that happened.

Jael ducked her head, emotions rushing quickly towards her throat, her eyes, rising in her chest. 'You should be... mad at me. I promised you...'

Aleksander shook his head, listening to the roar of the falls behind them. 'You and Eadmund appear to be something made by the gods. How are you to refuse them?'

'I'm not sure I believe that,' Jael insisted, 'or this whole prophecy, sword, Evaine mess. If I could close my eyes and be back in Andala with you, and my father, before any of this happened, I would.'

Aleksander looked at her, squeezing her hand. 'No, you wouldn't.'

Jael frowned.

'Would it be easier? Of course. But you're happy here, I can see that. What Eadmund is doing, I've no idea. And perhaps he doesn't either. But don't forget who *you* are. That girl, Evaine? She's come to kill you. You can't forget that. This prophecy is important. I don't know how or why, but we'll find out. You can't falter yet. Not yet,' Aleksander urged. 'He's your husband. And you're a warrior. Are you really just going to walk away from this fight?'

Jael could feel the familiar heat of Aleksander's hand on hers. She didn't want him to let go. The memories, as they came, were fierce, and Jael found herself lost for a moment. But then she saw Eadmund's face.

Eadmund loved her, she was certain of it.

And she was not about to let him go.

***

Eadmund sat by the fire, holding his son as Evaine fussed over them both. He ignored her for the most part, distracted by Sigmund and the odd faces and gentle sounds he was making. It was a strange feeling to hold something so small and vulnerable; something, someone, who was his. 'Do you think he's hungry?' Eadmund wondered nervously, worried that he was going to drop the baby, who felt floppy in his arms.

Runa peered at Sigmund. 'Perhaps,' she said quietly, her eyes full of despair. 'Here, let me take him to Tanja for some milk.'

Evaine didn't argue or even look at Runa as she took her tiny bundle away to the young wet nurse Morac had found. She was relieved that he was feeding properly now, and not on her, although she was in agony waiting for her milk to dry up; her breasts throbbed painfully beneath the tight green dress which no longer fit her comfortably. 'Will you stay for supper, Eadmund?'

Eadmund shook his head. 'No, there's a lot to organise before tomorrow. We leave at daybreak, so I need to ensure my chest is packed.'

Morac watched from his chair, enjoying the change in his daughter now that she was back on Oss, in a proper house, with Eadmund again. She was simply glowing. 'I should do the same,' he murmured, standing with a groan. 'It's been a while since I looked at my armour.'

'You're going?' Eadmund asked, surprised.

'I am, yes,' Morac nodded. 'Your father asked me, and I've never missed a fight for Oss yet. No matter how things stand between us, I'll be by my king's side, as I've always been.'

Eadmund stood, looking for his cloak. 'Well, that's good to hear. We're going to need every bit of experience we have to get through to Skorro.'

'Mmmm, and your wife, it seems,' Morac said coolly. 'I hear she'll be commanding the fleet.'

Evaine glowered at her father, hurrying to help Eadmund on with his cloak. 'You will come and see us before you leave, won't you?'

Eadmund hesitated, then shook his head. 'No, I don't think so, Evaine. It's best if we say our goodbyes now.'

'I shall leave you to it, then,' Morac muttered, turning away.

'Oh, no, no,' Eadmund insisted quickly. 'No need, Morac. I'll see you when I return, Evaine. And we can talk to my father about what happens next, with you and Sigmund.'

Evaine frowned, gripping Eadmund's hands, wide eyes blinking, urging him to see her, to remember her, to remember how it once was between them.

'Take care of yourself, Evaine,' Eadmund smiled. 'And our son.' He opened the door, slipping through it before she could say another word.

Evaine stared mournfully after him.

'Do not worry, my dear,' Morac whispered, placing his hands on her shoulders. 'It's only the beginning. Be patient now.

Everything is falling into place.'

***

'I'm not sure about this, Eydis,' Eirik grumbled. 'Saala's not the place for you to be, especially with no one to look after you.'

'I'm old enough not to need anyone to look after me,' Eydis insisted as she packed her chest. 'Besides, I'll be taking Boelle. She looks after my things here, so she will look after me in Saala too. I won't need any more than that.'

Eirik glanced around the little bedchamber that Rada had decorated for their daughter. His only daughter. His heart broke at the thought of leaving her before he could ensure that she was safe. Married. Cared for. 'You will be fourteen-years-old soon,' he mused. 'Time to start thinking about a husband.'

'What?' Eydis' mouth gaped open. 'Father? Why do you say that? It's far too soon to think of marriage!' She shook her head. 'No! I don't want that.'

'We both know the gods want me. And soon. You've seen it yourself.'

Eydis' milky eyes rolled away from him.

'Of course, neither one of us wants it to be true,' he insisted. 'But I fear we can do nothing about it. And I worry about what will happen to you after I'm gone. I want to know that you'll be cared for.'

Eydis reached out for his arm, her eyes moist. 'Eadmund will care for me. And Jael,' she promised. 'I'll be safe now you've sent Ivaar away.'

It was not enough for Eirik, though. 'I want to find you a husband,' he said, the idea forming quickly. 'You'll not need to marry him for years, but you could become betrothed. Promised. To a good man. Someone I trust. Then I'll be able to rest easy.'

Eydis vigorously shook her head, but as much as she wanted to argue against the idea, she also wanted to please her father, to put his mind at ease. Sighing, she sat back on her heels. 'I will think on it,' she said eventually. 'For you.'

But Eirik wasn't listening. He was already scouring his memory for suitable candidates, wondering just who he could find to keep his most precious girl safe.

***

Jael wasn't looking where she was going as she wandered towards the gates on her way down to the beach. She'd been running over in her mind exactly how Haaron was going to line up against them. Whether he would attack first or sit back and wait for them to come, trapping their ships under a hail of arrows. Arrows! She needed to check on the fletchers, who were notoriously fussy and far too slow for her liking. Head down and buried under a mountain of half-remembered ideas, Jael ran straight into Eadmund.

He held onto her arms, forcing her to look up.

'What do you want?' Jael frowned, instantly annoyed.

'To talk to you,' Eadmund said quickly. 'Before tomorrow. We won't have time then.'

'About what?' Jael wondered coldly, her eyes meeting his with a crash. 'Your son again?'

Eadmund shook his head. 'No, he is warm and well-fed now. He's as safe as he can be. So, no, we don't need to talk about him. But we do need to talk about us.'

'Us?' Jael scoffed. 'Now you want to talk about us? *Now* is the right time?'

Eadmund glanced around. A gathering crowd of wide-eyed Osslanders stood watching them in the afternoon drizzle, ankle-deep in mud, whispering to one another. 'Come in here,' he muttered, pulling his wife into one of the guard towers by the gates.

Jael reluctantly went along.

There was no one inside the fusty smelling room. The guards appeared to be up on the ramparts.

'I'm sorry,' Eadmund said, closing the door behind them. 'I should have spoken to you before I left. I should have spoken to you at all, but when Morac told me about Sigmund...' Eadmund shook his head. 'Nothing felt the same. I didn't know what to think... what you would think.' He squinted into the darkness, desperately trying to see past the anger in her eyes.

Jael sighed. 'I understand that. I wish I could have had a minute to think myself but with Edela falling ill, leaving for Saala, and Aleksander... it was a confusing time for both of us.'

Eadmund's shoulders dropped, his eyes turning to the dirt floor. He didn't want the reminder.

'Evaine is trying to –' Jael began.

'Trying to what?' Eadmund snapped, lifting his head, suddenly on the defensive.

Jael saw it in his eyes, then, that instinct to defend the mother of his child, and she retreated. 'Nothing,' she said, shaking her head. 'Nothing.'

'Evaine just wants to be here,' Eadmund tried to explain. 'With her mother and father, in her nice house, with a wet nurse, being cared for. Feeling safe. That's all. She knows it's different now, that I'm married to you. That I love you.'

'Does she?'

'This isn't about Evaine, I promise. I left to see my son. I didn't plan to bring him here at all. I know what you think, what Eirik thinks. But he was so small and helpless, and Evaine was struggling in that filthy shack.'

'And Morana?'

Eadmund looked puzzled. 'Morana? She wasn't there. Evaine said she would often be gone for days, disappearing into the mountains, leaving her to fend for herself. She showed no interest in Evaine or the baby at all.'

Hearing footsteps, Jael glanced at the stairs. 'I need to go. I have to see the fletchers, finish packing my chest, find Fyn and Thorgils. And Eirik.' She headed for the door.

Eadmund hurried after her, grabbing her arm.

Jael turned back to him. 'Trust is like a sea of ice, Eadmund. It's unbreakable. Solid,' she whispered, leaning up to his ear, one eye on the stairs. 'But you leaving like that... now there is a crack in the ice. And I for one, don't know what will come of it.' She turned and left quickly, not wanting to talk anymore, feeling the crack widen, burrowing deeper into the water below.

CHAPTER TWELVE

Edela placed a small round stone in Jael's hand.

Jael looked down in surprise. 'What's this for?'

Edela shrugged nonchalantly. 'Just a small stone. Nothing more,' she said lightly. 'But do keep it with you, on you, at all times. Promise me.'

Jael rolled it over in her palm. It was a grey, smooth, ordinary-looking river stone from Andala. Familiar. But it had a symbol inscribed upon it that wasn't familiar at all. Jael stared at Edela, but her grandmother had already turned away towards Aleksander.

'I will not see you again,' Edela said sadly.

'What do you mean?' Aleksander asked, gripping her hands. 'Is there something I should know?' He felt strange.

Edela shook her head. She was still not fully recovered, and her thoughts were jumbled, hurrying out of her mouth in the wrong order. She laughed. 'No, no, I just meant that you will go back to Andala, won't you? Once it's all over.' She reached up, touching his face. He was not as thin as he had been, she was pleased to see, but his cheekbones still jutted out sharply, and his eyes had a sad, hollow look about them. Edela suddenly felt worried.

Who would care for Aleksander if she stayed on Oss?

'Well, I hope that's true, and you're not keeping something from me?' Aleksander smiled, but it didn't reach his eyes. 'If I'm about to meet Vidar, I wouldn't mind some warning!'

'No, I'm not,' Edela said, feeling the clanging bells of uncertainty ringing in her ears. 'And no, you're not. Not that I can see.'

Aleksander leaned in, pulling her bony frame close. She felt cold. He felt sad. He would miss her company; miss helping her, cooking for her, caring for her. 'Thank you,' he whispered. 'For everything.'

Edela felt a rush of emotion as she stepped back and looked up at him. 'Oh, you'll have me weeping like the old woman I am in a moment, so you'd both better hurry up and leave. Biddy and I are looking forward to some peace and quiet!' Edela laughed, shooing Aleksander away before turning back to Jael. 'And you, my Jael...' She reached out for Jael's hands. 'You will be fine, I know it.'

'Oh, so you think you'll see *me* again, then?' Jael grinned, desperately searching her grandmother's eyes for any hint of uncertainty.

'I do,' Edela insisted. 'I wouldn't have risked the Nebbar Straights again if I thought there was no point!'

Jael hugged her grandmother tightly. 'I'm glad. But stay well. Don't go rushing around in the cold, and try to do what Biddy says!'

Biddy rolled her eyes at the likelihood of that happening.

'Keep her safe,' Jael whispered, wrapping her arms around Biddy. 'I know Evaine is after me, but she's dangerous. Keep Edela close.' She stood back and smiled quickly, her face tense. 'I've asked Askel to keep an eye on you both.'

'I can look after myself, Jael,' Edela grumbled, following them to the door. 'You wait and see. That little girl has met her match in me.'

Aleksander hugged Biddy goodbye as Jael bent down to Ido and Vella. They had been unsettled by Eadmund's absence, and their sense that something was not quite right was only growing. They rushed to lick Jael's face as she hugged them both. 'Look after Biddy,' she laughed, trying to avoid their wet tongues. 'I'll see you soon, I promise!' Jael stood up and took a deep breath, turning to Aleksander. 'Well, come on then, let's go and see Lothar!'

Aleksander's body slumped at the thought of that miserable fate as he followed her through the door.

Biddy bent down to snatch the puppies before they could race off after them. 'Goodbye!' she called, fighting the urge to cry as the door closed. They were like her children, both of them, going off to fight. She had cared for them all their lives. Her lips wobbled, then contorted as Ido and Vella started licking her face. 'Get away!' she cried, trying not to smile. 'Get away, you filthy creatures!'

***

'Are you sure?' Ivaar wondered again, his fingers teasing Ayla's nipples. 'You see me returning?'

'Yes,' Ayla shuddered, wishing he would stop. He had exposed her, admiring her body, touching it, exploring it as he chose while she lay there freezing, desperate for the furs, bored with his desires, longing for an end to his questions. She missed her husband. His touch had been soft. Loving. Welcome. 'I have dreamed of that. Of you with your son when he is older, as old as Selene, at least.'

Ivaar smiled, distracted by that image for a moment. 'I'm pleased to hear it,' he sighed, leaning down to kiss her full pink lips. 'But you must behave yourself while I'm gone. And keep your mind on Oss. Always. I want to get back there soon.' He lifted himself on top of her, his face almost touching hers. 'Once you help me find a way out of here and onto that throne, Ayla, you will have your freedom, I promise.' He eased himself inside her, not noticing her grimace of discomfort as she turned her head to the side.

***

It was not much, Jaeger thought as he surveyed Skorro's stone fort from the ramparts. But it would be enough. Enough to keep the Islanders at bay. He did not have a large fleet as the bulk of Haaron's men would be trekking through Vidar's Pass with Haegen and Karsten, but they had arrows. Plenty of arrows. He had checked the stores himself.

Skorro was a small island whose prime position in the Adrano Sea made it one of Hest's most valuable possessions. It sat between the high cliffs of Osterhaaven and the even higher cliffs of Hest. Any ships that made it through the Widow's Peak would face a barrage of arrows from their fleet and the Tower. There was no way through. No way that anyone had found yet. But if they did, they'd have to sail past Skorro where he would leave a well-armed garrison ready to make a final stand.

Once he claimed victory, Jaeger was confident that his position would change. Or would it? Would his father merely blink and continue to ignore him, berate him, humiliate him, as he had always done? He thought of Meena, wondering if she had discovered anything more about the book for him.

Probably not, knowing the strange girl.

Berard stood anxiously beside his brother, watching as their ships bumped gently against Skorro's short pier. He didn't like it here. Too many men. Drunk and angry and full of pre-battle bravado. They looked down at him with obvious scorn. Berard didn't blame them. He was small and his body hunched over, his shoulders having decided many years ago that they would not sit straight and proud. But, he tried to convince himself, there were more ways to win a war than with a sword. And he would just have to find them. 'When will they come, do you think?'

Jaeger turned away from his view of the Widow's Peak. Those ship-wrecking stones had provided Skorro with much protection over the years, but the Islanders knew them; they could navigate the dangerous waters in between. 'Four days. That's what Varna told Father. If she is right with her dreaming anymore, the stinking old bitch.'

Berard frowned. That was a long time to wait. 'And in the meantime?'

'We prepare!' Jaeger growled. 'The men have grown lazy, used to nothing but easy victories against whoever tries to claim this island. Father doesn't test them. The ones he leaves here have no one looking over their shoulders. Until now.' He stared down at his brother. 'Varna sees trouble for us, but we can turn that around. We have four days to prepare. The Tower will signal us as soon as they see the Islanders coming, so we'll need to be ready to spring our trap.'

Berard kneaded his hands together, wishing he was back in the relative calm of Hest; the castle, the food, the sunshine. Skorro was damp and dull, loud and dirty, and, according to Varna Gallas, about to become a very dangerous place to be. He glanced up at his brother, never doubting Jaeger's strength of will to get things done.

But still... fate had a way of finding even the most determined souls wanting.

**

Gant smiled at Axl. He reminded him of Ranuf, who had never enjoyed riding either. Horses got you places quickly, but after nearly six full days of sitting in an arse-numbing saddle, Axl's patience had worn through. His lips were turned down, his shoulders slumped in a self-pitying heap. He was thirsty, cold, tired of being wet, could no longer feel his legs, and was missing Amma.

'You look ready to cry,' Gant grinned.

Axl glared at him. 'And who wouldn't, after spending all this time listening to your terrible jokes. With no escape!'

'Ha!' Gant laughed. 'Going to battle isn't as exciting as you imagined, then?'

'This is hardly battle,' Axl sneered, ducking beneath a low-hanging branch.

'There's much more to battles than blood and glory,' Gant said sagely. 'As you're finding out. And be grateful you're not one of the men who's spent the last six days on his feet, or your horse, who's been carrying your ungrateful arse from daybreak till dusk.'

Axl felt a twinge of guilt as he glanced around at the columns of men struggling behind him, and his horse, who did indeed feel weary beneath his numb arse. None of them had a smile on their faces either. It had rained nearly every day of their journey, and no one was enjoying themselves, especially with Osbert in charge. He had no interest in pacing the men, and he'd pushed them harder than Gant would have.

It was not a promising beginning.

'We'll be in Saala soon,' Gant said encouragingly. 'And we can all rest under Rexon's roof while we wait for your uncle to arrive.'

Axl started to roll his eyes, then stopped, for Lothar would be bringing Amma, and suddenly her idea to come along didn't seem so terrible after all.

***

Thorgils stood next to Fyn and Jael as they considered their ships, which were mostly full now. Eirik's red banner of Ilvari, Ran's three-headed sea monster, breaking slave shackles with her terrifying teeth, flapped angrily from each mast. 'They look impressive.'

Jael wasn't so sure. 'Perhaps. But useful, certainly.'

'Will we have enough?' Fyn wondered nervously. 'They're so wealthy in Hest. Surely Haaron will have built many more ships than last time?'

'I'm sure he has,' Jael agreed. 'But a small army can always defeat a big one, and so the same follows with a fleet. It's all about tactics.'

'And we have some of those, do we?' Thorgils asked, nudging Jael.

'Maybe one or two.'

'I'm glad to hear it,' Fyn said, looking relieved. 'I don't want to die in my first battle.'

'Oh, really?' Thorgils lifted an eyebrow in his direction. 'Feeling picky about how things should go, are we?' he grunted. 'Perhaps you'd like to stay here and hide behind your mother's skirts? Keep your sister company?'

Fyn frowned, fixing Thorgils with a sharp-eyed glare.

He was getting tall, Jael thought, though he still only came up to Thorgils' chin. 'No, I just hope we stand a chance, that's all. I want an opportunity.'

'Ha!' Thorgils laughed. 'You'll have plenty of opportunities, my friend. Opportunities for getting an arrow in your arse, in your eye, or in your bollocks, if you don't keep your shield up!'

Aleksander wandered towards them, eager to get going. 'Nearly ready?' Conditions were perfect for sailing, and as much as he didn't want to say goodbye to Jael again, he didn't want to delay their departure either. In his short time on Oss, he'd discovered that the weather could turn foul in a heartbeat.

'I think so,' Jael murmured. She felt uptight. There were too many things on her mind, and she was worried that she'd missed something. Lives were at stake. Most of Oss' warriors were leaving the island.

And she would be responsible for bringing them back.

Jael spotted Sevrin talking to Otto. No doubt Otto was grumbling about her in Sevrin's ear. Sevrin was the more level-headed of the two, so hopefully, he wasn't taking too much notice. She needed to talk to him before they left. He would remain behind with a small garrison to guard the island, to keep the women and children safe, and, if needed, defend an attack from Haaron if they failed in their own. 'I'll be back,' she said, quickly heading across the stones.

Thorgils peered at Aleksander who was staring after Jael. 'So this is it? We won't see you again?'

Aleksander blinked. 'You'll see me in Saala, possibly. I'll be with Lothar when we arrive and no doubt he'll take a lot of looking after.'

'Well, I'm sure it's for the best,' Thorgils suggested carefully. 'Jael needs a clear head for what we're about to do.'

Aleksander wanted to scream, to shake off the heavy cloak of amenability he had been wearing for too long now. He closed his eyes, taking a deep breath. 'I imagine you're right,' he admitted reluctantly.

Thorgils glanced around. Fyn had wandered off, and they were alone. 'It's not an easy thing,' he said slowly, feeling his own dull heartache creep out from behind its heavily guarded door. 'To have the woman you love taken from you. Married to another man.'

Aleksander stared at him in surprise.

'My woman, Isaura...' Thorgils said sadly. 'I've been without her for eight years now. We were together all our lives and always wanted to be. But she's with a man, married to a man she despises, who is no doubt cruel to her. And she's had to have his children.' Thorgils turned to Aleksander. 'Knowing she's so unhappy and in so much pain? It's too much to live with sometimes. I would kill him, Ivaar, if he were not Eirik's son.' He shook his head. 'Jael was happy with Eadmund and will be again, once she kicks some sense into him. And if you love someone, I think that's all you can wish for them.'

Thorgils relaxed his frown, trying a lop-sided grin instead. 'But what do I know? We may all end up skewered to the bottom of the sea before long!' He shook away all thoughts of Isaura, hiding them back behind their door. Reaching out, he clapped Aleksander on the shoulder. 'Good luck, ' he smiled. 'I hope you Brekkans don't fuck it all up!'

**

Ivaar was gone, perhaps never to return.

Isaura shook her head. Surely that was too much to hope for? Her eighteen-month-old son hung onto her fingers, toddling beside her as she walked back into the hall. What sweet relief it was to know that there was no Ivaar to demand anything from her with those cold eyes of his. She allowed herself a small smile, then frowned. But what of Thorgils? If there was a chance that Ivaar might never return, there was also a chance that Thorgils might meet a similar fate. She felt her heart clench in fear, her eyes locking on Ayla who was playing with her three daughters at the back of the hall.

Isaura didn't like the woman. She wasn't jealous that Ivaar spent many more nights in Ayla's bed than hers these days; she was grateful for that. But why was she here? Why did she stay? The mystery of that had gnawed away at her for well over a year now. Isaura didn't trust her, but perhaps, despite all of that, perhaps Ayla could help her? She was a dreamer, after all.

Isaura patiently walked Mads down to the back of the hall. 'Ayla,' she called softly. 'May we speak?'

Ayla froze. Isaura never spoke to her. Ever. Unless it was to scold her. She looked up and saw the desperation in Isaura's eyes; the nervous twitch as she ran her fingers through her long golden hair. 'Of course, my lady,' she said quickly, bobbing her head.

'Girls, take your brother to Selda for me, please. Ayla and I must speak in my chamber.' Isaura handed Mads over to her eldest daughter, Selene, ignoring his grumbles.

Ayla found herself smiling sadly. In the end, no matter what someone thought of a dreamer, they would always come seeking advice.

***

Morac could see that no affection was forthcoming as he stood rigidly before his wife. Runa had barely looked at him since his return, and even less so since Evaine's. It saddened him, but his mind was on getting to Saala now. He would find a way to make things right with her once he returned. 'Take care of yourself, Wife,' he said, nodding curtly before stalking away to where Eirik stood, helping Eydis into *Sea Bear*.

Runa was relieved Morac was leaving. She felt nothing for him except hatred for what he had done to Fyn; for the way he had treated *her* son. In the past, she had given in to her own guilty feelings, thinking that Morac had a right to treat the boy badly because of his own hurt over her betrayal. But no more. Fyn was her only family now. Morac and that evil little witch had brought them nothing but pain.

'I have to go, Mother!' Fyn called, hurrying towards her. He'd barely slept and had been desperate to leave since first light. He just wanted to get underway, hoping that his nerves would ease once they were out on the water.

'Yes, I know,' Runa cried, pulling him to her, trying not to think about all the things that could go wrong; all the reasons that might stop him from returning to her. She squeezed Fyn tightly, feeling the strength in his arms, sensing his desperation to escape her embrace. He was a man now, she knew, but she could feel fear coursing through his limbs as she clung to them. 'Please, my darling boy, please come back to me.'

Fyn tried not to look at her tears as they cascaded down her anxious face. 'I will, Mother, I promise I will,' he said with more certainty than he felt. He had never been so nervous about anything in his life. It was going to be his greatest test.

But what if he failed it?

***

They sat on opposite sides of the only table in the room.

It was a warm, intimate chamber, and Isaura had made it hers alone. She spent many peaceful afternoons here; the children playing at her feet on thick furs while she sat at the table, stitching colourful patterns onto pieces of cloth. Sometimes they would be turned into a hanging for one of the walls, other times it was for no purpose at all. It helped to focus her mind on something useful and stopped it from wandering back to Oss.

'You are loyal to Ivaar,' Isaura began, staring at her clasped hands, uncomfortable in Ayla's presence. 'Perhaps you will tell him about this conversation?' She looked up, blinking nervously.

Ayla sat completely still. Her sleek dark curls hung unbound over her simple blue dress as she studied Isaura. 'No,' she said plainly. 'I will not tell him. He is not here. He will not know unless someone else tells him.'

'If he returns...' Isaura stared hard into Ayla's eyes.

'He will return,' Ayla promised her calmly.

Isaura sighed, listening to the children argue through the wall. They were getting older so quickly, picking at each other constantly. She dreaded to think that any of them would turn into Ivaar. 'I imagine so. How could he not?' She shook her head, reaching for her cup of small ale. 'But I did not wish to speak to you about Ivaar. I can do nothing about him.' She lowered her voice. 'It's Thorgils I want to know about.'

Ayla was not surprised. She had seen the way Isaura had looked at the large red-headed man while they were on Oss. 'What did you want to know? I have seen nothing about him in my dreams.'

'No?' Isaura said sadly. 'Oh.'

'Which is a good thing,' Ayla rushed to reassure her. 'I don't see his death, if that's your question? But then again, I wouldn't dream about him at all, unless it was for a reason.'

'But could you?' Isaura wondered quietly. '*Would* you? To see if he's safe?'

Her eyes were wide with pain and Ayla couldn't deny her.

'I have this,' Isaura said, pulling a bright red curl from her purse. It was tied to a thin leather strap. Thorgils had given it to her before she left Oss all those years ago. 'Will it help?'

Ayla took the strap from her, slipping it inside her own purse. 'It will. But I cannot guarantee anything. I can only try. If there is nothing the gods want to show me about him, then I'll not see anything. But I will try.'

Isaura nodded, tears stinging the corners of her eyes. As much as she was desperate to know what Ayla saw, she was just as terrified to find out what would happen to Thorgils.

***

Jael nodded at Eadmund as he turned towards her. It was as much affection as she could summon; she was far too distracted for anything more. He looked sad as he nodded back, hoisting himself into *Ice Breaker*. She chose not to feel guilty for that, Eadmund being the one who had left her without a word.

Jael turned away. Her attention needed to be focused on leaving now. As much as Eirik was the king, he had put her in charge of a band of ornery old helmsmen, most of whom had no inclination to follow her at all, and somehow she had to get them all working together under her leadership.

'Are we ready for this, do you think?' Eirik asked, inhaling the salty air as he and Eydis joined her in *Sea Bear's* stern. The ships were in the water, rocking expectantly, waiting for her signal for the oars to dig in.

'I hope so,' Jael said briefly, running her eyes over their fleet. She swallowed, unfamiliar with the nerves fluttering in her chest. She heard her father's voice then, booming in her ears. 'Well, it's what you wanted, isn't it? To be the leader? So lead, Jael. And hurry up about it!' Smiling, Jael turned to Eydis who looked equal parts terrified and excited as she clung to Eirik's hand. 'Are you ready, Eydis?' Jael asked, signalling Beorn, *Sea Bear's* helmsman, to get them underway. She waved at Thorgils who was watching from *Fire Serpent*, two ships along, and he signalled on down the line. Oars went up and into the water in quick succession.

Eydis nodded, stumbling as the ship backed up into the gentle waves. Eirik grabbed hold of her arm to steady her.

'Have you ever been to sea before, Eydis?' Jael wondered, reaching for the gunwale to steady her own feet. She thought of Tig, then, hoping that she would see him again soon.

'Yes,' Eydis said with wide eyes. 'But not very far out.'

Eirik smiled, happy that she'd finally convinced him to bring her along. He didn't want to let her out of his sight. Not anymore. 'Let's sit you down here, on my chest,' he murmured gently. 'It's a good place to be until you find your sea legs.'

Jael watched as Eirik eased Eydis down onto the chest, tucking her cloak tightly around her. She took a deep breath, pushing all thoughts of Eadmund and Evaine far behind her as Oss grew further and further away, promising herself that she

would bring their men back.
>	She had to. There was no choice.
>	They couldn't be defeated.

PART THREE

Saala

CHAPTER THIRTEEN

The vast horde of Hestian warriors stood in columns that stretched from one end of Hest's cobblestoned square to the other, their polished mail and armour gleaming in the early morning sun.

Haaron stood at the bottom of the castle steps taking in the impressive sight. He was pleased, confident that they had enough men to keep the ambitious Brekkans at bay. 'You must show Lothar that his desire to conquer us will never be fulfilled,' he said pointedly, his eyes snapping to his heir who jiggled impatiently beside him.

Haegen nodded, squinting into the glare of the sun. 'I understand, Father. We will crush them.'

'Don't just crush them, humiliate them, and if there's an opportunity to take Lothar, do it,' Haaron said. 'I would enjoy that. A Furyck prisoner?' He smiled for a moment, but his eyes quickly lost any hint of amusement. 'But make sure you keep Karsten under control. He's too reckless with those axes of his.'

'Agreed.'

'Well, say goodbye to your wife, then, and get going.' Haaron clapped his son on the shoulder and turned to leave. 'I shall head for the Tower and await word of your success. I don't expect you'll have any trouble, but I will have men... if you need them.'

Haegen nodded to his father and turned to Irenna, who was hovering anxiously nearby. He cupped her small face in his hands, noting how swollen and red her eyes looked. 'You've no need to worry, my love,' he smiled reassuringly. 'They can't get through the pass. They won't. You'll be safe here. We'll protect Hest. I promise.'

Irenna sighed, nestling into his thick mail-clad chest, her head under his bearded chin. 'That may be so, but I'm not foolish enough to think that war does not mean victory without death. And I'm not worried about my safety as much as I am about yours. I know you, Haegen, always wanting to prove something to your father. You're all the same, you Dragos men. You'll put yourself out in front, where the most danger lurks.'

Haegen held her close. She was tiny in his arms; fragile but fierce. 'True. I will, of course. I must. No real leader fights from the rear or asks his men to do what he will not. But we've done this before,' he said calmly. 'We're Hestians, and I will be king here one day. Varna sees that. You shouldn't worry about this one battle.'

But Irenna's mind did not ease. She pulled back and glanced at Karsten, who was kissing his young wife goodbye. 'Don't listen to Karsten, whatever you do,' Irenna warned her husband. 'He is not the same since he lost his eye. And he was never right before it.'

Haegen stared at his brother, who broke away from Nicolene and headed towards him. '*I* am in charge, Irenna,' he whispered hoarsely. 'Nothing happens without me deciding it, I promise.'

'Shall we go then, Brother?' Karsten smiled. He was barely able to contain his excitement. He had spent days sharpening his axe blades, and although he might not be able to wield them at Jael Furyck this time, Karsten felt confident that there'd be Furyck blood on them before the battle was done. *If* he could shake off the leash that Haegen was surely planning to keep him on.

Haegen... his father's favourite. For now.

Karsten looked back at Nicolene and smiled.

***

Lothar took ill on their sea journey, and Gisila was able to enjoy his lack of interest in anything but the bucket he bent over.

She had happily left her incapacitated husband in the stern, spending her time alone with Amma in the bow. But their arrival in Saala had roused Lothar's spirits and stopped the steady stream of ear-piercing retching they had all cringed beneath for two days. And he was once again by Gisila's side, pressing himself firmly against her as he clasped the Lord of Saala's arms.

'It has not been such a long time, my king,' Lord Rexon Boas smiled at Lothar, his lips tight with tension. Saala's proximity to Hest had always made it the perfect base for Brekkan kings to attack or defend from; as it was again now, and had been many times since Lothar had stolen the throne.

Rexon was a pragmatic, fair leader, made lord by Ranuf Furyck six years ago. He had admired Ranuf enormously, and, like most, had assumed that Jael would succeed her father. His disappointment that she hadn't still lingered and he found it almost impossible to look at Lothar without obvious distaste. Lothar had proved a selfish, reckless king, especially for the Saalans whose land bordered Hest, and whose fort and warriors were regularly commandeered by Lothar to launch his assaults on the Hestians.

'No,' Lothar admitted, ignoring the lack of warmth in Rexon's greeting. 'But, I am a Furyck, and we do not give up easily! In order to secure Brekka's safety and defeat Haaron once and for all, we must keep going. I'm sure you agree that conquering Hest will be a gift to your people. The gift of peace for years to come!'

It was clever for Lothar to twist his motives in that way, Rexon thought as he turned his pale-blue eyes towards Gisila; a woman whose figure was once widely admired, but who now looked a barely-there shadow of her former self. 'My lady,' he said, bowing respectfully.

'Rexon,' Gisila smiled. Rexon had become part of Ranuf's household before there was any hair on his face, and he had grown into a powerful man; a good man. She could see the displeasure in his eyes at the position Lothar was putting him in again.

Lothar grunted, annoyed that Rexon had saved his manners for his wife. 'You have met Osbert, of course, and this is my youngest daughter, Amma.' He coughed, shunting an embarrassed looking Amma forward. 'I shall require your best lodgings for the women and their servants.'

Rexon nodded briefly, turning to whisper to his steward. 'Helvig will take your ladies to their quarters, and perhaps you'd like to join me in the hall, my lord? Your men are welcome to stay there. And we have barns, and plenty of Saalans ready to take them in, as always. The rest will need to make their camp outside the gates.'

Lothar nodded, his empty stomach growling, spurred on by the smell of roasting meat wafting through the open doors of the hall. 'Well, I shall leave that to you, Osbert,' he said with a dismissive flick of his hand.

Osbert glowered at his father as he hurried off with Rexon, oblivious to everything but the call of his empty belly. He watched Amma and Gisila disappear into a large house near Saala's new hall. Osbert could hear the grumble of his own empty belly. 'You see to it, Gant,' he muttered. 'Axl can help you. It's best if I go and assist my father.'

Gant watched him go with a cynical grin, relieved to be rid of the little bastard.

'That smells good,' Axl sighed beside him.

'It does indeed,' Gant agreed. 'But we are not Osbert,' he said quietly, his eyes on the disappearing heir to the king. 'So we will look after our men first.'

***

Saala's hall was small, only a quarter the size of Andala's King's Hall. It had been rebuilt the previous summer, Haaron having set fire to it during Lothar's last failed attack on Hest. Rexon still hadn't forgiven him for that. He had lost a lot of men during that campaign; buildings too. It was hard not to feel bitter when tied to the whim of a foolish, vain king like Lothar; hard not to think back to a time when they had been ruled by one who wasn't.

There were Islanders everywhere. Lothar's fleshy shoulders heaved in resignation. There was no Eirik, so he would have to talk to them. He glanced at the pig roasting on the spit as he walked down the centre of the hall, trying not to lick his dry lips. His empty stomach was growing painful now, but he was a king, and there were some things he could simply not ignore.

Rexon led him to the high table, which was barely long enough to accommodate the six well-dressed lords who sat there, elbow to elbow. The men, most old, some less so, were wrapped in new furs, gold rings on their fingers, silver nuggets braided into their well-oiled beards. They had come dressed to impress, that was obvious, but still, they were only lords; lords of tiny islands, belonging to a self-made king with no lineage. They puffed up their chests as Lothar considered each one in turn, but he saw nothing to be impressed by. He nodded briefly, his lips weighted down with disdain.

'You won't know anyone here, of course, my lord,' Rexon said as each of the six men rose – some more easily than others – to their feet. 'But these are Eirik's lords. Most of them.'

For all their attempts at finery, they were a rabble of hard men, none used to setting foot in the royal kingdom of Brekka; not invited at least. Each one appeared awkward in the presence of the Brekkan king.

'Which one of you is Ivaar Skalleson?' Lothar muttered through barely moving lips, deciding that there was no point in bothering with any but Eirik's son.

'The Kalfans have not arrived, lord king,' Hassi of Rikka spoke up, his feet still unsteady after a days sailing. 'I expect they will be here this afternoon, along with the Osslanders. On a wind this stiff, they're sure to land before nightfall.'

Lothar grunted. 'Well, as I've only just arrived myself, I require ale and some of that suckling pig you have turning over there, Rexon,' Lothar grinned, shifting his attention to a timid serving girl who quickly handed him a silver cup. Lothar inhaled the heady scent, relieved to experience a sensation that wasn't nausea. 'Well, this is a good start!' He looked around the freshly cleaned hall, and, spying Rexon's freshly made, fur-covered chair, he promptly ignored the lords and went to make himself comfortable while he waited for his food.

The lords raised surprised eyebrows at each other, uncertain what to do, but as King Lothar Furyck appeared to be paying them no mind, they slowly sat back down and picked up their cups, returning to their conversations, happily paying him no mind in return.

***

Jael felt relieved to see Saala appear from underneath the low clouds in the distance. She was not a sailor, much like Tig. The thought of digging her boots into earth again, be it mud or sand, lifted her spirits. She shivered, wrapping her fur cloak tightly around her chest. The bracing wind had helped them fly around the islands, but she was looking forward to getting out of it.

'No doubt Lothar will be wondering where his little spy has disappeared to,' Eirik chortled as he stumbled over to Jael, one hand on his long beard which had been flapping about like a sail. 'What do you think I should tell him?'

Jael frowned at the memory of that vile slug, Tiras. His big mouth had nearly gotten both her and Fyn killed. Her only regret about killing him was that she hadn't done it sooner. 'I would say as little as possible,' she said, turning to him, watching as the seabirds started calling and diving above their heads. 'There were so many storms over the winter, it's a surprise more men weren't lost, wouldn't you say?'

Eirik laughed, enjoying the simple pleasure of sailing on a determined wind, *Sea Bear's* red-and-white striped sail snapping above his head, his men chatting quietly to each other as they sat huddled beneath rows of shields arrayed along the gunwales. He looked towards the bow where Eydis and Fyn were talking. Frowning suddenly, he leaned into Jael. 'I want to find Eydis a husband.'

Jael spluttered in surprise. 'But she's a child!' she whispered hoarsely. 'You can't do that!'

Eirik's beard escaped his hold, flapping up into his face. He brushed it away in a sudden burst of irritation. His daughter-in-law had a way of flattening every one of his plans, like a boulder dropping from the sky. 'I want to ensure her safety,' he insisted indignantly.

'She doesn't need a husband to be safe,' Jael scoffed. 'Having a husband could just as well make her less safe, don't you think? She's too young!'

'Well, of course she is,' Eirik muttered, conscious of keeping the conversation private. 'But I won't be around much longer to guide her, will I? To help her make the right choices. It may be the last thing I can do for her, seeing her betrothed to a good man. One she can marry when she is older.'

Jael's scorn softened as she saw the real fear lurking in Eirik's watery eyes. It was no secret that his death was coming and she didn't blame him for wanting to make sure that Eydis would be looked after. But still... 'What if she doesn't want to marry? Ever?'

'She will,' Eirik said confidently, watching Eydis laughing with Fyn. They were the youngest on board and had drawn themselves together once the sail had gone up. 'She's not like you. Not about to defend herself with a sword and a boot.'

Jael smiled. 'No, but marriage –'

'Marriage can make you happy!' Eirik insisted. 'To the right person. And, marriage is security. I know you believe that you and Eadmund will take care of her, but look at what is happening with him,' he sighed, trying not to let the worry of that situation gnaw away at him further. 'A man betrothed to Eydis would be beholden to care for her until his death. To keep her safe.'

Jael didn't want to agree, but she could understand Eirik's desperation to protect his only daughter. In his eyes, she was blind, and that made her helpless. He couldn't see how strong and independent Eydis actually was.

'What about Fyn? She seems to like him,' Eirik suggested slyly.

Jael didn't know what to say.

'You don't think he's a good man?'

'Fyn?' Jael glanced at her young friend. His cheeks were flushed red, but from the bitter wind, or from talking to his companion, she couldn't tell. 'Fyn's not quite a man, but he will be soon enough,' she began. 'Though I'm not sure he'd like me volunteering him for marriage just yet! Even to someone as lovely as Eydis.'

Eirik ran a hand over his damp, salty moustache. 'Perhaps you could speak to him? He seems like a fine boy to me. Someone to consider, at least. If he lives through this battle, of course!' And mumbling away to himself, Eirik swayed and stumbled down to the bow to see his daughter.

Jael sighed, thinking about Eadmund.

Marriage was much like sailing, she decided. Sometimes the skies were dark, the waves fierce, and your stomach lurching as you were buffeted about. Other times the sea was so flat you were ready to pull out your hair. But then there were those perfect days when the sky was clear, and a fresh breeze was filling your sail, and you wouldn't have wanted to be anywhere else.

***

Somehow Eadmund had ended up with Morac.

There were better men to have for company on a two-day sea journey, but Jael had ensured that those men had been spread around the fleet. She needed an ally on every ship to keep an eye on the old helmsmen who didn't like her very much. Eadmund understood that. But Morac?

He supposed it was a fair punishment for what he'd done.

The guilt of his disappearance to Rikka had sailed alongside him. He still couldn't understand why he'd done such a thing. Left Jael without even a word? He shook his head, furious with himself.

'Nearly there,' Morac sighed, the relief of their voyage being near its end clearing his usually stern face. 'We've made good time indeed.'

'We have,' Eadmund murmured, not really listening. He'd had two days of the voice in his head taunting him. Two days of being tormented by Jael's hurt face. He closed his eyes and took a deep breath, trying to clear the confusion that swirled around him in thick clouds. But all he saw in the darkness was Sigmund.

'Are you unwell, Eadmund?' Morac asked with concern.

Eadmund opened his eyes. 'Just a sore head,' he said lightly. 'I've not slept well lately.'

'No, I expect there is much on your mind,' Morac sympathised. 'And not just Hest, either. Your wife is not happy with you. I know how you feel.'

Eadmund didn't want Morac commiserating with him. His attempt at friendship only served to make Eadmund feel worse. 'My wife has every reason not to be happy with me,' he said shortly. 'As does yours, I'm sure. In marriage, I've discovered, it's usually only the woman with any sense.'

Morac's laugh was a little too forced to be genuine. 'Indeed,' he smiled, reaching into his pouch and pulling out a stone. 'I forgot... Evaine asked me to give you this. It's a good luck stone she's had since she was a child. Runa gave it to her on her eighth birthday, I remember. Evaine has kept it close ever since.' He handed Eadmund the stone. 'She wanted you to have its luck and protection, so you could stay safe and come back to her and Sigmund.'

Eadmund stared at the small grey stone. It was flat and smooth, inscribed with a symbol he didn't recognise. He tucked it into his pouch without another thought for it or Evaine. 'That was kind of her.' Eadmund didn't know what else to say. He would have happily tossed the stone into the sea. It wasn't Evaine he had gone to Rikka for. It was his son. But why had he done it without talking to Jael first? He couldn't understand what had happened. His head was a thick haze of guilt and regret.

He felt so utterly confused.

***

'Now *that* was a good journey!' Aleksander smiled at Jael as they met on the foreshore. Their men were busy pulling all the ships up onto Saala's long beach. Rexon had one short pier, and it was already full.

'Better than six days on a horse?' Jael wondered.

Aleksander nodded. 'I can't feel my face, but at least I can feel my arse!'

Jael laughed as they wandered along the black sand towards Thorgils and Fyn, who were telling the tales of their journey to Torstan and Eadmund. She sighed, happy to see her husband, eager to talk to him again. They would be going into battle soon. She didn't want to leave things like this.

'I hope they've saved some food for us!' Thorgils called to her.

Dusk was slowly turning the clouds a deep blue, and the air was cooling down. Jael yawned, unsteady on her feet. She was ready to lie down, but the thought of something hot in her belly spurred her on. 'Well, if Lothar's been here long, I'd say you have no chance!' she called back. 'He could eat an entire farmyard in one sitting!'

Eirik, Eydis, and Morac came walking over to the group.

'Let's get to a fire!' Eirik cried to the cheers of his cold and weary men. 'I hope this Rexon has a good supply of ale.'

'From memory, he does,' Aleksander said as he led them towards the gates of the small village. 'But it's his wine you should ask for. Unless, of course, he's hidden it from Lothar!'

Jael cringed. She was dreading seeing her uncle again, but hopefully, it wouldn't be for long. The Brekkan army would march in a few days, aiming to trap Haaron's men in the pass. Although, according to Edela, there was little chance of it making any difference.

They were all doomed to fail.

She glanced at Eadmund, who ignored her. His eyes remained focused on Torstan, who was talking animatedly to him. Jael frowned, puzzled, her attention drifting to Aleksander who was sneezing beside her. 'I suppose you'll slip away now?' she asked quietly. 'Go over to the Brekkans?'

Aleksander felt the odd, rolling sensation as he adjusted to land again. 'Well, there'll be a lot to organise. I imagine Lothar and Osbert will have left everything to Gant, so he's going to need some help.'

'Make sure you stick Osbert out in front when the time comes,' Jael grinned, wading through the soft sand beside him. 'He has a way of sliding to the rear like a cowardly little worm.'

Aleksander laughed. 'I'll try my best!'

Jael turned towards the leaning wattle gates that led to the village, where Gisila stood, watching with Axl. She felt an unexpected burst of emotion as she hurried towards them.

'Jael!' Axl's smile was bright as he took her in his arms,

hugging her tightly.

'You're even bigger!' Jael exclaimed, stepping back to look him up and down. It was getting dark, but flaming torches along the fence line shone some light their way. 'How is that possible?'

'Perhaps you've shrunk?' Axl suggested cheerfully. There wasn't even a hint of the resentment that had been there when they'd said goodbye. He had changed a lot in the time she'd been gone.

He had grown up.

'Could be,' Jael admitted. 'I am getting old!' She turned to her mother, who stood next to Axl, shaking, her eyes brimming with tears. Gisila may have looked like a queen again, with her fine new cloak and her neck draped in jewels, but she appeared thinner than ever and utterly morose.

Jael walked towards her and Gisila held out her arms, tears running down her face now. Lothar wasn't there. Nor was Osbert. They hadn't left the hall. She could be herself; for a moment, she could completely be herself.

Stepping into Gisila's embrace, Jael could feel her mother's chest heaving as she sobbed against her. 'It's alright, Mother, it's alright,' she soothed as Gisila wept; all the terror and misery and unhappiness pouring out of her in a great flood.

Aleksander was there too, and when Jael released Gisila, he leaned in and hugged her gently. Jael looked at Axl and saw the tears in his own eyes; his worry for their mother furrowing his brow.

'Where's Lothar?' Jael wondered.

'In the hall with Rexon and the Islanders,' Axl said. 'And Osbert.'

'Good,' Jael said quickly. 'While everyone else is going to the hall, let's slip away somewhere. We can talk about everything that's been happening before Lothar wonders where we are.'

Gisila smiled, wiping her eyes. She felt a release of tension, a sense of hope that she hadn't experienced in a long time. Jael was here, and for a moment, she didn't need to think about being strong. Gripping her daughter's arm, Gisila followed Jael, Axl and Aleksander, as they slipped through the village.

Eadmund and Thorgils watched the family reunion from a distance.

'We should go,' Eadmund muttered, nodding towards their men who were heading into the village.

Thorgils blinked at him. 'You don't want to go and see Jael's family?'

Eadmund shook his head, walking away from him without a word.

CHAPTER FOURTEEN

'But where did you get it?' Dalca wondered. '*How* did you get it?'

Her sister smiled darkly. 'You wouldn't believe me if I told you.' She shook her sleek hair, turning her attention to the book, stroking its fine leather cover. 'It doesn't matter, does it? What matters is what it can do for us.'

'*Do* for us?' Diona asked hesitantly. She glanced around. It was just a book, but her sister was acting as though they were doing something wrong. She swallowed, listening for footsteps. They were alone in their house, upstairs in their shared bedchamber, but Diona was nervous, worried that a dreamer would see what they were doing.

What *were* they doing?

'It is a book of magic,' the girl with the dark hair whispered. 'Spells, potions... every way you could imagine to exact our revenge is in here.'

Diona looked horrified. She shook her head firmly. 'No!'

'Don't you want to make them pay for what they have done to us?' her sister demanded angrily, her voice rising.

'Stop it!' Dalca hissed. 'Both of you. Stop arguing. And tell us what you mean, Sister. What do you want to do with this book of magic?' She was the wisest of the three; the eldest.

'I want to make them suffer for what they did. The Tuurans, the Furycks... they destroyed our family. And with this book,' she smiled, her beautiful young face alive with hope, 'we will be able to exact our revenge and destroy them all.'

Diona gasped and looked at her sister. 'All of them?'

'*All* of them.'

***

Edela woke up slowly, puzzled.

She had fallen asleep in a chair by the fire, almost submerged under a heaping pile of furs, both puppies on her feet. She felt warm and cold at the same time.

'Are you alright, Edela?' Biddy wondered as she walked inside, her broom thick with cobwebs. 'Shall I get you some water?'

Edela grimaced, her neck tight from sleeping in an odd position. 'Yes, I would like that,' she murmured throatily.

What a strange dream it had been. So different than any others. So clear. And that girl was there. The one she had dreamed of before. She was quite mesmerising, but there was something about her eyes that troubled Edela.

And, of course, she had the book.

'Here you are,' Biddy smiled, handing Edela a cup. 'Was it a bad dream, then?'

'No,' Edela yawned, taking a long drink of water. 'No, it wasn't, which was a nice change. It was about that girl again. You remember, I told you about her?'

Biddy nodded, shooing the puppies away from Edela's feet.

'She has sisters...' Edela frowned, trying to tease out a memory. Her eyes widened. 'Those girls... her sisters... they were the ones I saw in my dream! The beheaded ones!' She shook her head slowly, her mouth hanging open, her mind whirring. 'I'm certain of it,' she shuddered, thinking of those poor young girls whose heads had been severed and stuck on pikes.

But who were they and what had they done?

And more importantly, what had happened to their sister and the book?

***

Rexon's hall was not large enough to accommodate such an influx of people. Most had to camp in a hastily constructed tent village, just outside Saala's wooden walls. But they had ale and food and stories to share as they sat around the fires, laughing and drinking together.

Rexon was not laughing as he watched Lothar Furyck devouring his food, and draining his barrels of fine wine. He grumbled to himself, wishing he'd hidden them away.

'Missing Ranuf?' Gant whispered, stopping beside Rexon who was leaning against the door, surveying the scene with an ever-deepening frown.

Rexon laughed. 'Not at all. Lothar is my king now, old friend.' He stared at Gant, his hooded eyes barely concealing how false his words were.

'Indeed,' Gant nodded, continuing to stare at the high table where Lothar and Osbert sat with Eirik and Eadmund Skalleson. Thankfully, Lothar had not even noticed that Gisila wasn't there.

'But, of course, anything can happen in battle,' Rexon mused, rolling a toothpick around his mouth. 'Can't it?'

'That it can,' Gant agreed slyly, checking behind them. 'I'm sure Haaron's had his fill of the Brekkans by now.'

'Well, some of them anyway,' Rexon smiled.

'I'm going to go and find Gisila and Jael before Lothar gets stroppy and wonders where they are,' Gant whispered. 'Keep an eye on him for me.'

Rexon nodded as Gant slipped out of the hall.

***

The Furyck women had been sequestered in a warm, accommodating house close to the hall. There was a separate bedchamber and enough chairs and stools for them to sit around the fire in the comfortable main room. Amma was there too, and Jael had brought Eydis along to save her from having to be stuck in the hall with all those loud drunken men.

The fire was warm, but there was little joy on the faces of those who sat around it, sipping from cups of small ale that Gunni, Gisila's servant, had handed around.

'What about your husband?' Gisila wondered into the awkward silence. 'How is he? *Where* is he?'

Eydis looked troubled.

Jael looked confused. 'He is... good.'

'Good?' Axl was also confused, remembering the bloated mess of a man he had left swaying beside Jael on Oss' quickly freezing beach.

'It's too complicated to talk about now,' Jael grumbled, feeling the rising irritation of Eadmund's absence crawl under her skin; annoyed that he'd hurried away without even a look towards her or her family.

Aleksander could see that Jael was getting tense. 'There'll be a lot to do in the coming days. We'll not have much time to say anything to each other, so, best we say it all now.'

'Mother, you have to stay strong,' Jael said quickly. 'And be patient. We can't make any plans until after this battle.'

Gisila hung her head. 'And if you all die?' she breathed. 'Edela saw that this would be a failure, that Lothar would not succeed again. He will not get through Valder's Pass. And if you all die, what will Amma and I do?'

Jael glanced at Eydis; she didn't need to hear this. 'Mother, the gods will decide our fate,' she tried. 'You know that. And whoever is still standing at the end of this, that person will take care of you, I promise.'

Axl nodded. 'All of you.'

'I'll find Rexon and speak to him,' Jael added. 'He's a trusted ally. He will protect you if there's no one else.'

No one looked especially reassured.

'Eydis is a dreamer,' Jael tried. 'She hasn't seen anything bad coming, have you, Eydis?'

Eydis squirmed uncomfortably. There were too many new people for her to feel confident about speaking at all. 'No,' she whispered.

Amma reached out and kindly squeezed her hand.

'And remember, Mother,' Axl said, wrapping one arm around Gisila's shaking shoulders. 'Edela didn't see anything bad either, did she? She didn't see any of us dying.' He swallowed, hoping that his grandmother hadn't hidden the truth from them. He knew he had to come back to keep his mother and Amma safe.

***

'Are you sure you're alright?' Thorgils wondered again, shovelling a fat slab of gristly pork into his mouth. After two days at sea, he was too hungry to be particular about the overcooked food on offer.

Eadmund looked at him blankly. 'Why do you keep asking me that? Jael doesn't need me interrupting her family reunion. Not the way things are right now. Besides,' he murmured, leaning towards his friend, 'I don't want to miss Ivaar's company, do I?'

Thorgils' jaw clenched as he looked along the table towards Eadmund's older brother, Ivaar Skalleson; the biggest turd he'd ever had the misfortune of knowing. Ivaar was a complete cunt, married to Isaura, Thorgils' woman; Lord of Kalfa, but never, Thorgils swore to himself, never the King of Oss. Oh, how he'd like to aim one of those sea-fire jars at Ivaar and give Eadmund a burning arrow. Together they could make him disappear from all their lives, in one great ball of fire. Just the thought of that put a smile on his face.

'You look happy,' Jael noted, peering down at Thorgils.

Thorgils blinked himself awake, leaving thoughts of firing Ivaar into the sea for another day. 'Well, you took your time,' he grumbled. 'Having a lie-down, were we?'

Jael ignored him and Eadmund, and instead wandered over to Eirik, who already looked a little worse for wear as he motioned her over. She nodded at Osbert and Lothar, whose drunken eyes barely acknowledged her, and bent her ear towards the king.

'Is Eydis alright?' Eirik wondered anxiously.

'She's fine. I left her with my mother and cousin,' Jael assured him. 'They'll care for her, you needn't worry. There's plenty of room for her to stay with them.'

'Good, good!' Eirik called, surprising Jael with a loud belch.

Lothar laughed, joining in.

Jael frowned, turning to the man whose presence she'd suddenly felt as he crept up behind her. 'Hello, Ivaar,' she said, glaring at her brother-in-law.

'Jael,' Ivaar purred. 'You look well. Still not pregnant, I see.'

Jael didn't even blink. 'No, I thought I'd leave that until after I'd killed you,' she whispered.

Ivaar flinched, surprised by the ferocity of her words and the anger in her eyes. 'Well, it appears that time has not softened you. Nor me, I must confess. We have, it seems, become enemies.'

'Hardly a surprise when you wish to take everything from me. How could we be anything but?'

Eadmund and Thorgils were watching; Jael could sense that out of the corner of her eye. It was a public place and no time for threatening people she was going to be fighting alongside. She was exhausted and hungry, her throat salt-dry. There would be plenty of time to trade insults with Ivaar later.

Ivaar studied Jael with a tense sigh. She was infuriatingly

smug, and he was annoyed to find that his body still responded to her intoxicating eyes. 'Well, perhaps that's so, but I'm not the only one who wishes to take everything from you, am I?' he breathed in her ear. 'I hear that Evaine Gallas has returned to Oss with Eadmund's son. I can only imagine how you must feel. But then, I suppose, now you can lean on Aleksander for comfort.' And deciding that that was enough to leave her with, for now, Ivaar slid away to talk to his father who was frowning in his direction.

'Jael,' Fyn murmured, stopping beside her. 'I think I should find somewhere to sleep.' After his years of abuse by Tarak, he felt permanently on edge around other men, especially large, bullish ones with too much ale in them, and the small hall was full of those.

'Already?' Jael asked, sensing his awkwardness. 'Where?' She caught sight of her brother chatting to a familiar Andalan face. 'Axl!' she called. 'Where are you sleeping?'

'In the tents,' Axl mumbled between sips of ale. 'With Gant.'

'Do you have another bed for my friend Fyn?'

Fyn looked uncomfortable, not wanting to be handed off to complete strangers like a child. He made protesting sounds, staring at his boots.

'Just until tomorrow,' Jael assured him. 'We can figure everything out when it's light. You'll be safer there with Axl and Gant than in here. You can trust them.'

Fyn shrugged, and Jael smiled as Axl approached. They certainly did look alike, Axl and Fyn. Tall, floppy-haired, determined to prove themselves. Young...

'Fyn's under my protection,' Jael said firmly to her brother. 'Anything happens to him, and I'll come looking for you.'

Axl laughed. 'Well, I'm sure you'll know where to find me!' He nodded at Fyn. 'Come on then, I'll show you where to go.'

Jael sighed, relieved, wondering if she should follow them, but her eyes accidentally caught Lothar's as he rose from Rexon's chair, his arms outstretched.

'My niece!' Lothar slurred loudly as Jael squirmed before

him. 'It has been so long, and yet, I would have to say, not long enough!'

Osbert couldn't help but snort as he swayed behind his father.

Jael cringed, noticing that Eadmund had his head down, avoiding her entirely. That was surely a far worse problem than the drunken fool of a king wobbling towards her.

'I've heard that Eirik put you in command of his fleet!' Lothar boomed, grabbing her arms and kissing her cheek.

His breath was overpowering, his lips wet on her face. Jael swallowed, pressing her boots onto the floorboards, forcing herself not to step away. 'Yes, Uncle,' she said without emotion. 'I am.'

'And how do his men feel about that?' Lothar bellowed, waving his hand towards the island lords, who had their heads together, having been moved to a smaller, lower table now that the kings and their families had arrived. 'How do the lords of the islands feel about a woman in charge of their destiny?'

Eirik frowned. Lothar's lips were as loose as his trousers after he'd removed his belt. He turned to Rexon, who he'd quickly realised had more sense than Lothar and his son put together. 'I think your king might need his bed,' he murmured.

Rexon nodded slowly. 'Yes, I think so. But whether he's going to let anyone take him there, I don't know.'

Lothar was teetering on his feet now. Jael glanced at Osbert, but he didn't appear in any state to save his father from further humiliation. It would do no good for him to continue in this way; to make a fool of himself in front of everyone he wished to follow him. 'Well, if they have any problems, they can speak to their king,' she said quietly, eager to change the subject. 'But in the meantime, I wanted to wish you congratulations on your marriage. My mother has been telling me all about it.'

Lothar's eyes bulged, his head spinning, realising for the first time in a while that there was still no Gisila. 'Ahhh, yes, my beautiful wife,' he sighed wistfully. 'And where did you say she was?'

Jael thought quickly, not wanting to send Lothar to prey on her mother in this state. 'She is asleep, with the other women. With Amma, and Eirik's daughter.'

'Oh,' Lothar frowned. 'Well, we shall have to change all of that tomorrow, I think, once we are properly set up.' His mind wandered as the hall started to blur around him. 'I must have my wife by me, in my bed! She is my wife!'

'My lord,' Gant said softly as he approached. 'I'm sure Gisila would want you to head to bed now, so you may breakfast with her in the morning.'

Lothar frowned, annoyed at being coddled like a baby, but he did feel ready to drop. 'Very well,' he slurred, promptly slumping into Gant's arms. 'We shall talk tomorrow, Eirik!' Lothar called over his shoulder as Gant manoeuvred his slumberous king through the tables, towards the bedchambers at the back of the hall.

Eirik could barely keep his eyes from rolling.

That man was likely to get everyone killed.

'An interesting alliance you've made there, Father,' Ivaar sneered. He had no reason to impress Eirik anymore. He didn't see any way back to the throne while his father was alive. 'It never breeds much confidence to be led by a drunk.' He glanced at Eadmund as he spoke.

Eirik frowned, pushing away his cup. It didn't feel late, but he'd had enough of the day now. A clear head would serve him better in the morning than a regretful one, he decided. 'No, it doesn't,' he agreed. 'Nor does it breed much confidence to be led by someone who wouldn't hesitate to murder his entire family to satisfy his own ambition.' Eirik was not quiet, and more than a few heads snapped towards them.

Ivaar tried to turn his grimace into a smile, but it merely twisted his narrow face into a scowl. 'Shall I help you to your bed, Father? You seem a little unsteady on your feet.'

Eirik batted him away with one hand. 'You may think me old, Ivaar, but I'm still the King of Oss, and you are not. And the

King of Oss does not need anyone to help him to his bed!' And with one, final, bitter look at his bitter son, he walked towards the back of the hall, to the bedchamber where Rexon had placed his chest.

Ivaar watched his father stumble away, feeling the heat of embarrassment on his cheeks; sensing the smirks, and the gossip that was already beginning to flow around him. He didn't care; he dismissed it entirely, for Ayla had seen him as the King of Oss.

And soon.

***

Jael wedged herself in between Thorgils and Eadmund. She wanted her bed, but she also wanted to take her husband with her. He had been drinking steadily since their arrival. It was unlike him, and she felt too worried to be mad anymore.

Thorgils eyed her over the top of Eadmund's drooping head. He looked as anxious as she felt.

'Shall we go?' Jael asked lightly.

Eadmund turned to her, puzzled, his face completely blank, his eyes hazy. 'Go? Where?'

'To find a bed,' Jael suggested. 'We're still married, I believe. So, we could find a bed together.' She had missed him and was ready for it all to be over. There were far too many important things coming now to be fighting about a bad decision and a trouble-making bitch.

Eadmund shook his head. 'No, you go,' he sighed. 'I haven't even touched the sides of this cup, and besides, it's better if I just sleep here.' He turned towards his ale, studying it closely.

Thorgils' eyes widened. 'I hardly think you'll find any room in here tonight, my friend. Not unless you plan on cuddling up with me!' He tried to get Eadmund's attention but Eadmund continued to stare at his cup.

Jael put her hand on her husband's knee. 'Eadmund,' she urged. 'Let's go. You've had enough for tonight.'

He looked at her then, his eyes absent of any feeling as they tried to focus on her face. 'Enough?' he frowned. 'No, I don't think I have.' And picking up his cup, Eadmund drank deeply, not stopping until it was empty. Wiping a hand across his coppery beard, he staggered to his feet and without a word, he pushed past Thorgils, wandering off in search of more ale.

They watched him go, numb, confused, unable to move.

This was different and not in a good way.

Something was terribly wrong with Eadmund.

CHAPTER FIFTEEN

In Amma's fervent desire to take care of Eydis, she had buried her beneath a mountain of furs. Eydis had not slept well, tossing and turning, waking frequently, confused by the strange sounds coming from outside the bedchamber, and the unfamiliar ones inside it.

She closed her eyes again, stretching her hot feet as far as she could towards the end of the bed. Her legs wouldn't stay still, though; they twitched constantly. Eydis sighed, letting her head fall back into the pillow, imagining herself sinking. That was something Ayla had taught her: the idea of sinking back into the clouds; falling into their comforting embrace, into the dreams that awaited her.

Eydis' breathing slowed, her chest rising high and falling deep, her body finally unwinding, her legs still. And then, in the darkness, she saw it: Ivaar's face. And she gasped.

For he was smiling.

***

'Evaine!' Runa called impatiently as she tried to burp Sigmund over her shoulder. 'Where are you going?'

'I told you,' Evaine grumbled, wrapping a fur around her shoulders. It had snowed lightly during the night, and she shivered as she dressed. 'I must see Sigynn about getting a new cloak made for summer.'

'In *this* weather?'

'I have nothing to wear!' Evaine exclaimed as she slipped on her gloves and hurried to open the door. 'Nothing that isn't worn through and if I am to be...' Her voice trailed away.

'If you are to be what?' Runa frowned, unsettled. 'Leaving soon?'

Evaine spun around. 'Is that what you want? To throw me out? Send me back to that place, with that woman?'

Runa rubbed Sigmund's tiny back. 'Me? None of this has anything to do with me, Evaine. But surely it does have something to do with your son, who I don't believe you've even looked at today.'

Evaine huffed her way back over to the baby as he gave a loud burp, rivers of milk streaming from his mouth. She grimaced. 'I need to get my strength back. And you have so much more experience than me. He needs your care more than mine right now, wouldn't you say?'

Runa couldn't argue with that. It was obvious to her that Evaine saw motherhood as simply a way to hook her claws back into Eadmund's heart. If they had ever been there at all. 'Well,' she said tightly, 'perhaps you're right.' She didn't want to stand in the way of Evaine leaving the house. It was all Runa desired. And Sigmund was far better company.

Evaine smiled triumphantly, turning back to the door. 'And you needn't worry. I won't be leaving Oss. Neither of us will.'

***

THE BURNING SEA

Eadmund rolled over. His head was aching.

He frowned, annoyed with himself. He couldn't remember the last time he'd lost himself in drink. Not since before the tincture. He couldn't understand what had happened. Why had he lost control? Why now?

He tried to open his eyes, but the sharp pains in his head closed them quickly. The narrow bed he'd managed to secure for himself creaked as he shuffled around, trying to find a more comfortable position. It seemed like an impossible quest, though. He groaned instead, trying to swallow.

Saala's cold hall was coming to life around him, but he was not ready to be awake yet. He was half asleep, still thinking of Evaine. His dream of her had felt so intense, as though it had actually happened. Eadmund grimaced, feeling an unsettling mix of desire and guilt.

'Had a nice sleep?' Thorgils grumbled as he shoved Eadmund over and sat down, squeezing his wide rump onto the edge of the tiny bed. 'Better than most in here I'd say, by the look on your face. Must have been all that ale you had?'

Eadmund tried to sit up. 'You're getting more like Odda every day,' he croaked moodily. 'No wonder your father spent all his time trying to divorce her.'

'That's a nice greeting for your best friend,' Thorgils muttered. 'And here's me, bringing you a cup of water. I may as well drink it myself.' He lifted the wooden cup to his great frothing beard.

Eadmund leaned over, snatching it out of Thorgils' hand. 'I'll take it.' He drained the cup quickly, cleared his throat and tried to smile, ignoring the thunderous pounding between his eyes. 'Thank you. I needed that.'

'Well, you see, that's what being a friend is... thinking of others,' Thorgils murmured. 'Looks like you're going to have to start remembering that. Being a friend... being a husband.' He leaned in, watching as the servants brought the large fire in the centre of the hall back to life. 'There aren't many around here impressed with your wife, you know. Ivaar is weaving all sorts of doubts into their minds, helped along by Otto, of course. I think Jael could do with all the friends she could get right now.'

Eadmund swallowed, wishing there was more water. His shoulders sagged; he didn't want to think about Jael. 'Well, perhaps you and I need to work our way through the Islanders? Make sure their loyalties are intact before we leave.' He eased his way to the edge of the bed. 'We can't have their heads being turned before the battle.'

Thorgils looked pleased. 'That's the most sense you've made in a while!' He stood up, grabbing Eadmund's cloak and swordbelt. 'Come on, then. It'll be some time before there's anything for us to eat by the looks of it. Let's go and see who we can find.' He glanced around, lowering his voice. 'I'm not about to let Ivaar defeat Jael, or us.'

Eadmund threw his cloak around his shoulders, trying to blink himself back into the present, but all he could see were images of Evaine's naked body as it writhed beneath him.

***

The house was not warm. And as for the bed...

Jael shook her head at how soft she had become as she stretched her arms and yawned. It was not so long ago that she'd been squeezed into that tiny little cottage in Andala with Biddy and Aleksander. But now she couldn't stop her mind from wandering back to the house on Oss and the bed she had shared with Eadmund. And the puppies. She sighed, rolling over.

There were so many things to organise, but all she could think about was what was wrong with Eadmund. Was it because of Aleksander? Or his son? Had the tincture suddenly stopped working?

Was it Evaine?

'Jael?' Eydis whispered as she felt her way around the dark room.

Light was seeping under the door, and it helped Jael to see, but for Eydis, it was always night.

'I'm here, Eydis,' Jael whispered back. 'Follow my voice.'

Eydis found the bed and Jael grabbed her hand. She felt warm. 'Are you feeling unwell? You're very hot.'

'I had too many furs,' Eydis murmured as she sat down, not wanting Amma to hear.

'Ahhh, so that's where they all went,' Jael laughed, noticing that both her mother and Amma were awake and talking now. 'No wonder I was so cold!'

'Well, I didn't want Eydis to freeze,' Amma said sleepily. 'It's not a very warm house.'

'No, it isn't, but we could be in a tent with Axl and Fyn,' Jael pointed out. 'I'm sure they'd happily change places.'

'And why are *you* here?' Gisila wondered, wrapping her cloak around her nightdress as she walked over to poke the thoroughly dead embers in the brazier. 'I thought you'd be with your husband by now?'

Jael's face fell. 'And miss listening to you snore all night, Mother?'

'What has happened?' Eydis asked softly. 'Something's wrong with Eadmund, isn't it? I feel it.'

'Do you see Eadmund in your dreams?' Jael wondered as she grabbed a fur, draping it around them both.

'I see Ivaar in my dreams,' Eydis whispered. 'He is so happy.'

'Ivaar?'

Gisila had disappeared into the main room, looking for Gunni. Amma was hurriedly dressing.

'I'm worried, Jael,' Eydis said, her bottom lip quivering. 'I don't want anything to happen to you. Or Eadmund.'

'Eydis,' Jael said gently. 'I must certainly survive this battle if I'm worthy of having a prophecy written about me. There must be something important I'm supposed to do, and I don't imagine this is it.' She squeezed Eydis' hand. 'And you know that I'll do everything in my power to keep everyone safe, including Fyn.'

'Fyn?' Eydis blushed.

Jael smiled. 'Well, that's good news.'

'What?'

'Your father is thinking of betrothing you to Fyn, so I'm glad to see that it wouldn't be such an unwanted thing.'

'He wants me to marry Fyn?' Eydis' mouth fell open.

Jael laughed. 'Come on, let's find your clothes. I want some breakfast before Lothar and Thorgils eat it all. There's plenty of time to talk about Fyn later.' She stood up, reaching down for Eydis' hand as she sat there, horrified, too shocked to even close her mouth.

***

Meena woke up sobbing, her pillow soaked in tears. She shivered as she lay there, pulling her thin blanket up to her face, rocking back and forth, terrified. Her little bed felt so lonely, tucked into the corner of Varna's dark chamber. She thought of her father, who had been dead for so many years now; her mother, who she couldn't even remember. Now there was only her grandmother.

And Meena was terrified of her.

But she had to do something.

She couldn't take another night terrorised by those nightmares.

***

Biddy was not about to let Edela go wandering off by herself. Not after the surprise dump of snow overnight. Well, not really a dump, she supposed as they shuffled across the square together. More a generous sprinkling.

Ido and Vella were happy with it, though, sniffing the freezing white powder as they raced around the two women, urging them to hurry up.

'Could we go faster?' Edela grumbled. 'I am not a toddler learning how to walk!'

'It's slippery,' Biddy said sternly. 'So no, I don't think that would be a good idea.'

'At this rate, we'll be at Entorp's for supper!' Edela huffed, trying to speed up but Biddy had a firm grip on her arm, and, being nearly twenty years younger, she had a good deal more strength on her side.

They tussled as they walked, until Edela finally gave in, both of them laughing. Biddy's face froze quickly, though, as she spied Evaine walking towards them, her long white cloak swishing across the snow-touched ground.

'Hello, again!' Edela called out, already pulling a reluctant Biddy in Evaine's direction. The puppies, seemingly on Edela's side, raced towards Evaine, their tails wagging as they jumped up at her cloak.

Evaine stopped, cringing, trying to push their dirty paws away.

'Ido! Vella!' Biddy cried.

The puppies ignored her, then suddenly sat back on their haunches, low growls building in their bellies. Evaine stumbled backwards, surprised.

Biddy smiled, leaving them to it, much to Evaine's displeasure.

'Those are Jael's dogs, aren't they?' she asked, trying to mask her irritation.

'Jael and Eadmund's, yes.'

Evaine ignored the disdain on Biddy's face. 'They don't seem to like me very much, do they?' she laughed nervously.

'No, well dogs have a good sense about people,' Biddy said coldly. 'They can tell a lot more than we can about somebody's true intentions.'

The smile froze on Evaine's face, and she quickly turned her eyes away from Biddy. 'And how are you feeling, Edela?' she wondered, trying her best to appear concerned. 'You look much better than when I last saw you.'

'Thank you,' Edela said cheerfully. 'I am much improved. And ready to do what I came here for.'

Biddy gripped Edela's arm tightly, but Edela refused to move or even look her way. She wanted to warn the girl, to show her that she was not unopposed here on Oss. That her plans for hurting Jael stood no chance for success.

'And what is that?' Evaine asked carefully.

'I am here to stop you,' Edela said firmly, staring into Evaine's eyes, ignoring Biddy's surprised gasp. She smiled confidently. 'You may flutter your pretty eyelashes, but know that we know what you are doing. More of us than you might think. We are watching you, and neither you, nor your mother will succeed.'

Evaine backed away, too shocked to speak.

The puppies' growls reached the back of their teeth.

'I, I,' Evaine stammered. 'I don't know what you're talking about. I must be going. I don't know what you're talking about.' And she hurried to turn around, walking away as quickly as her delicate feet would carry her.

Edela's knees almost gave way as Ido and Vella bounded back to her side.

Biddy grasped her arm to steady her, swallowing repeatedly, speechless.

'Well, come on then,' Edela said, clearing her throat, trying to find her voice again as she straightened her spine. 'We don't want to keep Entorp waiting, do we? There is much we need to discuss!'

***

Evaine slammed the door and rushed up the stairs without removing her cloak and boots. She didn't even acknowledge Runa who was still sitting by the fire, Sigmund asleep in her arms.

She hurried to the far side of the mezzanine where her double-sized bed stood, piled high with luxurious furs and pillows. Sitting down, Evaine tried to breathe, tried to think, but she was too panicked to see anything clearly.

What did Edela know? What *could* she know?

'Evaine?' Runa called up to her. 'Has something happened?'

Evaine shook her head, frantically trying to clear Edela out of it. She had no time to be distracted by an old woman's ramblings.

She would have to work fast.

***

Fyn sat down next to Jael and Eydis, yawning.

'Didn't sleep much?' Jael wondered, swallowing a lump of warm porridge and honey.

'Your brother snores,' Fyn groaned, rubbing his swollen eyes which were already considering the generous spread of food before him.

'Must run in the family,' Jael smiled. 'Perhaps I should swap places with Axl tonight? That way, we can both sleep!'

Fyn grabbed a flatbread and a slice of cheese. 'What about Eadmund?' he mumbled, shovelling everything into his mouth with speed. He nodded towards Eadmund, who was talking with Thorgils and Eirik on the opposite side of the hall.

Jael ignored his question and changed the subject. 'You should grab as much food as you can before it's all gone,' she grinned, noticing the influx of Islanders and Brekkans as they ambled in through the doors, their bulky frames and booming voices suddenly filling the hall with noise and earthy odours.

Fyn eyed the men and hurried to grab some fruit and cheese from the tray in front of them. 'What's the plan for the day, then?' he asked, popping a handful of berries into his mouth.

'Today, we prepare and talk. *A lot.*' Jael glanced at Eirik who motioned her over. 'Best keep yourself busy with Axl, sharpening everything you've got. Perhaps you could take Eydis with you? See if you can find my cousin Amma. Axl will help you find her. She'll look after you, Eydis.'

Both Eydis and Fyn appeared ready to protest, but Jael left too quickly for either one to even form the words. They sat silently next to each other, neither knowing what to say.

Jael smiled as she wandered over to Eirik.

'Did you sleep well?' Eirik wondered brightly.

'Not really,' Jael said, glancing at Eadmund, who appeared to look right through her. 'Nothing could compare to my bed on Oss.'

Eirik was pleased to hear it.

'Well, at least you *had* a bed,' Thorgils grumbled, his hair shuddering as he scratched his nose. 'I had the floor, and not much else.'

'These are hard times,' Eirik said, trying not to laugh. 'And where is your uncle?' he wondered, nodding at Rexon and Gant who joined them.

'Lothar is just up,' Gant said. 'He'll be here shortly, I'm sure.'

Eirik was relieved to hear it. He felt a rush today. He'd slept well and didn't feel too ill, which was surprising given how much wine and ale he'd consumed. He was so pleased to be preparing for battle that he happily ignored his familiar old-man aches and pains. He'd already been out for a walk around the fort and seen that the sky was hidden behind iron-grey clouds, but there was blue lurking just behind them, and he was looking forward to a productive day. They would set sail the day after tomorrow, and

Eirik couldn't wait.

'We'll hold a ritual tomorrow night,' Rexon announced, nodding at some of Eirik's lords as they made their way into the hall, looking very much the worse for wear. 'I've spoken to Lothar about it.' He tried not to let the scorn from his tongue show on his face. 'He's not very interested, but I know that my people would appreciate Furia's blessing before we depart.'

'I'll take any luck I can get!' Eirik agreed. 'But along with luck, we need a solid plan. So as soon as Lothar and Osbert are here, we must begin the arguing and compromising.' He glanced at his six lords and Ivaar, knowing how these things went. 'You have a map?'

'Oh, yes,' Rexon said wryly, causing Gant's serious face to break into a smile. 'This is not the first time we've done this.'

Eadmund was barely listening as he looked on. As soon as Ivaar had entered the hall, all he could think about was killing him.

How he would do it. When.

Perhaps in this battle...

It had been rewarding, turning fat into muscle, honing his skills, increasing his strength, becoming faster and sharper than he had been in years. But all that work hadn't been for Hest; it hadn't been for his father, or even for Jael.

Eadmund knew that everything he had done over the past few months had been for one thing only.

To help him kill his brother.

***

'Please, Grandmother!' Meena wailed, cowering on her knees by Varna's chair. 'Please, make it stop. I will do anything. Anything!' she sobbed in despair. 'Please make it s-s-s-stop!' Her eyes were swollen, raw from crying. She had barely slept in three nights, driven mad by nightmares; nightmares so gruesome she wanted to vomit. Terrifying hounds, with blood, and death and darkness and beasts and murderous men, half-dead, with knives and...

She shook all over, tapping her foot as she stooped even lower, wanting to curl up into a ball.

Desperate to feel safe.

Varna rose from her hard wooden chair, standing over her. 'You have learned your lesson, then?' she rasped, her teeth bared. 'You have learned who you must be loyal to above all others?'

Meena resisted the urge to shrink away. She started nodding.

'You have seen what will happen to you if you are not?' Varna asked, bending so close to Meena that her ice-cold breath devoured her granddaughter's shivering frame. 'What will come for you in the dark?'

Meena's eyes widened. 'Y-y-y-yes,' she stuttered.

'And you will show me what it is that Jaeger Dragos has you scurrying about for?'

'Y-y-y-yes.' Meena didn't hesitate. She wanted to be loyal to Jaeger, but not as much as she wanted to feel safe again. To know that she could close her eyes and not see the evil emerging from the shadows her grandmother was tormenting her with.

Varna smiled. 'Well, then get up, my child. Come, sit by the fire, and we shall talk, you and I.'

CHAPTER SIXTEEN

'Where have you been?' Jael frowned.

Aleksander smiled, happy to see her, despite her grumpy face. 'Been?'

'I haven't seen you since last night,' she said, coming to a stop in front of him. 'You missed our meeting, and Lothar's looking for you.'

'There's a sickness spreading through the camp.'

'What? *Already*?'

'Well, according to some of the men I spoke to, it started on the march from Andala, but no one said anything about it.'

'And now?' Jael wondered as she started walking back to the hall, enjoying the heat from the sun which had finally emerged from behind the clouds. 'How many men are we talking about?'

'I counted twenty-three.'

'*Twenty-three*?'

'Mmmm, not such a small amount,' Aleksander said seriously. 'Avilda and Pria are with the sick.' He nodded at Gant, who was approaching. 'That's where I've been, moving them away from the rest of the men.'

'What is it?' Gant asked, noting the tension on Aleksander's face. 'Where have you been?'

Aleksander explained the situation as they continued into the hall, where Lothar had once again made himself comfortable in Rexon's chair. Eirik stood beside him, talking animatedly to Frits

Hallstein from the island of Bara, who had not been convinced by Jael's plan for their attack. Jael eyed him moodily. None of the lords had thought much of her ideas. Then again, they hadn't seen Aleksander's demonstration of the sea-fire. Let them grumble, she thought to herself, trying not to let it unsettle her.

But it was not only Frits who had a problem with Jael. Eirik's other lords were griping as well, talking amongst themselves, heads together, eyes furtive as they shot her barely-concealed looks of distrust; no doubt stirred up by Ivaar, who appeared to be going from one lord to the other, his lips always a hair's breadth from one of their ears.

Jael turned towards the more urgent discussion of the camp sickness.

'Sick men will do nothing for morale,' Lothar was muttering. 'Nor will they do anything for my defenses!' He glowered at Aleksander. 'And they are far away now? From the healthy men?'

'Yes, lord,' Aleksander nodded.

Lothar turned to Osbert. 'Didn't you notice anything on your march? Didn't you wonder what was happening when your men were squatting in the bushes and shitting their breeches?'

Osbert swallowed, wanting to turn his father's bulging eyes towards someone else. 'Gant was in charge of the columns of men –'

'Gant?' Lothar sneered, his thick head making him thoroughly irritable. 'Gant Olborn is not my heir, the one who wishes to be king! Gant Olborn was not leading my men, *you* were, Osbert!' He slapped Osbert on the side of the head. 'And *you* should remember to check on your men!'

Osbert was too horrified to speak. His eyes flared before quickly finding the floor. Rage rushed up into his throat; rage he quashed in a hurry. He had to; they were all looking at him: the lords, the Skallesons, Jael... 'Of course, Father,' he muttered. 'I shall go and see how they are faring.'

'Yes, you will!' Lothar barked as Osbert hurried towards the doors, desperate to escape. 'But you will not get close, do you understand me? Whatever evil is lurking in those men's guts, I do not wish it brought back here!'

Gant turned to Aleksander. 'How bad are they?'

'Unable to walk. Very ill.'

'So we may lose some?'

'I would say so.'

'Well, this is terrible timing, wouldn't you say, Eirik?' Lothar groaned. 'Not good at all.'

'Yes, I agree,' Eirik said, turning away from Frits, who had left surly and unsatisfied. He had not realised how popular Otto was, nor, perhaps, how unpopular a decision putting a Brekkan in charge of their fleet would be, and a woman at that. But Eirik was confident that, eventually, they would see what he saw in Jael. 'There's no going back now, though. Haaron knows we're coming, and soon his ships will leave his harbour. We cannot change course.'

'Nor would we want to!' Lothar growled happily. 'When we have come so far and with so many men? We'll surely not miss a handful.'

Aleksander looked doubtfully at Gant and Jael. From what he had seen of the state of the sick men, they would be lucky if it stayed a handful for long.

***

Varna had dragged Meena around the castle towards Jaeger's chamber on the second floor. No one had even glanced their way; most being too afraid of Varna to say a word, and none having any affection for Meena anyway.

She was a strange girl.

Varna yanked her granddaughter into the chamber, quickly shutting the door behind them. 'Where is it?' she hissed impatiently.

Meena swallowed. It felt as though the sharp claws digging into her arm were digging into her very soul.

There was no fire, and, despite the window that overlooked the harbour, there was little light. Meena frowned, peering around. 'He kept it over there,' she mumbled, pointing towards the table that stood near the empty fireplace, in the middle of the room.

'What?' Varna barked. 'Speak up, little mouse! Or is it that you're changing your mind already? Worried about what your lover will say?'

Meena cringed. 'He is not my –'

Varna didn't care. '*Where* did he keep it?' she snarled.

Meena tapped her head. 'On the table. Un-un-under a cloth.'

Varna was already at the table, but there was no cloth. There was nothing on the table but a goblet and a jug; both empty. The chamber appeared to have been recently cleaned. But, of course, she realised; Jaeger could not be a complete idiot, or he wouldn't have found the book in the first place. Spinning around, Varna scurried towards Jaeger's bed at the far end of the long chamber. 'Get under there, girl!' she ordered. 'See if it's there!'

Meena hurried to do as she was bid, crawling around on the ice-cold flagstones, scraping her knees. It was too dark to see anything much, but she felt around anyway. There was nothing there, apart from a goblet that had rolled under the bed, and a mouse who scurried away from her. Part of her felt relieved. The other part of her realised that her grandmother was unlikely to release her from her spell until she produced the book.

Varna had torn off the bed furs and thrown them onto the floor. She was breathing heavily, her bent shoulders aching from the effort. Nothing. She peered around in the dim light as Meena emerged from beneath the bed, shaking her head. 'Well, keep looking!' she panted, shuffling over to the decorative iron chest at the end of Jaeger's bed. It was not locked, so she eased open the heavy lid, sifting through its contents with an increasingly irate desperation. Nothing! Nothing but women's clothing and jewels.

His dead wife's chest, she realised with a groan.

Meena came back to her grandmother, empty-handed. She glanced around.

They had looked everywhere.

Varna sat down on the bed, working her jaw. 'Who else knew about it, do you think? His servant? That fat little man, what's his name?'

'Eg-eg-eg-Egil,' Meena spluttered. 'I don't know.'

'Well, someone must know! Someone must have given that book to him. He did not go digging about for it himself, did he?'

Meena kept her eyes on the floor, worried about what her grandmother would do next.

Varna's head snapped around, surveying the room. 'Find something of Jaeger's. Clothing, an arm ring. Anything!' she rasped. 'There are other ways to find out what we need to know!'

***

Eydis felt odd. Being around so many strangers was unsettling. And Fyn. She wasn't sure which was worse.

'Eydis?' Fyn peered at her. She was sitting on his chest, a worried look furrowing her brow. 'Are you alright?'

Eydis turned towards Fyn's voice. She could hear him scraping his whetstone down the blade of his sword; sharpening it, as he had been doing for most of the morning. She sighed. 'Yes, as I said a moment ago, I'm fine.'

Amma laughed. 'Perhaps it's just that it's so very dull to sit and listen to that dreadful noise all day!'

Fyn looked at Axl, who was doing the very same thing.

'Well, would you rather our swords were capable of killing a man or just tickling him a bit?' Axl snorted at Amma, barely looking up from his own sword, which gleamed in the sunshine.

Amma rolled her eyes. 'Come on, Eydis,' she said. 'Why don't we go for a walk? I can tell you all about Saala and what I can see. It's not a very large place,' she said, 'but it's far more interesting than staying here with these two!' She smiled tartly at Axl.

'I'd like that,' Eydis said eagerly. 'I'd like to see what is happening.' She shook her head, reaching for Amma's hand. 'With my ears, of course.'

Fyn didn't look happy. 'I promised Jael –'

'Jael will be fine with Amma looking after Eydis,' Axl assured him. 'Amma wouldn't dare cross her, would you?' he smiled.

'Jael?' Amma laughed. 'No, I'd like to see Andala again!' She helped Eydis out of the tent. 'Don't worry about us. We'll stay far away from anyone who looks too hairy and mean!'

'Make sure you stay away from the quarantined area, too,' Axl reminded her.

Amma rolled her eyes, turning after Eydis, her cloak swirling around her like a sail. Axl watched her go, distracted.

'Is she your... woman?' Fyn wondered shyly. 'Your cousin?'

Axl blinked, quickly clearing his face of anything other than irritation. 'My woman?' He shook his head, suddenly very interested in one particular area on his blade. 'No, she's just my cousin.'

'You think I'll tell Jael?' Fyn asked quietly. He had started to enjoy Axl's company after an awkward start. He wasn't sure he'd ever had a friend his own age before, and though it was strange, it wasn't unpleasant.

Axl peered at him. 'You wouldn't? But you're loyal to her.'

Fyn's face was suddenly serious. 'I would do anything for Jael,' he said fiercely. 'Anything. She saved my life. Changed my life. Everything. I owe all of it to her.'

Axl wasn't sure if he should feel proud of his sister or annoyed that she'd worked so hard to help someone who wasn't him. 'Is that so?'

Fyn nodded eagerly. 'When I met her, I couldn't even hold

onto a sword, let alone use it properly. She trained me.'

'Well, you must be a good warrior, then,' Axl decided. 'I don't imagine she'd keep you around if you weren't.'

Fyn smiled, hoping that was true.

'And as for Amma,' Axl murmured leaning towards his tent-mate. 'If her father or brother found out they would marry her off immediately. So, tell Jael, if you wish. I'm not sure she'd care either way. I know she wouldn't say anything. But no one else can know.' He swallowed. 'I must keep Amma safe.'

Fyn thought about Eydis, hoping she was alright. He frowned, then smiled, realising that he knew just how Axl felt.

***

'What do you think you're doing?' Bayla cried as she crashed into Meena Gallas, who was hurrying out of Jaeger's chamber. Her surprise only intensified when Varna came rushing out after her.

Meena gasped, turning quickly to her grandmother, her feet shuffling helplessly beneath her. She was desperate to run away from Bayla and Varna, both.

'We are looking for something,' Varna said boldly, her eyes challenging Bayla.

'In my son's chamber? What?'

'Something Meena left there when your son forced himself upon her!'

Bayla was surprised. 'Why would he do *that*?' She stared at the crumpled, hunched, twitching figure before her. Perhaps if she were tidied up, perhaps there was something worth looking at under all that wild red hair and those shapeless rags. But Jaeger would've had to look very closely to have seen it. 'Why?'

'Your son took advantage of my granddaughter!' Varna growled crossly. 'A girl who is not even right in the head. A poor, addle-brained girl!'

Bayla glanced at Meena, who was indeed tapping her head. 'Jaeger is the son of the king,' she sneered. 'But I suppose, even the son of the king can be drunk and desperate enough to settle for a hideous mess like this.'

Varna's lips curled venomously. 'Yes, I imagine that's what Haaron's father thought when his son chose to marry you.' She grabbed Meena's hand and hurried her away from Bayla's blanched face.

Bayla stared after them, too furious to even blink.

***

Eadmund was showing Torborn Sverri of Tervo – the smallest of Eirik's islands – around his ship. They had grown up together on Oss but were much changed from the carefree boys, or even the fearless warriors, they had once been. Both had heavy shoulders now, weighed down with the responsibility of their positions.

'Seven children?' Eadmund laughed. 'You're doing better than me, old friend!'

'Well, you're only newly married,' Torborn smiled. 'And perhaps your wife has her mind on things other than little Eadmunds?' His expression became serious as he glanced around, but the closest men were far down the beach, not within hearing distance.

'Jael?' Eadmund muttered, his smile fading. 'She's an excellent warrior, it's true.'

'So I hear, but commander of our fleet?' Torborn wondered, a reddish eyebrow raised at his friend. 'It seems as though your father favours her greatly. To remove Otto like that?'

Eadmund frowned, sensing where this was going. He leaned towards Torborn. 'Otto removed himself after our last attack on

Skorro and don't let anyone tell you otherwise. He'd still be there if he hadn't left so many Islanders sinking to their deaths in the Adrano while he ran back to Oss as quickly as he could.'

Torborn stood back. He was not as tall as Eadmund, nor as broad. And despite what may have happened to his friend since Melaena's death, he knew that the Eadmund of old had returned now and that Eadmund, from memory, was not a man to be trifled with. 'Well, as you say, Otto has no reason to complain, I see that. But,' he began diplomatically, 'why didn't Eirik think of you to replace him? Are you happy he chose your wife over you?'

Eadmund turned towards the sinking sun. Images of Evaine and Sigmund flashed before his eyes, and, distracted, he hoped they were both well. He thought of Jael. Jael fighting Tarak. Jael fighting Aleksander. Finally, he shook his head. 'My father favours her for good reason. She is Furia's daughter, and just as fierce as that war goddess. He could not have made a better choice, I promise you.' Eadmund said it without thinking, without feeling, and frowning, he turned back around. 'And make sure you tell all the lords that. I know what Otto and Ivaar are doing with their whispers, but I promise you, Torborn, my father will not hesitate to remove any man who doesn't follow Jael. As would I, in his place.'

***

'This will be the first time we've fought without each other,' Aleksander said as they stood on the sand, watching Eadmund talking to one of the lords on *Ice Breaker*.

Jael blinked at him, surprised. It was true. 'Who will watch my back?' she wondered with a sad smile.

'You seem to have a few new friends,' Aleksander said, with only the smallest hint of jealousy.

'I do,' she supposed. 'And you?'

'Well, I'll have Gant and Rexon. Not the worst.'

Jael laughed. 'No, not the worst. And there's always Axl too.'

'I'll keep Axl close if I can.'

'Good,' she said quickly. 'He'll need you. Remember our first battle? The sound and the smell and the horror of it all?' Jael shook her head, the memories surging back. 'It was a shock, no matter what had come before, no matter how hard we'd trained. It was so fast and loud and terrifying.'

'But we were together. With Ranuf. And Gant.'

'And Rexon,' Jael said nostalgically. 'Back then.'

Aleksander shrugged. 'We've done well to have survived this long, wouldn't you say? All of us.'

'I'd say so, but I'd like to survive a bit longer, I think,' Jael mused. 'I have a prophecy to fulfill.'

'Apparently.'

They laughed.

'If anything happens to me...' Aleksander's voice drifted away.

'Don't say that.'

'I want to say some things.'

'Why? You don't need to,' Jael insisted awkwardly, looking away.

Aleksander reached for her hand, his eyes on Eadmund in the distance. 'I'm not mad at you,' he said quietly. 'In case you think that. I'm not.'

Jael's shoulders heaved. 'But...'

'No, Jael,' Aleksander insisted, 'I'm not. I wish it were different, of course, but I don't blame you for anything. I know you'd never try to hurt me.'

Jael couldn't meet his eyes. It was all a mess. She didn't even want to begin to make sense of it. She changed the subject. 'There's no glory in dying for Lothar, you know.'

'You think I'd throw myself in front of that piece of shit?' Aleksander laughed, shaking his head. 'Take an arrow for him?

No, I promise you this... if Lothar is determined to kill himself, I won't stand in his way. And he can take his turd of a son with him. I'll grab Axl and retreat.'

Jael grinned. 'I'm glad to hear it.'

'I think Gisila would thank me.'

'I agree. She looks terrible.'

'Well, not everyone falls in love with the husband they're forced to marry.'

Jael rolled her eyes, but it was hard to keep the sadness out of them.

'You can talk to me if you like,' Aleksander suggested, nodding towards Eadmund. 'About what's happened.'

'No.' Jael shook her head. 'Never.' And inhaling a deep breath, she turned away from the beach. Eadmund had left the ship and was making his way towards them. 'We should go. There's a lot to do. I need to meet with the lords again. I have to get through to them somehow. They're such a difficult bunch of bastards, though!' And, muttering to herself, Jael hurried away, not waiting for him.

Aleksander watched her go, before sighing and trudging after her.

***

'This was certainly a good idea, don't you think?' Lothar panted as he rolled off Gisila, sweaty and happily undone.

Gisila grimaced as she eased over to her side of the bed, gasping for air. Lothar's great lumping body was getting bigger by the day, just as hers was shrinking. Soon, she was certain, he would snap her bones. 'Yes, of course,' she said mutely, pulling the furs up to her chin, desperate for some warmth. Being so close to Hest, Saala was a warm place, but as soon as the clouds covered the sun, it was like being back in Andala.

'Just what I need to set me right again,' he sighed, stretching out sleepily.

'Don't you need to go back to the hall, my love?' Gisila asked gently. 'Isn't there a ritual tonight?'

'No, no, that's tomorrow,' Lothar yawned. 'It appears that Rexon's people are as superstitious as Ranuf was. He wants to sacrifice something in the hope that it will bring us luck.'

'But that can't be a bad thing, can it?' Gisila murmured, thinking of her family. 'Whether you believe in it or not, having the gods on our side was always helpful to Ranuf.'

'Yes, I suppose so,' Lothar said quietly, his eyes heavy. He had eaten two full meals, and his recent effort with Gisila had taken him over the edge. 'But enough talk, for now, my sweet, I shall just close my eyes for a moment.'

He was snoring within seconds, much to Gisila's relief.

She lay there, next to her husband, desperate to be anywhere else, praying that Furia would kill him in the battle.

She had no wish for him to return.

***

Rexon slowly kissed his wife goodbye, his hands on either side of her rounded face. Demaeya Boas was pregnant; heavily so. He had thought to keep her with him as they had lost their first child, but now, with the sickness spreading, Rexon knew that he had to get her out of Saala fast.

'Have your aunt send word,' he insisted, his breath warm on her cheek. 'As soon as the child is born.'

'Child?' Demaeya laughed, wrinkling her freckled nose. 'The size I am, I'm certain there's more than one in there!'

Rexon didn't think that sounded such a bad idea.

Demaeya frowned. 'Please, whatever you do,' she whispered, glancing around from her position high atop the wagon. 'Please don't let that man destroy you or our people. Or our home. Not again. Please.'

'I promise,' Rexon smiled with as much certainty as he could imagine when thinking of Lothar. 'You will return and not even notice that we've been in a battle.'

His wife did not look convinced.

'And you will return with our new children!' he laughed. 'All three of them boys!'

Demaeya smiled as the driver impatiently clicked the reins. 'Be safe, my love.'

'And you.' Rexon held up a hand, watching as the small wagon wobbled away, his eyes never leaving his wife's face as she disappeared slowly into the dusk-covered distance. He felt an unsettling emptiness, suddenly deprived of what he loved and valued most in the world. He could not allow Lothar to endanger that; to destroy his future and the future of his people with his reckless ambition.

'I've got some news,' Gant announced as he approached. 'About the sickness.'

Rexon's eyes were still on the wagon. 'What?'

'A man has died. Two more about to follow. Seven more gripping their bellies.'

Rexon ran a hand over his lips, remembering the sweet taste of Demaeya's cheek. 'I'll have my men build the pyres.'

'It's a bad sign.'

'It is, my friend.'

'No good will come from Lothar's push into Hest,' Gant murmured, his eyes everywhere. 'That's what Edela warned.'

'Did she?' Rexon was surprised, then troubled. 'Lothar failed to mention that part.'

Gant said nothing, conscious of their very public location.

'It's time Brekka had a new king,' Rexon whispered, narrowing his eyes as he turned to his friend. 'Wouldn't you say?'

Gant stilled.

He stared at Rexon, his wary eyes communicating as much as he dared.

CHAPTER SEVENTEEN

Jael felt sick as she watched Eadmund from across the hall.

His eyes never drifted towards her. They hadn't drifted towards her once since their arrival in Saala. He'd not spoken to her either, quickly disappearing whenever she approached him.

'It must be Evaine,' Thorgils murmured, coming up behind her. 'She's done something to him, wouldn't you say? Her or Morana?'

Jael swallowed. 'Yes, I think so.' She shook her head. 'But we've no time to find a solution now.'

Thorgils frowned, his eyes boring into Eadmund as he sat drinking with Torstan and Torborn. 'No, no time at all, for Haaron's ships will be in the water soon, and you, my friend, have many problems.'

It was Jael's turn to frown. 'What do you mean?' she wondered, sipping slowly from a cup of Rexon's excellent wine.

Thorgils inclined his head towards the doors. 'Let's go for a walk, and I'll tell you about my day.'

Jael put her cup on the nearest table, and with one last, worried look at Eadmund, she followed Thorgils outside.

***

Ayla had felt lighter since Ivaar's departure. She could wander wherever she chose, sleep fully clothed, in peace, undisturbed. And as deeply unhappy as she still felt in her heart, the absence of Ivaar had brought a welcome sense of relief, and she was determined to make the most of it before his return.

He would return. She had seen it.

Every night she went to bed with a collection of things now. She had one of Ivaar's arm rings that he'd left behind to help her dream for him. There was Thorgils' red curl from Isaura, and one of Eydis' brooches which she'd taken before she left Oss, determined to keep one eye on her. Ayla smiled sadly. It was a weight to carry, but also an opportunity to peer into the future; to find hope, even though she was worried that none truly existed.

Dusk was slowly turning to night as she made her way back to her cottage with a basket of food from the hall kitchen. She didn't want to eat with anyone, despite Isaura's kinder approach to her now. Ayla just wanted to be alone with her thoughts, her sadness, and her pain; free to grieve for all that she had lost; free to pray to the gods for all that she wished to reclaim. She had that in her basket too: herbs, mushrooms, stones, bones, even a jar of fresh blood. All the things she would need to reach out to Lydea, the Tuuran Goddess of Dreams.

She was desperate for some help.

Strict rules applied to what Ayla could do with her gifts, but her aunt had not believed that the temple was the only source of wisdom in Tuura. She had taught Ayla that her gifts as a dreamer could open doors that the elders kept locked.

Doors into dreams that weren't even hers.

Doors to the gods, the Old Gods, the Tuuran Gods.

And Ayla needed their help.

***

Jael and Thorgils walked along the soft sand, which made a nice change from Oss' slippery stones. The noise from the hall and the village followed them at first, but as they walked further down the beach, they left more of it behind.

'Ivaar's sowing seeds,' Thorgils said quietly. It was dark now, thick clouds hiding the moon and stars, and there was little way of telling who was lurking around the ships they passed.

'Of course he is,' Jael murmured. 'He'd be foolish not to if it's the crown he still wants.'

'Which, of course, it is.'

'But he needs support to win it back,' Jael suggested with a frown. 'So how many of the lords are with him, then?'

Thorgils stopped, turning to her. 'All of them.'

'What?' Jael was stunned. '*All* of them?'

'Yes, I spoke to half the lords today,' he said. 'Eadmund talked to the others. Viktor and Ador both implied that Ivaar had the support of all the islands.'

'And they just *said* this to you? Not caring if you told Eirik or Eadmund? Or me? They don't care if their king knows that they're not loyal to him? They would say that so openly?' Jael shook her head in disbelief.

'It's a bad sign,' Thorgils agreed. 'They could join together to defeat Eirik, or Eadmund after Eirik's death. I didn't get the feeling that any of them had the stomach to remove their king now, though. They all owe their lordships to him.'

The wind was rising. It was cold in the darkness and Jael shivered. 'And they feel no loyalty towards Eadmund at all? None of them?'

'Well,' Thorgils sighed, 'they like Eadmund, sure, but in Ivaar they see the next Eirik. They don't see that in Eadmund. Or perhaps they forgot who he was after all those years of him being a useless drunk. They look at Ivaar and see a ruthless and hungry man, just as Eirik was when he called himself Eirik the Bloody. And...'

'And?'

'They don't like you. You're a Brekkan. A Furyck. Their sworn enemy.'

'Oh.'

'So you can imagine they don't like that Eirik chose to make you their commander.'

Jael clenched her jaw. 'For what we need to do, everyone must follow my orders. We can't be a fleet in disarray. It would be catastrophic.'

'Then we have some more talking to do, it seems, Eadmund and I.' Thorgils grabbed his cloak as it fluttered away from him, pulling it around his giant frame. 'We have one more day to turn it around.'

'Well, if anyone can sweet talk a bunch of grizzled old men into following me, you can,' Jael grinned, trying to cheer them both up; ignoring the loud voice clanging in her ears that warned her he was wasting his breath.

***

'You needn't worry about your brother,' Eirik whispered, squeezing Eydis' hand. 'Ivaar will not get near Oss. I will not let it happen. Jael and Eadmund will not let it happen.'

But Eydis' frown did not relax. The heady din of Rexon's hall was overpowering her senses, drowning her in confusion.

'You have made a friend, I hear,' Eirik said, trying to make her smile with a new subject that didn't involve her eldest brother. 'Jael's cousin?'

'Amma,' Eydis nodded. 'Yes, she is nice.'

'You'll have company, then, when we leave.'

'And Gisila,' Eydis mumbled. 'She will look after me too.'

'I'm glad,' Eirik said, distracted, watching Otto and Morac with their heads together; two old problems he needed to attend to, amongst so many others. He sighed, his eyes drifting towards Eadmund, who was laughing with Torstan. More problems than he could keep track of. But at least Eydis was in good hands. 'I have to go and speak to some of my men,' Eirik murmured. 'I'll take you to Amma. She's yawning like you, so perhaps you'll both need your beds before long.'

Eydis was ready to protest, but another yawn crept out of her mouth, and she realised that her father was right.

Eirik led her towards Amma, past Eadmund, who nodded briefly at him over the top of Torstan's head, a cup of ale in his hand. Eirik frowned, not wanting to give thought to the very real possibility that everything was about to unravel entirely.

Eadmund ignored his father's disapproving frown and laughed, slapping Torstan on the back as they stood whispering to each other by the fire. 'Ha! But what if Gunter finds out?'

Torstan squirmed. 'And why would he find out?' he wondered quietly, glancing around. 'She'd never say a word.'

'You did tell Thorgils, though,' Eadmund reminded him as he emptied another cup.

'He promised not to say anything,' Torstan mumbled, suddenly anxious.

'Here's hoping Thorgils doesn't get too many ales in him tonight,' Eadmund smiled. 'You and Gunter will be sharing a ship soon, and there'd be nothing to stop him tipping you into the Adrano. In the midst of battle, no one would notice a thing!'

The look on Torstan's face had Eadmund laughing again.

'You *are* enjoying yourself tonight, Brother,' Ivaar murmured as he and two of the lords joined their conversation.

Eadmund nodded at them, ignoring Ivaar. 'Hassi. Viktor.'

Both men returned tight smiles. They were similar in age: Eirik's age. Loose-skinned, leathery sailors of long ago. Hard men, who had never lost the look of hunger and starvation they had endured as slave children on Oss. Eirik had freed them, as he had all of his people, and they had been loyal to him. He had made them lords. And they owed him a great debt. But they also owed their people a future that would last long after the death of Eirik Skalleson.

'Hassi and Viktor were talking about how well you looked,' Ivaar smirked. 'So different than when they last saw you. There's so much less of you to see now.'

Torstan blinked rapidly, desperate to leave and have a word with Thorgils, but the look on Ivaar's face made him keep his boots where they were: right next to Eadmund's.

Eadmund had no interest in games. There would be time for him to speak to Ivaar, he knew, and he would prefer to do it with a sword in his hand, rather than an empty cup of ale. 'Indeed.' His lips were set in a straight line. 'I am myself again.'

'It's good to see, Eadmund,' Viktor of Mor said gruffly. 'Oss will need a strong leader when Vidar comes for your father.'

Eadmund didn't like the smile on Ivaar's face or the doubts in the old lords' bloodshot eyes. 'Well, you'll be pleased to know that there will be two. Eirik has named Jael as his heir as well.' He frowned; it felt odd to say her name.

Hassi of Rikka snorted.

Eadmund glared at him. 'You disapprove of his decision?'

Hassi pulled on the ends of his long white moustache which hung down to the middle of his chest. 'You think we Islanders should be happy to have a Brekkan lead us?' He coughed, clearing his throat. 'That we should *embrace* such a decision? And not just any Brekkan, but one who killed many of our men alongside her father. One who wasn't worthy of the Brekkan throne, but somehow, she's good enough for Oss'?'

Torstan swallowed, turning to Eadmund, who didn't even blink at the insult. 'It's a good thing my father can't hear you, Hassi,' he scowled, lowering his voice, 'because just as enemies can become friends and family, family and friends can quickly become enemies, isn't that right, Ivaar?' He smiled evenly at his brother. 'Especially ones who stir up trouble on the eve of the biggest test our kingdom has ever faced.'

Hassi blanched, looking at Viktor.

'One led by your wife,' Viktor grumbled, his broad red face glowing hotly in the flames of the fire they stood around. 'How are we to have confidence in her as our leader, when, as Hassi says, her own father did not?'

'You can choose not to have confidence in Jael,' Eadmund said firmly. 'That's your right. But your confidence in my father's decision to decide the commander of our fleet should not waver. Eirik is not easily fooled. Nor is he prepared to put up with failure. And Otto was a failure.' He looked up to see his father approaching their small group. 'But here he comes, so why not tell him your concerns?'

Hassi and Viktor glanced at each other, before moving away, merging into the crowd; neither one prepared to face their king with the truth of their feelings. Not without a few more cups of ale in them.

Eirik frowned. 'Is it me?'

Eadmund grinned. 'I think so.'

'I didn't realise so many of my lords needed hand-holding before the battle.'

'They don't like Jael.'

Eirik glared at Ivaar. 'So I hear.'

'Don't look at me, Father,' Ivaar said indignantly. 'The lords' feelings for Jael Furyck are not new. She's been killing Islanders for years. They have no wish to see her on the throne of Oss one day.'

'Well, then,' Eirik murmured, 'perhaps it's time I look for new lords? Men prepared to embrace the future that *I'm* choosing for the islands. I am more than happy to discuss removing any who don't agree with me or my choice of commander.' He took the goblet of wine a servant offered him, inhaling its sweet fruity scent; Rexon Boas really did have the best wine he'd ever tasted. 'And that includes you, Ivaar.' He stared at his son, all humour gone now. 'You may wish me dead, and your brother, maybe even Jael. But none of us will survive Haaron's fleet if we do not follow *one* leader into battle. If you continue to stir up trouble or sow any more seeds of rebellion in my lords' heads before we take to our ships, then you will no longer be the Lord of Kalfa, do you understand? You will be Lord of the Nothing,' he spat. 'And I shall send Thorgils to Kalfa to inform your wife of your tragic loss.' He glared at Ivaar, his old eyes hard and bitter. 'I'm sure he'd enjoy that enormously.'

Ivaar shook with fury, his lips thin and white as they clamped together, his hands at his sides, pulsing against his legs. He nodded. 'As you wish, Father,' he muttered, at last, feeling the thud of his heart, like the angry beat of a drum inside his chest.

Eirik didn't move as he watched his eldest son walk stiffly away. Perhaps he had been too harsh? Said too much? But he would not let Ivaar destroy Oss or their chance of victory, however slim it might be.

***

Ayla's head had barely touched the pillow before she was lurching back up, gagging for air.

She sat there, trembling in the darkness, listening to the frantic rhythm of her breathing, her eyes flicking around as pieces of her dream flashed before them.

Panting, she tried to think of what to do.

What *could* she do?

And then she saw Eydis' face.

***

'Are you alright?' Jael wondered as Eadmund stumbled. He

didn't look drunk, but Torstan had muttered that maybe she should go and check on him, before hurrying Thorgils away for a quiet word.

'I just slipped,' Eadmund said crossly, looking to leave.

Jael grabbed his arm, imploring him to come back to her with her eyes, but his would not meet hers.

'I just slipped,' he said again, resisting the urge to shake her off and walk away; he didn't need her fussing. 'The floor is covered in ale. And not mine either. I've only had a couple of cups. No need to worry.'

Jael looked worried.

She was just about to try and get his evasive eyes to focus on hers when two men burst through the doors of the hall, forcing their way through the crowd of men and women gathered around the fires, their dirty wet cloaks flapping behind them.

Rexon, sitting next to Lothar at the high table, was quickly on his feet, striding to the fire to meet the men. His scouts.

'My lord.' The two men bowed their heads.

'You have news?' Rexon asked, his voice suddenly loud in the hushed hall.

'Yes, lord,' the older of the two men said breathlessly. 'Haaron's sons are on the march with a large army. Well over a thousand men. They should be at the pass in a day.'

A surprised murmur swept around the hall. That was much earlier than they had anticipated and would likely put an end to their plans for trapping the Hestians in the pass.

'And Haaron?' Lothar bellowed. 'You saw him?'

'No, my lord,' the older man replied, shaking his head. 'But Haegen and Karsten Dragos were there, leading their forces.'

Lothar frowned, glancing at Osbert. He'd had his heart set on defeating Haaron, but where was he?

'Perhaps he's gone to Skorro?' Osbert wondered, reading the perturbed expression on his father's face. 'To command their fleet?'

'Well, perhaps that's a good sign?' Lothar decided, voice

booming. 'Perhaps he fears what we're about to deliver to both his doors?' He wasn't feeling the confidence of his words, though.

'We'll need to leave in the morning, my lord,' Rexon said, turning to his king. 'If we're to have any hope of reaching them before they get through the pass, we can't delay.'

'Mmmm,' Lothar agreed, looking for Eirik, who was trying to make his way back to the high table. 'I would say so.'

'Therefore, lord,' Rexon continued. 'We must hold the ritual now. There will be no time tomorrow.'

Lothar farted, flicking a hand at Rexon. 'Go ahead, then,' he muttered, before turning to address the hall. 'I suggest we all say our goodbyes this evening! Ensure your swords and spears are sharp, your ships are loaded, and your bellies are full. And whatever you do, stay away from those sick men! We are going to need all of you to defeat Haaron and his sons!'

Rexon hurried to organise food and ale for his weary scouts as Eirik and the island lords joined Lothar and Osbert.

Eadmund turned to Jael. 'We should go. You don't want to be left out of that discussion.' And without waiting for her, he made his way through the crowd towards his father.

Jael hesitated, unsettled by Eadmund's strange behaviour.

Aleksander stopped beside her. 'I imagine Eirik will want you up there to keep those old goats in line,' he grinned. 'Come on.'

Jael felt happy to see his familiar face. 'Yes, I suppose so,' she smiled back, following him through the crowd, the aching hole in her heart growing wider and wider.

***

Ayla rummaged urgently inside the chest.

She had placed a lamp beside her on the table in Isaura's

private chamber. It was not enough light to see by, not really, not inside a dark chest. The night was stormy, and the moon was only visible in occasional flashes. She sighed impatiently, frustrated, but at last, her fingers touched hair. Gripping hold of it, Ayla yanked the doll out of the chest, holding it to the flame.

It was the right one. She smiled, turning to leave.

'What do you think you're doing?'

Ayla jumped in surprise. 'I, I...'

Isaura walked towards her, frowning, holding her own burning lamp. As she came closer, she saw the wooden doll Ayla held in her hand. Selene's doll. 'What are you doing, Ayla? Why do you want my daughter's doll? Do you mean her harm?'

Ayla shook her head. 'No, I don't,' she insisted. 'Never. It's just that I... need it.'

'For what?' Isaura's body was tense, her eyes suspicious.

Ayla didn't have time to convince Isaura of a story; there was barely enough time for the truth. 'I had a dream.'

***

They gathered by Alfnir's Tree, Saala's oldest tree. Ancient and mysterious, it had drawn Brekkans to seek its luck and protection for centuries.

The Tree of the Oster Gods, they called it.

The moon was bright, illuminating Rexon as he strode through the middle of his men, holding the sacrificial copper bowl; walking towards the stone at the foot of the tree where his volka, Huba, stood waiting.

Jael frowned. She glanced at Aleksander, and he turned to her, sharing in her discomfort. They could hear the horse as he was brought forward. Jael thought of Tig. She thought of her father. This was a ritual he had carried out as king. He had taught it to Rexon. It was older than any of them.

Jael wanted no part of it, though, certain that Furia did not need a horse to die to bestow her luck upon them. How could a warrior, a Brekkan warrior especially, wish for the death of such a noble creature? Her father had said it showed the ultimate sacrifice; that a Brekkan would give up one of their beloved horses to honour Furia. Jael shook her head, choosing to disagree.

Aleksander wanted to reach out and grab her hand. He'd always hated it as much as she did. He could hear the anxious terror of the horse as he skittered, pulling against the man who dragged him forward.

But Rexon was like Ranuf. Like Gant.

They believed that the gods would only bless them if they spilled blood before the tree; whether it was Alfnir's Tree in Saala or Furia's Tree in Andala.

A sacrifice needed to be made.

Jael turned her eyes to the ground, not wanting to see it.

Eadmund was beside her, looking on. Thorgils beside him. She wanted to leave.

The volka was chanting, the horse whinnying.

She couldn't look.

The horse squealed.

They heard the blood as it gushed into the bowl; the horse's body as it slumped to the earth.

Jael felt the sudden loss and closed her eyes, imagining his spirit running free as the volka started to cry and wail imploringly to Vidar; to his daughter, Furia. Dipping his hazel switch into the bowl, he walked through the gathered men, flicking them with warm blood; blessing them with the luck they would need for the coming battle.

Lothar mumbled loudly throughout the volka's call, which made Rexon irate and distracted everyone present. Both Gant and Gisila glared at him, but he was oblivious as he yawned and scratched and farted, not caring if Furia looked favourably on him at all.

Lothar had no need for her luck.

He felt confident enough in his own.

***

They had hurried to Ayla's cottage and were now crouching around the small fire. It was a cold, wild evening, snow still on the ground, but neither woman noticed their shivering; they were too intent on what they had to do.

'You need to tap the drum, Isaura,' Ayla said in a hushed voice. She stared into Isaura's worried eyes. 'Slowly and rhythmically. Don't stop. I will leave you and go into my trance, but I need your drumming to help me stay there.'

Isaura, on her knees, nodded. She held the drum awkwardly, never having used such a thing before. It was a simple enough instrument – a wooden frame with rawhide tightly pulled over it – but Isaura felt all at sea. 'Like this?' she wondered nervously, tapping the skin with her palm.

'Yes, that will be fine,' Ayla murmured distractedly, checking she had everything. She'd placed candles around the circle she had drawn in blood, mixed with hair from the doll. Ayla had remembered that Eydis had given the doll as a gift to Selene; a doll made with Eydis' own raven-like hair.

Unwrapping her small bundle of herbs, Ayla inhaled slowly before throwing them onto the flames. She turned to Isaura. 'Start drumming.'

***

'Your uncle is ready for his bed, I think,' Eirik whispered to Jael.

Jael rolled her eyes. Lothar was ready for his pyre, she thought to herself. If only the gods would send the message that Brekka was ready for a new king. Surely, in their wisdom, they could see the destruction Lothar Furyck was causing to the first kingdom of Osterland. 'I'm sure he is,' she whispered back. 'But I don't imagine my mother wants him in her bed until he's completely unconscious.' She nodded towards Gisila, who looked utterly miserable, trying to push her slumped husband away from her.

'Ha!' Eirik sniggered, handing his empty cup to a passing servant. 'The poor woman. I can only imagine...'

Jael's eyes met Eadmund's, and he looked away, back to Thorgils and Fyn. There was no cup in his hand, which was something at least.

Thorgils winked at Jael, trying to cheer her up.

'Tell me he's not slipping away again,' Eirik said, suddenly serious, his eyes on Eadmund. 'Back to that place.' He turned to Jael. 'Has the tincture stopped working?'

Jael shrugged. 'I don't know.'

'But something is wrong?'

'Yes.'

Eirik sighed.

'You don't need to worry,' Jael insisted. 'You never need to worry about Eadmund. Whatever has happened to him, I can fix it. I just need to get this battle with Haaron out of the way first.' She smiled at Eirik with more confidence than she felt.

Eirik looked into those fiercely determined green eyes and relaxed his shoulders. 'Well, Jael, I said I had faith in you, so I can hardly give up on you now, can I? Not when you're about to show me all that you can do.' He smiled, his attention shifting to his lords, his men, Lothar and his son. 'You mustn't let any of them get the better of you, with their words or their doubts, because I believe in you and you're *my* commander. *My* heir. Don't you forget that,' he said firmly, placing his hands on her shoulders. 'And you have a job to do. For me.' And kissing her on the cheek, he walked away, through the crowd, back to those lords, those men, that king and his son.

Jael watched him go, standing just a little bit taller.

He was right. She shook her head. Eirik was right.

She had a job to do.

CHAPTER EIGHTEEN

'Sleep well,' Amma smiled as she headed for the door. She was desperate to see Axl one last time before he left. They had arranged to meet amongst the trees, just outside the gates, but she needed to ensure that Eydis was safely tucked in bed first.

'You're not staying?' Eydis asked anxiously from her bed.

'No, I...' Amma stalled, guilt flooding her veins as she caught a glimpse of Eydis' worried face in the faint glow of the brazier. 'I won't be long, I promise. The servants are just outside the door. And Jael will be here soon,' she said reassuringly.

'Alright,' Eydis sighed, not feeling that reassured, but lying down anyway. 'Goodnight.'

Amma slipped through the door, closing it quietly after her. She turned around with a jump.

'Where are you off to, then?'

'Ahhh, I, ahhh,' Amma stumbled, nervous under Jael's interrogating glare.

'You're leaving Eydis? Alone in there?'

'Well, I wasn't going to be long,' Amma insisted, her eyes sweeping the rugs on the floor. 'And she's not really alone with the servants here.'

Jael had to admit that she was right. Eydis had her servant, Boelle, and Gunni was there too. Jael could see them preparing for bed, whispering to each other as they banked the fire. 'But where are you going? This late? By yourself?' Her cousin's face was so coloured with guilt that Jael knew she was hiding something.

Amma didn't see what else she could do but tell the truth. Jael's eyes told her that she was not in the mood to receive anything else. 'I'm going to say goodbye to Axl.'

Jael frowned, puzzled, but Amma looked at her with such feeling that realisation dawned quickly. 'Oh.'

Amma shrugged guiltily, a small smile on her face. 'Yes.'

'Does anyone know?'

'A few people,' Amma mumbled.

'But if Lothar or Osbert find out...'

'Yes, I know,' Amma sighed, dropping her head. 'We know what will happen.'

'Then hurry and say goodbye to him,' Jael urged. 'But be quick and don't be seen. Your father will not take it well if he discovers you sneaking around with Axl. Not tonight.'

Amma nodded, hurrying out of the house, hoping that Axl would still be waiting for her.

Jael watched her go, smiling, for she had suddenly realised why Axl seemed so grown up.

He had fallen in love.

***

Varna groaned as she sat, her breath hissing out of her from the sheer pain of bending in such an unnatural way. She was far too old to be sitting on the floor. Her ancient limbs would not flex, but she could not sit on the bed or a chair; not for what she planned to do. 'You will drum for me,' she instructed with a growl, batting away Meena's attempts to help her get comfortable. 'Do not think of stopping. Not till I return.'

'Yes, Grandmother,' Meena mumbled, shaking as she sat beside her. It was cold on the flagstones, and the fire in front of them was struggling, giving off little heat. Meena gripped her drum – the instrument she had used to help her grandmother since she was a little girl – and waited, swallowing repeatedly as saliva flooded her mouth.

Varna leaned forward, grimacing at the discomfort, shuffling around until she found the most bearable position. She picked up the herbs and bones Meena had gathered, and a torn piece of clothing they had taken from Jaeger's room. And, throwing them all into the fire, she sat back, her eyes closed.

Meena started drumming, looking on in horror as the herbs and cloth sucked all life out of the fire. She watched with an open mouth, her drumming hesitant and sporadic, waiting to see what would happen.

'What are you *doing*?' Varna snarled, wrenching one eye open.

The flames emerged from under their heavy load then, crackling and bursting into life.

'I'm sorry,' Meena whispered, drumming more steadily now.

Varna took a deep breath, turning towards the flames as she closed her eyes again, inhaling the acrid smoke.

Meena wrinkled her nose, trying to push the smoke out of it. She knew better than to gag; that would only incur her grandmother's wrath again. Quickly closing her eyes, she let the smoke take her away too; calming her nerves, easing her shoulders down from her ears, steadying her hand as it tapped the drum.

And together they drifted away in search of answers.

***

Eydis skipped along the edge of the cliffs towards Oss' harbour; its dark stone spires sharp against a serene, pale-blue sky. She stopped suddenly, surprised to see Ayla running towards her.

'Ayla!' Eydis smiled.

But Ayla's face was serious as she reached Eydis, and suddenly the sky darkened around them both; threatening storm clouds swamping the light.

'Eydis!' Ayla grabbed her arms, out of breath. 'Eydis, listen to me!' She stopped, trying to calm herself down. 'Your father,' she gasped. 'He's about to die! You must hurry. You must hurry, Eydis. Wake up, Eydis! He's about to die now!'

***

'So now Jael knows.' Axl rolled his eyes, sighing dramatically.

'She's not going to tell anyone,' Amma insisted quietly, glancing around as she gripped his hand. 'Is she?'

Axl shook his head, on edge. 'No, of course not.' They were standing in the shadows, behind a large tree, not far from Saala's gates. It was not dark enough for his liking, though. There were too many people milling about. Many were up late, making last-minute preparations for their unexpected departure in the morning. He could hear rustling in tents, mumbled voices, weapons clanking, humping.

Too many people.

Amma could sense his tension. 'I won't stay long.'

Axl pulled her into his arms. 'Just long enough for me to remember everything about you,' he smiled, kissing the top of her head. 'Every smell and taste. Every sound.'

Amma laughed quietly into his warm chest. 'Sound?'

'You don't think you make sounds?'

Amma frowned. 'Not memorable ones, I hope!'

Axl squeezed her tightly. 'How little you know.' He bent down, kissing her quickly.

They didn't have long.

Osbert watched them from near the gates. He had spied Amma escaping the house she was sharing with the women; scurrying away into the night. As drunk as he was, the surprise of that had cleared his head, and he had eagerly followed her.

To Axl.

It had not been such a surprise, he supposed, as he stood there, his bladder bursting, knowing that he had to leave quickly before he pissed himself. But it was simply impossible not to watch how happy they were.

Oh, what a trap Amma had placed herself into. Her and that idiot boy.

His father would be furious.

***

Eirik turned towards the bed.

He felt a familiar mix of excitement and anxiety tingling in his limbs. Battle joy was stirring. His last one, he supposed; there seemed to be little doubt about that. But he felt more at peace than he had in a while. The idea of a battle death was more than he could have hoped for.

If it were to be so.

The bed was not a comfortable one, nor was it particularly warm, but the fire was, so Eirik turned towards it instead, grabbing a goblet from the bedside table. He sniffed it. Rexon's wine. He smiled. That was a much better choice than a hard, prickly, lonely bed.

Yawning, Eirik made his way to the fire, adding another log from the small stack nearby. He settled down into a low chair draped with thick furs, and made himself comfortable, enjoying the silence, inhaling the sweet, fruity scent of the wine as it called to him.

***

Eydis woke up crying, tears streaming down her cheeks. 'Jael!' she yelled into the silence. 'Jael!'

Jael jerked awake, upright, her eyes closed, knife in hand. 'Eydis?' She spun around, her heart racing, hearing the panic in Eydis' voice. 'Eydis?' She hurried towards the small bed in the corner of the room.

'My father! Quick, Jael! Quick! You must hurry! Go! Save him! *Please!*'

Jael didn't wait. Without stopping for her cloak, she ran into the main room, fumbling with the unfamiliar handle of the door, then, pulling it open, at last, she disappeared into the night.

The house wasn't far from the hall, but it was far enough for Osbert to stumble into her path. Somehow, despite her speed and his dulled senses, he managed to grab the sleeve of her tunic as she flew past.

Jael spun, furious with him. She swapped her knife into her left hand and punched Osbert with her right. He staggered backwards, toppling to the ground. Jael didn't wait. Ignoring the pain in her hand, she swapped her knife back and ran into the hall.

'Eirik!' Jael screamed, pushing the drunken, sleepy men out of her way. Rexon was busy with Gant, trying to usher their men to bed. Their heads went up, and they gripped their swords, rushing to follow Jael as she ran for the bedchambers, screaming. 'Eirik!'

Eadmund was after her in a flash, his heart stopping, his body clenching in fear, Thorgils close behind him.

***

Ayla jerked forward, sucking smoke into her lungs, coughing, her eyes blinking open. Isaura dropped the drum and rushed to get her some water.

Ayla turned to her, still kneeling on the floor. She took the cup, tears filling her eyes; whether from the putrid smoke or something terrible, Isaura, with her foggy head, couldn't tell.

***

'Oh my,' Varna smiled through a series of rib-rattling coughs. 'He does keep his secrets buried deep, doesn't he? Aarrghh!' She cried out in agony as Meena helped her to her feet.

'You have seen the book, then?' Meena wondered anxiously. She wasn't sure which answer she would feel more comfortable with. Probably none.

'Seen it?' Varna smiled. 'Oh yes, I have. And tomorrow you will need to find a spade, my girl, for we are going digging.'

***

Jael flung open the door to Eirik's bedchamber.

He was there, sitting in a chair, his eyes wide with surprise at her sudden arrival. Then his hand shook, and the goblet he had been holding fell to the floor, red wine running out of his mouth, through his long white beard like blood. His eyes opened even wider as he felt it: the burning in his belly, the loss of breath, the sharp grip around his throat, the sudden, thunderous stutter of his heart.

'Eirik!' Jael cried as he slumped forward.

'Father!' Eadmund was behind her now. He froze. He had been here before. Memories of Melaena's death lurched out of the shadows. 'No!' he bellowed, running to his father.

Jael was at Eirik's side, her arm around his shoulder, trying to hold him up. His eyes were closing, his breath strangulated, pain contorting his face. 'Get Avilda! Get Pria!' She turned, yelling at Thorgils, Rexon, anyone. 'Quick!'

'Eydis –' Eirik rasped, quietly, slowly, his mouth hanging open, a gasping, gagging plea as he lost his breath, his eyes bulging in terror, then slowly glazing over, retreating.

Lifeless.

'Father!' Eadmund cried, gathering Eirik's body into his arms, kneeling beside him as he slumped in the chair.

The room was suddenly full. The lords were there, with Morac, and then, Eydis, holding onto Boelle's hand. 'Father!' she screamed frantically, terrified, desperate to reach him.

Boelle, her face pale with horror, guided her quickly towards the chair.

'Jael? Eadmund?' Eydis sobbed. 'Please, no! Father!'

Jael wrapped her arms around Eydis. 'I'm so sorry. I was too late, Eydis. I'm so sorry.'

'No!' Eydis screamed, pounding her fists on Jael's chest. 'No!' she cried, her heart shattering. 'Please, no! Jael, you have to save him! *Please!*'

Eadmund was motionless beside her, clinging to his father's body as everyone looked on. He stared helplessly at Thorgils.

Thorgils looked bereft, his eyes filled with tears.

Jael's mouth was open. She couldn't think.

Eirik was dead. She couldn't think.

She turned to the doorway and saw Ivaar standing there. He looked shocked. She felt Eadmund still beside her. He had seen Ivaar too.

'You!' Eadmund screamed at his brother. '*You* did this!' He made to get up, but Jael grabbed him quickly, inclining her head towards Eydis who was sobbing next to her; to his father, whose dead body he was supporting.

Thorgils went for Ivaar. 'It's best if you left,' he growled, his hands on Ivaar's chest, butting him towards the door.

'He's my father too!' Ivaar insisted furiously, but Thorgils' towering frame and tear-stained face had him backing away. 'I didn't kill him,' Ivaar insisted, blinking rapidly. 'Whatever Eadmund is thinking, or you, or anyone... I didn't kill him!'

Rexon had rushed to find the two old Andalan healers, Avilda and Pria, who had been tending to the sick men outside the village. The sisters were there quickly, breathless but eager to see what they could do. Rexon ushered them through the crowded room.

Jael moved aside, clinging to Eydis, who was sobbing in her arms, her small body heaving in waves of despair. 'Let the sisters look at your father now,' Jael said gently. 'Let them see what's happened.'

'We need to give them some room!' Rexon called over the noise, nodding at Jael. 'Everybody back to the hall!'

Jael shook her head, still in shock, feeling tears coming now. Why hadn't she been quicker? Why had Osbert been there? *Why*?

'What is going on?' Lothar bellowed, bustling into the chamber with Gisila; Osbert next to him, a hand over his swollen eye. All three faces registered complete horror at the scene before them.

'It is poison,' Avilda said, standing up with a frown. 'Pinweed. Hard to smell, but the residue is there. I can see it. Smell it too... if you know what you're looking for,' she muttered, holding the goblet out to her sister. 'The king would not have known when he drank it. The wine's scent is far too overpowering.'

Eydis screamed in despair and Eadmund reached for her, tears burning his eyes. His mouth opened and closed but his head was a whirling mess of confusion. He couldn't make sense of anything, except to think of Ivaar. 'Eydis, you stay with Jael,' he said quietly, his teeth clamped together. 'I need to go and find Ivaar.'

***

'And why shouldn't Ivaar be allowed in there?' Frits growled, annoyed at Thorgils' continued attempts to keep Ivaar out of the chamber where their king lay dead. 'He's Eirik's son! Who are you to stop him?'

Aleksander was there now, next to Thorgils, lining up with him against Frits and Ivaar and the other lords, none of whom looked pleased with the situation.

Rexon and Gant joined them. And Fyn.

It was almost an even contest.

'Perhaps Ivaar could put his sister first, and let her grieve for a moment before he decides to start a war with his brother,' Thorgils said coldly, eyeing Ivaar, his chest puffed out, his lips set in a hard line. His whole body was trembling, and he wanted to weep, but Ivaar didn't need to know that. 'Besides, who's to say that Ivaar wasn't the one who did this? It makes sense, him having experience with such matters before.'

The lords grumbled, frowning at one another as memories of Melaena's poisoning were revived.

'I would never!' Ivaar insisted loudly, turning to them. 'Never!'

'Ha!' Thorgils laughed, stepping forward. 'This all sounds very familiar, Ivaar.' He could feel his blood boiling, then the firm hand of Aleksander on his arm, steadying him. Thorgils glared at him, but Aleksander's face was so still and measured that he hesitated and took a moment to breathe.

Eydis.

'You may see your father,' Thorgils said evenly, stepping back into line with the others. 'Of course. But give your brother and sister a chance to be with Eirik first, they being his favourite children. The ones he *actually* loved.' He couldn't help it, sneering as he stood there, watching as Viktor grabbed Ivaar's arm and pulled him away.

***

Jael listened to the commotion outside. She was relieved to hear Thorgils' voice, loudest of all. In the midst of her grief and panic, her mind started to wake up. 'No!' she called to Eadmund, realising that he was heading for the door. 'You can't go after Ivaar!'

Eadmund stopped, turning back to her. He caught a glimpse of his father's body and sobbed. 'Why? He did this! You know Ivaar did this!'

'Ssshhh!' Jael hurried to him, grabbing his hand, leaving Gisila to comfort Eydis. 'Eadmund, wait, you can't do this now. Not when we have to leave tomorrow. Not when we need all those lords out there to follow us.'

'*What*?' Eadmund was incredulous. 'You think we can still *go*? In the morning? A few hours from now?' He shook her hand away.

'Your wife is right,' Lothar muttered as he waddled towards them, pulling his cloak around his commodious nightshirt. 'We must not delay. And I cannot imagine your father would have wished us to, either. You are the king now, Eadmund. And your wife is queen. But I promise you, Haaron and his sons won't give a fuck who they're fighting. Their ships will be in the water, and their men will be in the pass, and if we don't act, they will be at Rexon's gates ready to slaughter us all!'

Gisila glared at her indiscreet husband, covering Eydis' ears.

Jael couldn't believe her own ears; Lothar was agreeing with her. 'It's true,' she said. 'Those lords out there are one step away from siding with Ivaar. He's wormed his way into their trust. None of them are really going to believe he killed Eirik, are they? And if they do, they're unlikely to break their own alliance. And if they unite behind Ivaar, they could defeat us,' she whispered hoarsely. 'They have the men and the ships.'

Eadmund couldn't breathe. His ears were ringing. It was

all too much to take in. He couldn't think. His father... he put his hands to his head, feeling the sobs rising up in his chest. 'He killed him!'

'What proof do you have?' Jael asked, looking around. Avilda and Pria shrugged, shaking their heads. 'There's no proof. There's no time to find any either. All you have are accusations. Unfounded. And you can't kill a man based on those, not if you're to rule as a fair king, as your father wanted.'

Eadmund turned to his little sister, his thoughts crystallising. He had to keep her safe. His shoulders sagged. 'Alright,' he muttered, walking back to Eydis whose plaintive cries were rising. 'We leave after we burn his body.'

Jael nodded, still in shock. She couldn't believe it; couldn't believe that she had been so close to stopping it from happening.

But had Ivaar done it?

She didn't know what to think, watching as Eadmund and Eydis clung to one another, united in grief.

'So, now you're a queen,' Lothar whispered in her ear. 'Queen Jael of Oss.'

Jael cringed at his sudden closeness.

'Not such a bad result for you,' he smiled.

'Well, it helps you, doesn't it, Uncle? A Furyck on the throne of Oss?'

Lothar narrowed his eyes. 'It does indeed. A good idea my alliance with Eirik turned out to be. For both of us.'

'But it may not last for long if you don't have a word with those Islanders out there,' Jael said quietly, not wanting Eadmund to hear. 'If they think there's a reason to stand behind Ivaar and support *his* claim to the throne, then there'll be no alliance, and we'll all be slaughtered come tomorrow.'

Osbert edged his way into the conversation, looking crossly at his cousin.

'What happened to your eye?' Lothar asked, suddenly noticing the bruised, swollen lump where his son's right eye used to be.

Osbert glared at Jael. 'She punched me.'

Lothar tried not to laugh as even he could see that it wasn't the place or time for humour.

Jael wanted to grab Osbert by the throat and do more than punch him. It was his fault that she hadn't been able to save Eirik. 'Why did you try and stop me?' she growled, baring her teeth.

'I didn't know what you were doing,' Osbert insisted. 'How did you know he was about to die?'

Jael looked towards Eirik's body. 'Eydis had a dream.' It was as though he was sleeping in his chair. She shuddered. 'But I was too late.'

***

'So Ivaar will become the king now?' Isaura wondered slowly, swallowing the bitter taste of smoke, still thick in her throat.

They were sitting on Ayla's bed, the door of her cottage wedged open, despite the cold night lurking outside. It was a relief to feel some fresh air as it rushed inside, clearing out the fetid stink.

Ayla shook her head sadly. 'I've seen Ivaar as the king many times, but not tonight. I don't know when it will happen, but Eadmund is the king for now.' She felt weak, light-headed, only half of her present.

Isaura had no love for Eirik Skalleson. He had sent her off to marry Ivaar, to be exiled with him on Kalfa. He had been responsible for ruining her life, for taking her away from Thorgils. But at that moment, as she reflected on his death, she thought of her children who had lost their last grandparent, and Eadmund and Eydis who had lost their father. And she remembered her time on Oss over the winter, when she had organised Vesta with Eirik and found a way to become almost friends. Tears filled her eyes then.

Ayla looked away from Isaura, staring into the flames, wishing she could see more. If Ivaar did not become the King of Oss, her life would never be hers again.

But if he did, she feared what that would mean for everyone else.

CHAPTER NINETEEN

Eadmund felt numb as he walked along the beach. He was without his cloak, which he'd taken off to sleep, but his tunic wasn't warm enough, and he had started shaking.

He didn't notice.

Jael curled her hands into balls, trying to warm her frozen fingers as she walked alongside him.

They had been desperate to escape the hall, the people, and their pity. Eydis had finally cried herself to sleep on Eirik's bed, with Amma and Gisila watching her. Gisila was happy to avoid Lothar for the rest of the night, much to his annoyance, but she had promised Jael that she would stay with Eydis while she slept, and there was little Lothar could do about that.

Eadmund saw the first hint of dawn in the distance.

Soon they would burn his father's body. He shook his head, again resisting the urge to take his knife to Ivaar's throat; Ivaar, who had taken so much from him.

And now this.

Jael gripped his arm. 'We should get some sleep,' she murmured, trying not to yawn. 'We need to be able to think when the sun rises. There'll be so much to do.'

Eadmund sighed and nodded, allowing her to lead him back to the village. Jael was right, his eyes stung; he could barely keep them open. But now he was the king, and she was the queen, and somehow, between the two of them, they had to take their people to war.

***

Jaeger couldn't sleep.

He'd forgotten how much Berard snored, and once woken, he found himself just staring into the darkness. It had been that way since Elissa's death. He had loved her: the smell of her; the softness of her golden, freckled skin; her warmth. It had been unexpected to find happiness and love when all he'd imagined marriage would provide him with were sons and ceremony. Jaeger pulled the pillow over his ears, wishing for a different night, and a quieter sleeping companion.

They were ready now; he was certain of that. Varna might think that the sea battle would test them, but Jaeger couldn't see how. Their ships were prepared; their men experienced and hard. They had the support of the Tower whose archers were expertly drilled in destroying enemies on the sea. And they were well-stocked for a siege, with healthy stores of both food and weapons.

If it were to come to that, Jaeger smiled confidently.

Berard groaned, rolling over, his snoring coming to a rumbling halt. Jaeger sighed in relief and rolled over himself, towards the wall. It was the biggest chamber in the fort, but there was barely enough space for their two narrow beds. Its stone walls were damp and cold, windowless and dark. There wasn't a hint of comfort about the place. Jaeger had tired of it quickly, desperate to return to Hest, to Meena, to find out what she had discovered in his absence. Or whether, as he suspected, she had simply turned him in to Varna.

He closed his eyes. There was still more than enough of the night left for him to claim some sleep, and he would need it, for tomorrow they would take to their ships and sink their enemies to the bottom of the Adrano Sea.

***

Ivaar felt an unexpected sense of loss. His father had made it abundantly clear how little he thought of him, it was true, but still, a part of him felt empty. And frustrated. There was no victory to claim. No hope of ever being able to show his father that he was worthy of his respect. Or more.

He shook his head as he sat on the bench outside the quiet hall. In the hours since Eirik Skalleson's death, most had drifted away to find sleep. Lothar had spoken to the lords and dampened any hint of rebellion, and for a usually ridiculous man, he had actually made a lot of sense. Haaron had to be their focus now. There would be time to conquer other enemies and make new alliances once they had defeated him.

Ivaar thought of his mother, who he'd loved dearly, humiliated by his father, who he wished had loved him at all.

He was cold. And far too awake. He needed to find some sleep, or a distracting woman like Ayla. She had seen that he would be king. But he wasn't. He frowned, staring into the darkness. They were going to sea to fight the biggest battle of their lives, and there was certainly a chance that the new King and Queen of Oss might not survive.

Ivaar smiled; perhaps Ayla wasn't so wrong after all?

'Maybe they're right about you?' Osbert laughed, sitting down next to Ivaar with a groan. He had come out of the hall, desperate to escape the stink of farts, stale ale, and smoke. 'Sitting here smiling, your father's body still warm.'

Ivaar glared at him. 'Should I care what *you* think?' he snorted. 'You don't know me. You didn't know my father.'

'No, and now I won't, since we're about to cook him for breakfast.'

Ivaar reached out and seized Osbert's throat, leaning over him. 'You need to learn some respect, boy,' he growled throatily. 'My father was a king!'

Osbert spluttered, his one open eye bulging, realising that tiredness had thickened both his head and his tongue.

Ivaar released him, shoving him away. 'You Brekkans think you're better than us,' he spat. 'And though we weren't made by Furia and our line is short, we're no less than you. We never have been. We all came from Osterhaaven. We all share the same gods.'

Osbert coughed, feeling his throat. 'Well,' he coughed again, 'it's true that some Brekkans look down on the Islanders. But not all. And not me.'

Ivaar raised a tired eyebrow at this small, swollen-eyed man, wondering what he wanted. 'I doubt that,' he scoffed, taking a deep breath as he leaned his head back against the wall. 'What happened to your eye?'

'A mutual enemy of ours punched me,' Osbert said, leaning in closer. 'We have much more in common than you realise, Ivaar Skalleson.'

***

Eadmund had wept for his father, holding Jael in his arms. And both of them had slept, restlessly, and now they lay there, face to face, the first rays of sun seeping under the bedchamber door.

They were alone.

'I let him down,' Eadmund said haltingly. 'So many years of embarrassing him. Of being less than a man, just a fool. And he endured it. All those years, he endured it. His heir, the one he had chosen. A fat, drunk, useless fool.'

'But you changed,' Jael whispered, running her hand through his beard. She had missed the feel of him; missed his eyes and his closeness. 'He saw that. You came back to him. He was happy. He had hope again.'

Eadmund sighed sadly, kissing her. 'Because of you.'

'No,' Jael insisted. 'You picked up the sword. You made the choice.'

'Well, I think after that tincture, I didn't have any choice at all, did I?'

'Possibly,' Jael admitted. 'But it doesn't matter, does it? Why or how? Just that you did and that he saw you come back. He believed in you again.'

'In us.'

'In us, yes,' Jael murmured, remembering Eirik's last words to her.

Eadmund frowned. His throat was dry. He couldn't make sense of his thoughts at all. He closed his eyes and this time he didn't see Evaine. He saw his father, slumped in the chair, his eyes wide with shock. 'I don't want to go anywhere,' he murmured, running a finger across Jael's scar. 'Nowhere, without you. Not again. I don't know why I went to Rikka like that. I don't want to lose you, Jael.'

Jael swallowed, her body tense. He was there again; he'd come back. 'There's so much I have to tell you,' she whispered. 'About Evaine. About what she's trying to do.'

Eadmund squirmed. 'No, not now. Please, Jael. Not her, not now. Let *us* just have a moment. Perhaps after today, we won't have another. Don't bring her here when it's just us.' He leaned forward, kissing her desperately, relieved that she was with him again. He felt the empty hole of his father's death as it dug deeper into his heart, but they were together, and for a moment, he could forget about all that had been, and all that would come.

***

Rexon had put his people to work quickly. Morac had offered his assistance, and together they had worked through the night to ensure that a pyre was built on the beach; tall and thick with tightly stacked, dry wood. A pyre worthy of a true king. One whose smoke pillar would rise high, sending Eirik Skalleson onwards, to Vidar's Hall, where he would sit and drink and fight for eternity alongside the King of the Gods and his faithful companions.

Eirik had been dressed in his battle-gear. His loyal steward, Gurin, had washed his face and combed his hair, braiding more silver nuggets into his long white-and-gold beard, pushing polished arm rings over his tunic sleeves. He had been wrapped in a thick bear-skin cloak, his simple silver crown sitting gently atop his head.

They came to say their farewells, then. First, his lords, the ones whose loyalties appeared so confused now. Their guilty faces were solemn as they stopped to take a last moment with their king as he lay lifeless on top of his pyre. And then his warriors, the men who had fought alongside Eirik throughout his long reign; men he had freed, those whose fathers and mothers had been born slaves, living under the terrifying rule of Grim Skalleson.

Eirik had released them all, just as he had set himself free, turning the Slave Islands into a kingdom worthy of an alliance with Brekka.

A kingdom about to go to war.

The sun was rising above the sea, and it was big and gold and warming after a desolate night, when many had not slept at all. Thorgils sighed, staring sadly at the familiar figure lying before him. Eirik would enjoy watching their victory over Haaron, he told himself, not wanting to give in to the sadness that was trying to consume him. They would all give him that. Eirik could raise a cup to his men as he sat in Vidar's Hall; to his family, to all of the Islanders as they claimed the prize of Hest for him.

'Are you happy?' Rexon asked.

Thorgils blinked back the tears he could feel coming again. 'Happy?' he looked confused.

'With the pyre,' Rexon muttered, almost apologetically. 'Is there anything else you think it needs?'

Thorgils looked it over. Eirik had his sword in his hands, his helmet and shield on either side of him. A small wooden bucket filled with gold and silver coins sat at his feet, along with a jug of Rexon's best wine and trenchers of food for his journey.

Thorgils glanced at the gathering crowd. He saw Eydis coming through with Fyn, Amma, and Gisila. His heart broke for her. She was carrying a wooden doll, her face turned towards the sand. He took a deep breath, steeling himself for what they were about to do. 'Yes, it's fine, I think,' he croaked. 'But let's see what Eadmund says when he gets here.'

Rexon nodded, stepping back into the crowd. There was much to do, but nothing more important than this, he knew. The Islanders needed to say goodbye to their king, to inspire their victory, for, without them, all of Brekka was doomed.

***

Eadmund stood staring at the wall as he tied his swordbelt around his waist.

He had been out to check on proceedings, relieved to see that Rexon and Morac had everything under control and that Thorgils was there, keeping an eye on them both. He had gone back to the house with Jael, to take a moment to prepare himself for what he must do next. He needed to lead, just when he wanted to sink into a hole of utter despair. But he was the king, and, he smiled to himself, remembering his father's words: a king must put his people first.

'Shall we go?' Jael wondered, stopping behind him, resting a hand on his back.

Eadmund flinched, turning around to scowl at her. Jael was

surprised, catching a flash of anger in his cold eyes.

He had gone.

She sighed, her body sinking at the unexpected loss of him again.

'Yes,' Eadmund said blankly, wishing he had Evaine's warm body wrapped inside his arms; certain that her presence would make him feel better. Hers and their son's. He smiled wistfully. 'Let's go.' Eadmund didn't look around as he headed for the door.

Jael pushed back her shoulders, waiting for a moment.

She remembered Eirik's face: the shock on it as death came to claim him; the surprise in his eyes that it had happened like that. Was it Ivaar? Jael didn't know. But she did know that Eadmund had gone, Eirik had gone, and somehow she had to keep Oss out of Ivaar's hands.

Taking a deep breath, Jael placed her hand on the cool moonstone pommel of her sword and followed Eadmund outside.

***

Evaine smiled as she watched her son sleeping next to Tanja in the small cot on the opposite side of the mezzanine.

Now that Sigmund was well-fed and being cared for by his wet nurse, she could finally get more sleep, and the joy of her body belonging solely to her again was overwhelmingly pleasurable. What wasn't pleasurable, however, was worrying about Eadmund and what would happen to him in the battle. Morana had assured her that they were meant to be together; that he would survive and return to her. And while there was comfort to be found in that, there was no certainty. Not until Eadmund was back on Oss would she be able to truly relax again.

Evaine yawned as she slid out of bed and tip-toed over to her chest. Grabbing her white fur cloak from the nearby stool, she wrapped it around her shoulders and held her breath, lifting the lid of the chest. It creaked. She cringed. It was her father's chest, old and fusty smelling, and despite having Respa oil it regularly, it continued to groan every morning when she got up to go through the ritual.

The servants were not awake yet. Morning was coming, Evaine could see that, as faint rays of light leaked through the smoke hole above her head, but there was still time, she knew, before anyone would see what she was doing.

Runa stirred, still mostly asleep. The creak had woken her, as it had for the past few mornings. Her body was getting into a rhythm now; the same rhythm as the person opening the chest with a surreptitious creak just before dawn. Runa was desperate to know what Evaine was doing up there, but there was no way to find out. The mezzanine was only accessible by the stairs, which were louder and creakier than the chest.

Runa kept her eyes closed as she listened to the shuffling footsteps, wondering about Fyn, wishing it were Evaine about to face her death instead of him. She felt a stab of guilt, having raised Evaine as her own daughter, but she had always been slightly terrified of her, never feeling safe when she was around.

Because Evaine was Morana's daughter.

And Morana Gallas was most certainly a witch.

***

Varna had woken early and now stood fully dressed, hidden beneath a shabby brown cloak, prodding Meena with a rough, cold finger. 'We don't have time to lie in bed all day!' she grumbled hoarsely.

Light was barely straining through the tiny window in Varna's chamber; dull, blue morning light. It was too early, and

Meena yawned, not ready to get out of bed yet. She had been dreaming of Jaeger, and the tempting, teasing visions were so vivid that she didn't want to leave them behind.

Varna poked her again. 'If you don't want a slap, you'd better rouse yourself quickly, my girl!'

Meena shuddered, cold beneath the thin blanket that was all she'd been given; uncomfortable on the old, straw-stuffed mattress that Varna had handed down to her. It stunk of piss, like her grandmother. She thought of Jaeger's luxurious bed, then blushed and blinked, shaking her head, banishing the ridiculous dream and all thoughts of him, both terrifying and oddly exciting.

'Well?' Varna loomed over her. 'Are you ready? I cannot dig this book up without you, Meena.' She shuffled away to the door. 'And if you can get it out of the ground quickly enough, I will let you have some breakfast!'

Meena frowned, feeling her fingers twitch, in anger, not anxiety.

That was new.

She was twenty-eight-years-old now. Not a child. Not someone who should have to beg for food or a blanket. But as her grandmother turned and glared impatiently at her, she found herself shrinking in fear.

That was not new.

***

'How is he?' Thorgils whispered as Jael stopped beside him, leaving Eadmund to go to Eydis.

Jael blinked, trying to avoid the pyre. The sun was still low in the sky, shining right in her eyes. 'He is...' She shook her head. 'I honestly don't know. He was there for a while, but he has gone again. I'm sure Evaine has done something to him,' she sighed.

'But what and how, I don't know.'

Thorgils frowned, nervously twisting the ends of his red beard. 'Well, it makes sense of the way he's been. It's like talking to an open window. There's nothing there most of the time.'

'Perhaps she's controlling him, but how?' Jael murmured, shaking her head. 'I wish Edela were here.'

'My mother would often talk about Morana Gallas, of the things she did to people before Eirik got rid of her,' Thorgils mused, digging into the dusty corners of his memory. 'She used to say that Morana had put a spell on Eirik to make him love her, which is why he was blind to her evil ways for so long.'

Jael's eyes were sharp now, feeling another rush of grief as she remembered her conversation with Eirik about Morana. 'Well, if that were true, it's knowledge she could have passed on to Evaine. But there's nothing we can do about it now. Not till we get back to Oss and Edela.'

'Mmmm,' Thorgils nodded. 'All we can think about now is what we have to do today.' He glanced at the pyre, which was ready; ready for something that none of them were prepared for. He waved at Torstan, Fyn, and Axl who came to join them. 'It won't be an easy morning for anyone.'

'No,' Jael said quietly. 'Especially Eydis.' Her eyes drifted to Eadmund, who was comforting his broken-hearted sister.

'She seems to like Amma and Gisila, though,' Fyn said softly. 'They're taking good care of her.'

Jael smiled at him. He looked unusually pale. She had almost forgotten that they were leaving for battle soon. Fyn's first. 'Are you alright?'

'Oh, Fyn here has spent most of the morning in the latrines with your brother,' Torstan smiled, slapping the much taller man on his back.

Both Axl and Fyn glared at Torstan, who looked to Jael and Thorgils for support, only to be met with frowns.

'Not really the time for joking,' Thorgils grumbled. 'Not in front of your new queen at least.'

Torstan's smile slipped as the realisation of that sunk in.

Jael swallowed uncomfortably, looking towards the pyre, at last, remembering Eirik's eyes, so filled with shock as she'd run for him. If only she had run faster.

If only Osbert had not been there.

Axl peered at his sister, his face as ghostly and anxious as Fyn's. 'Queen of Oss? I'm not sure how Father would have felt about that.'

Jael smiled sadly, imagining Ranuf Furyck's stony face upon hearing that news. 'Well, I suspect that if he'd gotten to know Eirik, he would have thought it was an honour.' Tears were coming; she could feel them. The depth of sadness and loss she felt surprised her. But, she realised, Eirik had quickly become more than a friend. He was someone she had respected. Someone she had wanted to impress, much like her own father. To prove herself to him. And he had given her the chance to do just that.

And now he was gone.

'I'm going to see Eydis before we begin,' she mumbled, quickly walking away.

Thorgils watched her go, trying to raise herself up, keeping her head high. Queen Jael. 'It will be a hard day for your sister,' he said to Axl. 'She thought a lot of Eirik. And he put all his hopes for Oss in her.'

'She won't let him down,' Axl insisted. 'She'll make a good queen.'

Thorgils nodded, pulling his own broad shoulders back, determined to let the sadness go for now. They would have to gather themselves together quickly, for today they had to take Skorro. 'Let's go and say goodbye to our old king, then. It's time to send him to Vidar.'

***

Hest's magnificent castle, built out of the stones it sat nestled amongst, shimmered in the morning sun. The vast cobblestoned square that joined the castle steps to Haaron's six long piers was empty, apart from a handful of armed guards who shuffled around yawning, waiting to be relieved from their night shift.

Varna hurried Meena across the square, ignoring the guards, who dared not make eye contact with her. She shooed away a few chickens who were pecking between the stones, in no mood to be delayed.

Meena carried a spade beneath her worn grey cloak, which made walking difficult. Not that her grandmother noticed, gripping her hand tightly and almost dragging her along in her desperation to get onto the path that led away from the square before the city came to life.

They could have gone through the castle, winding their way around the maze of corridors, down into the kitchen and scullery, and through a side door, but that would have aroused far more attention than simply walking straight through the front doors. And Varna was in no mood to run into Bayla Dragos again. Though, she supposed, Bayla was hardly likely to have dragged her ageing bones out of bed this early in the day.

Varna frowned suddenly, wobbling to a halt. They were on the path now, heading past the large sheds where Haaron stored his ships. Varna turned her head back towards the piers as Meena stared at her in confusion.

Someone was coming.

'Grandmother?' Meena whispered anxiously, wanting to rip her hand out of Varna's, desperate to tap her head with it. 'What is it?'

But Varna didn't reply as she watched the figure approach, hooded, just as she was. She sighed as the figure shuffled urgently towards them.

Meena squinted, her heart thudding. 'Who is it?'

Varna didn't smile. 'That, I believe, is your aunt.'

***

Eydis stood between Jael and Eadmund, shaking uncontrollably. Her eyes ached from near-constant crying, as did her head, which was confused and sleep-deprived. She had slept, she knew, at times, but there had been pain, even in her dreams.

She had seen Ayla again.

It was not the same as before, though. She had watched Ayla and Isaura desperately trying to help Eirik. And she had seen her father, but that was not a dream, it was a nightmare, repeated over and over; watching as he died, whispering her name. She imagined how it must have felt for him; the shock, so sudden, after all this time of waiting.

Eadmund gently tugged his sister forward. Eydis had a doll in her hand, one that her father had carved for her when she was small, made with her own hair; black, just like her mother's. And now she had lost them both. Sobs rose up into her chest as she approached the pyre. Eadmund lifted her up, and she leaned towards their father's body, feeling around, tucking the doll into the side of his arm so that part of her would go with him to keep him safe on his journey.

Eadmund placed her back on the sand, bending down to wipe away the tears that ran so freely down her young face. She reached up and did the same to him, then fell into his arms, desperate to escape the terror that was consuming her.

They were waiting, all of them, for Eadmund to say something, because he was their king now; because his father lay dead on the pyre. But Eadmund didn't even know where to begin. He wanted to sit, alone, and sob until it felt real. That, or charge at his brother and rip out his throat with his bare hands. How did Ivaar have the nerve to just stand there, attempting to look as upset as the rest of them, when *he* was the one who had done this to *their* father?

Eadmund could feel himself shaking in fury, his ears ringing, his breath coming in short, ragged bursts as Jael stepped up and stood beside him, holding his hand. She stared at him intently, and he sighed.

There was no time for anything other than this.

'My father was a self-made king,' Eadmund began, his voice weak at first, straining as he sought to raise it above the seabirds searching noisily for their breakfast. 'And he often saw that as a black mark against his kingdom. Because he didn't have a royal line going back centuries. Because his ancestors were slaves, not gods.'

Lothar tried hard not to nod in agreement.

'But what he did do was change the lives of all of us who would have been born and raised as slaves, prisoners of wealthy, cruel men. He made us free. He set us free to live as we chose.' Eadmund stumbled, his voice faltering. He looked at Jael, and she smiled encouragingly at him. 'And you all chose to follow him. For over forty years, you followed him as he built our kingdom up from nothing, kept us safe, made sure we thrived and survived every winter, through every sickness, and every loss. And before he died, he chose Jael and me to carry on after him, as his heirs.' Eadmund frowned at the raised eyebrows and whispers that were exchanged between a few of the lords. 'I know there have been questions and doubts about that. About me, and who I let myself become, or my wife, who you don't know well enough to respect as he did and I do. But I am your king now, and Jael is your queen. And we are here to lead you to victory over Haaron Dragos! We will take Skorro in the name of Eirik Skalleson and his islands. Our islands! This victory today, *our* victory will be for my father!' Eadmund swallowed. He had said enough, and now he wanted it done before he changed his mind and simply threw himself onto his father's body instead.

Most of the men and women gathered cheered in return.

'Wait!' Eydis cried, stepping forward. 'Wait! Please, Eadmund!'

'Eydis?' Jael frowned, reaching out to grab her but Eydis shook her off. 'I want you to know that I will come for you in my dreams!' she called in a shaking, but determined voice as her head spun around, blindly searching the crowd. 'I will find you! The one who did this to my father! I will find you in my dreams because my name is Eydis Skalleson and I am a dreamer!'

Gasps and shocked faces followed that announcement.

'I saw that my father would die,' she continued. 'But I did not see who would kill him, so I couldn't stop it. I couldn't save him!' Her voice broke as grief overwhelmed her. Eadmund pulled her to him and she sniffed back tears, her body shuddering with barely controlled fury. 'But I will find you. I will find who did this, and Eadmund will cut out your heart!' She collapsed then, burying herself into Eadmund's chest.

Eadmund kissed the top of his sister's head, inhaling the cool morning air, nodding at Morac. A breeze was building, and the flame fought the wind as Morac came forward to pass the torch to Eadmund. He took it in one hand, grabbing Eydis' cold hand in the other, and together they stood next to their father as Eadmund bent to light the pyre.

Jael walked up and stood beside them as the wood started to catch. Eadmund tried to blink away his tears as he turned towards the lifting smoke.

Jael thought of her own father's pyre nearly three years before; a heartbreak she had still not recovered from. Eydis, as she cried, remembered saying goodbye to her mother when she was barely five-years-old. And Eadmund felt the sudden loss of his own mother, so long ago now, but the pain of her death was refreshed by this one.

As the smoke billowed and the flames grew, Eadmund squeezed Eydis' hand tighter, pulling her back, away from the flames, back to where Morac stood with Thorgils and Torstan. He knew that Ivaar was there, lurking further behind them with the lords, but it was not something he needed to acknowledge. Not now, when his father was leaving to be with the gods.

Leaving him.

As the King of Oss.

CHAPTER TWENTY

'Hello, Mother,' Morana smiled, her dark eyes hooded and hostile as they glared at the old woman who waited for her.

'Morana,' Varna growled, cringing at the sound of that name after so many years. 'It has been a long time.'

'*Long*?' Morana laughed, a cackling snigger as she shuffled forward. '*Long*?' She pulled back her hood, shaking out her matted black-and-white hair, staring at the girl. 'Who's this?'

'Morten's daughter,' Varna said shortly.

'Morten?' Morana looked surprised. 'He lives?'

Meena dropped her eyes, not wanting to be inspected by this peculiar woman, whose black eyes were roaming all over her.

'No,' Varna said quickly. 'He died years ago. Him and his wife, both. I have raised the girl.'

Morana barely blinked. She was frozen; worn through. Her sea journey around Osterland from Rikka had taken many more days than she'd wished, but she had not wanted to stumble across the Brekkan army as it marched towards Saala. Instead, she had taken a ship and suffered on the sea for far longer than was comfortable. 'I need food,' she said irritably. 'Then we must talk.'

Varna thought on that, digging a frown deep into her crumbling forehead. 'Why have you come? Why now?'

'You know as well as I do, Mother,' Morana snarled. She glanced around as the square started to fill up; merchants and their slaves hurrying to prepare their market stalls for another day. 'And that is not something we should discuss out here. Not if you still want to keep me your little secret.'

Varna sighed. Morana had not come all this way for nothing. There was no point in trying to hide anything from her. Not anymore. 'You may as well come with us, then. There is no food, but you look well fed. I'm sure you'll survive until we return.'

Morana frowned at her mother, then caught a glimpse of the spade poking out of Meena's cloak. One eyebrow rose, as did one corner of her thin, blue lips.

She smiled greedily.

***

Lothar wasn't pleased by the sudden shift of power.

'Hostages?' he grumbled.

'It makes sense,' Jael insisted, glaring at Osbert, hoping to get through to one of them at least. 'It's a bargaining tool. And you might need one.'

Lothar snorted. 'I think all that crying has addled your brain. Or you've been listening to that grandmother of yours again.'

'And when has that ever been a bad idea?' Jael retorted. 'When did *you* stop listening to dreamers?'

Gant stood quietly to Lothar's left, making no move to cool Jael down. She was a queen now, he thought; let her say what she liked. With Jael leading the Islanders, Lothar would stand no chance if he stood in her way.

He tried not to smile.

Lothar looked far less pleased. 'When they got too old to make any sense!' he sneered, glancing at his son for support.

Osbert did not provide any.

Jael tried again, her lips barely moving. 'If one of us succeeds, the other will need to be in a good position, or we'll both end up compromised. So, if you can, Uncle, take hostages.' She turned to Gant. 'Signal us when you get to the rise. We'll set off then.'

Gant nodded.

'Good luck,' Jael smiled quickly, then turned to Lothar. 'We're in this together,' she said firmly. 'As an alliance against Haaron. And an alliance will not win anything if its members are on opposite sides. We must be united in our purpose.'

Lothar gave her a look of bored disdain. 'Naturally.' He lifted up his cloak, resettling it over his shoulders, trying to appear more regal as he stood there under the glare of his tall niece. 'I wish you Islanders luck. We will see you in Hest.'

Jael swallowed, hearing Edela's warning, loud in her ears. It would not go well, Edela cried over and over again. 'We shall see you in Hest,' Jael said with a confidence she did not feel. And with one last glance at Gant, she left to find Axl and Aleksander.

'Your cousin has eased herself into her new role rather quickly,' Lothar spat, turning to Osbert, wishing his son was taller. 'Eirik's bones are still burning on the beach, and there she is, running about, issuing orders as if her husband didn't even exist!'

Osbert didn't know what to think. Jael in power was dangerous for his father, he knew that. But he also knew that they needed her if they were to conquer Haaron. But, he mused, squirming in his thick mail shirt, once that was achieved, they would surely have to remove her before she became a problem.

'Hopefully, you'll have the decency to wait until my ashes are at sea before you start smiling!' Lothar grumbled and stalked away, his mind already turning towards Gisila. He'd wanted a better goodbye than a broken night's sleep and an early start, none of which had included her naked body beneath him.

***

Gisila couldn't stop crying. As much as she knew it wasn't helping, she couldn't hold back the tears that had been streaming down her sunken cheeks since Eirik's funeral. The night had been so disturbing, with the king's death and trying to comfort poor Eydis, that she was simply beside herself at the thought of losing Axl, Jael, and Aleksander all at once.

'Mother,' Axl said gently. 'I must go.'

Aleksander reached in to help extract him from her desperate arms. 'We must go, Gisila,' he insisted. 'We need to be at the front of our column, leading our men.'

They were fully dressed for battle now, helmets on, weapons secured, and Axl looked ready to vomit. Aleksander needed to get him with the men and away from Gisila before she eroded the rest of his rapidly dwindling confidence.

'Mother, Aleksander's right,' Axl murmured gently, pulling himself away at last. 'We need to leave.'

'Not yet, you don't,' Jael said, smiling sympathetically at the sight of her brother's ashen face. He looked petrified. She remembered how that felt. 'Not until you say goodbye to me.'

Axl leaned forward to hug her. 'Good luck,' he whispered in her ear. 'Father would be proud of you.'

That unsettled Jael entirely. She stepped back and frowned at him. He looked ready, she supposed. As terrified as his eyes hiding beneath the rim of his helmet appeared, his body was strong and well balanced; not such a dangling mess of disjointed parts anymore. There was weight to him. Strength. Now he just needed belief. 'And you,' she smiled. 'You look like a Furyck. And you know what they say about Furycks...'

'That they've never been killed in battle?' Axl sighed, brushing away the reminder. 'I wonder if the gods are laughing right now, thinking about changing their minds?'

Gisila looked horrified as Axl kissed her cheek.

Aleksander smiled, grabbing Jael before she could argue. He held her in his arms, not wanting to let her go. It was the single nicest feeling he could remember since he'd last held her. She was rigid, as she often was, but suddenly sunk into him, almost hugging him back. 'I'll look after your brother,' he promised.

'And yourself?' she wondered.

'Of course,' Aleksander said quickly. 'One can't happen without the other.'

Jael slipped out of his arms, her eyes not leaving his.

'Jael?' It was Thorgils. 'The men are waiting.'

She turned around, catching a glimpse of his perturbed face.

'You go,' Aleksander said, suddenly worried that this might be the last time he saw her. 'And take care of yourself. I won't be there to save you when you get in trouble.'

'I suppose we'll both have to save ourselves, then,' she smiled. 'I'll see you in Hest, Aleksander Lehr.' Jael stared into his eyes before turning away.

'I'll see you in Hest, Jael Furyck!' he called after her.

Jael's smile quickly turned to a frown as she walked up to a scowling Thorgils. 'Don't say a thing,' she huffed, stalking straight past him.

***

Runa waited for some time after the door had closed before calling Tanja, the wet nurse, over. Tanja had fed Sigmund and was burping him gently over her shoulder as she walked around the kitchen.

The young girl looked nervous as she came to sit by the fire.

Runa put her arms out for Sigmund, who she'd quickly formed an attachment to. He was a lovely, placid boy. He reminded her of Fyn. She rested the baby over her own shoulder and leaned towards Tanja. 'I was wondering what you think of Evaine?' she began nervously.

Tanja's tired cornflower-blue eyes popped open. She was

barely eighteen-years-old, timid and small, and had recently lost her own son within the first month of his life. It was both torturous and healing to have another baby to care for, to feed and nurture, but she had been on edge since moving into the Gallas' home. Evaine had never said a kind word to her, and she lived in constant fear of displeasing her, working hard to keep the baby quiet at all times.

Runa smiled, lowering her voice. 'Perhaps you think I'm going to be cross or tell Evaine what you say?' she wondered gently. 'But I assure you, that's not why I ask.' Sigmund burped loudly, and both women couldn't help but smile. It relaxed Tanja slightly, and Runa hurried on. 'I'm worried, you see, about what Evaine might be doing. Why she has come back here.'

Tanja looked puzzled, unsure how she could help. She didn't say a word, though, desperately avoiding Runa's searching eyes.

'I hear her every morning, opening that chest,' Runa said, continuing to rub Sigmund's back. 'Rustling around up there, the floor creaking, mumbling to herself. She's doing something, and I need to know what it is.'

Tanja stared at her chapped hands, squeezing them together, her mouth opening and closing. 'But if I were to tell you...'

Runa edged forward. 'I would keep you safe from her, I promise. And I will pay you, of course. Double what you're earning now.'

They heard a noise outside, both of them glancing nervously at the door.

'It's very important, Tanja,' Runa went on as she brought Sigmund down into the crook of her arm. 'I need to make sure the baby is safe, and that Evaine is not doing anything that might cause him harm.'

Tanja blinked, staring longingly at the little boy who she'd fallen desperately in love with. Eventually, she shrugged, resigned to her fate. 'There is something... something strange in that chest.'

***

They had time before Gant would signal them on the march to Valder's Pass. On his signal, the Islanders would take to their ships, light now by the handful of men who were sick, or had already died of the sickness that was sweeping through the camp. Jael hoped they would not come to regret those missing hands during the battle, when they needed more power in their ships, or arms to wield swords. She shook her head, knowing there was nothing she could do about that now. They could only prepare themselves to try and come together; to fight as a united force. But by the looks on the faces of the men before her, a mix of shock, confusion, and deep-rooted scepticism was already plaguing their mission.

'We need to be a floating shield wall!' Jael called to the rows of Islanders arrayed before her on the beach. 'Sailing as one! Which is why the flags are so important.' She held up a red piece of cloth. 'Choose one person on your ship to be the flag carrier. That man will be responsible for passing the message along to each ship. It's the only way we'll be able to work in unison!'

Eadmund could see the doubts weaving themselves through the minds of the lords and their men as they frowned at each other, scratching their beards and narrowing their eyes. 'We'll likely have more ships than Haaron, but that alone won't save us!' He added his voice to Jael's, grimacing at the pain in his head as the sun seared itself into his swollen eyes. 'Do you remember our last attack on Skorro? How many men we lost? How many ships? And did it make any difference that we outnumbered them then, as we likely will now? No!' he cried passionately. 'That sort of thinking will not save us. But we've a chance for success if we follow this plan of working together as a shield wall to defeat them!' He glanced at Jael. 'And a shield wall is only strong if it remains intact, which is why these flags are so important.'

Ivaar was standing near Jael. The lords had rallied behind

him, supporting him in the wake of Eadmund's accusations. 'It makes sense!' he agreed loudly. 'Surely none of us want to end up at the bottom of the Adrano because we were too stupid or arrogant to think we knew better!' He nodded at Jael, who blinked in surprise to receive his support. 'We will no longer be lords at the bottom of the sea!'

There were a few cheers at that, a few nods, and the odd reluctant grunt of agreement.

'And you want Eirik to be given a true send-off, don't you?' Thorgils bellowed beside Eadmund. 'For him to taste the victory of Haaron's defeat that we'll deliver to him?'

Fyn gulped as he stood next to Jael. His nerves were getting worse, and his belly was griping again. He hoped it wasn't the sickness, just a bad case of pre-battle terror. He held firmly onto the sack of flags and looked at Jael.

'Fyn and Thorgils will give you your flags and talk you through what each colour means!' she said loudly. 'Make sure you all know because we'll need to keep going, no matter what happens. Someone on your ship must follow our orders!' She caught a glimpse of Eydis coming down onto the sand with Gisila and Amma; all three of them looking utterly morose. 'Prepare yourselves and your ships! We'll be leaving soon!'

Jael inclined her head towards Fyn, urging him after Thorgils who was heading for the men. He swallowed and loped after him, still awkward in his new mail. His body was suffocating under its cumbersome weight, and he walked oddly because of it. Jael smiled, watching him go before turning to Eydis whose bottom lip was quivering.

'I need something of yours, Jael,' Eydis said urgently. 'To keep, so I can dream. So I can see how to help you. To see how you are.'

'Well,' Jael frowned, thinking, 'you can have this.' She reached inside her cloak and slipped a coiled gold ring down her arm. She placed it into Eydis' small palm, rolling her fingers over it. 'That's the first arm ring my father gave me,' she smiled wistfully.

Eadmund wasn't wearing any arm rings. 'Here,' he mumbled, twisting off his wedding band and handing it to Eydis. 'Take this.'

Jael was surprised, but Eydis seemed pleased to have something from each of them, so she didn't make a fuss as she bent down to her. 'Gisila and Amma are going to take care of you, Eydis,' she said softly. 'And Eadmund and I will be back as soon as we can.'

Eydis didn't look reassured. In fact, more tears quickly flooded her eyes. 'And what if you don't? What if Ivaar is the only one who comes back?'

Jael pulled Eydis into her arms, placing her mouth next to her ear, lowering her voice. 'You remember what we talked about? About the prophecy?' she breathed. 'You know that I'll return. Someone wrote that down. A dreamer saw it. I'll come back to you, Eydis, and I'll bring Eadmund with me.' She kissed Eydis on the cheek and let her go. Standing up, she spoke to Gisila. 'You need to keep her safe, Mother,' she said sternly. 'Especially after what you said, Eydis. Anyone evil enough to murder your father won't think twice about trying to hurt you.'

Amma shuddered, wrapping her arm around Eydis' shoulder. 'We'll both look after her,' she said. 'I promise.'

Eadmund was barely able to keep to his feet. He knew what was facing them, but most of him was desperate to just drift off with his father; to lose himself in the grief that was slowly consuming him. 'Jael's right, Eydis,' he said, taking a deep breath. 'You need to stay safe until we return. Then we can all go home together.' His mind flickered quickly to his son and Evaine. He looked at Jael, confused. It was as though she was a stranger to him now. He shook his head, pulling Eydis close. 'Try not to worry, Little Thing. We'll go home soon.'

Eydis sighed, grateful for his arms, which felt strong, and his voice, which was reassuring. But it was not enough. None of the people she loved were safe.

Not anymore.

***

'She needs some help!' Varna snapped at her daughter. 'You take a turn.'

Morana looked horrified as she stared at Meena, knee-deep in a hole and covered with dirt, her red face dripping with filthy sweat. She glared at her mother.

'Do you expect *me* to jump in the hole and dig?' Varna snorted indignantly. 'At my age?'

They were standing in a towering copse that surrounded the oldest tree in Hest. Skoll's Tree. An enormous ash, thousands of years old; its roots bursting out of the earth, crawling over the land like long wooden worms. It was the tree Varna had seen in her dream; the one Jaeger had buried the book beneath.

Morana clenched her jaw and jumped into the hole, snatching the spade out of Meena's blistered hands. 'Fine,' she grumbled, shaking off her cloak. She wanted that book more than any of them. It didn't matter what she had to do to get it.

Meena sighed in relief, heaving herself out of the hole, her back aching as she fell into a heap on the cool grass.

Varna didn't even look her way. Her glazed eyes remained fixed on the hole, and what she'd dreamed was hidden inside. That book, after centuries, was about to be unleashed upon the world again. And whoever possessed it, whoever had the knowledge to master its dark magic, would wield a power worthy of the gods.

And Varna was determined that that person would never be Jaeger Dragos.

***

'She lights a candle,' Tanja whispered, her eyes never leaving the door. 'She takes it out of her chest. The same one, I think, as it looks smaller each morning.'

'You've *seen* it?' Runa asked breathlessly, her eyes wide.

'She leaves it to burn for a time,' Tanja went on, nodding. 'Saying words, the same ones, over and over again. Just mumbling though, my lady,' she hurried to explain. 'I couldn't tell you what she was saying. But it sounds the same.'

'And then what?'

'Well, she does that for some time, then she blows out the candle, puts it back in the chest and goes back to bed.'

'And you don't know what else she has in there? Just the candle?'

'I only see the candle, my lady,' Tanja insisted. 'There may be other things. It is quite dark.'

Runa glanced up at the mezzanine, then back to the door. She didn't know where Evaine had gone, but she needed to know more while she was still away. 'Here, take Sigmund upstairs. Put him on the bed, change his cloths. I think he's wet through,' Runa said carefully. 'I will watch the door. I need you to check inside that chest.'

Tanja blinked in horror. 'I, ahhh...'

'Go now,' Runa ordered, handing the baby to her. 'Quickly! You have an excuse to be up there, don't forget. But I don't. I'll stay here. Be as quick as you can!'

Tanja realised that she couldn't argue. She clutched Sigmund tightly to her chest and hurried up the stairs.

***

Morana screamed in ecstasy as she pulled the sack from its dirty grave. Clambering out of the hole, her long hair clinging to her sweaty face, she rushed to her mother who had collapsed next to

Meena, worn out by the waiting.

Varna leaned forward, her body more alert than it had been in years. 'Is that it?'

Morana stumbled to the ground, her crooked teeth bared as she laid the filthy sack on the grass. Hands shaking, she tore it open to reveal a leather-bound book. 'What else could it be?' she growled gleefully. 'What else could bring us both here, to this very spot on the same day?'

Meena blinked, her head cocked to one side as she considered the book. She frowned. That wasn't the book she remembered. Then she thought of Jaeger and smiled, her toes tapping in delight.

Varna caught her dreamy look and glared at Morana. 'Open it!' she ordered.

Morana was happy to. She wiped her hands quickly on her black dress before turning the aged cover. The vellum pages inside the book were old and crisp, and its contents... Morana frowned, scowling. 'Recipes?' She turned page after page. 'Pigs feet? Chicken and turnip pie? Grrrr!' she screamed, throwing the book into the bushes, rocking back on her heels in frustration. She caught Meena's nervous, barely hidden smirk. 'You knew this, girl?' she bellowed. 'Knew this book was not the one we were after and yet you dug for it? Let *me* dig for it? Wasted our time?' She lunged at Meena, grabbing her by the throat. 'Where is it? Where is the real book?!'

Varna didn't rush to Meena's aid.

Meena gurgled, her legs flailing under her aunt as Morana slapped her across the face, pinching her throat harder, smacking her head into the ground.

'Where is the *real* book?' Morana screamed. 'Where is it?'

Varna let her own annoyance dissipate; how could she compete with Morana? 'Take your hands off the girl,' she said slowly. 'We will not find the book if you kill the only person who might know where it is.'

Morana didn't appear at all ready to hear reason, but as Meena's eyes bulged urgently and her chest rose in panic, she reluctantly gave in, letting Meena scramble away. 'How is it possible?' Morana panted. 'How could we both have dreamed of this book? I don't understand.' She shook her head. 'Why? Why would we have seen him burying the book here?'

Varna was more measured, quicker to put the puzzle together. 'Because that is what he wanted us to see, of course. He buried this book to distract us. He must have known the stupid girl would not be able to keep his secret.'

Meena was still gasping for air, her throat raw. She could barely hear anything her grandmother was saying over the ringing in her ears. If Varna was horrifying, then Morana was doubly so.

She wanted to run and hide from them both.

'So, my girl,' Varna cooed, turning to her granddaughter. 'We must find a way into the Bear's head. We must see what he did with the real book before it takes hold of him.'

Meena frowned. Takes hold of him? She shivered.

What did that mean?

CHAPTER TWENTY ONE

Berard vomited over the side of the ship.

It wasn't that the sea was choppy, nor the weather foul, he just felt ill. An approaching battle always had that effect on him, whether on sea or land. He wiped the back of his hand across his mouth, wishing he had a cup of wine to wash away the bitter aftertaste.

'Better now?' Jaeger laughed at his green-tinged brother as he swayed back to the stern of *Death Bringer*, Haaron's newest warship. They were under sail, in a light, but freshening wind, his men hunkered down against the shield-laden gunwales.

Berard coughed, saying nothing as he debated going back to the side of the ship. He looked towards the Widow's Peak in the distance, trying to take his mind off his surging nausea. 'No sign of them.'

'No,' Jaeger said cheerfully. 'But they'll come. Their scouts would have seen our men on the march.'

'And when we get near the Tower, we'll just wait?'

Jaeger smiled, his eyes narrowing to slits in the glare of the morning sun. 'Yes, we will wait, and they will come, and we will sink them all.'

***

They had seen the signal from high atop the mountains that towered above Saala, the place where Rexon had a lookout; where a fire would burn as soon as there was any sign of attack. But this time the flames were burning for their own attack, the attack that none of them really wanted. No one but Lothar.

Saala's beach was full. The men were saying their goodbyes to the women they had brought with them, for they would stay behind now and wait for word to come.

Jael had said her goodbyes and was starting to shut everyone out of her head: Eydis, and her mother, Axl and Aleksander. She had to think about what they needed to do now. The Islanders. Their fleet. Her men. All of them.

She turned to Eadmund, who had barely spoken all morning. 'Shall we go, then?'

He looked away to where the men were filling the ships. 'We should,' he said simply, turning to leave.

'Wait, Eadmund!' Jael called, grabbing his arm. 'Wait!'

He turned around, almost impatiently, his eyes skirting hers.

Jael was not deterred, though. She took his face in her hands, leaning towards him. 'You're still in there, I know it, Eadmund. And I know you love me, no matter what she's done to you.'

Eadmund shook her away, confused and annoyed at what she was implying.

Jael didn't care. There was no guarantee that she would have the chance to say anything ever again; Eirik's sudden death had taught her that harsh lesson. 'You love me, and after we defeat Haaron, when we're back on Oss, I'll find a way to stop this and bring you back to me.'

Eadmund frowned but didn't leave. He stared into her eyes, which looked tired and swollen, but green, so green and deep, and for a moment, he remembered her. He reached out a warm hand and laid it on her cold face, his eyes lost in hers.

Jael rushed to kiss him before he could move. 'I promise you, Eadmund, I'll bring you back.' And with that, she started walking towards *Sea Bear*, where Fyn stood waiting nervously next to

Beorn.

Eadmund watched her go, feeling the sudden loss of her, resisting the intense urge he felt to go after her. He blinked, shaking himself away from those eyes and back into the moment. Opening up the pouch hanging from his belt, he touched the small blonde curl of his son, and the stone Morac had given him from Evaine. Settled again, he took a deep breath and walked away to his own ship, trying desperately to clear the stench of his father's burning corpse out of his nostrils.

Thorgils wandered over to Jael as she reached the water's edge. 'And what about me, then?' he smiled cheerfully, but his eyes were anxious. 'What if this is the last time we see each other?'

'What was your name again?' Jael asked with a serious face, happy for a distraction.

'My name?' Thorgils bellowed, puffing out his chest. 'My name is Thorgils Svanter, and I am your servant, my queen!' he bowed. 'Your loyal oathman,' he added, looking up. 'And I'm about to deliver you a great prize. A fleet of Hestian warships!'

'Well, then, you should certainly receive a reward for that,' Jael smiled. 'Perhaps a new arm ring?'

Thorgils' eyebrows dismissed that with speed.

Jael laughed. 'I suppose I could stretch to two.'

'Ha!' he snorted. 'Perhaps I should go and declare myself for Ivaar?' He glanced around quickly, relieved to see that Ivaar was already on board his ship. 'He might have better prizes on offer.'

'Ivaar?' Jael sneered. 'Well, I suppose he'll need all the help he can get if he makes it through this battle. We won't be able to keep Eadmund away from him for long.'

'True,' Thorgils grinned. 'But still, you'll never last as queen if you're going to be that miserly.' He wrapped his fish-like arms around her. 'Two arm rings? You're lucky I'm such a loyal man!'

'Indeed, I am,' Jael said, letting him hug her. There had been far too much affection already this morning, but Thorgils' big arms and thick chest enclosed her with such warmth that she felt like a child for a moment. Safe. Protected. It reminded her of being in her father's arms. 'Well, I might think of a more suitable reward,' she mumbled into his shoulder.

'Glad to hear it,' Thorgils smiled, letting her go. 'You protect your queen!' he called to Fyn. 'I'll need her alive if I'm to collect my prize!'

'And you keep an eye on Otto,' Jael urged quietly. 'If he steps out of line, knock him on the head.' She said this with one eye on Otto, who was deep in conversation with Torborn and Hassi. Jael shook her head, turning towards *Sea Bear*, the ship she had spent the past few months getting to know intimately. Beorn had taken her and Fyn out sailing regularly, testing and tweaking. She was a wild beast, finely crafted, and, Beorn had admitted to her, his favourite.

Jael stepped into the freezing water, raising one hand to Torstan who stood in the bow of *Dragon's Tooth*, looking as though he wanted to rush back to the latrines. She smiled, and her eyes met Ivaar's. He glared at her, unblinking as he stood grasping the prow of one of his Kalfan ships, watching as the last of his men clambered aboard.

Jael frowned as Ivaar turned away. She had saved him from Eadmund's revenge for now, but would that come back to haunt her in the end?

***

Biddy opened the door, her eyes rounding in surprise. 'Runa?'

Runa was out of breath, blinking rapidly. 'May I come in?'

'Of course, of course,' Biddy said, ushering her inside. She peered behind her, smiling at Askel, who was shooing the puppies away from a pile of dung he was making, before closing the door.

Edela was pulling on her gloves as Runa walked into the main room. She smiled politely, then frowned. Something was wrong.

'This is Runa Gallas,' Biddy smiled, gently pushing Runa towards Edela. 'Fyn's mother. Evaine's... mother.'

They both stared at Runa, who swallowed nervously.

'What has happened?' Edela asked, sensing Runa's distress. 'Why don't you sit down and tell us?'

'No, no,' Runa mumbled, noting that both women were wearing their cloaks. 'You are going somewhere. I should leave, come again another time.'

'Is it about Evaine?' Edela wondered softly.

Runa's eyes widened in fear. She looked at the women, desperate for some help. 'Yes,' she sighed. 'Yes, Evaine is doing something. Every morning. She is doing something... magical.'

Edela's blue eyes sharpened as she glanced at Biddy. 'Perhaps we need some tea?'

***

'Who is that?' Irenna wondered with a frown as she braided her eldest daughter's hair on the balcony. The spring warmth had encouraged the Dragos women to take themselves outside to sit and drink tea while the children played. 'That woman, with Varna?'

Bayla was immediately alert, hurrying over to the edge of the first-floor balcony. She didn't recognise the figure whose long black-and-white hair flapped behind her as she hurried across the square next to Varna and that stupid girl. 'I have no idea.'

'Looks like one of The Following to me,' Nicolene sneered, helping herself to another piece of apple cake. 'With that strange hair? They all look filthy and unhinged.'

'Nicolene!' Irenna chided, glancing around. 'They're hardly the people to be insulting, are they? With the knowledge they have? Who knows what they could do to you or your children?'

Bayla laughed as she came to take her own, fur-lined seat. 'Irenna,' she smirked. 'You really think *we* have any reason to be worried? We are the royal family, and they are...'

'A secret society of powerful dreamers?' Irenna suggested with a wry smile, turning her daughter Lucina around so everyone could admire her hair.

'Ha! If they're so powerful, then why do they creep about in the shadows, pretending they don't exist?' Bayla sipped her lukewarm dandelion tea with a grimace, wishing it was wine. 'Why keep their supposed magic to themselves?'

Nicolene's eyes were alert. She was fascinated by The Following, especially Varna Gallas, who crept around the castle with constant threat in her rheumy eyes. She looked like a decrepit crone, but Karsten had warned her that, although Varna was old, she would never be weak.

'Probably because they like it,' Irenna suggested, handing Lucina a piece of cake. 'They like the mystery and secrecy of it all. It keeps us watchful. Far away from them and their plans.'

Bayla thought about Varna, wondering what she had really been doing in Jaeger's chamber with that ugly girl. She was up to something.

Bayla was certain of it.

***

Runa told them everything she knew, from the beginning. All about Morana and Morac and Evaine. All the suspicions and fears she had harboured over the years. She was relieved to let it out; to have someone to talk to at last.

'And now?' Edela wondered carefully. 'You say that you are worried, but why? What is she doing now to make you feel so?'

Runa had been wringing her hands, but she suddenly stopped and looked up. 'She is different.' She swallowed, trying to find the right words. 'Before, Evaine was desperate, childish. She would have tantrums because she couldn't be with Eadmund. She was so impatient and angry, but now...'

'Now?' Biddy wondered anxiously, perching on the edge of her stool.

'Now, she is confident,' Runa said, shuddering. 'So confident. Smiling. Calm. And that is not the Evaine I know at all.' She reached her hands out to the flames, suddenly cold. 'She is doing something every morning before the sun is up.'

Edela's eyebrows rose. She took a sip of elderflower tea and creaked forward.

'She has things in her chest,' Runa went on. 'I have spoken to her wet nurse, and she tells me that every morning Evaine lights a candle and mumbles words, the same ones, over and over again, then blows it out and puts it away.'

'Oh,' Edela said breathlessly. 'I see.'

'I asked Tanja to look in the chest before Evaine returned,' Runa said nervously. 'And she found stones in a bag, five of them. Each one with a painted symbol on it. And the candle, it had symbols scratched into the wax. She didn't recognise them.'

Edela peered at Runa with concern. 'Well then, I think it best that you come along with us. We can talk more at Entorp's house.'

'Entorp?' Runa looked surprised as Biddy and Edela stood.

Edela smiled. 'Yes. We are going to get Biddy tattooed. And I think it's best if he works on you as well. It sounds as though that girl is trying to cause a lot of trouble, and we will have no hope of stopping her if we don't protect ourselves first.'

***

'The look on your face tells me you don't agree, Brother?' Haegen grumbled, his irritation with Karsten ready to burst like a bloody boil. Karsten had been niggling away at him since they'd left Hest; picking at him, criticising his plans, and he'd finally had enough. *He* was in charge of their men, not his younger, loose-lipped, revenge-obsessed brother.

'Well,' Karsten mused, walking his horse alongside Haegen's, gnawing on a piece of salt pork. 'It's a predictable attack. They'll expect it. Anyone with half a brain would.'

'Is that so?'

'Not all Brekkans are as stupid as their king,' Karsten insisted.

'But they'll expect to find us still in the pass, thinking they can trap us in that narrow space between the cliffs,' Haegen pointed out, tugging his reins to the right, steering his horse around a boulder. 'They'll not be prepared for us to come upon them so quickly, *before* they reach the pass.'

'True,' Karsten agreed. 'And we'll kill a great many of them because of it, I'm sure, but... imagine how many more we could kill if we did things *my* way?' He turned to look at his brother. Haegen was almost as tall as Jaeger, but despite his best efforts, never as menacing. 'Surely you want to deliver the best outcome possible to Father? A victory so bloody and final that the Brekkans will never trouble us again! We'll likely have fewer men than them. Less chance of that happening unless we do it my way.'

Haegen, who was not inclined to listen to anything Karsten had to say, suddenly hesitated. Haaron had never been impressed by anything they had done. Ever. And this was their first time going into battle on their own. Leading the men of Hest against the might of Brekka, without their father. His judgement of the outcome was bound to be harsh, whether they were victorious or not.

Haegen peered at Karsten, ignoring Irenna's voice as it warned him to stop. 'Tell me again,' he said slowly. 'What are you suggesting?'

***

Morana ran her black eyes over Varna's stark chamber. It was larger than her entire cottage, but there was no warmth or comfort in its cold stone walls or its cold stone floor. It had one tiny window, high up near the rafters; one blackened fire pit in the middle of the room, sitting beneath one smoke hole; two simple, wooden chairs; two narrow, low beds, and now... three of them to share it all.

Meena wanted to disappear as she stood with her back wedged into a corner of the chamber, hoping to go unnoticed. Her neck ached where Morana had gripped it, and she was so overcome with anxiety that she could barely breathe. She tapped the side of her head repeatedly, wriggling her toes inside her boots, unable to stand still.

'Does she ever stop?' Morana wondered irritably, glaring at the shaking woman.

'No,' Varna said plainly. 'And you will leave her alone, for she is the one who will help us get the book.'

'Why? Why her?' Morana sneered, sitting on the edge of her mother's bed, her stomach growling angrily.

'Meena has seen the book,' Varna murmured, lowering herself into her old chair. It was as wobbly on its feet as she was. 'She has seen the texts written in Raemus' own hand. And *he* can't read it. Not without my help.'

'You think you're the only one who can read the symbols of the Old Gods?' Morana spat.

Varna stared at her.

Her daughter.

It had been eighteen years since she had last seen this snarling creature.

She had not missed her.

'Perhaps there are others,' Varna conceded wearily. 'But none of them will have the book, will they? Only I will, once Meena brings it to me.'

Meena, shuffling her feet, gulped.

Morana didn't look pleased.

'We have always known what we needed to do, Daughter,' Varna reminded her. 'Always known our part in the prophecy. We must stop Jael Furyck, which is what I thought I had instructed *you* to do.'

Morana clenched her jaw, wishing there were flames in the fire pit to warm her numb hands. 'And I am!' she snapped. 'Evaine is hard at work. We have nothing to worry about there.'

'And yet, here you are, sticking your nose into *my* business. My business, which is the book!' Varna hissed, suddenly noticing the lack of flames herself. 'Go and get some wood, girl!' she called to Meena, who looked relieved, scurrying out of the room as quickly as she could.

'How many years did you search for that book?' Morana scowled. 'I thought that perhaps you had lost your abilities, Mother. That you would be grateful for my assistance.'

Varna inhaled a raspy breath, eyeing her daughter whose face was all but hidden behind the cascading nest of hair that fell down to her waist, swamping her small frame. 'It will not hurt, I suppose, to put our two heads together. I had not expected the Bear to find it before I did.'

'And The Following?' Morana wondered. 'What will you tell them?'

Varna's head jerked up, her hairy lips twitching with distaste. 'The Following? They will be ready when we are. But until we have that book, there is nothing anyone can do. We must find it.'

***

Axl couldn't stop sweating. The long morning hike into the

mountains wearing his mail had been exhausting. The terrain was challenging, and they had left their horses behind in Saala; all but Lothar that is, who rode near the back of the first column, protected by two heavily armed bodyguards.

Hest was a barren, warm place; a land of stone and red dirt, dry and inhospitable. The path had grown increasingly dusty and sharp-edged the higher they climbed. Axl found himself slipping on gravel as they shrunk into narrower and narrower columns. Walls of angular, angry rocks peered down at them, closing in around the Brekkans as they struggled along under the heat of the midday sun.

Axl had tried not to empty his water bag too quickly. No one was waiting for those who hopped out of line to piss in the dust.

'Are you alright there?' Gant wondered, looking as cool and calm as when they'd left Saala.

'Fine,' Axl panted, his red face dripping with perspiration. 'Nothing a dip in the Adrano wouldn't cure.'

'Well, don't wander too far off the path or you might find yourself swimming about in there by mistake!' Gant smiled, covering up the fact that he was just as ready to lie down as Axl. The weight of his mail and the length of the march was not new to him – Lothar had driven them up a similar path last summer – but he'd barely slept since they'd arrived in Saala, and if he were honest, he'd barely slept since Lothar had forced Gisila to marry him. Guilt and memories of his promise to Ranuf kept him awake most nights. He was happy that at least Gisila would have some respite from her odious husband while they were away.

'Having fun?' Aleksander puffed, falling into line with them. He had grown fed up of walking with Osbert at the head of the first column. Osbert had started complaining as soon as they'd lost sight of Rexon's village, and Aleksander was desperate for someone else to listen to. He looked almost as red as Axl but much more cheerful.

'Why do *you* look so happy?' Axl grumbled. His belly was griping; with hunger or discomfort, he couldn't tell. His eyes rushed around anxiously, scanning the cliffs on either side of them, waiting for an ambush.

'We have scouts, you know,' Aleksander smiled, noting the path of Axl's eyes. 'They're up there, and ahead of us. Behind us too. Watching all sides. We'll know when they're close.'

Axl sighed, embarrassed at feeling like such a novice. He expected he wouldn't feel like that much longer.

'The main thing to remember,' Gant said in a low voice, 'is to hold your sword and your head at the same time. And aim to kill with every strike. It will be loud and fast and not at all like any training we've ever done. Nothing can replicate the shock you will feel at first.'

'Gant's right,' Aleksander agreed. 'The noise will disorient you quickly. And you won't be facing one man but three or five, all from different directions, all at once. So kill quickly. And if you can't kill with your first blow, get them down to the ground in a hurry, then finish them off and move on.'

Axl swallowed nervously, thinking about his promise to Amma; his desire to prove himself worthy of his Furyck name. It all felt so childish now. He would quite happily turn around and go home.

Or would he?

'It will be both better and worse than you're imagining,' Gant assured him, watching Axl frown. 'And when it's done, you'll know more about yourself and what you're capable of. It's what you need.'

'If I live,' Axl murmured, almost to himself, his eyes fixed on the mail-clad back of the man in front of him. He didn't know his name.

'Well, best you offer up a prayer to Furia while you're marching,' Aleksander suggested, jiggling his spear in his right hand. 'Remind her that you're a Furyck, that you need her protection.'

Axl gulped, staring up at the steep, red-dirt ridge they were about to climb, thinking that sounded like a good idea.

He could feel it now.

They were getting closer.

***

Haaron had not slept. Excitement surged through his veins as he peered through one of the Tower's long windows, down to the Adrano, watching as his fleet sailed slowly into place. There had been little wind throughout the morning, but he was relieved to see that it was picking up now as his ships moved forward with more urgency.

Haaron turned around, checking on his archers who were clustered in groups before each of the windows around the Tower's cavernous stone hall. They were talking quietly amongst themselves, fingering their bows, eager for the arrival of the enemy. Great buckets of iron-tipped and pitch-soaked arrows waited behind each group; blazing braziers nearby.

The Tower.

Valder Dragos had built the formidable, three-storeyed defensive structure into the side of an overhanging cliff. In the centuries since his death, it had slowly become part of its rocky home, half-hidden and half protruding over the Adrano Sea. It was the perfect place to attack any ship who would dare come through the Widow's Peak and threaten his kingdom.

From here, Haaron would watch as his youngest sons battled against Eirik Skalleson's Islanders. If last time was any indication, it would not be a good day for the Islanders. But then again, Varna had seen trouble for Jaeger; that things would not prove as straightforward as they might expect. Haaron had no desire to lose ships or men, but the thought of losing his youngest son kept his eyes alert, and his mood eager.

He smiled, enjoying the cooling breeze as it wafted through

the window. He was ready. He only hoped the same could be said of his sons.

PART FOUR

The Burning Sea

CHAPTER TWENTY TWO

'There they are!' Jael cried, her eyes snapping to the fleet of Hestian warships strung across the Adrano.

The Islanders were still navigating the narrow passes between the colossal stones of the Widow's Peak, but they could all see what was waiting for them when they emerged.

A blockade.

Smaller than Jael had imagined – she quickly counted fifteen ships – but exactly where she'd hoped. She turned to Fyn, who was pale and wide-eyed beside her. 'Ready?'

He tried to look confident, but his shoulders were up around his ears, and he was barely breathing. 'Yes,' he croaked, wondering when he'd last had a drink; his mouth was painfully dry.

Jael squinted, staring far into the distance. Once through the stones, they would be in open water, underneath Haaron's Tower.

And then the arrows would come.

***

There was a scream.

All eyes went up, hands clutching hilts, sweaty fingers curling around shield grips, heartbeats racing, heads swivelling.

Gant surged to the front of the second column with Aleksander, his eyes scanning the ridge to their right, Axl stumbling in their wake. They were in a shallow ravine, boxed in by the rocky terrain.

More screams. Horses roaring.

Then the scouts were racing towards them, scrambling over the ridge. Four of them; bleeding, tripping, falling, not getting up.

No horses.

'Shield! Wall!' Rexon yelled from the rear column, sensing, rather than seeing the rumbling of Hestian warriors he knew were coming.

'Shield! Wall!' Gant turned and cried to his men in the middle column. 'Four sides! Spears in behind!'

Aleksander caught the sudden panic in Axl's eyes as their men slapped their shields together, hurrying into formation. 'Don't break the walls till I come back!' he growled. And dropping his spear, he hefted his shield up to his shoulder and pushed himself through the wall. Running to the nearest fallen scout, Aleksander grabbed him by the mail, dragging him across the dirt, back towards the column.

Gant rushed out after him, grabbing another. The others, they could both see, were clearly dead.

'Open!' Aleksander yelled, and the shields parted as they pulled the scouts inside, closing quickly around them. 'Where are they?' he panted, rolling the man over.

He was Saalan. Aleksander didn't know his name. He had an arrow in his shoulder, another in his thigh, one in his neck. His eyes could barely focus. 'Here,' he gurgled, trying to breathe through the blood bubbling from his mouth. 'Rear... flank... here.'

Aleksander looked up at Gant, who blinked quickly and strode to the right wall of their column, searching the ridge, listening. He spun around suddenly; Lothar was coming.

'My lord!' Gant yelled, surprised to see him still on his horse. 'They're coming from the rear. On our right flank! Get Osbert's men into a shield wall! Four sides!'

Lothar looked startled as he tried to dismount, his boot catching in a stirrup as his horse skittered in terror. He fell to the ground, dangling there, ensnared. Lothar's bodyguards rushed to his side and unhooked him, hurrying their king behind the hastily formed walls of Osbert's first column.

They waited in the ravine behind their shields, hearts pounding, ears open.

Three long rectangles. A thousand men in each.

Trapped.

The rumble grew louder. Men were coming. Dust filled the sky over their heads.

The Brekkans shuffled their feet, looking for purchase in the dirt. Elbows braced against shields, hands rolling spears, they desperately searched the ridges above them; some wishing they'd been able to afford helmets, others regretting that they hadn't taken the time to tighten the strap on theirs. But it was too late, all hands were now full.

And then the beating of swords on shields.

'Here they come!' Rexon yelled from the rear column, watching as the Hestians poured over the ridge towards them. He clenched his jaw, screaming at his men. 'Shields together! Brace yourselves! Spears!'

Rexon's first rank of shields was locked together across the front of their column. The second rank angled shields over their heads, and the third rank was all spears. They surged forward, jabbing their sharpened spearheads through the gaps in the walls.

Waiting.

Gant saw a flash out of the corner of his eye. 'To the right!' he yelled, spinning as a frothing mass of screaming Hestians rushed over the rocky outcrop nearest their right flank. 'Spears to the right!'

'Brace yourselves!' Aleksander cried, tightening the grip on his spear as the Hestians threw themselves off the rocks and onto their shields, hacking and chopping with axes and swords. He crunched his boot back into the gravel, balancing himself, jabbing between the shields with his spear. 'Hold!'

They had to stay together if they were to stand a chance.

***

'Now we see if the lords will play my flag game,' Jael muttered. 'For if they don't, we're going to find ourselves in a dark place very quickly.'

That wasn't what Fyn wanted to hear as he stood alongside her, holding the sack of flags, his guts twisting with every rhythmic slap of oars into the sea.

'They will!' Beorn growled, gripping the tiller harder, his eyes skimming the sea, searching for any rocks that would threaten his hull. 'Otherwise, they'll be gobbled up by Ran, and that goddess can be a real bitch!' Thankfully the sun had been masked by clouds now, and he could see better than he had all day. With the help of two men who were crouching near the catapult, checking for shadows in the water, they had navigated *Sea Bear* through the Widow's Peak without a scratch; sail furled, under oar.

Jael smiled, exhaling in relief as they finally emerged from the stones into the vast expanse of the Adrano. It lay before them, dark and threatening under the increasingly moody sky. She glanced around, relieved to see the rest of their fleet appear from behind the stones. Thorgils waved to her from the bow of *Fire Serpent* on her right, his face as cheerful as ever.

'Light the braziers,' she nodded to Fyn. 'Let's get ready.'

Fyn dropped the sack of flags, fumbling with his tinderbox as he headed inside the wooden house. His fingers were numb from the cold, shaking with nerves. He hoped Jael wouldn't notice.

'Check our distance, Arlo!' Jael called to her head archer who stood expectantly along the gunwale with his men. There were eight of them in all; eight men who knew a bow better than a sword; whose eyes were sharper and arms stronger than any on board.

Arlo drew an arrow from his quiver, held his face up to the quickening wind as it flapped his shoulder-length braids, nocked it, and drew back his bow. All heads turned towards the sky, watching as he released the arrow, following its arc as it soared through the clouds and dropped, with a silent plop, into the sea, some distance from the enemy's fleet.

Jael looked at Beorn. 'We keep going.'

Beorn nodded tightly.

'Helmets on!' Jael cried. 'Check your bow and arrows are nearby! Know where your shields are! Make sure all those buckets are full of water! Listen for my signal!'

Not long now.

***

Blood splattered into Osbert's eyes. The man to his right screamed, an axe cleaving open his cheek. Osbert cringed, looking away. He was in the third rank of the front column, working with his sword to stab anyone who tried to throw themselves over their walls. Of which there were many contenders.

The Hestians roared as they smashed onto the shields; their axes and swords thumping and crashing down in a furious attempt to break up the Brekkan formations as quickly as possible.

Karsten was wild, his eyes glazed, his teeth bared as he swung his twin axes in a blood-making frenzy. He was bare-chested, angry, kicking out at the wall of shields before him. 'Go low!' he cried impatiently, slashing into the ankle of a Brekkan who yelped in agony, toppling to the ground. 'Cut their fucking legs!' He chopped his axes down onto the spears that were keeping his men at bay, breaking off their deadly tips. 'Take their spears out!

More! More!' he yelled. 'Kill them!'

Lothar looked on with bulging eyes from the centre of the first column, sweat dripping down his back, his bodyguards on either side of him keeping him safe. Osbert had skewered a Hestian who had thrown himself up onto their shields, but his sword was now stuck and wouldn't come free. He yanked and pulled, gritting his teeth in desperation, but the sword was stubbornly lodged into the Hestian's shoulder. Lothar hurried to his son, adding his substantial weight, and the sword slid out, at last, in a big rush of blood. Osbert pulled his shield away, and the dead Hestian fell down onto the pile of bodies at his feet.

Osbert and some of his men dropped to the ground now, stabbing the Hestians trying to cut the shield bearer's legs. 'We have more men!' he shouted urgently, sensing the panic in his men's eyes that mirrored his own. The Hestians were overpowering them with their deafening noise and surging rage. The threat of their spears was being undermined by the number of axes swinging to destroy them. It was unsettling, sapping their confidence quickly. 'We have more men! Hold the walls!'

Osbert's voice was lost amongst the screaming warriors whose swords and axes clanged off the Brekkans' shields, driving a whirlwind of noise into Axl's head. He couldn't hear, couldn't think, could barely breathe as he fought, elbow to elbow with Gant and Aleksander, in the third rank of their middle column. Shoulders pushing against the shield holders before them, they worked the gaps relentlessly with their spears.

'Go low!' Gant urged, his voice hoarse, watching the Hestians move their attention. 'Spears to the ground!'

Half the spear holders crouched, stabbing through the narrow spaces between legs; legs that were shaking from the strain of holding the line against such an overwhelming onslaught. They were starting to slide backwards now, pushed by the Hestians driving their shields into the Brekkans with force; butting and jamming and smashing with gritted teeth. They had fewer men but had taken the advantage with their surprise attack.

They were causing chaos.

Karsten smiled as he swung his axes into a shield, shattering it in two. They would not hold on much longer. Soon their walls would break, and the Brekkans would scatter like terrified mice.

***

Thorgils glanced over at Jael, vibrating with excitement and nerves as he fiddled with the soft white feathers fluttering at the ends of his arrows.

No flags were flying from her ship yet.

'What is she *doing*?' Otto grumbled next to him. 'We should have stopped by now. She'll have us under the Tower!'

Thorgils turned to glare at the pinched face of the balding man, whose scant wisps of grey hair blew angrily across his head. And not for the first time since they'd left Saala. 'We need to get close enough to hit them with the sea-fire. There's no point in us sitting here! How will it help us if we're firing into the sea?' he grumbled back. 'The waves aren't going to break the jars!'

Otto frowned, rolling his eyes at Borg, *Fire Serpent's* helmsman, who stood to their right, one hand on the tiller, watching as their men pulled tirelessly on the oars. He glanced up at the clouds rolling in, suddenly anxious. The sea would turn soon and then all of their plans would be sunk.

'Light the braziers!' Thorgils bellowed, ignoring Otto and his rolling eyes. 'We're getting close!'

Otto huffed and stumbled towards the wooden house that ran from the stern to just before the catapult. Their sail had been furled, stored with the yard, between the sea chests and the house. Rows of shields lined the gunwales. Fifteen per side. They would help protect the oarsmen when the arrows came.

For when they came, it would rain death.

***

Aleksander thrust his bloody spear through the gaps in the wall, driving his shoulder against the man before him, helping him to hold his place.

Axl was next to him, low to the ground, jerking his spear back and forth, teeth gritted, blood and sweat dripping into his eyes. Suddenly his spear snapped. He felt the weight of it lighten as half his spear stayed outside the wall. Pulling back the broken shaft, he stared at it in shock.

'Sword!' Aleksander yelled at him.

Axl blinked, waking himself up. He threw the broken shaft away, trying to ignore the pained wails of the men being stabbed around him; the blood that was flying, the stink of shit in the air. The Hestians pushed harder and harder against their shields, hooking some out of the wall with their curved axe blades, exposing gaps that were hastily filled. Axl unsheathed his sword, thought of his father and stood up, squeezing his way in between two men, one who was grasping his bleeding neck, wavering slightly, his shield dropping. Axl bumped against him, shunting him upright.

Aleksander could feel the heat of the Hestians' fury as they came pounding and chopping at their shields again and again. He pulled back his spear and drove it through a gap. The Brekkan in front of him screamed as a sword tip pierced his eye. Aleksander pushed him out of the way, yanking the man's hand out of the shield grip and slipping his own through it. He dropped the spear now, unsheathing his sword, eyes everywhere. 'Hold the walls!' he screamed. 'Shields together! Hold!'

Osbert was panting, grunting, his sword slick with blood as he fought off a continual stream of Hestians who were attacking their shields from all four sides. Their walls were moving now, moving and sliding about; boots skidding on blood-soaked dust as wounded men lost both strength and resolve.

'Hold the walls!' Lothar panicked, stabbing forward with his sword, sticking a warrior in the neck as he flew up onto a shield. 'Do not break! Kill them! Kill them!'

Screaming, raging, berserking Hestians on all sides assaulted their shields with axes, hammers, and swords, whipping themselves into a killing frenzy. Lothar's men's eyes darted about anxiously. Most were seasoned warriors, but their minds were starting to work against them now.

'We have more men!' Lothar cried desperately. 'We can keep them out! Hold!'

'Aarrghh!' Axl screamed as a knife slid into his hand, ripping his skin, blood coursing down his fingers, loosening his grip on his sword. Teeth clenched against the shock and pain, he forced his fingers into a fist and lunged forward, angry now, pushing his blade into a Hestian's chest. The dying man was pulled back quickly and with him, Axl's sword. He looked around blankly, scrambling in the dirt, crawling over the dead body of a boy he knew; his eyes lifelessly staring towards the sky, his throat leaking blood.

Axl blinked away everything but what he needed to do: Get. A. Sword.

Gulping, he snatched one out of the boy's bloody hand.

Haegen was too busy to notice what Karsten was doing. There were three columns, each one wrapped in four thick walls of shields, all proving hard to break down. Naturally. The Brekkans were the toughest warriors he had fought, but without Ranuf and Jael's leadership, they were weaker, less organised. They would break, and soon, he was certain of it. He could see the doubt in their eyes; the doubt that was working its way into their heads and their guts. Before long, they would collapse. 'Kill them all!' Haegen roared, chopping his sword onto the shield of Rexon Boas; a good warrior, he knew, and one he needed to kill. Chaos reigned when leaders fell. 'Jump! Jump over them! Pull down their shields! Get over their walls!'

Rexon hurried to react. 'Spears to the centre!' he panted

loudly. 'Stab them if they try it!' He eyed Haegen Dragos through the gaps in the wall, narrowing his gaze until there was nothing but hatred and fury left. Digging his boots into the dirt, he pushed against his shield with his left shoulder, thinking of his wife and their unborn child. He needed to survive to ensure their safety. 'Keep your shields together!'

Karsten had no time to get the blood out of his mouth. He spat, but the wind blew it straight back into his face. 'Aarrghh!' he bellowed, throwing himself up and over the shields. Lothar Furyck was in there, he could see him. The prize his father so desperately wanted. But Karsten had no intention of giving him to Haaron alive. He screamed, cleaving his axe into the scalp of the Brekkan whose shield he'd just shattered.

Lothar gaped as Karsten Dragos, mad-eyed, half-naked, and wet with blood, lunged over the shields, tumbling onto the dead bodies before him.

'With me!' Karsten shouted to his men, his voice carrying over the clattering of weapons, and the howls of pain. 'I have the king! With me!'

'The king!' his men roared, charging into the collapsing shields. 'Get the king!'

Haegen's head was up.

He frowned, stepping quickly out of Rexon's reach, and ran, past his bleeding, stumbling, skewered men, towards the sound of his brother. 'Karsten! Karsten!' he screamed, jumping over the bodies that lay scattered around the walls. 'Karsten! Wait!'

***

Fifteen ships. He could only count fifteen ships.

Ivaar frowned. Last time they'd attempted this, the Hestians had come at them with a lot more than that. Perhaps Lothar's plan was going to work after all?

Ivaar stood gripping the carved neck of *Shadow Blade's* dragon prow whose face looked as angry as his. He had been relegated to the second row behind Jael's five ships. Thorgils was to the right of her, commanding three more. Ivaar and his two ships, along with the other lords and theirs, followed torturously in their wake.

Waiting.

His father was dead. *He* should be the king, leading the line, defeating Haaron.

And if today went as he hoped, by the time the sun went down, he would be.

***

Lothar's one remaining bodyguard threw himself in front of Karsten. Osbert stumbled, rushing to protect his father. Karsten twirled his bloody axes, lunging at the bodyguard, who ducked and swung his sword at the shieldless attacker. Karsten's eyes narrowed, and he smiled, baring his teeth, kicking at the guard, knocking him down, hacking into his neck with three short blows.

There were other men now, Karsten's men, surging through the shields as they collapsed, parting under the sheer weight of the Hestian onslaught. Axes and swords glinted in a burst of sunshine, slashing through the air towards Lothar and Osbert.

Gant watched it unfold through gaps in shields, the urgent thudding of his heart pounding in his ears.

Torn.

Lothar could die. Osbert could die. Axl would be king.

They would try to protect Axl, keep him safe. But could they? Could he live with himself for not even attempting to save his king? A Furyck?

Probably.

But if Lothar was defeated, the men's morale would surely follow and what would happen to Axl then?

Gritting his teeth, Gant screamed to the gods and peeled away from his position, running towards Aleksander and Axl. 'We have to help Lothar!' he cried, certain now despite the bitter taste of the words on his tongue.

'What?' Aleksander was puzzled, but he didn't look around as he thrust his sword at the mail-clad chest of a Hestian warrior. He missed and turned to Gant, stepping back quickly. '*What?*'

'Lothar's under attack, their walls have broken,' Gant said quickly, glancing around at their own twisting walls. 'We have to help him! If he falls, none of us will stand a chance!'

Aleksander hesitated for a moment, but only that; there was no time for more. He nodded, swallowing. 'With me!' he yelled to their men. 'We must save the king!'

'Break the walls!' Gant roared. 'Rexon, you hold! We're going for Lothar!' He wasn't sure if Rexon had even heard him, but he turned and ran towards the shields anyway. 'Break! Break the walls! Follow me!'

His men didn't hesitate to scramble to their feet, clutching their battered shields up to their aching shoulders, limping, running and panting after their leader.

Hoping to save their king.

***

The arrow hit the deck.

Jaeger blinked, pleased, his smile growing as he turned to his brother. 'Here we go! Grab your shield, Berard!'

Berard gulped, stumbling down the deck, scurrying away from the arrow, its white fletching fluttering innocently in the breeze behind him.

'Archers!' Jaeger cried. 'We have the range now thanks to the Islanders!' He nodded to his head archer. 'Kill them!'

***

'Into the houses!' Jael yelled as Fyn fumbled with the flagpole, pushing it through a small hole in the roof of the wooden house he was already sheltering in. He'd attached the yellow flag.

Shelter.

They rushed into the houses; every man on every one of the ships in the first row. The Islanders in the second row were not within range. Not yet.

Jael squeezed in between Beorn, and Fyn, who looked ready to throw up all over her. 'Poles ready! Bows ready!' she called to the archers who had positioned themselves under the flaps, and the four pole-men who waited next to them. 'Let their first wave come, then you'll be up. Wait for my call.'

They heard it then, the terrifying whistle as the arrows flew towards them.

'Nock,' Jael said calmly, waiting for the impact.

An explosion of arrows struck the deck and the walls of the house. They heard splashes as some hit the water. The house remained intact.

Fyn sighed in relief.

The archers moved, ready to go.

'Wait!' Jael cautioned. 'Wait for the Tower.' She listened for another wave, waiting. Waiting.

Nothing.

'Black flag, Fyn.'

Fyn tried to steady his shaking hands as he pulled the pole down, adding the black flag to the yellow one.

Arrows.

'They're waiting for us,' Jael grumbled, glancing at the archers, who looked eager to go. 'Draw! Open!' The pole-men shunted the flaps open, the archers quickly standing, bows at the ready. 'Aim!' Their eyes snapped to the Hestian ships in the distance as they angled their bows to the sky. They had checked for wind and distance while they waited, but this would be the first real test. 'Release!' Jael called. 'Down!' The flaps banged shut as the Tower's arrows shot towards them, sticking and stabbing into the house; one arrow shooting through the wall near Fyn's side.

'Away from that wall!' Jael ordered. She peered through the end of the house, watching the arrow storm as it buffeted the rest of their ships.

The Hestians would have more arrows than ideas, she knew.

And she needed to use them all up quickly. 'Nock!'

***

Axl spluttered, choking, as the man on top of him squeezed his throat, foaming at the mouth, spittle flying everywhere. Axl hit out at him with his leather arm guard, smashing it into the bridge of his bulbous nose, knocking him away. Scrambling to his feet, gasping for air, Axl rammed his sword into the man's neck. He pulled it out, ignoring the spurting blood and the scream of agony, spinning to hit the next Hestian on the shoulder. He was a thick-necked mountain and didn't even sway.

'One shot, Axl!' Gant growled, fighting his way towards Lothar, who was cowering behind Osbert, who was trying to avoid being cut to pieces by Karsten.

Haegen was there. 'Karsten!' he screamed angrily, trying to force his way through the tangle of warriors; trapped, unable to get any closer. 'Karsten, wait!'

Karsten Dragos smiled as he drew back his axes and lunged, hearing nothing but the ringing call of Vidar in his ear, telling him to kill Lothar Furyck.

CHAPTER TWENTY THREE

Edela jerked awake, spilling her tea on the floor. Vella, who had been lying at her feet, scrambled away, shaking the warm liquid from her fur.

'Edela!' Biddy cried, hurrying to the chair. 'I didn't notice you'd fallen asleep. I should have taken your cup!'

Edela frowned as she tried to catch her breath, letting Biddy remove the cup from her shaking hand.

'What has happened? What did you see?' Biddy asked. 'Is it Jael?'

Edela shook her head, half-trapped in her dream. 'No, not Jael. It's Eirik Skalleson.' She swallowed, staring into Biddy's worried eyes. 'He's dead.'

Biddy gasped, covering her mouth in shock, her mind whirring through the ramifications of that. 'Eydis...' she said sadly. 'Poor Eydis.'

Edela turned to the fire, its hypnotic flames twisting and sparking before her. 'He was murdered,' she said quietly, slowly, watching Eirik's death in the fading shadows of her dream. 'And I saw who did it.'

***

The wooden houses had been a good idea of Jael's, Thorgils decided, watching as more arrows drove themselves into the wall in front of them. Good, but not going to last much longer if the Hestians didn't run out of arrows soon. He leaned back and peered down the end of the house towards Jael's ships. Their flags were still black.

Arrows.

'Nock!' he called to his archers, ready to run the drill again.

He was waiting for the red flag because red meant sea-fire.

***

'Grrrr!' Haaron roared, slamming his palm against the stone wall. It hurt, but he didn't care. He shook his head, clenching his fists in frustration, stalking across the flagstones, muttering to himself. 'Are they planning on just *sitting* there? *Waiting* to die?' He blinked rapidly, scratching his forehead, trying to decide what to do before turning back to the window. '*Why* are they waiting?' he barked at the man closest to him.

The archer hesitated, bow in hand. 'They want us to use up our arrows, my lord?' he suggested nervously.

'Well, obviously!' Haaron spat, squinting at the ships in the distance. 'They think they can survive long enough to see us emptied of arrows. And perhaps they can in those ridiculous shelters, so Jaeger needs to attack them. Draw them out! They'll have no choice but to come out of their hiding holes once our ships are bearing down on them.' He glared around the room, his eyes dark and determined. 'No more arrows! Let's watch and see what my son can do!'

***

Gant's boot slid, but he kept to his feet, his long sword scything menacingly, his shield clutched tight, protecting his chest.

Karsten screamed in frustration, furious at this old man who'd fought his way in between him and the Furycks. He remembered this man. He'd been standing next to the bitch when she'd taken his eye. Karsten lifted both axes, swinging them above his head like an arrogant fool.

Gant lunged quickly, slicing Karsten's armpit.

Karsten jerked away, bleeding. 'Fuck!' He swung with one axe, missing, as Gant jumped back. Karsten spat, cursing again, his other axe cutting nothing but air. 'You want to die today, old man?' he sneered. 'You look ready to die to me!' He sprung forward, screaming. 'Get out of my way!'

'*Me*? In *your* way?' Gant wondered coolly, his breath coming in short bursts as he ducked and spun, avoiding the glinting axe heads carving towards him. 'Can't you see with one eye, Karsten Dragos? Perhaps I should remove the other if you've no need for it?'

'Karsten!' Haegen called desperately, still trying to find a way through but the Brekkans were regrouping now, forcing the Hestians back.

Karsten ignored his brother, and kicked out at Gant, taking him by surprise, but Gant's reflexes were still sharp, and he skidded quickly to the side, missing most of the impact as he stumbled over the bodies of Lothar's guards.

Lothar was behind him, his sword long gone. Osbert, bleeding from both arms, was trying to protect him against Karsten's men with just his short sword. Aleksander was there, on his other side, Axl as well. They had surrounded Lothar and would fight off any Hestian who tried to claim their king.

Weak and foolish though he may be, Lothar was a Furyck, protected by Furia.

His death would not come at the hands of a Hestian.

***

'We need to get closer,' Jaeger muttered irritably to his helmsman. 'We need to move!' He felt his father's scowl crawling out of the Tower across the dark sea to claim him. Jaeger knew how scathing Haaron's disappointment would be; how loud his curses as he hurled them from the windows.

Eirik Skalleson had decided to play a different game this time, but in the end, he would be no match for the fleet they had assembled. 'Blow the horn!' he yelled to the man hanging from the prow. 'It's time to make them piss themselves!'

***

'At last!' Ivaar sighed as the Hestian fleet finally started advancing. The onslaught of arrows had stopped, but the Islanders in front of them were still hiding in their houses. He scowled; this was no way to fight. A true king did not hide like an old woman. He could see the doubt and confusion in the eyes of the men around him; his men, who stood impatiently, watching everything unfold before them.

Without them.

If Jael's mistakes meant that she had to die, though, he saw no reason to intervene. Not yet. Not until the ships in his line were threatened. 'We hold and wait for the flag!' he cried. 'Wait for the flag!

***

Haegen surged forward with his men, at last, throwing his arm around Karsten's throat, yanking him backwards, trying to avoid his brother's flailing axes, his spitting mouth. 'Stop!' he cried. 'Stop!' He was furious; furious that Karsten was so lacking in self-control that he would try to kill Lothar, *and* his son, against their father's orders.

The Hestians rushed past the Dragos brothers, swarming over the Brekkans as they fought to keep their king safe. Gant was pushed to the ground, battered by boots as men stumbled over and around him. He groaned, wincing, covering his head with his hands as he tried to protect himself.

Aleksander backed into Axl who was struggling to fend off three attackers, stabbing to the right with his sword, batting away a Hestian with his left arm. But it was useless. Osbert was on the ground, Lothar almost sobbing behind them.

There were simply too many of them now.

Karsten pulled away from Haegen, his body jerking with rage, his mind clear of any reason. He growled, teeth clenched, then stepped back. Reluctantly. Screaming. Lunging at an escaping Brekkan, he chopped viciously into his neck, not even bothering to watch as he fell. His eyes remained fixed and furious... on his brother.

Haegen turned back to Lothar who was being restrained by two of Karsten's men now. Blood was dribbling from his nose and mouth, much like his son who was on his knees beside him. Osbert's legs had given way, his arms thick with blood, his face so pale that he looked ready to pass out.

'We have your king!' Haegen shouted to the Brekkans who were still trying to hold on, even as they were being overcome by ever-increasing numbers of Hestians. 'We have your king! We have his son! Surrender now, or we'll kill them both! Throw down your weapons! Now!'

***

'Here they come!' Jael cried, her eyes trained on the enemy fleet. She blinked, squinting, staring again. 'Here they *all* come!'

Edela had stopped Jael before she left Oss, pulling her quickly to one side. 'I've had a dream,' she'd whispered in her ear. 'Hest's fleet will be small. They will not have the men to launch all their ships, so Haaron will seek help from Silura. More will come. I see the leaping fish banner of Aris Viteri flying from many ships. You will need to plan for that. They will not reveal their true strength. Not at first.'

Jael smiled, shivering with nervous energy. She had indeed planned for that, and here they were, just as Edela had promised. 'Change your arrows,' she instructed, watching the ships grow into a thick, layered mass of angry prows, all surging towards them on a building sea. 'Now we're going to shoot fire,' she said calmly. 'Catapult crew to the front. Wait for my call. Red flag, Fyn.'

Sea-fire.

***

'Where have you been all day?' Evaine asked sharply as Runa closed the door. 'Tanja didn't know where you were. Nor Respa. You just disappeared.' She rounded on Runa, her blue eyes like icicles, frozen with menace. 'Is something wrong?'

Runa floundered under Evaine's intense scrutiny. 'Wrong?'

'You look in pain,' Evaine murmured, peering at her. 'Are you unwell?'

Runa wanted to believe that Evaine couldn't possibly know what she'd been doing; that she couldn't possibly know about the tattoos. But, of course, even if she hadn't acquired some magical skill that meant she could read minds, someone might just have told her. 'I am,' Runa said weakly, wanting to get away from those venomous eyes. 'I think I shall go to my bed. I've been visiting Edela and Biddy, and I feel quite tired.' It was best not to stray too far from the truth, she decided.

Evaine's pale eyebrows rose in surprise, following Runa as she hurried to her bed. 'Oh?'

'Yes, I went to see how Edela was, to see if she was recovering,' Runa said quietly, lying down, grimacing at the ache in her upper arms where Entorp had tattooed her. She didn't mind, though. She was terrified; desperate for any form of protection, no matter how painful it had been.

'I didn't realise you knew her,' Evaine murmured, her nose wrinkling. 'What is that stink?'

Runa thought quickly. 'It's a salve. Biddy applied it when I said I was unwell. I think it best if I just close my eyes awhile and try to sleep.'

Evaine stood watching as Runa tucked herself under a pile of furs, turning her face to the wall. She frowned, her eyes bright with irritation.

Edela, Edela...

What was she going to do about the problem of Edela?

***

'How many are there?' Morac gasped, amazed at the size of the fleet amassing before them now. It was no surprise, though, not to Eadmund's flotilla of four ships, as they waited, hidden amongst the giant stones of the Widow's Peak, holding their position.

'Enough to destroy us all and more,' Eadmund breathed, his focus sharpening. He'd barely spoken since they'd left Saala, too numb to feel anything, but he knew what he had to do now.

He had to save his people.

'There's the red flag!' cried a man in the bow, peering through the rocks. 'Sea-fire!'

'Send up our flag!' Eadmund called, turning to Villas. 'Take us out!'

***

Jaeger smiled, turning to admire the vast formation of ships assembled behind him now, rowing in unison towards their enemy. His smile faded quickly, though, as he turned back around, watching the catapults being loaded ahead of him. 'Archers!' he screamed. 'Kill those men!'

***

Haaron's eyes twitched as the Islanders scrambled out of their houses and rushed to load their catapults. 'Archers!' he yelled furiously. 'Light your arrows! Kill those men!'

***

'Release! Back to the house!' Jael cried to her catapult crew, listening as the jars of sea-fire crashed onto the Hestian ships.

The arrows wailed, hurtling towards them from the Tower,

but her men made it back to the shelter before the walls of the house were peppered again.

Jael peered through the gap near the roof, watching fire bloom. 'Fire on deck! Sigthorn! Darri! Get those buckets out there! I need men with shields! Siegbert, Mats, cover them! Go! Load the catapult! Fire at will! Archers ready!' Jael held her breath as her men rushed into the bow and prepared the catapult for launch. They carefully placed another jar into the cradle, released the tension, and hurried back into the house as the arm swung back, lobbing the sea-fire jar into the air. 'Archers! Nock! Light your arrows!' Jael watched as the archers turned and dipped the pitch-soaked arrowheads into the braziers. 'Draw! Open! Aim! Release! Down!' she called, checking on the flames which had quickly been doused. 'Load the catapult! Again! Fyn, take those buckets up to the door.'

Jael's eyes widened as the sea-fire suddenly exploded in the distance. She could hear the panicked screams as flames burst into life on one, two, three Hestian ships; rising out of the sea. She watched as the wind caught the flames and fanned them from ship to ship, fire sparking as the burning vessels tried to turn around.

Now they had to trap them.

'Here comes Eadmund!' Fyn cried, peering through the hole near the roof as Eadmund's ships emerged from behind the tall stone spires of the Widow's Peak.

Jael glanced to the right as Thorgils' small flotilla hammered the Tower with sea-fire, showering it with flaming arrows.

That would keep them busy for a while.

***

'Turn!' Jaeger screamed through the flames. 'Turn the ships

around! Now!' His voice, urgent and demanding, was lost amidst the rising panic as his men caught fire, screaming, trying to flee. The two ships to his right were already burning. The fire was spreading, blazing across his fleet. Desperate men threw themselves into the sea, oars abandoned, sails flaming, wood catching.

The catapults kept firing, splashing the thick black liquid all over them.

The sea was on fire. Everywhere Jaeger looked, he saw flames.

'Turn!' Jaeger yelled helplessly, his head reeling, watching as his fleet tried to head to the right. Then he saw them. More ships. Islanders.

Islanders with catapults.

Coming for them.

***

Haegen bent down and grabbed Lothar by his mail shirt, yanking him to his feet. 'Do you want your king to die?' he bellowed, bringing his sharp knife up to Lothar's soft neck. The sky was grim now, but Haegen's eyes bulged, bright in the gloom. 'Because I can kill him now! I can kill his son! And then we can kill all of you!' He looked at the dirty, bloody faces of the Brekkans who stood waiting, hands on swords, eyes on their king, confused. 'I can slit his throat!' Haegen yelled. 'Just like that! Should I?' He spun Lothar around, showing him to his men, listening to him snivel and grovel, ignoring Karsten's petulant face.

'No! No!' Lothar cried, trying to pull himself away from the razor-sharp edge of Haegen's knife. 'No! Put down your weapons! Throw down your swords! We are overwhelmed! We must surrender!' He was too panicked to sound disappointed. 'I surrender!' There would be a way out of this, Lothar was sure, if he could just stay alive.

He had no intention of being the second king killed in Osterland that day.

***

'Again!' Eadmund screamed at his catapult crew, now one man down. The loader had an arrow through his side, and he was lying at Eadmund's feet, his eyes glazed, his breathing laboured. 'Load!' He turned to his archers. 'Nock! Light your arrows!' He glanced at the ships to his right. Jael's ships. They had the Hestian fleet on fire. And beyond them, Thorgils' ships had the Tower under siege; flames bursting out of every window.

Eadmund could see the Silurans turning away. He had to stop them from running. He had to burn as many as he could; destroy their enemy's fleet before they escaped the flames.

Before the wind came.

***

'Do something!' Haaron yelled to his commander, who stood frozen next to him. But the man was reluctant to move any closer to the searing flames. The liquid that had exploded inside the Tower was on fire, everywhere they looked.

'Water!' Haaron cried, taking charge. 'Bring in the water!'

'But my lord,' his commander muttered helplessly, 'the sea is on fire below. 'I don't think water will stop the flames.'

Haaron blinked, wanting to slap the man, but he wasn't wrong. He pulled his cloak tightly around his mail chest, stepping away from the blazing heat, shaking his head. How? *How* was the sea on fire? 'Get to the other windows!' he implored. 'See what you can do from there!'

But no one moved.

The fire was growing taller and wider; a sheet of flames threatening anyone who attempted to go near the windows. And then another jar flew inside, shattering its liquid contents near their feet, another round of flaming arrows shooting in after it.

'Back! Back!' Haaron shouted as their buckets of arrows were swallowed by the flames. His men had been too surprised, rendered too stupid, to think about grabbing those in time. 'Get out!' he bellowed hopelessly, his voice fading away, drowned out by the heady rush of fire, the urgent cries of his men as they tried to rescue those who had caught alight; the screams from below as his fleet exploded on the sea.

If Jaeger and Berard were being burned to a crisp down in the Adrano, his heirs would halve. He could only hope that Haegen and Karsten weren't making such a mess of the pass.

***

Gant hung his head as Karsten kicked him in the groin. He groaned, trying to absorb the pain without letting it consume him; his head bent, his jaw working, his mind clearing.

He would gut that little shit one day.

Haegen eyed his brother, wanting to reprimand him again. He doubted there was any point to his words, though; Karsten wasn't listening to anyone. 'We have a long march ahead of us, Lothar Furyck,' Haegen warned the Brekkan king, smiling as he stumbled before him. 'Best you get waddling!'

His men laughed, and Haegen grinned, happy that he would return to the Tower with such prizes: two Furycks, the Brekkan army, and few losses. His father would surely be impressed by that effort.

Osbert fell to the ground, his face skidding into the gravel.

No one made a move to help him.

'My son?' Lothar turned to look at Haegen, the least volatile of the brothers, it seemed. 'He's badly injured. He needs to be helped!'

'Helped?' Haegen wondered coldly, trying to muster any sympathy for the pathetic man curled into a ball in the blood-dust. He sighed. 'Yes, I suppose he does.' He nodded to two men nearby. 'Osbert Furyck is yours to care for. Ensure he gets to the Tower still breathing.' The men picked up their prisoner whose sleeves dripped with fresh blood, his head lolling as they lugged him forward.

'Can we not tend to his wounds before we march?' Lothar wondered feebly.

Aleksander wished that Lothar would shut up. Karsten Dragos looked ready to take his axes to him. He reached instinctively for his swordless scabbard, brushing past his knifeless belt, hoping that Jael was having better luck.

***

'Berard!' Jaeger called, trying not to swallow any more water. 'Quick!' His brother was not a strong swimmer, but Jaeger was. He reached out and seized Berard's arm, too enraged to notice the sharp bite of the sea as it froze his limbs. It was burning all around them, burning their ship to cinder and ash, but Jaeger had seen another ship, untouched by flames; a way out, if only he could reach it in time. 'Help!' he screamed hoarsely, trying to keep himself afloat as the additional weight of Berard threatened to sink them both. 'Throw out a rope! Help!'

A man in the bow saw his commander sinking into the sea. 'My lord!' he cried, turning and rushing towards the stern. 'Quick, it's Jaeger and Berard! Throw out a rope!'

The helmsman, one of Haaron's oldest seamen, frowned, less than eager to stop. He shrugged, certain that Haaron would not reward him either way. 'Hold water!' he grumbled to his oarsmen, who quickly lifted their oars out of the burning sea. 'Eilif, throw that rope over the side! And be quick!'

Jaeger dug into the freezing water with his left hand, dragging Berard behind him with his right. He needed to get to that rope.

He had to make it back to Skorro.

***

'Who?' Biddy wondered desperately, kneeling before Edela, clasping her hands. 'Who murdered Eirik?'

Edela was alert now, alert and focused, her mind sharp to the threat that was growing. She could feel it like a cloud descending, sinking, submerging them entirely. 'I don't know his name,' she said slowly. 'But I've seen him in my dreams. I've seen his face, and I can feel the depth of his hatred. He loathed Eirik Skalleson, despised him all his life.' She stood up and took a deep breath. 'And now he will try to claim the throne. And we must hope that Jael can stop him before it's too late.'

Biddy frowned, remembering Eydis' dreams.

Ivaar.

CHAPTER TWENTY FOUR

Eadmund gripped the simple wooden box in both hands, biting back tears. He thought of his son as he held the box to his chest; his son, who might one day stand holding his warm ashes, as he held his father's.

There was time, a moment, he knew, before the next assault would begin. They were chasing the only two unscathed Hestian ships back to Skorro. The Silurans were not wasting any more of their men or ships. They had extracted their few surviving crews from the flames and appeared to be heading far away from them all.

Morac came up next to him. Eadmund wished he would stop lurking about, but quickly felt guilty for his petulance; Morac had known his father far longer than he had. He knew that, despite their differences, they had been like brothers for most of their lives. He nodded to Morac, and together they stepped towards the stern, away from the men who sat against *Ice Breaker's* gunwales, preparing themselves for what would come next; away from the archers who were huddled in the wooden house tending to their wounded.

'He would have liked today,' Morac smiled sadly, watching the flames dance across the sea, growing, bursting, fanned by the wind; a wind that had thankfully remained steady but not overwhelmed them yet. He looked to the burning Tower that had terrorised them on their last attack. 'Eirik would have enjoyed it.'

But Eadmund wasn't listening; he was remembering his father handing him his first sword, smiling at him, that twinkle in his eye, maybe a tear too. He had been so proud of him. Once.

Eadmund felt the sharp sting of the cold wind as it battered his face. He turned away from it, opening the box over the stern, letting the wind carry his father away to Vidar's Hall, where he would drink with warriors of the highest order. Because he was Eirik Skalleson, first of his line.

King of the Slave Islands.

His father.

***

They had two wounded men. Two. After all those arrows, which had torn into their wooden house, making it look like the back of a hedgehog. Just two.

Jael sighed, pleased. It was a start.

The burning ships; that was a start too.

The sight of Haaron's Tower consumed by flames was also pleasing, but Jael could see the ships ahead, pulling away, streaking towards the safety of Skorro's fort; the fort they needed to claim for any chance of victory. Two ships were nothing against their fleet of twenty, all still intact, but she had no idea how many men had been left to guard that fort.

Enough, Jael was certain. There would be more than enough.

Fyn looked slightly more confident now, relieved to have survived the arrow storm, his mind dwelling only occasionally on what lay ahead. He was transfixed by the fiery carnage of the ships they passed, trying to block out the terrifying cries of burning, drowning men. The smell of their sizzling flesh reminded him of Eirik's pyre that morning.

'I've never been to Skorro,' Jael told him quietly as she came back to the stern. 'But I can imagine it. They knew we were coming, so it will take some breaking into.'

Fyn swallowed, reaching for the pommel of his sword. It still didn't have a name.

'You're ready,' Jael said, staring into his anxious eyes. 'I know it. And soon, you will too.'

Fyn let out a long sigh and turned away from the flames, towards the island they were quickly approaching.

He hoped she was right.

***

'Faster!'

Jaeger stood in the packed bow, leaning forward, watching the ship cut through the dark sea beneath him, urging it on. He kept turning, certain that the Islanders were gaining on them.

His exhausted men lay scattered around the deck; wet through, bloodied and burned, their arms weak from swimming, shaking from the freezing cold water. Jaeger growled, annoyed to be running away.

Like a dog.

But if they could reach Skorro in time, he knew they stood a chance of still emerging victorious. Jaeger was not prepared to let his brothers gloat over his failure, nor his father hound him for the rest of his days. He glared at Berard who sat shivering near his feet.

He'd made mistakes; too many, so far. But there was no way he was letting those Islanders into Skorro's fort.

For that was where he'd hidden the book.

***

Aleksander hadn't noticed the cut on his thigh, but it was leaking blood through his trousers now as he stumbled, prodded in the back by one of Haegen Dragos' men. He bit his lip, resisting the urge to turn around and kick him in the side of the head.

Aleksander glanced at Axl, who had a few cuts on him but otherwise appeared whole. He looked morose, though, his eyes turned down towards the well-worn path they trudged along. The Hestians didn't appear to know that he was a Furyck and Aleksander hoped that Lothar was smart enough to keep it that way. Prisoners were weapons that Haaron would unleash upon Jael, depending on the success of the sea battle.

He grimaced, already regretting saving Lothar's life, although, he was sure that Jael would have done the same. It didn't matter how much they hated Lothar; he was their problem to solve, not Hest's. Brekka had to stay strong. The Furyck line had to continue, safe under Furia's protection.

It was everything to their people.

Aleksander smiled, peering over the cliffs as he walked, watching the Islanders chase the Hestians across the sea. He wished he was down there, standing on *Sea Bear* next to Jael, far away from the endless moaning of his pathetic king.

Lothar was demoralised as he shuffled in front of Haegen Dragos. Despite the clouds, it was warm, and he was suffering, never having walked so far in recent memory.

'Move your feet!' Haegen grumbled, poking him with the butt of his spear, as he had countless times already. 'I plan on getting to the Tower before dark! Unless, of course, you'd like to sleep in the bushes tonight?'

Lothar lifted his aching feet, motivated by that miserable fate, peering at Osbert, who limped morosely beside him, pain etched onto his pale face.

Karsten simmered beside his brother.

'You think Father would have been happy to see us return with just a couple of heads?' Haegen wondered calmly, enjoying his brother's sulking. 'He sent us to destroy them. To bring him prisoners!' he smiled, motioning to all the Brekkans they had captured. 'And look how well we have done. Better than Jaeger down there!'

It was true, Karsten realised, his eyes wandering to the edge of the cliff. They were sheltered from a sheer drop by a waist-high wall of red rocks that most eyes were trained over as they walked, fixated on the unfolding chase below.

'You think Jaeger and Berard are on one of those ships?' Karsten wondered, his head suddenly clearing.

'I've no idea,' Haegen admitted. 'I can only hope so. Although, after the disaster down there, I'm sure Father won't agree with me!'

'No,' Karsten said. 'But, as you say, at least *we're* returning him half a victory.'

Haegen laughed at his brother's abrupt turnaround. 'So you've come back, then?'

'I suppose so,' Karsten shrugged. 'Although, I may be tempted to push one of these worthless pieces of Furyck shit over the cliffs.'

Lothar swallowed, his ears open to the conversation behind him, his eyes darting to the left.

He had no desire to end up in the burning sea.

***

The afternoon was not over, but the sky had already darkened, turning the day even colder. Ayla dipped her toes in the water, her body heavy with pain.

Trapped. She was trapped on Kalfa.

And nothing she dreamed showed her the way out.

'Why did you do it?' Isaura asked gently as she walked beside Ayla, her own bare feet braving the icy water, just as desperate to clear the smoke out of her head. 'Why did you try to save Eirik when you are loyal to Ivaar?'

'Because it was the right thing to do,' Ayla murmured. 'For Eydis. For the king.' She shook her head, feeling sad. 'But it was not meant to be. The gods made sure of that.'

'You mean Ivaar did.' Isaura pulled fly-away strands of golden hair out of her mouth, tucking them back inside her hood.

Ayla didn't answer as she searched the bare horizon, where stone-grey sky met stone-grey sea.

Isaura sighed. 'Why are you here, Ayla? Why do you stay on Kalfa? If you don't want to be with Ivaar, loyal to him, why not just leave while he's away?'

Ayla dropped her head. Isaura's questions were fair and kindly asked. Perhaps, perhaps it would be nice not to feel so utterly alone. 'My husband,' she whispered at last. 'My husband is here.'

***

Thorgils stood in the bow, next to the catapult, willing his ship on as it skimmed the deep, murky water. They were gaining. And, for the first time, Otto was quiet. Not just quiet, though, he was barely noticeable as he watched the chase from the stern, muttering conspiratorially with their helmsman. Thorgils had long since realised that whichever part of *Fire Serpent* Otto was in, he was best to stay on the opposite side. It was easier to resist the temptation to tip him overboard.

'Come on!' Thorgils bellowed to the wide red sail curving taut and full as it soared above him, his right hand twitching over the iron pommel of his sword. He smiled broadly, enjoying the sharp bite of the wind as it numbed his face, the cool spray of seawater on his dry lips, savouring their first taste of victory.

But now was the real test.

Could they take Skorro? Capture Haaron's prize?

Soon they would find out.

***

Eadmund turned to Villas. 'Bring us alongside *Sea Bear*,' he instructed his helmsman, his eyes never leaving the ships in front of them. They had gained significantly over the stretch of sea between the Widow's Peak and Skorro, breathing down the Hestians' necks, urged on by the chase and the sense that victory was now within reach.

Skorro was not a large island, but its fort appeared mighty; Eadmund could see that clearly enough in the fading light of the afternoon. Thick stone walls crowned with heavily patrolled ramparts rose out of a rocky mound. Two tall, solid wooden gates. And a garrison within.

Eadmund knew what that meant: more arrows.

It was time to slow down and wait.

***

'Quick!' Jaeger screamed. They needed to disembark with speed, to get all their men off the ships and into the fort before the Islanders landed. He knew they were prepared for a siege.

If they could just get inside in time.

'Berard!' Jaeger grabbed his brother, pulling him up from the deck. 'Get ready!' he demanded, his eyes enraged at the defeat he saw in his brother's. 'We have a chance for victory!' he yelled insistently, loudly, so that everyone could hear. 'We will not lose Skorro! You know how secure the fort is! We have men! We have weapons, arrows, everything we need to defeat those bastards! To take revenge for what they did to us! For what they have taken from us today!' Jaeger shook with fury and cold, but also determination. He would not be defeated. Not here, not in front of his father, his brothers, his men. He would not give in without a fight. Because he was going to be the King of Hest.

And Dragos kings were not defeated by nothing Islanders.

***

Gant kept his eyes down, not wanting to accidentally make eye contact with Axl. He didn't want to lead Haegen or his dolt of a brother to any conclusions about Axl's parentage. He was not surprised to see that Aleksander was employing the same tactic.

Despite the precarious nature of their situation, Gant had seen enough of what was happening down in the Adrano to realise that the Islanders' fleet was about to attack Skorro. The only hope the Brekkans had that he could see was that Jael and her men would be victorious. And that Lothar and Osbert would keep their mouths shut for long enough not to get them all killed.

***

Jaeger didn't wait for the ship to be grounded. He jumped into the water, ignoring the cold as it quickly soaked him to the bone again, wading towards the foreshore, his swords in the air. Berard gulped and jumped in after him.

Jaeger looked past the men who gripped the sides of the ships and started pulling them towards the beach; past the men who were still clambering into the water, swords, axes, and shields raised, hurrying to the fort. They were there, Jaeger saw, the Islanders. Waiting, just out of range, he was sure. 'Open the gates!' he roared, hurrying towards the narrow beach that was mostly rock and very little else. There were three ships moored to a small pier. He was relieved to know that he'd left such a large garrison in place. One hundred men were inside, ready to help them repel their attackers.

The gates creaked and groaned open as the ships were quickly abandoned on the foreshore.

'Inside!' Jaeger yelled as his sodden men stumbled past. 'Get inside! We need to close the gates! Archers to the ramparts! Hurry!'

***

Villas eased *Ice Breaker* in beside *Sea Bear* as their crews hurried to bring down yards and furl sails.

Jael nodded at Eadmund, relieved to see that he was alright.

'After you!' he called, motioning to the fort.

She looked up at the darkening sky as arrows from the ramparts shot towards them, burrowing into the water some distance from their ships. Turning around, Jael was pleased to see the rest of their fleet gathering behind them. 'Let's close in, just a bit!' she called to her men who were busy slotting oars into holes, nodding at Beorn on the tiller. 'At my signal get back to the house, though. No point in dying till you've got a sword in your hand!'

Fyn took a deep breath, his stomach churning, his eyes accidentally meeting his father's as he stood next to Eadmund. Morac scowled and looked away, turning his attention towards the fort as *Ice Breaker* eased forward.

Jael swayed down to the stern, watching the rest of their fleet follow them in. There were no smiles that she could see, only faces tight with tension, minds flooded with impatient bloodlust, arms itching to wield swords, feet desperate to feel the earth again. They wanted battle and victory.

The time for hiding was done.

***

'Your husband is here?' Isaura's mouth hung open. She looked around. '*Where?*'

Ayla sighed, suddenly wondering whether she should have said anything at all. It was too late now, though. But she didn't know where to begin.

Isaura shivered, curious but cold; she couldn't feel her toes anymore. 'Let's get back to the hall. We can go to my chamber.'

'No!' Ayla cried anxiously. 'No, it's better if we talk here. There are no spies out here.'

Isaura nodded. 'Alright, but I must get my boots first,' she smiled, heading for the rock she'd left them on.

Ayla followed her, waiting silently while Isaura sat down, pulling her socks and boots over her wet, frozen feet.

'So, why?' Isaura asked, standing up, wiggling her toes, trying to feel them again. 'Why did you come here?'

Ayla ducked her head and started walking, her eyes scanning the shore, but there was still no one about, on the beach at least. She could see people near the fort, but with most of the men gone now, it was a quieter, more subdued atmosphere. Almost pleasant.

'My husband, Bruno,' Ayla began. 'He was from Silura. A merchant. He charmed me when he came to Tuura. Refused to leave until I married him.' She smiled, warmed by the memories for a moment. 'Which I did.'

'Because you wanted to?' Isaura wondered, walking carefully across the stones beside her.

'Yes,' Ayla nodded eagerly. 'I loved him. I had seen him in my dreams for many years. I knew that he would come for me, and I was desperate to leave Tuura. So I went with him, as his wife. Willingly,' she sighed. 'We travelled everywhere together for years, and although we were happy, I was ready to stop and find a home. Bruno promised that we'd return to Silura. But first, he wanted to sell a large shipload of furs he'd bought in Alekka, so we came to the islands. And that's how we met Ivaar.'

Isaura frowned. 'I don't remember you coming.'

'You had only recently given birth to Mads,' Ayla reminded her. 'You were very ill, remember? In bed for weeks.'

Isaura nodded. 'That's right, and when I emerged, you were there. But just you. All of a sudden Ivaar had a dreamer. But where was your husband?'

Ayla opened her mouth, then closed it, trying not to cry. 'Ivaar entertained us lavishly when we arrived. He was making deals with Bruno, but his eyes were all over me. Bruno could see it, of course, but he thought that we would just take his money and leave,' she said sadly. 'But then, one night, he drank too much... talked too much. He told Ivaar that I was a dreamer.' She stopped suddenly, struck by the memory, still so fresh, of when Ivaar had first grabbed her, threatened her, touched her.

Isaura stopped; they were getting too close to the fort.

'He took Bruno as his prisoner... to force me to stay here,' Ayla said quietly. 'He's in one of his prison holes. Still. After all this time!' she cried. 'And I'm allowed to see him once a month. Nothing more. Not until I get Ivaar on the throne, and then he will release him. But I don't believe him!' she sobbed. 'I don't believe he'll ever let Bruno out. That he'll ever set us free. I can't see anything ahead for me. There's nothing in my dreams but Ivaar.'

Isaura held Ayla's hand, her eyes full of sympathy. 'I'm so sorry,' she said. 'I'm so sorry for you.'

'He forced me!' Ayla wept. 'I do not wish to be in his bed, you must know that.'

'Of course,' Isaura soothed. 'Of course, neither do I!' She tried to make Ayla smile, but the dreamer was barely listening as tears streamed down her cheeks. Isaura leaned forward, pulling her into her arms. 'And do you?' she wondered quietly. 'Do you really see Ivaar on the throne?'

'I did,' Ayla sniffed, pulling back, wiping away her tears. 'I did. Once. But now it's very clouded. I'm afraid that he'll become the king and hurt a lot of people. Afraid that he won't, and I'll never be with Bruno again.'

Isaura narrowed her eyes. 'Ivaar Skalleson has taken far too much from both of us,' she said firmly. 'Far too much over all these years. There must be something we can do?' She looked at Ayla, desperate for a sign of hope. 'Together?'

***

Lothar's aching body slumped as he was butted towards the gates of the Tower by Haaron's mountainous son. *He* was meant to be the victorious king; him and Eirik Skalleson, both. Now Eirik was merely drifting ash, and he was a prisoner, humiliated, ready to fall to the dirt, expected to beg for mercy. Lothar trembled, exhausted, but he forced himself to straighten his aching spine. He was a king. *The* king, the most powerful king from the oldest line in all of Osterland. And his niece was out there on the sea with a large fleet behind her, ready to attack Skorro.

All was not lost. Not yet.

It was the strangest twist in fortunes, Lothar thought, that he found himself praying to Furia, hoping she would protect Jael, and see her victorious, so that Jael could then save him.

Osbert sighed, relieved to be at the Tower, at last, his stomach cramping with discomfort, his body ready to collapse. His wounds had been hastily wrapped in scraps of cloth, and much of the blood had clotted, but now he was left with the pricking, stinging pain of it all, and the worry of what was about to happen. He doubted that his father had the quick mind to talk them out of the dire situation and he could barely see straight, let alone think of how to help him.

Haaron strode through the wooden gates, the Tower aflame behind him, his black cloak flapping angrily with every determined stride. He nodded briefly at his sons. 'You have brought me better news than your brothers, I see,' he growled, not bothering to acknowledge Lothar.

Not yet.

'Father!' Haegen could barely keep the smile off his face. His pride in their victory, in the prizes he had managed to retrieve from Karsten's murderous axes, painted his face with a youthful confidence he had not felt in years.

His father scowled, not sharing his good mood.

'Lothar Furyck,' Haaron sneered, turning towards his bloodied and bruised enemy. No, Haaron reminded himself, his *prisoner*. 'What trouble you keep causing for me, you and your family.' He frowned, circling the dishevelled man who he could see was so desperately trying not to look as compromised as he actually was. 'So much trouble. What your little friend Eirik Skalleson did out there to my fleet... my Tower...' He shook his head, his steely eyes bursting with anger.

'Eirik is dead,' Lothar said bluntly.

Haaron's eyes registered shock at that, as did his sons'. They all turned to peer at Lothar. 'When? When did he die?'

'This morning. Last night. In the night.' Lothar shook his

head, stumbling over his words, too exhausted to think clearly. It was late afternoon now, but he felt as though he had not slept for days. 'Poisoned.'

'*Murdered*?' Haaron was intrigued. 'By who?'

Lothar's mouth was so parched that it hurt to speak. He coughed, hoping to subtly convey his urgent need for something to drink.

Haaron ignored him, waiting on an answer.

'I don't know,' Lothar rasped irritably. 'There was no time before we left to discover who had done it. Although, there were suspicions that it was his son, the eldest one.' He coughed again.

Haaron was surprised, though he wasn't sure he should be after what he'd heard about Ivaar Skalleson. 'Well, it appears the gods have punished Eirik for what he did to his own father,' Haaron mused, narrowing his eyes on the rapidly expiring Brekkan king. 'Who led his fleet out there against my sons, then?'

'Jael,' Lothar croaked.

Karsten looked furious. 'Jael?' That bitch.

'And now she may be about to take my island too,' Haaron muttered, ignoring more coughing from Lothar, as well as the rumble from his royal prisoner's empty stomach. 'Although, as we both know, a secure, well-stocked fort can hold out against most enemies. And there are not many better than the one I built on Skorro.' He rose up on his toes until he was towering over Lothar. 'It has never been taken.'

'Of course,' Lothar conceded, annoyed by the lack of courtesy he was being shown. 'But if it is? Perhaps it would make sense to begin some preliminary... negotiations?'

Gant and Aleksander glanced at each other.

Osbert's one open eye bulged.

'*Negotiations*?' Haaron eyed Lothar curiously, then laughed, smiling at his sons. 'You are aware that you are *my* prisoner? That all of your men are *my* prisoners? That I can kill you, should kill you, as you stand there dribbling and stinking before me? Pathetic and meagre and conquered! By my sons! By me!' His voice rose loudly until he was bellowing at them all as they stood near the edge of the cliff, the smell of burning sea-fire a bitter stink in their nostrils; the Tower, swallowed by smoke and flames behind them. 'Because of you and your foolish ambition, my fleet is sunk, my Tower is on fire, entirely useless, and my youngest sons, if they still live, are about to be attacked by your niece. So why do you think that *you* have anything to say that *I* would wish to listen to?!'

Lothar could feel the hot anger rising from Haaron, the spittle flying from his mouth, twisted in fury as it was, but he didn't waver, nor shrink in the face of it. Because Jael was Ranuf's daughter and, just like his brother, he knew exactly what she was capable of.

CHAPTER TWENTY FIVE

'Remember what I said... it's all about what you do up here.' Jael tapped the side of Fyn's helmet as he shook beneath it. 'Stay calm. Keep thinking.' She sought his eyes quickly. It was time to begin.

Fyn nodded, attempting a smile, gripping his sword, reminding himself that he could do this. He closed his eyes and saw Thorgils' face urging him on.

Jael turned to Arlo. 'How many arrows left?'

'At least a hundred, my lady,' he said with certainty.

She cringed, not wanting the reminder that Eirik was dead. That she was suddenly a queen. 'And jars?'

'Six.'

'That's enough to start a fire or two, I'd say. Light the braziers and let's test the range again!' Jael called to her archers before turning to her men whose hands were gripping the oars, itching for their swords and axes. 'I'm getting hungry, aren't you? Ready for a nice jug of ale to toast our victory!' Her eyes wandered up the imposing stone shell of the fort. 'I'm sure Haaron has a good store of food in there too!'

They had slowed to a stop, lurching in a choppy sea, the clouds sinking around them. Jael knew that they didn't have long to get into the fort before night came to snuff out their plans.

Arlo's arrow went straight through the cheek of a man standing on the ramparts. He screamed, grabbing his face, and pitched forward, falling onto the death-making rocks below.

'Stow the oars! Into the houses!' Jael cried. 'Two flags up, Fyn! Yellow and red!'

***

Jaeger threw up his shield as the first jars of sea-fire arced over his head, smashing onto the ground behind him. A thick shower of burning arrows followed. Men on the ramparts and those standing around the inner fort below – those who had not been out on the sea – froze, blinking in surprise, watching as the liquid caught, exploding into flames.

'Water!' Jaeger yelled down into the fort. It seemed a futile order, he knew, but something had to stop the fire from spreading. 'Berard! Try anything!' he implored. 'Get that fire out! Now!' He turned back around, watching as the catapults were pulled back again. 'Archers! Aim for those men!'

Berard froze in front of the flames, panicking as men rushed before him with buckets of water. It made no difference at all; if anything, it seemed to be helping the fire to spread. And quickly. 'Flour!' he yelled suddenly to one of the cooks who was rushing out of the kitchen, ferrying water in a cauldron. 'What about flour?'

The cook, an elderly man, looked at him incredulously. 'You think I've enough flour in my kitchen to throw on *that*?' he cried, pointing to the towering flames blowing towards the wooden walls of the bedchambers and storage rooms.

The fort's shell may have been made of thick stone, but many of its interior walls were wooden. Flames were already licking the poles and posts that held up the ledge running around the ramparts.

Berard glanced around anxiously, stepping away from the heat of the flames as they surged towards him. There had to be something he could do. But what?

'Berard!' Jaeger yelled as another batch of jars sailed overhead. 'Get out of there! Quick!'

***

'Aim for the gates!' Jael called. 'The sea-fire is so thick, it'll stick. Aim high and let it run down. Just one jar!'

The arrows flew towards them from the top of the ramparts, stabbing more holes in their shelter.

'Wait!' Jael called, sensing the danger. 'Four shield men, go with Bjorr and Alek! Quick!' She turned to her archers. 'Nock! Light your arrows!' Jael watched as the archers dipped their pitch-soaked arrowheads into the braziers before stepping back into position; her eyes jumping to the catapult crew crawling around the bow, protected on all sides now. 'Load the catapult! Fire at will! Draw! Open! Aim! Release! Down!'

There were a lot of men on those ramparts. Two went down, tipping back into the flames she could see rising from behind them now.

Two more quickly took their place.

Jael heard a scream as her catapult loader went down, an arrow through his arm. Another man rushed out to take his place. She frowned. 'I'll be right back! Fyn! Run another drill at those gates!'

Fyn gaped after her but did as she asked, his voice wavering, but his pace steady.

Grabbing two shields, Jael hurried through the rear of the house, towards the stern, trying not to attract much attention. Ivaar and the lords stood in the bows of their ships, waiting. 'Ivaar!' she cried. 'Lead your line! Bring your ships in range! We need every bow you've got! Take those men on the ramparts down!' She ducked back into the house quickly as the Hestian archers turned their bows towards her, firing off a whistling volley of arrows.

'Well, your shield works fine,' Jael smiled crookedly at Fyn, handing it back to him, decorated now with three arrows. 'Perhaps we'd better swap?'

***

Thorgils turned to Otto as they crouched in their house, which was quickly becoming more holes than wood. 'Nothing to say?' he taunted the mumbling old man as he squeezed his helmet over his huge nest of hair. 'I'm not sure what to make of all this peace and quiet? You have me worried!'

Otto tugged on his leather helmet strap, avoiding Thorgils' eyes. 'You need to watch those jars,' he grumbled. 'We don't have many left.'

'No,' Thorgils agreed, watching another jar fly. 'But hopefully, we won't need to use too many. It's not a big fort, is it?' He nodded to the two men who stood nearest the catapult. 'Follow *Sea Bear's* lead,' he ordered. 'Archers! We need to burn the bollocks out of those gates, so stick your arrows through that wood!' He jumped back as an arrow flew into the wooden house, screaming straight past his nose. 'I might need a new pair of trousers when we're done!' he smiled. 'Now fire that fucking catapult!'

***

They were running low on arrows.

Eadmund watched as the gates burned, and the ships behind him decimated the men on the ramparts, their line growing smaller and smaller under the constant pressure of the Islanders' arrows.

Behind those men, the flames grew, and before them, the rocks beckoned. Neither fate looked appealing to the men trapped on the ramparts.

And then, as Eadmund looked on, they disappeared entirely from view in one, enormous, clattering bang.

***

They were far away now, and it was getting too dark to make out much, but the fire was obvious enough. It was a good sign, Aleksander thought to himself as he glanced at the demoralised faces of the men around him.

Jael was their only hope.

They all knew that.

All of the Brekkans who crouched and sat and lay on the rough, gravelly dirt in the dim light of the gloomy afternoon knew that if Jael didn't take Skorro, they were all dead. Because if they could not capture the island or either of those two Dragos sons – if they lived – then Lothar would have nothing to bargain with.

The blood from Aleksander's leg wound had congealed, forming an encouraging shield over his cut. He was relieved. Many of the men around him were not as lucky. They gripped bellies and arms that still oozed, worsened by their long trek to the Tower. His tunic was in tatters, having ripped so many pieces from it in the hopes of staunching his men's bloody wounds. Some were luckier than others. Two had died since they'd been left on the dusty ground beneath the burning Tower to wait – without water or food – guarded over by rows of axe-wielding Hestians, while Lothar and Haaron and their sons negotiated.

Negotiated what?

***

'Jaeger!' Berard yelled, racing to the fallen men, only some of whom were scrambling out of the broken ramparts, burning poles and sparking flames all around them. He reached for his brother's hand, coughing uncontrollably, trying to drag him away from the fire.

Men rushed to join him, trying to rescue those yet to be consumed by the flames; trying to ignore the terrifying screams from those who had.

'We have to get out of here!' Berard panicked. 'The fire is everywhere! We should surrender!' He coughed, gagging on the thick smoke that rose up in billowy clouds, threatening to suffocate them all. Sweat dripped down his forehead, settling into his furrowed brow.

Jaeger hadn't noticed the smoke on the sea, but here, enclosed within the thick stone walls of the fort, its throat-clogging, ashy tang was making it impossible to breathe. He glanced around, awareness dawning as he watched the flames spread towards the bedchambers, racing for the wooden doors of the hall.

The book!

'Berard, come on!' Jaeger called, running to the hall. 'We must get the book!'

'But...' his brother tried, looking around at the men trapped between the gates and the flames. Their screams rose the hairs on his arms, and Berard's mouth hung open in confusion.

But ducking his eyes away from theirs, Berard ran after Jaeger.

***

The flames sparked and spat as the wind rose, and the night fell.

'We may as well get comfortable,' Jael said to Beorn. There were no arrows coming for them now. No men waiting on the ramparts. They could hear their screams as they stood and watched the fire consume the fort's interior. The stones would stand, and they would have to wait to find out how much damage they had done inside.

'That fire does like to burn,' Beorn noted wryly. 'Rather useful stuff your grandmother made.'

Jael nodded. It wasn't pleasant, listening to the terror they had caused, and she didn't smile. Better that it wasn't the screams of her men, though; better that she took them home to their wives and mothers and daughters and sisters.

Most of them. If she could.

'We should eat and rest now!' she called to her men. 'We're not going anywhere until that fire dies down.'

Weary shoulders slumped around her, tension releasing for the first time all day. And it had been a long day. A day of fear and death and loss.

The loss of their king.

'Are you alright?' Thorgils bellowed cheerfully over the side of *Fire Serpent*. 'Have you lost any men?'

'No!' Jael shook her head. 'You?'

'No, but we've a few arrows to remove!' Thorgils smiled back. 'I don't think they'll be able to say the same!' He nodded at the fort, cringing at the screams from within. He didn't envy that fate: dying on a nothing island, trapped in a stone bowl of fire. For what? Ambitious kings? They were all the same; playing with the lives of men who meant nothing to them. Thorgils shook his head. 'So we wait?'

'We have no choice! There's nowhere for them to go!' Jael called. 'And we can't get in till the fire burns itself out. Tell

Torstan. I'll talk to Eadmund and Ivaar.'

Thorgils frowned, peering at Ivaar waiting by his prow for news. 'Rather you than me,' he growled, walking away.

***

Haegen turned from the flames in the distance towards his father's sullen face. His victorious mood had been entirely consumed by fire; the fire smouldering in the Tower; the fire that had destroyed their fleet; the fire they could all see still burning out there in the black sea.

Lothar's mood had improved over the course of the afternoon. He was still thirsty, hungry, and sore, but he had begun to feel optimistic. 'It seems to me that your men are struggling out there,' he suggested.

Haaron glared at him as they stood outside the stables, inhaling a stomach-churning mix of horse shit and smoke. The smoke that scratched the back of his throat was so bitter and pungent; like nothing he'd ever smelled before. His face contorted with rage as he strode back and forth in front of his prisoners. Irritated. Thinking. It certainly did not look as though his men were having any luck on Skorro. But how could he expect them to against that fire?

'Your confidence is charming,' Haaron spat. 'But how do you know who burns in that fire, Lothar Furyck? How do you know it's not your ships, and your niece being consumed by the flames? From *this* far away? In *this* light? It could be anyone.'

Osbert glanced at his father, willing him to keep his mouth shut. He sat on the ground, resting against the stable wall, trying not to move; his limbs weak, his mind working hard to ignore the pain. But he had not gotten any worse, and his wounds were not leaking as they had been earlier. He would recover. He cringed, adjusting his back, watching his father.

Haaron looked ready to kill him.

'True,' Lothar smiled, swallowing, desperate for a jug of ale to wet his desert-like throat. 'But perhaps unlikely, wouldn't you say?'

Haaron bit down on his teeth again, twisting the rings on his left hand. What did he care for Skorro? Really? It was a useful island, or had been. But did he really need it?

And as for his sons...

If they lived.

'We will sleep here tonight,' he grumbled at Haegen. 'You may have secured a victory for us today, but it is ash-thick and burned down by whatever catastrophe your brother has led us into out there.' He attempted a smile, but there was no joy in his heart, so it warped into a pained sneer. 'We will march back to Hest at first light!'

Lothar's shoulders slumped. Hest was at least two days away by foot.

That didn't sound like a good idea at all.

***

It was bitterly cold out on the sea. Despite the hot flames being fanned all around the fort, the wind blew icily into Eadmund's face.

He didn't notice.

The minds of his men were weary after the long day, but their bodies weren't. No eyes were closed as they sat hunched against the gunwales, arms crossed, chatting quietly to one another, waiting for the flames to die down. Most of them, having sat out the battle, were eager to play their part. They had not spent hours sharpening their blades just to watch the archers impress the gods.

Eadmund lay his head against the high rise of the stern, wishing he had one last chance to speak to his father. There was so much he needed to say. And now there was nothing but the memory of his ash as it rose into the sky and drifted across the sea, far behind them.

And his murderer still lived.

***

'I shall lie with you,' Amma insisted for the third time, tucking the furs around Eydis. 'You shouldn't be alone.'

Eydis' eyes hurt. They felt thick and heavy, swollen from crying, and ready for sleep. She needed time, silence, a chance to escape into her dreams and find answers. And Amma Furyck couldn't help her with any of it.

'Come away, Amma,' Gisila said gently as she sat sipping wine by the fire. 'Eydis is not used to so much fussing, I'm sure. We are not far away, are we, just over here?' Despite her worries and fears for her children, she felt surprisingly calm. Perhaps it was the wine? No, she had barely sipped her way through half a cup. It was most certainly the absence of her husband and the stench of his warm breath as he grunted over her as he had done every single night since their marriage.

Gisila felt a relief in Lothar's absence that was as sweet as a cool breeze picking up on a hot day. As strange and unsettling as everything was, there was freedom in the quiet of the evening; an evening without Lothar, who she hoped was lying abandoned in a ditch, his dead body being feasted on by creatures of the night.

'Gisila?' Amma murmured, concerned by the strange look in her step-mother's eyes. 'Are you unwell?'

Gisila blinked away her fantasies, shades of guilt rushing

across her face as it glowed warmly before the flames. 'No, I was just thinking of Axl and Jael, and Aleksander,' she said quickly. 'Wondering how they fared today.'

'You mean if they still live?' Amma asked, shuddering.

'Yes,' Gisila whispered, feeling the familiar twinge in her stomach that had gotten considerably sharper over the course of the day. 'We can only hope and pray that Furia protected them all.'

'I wish Edela was here,' Amma sighed. She grabbed a fur from the nearest bed and perched on a stool in front of the fire. 'She would see what's happening. If anything had... gone wrong.'

'I wish she was here too,' Gisila agreed. 'But remember, she was not worried, not that I saw. Not that she said. We must take comfort from that.'

'Perhaps,' Amma murmured, thinking about Axl. Worrying about Axl.

Eydis rolled over, trying to shut them both out. She had not wanted to sleep in the other room, in the bed she had slept in when Ayla had come to warn her. She didn't want the memory. Eydis just wanted sleep, desperately. She needed a chance to rest. And once she had recovered, she would try to dream and find her father's killer.

***

Ivaar stared at the fort, wishing the flames would disperse, but they burned with as much vigour as they had for the past few hours. It appeared that the Islanders would still be waiting when the sun rose, but would there be anyone left to fight?

He scratched his short beard, thirsty for ale, but at the same time desperately aware that he needed to keep a clear head. Whatever happened when the new day broke, he was certain that

Eadmund was going to try and kill him.

King Eadmund, the man who wore the crown meant for him; the crown given away by a bitter old man. A dead old man now, Ivaar smiled sadly, feeling a pang of loss, but his hatred built again, and he frowned, his mind whirring away.

He needed to think of a way to escape before it was too late. He had to get back to Ayla and see what her dreams told her would happen next.

***

It had been a horrible day, with an early start and a strange visitor, and in between everything had turned upside down and nothing was ever to be the same again, Meena was sure.

A chill settled over her as she stared up through the smoke hole, counting the stars, wondering if Jaeger lived. She shuddered and looked down, back to the fire she was supposed to be attending to.

'Are we to freeze to our very bones, girl?' Morana spat, blowing on her blue-tinged fingers. 'While you gaze at the moon, pining for your love?' She laughed, and it cackled around the tall stone walls, running down Meena's spine.

Varna sighed, wishing away the sharp sound of her daughter's hateful voice. Her return had been an unwelcome intrusion. Varna had given Morana and Morac away many years ago; sold them to Grim Skalleson when they were small children. She'd had no desire to be a mother, so it was easy to ignore their weeping little faces as they'd begged to remain with her. Although, she had softened somewhat by the arrival of her third child, Meena's father, Morten.

She had kept him.

'Leave her be,' Varna grumbled. 'I have told you that we need her. She will lead us to the book.'

'But not if we freeze to death she won't,' Morana muttered, rolling her eyes, thinking that the sparse fare her mother had provided for their supper had barely been enough for one mouthful, let alone the first proper meal she'd eaten in days. For all that Varna Gallas had the ear of the King of Hest, she appeared to live in utter poverty.

'And what of your daughter?' Varna asked loudly, wanting to get Morana's mind away from torturing Meena, at least until she brought the fire back to life again. 'How is *that* plan unfolding?'

Morana smiled, leaning towards her mother. 'Better than you could have imagined. She is lovesick for Eadmund Skalleson. Obsessed. Desperate to have him for herself. Her motivation is strong.'

'And you have taught her how to claim him, then? Seen that she has? That he is hers?'

'Oh yes, it's working.' Morana bared her teeth as the flames burst into life between Meena's carefully stacked logs. 'She has his son, and now she is taking him away from her. It will be done. Soon Jael Furyck will lose Eadmund forever.'

CHAPTER TWENTY SIX

The water rippled under the slowly rising sun. It was cold as Jael jumped down into it, gushing into her boots, icy and wet between her toes. She shivered, but it was more in anticipation, listening as her men splashed down behind her; some well-rested, most on edge. Tense hands gripped swords and axes, all eyes fixed on the entrance to the fort.

Ashy smoke had wafted towards them as they rocked gently on their ships all night, but now, as they approached the jagged shore and stared up at the towering stone fortress, its stench was overpowering.

There were no flames.

No gates, either.

Eadmund waded up onto the beach, frowning at his wife. 'What do you think?'

He looked tired, Jael thought as she listened for any sign of life. More men surged forward onto the narrow stretch of beach that sat beneath a lip of overhanging rock. There was a short path leading to the smoke-filled hole where two wooden gates used to be.

They heard nothing but themselves.

'It's made of stone,' Jael said quietly, nodding at Thorgils who yawned as he approached, ignoring Ivaar and the other lords, who stood at a distance, talking amongst themselves. 'And the stone is still standing, so they're in there. Somewhere.'

Eadmund nodded, cracking his neck from side to side, flexing his fingers around his sword. 'Well, then,' he smiled tightly. 'Shall we?'

***

Axl yawned in the dawn light, his body aching as he rolled over, stiff and uncomfortable in the gravel. He had dreamed of the battle; disturbed dreams of the men he had injured or killed. In most instances, he wasn't completely sure. He'd seen their eyes, the shock in them; wide-eyed terror and then nothing. Axl felt different, certain that he was changed as he lay there, flexing his injured hand, not wanting the day to begin. At least in his dreams, there was a chance to escape the reality that they were Haaron's prisoners.

Their fate lay in his hands now.

His and Lothar's.

'It is very kind of you,' Lothar mumbled to Haegen in between mouthfuls of warm ale, relief easing his throbbing limbs as he sat back against the stable wall. It had been a night of aches and pains and frantic conversation as he and Osbert conspired to find a way out of this mess.

Osbert, drinking from his own cup, looked equally grateful, his body collapsed weakly next to his father's.

Haegen glared down at them both, frustrated that they found themselves in this position; unsure where they went to from here. But any decision his father made about what to do with all the Brekkans would have to wait until they heard from Skorro.

'Why are you giving them our ale?' Karsten grumbled from behind his brother.

'You think they shouldn't drink?' Haegen snorted. 'That they can make it back to Hest without drinking anything? That's how you'd treat your prisoners, is it, if you were king?'

'If *I* were king,' Karsten spat, lowering his voice, 'I wouldn't keep prisoners. What's the point? Feeding them, watering them, housing them?' He kicked out at Osbert's bandaged legs. 'Fuck them! I'd leave them to the birds.'

'Well, that's good to know,' Haaron murmured as he approached, his face taut with irritation. 'I shall make a note of that, my *second* son. Perhaps now, my youngest son?' He shrugged his aching shoulders, unsure how he felt about that. He didn't despise Berard in the way he did Jaeger. But Berard was almost entirely useless, so he'd be no real loss.

Except to Bayla. And she would blame him.

'Jaeger wouldn't have just given up, Father,' Haegen assured him. 'You know that.'

Haaron inhaled, frowning, wanting to smell something other than smoke. 'I don't imagine he would have. He is a Dragos, after all.'

***

'Ivaar!' Jael called reluctantly. 'Do your archers have many arrows left?'

Ivaar came over with the other lords. 'They do.'

Torborn and Frits nodded in agreement, their faces more amenable as they looked towards their queen now.

'Send them to the back. We'll all go in with shields. Have your archers ready to provide cover. We've no idea how many are left in there.'

The fort's gates may have burned into a crumble of ash and charred wood, but there was nothing to see beyond them which provided any further information.

Just thick clouds of eye-watering, stinking smoke.

Jael smiled encouragingly at Fyn, who stood nervously next to Thorgils and Torstan. 'Archers to the back! Shields to the front and sides! Eyes everywhere! There may be no one left alive, or just as easily hundreds in there, hiding in the smoke!' she shouted to the waiting, jiggling, eager men. 'Kill anyone, except a Dragos! We need them whole. A head on its own won't do!'

Thorgils elbowed Fyn. 'Time to show your shit of a father how wrong he was about you, wouldn't you say?' he whispered in his friend's ear, smiling widely at the morose face of Morac who hovered near Eadmund.

'Let's finish what we started!' Jael yelled, sliding *Toothpick* out of his warm, sheepskin-lined scabbard, lifting him up to the sky that was quickly brightening above them. She turned and walked up the path, Eadmund and Torstan on her left, Fyn and Thorgils on her right, Ivaar and the lords behind them. Her eyes raced ahead, checking for any sign of movement in the dense smoke. 'Let's take this island for Eirik Skalleson!'

Eadmund glanced at his wife, but her attention was elsewhere, searching for the threat they all could sense lurking within the walls of the silent fort.

***

Haaron sat upon his horse, his head turned towards the sea. Whatever had happened, he knew, word would be taken to Hest. And so he would have to wait before making any decisions about the Brekkans' fate. He had sent a man ahead on a fast horse to warn Bayla. He wanted her to be prepared for whatever news might come before his return.

Why, he wondered, as he so often did... why did he care so much about her feelings, when she cared so little for him?

Haaron shook his head, smiling suddenly at the sight of

Lothar Furyck huffing and puffing beside him. It was not an easy march back to Hest, but soon they would reach the summit and then it would all be downhill. His smile was brief, though, quickly replaced by a frown. If Jael Furyck was in command of Skorro, would she be so inclined to hand it back in return for her uncle and cousin? He doubted it. Lothar was not her father and certainly not a man worth sacrificing anything for. But he was her uncle and a Furyck. Perhaps she would see the importance in that?

'Axl!' one of the Brekkans yelled.

Haaron turned around sharply, in time to see a young man stumble near the edge of the cliff. Karsten stood nearby, looking guilty as others raced to grab the man before he tipped over the side.

Axl?

Haaron blinked, staring at the young man with fresh eyes.

***

They strode into the smoke.

Jael nodded for Eadmund and Torstan to lead their men to the left, Thorgils and Ivaar to the right. She ignored the roll of Thorgils' eyes and stayed with Fyn in the middle as they all slowly filled the entrance to the fort, silently, apart from the coughing which was impossible to repress. The smoke tickled the back of their throats, stinging their eyes as they bent, crouching behind shields, searching for their enemy; the archers behind them, arrows nocked, bows drawn in anticipation.

'Aarrghh!'

They heard the whistle, then the sudden, dull thudding against shields.

One man fell to the ground.

'Shield wall!' Jael yelled, slapping hers over Fyn's as the Islanders rushed into a line across the smoky fort, forming opposite their enemy. 'Archers! Find your targets!' That was an impossible request, she knew; they couldn't see a thing.

The archers released volley after volley of arrows into the smoke. There were a few cries, then a quick return.

A gust of wind blew through, at last, and there they were, perhaps a hundred Hestians, lined up, shield to shield, archers standing in behind, aiming straight at them.

'Archers! Aim and loose!' Jael bellowed, ducking out of the shield wall, the men on opposite sides of her coming together to fill her space. She hurried over to Eadmund, who came out of his place in the wall, crouching beside her, coughing. 'They have nowhere near as many men as we do!' she called over the noise. 'I say we leave the archers here behind a row of shields, get the Hestians to focus on them, and the rest of us go around the flanks. We can break their walls easily, finish it quickly.'

Eadmund nodded. 'I'll send half my men to wait with the archers until they run out of arrows, which won't be long.'

Jael nodded, hurrying back to Fyn, flinching as another wave of arrows thudded into the Islanders' shields. 'Let's go,' she whispered to him. 'Follow me. And whatever you do, don't let go of your sword!'

***

'Your sister can't think much of you, can she?' Haaron mused as Axl trotted to keep up with him and his horse. 'After all, your father left you what was supposed to be *her* throne, before your uncle then stole it away from you.' He enjoyed the indignant scowl on Lothar's sweaty red face as he struggled along beside Axl.

Axl didn't know what to say, having just become an unwilling pawn in this game of kings; this battle of kingdoms. But, he surmised, Haaron was right about one thing: if Lothar hadn't stolen the throne, *he* would be the one negotiating with him now. So it was time he figured out how to do it and quickly. 'My sister,' Axl said, imagining Jael's face. 'My sister burned your ships and your island. And soon she will come for you and your sons. The ones who still live, that is.'

Lothar looked horrified. He glanced around at Osbert who was leaning on Gant, limping, struggling to keep up. That was no way to get around Haaron Dragos.

But Haaron laughed, slapping his leg. The Furyck fire. Perhaps this one wasn't as limp as was loudly rumoured, he thought, staring at the stubborn frown on the tall, young man's face. 'You think she will try to take Hest?' he asked sharply. 'And how do you know she's even taken my island? That it's not *her* ships burning? *Her* men sinking into Ran's evil arms? You may know your sister, Axl Furyck, but you do not know the runt of my litter. He would rather die than allow that bitch to take anything of his. Of ours. So, do not be so quick in your assumptions, pup. Who knows what we may have to discuss when we return to my castle.'

Haegen, who was riding behind Haaron, blinked. There was almost a hint of pride in his father's voice. That would have had Jaeger choking in surprise.

***

'They're coming!' Jaeger called to his men as the Islanders' battle cries grew louder, rumbling towards them from both flanks now. He nodded to Berard who stood, singed and nervous next to him, his shield up to his nose, his sword shaking in his hand. 'Shields to the flanks! Hold your line! Dig in!' His voice was barely there, smoke-dry and weary after a night spent hiding in the kitchen, grateful that his father had thought to protect it with thick stone walls; the only thing that had kept his men safe from the flames that had choked and tortured them all night long.

Many had died; burned, unable to breathe. Screams of agony still rang deep inside Jaeger's sleep-deprived head. And as the smoke slowly cleared, he could see the truth of their situation. They did not have nearly enough men. The Islanders swarmed inside the fort, rushing towards them; hundreds more men than they had standing.

But they would fight.

'Run!' Jael yelled. 'Finish this!' And with one last look at Fyn, she kicked out at the nearest shield, dropping down to the dirt to slice across the legs of the shield holder as he held his line. He screamed, faltering, tipping forward, pushed out of the way by the Hestians in the wall as they hastily replaced him. Jael stuck her sword through his throat, sliding *Toothpick* out quickly, her eyes back on the wall of shields she needed to break.

Fyn was beside her, striking out with his own sword, still nervous but focused now, his grip firm. The arrows flew over their bobbing heads as each side's archers battled to strike down the other.

'Axes! Break the walls!' Jael cried, and the men with great, hefting axes pushed forward, muscles taut, straining for every bit of strength as they swung, chopping into wooden shields, hooking their iron rims. The men of Skorro braced themselves, praying they would not shatter.

Some did.

'More shields!' Jaeger croaked, but it was a hopeless request as many had been lost in the flames, destroyed by the thick, spreading, sparking liquid before there was any time to rescue them. He thrust his sword through the gap between his and Berard's shields, fighting back against the surging invaders, his teeth clamped together, desperate to survive. He needed to get out of here alive.

The wind was rising. Jael's braids whipped around her head as the smoke continued to dissipate. 'Push down their walls!' she yelled along the line. 'Everyone get in behind and push down their walls! We outnumber them! Let's break these fucking walls!'

The Islanders rushed up behind the men who had been trying to force their way through the shields, and leaned in, pushing with all their weight, shields against backs. Over and over, more men came into the line, heaving themselves forward.

Jaeger screamed as his foot skidded helplessly, his arm shuddering with the effort of keeping his shield upright. 'Aarrghh!' It was no use. He gritted his teeth, willing his feet to stop moving as his exhausted men slid and fell around him, overrun, scrambling for dropped swords, abandoning shattered shields.

Jaeger stumbled, the tide of Islanders swarming straight past him, breaking the wall all around him. He spun, shieldless now, drawing out his second sword, roaring.

Ready to fight.

***

Lothar had abandoned trying to keep up with Haaron.

Haaron had been too busy plying Axl for information to even notice that he had slipped back, panting and hobbling, only just managing to keep up with Osbert as he limped along with a stick Gant had found. Despite having wounds all over his body, he was still more able than his suffering father.

'Surely, he should rest soon?' Lothar panted. Clouds were darkening above them, and despite a steady breeze, it was unbearably warm. Lothar had squeezed out of his mail, reluctantly leaving it behind at the Tower. There was no way he was going to be able to carry it for two days.

'He doesn't appear too bothered,' Osbert sighed, the pain rendering him mostly silent. As much as he was desperate for a drink and a bed, he didn't have enough strength left for moaning.

'Mmmm,' Lothar agreed crossly, his shoulders curling in humiliation. 'It should be us on horses, leading them back to Saala to negotiate.'

Osbert's eyebrows rose, and his voice dropped. 'You really believe he will listen to you?'

'Of course,' Lothar huffed. 'Our freedom for his island... if Jael has indeed taken it.'

'And if she hasn't?'

Lothar grimaced, distracted. The hole in his right boot had grown so large that there was now gravel rolling around beneath his sweaty heel. 'If she hasn't, well, as you said, there's always your sister, isn't there? As long as Jael hasn't killed her prospective husbands!'

***

Jael glanced over at the towering man who had everyone's attention. Not as big as Tarak, but still... he wasn't going down without a fight.

Jaeger swung his long sword at an Islander, who jumped back, skidding on a slick patch of blood. Recovering his balance, the man spun away, just managing to avoid Jaeger's second sword as it came in behind.

'That's Jaeger Dragos!' Jael yelled, hoping that someone would hear. No one seemed to be listening, though. The fort rang with a heady din of screaming men, clashing blades reverberating around its blackened stone walls.

Jael had to get to him, but first, she had to escape a spitting

Hestian, bleeding from a deep gash in his soot-covered head. He seemed oblivious to the pain, his eyes wide, mad, almost delirious. She kicked out at his chest. He stumbled, off-balance, his ankle twisting. Shaking away the pain, he lunged at her, hacking his axe towards her neck, but Jael was too quick, ducking out of its arc, swinging her boot into the side of his head. He fell heavily to the ground and Jael jumped towards him, *Toothpick* through his throat.

She was up again quickly, turning back to check on Fyn who was still clinging to his sword, fighting off a man almost as big as Jaeger; a man who looked a little too much for him. 'Thorgils!' Jael called, nodding urgently at Fyn.

Thorgils headbutted the man before him, knocking him out cold and turned to Fyn, who didn't have time to look as relieved as he felt. 'Shall I show you how it's done?' he smiled, lashing out with his shield.

Fyn stood there as the man charged at Thorgils, his axe swinging.

'What?' Thorgils bellowed at Fyn, never taking his eyes off their opponent as he stabbed him straight through the shoulder. 'You're not going to help? Come on, then! Show me you remember how to use that thing!'

Fyn speared his sword through the Hestian's boot, pinning him to the ground.

The man looked from one to the other, in shock, unable to move.

'Good idea,' Thorgils grinned, then frowned. 'But you'll be needing your sword back.' He swung his own sword into the man's neck, quickly turning away from the horror in his dying eyes. They had a job to do.

Eadmund spotted a small man creeping away. He threw his small knife at him. It missed, clattering onto the stones behind him. Eadmund shook his head. Still rusty. The man looked as though he'd just pissed himself, though, as he turned and ran. Eadmund, leaping over a heap of fallen bodies, hurried after him.

'Berard!' Jaeger yelled, shunting a dying Islander to the ground, retrieving his sword from his opened belly. 'Berard!' He turned to run after his brother.

'Hello, Jaeger,' Jael smiled, stepping in front of him, her shield over her chest, *Toothpick* blood red in her hand. 'Not running away, are you?'

Jaeger didn't wait to talk; he needed to end Jael Furyck and find Berard. He stood before the tall, dark-haired woman, with only one sword now, but that sword was significantly larger than hers, and he swung it at her with every bit of strength he had left.

Jael skipped to the side, letting his sword hit the charred dirt as he stumbled after it. He reminded her of Tarak, but not as dumb. 'You've lost, Jaeger,' she taunted. 'Can't you see? Your men are dying. Needlessly. End it now. Surrender to me –'

Jaeger didn't wait for her to finish as he lunged, hacking his giant sword into her shield. Jael felt the shock of its weight reverberate up her arm.

'Surrender?' Jaeger laughed hoarsely, smashing her shield over and over again until she threw it away, spun around, and kicked him in the neck. Jumping back on one foot, Jael dropped to the ground and took out his legs. Rolling away as Jaeger fell, his sword clattering out of his hand, she whipped out her knife and stabbed it into his right ankle. Jaeger screamed. Jael sliced across the other ankle with her knife and was up and over him, *Toothpick* across his throat, shunting her knee into his ribs.

'Kill me!' he dared, spitting in her face.

'Jaeger! No!'

Jaeger blinked away his rage, jerking his head towards his brother's voice. He could see Berard, standing there, captured, sword against his throat, just as he was.

'Oh, look,' Jael panted. 'A family reunion. How wonderful.' She leaned in closer, *Toothpick's* blade nudging Jaeger's pulsing neck. 'As I was saying, surrender to me and my husband won't slit your brother's throat.'

'Your husband?' Jaeger glared at Eadmund who was

breathing heavily after chasing a very wiry and fast Berard Dragos all around the fort. 'Eadmund Skalleson?' he sneered.

Jael pushed on *Toothpick* until Jaeger's neck bled. '*King* Eadmund Skalleson,' she said coolly. 'Now order your men to throw down their weapons, or they can keep going, and while they take their last breaths they can watch me cut out your brother's eyes! Perhaps I'll send them as a gift to Karsten? He could no doubt do with another.'

Jaeger screamed to the gods, banging his head against the ash-covered earth.

He closed his eyes.

It was done.

PART FIVE

Hest

CHAPTER TWENTY SEVEN

'You do stink, Brynna Halvor!' Edela chuckled as they strolled towards the square, appreciating the noticeably warmer air and drier ground that greeted them.

Biddy cringed, unused to the formal sound of her real name. She had been nicknamed Biddy by Jael when Jael was just a toddler, and it had stuck. No one ever called her Brynna anymore. 'Blame Entorp, not me. It's his salve!'

'Well, there's no helping that, then,' Edela smiled cheerfully, 'for Entorp's salves work wonders!' She felt well-rested for the first time in days. Her body was freer, her step lighter. It had been a relief to sleep through the night without terror, without dreams of any kind. She frowned, pensive all of a sudden, reminded of Eirik Skalleson's death. 'It will all change, you know,' Edela said solemnly, her mood darkening like a sudden rush of clouds across a clear sky.

Biddy shook her head, unable to keep up with her. 'What do you mean?'

'Around here,' Edela murmured, inclining her head towards the square which was much emptier now that most of the men, including Ketil, had left to fight the Hestians. There was no meat cooking in the fire pit anymore, no clanging blades in the Pit; barely a noise at all apart from the grunting and squawking of animals and children. 'I saw Oss becoming such a bleak place after Eirik's death.'

'Bleak?' Biddy looked confused. 'You mean because everyone will feel so sad? They will. Eydis and Eadmund. Jael too. She was very fond of the king, you know. He was well-loved, much like Ranuf.'

'No, not that,' Edela said, shaking her head. 'It is something more. As though what claimed Eirik will spread, like a worm in the wood, weakening everything inside before it collapses around itself.'

Biddy stopped and stared at Edela, who had gone from sunshine to stormy in a few steps. 'Edela!' she said firmly, gripping her arm, staring into her eyes. 'Are you alright? Are you here?'

Edela shuddered. Disoriented. She often felt as though she existed somewhere between what was real and what was yet to come, and sometimes it was difficult to determine exactly what was what. 'Yes,' she sighed, trying to smile. 'Yes, I just have gloomy feelings today, which is surprising, it being such a pleasant morning.'

'Well, think yourself lucky,' Biddy muttered quietly, glancing around. 'Imagine if you were Runa, stuck in that house with Evaine all day and night. She looked terrified yesterday. I wouldn't have wanted to go back there last night.'

'She's right to be terrified,' Edela murmured as they came to a stall selling fruit and vegetables newly delivered from Alekka, her eyes widening at the sight of wild plums. 'That girl is growing powerful, I can feel it. She is so determined to take Eadmund, certain that she will. I doubt she plans to let anyone stand in her way.'

'Well, I'm sure she'll have a fight on her hands when Jael returns,' Biddy said defiantly. 'Jael will stand in her way.'

Edela smiled, relaxing away from her dark mood. 'Yes, I should like to see what Jael does with Evaine Gallas now that she is the Queen of Oss. Imagine poor Evaine's face when she finds *that* out!'

***

Sigmund had cried off and on all night. Despite Tanja's best efforts to soothe him, Evaine had barely slept, and she was in a foul mood because of it.

'Don't hold him like that!' she grumbled, sipping a cup of milk. 'You'll make him sick, and Tanja's only just changed him.'

Runa frowned, wondering what Evaine was talking about. The baby was gurgling happily in her arms; the baby Evaine had barely noticed since Tanja had come to stay with them. She handed Sigmund to his mother. 'Here, you take him, then, I'm going to visit the market,' she said quickly, desperate to escape. 'Another ship arrived from Alekka this morning. It will be nice to have something different to eat tonight.'

Evaine frowned as she grabbed Sigmund under his arms and lifted him onto her knee. She instinctively looked up at the mezzanine to see where Tanja had gotten to. 'Well, I'll be glad to be rid of that stink for a while. I'm not sure anything has ever smelled worse!'

Runa grimaced as she lifted her cloak over her shoulders. The ache of her arms was unbearable, but the relief she felt in knowing that there was a barrier between her and Evaine now was worth all the pain and more. 'You're right, I'm sure,' Runa said, barely listening. 'I may go and see Edela and Biddy again,' she added, 'so you'll be able to enjoy the fresh smelling air all morning long.'

Evaine frowned, irritated and helpless all at the same time. There was no Respa, she couldn't see Tanja, and Runa was leaving her holding the baby. A burst of fire surged up into her chest. 'Father and Eadmund will return soon,' she snapped as Runa grabbed her basket and hurried to the door. 'And everything will be different then, I promise.'

Runa swallowed, pulling the door open and hurrying out into the sunlight, desperate to escape the chill of Evaine's words.

***

It was not going to be an easy place to hole up, Eadmund decided, glancing around at the charred walls of the cramped hall. Skorro had been designed as an island of minimal comfort and maximum strength. The Islanders had certainly tested the latter, and Eadmund decided that he was not so enamoured with the former. He turned to his wife, who was dabbing a wound on her forearm. 'How's your arm?' he wondered hoarsely, his throat raw from inhaling so much smoke.

'It's not deep,' Jael said dismissively, her voice rasping just as throatily as his. 'Is Thorgils ever going to find their ale stores? I need something to drink.'

'The Dragos' aren't being especially helpful,' Eadmund muttered, nodding towards Jaeger, who sat tied to a chair in a corner, towered over by Thorgils. 'But I didn't mean that, I meant your whole arm. Tarak did break it only a few months ago.'

Jael smiled, her teeth black with soot. She hadn't remembered, not till now. All of her ached from crouching in the wooden house the day before. 'I forgot.'

'Well, it's a good thing it ended so quickly, then.'

'I'm not sure everyone would agree with you.' She nodded towards some of the men who still looked ready for more; Ivaar's men, Torborn's men. 'They didn't really see much action, did they?'

'No,' Eadmund frowned, sitting down next to Jael. He lowered his voice. 'And that could be a problem. We should have stuck them out in front, before Jaeger's archers. They could have picked off any dissenters.'

'You think they'll support Ivaar to take the crown from us?'

'There's a chance.'

Jael sighed, leaning into Eadmund, inhaling him. She'd missed him. 'But don't you have plans to kill Ivaar? Surely they know *that's* coming? Makes no sense to put your swords behind a man about to die.'

Eadmund stared at her, confused, his head awash with memories and feelings, none of which made sense anymore. He was certain he loved Jael, that he'd missed her, but as close as she was to him right now, with those eyes of hers staring into his, he felt nothing at all. Eadmund shrugged himself away from her, uncomfortable. 'Well, there's not a lot of sense in most people's heads, I find.'

Jael saw the tension in his eyes; he looked barely present. 'We need to drink to your father. All of us do,' she said sadly. 'To him and our victory. Leave Ivaar for another day.' She smiled as Thorgils returned to the hall, rolling a large barrel, basking in the throaty cheers of the thirsty men who crowded around him, desperately waving empty wooden cups. 'Besides, we need to get home first. And we can't do that until we find out what position we're in here. After what Edela warned, we've no idea what disaster Lothar might have led everyone into.'

Eadmund nodded, eager for a cup of cold ale to wet his dry throat. He groaned as he stood, stretching out his back. 'Well, hopefully, we'll hear something soon, before someone tries to kill our prizes!'

**

'Runa!' Edela smiled as they bumped elbows in front of a stall selling jars of amber-coloured honey and twists of fragrant spices. 'And how are your arms faring today?'

Runa rolled her eyes at Biddy, who nodded in sympathy. 'Not very well, I must admit. It was hard to get any sleep last night. Although,' she surmised quietly, 'that may have been because of Evaine.'

'You can come and stay with us, can't she, Edela?' Biddy said encouragingly.

'Of course,' Edela smiled, handing over a silver coin to the toothless merchant who placed a jar of honey into her basket. 'But perhaps that will just make things worse?'

'I think it would,' Runa said nervously, her eyes ferreting about. 'Besides, I'm not sure Evaine is being particularly attentive to the baby at all. It seemed just an act she put on while Eadmund was here.'

Edela led them away from the traders and their open ears. 'I wouldn't be surprised. But you must remember that you are not her enemy, not unless you do something to come between her and Eadmund. You see, that is her only goal. To have him all to herself, as Morana has promised she will.'

Runa sighed, walking with her eyes down, wondering how she'd ever been talked into taking Morana's baby all those years ago. She had Fyn and did not want another, especially the offspring of an evil witch. But, in the end, her guilt had overwhelmed her reason, and she'd gone along with Morac. After all, Fyn wasn't his, and she felt she owed Morac a child he could truly love.

But what would that decision cost them all now?

'Is there nothing we can do to stop her?' Biddy wondered. 'While she is binding Eadmund to her like this? With that candle and those stones and whatever else she has done to him?'

'Perhaps when he returns we'll be able to get him tattooed?' Runa suggested hopefully. 'Won't that protect him? Stop Evaine from turning his heart towards her?'

Edela shook her head. 'No, that will only help someone before something happens. It is not a cure. When Eadmund was here, I was barely awake, so it's hard for me to see what has happened, but I will dream on him tonight. I will try and see what Evaine has done to him.'

***

They were drunk now.

Jael watched, frowning as the Islanders taunted Jaeger and his brother, who had been separated but equally jeered at.

As long as they left it at that.

There were no women on the island and nothing to do but drink and wait and search for any food that Jaeger may have hidden away. With nearly six hundred thirsty, hungry Islanders, it would not be long before all the food and ale was gone.

'Not happy?' Thorgils smiled, plonking himself down onto the bench Eadmund had just vacated. 'After what you did?' He slapped her on the back.

'Me?' Jael looked confused.

'Leading us like that,' he mumbled between slurps of ale. 'With the houses, and the fire... and the catapults.' Thorgils leaned his big bushy head towards her, his eyes wide. 'And the victory!'

'Victory?' Jael had drunk a few cups of ale herself, but despite overwhelming exhaustion, she was unable to relax at all. 'This island?' She shook her head. 'Hest would be the real victory,' she said quietly. 'But if Lothar hasn't defeated Haaron, then we're just a target or a pawn.'

'But we have our prizes!' Thorgils insisted, ale slopping over the side of the cup which wobbled unsteadily in his sooty hand. It was terrible ale, but no one cared. 'Bargaining power,' he winked.

'Mmmm,' Jael mumbled, looking at Jaeger and Berard as Thorgils turned away to knock his cup into Fyn's. So many rumours had flown around over the years, but the one sticking in her head now was about Haaron's youngest sons and how he did not favour them at all.

***

There was no spoon, so Lothar ate the stew with his hands,

humiliated, but happy to have food in his desperately empty belly at last. By the time his bowl had been dished up, it was long cold, but he didn't care.

He was sure that he'd not endured a more horrendous day in his life: trekking through rugged mountains on blistered feet; boots worn through; barely a drop of water, or rest.

Haaron was a miserable, vengeful king, Lothar decided, certain that he would not have treated him in such a disgraceful way if their positions had been reversed. But Haaron was the only way he was going to get out of this mess alive, and somehow, he needed to find common ground; somewhere to begin their negotiations, which, so far, Haaron had completely refused to entertain.

Lothar refrained from licking the bowl, which he would have done if he weren't a king, in full view of his men and his enemies. Instead, he belched loudly and struggled to his feet, his body creaking with the effort, convinced that he wouldn't be able to get through another day like this.

He had to try and talk Haaron around now.

If things went well, perhaps there was even the chance of a horse?

***

'Tell me about your father,' Jael demanded for the second time. Jaeger clamped his blistered lips shut and looked away. She had expected that, and didn't even frown as she stood before him, trying to make herself heard above the noise of the tightly packed hall. 'Listen,' she said firmly, leaning forward. 'I'm sure you want to live...'

Jaeger spat in her face. 'Get away from me, bitch!'

Jael didn't flinch, but a few men around her did.

Eadmund strode up to Jaeger and slapped him on the back of the head. 'You don't talk to the Queen of Oss like that,' he warned. 'There are a lot of men here who will have a big problem with you if you do. And we'll be helpless to stop them, I'm afraid.'

'*Queen*?' Jaeger sneered. 'You must be getting desperate if you couldn't find anyone better than this Brekkan whore to replace your dead father!'

Eadmund punched Jaeger in the eye, clenched his jaw, and walked away.

There were cheers as Jaeger's head lolled about helplessly, his arms tied to the chair. He couldn't move, and when he tried, the coarse ropes chewed through his skin. He bit down on the pain searing through his eye, which was not as bad as the pain in his bleeding ankles, and lifted his head, staring defiantly at Jael with the one eye still open.

'As I was saying,' she continued, her expression unwavering, 'I'm sure you want to live, but as we both know, your father doesn't care if you do, not really. Neither you, nor your brother over there.' She nodded towards Berard, who was being taunted by some of Ivaar's Kalfans. 'So, I wouldn't rely on Haaron to save either of you.'

'Why not kill us, then? Why keep us prisoner? What use are we to you?'

Jael wasn't sure she had an answer, but Jaeger didn't need to know that. She shrugged. 'You'll either help us get what we want, or you'll fetch a good price as a slave, I'm sure. Although your brother, perhaps not so much.' She watched the smallest hint of panic flicker across Jaeger's face, but it disappeared quickly, and she was left facing an amber eye so ruthlessly cold that Jael wondered if she'd seen it at all. 'Either way, we'll find some use for you both, I promise.'

***

They had thankfully found a wide, flat clearing to sleep in. Well, it was not that wide, nor especially flat, but it was a vast improvement on the narrow cliff-hugging paths they had stumbled up all day long, and Lothar was pleased about that.

Haaron's men had erected a tent for their king, complete with a bed and furs. The rest of them would sleep in the dirt, it appeared; even the King of Brekka, Lothar grumbled to himself. He was a Furyck, raised by a king, brother to a king, and finally, one himself. He was not a man used to lying in the dirt.

'You have eaten, I see,' Haaron noted disinterestedly as he approached. 'It's so peaceful now that we don't have to listen to your fat guts griping.'

Lothar frowned, letting the slight slip away unanswered. 'I have, yes. Perhaps now would be a good time for us to speak? In private?'

It was Haaron's turn to frown. He flicked his tongue over his teeth, working out the bits of stew stuck between them. 'What did you want to talk about, Lothar, King of Nothing? Your death, and when I will claim it?'

Lothar tried not to shudder, but Haaron's face was sharper than the tip of a blade as he leaned towards him, sneering. 'No, I thought we could discuss your island and whether you wanted it back? But more than that... there are other matters we must discuss. Matters that, if agreed upon, would, I'm sure, prove beneficial to us both.' He pushed his shoulders back as far as he could, grimacing at the ache in them. Even his hair hurt as he stood there in the approaching darkness, on the high cliffs overlooking the Adrano.

Haaron's curiosity was piqued. 'Well, let us walk, then, and you can tell me what you have to offer that I would find beneficial,' he smiled. 'I am weary after the day, and would appreciate some amusement.'

Gant watched as Lothar and Haaron fell in beside one another, disappearing into the night. He had been the one who decided to save Lothar. They could have left him to die, perhaps should have.

And now?

He didn't imagine that Lothar was plotting to save anyone but himself.

***

The laughter washed over her like a wave, threatening to drown her in despair.

Gleeful, hysterical, victorious laughter.

Edela was desperate to hold her hands over her ears, but she couldn't move. Why? Why couldn't she ever move in these dreams? She felt trapped, as though she was buried beneath the earth; locked in an airless chamber of darkness; approaching death, the loss of all hope.

The laughter grew louder and louder and then abruptly stopped, its echo continuing to vibrate around Edela as her body shook in time.

'I wish you could see what I can, Edela!' the voice crowed happily. 'She doesn't realise who she has in her hands... *what* she has. So near... her prisoner. Ha! She doesn't realise that she could stop it all now. End everything. Now. No prophecy. Nothing. Nothing would happen if she finished him. And she could. He's right there. She has the sword...'

Edela frowned. Her chest ached as though her heart was being squeezed by a strong hand. Pain shot up her arms. Her breath struggled from her lungs.

What did she mean?

What did she want?

'But she doesn't see it, just as you don't see it. And you will all live to regret that soon!'

***

'We'll find out in a few days where we go from here, once we get word back from Hest!' Eadmund called above the noise. 'But for tonight, we celebrate our victory! The victory of a small group of islands against the might of Haaron Dragos! Revenge for all the lives and ships he took from us four years ago!'

The cheers were deafening in such a cramped hall; deafening too because the Islanders were drunk with success. They had never known a victory like this. Nothing so comprehensive, so utterly devastating. And with barely any losses.

This was a victory the gods would applaud.

But still, it was tinged with the bittersweet memory of their king's death.

Eadmund raised his cup, waiting for the men to quiet around him, wondering if he trusted himself enough to keep going. He'd felt numb since it happened, but the ale had broken through the walls around his heart, and he felt himself becoming more and more morose. 'My father,' he began, and his voice shook, his lips wobbling. Eadmund dropped his head, inhaling a quick breath, tears stinging his eyes. 'My father will be smiling in Vidar's Hall tonight!' he cried to the sooty, bloody, drunken mess of men before him. 'Proud of his Islanders! Proud of our victory!' More cheers as cups and hands banged on tables. 'Proud too, of the woman he chose to lead us.' There was complete silence as Eadmund turned to Jael, who stood next to him, suddenly awkward. 'He put all his hopes in you. He believed that you would lead us to victory. And you didn't let him down. Or any of us. You made this happen, Jael.'

Jael blinked, swallowing, surprised by this public show of... she wasn't sure what. She felt so uncomfortable. It was surely about Eirik, not her.

But the men seemed to disagree; at least most of them did. She didn't see Ivaar amongst the cheering Islanders who raised their cups and thumped their chests, calling her name, nor all of the lords either, but there were some there now, some who had scowled at her before – Torborn, Hassi, Frits – they were smiling.

Jael sighed, a lop-sided grin forming at last. 'Well, I didn't know your king long,' she said, trying not to picture Eirik's face as he lay dying before her. 'But Eirik Skalleson was a true king, a king to be proud of. He cared more about all of you than he ever cared for himself. And Eadmund and I will do everything we can to give him all that he wished for... for Oss, and all of the islands. But first, we have to take this victory back home. And to do that we need to stay sharp. Until we find out what's happened with Haaron and Lothar, we need to protect our prisoners and keep our heads. So, one more drink, then go get some sleep!' She tried to keep a straight face, watching the horror grow on theirs.

They were on their feet then, booing, bellowing, turning their smiling faces towards Jael and Eadmund, cups in the air.

Eadmund looked at the affection on the men's faces as they cheered his wife. He had said what was right, what needed to be said. And it was all true. But as he stood there, exhausted, broken-hearted, and grieving, all he could think about was how quickly he could get back to Evaine and their son.

***

They sat by Haaron's fire, and Lothar was grateful for its warmth, for, despite the temperate climate in the South, the nights were proving bitterly cold.

'And you think you have something I want? *You*?'

'Besides your island, you mean, or perhaps your sons?' Lothar smiled, his confidence growing.

Haaron frowned. 'You do not know me, or you would not make such an assumption.'

Lothar was not to be deterred. 'We are no longer young men,' he suggested, swallowing the insipid small ale Haaron had grudgingly provided. 'And perhaps the time for endless battles is now better replaced by forging alliances and negotiating agreements?'

Haaron raised a woolly eyebrow. 'And what do you have to offer me?' he sneered. 'My kingdom's wealth outstrips yours. Merchants flock to my piers, desperate to trade in my markets. My coffers are overflowing. I have four sons,' he began, then stopped. 'I have at least two sons and the ability to rebuild my entire fleet within the year. I'm curious to know what you think I need? From you?'

The night was quiet as they sat, listening to the sound of Lothar's endlessly gurgling belly and the crack of the fire.

Lothar grimaced as he leaned forward, his eyes straining to make out the shadowy figures lurking around the edges of their conversation. 'I know you want land. Fertile land. Not just rocks. You may have a castle and ships, and you can sail to the Fire Lands, but you cannot grow your own food. Not enough to sustain your people, from what I hear. Why else would you keep trying to claim my land?'

Haaron pulled on his short grey beard and sighed. He felt older and wearier than he wanted to admit. 'Are you offering me some of your land?'

'Brekka?' Lothar laughed, his sides aching with the strain. 'No. Never. And you will not offer me Hest, will you?'

It was Haaron's turn to lean forward. 'What, then?'

'I'm suggesting we claim Helsabor. Together. An alliance that would increase the size of both our kingdoms. And an agreement for free access through the Widow's Peak for my men, so that we may finally trade with the Fire Lands ourselves.'

Haaron laughed. 'Helsabor?' He shook his head. 'It's heavily fortified, walls on three sides. Wulf Halvardar has spent sixty years building those fucking walls! His army is too large, even with both of ours against it, surely?'

'Not with the Islanders as well.'

Haaron narrowed his gaze. 'And you think your niece will continue the alliance with you? You who took her father's throne? Who sold her to the Skallesons?'

'My niece is a queen now and, from what I've heard, very happy in her marriage. She would not have been so if she'd remained in Brekka,' Lothar insisted, puffing out his chest. 'I see no reason for her not to be grateful for that.'

Haaron was intrigued. Helsabor sat between Hest and Brekka, on Osterland's western coast. Most of it was rich and fertile, and that tempted him. But Wulf Halvardar had spent his entire reign breeding warriors to stand on his towering walls and kill anyone who dared come close.

It was not something he had ever considered. Until now.

A bug flew into Haaron's mouth, and he spat, coughing, taking a quick sip of ale. 'Or I could just kill you, your son and your nephew and then go and kill your niece, wife, and daughters. And that would be the end of the Furycks,' he mused.

Lothar tried not to shudder at the real possibility of that happening.

For all his bravado, he knew that their position here was desperately fragile. One wrong move and Haaron would take everything he had and destroy it all.

***

'How?' she asked into the whisper of flames, her thick white breath twisting before her. 'How will I do it?'

The woman smiled menacingly, her eyes glowing like embers. 'I will show you. He won't even know. It will not be easy, though. He loves her very much, I can feel that. But you will have two ways to bind him as soon as your son is born. Do not fear, you will take him and become his queen. I have seen it. And without him, she will never succeed.'

Evaine couldn't have looked happier as she sat, huddled beneath a fur, rubbing her hands gleefully over her large belly.

Edela frowned, desperate to hear more, but the vision faded into the night, leaving just the flames glowing in the distance.

He stood by himself, alone, watching her.

Eadmund.

Edela walked towards him, hurrying, calling his name, but her voice disappeared before it reached the tip of her tongue. He looked right through her, so lost, his face pained in despair. She could feel the weight on his shoulders, see the grief in his eyes.

Then Evaine was there, holding her hand out to him. Eadmund took it, his eyes on hers, and as she reached up to him, kissing his lips, the flames grew in front of them, separating them from Edela.

And she couldn't move. Couldn't warn him. Couldn't save him.

The flames weaved and twirled into a symbol that wrapped itself around Eadmund and Evaine, enclosing them inside its glowing, amber light.

A Tuuran symbol.

Edela blinked. She recognised it.

CHAPTER TWENTY EIGHT

The man scurried towards the dragon throne.

Bayla watched him, her back rigid, her hands twitching in her lap. She had heard rumours of the fire, smelled the smoke, and seen the sky turn hazy, and it had clenched her heart. But what it all truly meant, she didn't know.

Not yet.

The man stopped just before the throne, kneeling, out of breath. 'My lady,' he panted, his eyes dropping to the flagstones.

'Up!' Bayla demanded sharply, clearing her throat. 'What has happened? Tell me.'

The man, one of Haaron's scouts, had been ordered to Hest as soon as Skorro had burst into flames, to warn the queen of what might come. He had not welcomed such a mission. Bayla Dragos was not a woman anyone wanted to upset. 'The king...' he began nervously, his eyes struggling to aim anywhere near her emotionless face.

Bayla edged forward, one eyebrow arching at Irenna and Nicolene who had just entered the hall.

'The king sent me to warn you...'

'About?'

'The fleet was destroyed, my lady. By fire.'

Nicolene and Irenna both gasped as they hurried forward, eager to hear what had happened.

Bayla felt sick. '*Destroyed*?'

'Two of our ships escaped to Skorro. But then we watched as Skorro was set alight, too.'

Bayla shook her head, not wanting to let her mind wander yet; not until she knew everything. Her throat tightened. 'And Haegen and Karsten?'

'They captured the Brekkan king, my lady,' the scout said. 'The Brekkans surrendered to them.'

'And they both live?'

'Yes.'

'But what about the Siluran fleet?' Irenna wondered urgently, her eyes blinking in fear. Relieved beyond words to hear that Haegen had survived, she was desperate to know what had happened to her father, Prince Aris of Silura who had led his fleet in support of the Hestian ships.

The scout shook his head. 'I cannot say, my lady. I believe some escaped, heading back to Silura.'

Irenna's mind was not eased. She had known that her father's alliance with Haaron would not end well.

Bayla frowned, irritated by her daughter-in-law's interruption. 'And you say that Skorro was on fire? A stone fortress? *On fire?*'

'Yes, my lady.'

'So, the Islanders have the fort, and your king has the Brekkan army,' Bayla mused, her mind whirring, her calm face belying the terror pounding inside her chest; the fear that her sons were dead. 'And now they will play a game of cat and mouse?'

'The king wanted you warned, my lady,' the scout said. 'He is marching to Hest but may not make it back before word comes from Skorro. I saw a ship leave the island. It will be here soon.'

Bayla swallowed. They couldn't be dead.

She wouldn't forgive Haaron if they were.

***

'Here, drink this,' Biddy said as Edela yawned by the fire, her feet warming near the flames.

It was still raining heavily after a wild night of thunder and lightning which had frazzled their nerves. Neither of them had slept well.

Edela took the cup, sniffing. 'Lemon balm?'

Biddy nodded. 'Your favourite, from memory.'

'Indeed.' Edela smiled, at last. Her dreams had been so vivid that she hadn't been able to stop frowning since she'd crawled out of bed. Her shoulders finally relaxed as she sighed. 'I'm so worried.'

Biddy sat in the chair opposite her, inhaling the steaming scent of the calming tea. 'You're not normally one to worry.'

'No, but I'm not normally the one who needs to rescue someone. Not like this.' She shook her head, feeling the warmth of the liquid through the cup. 'I am so old and hopeless now. How am I supposed to battle that girl for control of Eadmund?'

'Do you think there's a way to bring him back? To... release him?'

'Oh, yes!' Edela's eyes widened. 'That symbol. If I can just remember that symbol exactly as I saw it, we can work on unbinding him. There were many symbols and spells in that Tuuran book the elderman gave me. If only I had brought it with me when we left Tuura.'

'If you had, they may have sent more men after you.'

'Yes, which is why I left it behind in the end,' Edela admitted. 'I knew they would want Aleksander and perhaps try to come to Andala for him. Taking the book would have only made them more determined.'

'Can we take the candle and stones from Evaine?' Biddy wondered, smiling at Vella, who put her paws on her knee; she was missing Jael and Eadmund. Biddy placed her cup on the floor, picking her up. 'We could ask Runa or the wet nurse?'

'I've thought of that, but even if we could, I don't think it will be enough. And it would cause great problems for Runa.'

Edela frowned. 'Perhaps we should visit Entorp? He may be able to help me with the symbol.'

***

Ivaar spun around, lowering his voice, biting down on an urgent desire to yell. 'With him? With her? What does *that* mean, Hassi?'

Hassi of Rikka took a step away from Ivaar's venomous spittle. 'It means that Jael and Eadmund led us to a great victory. What reason do I have to go against them now?'

They had wandered down onto the beach, away from the fort and the thick-headed Islanders who were moping about in search of more ale in the dull light of the morning.

'We had an agreement.'

'No, Ivaar,' Hassi insisted, squaring his broad shoulders and glowering up at Ivaar's pinched face. It had started to rain, and he was eager to get inside the fort but not until Ivaar understood. 'We had conversations, not an agreement,' he said firmly, his pock-marked face turning red with irritation. 'And as it stands, I agree with Eirik. He's left the islands in good hands. After what we saw out on the sea? And here?' Hassi looked back at the fort, but they were still alone. 'It would make no sense to try and force a change now, especially if...'

'If what?' Ivaar snapped.

Hassi squirmed, knowing Ivaar's temper as he did. He pulled nervously on his long white beard. 'If you killed your father. If you did that –'

'I didn't do that!'

'But if you did, then Eadmund will kill you, and even if you didn't, I imagine he'll come for you anyway. It's only his wife holding him back now. Have you not seen the way he looks at you? Eadmund's ready to gut you.'

That was not news to Ivaar, not like Hassi's disloyalty, which had come as a surprise. Because of Jael. He shook with rage. 'And the others?'

Hassi shook his head. 'You'll have a hard time finding anyone prepared to go up against Jael and Eadmund now, Ivaar. That victory... it united us. That was the sort of victory that'll be sung about for generations. And we're all still here because of Jael, to see what happens next. For the first time ever we have a part to play,' he said proudly.

But Ivaar wasn't listening as he watched Hassi's old eyes gleaming with possibilities. If his support truly had dried up. If the lords were all leaning towards the new king and queen and away from his claim to the throne, then his position here, trapped on this tiny island, was looking very precarious indeed.

***

Conditions had quickly become treacherous as rain hammered the marching men, streaming into their eyes and mouths, drenching them through. The dry and dusty paths had turned to sloppy mud, their boots sucking into it as they walked; sodden, muck-coated boots on miserable, wet, shivering bodies.

This was the sort of weather that rusted mail and rotted feet. But there had been no stopping as Haaron marched them solidly from first light, impatient to get back to Hest before the messenger arrived from Skorro. He had watched the ship's journey from the island with one eye as he rode, certain they stood no chance.

Haaron tried to imagine what had happened, wondering whether his sons lived. He thought he would care less than he did. Perhaps it was his pride confusing his emotions? The idea that his enemy could attack him, destroy his fleet, take his island, and kill his sons? That was not something he could dismiss lightly, no matter how desperate he'd been to remove the threat Jaeger posed.

Bayla would be devastated, but he couldn't see a way around that.

If they were dead...

And then there was Lothar's proposal. If his sons lived, that was something to consider. Helsabor was an attractive proposition, indeed. He had no regard for the weakling king that was Wulf Halvardar; a man so pathetic that he refused to fight anyone. Ever. Except, of course, to defend himself; something he was especially skilled at.

Haaron wiped the rain out of his eyes for the hundredth time and sighed, turning to Haegen, who looked morose. 'Your wife will be upset with news of her father's demise.'

Haegen blinked, surprised; his father had barely spoken all morning. 'We saw a handful of Siluran ships turn. Aris may have been on one of those.'

'Well, you can only hope,' Haaron smiled happily, taking pleasure in irritating his son, despite the fact that Haegen was easily his favourite. 'I don't expect your wife will be very happy with you if not.'

Haegen shook the rain from his long sandy hair. 'I imagine not, but her father made an alliance with you. He could not refuse to play his part. Irenna will understand that,' he said without confidence.

'Alliances are certainly a way for us to build a bigger kingdom, wouldn't you say?' Haaron mused, watching his son's reaction. 'Before Aris and I came to an agreement, we fought and lost many men and ships. But trade has made us both richer and stronger. And, of course, you have Irenna and the children.'

Haegen nodded, turning to his father. 'I agree. But whether it is right in every instance, I'm not sure. It depends what is on offer.'

'Of course,' Haaron agreed. 'There would be no point in an alliance without a prize. But sometimes you need help to claim something you could only dream of achieving on your own.' Haaron's eyes wandered over the cliffs again as they rode along, side by side, but not for long. Soon they would narrow down even further as the mountain pass grew more challenging.

He could no longer see the ship from Skorro.

***

Eydis sat by the fire, stroking the purring cat Gisila had placed on her knee, hoping it would comfort her.

They were all being so nice to her – Gisila and Amma, her servant, Boelle, and even Gisila's servant – as they fussed about, making sure she had everything she needed. But she didn't want or need anything except her father.

Or a dream that would help her find his killer.

Eydis had come to despise her dreams, or, at least, her inability to manipulate them. She thought of Ayla and Edela often, wishing they were here to help her, to show her what to do. She had lain in bed for two nights, holding everything she could, trying to find a path to the answers she so desperately sought. She had to get the proof Eadmund needed to kill Ivaar before he tried to take Eadmund and Jael away from her too.

'Eydis?' Amma touched the sleeve of Eydis' light-blue dress. 'Are you ready for something to eat?'

Eydis jumped, then froze, her mouth hanging open in horror at what she had just seen.

Amma gripped her arm, worried. 'Eydis? What's happened? Are you alright?'

But Eydis said nothing.

What could she say?

***

Jaeger needed to piss. Urgently.

But the man guarding him had fallen asleep.

Jael kicked Torstan in the shin as she approached. 'It's you who are supposed to be watching him, not the other way round!' she grumbled as Torstan jerked awake. 'Go find a bed.'

'I, I, only closed my eyes for a moment,' Torstan insisted groggily, scrambling out of his chair.

'Well, go and close them somewhere else! I'll stay here.'

Torstan looked suitably remorseful as he trudged away, yawning, much like everyone else, who had drunk themselves into such a state that they were barely able to open both eyes at the same time.

It was, at least, welcomingly quiet.

'I need to piss,' Jaeger muttered.

Jael didn't blink as she took a seat. 'Don't let me stop you.'

Jaeger clenched his big hands into small balls, his knuckles turning white.

'Shall I get you some water?' Jael asked, setting her lips in a straight line, her eyes fixed on him.

He ignored her, looking away, his eyes roaming around the blackened mess of the hall, the stink of it still strong in his nostrils. 'And what do you think you'll do without your fire jars? Without your arrows? When my father comes?'

Jael leaned forward. 'For you?' she mocked. 'From what I hear, that won't be the case, and no doubt I'll have that confirmed soon. Hopefully, tomorrow. Although, I think he would appreciate your confidence in him, that he was successful against my uncle. That he would launch a rescue to reclaim you and your brother.' She smiled, then frowned. 'You forget that I've been fighting your family for ten years, so I know that Haaron doesn't have the slightest bit of interest in whether you live or die.' Jael eyed Jaeger coldly and stood up. 'I think I'll go and speak to your brother. So far he's been much more helpful than you.' And she wandered off to Berard, motioning for Fyn to join her. 'Get Thorgils,' she whispered. 'He needs a piss. Thorgils has plenty of experience with that!' And smiling to herself, she turned to Berard. 'And how's your bladder feeling?'

Berard blinked nervously, confused as Jael pulled over a stool and sat down in front of him.

Jaeger wanted to scream as he watched her. The bitch. The fucking bitch. He would kill her. She was making a mistake to even think about negotiating his release because he would kill her.

One day, he would kill her.

***

Aleksander's eyes widened as he spied the massive castle in the distance. It was larger than anything he'd ever seen.

Haaron's palace of stone. Lothar's longed-for prize.

And now, there was Lothar, stumbling behind Haaron's horse like a pathetic, drenched slave. An utter failure.

And they'd saved him.

Aleksander turned to Gant. 'What's he been plotting, do you think?'

Gant rolled his eyes, shaking his damp hair out of them. It had mercifully stopped raining, and now they were all starting to steam in their cumbersome battle gear. He fingered his empty scabbard, anxious about his sword which had been confiscated with the rest of their men's weapons. 'Something for himself, no doubt,' he muttered. 'Whatever deal he reaches with Haaron, it will benefit him alone, of that I'm sure. But the rest of us? Or the Islanders?' he sighed. 'I doubt there'll be much thought for anyone else.'

Axl groaned on his left. His blisters had burst, and the pain in his feet was unbearable; his wet boots rubbing away at the open wounds as he walked. Still, he wasn't seriously injured as some of their men were, and he was clear-headed enough to be grateful for that.

'And as for you,' Aleksander whispered, turning to Axl. 'The best thing you can do is nothing. However Lothar and Haaron plan to tie you up in this mess, you'd better keep your mouth shut. Leave it to your sister to try and sort it out.'

Axl frowned but didn't argue. He had a bad feeling about all of it. His feet throbbed, and his chest tightened as they followed Haaron down the hill towards the city.

***

'I...' Eydis started, then stopped, stroking the cat. 'I keep seeing my father's face,' she lied quietly. 'It's so hard.'

Amma hurried to sit beside her, wrapping an arm around Eydis' shoulder. 'I'm sorry,' she said sympathetically. 'When my mother died, I didn't think I'd ever stop seeing her death. It hurt so much, but one day I remember thinking that I hadn't cried for some time, and I realised that my heart had begun to heal. But that doesn't mean I don't think of her and cry often. I do, especially now. It just means that the pain becomes less raw. Time makes it so.'

Eydis could feel tears building. She hadn't wanted to speak of her father's death again. She just wanted to hide away from it, pretend it hadn't happened until Jael and Eadmund returned.

If they did.

'My mother died when I was five-years-old,' Eydis said slowly. 'She had seen her death coming. She knew she wouldn't survive the birth of my brother. She knew he wouldn't survive either, so there was time to say goodbye, to prepare things.' Eydis blinked away the tears that filled her eyes. 'And with my father... we knew as well that it would happen. But not when, and not how.' She sniffed. 'I was so busy trying to find out how to stop it that I didn't think about saying goodbye.' She started sobbing, unable to stop, forgetting all that she had just seen, burying it away beneath her own pain.

Amma pulled Eydis into her arms, tears rolling down her cheeks as she pictured her mother, missing her so desperately. She doubted she would feel any such grief when her father died.

***

'Your brother seems an angry sort of man,' Jael smiled at the jiggling Berard. She frowned. 'Are you alright?'

'I can't feel my arse,' he groaned. 'Or my hands.'

'Well, then, how about we untie you for a while?' Jael suggested, nodding at Klaufi, who stood nearby. 'Help me remove these ropes,' she said gently, deciding that someone like Berard would respond more helpfully to a kinder tone.

Berard looked surprised as the ropes around his hands dropped to the ground.

'Here,' Jael said, grabbing his arm. 'Stand up, let some feeling come back into your body.'

Berard's legs were still tied to the chair, so he could barely balance, but Jael held onto him. He was smaller than her, and light. Shaking too.

'You're cold?'

'A bit.'

'I'll find you a fur or a cloak,' Jael smiled.

'But not for my brother?' Berard asked anxiously, his eyes darting to where Jaeger sat, his head drooping.

'Your brother wants to kill me,' Jael said. 'He's too busy spitting in my face to listen to anything I might say.'

'Our father will be very disappointed in him,' Berard sighed. 'Jaeger is worried, I'm sure. He blames himself for this.' He nodded at the broken shell of the hall as the rain fell down; at their bloodied and burned men who sat outside, soaked through, guarded by armed Islanders.

Jael frowned. They were very protective of one another.

Good to know.

'Understandable,' she said. 'He wants to impress the king. It's hard to get noticed when you're the fourth son, I imagine?'

Berard nodded, his tongue loosened by her soft approach. 'This was his chance, but you ruined it with all that fire.' He shook from the memory of it. 'Our father will be furious.'

'He will.'

'If he survived,' Berard mumbled, his mind whirring. 'You did fire the Tower.'

'Well, we'll hear soon, I'm sure,' Jael said. 'Now, why don't you sit down and we'll tie up your arms again and loosen your leg ropes for a while. I'll leave you with Klaufi here. He'll help you, and I'll go and find you that fur.' Jael smiled at Berard, who blinked over to where Jaeger had suddenly disappeared from.

What had they done with him?

***

Bayla waited, stony-faced, flanked by Irenna and Nicolene on the wide, stone steps of the castle; grizzling, impatient children milling around their feet in the light rain. She watched as Haaron's servant hurried to help him dismount his horse.

He looked bedraggled, she thought, her lips twisted in disgust. Old too.

Bayla's eyes wandered to her two sons as they embraced their wives and children, relieved to see that they appeared unharmed, as did her own husband, who walked stiffly towards her. She could see the anxiety in his face as his eyes searched hers for answers.

She did not plan to give him any. Not yet.

'You've had word?' Haaron croaked, reaching for her, hoping for something in return.

Bayla noticed the Brekkans, then. The filthy mess of a man, who had to be Lothar Furyck, stared towards them with curious eyes, and she relented, allowing her husband to embrace her rigid body. 'They sent Eilo. He waits for you inside,' she said icily, her eyes barely resting on his. 'Skorro has fallen. Our sons live. Prisoners of the new King and Queen of Oss.'

Haaron couldn't decide what to think about that. He looked towards his two eldest sons, but they were too busy with their own families to notice him at all. Sighing, he turned away from Bayla's judgemental eyes and walked into the castle, but he could feel them, the cold threat in them, as they followed him every step of the way.

Those eyes would give him no room to manoeuvre.

***

Jaeger was making things difficult. Thorgils had slapped him across the face more than once, but Jaeger was still fighting him as Thorgils dragged him towards an ashy pit which had become a temporary latrine.

'What do you think you can do if you get away from me, arse? When you can't even stand?' Thorgils growled, eye to eye with the raging bear that was Jaeger Dragos. 'Swim back to your mother?' Jaeger pulled against Thorgils, who glared angrily at

Fyn. 'Do you plan on helping me at all, Fyn Gallas?'

Jaeger stopped all of a sudden, stumbling, his eyes darting to the boyish-looking man long enough for Thorgils to get a better grip on him, but it did not last long as Jaeger twisted and turned himself away from Thorgils again, elbowing Fyn in the eye.

'Need some help there?' Eadmund wondered, one eyebrow raised in their direction.

'No,' Thorgils grumbled, punching Jaeger in the stomach before grabbing one side of him, while Fyn hung onto the other. 'We have everything under control, don't we?'

Fyn nodded unconvincingly, one eye closed as he hurried after Thorgils, clinging onto Jaeger.

'But I think next time he can just piss himself!' Thorgils called over his shoulder. 'He's far too much trouble, this one. Perhaps we should just toss him into the sea? We only need one brother, don't we?'

Eadmund couldn't help but smile, as miserable as he felt. 'I think we'll keep him, if you don't mind! Once you're done, make sure you tie him tightly to his chair, then go find some more ale,' he sighed. 'Get him to tell you where the rest of their stores are, and he can have a cup too.'

Thorgils nodded, liking the sound of that, and he shunted Jaeger towards the pit, muttering threateningly in his ear.

Eadmund turned, deciding to look for Jael who had left to inspect the ships with Beorn. Instead, he saw Ivaar standing in the burned-out hole where the gates had once stood.

Ivaar hesitated, then stepped into the fort, walking straight towards his brother. He was not about to be cowed by Eadmund or his wife, no matter what Hassi had said. The throne should be his, and he was never going to take it back by being weak in the face of threat.

Eadmund's hands trembled with rage as he stopped, watching his brother, remembering his father's death: his eyes pleading for help, in shock, pain, then so quickly glazing over, lifeless. His heart thudded in his ears as he lunged at Ivaar, grabbing him by the throat.

Ivaar barely flinched, defying his brother's rage as it burned all over him. He jutted out his chin, clenching his jaw. 'You want to kill me, Brother?' he laughed. 'Go ahead, but know that you will be a king who killed an innocent man! Hardly the sort of king our father would have hoped for!'

Eadmund's eyes were mere slits. His breath pumped urgently through his nostrils; his mind filled with an almost uncontrollable thirst for revenge. He had waited so long to destroy his brother. The man who had killed the people he loved most in the world.

He squeezed tighter and tighter, his filthy fingers digging into skin, Ivaar's eyes bulging, his hands flapping at his sides as he struggled to breathe. Eadmund suddenly caught sight of Jael, frozen at the entrance to the fort, her mouth open as she watched him. His eyes flicked back to Ivaar, whose pulse he could feel quickening beneath his fingers.

Closing his eyes, Eadmund shoved his brother away, shaking all over, unable to speak. He stormed towards his wife, grabbing her arm.

'We need to talk.'

CHAPTER TWENTY NINE

'Hmmm,' Entorp murmured, shaking his head. 'No, I don't know it.'

They stood around his small table, staring at the scrap of vellum that was puzzling them all.

Edela had tried to replicate the symbol she had seen in her dream. She frowned, not satisfied with her effort. 'It's not quite right. Let me try again.' Closing her eyes, she tried to slip back into her dream, to where Evaine had wrapped herself around Eadmund, and the symbol had entwined itself around them both. Opening her eyes, she took up Entorp's quill, dipped it into the inkpot and began scratching again.

Standing back, Edela wrinkled her nose, unconvinced.

'No, I'm afraid I don't know it, Edela,' Entorp said thoughtfully. He wandered over to a battered wooden chest, and kneeling, creaked open the lid, rummaging through loose pieces of vellum and books that had been haphazardly stuffed inside over the years. His memory, Entorp knew, was generally poor, so he liked to keep notes of everything he discovered; records of all his experiments. Although, he conceded, it was probably time to build another chest.

'Here!' he announced, at last, pulling out a faded leather notebook and creaking back to his feet. 'This is my book of symbols. All that I know about them is in here.' He placed the notebook on the table and started thumbing through its pages.

It was not a large book, however, and it took no real time to look through it.

'It's not there,' Biddy stated rather obviously.

'No,' Edela sighed. 'No, it's not. But I know it was in that book from Tuura. If only I could remember it properly.'

'And what was this book?' Entorp wondered.

'It was a book of dark magic. Ways to stop it. To ward yourself against it.'

'Then what Evaine is doing to Eadmund is certainly dark magic,' Biddy breathed. 'He's under her control.'

Entorp looked just as worried as Biddy. 'Yes, it sounds likely, for that symbol is like nothing I've seen before. You just need to find a way back into your memory, Edela, to see that book again. To find the symbol.'

'If only it were that simple...'

'Well, I do have a salve that might help with that,' Entorp smiled with a twinkle in his eye. 'It always works for me.'

'Has it?' Edela looked surprised and suddenly, very hopeful.

***

Eadmund clamped his teeth together, trying not to scream.

'You can't kill Ivaar now,' Jael insisted. 'It's the wrong time, the wrong place. It would breed bad feelings amongst the men. We don't need that. Not now, when they're full of victory and hope. Our minds have to stay focused on what happens next with Haaron and Lothar, not creating tension we can leave for another time.' She grabbed her husband's arm, glaring at him, trying to break through his anger. 'Taking Skorro has shown the Islanders that we're worth believing in, especially the lords. Killing Ivaar now would undo all of that.'

Eadmund shook off Jael's hand, walking over the rocks,

down to the water. Of course, she was right, he could see that. But Ivaar was here. Ivaar the Murderer was here. Now. It would be easy to end him.

Why was she so determined to let him go?

Jael followed him, not willing to leave things like this; leave him like this. 'Eadmund, I know how much you want to kill Ivaar. And if he killed Eirik, he should die.'

'*If?*' Eadmund seethed, his teeth bared as he turned on her.

'It's always an *if* unless you have proof,' Jael reminded him. 'And so far there is none. He says he didn't. You say he did. There's no proof either way.'

'You don't even think he killed Melaena!' Eadmund cried. 'Why? Why are you always so quick to believe him?'

Jael wasn't sure. She didn't like Ivaar, but she liked to think that she could read people; that she could separate a lie from the truth. It was a game she would play with Aleksander when they were children: guessing which stories were lies, which were true. They would rope everyone in to play: Edela, Axl, Gisila, even Gant and her father, and she was never wrong.

Not even once.

The drizzle was turning back into rain as they stood there, damp and cold. 'I want to believe that Ivaar did it,' Jael insisted. 'That he killed Melaena and your father. It would be easier that way, wouldn't it? To make him guilty. To know that there wasn't someone else out there murdering people. But I don't believe he killed Melaena. He loved her too much. And I'm not sure he killed your father either,' she said slowly. 'Ivaar's clever. It makes no sense to murder Eirik like that, in front of everyone, knowing that he'd be blamed.' She looked at the murky sky as the white-capped waves started building in the breeze. 'Ivaar is clever,' Jael said again, almost to herself. 'Why would he do something so foolish?'

'And if it *wasn't* Ivaar?' Eadmund growled, barely wanting to admit that she might be right. 'Then who did it? Who killed my father?'

***

Lothar wanted to sink onto the stone steps and die. His weak, worn bones could barely hold up his aching, sagging skin as he stood there, waiting with his men, abandoned by all of the Dragos' who had disappeared inside their massive castle to discover the fate of Skorro.

Finally, he sighed and simply gave up, collapsing onto the nearest step, not caring whether it looked royal or not.

'Father?' Osbert limped towards him, sitting down with a grimace. 'What's happened?'

Lothar grimaced back. 'What's happened is that I'm fed up with standing, so I'm sitting! Is that not obvious, boy?' He turned to his only son in a burst of exhausted fury. 'It's hardly been the best few days. I can't even remember when I last ate!'

Osbert's head drooped. It was hard to disagree with that. But then again, he supposed, they had earned their punishment for such a weak display against Haaron's army. When he was king... he rolled that thought around his aching head, inhaling the putrid stench of his father, and himself, for that matter; soiled and filthy, riddled with blood-crusted wounds, damp and disgusting as they sat there, discarded by the victors.

Oh, how he prayed to Furia that Jael had survived to restore their reputations.

***

Irenna was sobbing, comforted by Nicolene, worried that her father had drowned along with his Siluran fleet.

Haaron kept glaring at her, his right eye twitching in irritation. 'Perhaps you need to take your wife away?' he muttered to

Haegen.

Bayla rolled her eyes, cringing at the sound of her husband's hissing voice; it had been a pleasant few days without him. 'Let her cry. We need to talk about Jaeger and Berard.'

Haegen glanced at his wife, feeling guilty that her father might have drowned helping defend his father's island. 'Mother's right. We need to think about how to negotiate with Jael Furyck.'

Karsten glared at Haegen. 'What? *Negotiate*? With her?'

'Well, who else should we be negotiating with?' Bayla spat.

'I'm suggesting that we don't negotiate at all, Mother!' Karsten growled. 'Hest comes before family. Jaeger and Berard know that. And since they failed to defend Skorro and lost most of our fleet, they'd certainly see it as a fair punishment.'

'What?' Bayla and Haegen were united in outrage.

'How can you suggest such a thing?' Bayla barked. 'Your own brothers!'

'We need to find out what they want,' Haaron said evenly, ignoring his entire family. 'They have the island. They have a large fleet. We don't. Not anymore. Perhaps they have more of that fire liquid? We need to tell them that we have the Furycks,' he sighed, as irritated as Karsten at the thought of having to negotiate. 'But whether Jael Furyck is going to be enticed by the idea of saving her brother or her pathetic uncle, I don't know.'

Bayla glanced at him, panic in her eyes.

Haaron turned to the nearest slave. 'Find Varna for me,' he ordered. 'Quickly! I will see if she has any insight. And in the meantime, Karsten, you will see to our prisoners. They need to be housed somewhere. Clear out the ship sheds. They can sleep there. We certainly won't be needing them for some time. Bring the Furycks into the castle, though. We'll put them in a chamber. They are our prizes now, and we need to ensure they remain in good order. And you,' he grumbled at Haegen. 'You will go and make your wife stop that awful noise!'

***

Fyn wondered if he was still in shock as he sat there, guarding Berard. He kept seeing the battle for Skorro and the men he had killed. Two of them. The sounds they had made were painful and high-pitched; pleading, whimpering, dying sounds. He felt guilty when he heard them; confused too, as he felt a small sense of pride that he had not just turned and run. He'd stood there and fought and killed, alongside Jael and Thorgils.

Fyn watched his father and Otto, heads together, muttering away as they stood by the fire, occasionally glancing in his direction. It made him uncomfortable. Morac's eyes were always following him, silently judging him. Despite all that he might have become away from his father, being around him had awoken old memories. It was hard to keep his mind here, in the present, where his fingernails still had blood underneath them. And not his, either.

Berard coughed. 'Water,' he croaked. 'Please.'

Fyn nodded, picking up the cup that sat at his feet. He was relieved to be away from Jaeger, who had already headbutted Thorgils and bitten Torstan.

Berard drank gratefully from the cup held to his lips, his eyes constantly darting to his brother, watching as Jael Furyck walked up to him again. He sighed. Anxious.

Fyn followed his prisoner's gaze as he sat back down with the cup. 'Jael won't hurt your brother,' he said quietly. 'She's not that sort of person.'

Berard blinked, looking down at his filthy tunic. Everything in the fort was covered in stinking soot and ash. He was desperate to bathe. To stretch. To be back in Hest. 'Her family had a reputation for fairness. Once,' he said, almost wistfully. 'Before her uncle claimed power.'

'But Jael has not changed,' Fyn insisted. 'She's not like him.'

'No, but she hates him, doesn't she?' Berard murmured,

watching as Jaeger growled, spitting at the new Queen of Oss again. 'Perhaps she'll see no point in keeping us prisoner soon?'

Fyn shrugged. He didn't dislike or fear Berard in the same way he did his brother, but he didn't want to offer false hope. Jael was fair, he knew, but she was also not afraid to make hard decisions.

***

Varna had been preparing herself all morning.

Her dreams had revealed how it stood: the Bear and the Idiot imprisoned, Skorro captured, and the Furycks held hostage. It was not unexpected, for her at least, but her reaction to it would catch Haaron by surprise, she knew. So, as she crept towards them, as they all stood in anticipation, gathered around Haaron's throne like hungry birds, Varna steadied herself, her wiry grey eyebrows sharp, her eyes unrelenting.

Haaron wrinkled his nose as the old woman approached; damp weather tended to worsen her stink, he found. 'Well, you saw there would be trouble on Skorro, and you were not wrong, Varna,' he growled, enjoying the sweet coolness of his favourite wine as he sipped from his goblet. 'But now you must tell me what you see next. We have the Furycks. They have Berard and Jaeger, and, of course, my island. A decision must be made.'

Haaron could feel Bayla glowering beside him, biting down on her indignation that anything should be up for debate. She wanted her sons. In her opinion, there was nothing more to discuss.

'Yes,' Varna rasped, her crooked frame tipping towards him. 'A decision must be made. The one best for all of Hest, not just for two sons or one mother.'

Bayla rose up on her toes, glaring down at the old dreamer.

'And?' Haaron edged forward. 'What do you see?'

'I had many dreams last night!' Varna announced, her voice rising dramatically. 'I saw Hest growing powerful, increasing in both size and strength. More land, more people, more wealth! Richer than you have ever dreamed!'

Haegen and Karsten stared at one another.

Haaron looked suitably intrigued.

'And to achieve that, you will need Lothar Furyck,' Varna breathed. 'And you will need Jaeger and Berard too.'

Haaron frowned, confused. Bayla sighed, relieved.

'You want me to trade the Furycks for Skorro?' Haaron asked coldly.

'And your sons,' Varna insisted. 'But you will get much more from this arrangement than Lothar Furyck ever will, do not fear. If you make an alliance with him, you can take Helsabor and then all of Osterland will be open to you. Once you knock down Wulf Halvardar's walls, what is to stop you from taking everything?'

Haaron swallowed, rolling his hands over the ridged dragon's feet at the end of his armrests. For years Varna had warned him that Jaeger was a threat to his reign, and now? Now he should save him? Was that just for Bayla's sake? 'Haegen, Karsten, take your mother. See to your wives,' he ordered, dismissing them with an urgent wave of his hand. 'I wish to speak to Varna alone.'

Varna's back ached as she stooped there, waiting for them to leave.

As soon as Bayla had been reluctantly led away, Haaron dragged himself out of his throne and strode towards Varna, his face close to hers, not wanting to be overheard. 'And the Bear?' he whispered, trying not to inhale. 'What of him?'

'He will be of use to you,' Varna murmured, smiling. 'I have seen it.'

***

Entorp frowned, inhaling the stink of manure as he scraped at the stable door. Ido and Vella stood nearby, watching him work, occasionally nuzzling his legs. He had quickly become their favourite visitor; there were so many interesting things to smell on him.

'This is a very good idea,' Biddy smiled, hanging a small linen bag filled with rosemary over the lintel. 'I can't believe we didn't think of doing it sooner. And next, the house?'

'Of course,' Entorp mumbled. 'Now, don't worry about me, you go inside. I won't be much longer, then I'll get to work in there.'

'Alright, but you must stay for supper,' Biddy insisted, clambering down from the stool. 'I have smoked fish, flatbreads, and a nettle soup bubbling away inside. Plenty enough for you. I've even made some honey cake!'

Entorp's eyes bulged at the thought of such a meal. 'Well,' he blushed, 'I would like that very much.' Ducking his head, he went back to work, carving an ancient Tuuran symbol onto the back of the stable door with a chisel and mallet. It looked like the intertwined petals of a flower, but sharper, more angular; a symbol of protection that would hopefully keep the horses safe from anything Evaine might have a mind to do; that and the rosemary, which was known to ward off evil spirits.

Biddy smiled, patting her leg for the puppies to follow her. 'Come on, you two!' she scolded. 'Leave poor Entorp alone. He has important work to do.'

Ido and Vella, deciding that it must be time for their own supper, hurried after her.

***

'You must eat,' Gisila insisted.

Eydis sighed, pushing her bowl away, her stomach lurching at just the smell of the roast pigeon, which both Gisila and Amma seemed to be enjoying. They had nearly finished their meals while Eydis had not even started hers.

'Perhaps tomorrow your appetite will return?' Amma suggested kindly, frowning as Eydis turned away from her. She had been acting oddly all afternoon. Amma wondered if something had happened to Axl, and not for the first time.

'I think I just need sleep,' Eydis whispered. 'My eyes hurt.'

'Well, that's an even better idea,' Gisila smiled. 'And perhaps tomorrow there will be some news?'

Amma glanced at Gisila, whose eyes reflected the unsaid fear in her own. Why hadn't they heard anything yet? Something was wrong.

Something must have gone wrong.

***

Haaron's castle was like nothing Lothar had seen before. It was no dark, wooden hall in need of repair. This was an impressive stone palace, with ceilings too high to clean, and walls decorated with thick glass windows, draped with dark-red curtains. It was cold, but it was grand, and his confidence in his own superiority deflated with each heavy step he took towards his host. Lothar forced himself to look straight ahead, focusing on Haaron's throne. It was not easy, though. He could barely contain his envy as he walked, Osbert and Axl on one side of him, Gant and Aleksander on the other.

They had been ordered inside the castle to begin negotiations. That was something, Lothar thought to himself. He was weak from lack of food, from the arduous walk, the constant discomfort. He looked at Haaron, resting comfortably on his ridiculous dragon throne and felt furious. But, he reminded himself, nibbling his dry lips, not all victories were quickly won. Some would take longer to achieve. And if he could secure Haaron's help to defeat Wulf Halvardar, it would be the beginning of Brekka's quest to claim all of Osterland, kingdom by kingdom. And that was something worth waiting for.

Karsten glared at the Furycks from one side of his father's throne. It was not in his nature to negotiate. He could barely contain his rage at what his father was about to do.

'My sons are being held hostage on Skorro,' Haaron began. 'I will send Haegen with one of your men, to take my terms for releasing you all.'

Lothar almost fell down in relief. But it was Jael who would have the final say, so he checked himself quickly.

'If your niece and her husband agree to release my sons and leave Skorro, then you and your men will also be free to return to Brekka.'

Osbert was incredulous as he stood there, leaning on his stick. But Jael? His shoulders tightened. Would Axl be enough to tempt her into giving up all that she had fought so hard to claim?

Lothar looked to his left. 'Aleksander will go with your son,' he announced. 'He knows Jael better than anyone. I'm certain he'll be able to convince her of your terms.' He eyed Aleksander with a fierceness that implied there was no choice in the matter.

'Good,' Haaron sighed. 'And once Jaeger and Berard are back, we can move forward with the wedding preparations.'

Everyone looked surprised by that, apart from Haaron and Lothar.

Lothar raised a weary eyebrow, resisting the urge to smile gleefully. 'You have come around to that idea, then, my lord?'

'Come around to it?' Haaron muttered irritably. 'Yes, I suppose I have. As much as it pains me to say so, I think you're right, Lothar Furyck. Our two kingdoms, plus the Islanders, united against Helsabor, will make us powerful allies indeed.'

'Agreed!'

'And why not both become rich in peace, rather than warring, losing men and ships, deprived of land and opportunity which could belong to us all?' Haaron said loudly, weaving his words so that his sons would begin to understand his logic. 'We will both prosper when the Halvardar's fall.'

Axl turned to his uncle, confused. 'Wedding?'

'Yes,' Lothar smiled happily. 'I decided to take Osbert's advice. I have found your cousin the perfect husband.'

Axl's mouth fell open in horror.

CHAPTER THIRTY

Edela inhaled the salve.

It was more than just a pleasant scent; it was soothing, warming her chest, unwinding her mind as she lay in her bed, listening to Biddy murmuring to the puppies, who could not decide where they wanted to sleep now that their bedtime companions had gone.

Edela felt at peace as she curled her body into a familiar position, relieved that Entorp had carved all the symbols around the house and the stables; hoping that his salve would unravel the secrets hidden in the depths of her memory.

She needed to see that book again.

Yawning, she closed her eyes, ignoring her cold toes, enjoying instead, the heat on her chest; her weary body sinking deeply into the mattress, the furs pulled up to her nose as she drifted peacefully off to sleep.

***

Eydis lay there, unable to sleep.

Perhaps it was partly because, as much as she was desperate to discover clues that would lead to her father's killer, she was just as fearful of seeing his death in her dreams. She didn't want to watch him die before her eyes again.

Her dreams were the only place she saw anything. But she was not even fourteen-years-old, and Eydis wasn't sure that she was ready to face what was waiting for her in the shadows.

***

Talking to Isaura had been pleasant, Ayla decided as she lay there, watching the embers glow from the banked fire. It was a welcome change not to feel so utterly alone. She had grown weary being enemies with the one woman who could understand how she truly felt. But what they could do with their newfound allegiance, Ayla wasn't sure.

For when she closed her eyes, she saw Ivaar coming.

***

Jael crept over to Eadmund. She knew he wasn't asleep.

The two beds that hugged the dank walls in the small chamber weren't wide, but they were wide enough. She nudged him over and slipped in beside him, pulling the fur over them both. The bed creaked in protest but held.

Eadmund looked both surprised and annoyed, but Jael didn't care. Evaine may have taken his heart or his mind, but he was still her husband, and she was cold and lonely. She reached up and stroked his face, leaning over him, kissing his lips.

Eadmund flinched, pulling his head away.

'You're in there, somewhere,' Jael whispered sadly, laying

her head on his chest.

Eadmund frowned, uncomfortable with her closeness, as much as he wasn't. He was confused, his mind and body at odds with one another. He reached up a hand, almost reluctantly, and placed it on Jael's arm, running it down the length of her sleeve. She was cold. He smiled, memories stirring inside his heart.

She was always cold.

Jael twisted her frozen feet around his, entwining them with hers, seeking his warmth, pleased when he let her. 'I'll bring you back to me,' she whispered, her hand over his heart. 'We are meant to be, you and me. That's what the gods say.'

Eadmund shuddered, at once desperate to kiss her, to taste her lips, to feel her on top of him, and then, just as desperate to push her away. Because of her. The woman he was certain he truly loved. Her face, her body...

Evaine.

***

Evaine's head hurt as she lay there, struggling to sleep. She felt unsettled. Sigmund had wailed all day long, and her nerves were frayed. She thought of her father, and of Eadmund, hoping they were both safe; confident that they were. But still, Eadmund was with that woman. Every day, every night.

Evaine had seen the way he had started to turn towards her before he left, but now he was so far away. Would Morana's spell still work? She wrung her hands together, glancing at Tanja who had Sigmund tucked in beside her, both of them snoring lightly in her little cot.

Lifting the flickering lamp from her bedside table, Evaine hopped out of bed, tiptoeing to her chest. Placing the lamp on the floor, she eased open the lid. She had rubbed fish oil over its rusted hinges that afternoon, desperate to ease its heart-stopping creak, so she was pleased to hear only a faint noise as she reached into the chest and pulled out a small package.

Laying it on the ground, Evaine unwrapped the cloth, removing her beeswax candle. She dipped it into the lamp and set it alight, pushing it into an iron stand, its base carved with symbols. Glancing around again, Evaine took a deep breath, feeling calmer. She picked up her five smooth stones and placed them around herself at even points, ensuring that the symbol painted onto each one was facing up.

Evaine closed her eyes, reminding herself that Eadmund was hers.

He was always going to be hers.

And leaning forward, she inhaled the sweet scent of the candle.

**

Eydis crept towards the door. It was slightly ajar, and the flickering light from a fire fell out into the night, making her feel less afraid as she bent, shivering in the darkness, trying not to make any noise.

Where was she?

Who was in there?

The voices were low and muffled, but she could definitely hear a woman.

'Once you kill Eirik, everything will change. Your power will be limitless. You will rule as you always wanted to. As you have always deserved to.' The woman spoke so quietly that Eydis found herself edging closer and closer to the door. 'You will have the crown you crave, I see it so clearly. But first, you must take his life and quickly.'

Eydis gasped, stumbling, frightened, backing away into the starless night. She turned, running, too scared to stop; not waiting for the information she needed, her breath rushing in terrified bursts from her mouth, her nightdress flailing behind her.

Into the darkness.

***

Edela stood inside the flames. Great towers of fire rose up on either side of her, but she felt no heat as she watched the buildings burn and the people flee.

Tuurans. She was certain they were Tuurans.

The screams echoed around her, vibrating straight through her as she watched Tuura burn. Thatch was catching quickly; horses whinnying, desperate to escape their stalls. She heard the cries of frantic mothers searching for their missing children.

Dark clouds swarmed above her, so ominous and low, sucking all light from the sky. And then she saw Jael, running towards the gates, a child in her arms, Aleksander next to her as they hurried to escape. Branwyn was there behind her, Kormac too; their sons, Aedan and Aron, pulling horses; Aedan's wife, Kayla, holding onto two children, tears streaming down her red cheeks.

And in the distance, the temple, towering above them all. It, too, was aglow, disappearing into the dark clouds, consumed by flames from the buildings around it as the wind fanned them higher and higher.

Edela turned, watching her family run towards the gates, fighting to escape, panic in their eyes.

***

The bed was not comfortable, as beds went, but compared to the rocks and dirt he had been curling up on for the past few nights, it was bliss.

If only Axl hadn't been too numb to notice.

Four of them had been sequestered in one room; a small, dark chamber on the first floor of the castle that smelled of disuse, like the inside of a bowl left out over winter. Osbert lay in one bed, against the wall; his father in the bed along from him. Axl had taken the other side, with Gant, desperate to get away from them and their scheming.

He needed to think and couldn't. He still saw the battle and heard the screams; still felt the despair of the march and the worry about being captured.

And now Amma.

Lothar had taken his throne, his mother, and now he was giving away the woman Axl wanted for his wife. To another man. A Dragos. To live in Hest with him.

Shuddering, Axl rolled over. Perhaps Jael could help? There must be some way she could stop this from happening.

Lothar's thunderous snores bounced off the cold stone walls as Osbert groaned, tossing and turning to escape the noise of his father and the agony of his wounds. Axl didn't notice as he lay there, trying to remember the last time he had seen Amma, when he'd promised to return to her.

He couldn't let her down.

***

'Ivaar's gone.'

Eadmund glared down at Jael as she sat shovelling thick porridge into her mouth.

She looked up, surprised. 'From the island?'

Eadmund nodded, too furious to speak. Why had he listened to her?

'Well, he's only going back to Kalfa, isn't he?' Thorgils mumbled as he fought his way through his own bowl of porridge. 'Whether you'd killed him now or later, it doesn't make much difference, does it?'

'No, but on Kalfa, he'll be protected inside his fort. It won't be as easy.'

'True, but he's made things clear for you now, hasn't he?' Thorgils smiled, wiping his beard and reaching for a cup of water. 'Only a guilty man would run.'

Jael frowned. 'Or a man who thinks he's about to be killed without reason.'

They both scowled at her.

'Why are you always so determined to find that bastard innocent?' Thorgils grumbled, admitting defeat against the unappetising lump of porridge. 'Does he have to be standing there, holding the bottle of poison for you to think he's done it?'

Fyn squirmed in between them, thinking that it was time to go and sharpen his sword.

Eadmund stood in front of Jael, waiting for her answer.

Jael looked past him. 'There's a ship coming,' she said quickly, dodging the question entirely. 'A Hestian ship by the look of it.'

Eadmund turned towards the burned entrance of the fort. 'Well, let's hope they have some good news for us. I'm growing sick of the sight of this island.'

'Mmmm,' Thorgils agreed. 'Especially now that we've run out of ale!'

***

'But you couldn't see who it was?' Amma asked as they walked down the beach in bare feet, enjoying the cool sand between their toes.

The sun was out, the wind barely a breeze, and they had both grown tired of sitting inside, waiting for news that never came.

'No,' Eydis said sadly. 'Just a voice. But it was so muffled and far away. I didn't recognise it at all. Or maybe I did? I don't know.' She shook her head in frustration. 'It was a woman. That's all I know for certain.'

'A dreamer?' Amma suggested. 'It sounds like a dreamer.'

Eydis stumbled in the soft sand and Amma reached out to steady her. 'I think so. But I can't believe that it was Ayla.'

'Perhaps you'll have another dream tonight?' Amma suggested. 'And more will be revealed?'

'I hope so,' Eydis sighed, feeling the heaviness in her eyes, the ache in her chest. She wanted to fall onto the sand and sob. She felt lost, adrift in a terrifying new world, without her father; desperate to hear his voice, feel his face, pull on his beard, kiss his cheeks. Eydis could feel tears coming again, and she shook her head, not wanting to cry anymore. Not yet, not till she knew that Jael and Eadmund were safe and coming back for her.

She had to be strong until then.

'Eydis,' Amma said suddenly, stopping and turning to her. 'You've seen something about me, haven't you?' She was shaking all over, afraid to even ask. 'I can see it on your face. Is it Axl? Has something happened to him?' She held her breath, watching Eydis for any sign that her instincts were right.

Eydis' shoulders slumped. She wanted to hide away from the question, knowing that any answer she gave would make Amma feel worse. She swallowed, listening as seabirds sung in great wailing tones in the distance. 'I have... had a dream about you.'

***

Aleksander came towards them first, and Jael sighed, relieved to see that he was alive and unhurt. She was far less pleased to see Haegen Dragos walking behind him.

Eadmund frowned to see Aleksander again.

Thorgils nudged Fyn in the ribs as they stood waiting, just behind their king and queen. 'Here we go again,' he muttered, rolling his eyes.

'Welcome to Skorro!' Jael smiled at Aleksander, ignoring Haegen. 'I thought you might bring some ale to celebrate our great victory, but you seem to have brought a Dragos instead.'

Aleksander grinned, happy that she looked well, if not filthy. The whole place stunk of sea-fire and smoke. The evidence of the destruction the Islanders had wrought was everywhere. 'Well, it's more that he's brought me,' Aleksander said ruefully. 'We're Haaron's prisoners.'

That wiped the smiles off everyone's faces.

'*All* of you?' Jael wondered anxiously, her shoulders tightening into knots.

'I'm afraid so,' Aleksander said with a shrug.

'We have come to negotiate with you,' Haegen said impatiently. 'I'm Haegen Dragos, my lord.' He nodded to Eadmund in a surprising show of respect. 'I'm sorry to hear of your father's death.'

Eadmund didn't even blink at him.

Haegen did blink as he hurried on. 'My father wishes to have his men and his island back, and his sons returned.' He looked around at the broken remains of the fort, at all the soot-covered Hestlans who sat slumped miserably together, waiting to discover their fate. 'I am told they still live?'

There was genuine concern in his eyes, Jael noticed; affection, she supposed. Perhaps Jaeger was someone you warmed to over time?

'Well, let's go somewhere more private,' Eadmund suggested, motioning to the hall, which had various private chambers leading from it.

Haegen walked ahead of them and Eadmund fell in beside him, leaving Jael with Aleksander. She shot him a look he knew well. Aleksander smiled, knowing that her mind was already working away, trying to come up with a plan.

***

Amma shuddered as she listened.

'I wish I knew what it all meant,' Eydis said again. 'I wish I could see things more clearly, but you were in pain, I know that. Heartbroken and scared. Alone in the darkness, praying to the gods. You needed their help, you said, over and over.' Eydis stopped, reaching out in her own world of darkness for Amma's hand, wanting to reassure her somehow. 'I'm sorry I can't tell you more, but I'll try my hardest to dream about it again.'

Amma gave Eydis her hand as she stood, swaying gently on the sand.

Terrified.

Was Axl dead?

***

The bulk of the Brekkan army had been imprisoned in Haaron's ship sheds. The rest had been penned into stables and stalls, watched over by armed Hestian guards. The Furycks – valued hostages now – were confined to their tiny chamber on the first floor under the watchful one eye of Karsten Dragos, who had an annoying habit of poking Axl in the ribs, hoping to provoke him into an attack.

Axl was tempted.

He was desperate for an outlet for all the rage that was surging through his body at Osbert and Lothar; especially Osbert, as everything that came out of Lothar's mouth generally originated in Osbert's conniving head.

'You know what happened to his first wife, of course,' Karsten crowed as soon as Lothar left the room with Haaron. 'She died giving birth to his son. Just a few months ago. Barely any time ago at all. Very sad,' Karsten said, looking anything but sad. 'The poor girl, she had no chance... being married to Jaeger. He has no self-control at all, you know.'

Axl was staring through the window, watching as rays of sun escaped the moody clouds that hovered over the busy harbour; as the merchants and their slaves hurried up and down the piers, transporting their goods to the markets. He didn't want to turn around. He knew Gant was there, with Osbert. He knew he needed to stay calm.

'His wife, Elissa, was close to my wife,' Karsten went on, smiling. 'Nicolene was there when she started bleeding all over the floor. Dying, right there in her chamber, the child trying to come too soon. Because he'd punched her,' Karsten said coldly. 'Right in the belly.'

A shiver streaked up Axl's spine, and his hands shook as he spun towards his tormentor. 'You talk a lot,' he said, gritting his teeth, glaring at Karsten's sour face. 'Is that because you don't want anyone to notice that my sister took your eye?'

Karsten lunged for Axl, grabbing him by the throat as Gant rushed in between them, shoving Karsten away. Karsten spat at Gant. 'Get away from me, old man!' he growled as Gant held his arms and forced him towards the other side of the room. 'Get the fuck away from me!'

Osbert watched in amusement from his chair by the fire, enjoying the torment in Axl's eyes, imagining the look on his sister's face when she found out who her new husband would be.

Gant glared Karsten down, both taller and stronger than the

one-eyed man. 'Your father wouldn't be pleased to come back in and find one of his prizes bleeding and broken, I'm sure,' he said forcefully. 'So perhaps you should get hold of your temper before he returns?'

Karsten was ready to smash his head into Gant's to break free of his hold, but Gant's words checked him, and he realised that he was, in fact, making a fool of himself. That would hardly impress his father.

Axl stood near the window, shaking with rage and fear in equal measure. They were all powerless to do anything but wait and hope that Jael would agree to Haaron's terms.

She had to.

He needed to get out of here and save Amma.

***

'You want us to release your brothers, all of your men, leave your island and go back home?' Jael asked incredulously. 'When we have claimed it for ourselves, destroyed your fleet, killed your men, and captured your brothers?' She eyed Haegen in amazement. 'And your father's terms are that we just give it all up for nothing?'

'Not for nothing,' Haegen sighed, turning irritably towards Jael, acknowledging her at last. 'You will, in return, have the Brekkan army released, which includes, of course, your uncle, the king.'

Jael smiled. 'And you're saying that without laughing?' She turned to Eadmund. 'These are not terms we can accept. Not to save Lothar.'

'They have Axl,' Aleksander reminded her.

'And who's to say that I'd give all of this up for him?' Jael growled, glaring at Haegen, ignoring Aleksander.

'You?' Now Haegen did laugh. 'It's up to *you*?' He looked at Eadmund.

'Yes,' Eadmund said plainly. 'It is, up to Jael, and myself. We rule together. She won this victory for us. She leads our forces. *She* will decide whether your offer is fair, so if I were you, I would look her way once in a while.'

Haegen swallowed, indignant.

Aleksander suppressed a grin.

'They've made an alliance, then? Haaron and Lothar?' Jael guessed.

Haegen inhaled sharply, revealing just what he thought of that. 'They have, yes. And as the islands are part of the alliance with Brekka, it follows that you are part of it as well.'

'And what is the purpose of this new alliance?' Eadmund wondered.

Haegen hesitated, so Aleksander stepped in. 'Haaron and Lothar will attack Helsabor together, with your men as well. A three-pronged attack. Hest and Brekka will broach his walls, and you'll destroy his fleet.'

Jael and Eadmund looked at each other. 'Helsabor?'

'And Amma is to be married to Jaeger Dragos,' Aleksander muttered.

Jael's eyes popped open in horror. 'Well, it seems that there has been much discussed in Hest,' she murmured, eyeing Haegen. 'But Lothar and Haaron becoming allies depends on whether we want to play their game, wouldn't you say?'

Aleksander fidgeted nervously. He knew that look.

'We have claimed a great victory here,' Eadmund said. 'Why should we give it up?'

'For your family, of course,' Haegen frowned at Jael. 'You can't tell me that you'd be happy to let them die at our hands? For Brekka to exist no more?'

'You think I care about any of them?' Jael lied, her eyes hard. 'I'd be more than happy for you to tip my uncle and cousin off a cliff. And as for my brother?' She shook her head. 'We've no real affection for each other, which Aleksander will attest to.'

Aleksander, put on the spot, nodded as convincingly as he could.

'Perhaps,' Haegen mused, looking far from convinced.

'We will need to discuss it,' Jael said sharply. 'You can go and see your brothers and let us speak to Aleksander.'

Haegen frowned, annoyed at being dismissed so abruptly, but he bit his tongue and nodded, leaving without another word.

Jael waited for Haegen to be far enough away, before hissing. 'We have to do something! Amma cannot marry Jaeger Dragos!'

CHAPTER THIRTY ONE

'What do you think she'll say?' Haaron croaked, reaching for his goblet, his throat still raw from all that evil smoke. 'If, indeed, she is the one who will say anything? Perhaps her husband has taken hold of her tongue, as he should.'

Lothar's very life was in Jael's hands.

She had all the power now.

He swallowed, almost sighing at the memory of the roast pork, which had been tender and moist, but not very plenty. 'Jael?' he attempted to sound casual, ignoring Osbert's fretful face. 'She will agree, of course. Why wouldn't she? We have an alliance with the islands. And you have her family.' He wondered at that, sticking his knife into a turnip. Honey roasted. Now he did sigh.

Osbert had no appetite. Although he was certainly hungry, he felt sick at the thought of Jael deciding their fate. She didn't really care for Axl, did she? Not enough to give up a great victory.

Not for nothing.

***

Jaeger could barely look Haegen in the eye.

'I don't imagine anyone could have held the fort against that fire,' Haegen whispered, trying to cheer up his brother.

'I'm sure Father won't agree,' Jaeger muttered morosely, his eyes turned towards his knees. His ankles, wrapped in torn pieces of blood-soaked cloth, oozed and throbbed where Jael Furyck had stabbed him. Just the thought of her and he was grinding his teeth together.

'I'm sure he won't,' Haegen smiled tightly. 'But the Tower looks much like this, and he was powerless to stop it.' He glanced over at Berard, who was happily chatting to a young man. 'And they've treated you well?'

'What do you think?'

'I think you must make a very annoying prisoner,' Haegen smiled, adjusting himself on the tiny stool he perched on before his miserable brother. 'Berard seems fine.'

'They're trying to get him to talk,' Jaeger growled.

'Talk?' Haegen looked confused. 'About what?'

Jaeger shook his head, easing the deep line between his eyebrows, waking himself up. He had barely thought of anything but the book since they'd made it back to Skorro. He needed to get it safely back to Hest.

Haegen's eyes drifted towards Aleksander who motioned him over. He stood up and smiled reassuringly at Jaeger. 'Well, just sit there quietly. Don't cause any trouble. We'll know your fate soon enough.' He left his grumbling brother behind, nodding at Berard, who looked up anxiously as Haegen passed, following Aleksander back to the chamber.

Jael and Eadmund stood next to each other, their faces unreadable as they waited for Aleksander to shut the door.

'We will not accept your offer,' Jael began. 'For us to leave Skorro with nothing is a bad deal. We *are* prepared to leave, to return your men and your brothers, but it will cost your father.'

'Cost?' Haegen frowned, his eyes darting to Eadmund, willing him to speak. 'Cost what?'

Jael smiled. 'Gold.'

***

'Well, you must keep trying,' Entorp insisted. 'Again. Tonight. That salve will work, but it is the gods who hold true power over your dreams, Edela. They alone will decide if Eadmund needs to be helped.'

'I agree,' Edela sighed. 'But what did I see last night? What happened to Tuura? Is that the prophecy? That Tuura will fall? Burn to the ground?'

Biddy was on her knees, laying a new fire. She sat back on her heels, brushing hair out of her eyes with the back of her hand, avoiding her soot-covered fingers. 'Well, if that is the prophecy, it doesn't sound as though Jael stopped anything from happening. Not from that dream. And where was Eadmund?' She felt anxious, desperately worried about everyone. It was hard not to know who was safe. Who would return.

Edela shook her head. 'I don't know,' she admitted. 'My dreams always seem to take place in the dark these days. It's hard to make anything out!'

There was a wry smile on her face now, and Biddy relaxed to see it. 'Well, it is a clue, perhaps?'

'But what does Evaine have to do with any of it, I wonder?' Entorp mused, leaning back in Eadmund's chair, more comfortable around them now.

'Or the Widow?' Edela wondered. 'She must be mixed up in it somewhere, don't you think?'

Entorp shuddered. 'Why do you say that? What do you know of her?'

Edela noticed the sudden change in him as he stiffened, his eyes blinking nervously. 'Of her? Very little, except by reputation, of course. The elders want to capture her, I believe. They must think she poses a serious threat to Tuura.'

Entorp shook his wild mop of hair, his eyes wandering far away from Edela. 'The Widow is dead, surely?' he almost whispered.

Biddy glanced at Edela. She too could tell that something had changed with Entorp.

'I should be going,' he mumbled, scrambling to his feet and heading for the door; not even bothering to grab his cloak. 'I shall come again tomorrow and see if the salve worked. Good day to you both.' Entorp almost tripped over the door frame as he hurried away, not looking back.

Biddy reached for her tinderbox, raising one eyebrow at Edela.

***

Haegen laughed. 'You don't know my father. He prefers to *acquire* gold, not give it away.'

'Not even for his sons?' Eadmund wondered.

Haegen's eyes revealed more about his father than any words would have done. They flickered for a moment, lost, like a small child waiting for a show of affection that never came. He inhaled sharply, remembering Berard and Jaeger. Prisoners. 'What amount of gold are you talking about, then?'

'One thousand pieces,' Jael said.

Haegen looked relieved.

'For each island,' Eadmund went on. 'And three thousand pieces for Oss.'

'My father expected you would ask for something, of course,' Haegen said carefully. 'However, one thousand pieces for each island?' He shook his head. 'That's far too much. He would never agree to it.'

'Well then, you'd better go back to Hest,' Jael said firmly. 'Find a way to *make* him agree to it. Deliver the gold, and we'll return your brothers.'

Haegen looked uncertain.

'Your father sits on a pile of gold bigger than anyone in Osterland, and you know it,' Jael said coolly. 'Perhaps the truth is, his sons are just dispensable. Those that don't bring him the victory he craves, at least. But surely he would like his island back, and his men?'

Haegen ran a hand over his salty lips. He wanted a drink. He wanted this done. He needed to get back to Irenna to see if there had been any word about her father. 'You can have the gold,' he said, at last, knowing that his father would spit and snarl but ultimately be pleased to have it resolved quickly.

There was more Haaron wanted to turn his attention to now.

***

Morana clamped down on the urge to scream as she sat in Varna's chamber, watching Meena tap her head. 'I don't see why you must hide me away like this,' she snapped. 'How can I do anything if I'm trapped in here?'

'And what is it that you plan on doing, exactly?' Varna wondered as she shuffled across the flagstones towards the fire, her toes clicking with every step.

Morana felt the tension in her shoulders as she sat, her eyes fixed on the irritating girl. 'There are other things we can try to find the book. Spells...'

Varna laughed loudly, her mouth wide open, almost toothless, as she eased herself down into her chair. 'Spells? You think that book can be found with *spells*?' She laughed again, so freely that Meena stopped tapping and stared at her in surprise. 'I didn't realise I'd bred such a fool!' Varna sneered. 'If that book could be found with spells, why did it stay hidden for hundreds of years? Hidden from even the gods themselves! From all of us who have spent our lives searching for it? Dreaming on it? But somehow *you* can find it now?' she snorted. 'With spells?'

'Well, how did *he* find it, then?' Morana spat, furious with her mother's mockery. 'How did Jaeger Dragos discover the book when no one else could?'

Varna frowned, disturbed by that very question. She truly had no idea. 'At this moment, how he got it is far less important than where he put it, wouldn't you say?'

'If it were me, I would not have left it behind,' Morana said, scratching her feral nest of hair.

'Exactly!' Varna smiled. 'Which is why it is essential he returns.'

Meena felt herself almost rise up from the bed, her hand frozen in mid-air, her heart thumping at the thought of Jaeger returning to Hest.

'Even though he wants to destroy your precious master?' Morana growled.

'My master is not Haaron Dragos,' Varna said firmly, 'as you well know. My master is the only master, the Father of Darkness. Our family has always guided the Dragos kings, hoping to find that book.'

'And now we have.'

'Almost.' Varna turned to stare at Meena whose wide eyes were bouncing back and forth, following the conversation. 'But in order to get that book away from the Bear, we are going to need to put our little Meena to work.'

***

'A wedding?' Bayla looked disgusted as she stood impatiently next to Haaron, watching Haegen's ship edging closer to the pier. 'He has only just burned his first wife!'

Haaron sighed. His wife's tongue had sharpened so much over the years that he wondered how he could feel any affection for her at all, which he did, of course; more than affection. His love for Bayla clouded his judgement, he knew, but he was imprisoned by the desire to please her in the faint hope that she would look at him as she once had. 'And now he will have another.'

'A Furyck,' Bayla sneered, her voice low and grating. 'Our people will not take to her.'

'Her father tells me that she is a very pretty, amenable sort of girl,' Haaron murmured. 'Furyck or not, they will take to someone worth looking at. Someone they can grow to admire. Hopefully, her husband will feel the same... in time.' He frowned, irritated by the thought of bringing Jaeger back, but what choice did he have? He needed Skorro, and Lothar's plan for taking Helsabor was too tempting to turn away from.

Bayla glanced at Haaron. She didn't really care what deals he had to make, what alliances he needed to forge to protect their family. If they could bring Jaeger home, she would happily endure his miserable sulking at the prospect of being married to a Furyck.

Anything to bring him home.

***

Jael eyed Jaeger with a frown.

He glared back at her, defiantly.

'I'm not going to miss that angry piece of shit,' Thorgils mumbled beside her, his stomach growling.

Food was becoming an issue with so many mouths to feed. The fort had been well-stocked, but that was before nearly six hundred Islanders descended upon it.

Jael was hopeful that Haegen would return with the gold

quickly. She was as desperate to get off the island as everyone else. She wanted to see Eydis, to take her home to Oss, to talk to her grandmother about getting rid of Evaine. But first, they needed to exchange prisoners and gold.

And suffer through a wedding.

'Mmmm,' Jael agreed. 'He looks ready to kill someone, doesn't he? Maybe that's what being the fourth son does to you?'

'His brother's nice enough,' Thorgils decided, nodding at Berard, who was chatting to Torstan. 'Perhaps he was conceived while Haaron was away?'

Jael laughed, turning to him. 'Let's walk down to the ships.'

Thorgils was instantly intrigued, so he ignored the roar of his empty stomach and lumbered after her.

Evening was settling over Skorro, a thick mist creeping across the sea towards them as Jael led Thorgils down the beach. 'When the gold comes,' she said quietly, 'we'll send the lords back to their islands. The gold should keep them happy, for a while at least. I want you to lead the rest of the ships back to Oss with our gold.'

Thorgils looked ready to protest, his eyebrows almost meeting in consternation.

'I don't know what Ivaar plans to do,' Jael said calmly, ignoring his busy eyebrows. 'I don't know how loyal those lords truly are, or what plans they may make without us there. So I need to know that Oss will be safe. And I need you to make it so. There's no one else for me to trust. Not anymore. Just you and Fyn.'

'What about Eadmund?'

Jael looked around, but there was no one about. 'That's not Eadmund.'

Thorgils nodded, his shoulders drooping. 'No, that's not Eadmund.'

'When we get back to Oss, we'll have to find a way to stop that girl, without losing Eadmund. But until then, we can't trust him.'

'Agreed.'

'And we certainly can't trust Ivaar, or Haaron, or Lothar, or any of the lords.'

'No.'

'But we can trust each other,' Jael insisted. 'So you need to get the gold back to Oss and hide it. Take Ivaar's share too. Bury it at Fyn's old hut, then secure the fort. Prepare to be attacked. We don't know what Ivaar is planning, but I'll send most of the ships back with you. We'll keep *Sea Bear* and *Ice Breaker*.'

'What if you're walking into a trap? Don't you want to take more men to Hest?'

Jael shook her head. 'Aleksander didn't seem to think so. He would've warned me if he thought there was a risk, I'm sure. But, if I am, you can come and rescue me!'

Thorgils laughed. 'I may, for a price.'

'How about some gold?'

'Well, now that you mention it, I may be taking on a family of five soon, if Eadmund has his way and kills Ivaar, so it could come in handy.'

'I'm sure Odda would love the company! Not sure how you'll handle that little howler, Mads, though.'

Thorgils sighed wistfully at the thought of such a noisy fate. 'Ahhh, I have my ways...'

***

They sat together, eating in a companionable silence. The children had finished their supper and were now rolling around on the furs, playing and arguing with each other; ready for bed soon, Isaura was sure.

Ayla watched them sadly, wistful for the children she had planned to have with Bruno before Ivaar had captured them both. She pushed a salted herring around her plate, distracted, her appetite gone.

'You're sure he will return? Soon?' Isaura asked. 'You've seen that?'

Ayla nodded. 'Perhaps tomorrow.'

'Does that mean they won or lost the battle?' Isaura wondered anxiously. More than fearing Ivaar's return, she was worried about Thorgils.

'Ivaar is alone,' Ayla murmured. 'Just him and his men. I didn't see anyone else coming.'

Isaura sighed, pushing her plate away, and picking up the jug of wine, she refilled their cups. 'I wish he wasn't coming at all,' she whispered hoarsely.

'He is not the king,' Ayla said. 'If he were the king, he would not be coming here. He is running.'

Isaura turned towards a screeching Mads who was trying to bite Selene, watching as one of the servants hurried to grab him. 'Do you think that's because he killed Eirik? *Do* you think he killed Eirik?'

Ayla felt muddled. Ivaar's absence had given her a glimpse of the life she'd once had; the freedom she had enjoyed. But without Bruno, it had felt empty. And now, Ivaar returning without his desired crown? That would surely mean bad things for them both. 'I don't know,' she admitted. 'He is anxious and angry, I feel that, and running, yes. Perhaps he did... but it would make no sense unless he had the island lords on his side.'

'If only we could leave before he gets here,' Isaura smiled sadly. 'It's been so pleasant without him. I can't face him coming back.'

'There's nothing we can do,' Ayla said blankly. 'We're both prisoners here. And only Ivaar will decide our fate.'

***

Fyn had become so friendly with Berard that he'd managed to wheedle the location of a hidden stash of ale out of him.

He was now the most popular man on the island, and Jael smiled as she watched him getting drunker and drunker as men lined up to share a cup with him. He was becoming more confident, but every now and then he would turn to her or Thorgils with a hint of anxiety in his eyes. They were watching him, though. They wouldn't let anyone hurt him.

Berard had been rewarded with unlimited ale himself, and he'd relaxed considerably, Jael noticed, as he sat there, smiling in front of her, barely aware of the fact that he was still bound to a chair.

'Your brother over there,' she started. 'Is he really as mad as he looks?'

Berard laughed drunkenly, peering over at Jaeger who was doing his best to ignore everyone. There was no ale for him. 'Jaeger is...' he sighed. 'Yes, he is angry but...'

'But?' Jael sat forward.

'But he cannot help it, you see,' Berard went on, suddenly very earnest. 'Our father has never liked him. He's always treated him badly, so I don't blame Jaeger for his anger. He has no choice but to be that way.'

Jael smiled. 'Your father must like you, though?'

Now Berard really did laugh, causing Jaeger's head to snap around furiously. Berard didn't notice. 'No, I don't think so.' He shook his head, chuckling to himself. 'But I'm no threat to him. I'm nothing in his eyes, neither good nor bad. The others... well, they all have ambitions, I suppose.'

'And you have none?'

Berard narrowed his eyes, trying to wind his way through the fuzz inside his head. 'Well, I wouldn't say I have none,' he murmured carefully. 'But I'm less... obvious about any ambitions I might harbour.'

'Sounds smart.' Jael topped up Berard's cup, raising it to his lips. He smiled gratefully, taking a long drink. 'Your father and my uncle have made an alliance. They're going to marry your brother to my cousin.'

Berard spat his ale straight back out.

Jael blinked in surprise. She put down the cup and wiped the ale out of her eyes.

Berard hurried to gather his thoughts. 'I'm sorry,' he apologised. 'It's just that... I was not expecting such a thing. My father, the Dragos family... we have always hated Brekka.'

'Yes, you have, and the feeling has been entirely mutual,' Jael assured him.

'And Jaeger especially,' Berard stumbled on. 'His wife...' He shook his head. 'She's only just died, in childbirth. He is still grieving for her.'

'Oh.' Jael frowned. 'And was he a good husband?'

Berard's eyes dropped to the ground. He could feel Jaeger staring at him, and his tongue tied itself in knots. 'I, ahhh, yes, I, ahhh, he loved her very much, I'm sure,' he said quickly.

Jael nodded. She didn't need to hear any more.

***

Edela stood within the flames, watching Tuura burn again.

But it was different.

Mothers and fathers ran, clutching sobbing children to their chests as the fire spread from hay bales to thatched roofs, spitting flames into the dark sky. Horses burst out of stables, chasing terrified sheep and bleating goats down the main street.

It was not the Tuura Edela knew, though. There were no towering walls or gates, no decaying houses. She frowned, confused, lifting her eyes to the temple as it stood, apart from everything, untouched; its elders and dreamers rushing around, hurrying to gather water with which to hold off any threat to the sacred building.

They were far away, but Edela could hear their anxious voices, raised in fear.

'What do those girls want?' one elderly woman cried, dressed in the long grey robes the elders wore. 'To destroy their own people? To destroy their home? They are Tuuran! How could they do this?'

'They want revenge upon us all,' another elder sighed, watching the people flee, desperate to run himself, but resigned to the fate that protecting the temple was his sworn duty.

The elderman walked forward, staring into the distance as a band of warriors rode out of the gates. 'They are in the thrall of the book,' he said. 'Their souls have been corrupted. But we know where they are now. We will capture them. We will punish them, and destroy that evil book, once and for all.'

Edela blinked as the temple faded into the night, flames rising, devouring everything before her. She sighed, desperate to turn away from the vision, eager to wake.

'But they didn't, did they, Edela?' came the crowing voice, winding itself into the dark flames. 'They didn't destroy the book. And now it has been found.'

***

The fire in the brazier gave off little heat, but it was better than nothing, Jael thought as she held her hands to the meagre flames. Her mind was busy with thoughts of Amma. She had never been close to her cousin, but she was desperate to think of a way to save her from Jaeger Dragos' bed. That was a punishment she was not prepared for anyone in her family to suffer. Jael shook her head, frustrated. She didn't see what they could do. Not yet. 'Are you alright?' she asked, turning to Eadmund who sat on the edge of his bed, staring at his hands. He'd barely spoken to her since Aleksander and Haegen had left.

Eadmund looked up. 'I don't think so.'

Jael walked over and sat down next to him. 'Are you thinking about your father?'

'Of course, and Ivaar, and you, and Hest, and my son. Everything. But it's different,' he sighed, dropping his head to his hands. 'I don't feel anything. Not as I used to. It's confusing.' He looked up again, shaking his head. 'I feel so strange.'

'It's been a hard few days,' Jael said gently. 'You can't expect to feel right. It will take time. My father has been dead for three years now, and I still don't feel right. Nothing feels as it should without him.'

Eadmund turned to her, staring into her eyes as though she were a complete stranger; surprised that she was even there.

Jael shivered. She didn't know what to say.

'I know how I'm supposed to feel,' Eadmund said blankly, turning his eyes away from her, towards the flames. 'Sad, in love, angry. And perhaps I think I feel these things, or I act as though I do, but really, I don't. I don't feel a thing. And I want to.' He frowned, reaching out to touch her hand. 'I want to feel something. I don't want to sit here, trapped on this island, in this black hole, waiting for gold. I want to go home,' he sighed. 'I need to take care of Eydis.'

Jael put her hand over his. Eadmund was right; he wasn't there at all. 'You will. We will. Soon,' she smiled. 'And when we get back to Oss, everything will be different. You'll feel more like yourself again. Edela will help. I know she will.'

Reaching up, Jael kissed him on the cheek. Eadmund frowned, confused, unsure whether he wanted more or not.

'Just close your eyes,' Jael said softly. 'Lie down, and get some sleep. In a few days, we'll be sailing for Oss. And everything will be better once we get home, I promise.'

CHAPTER THIRTY TWO

'Any luck?' Biddy wondered as Edela padded out of bed, eager for the warmth of the fire, her eyes barely open.

Edela shook her head. 'No,' she croaked. 'No sign of that symbol. But I did have another dream about Tuura.'

Biddy stirred the porridge before picking up a cup of mint tea she'd been steeping. 'Here,' she smiled. 'It might still be warm.'

Edela sat down, taking the cup, sipping slowly. 'Mmmm, it is, thank you.' She patted Ido, who had come to say hello, and grimaced, easing herself down into the chair, trying to ignore the aches and pains in her old bones. Now was not the time to feel weary and weak.

'What are you being shown about Tuura now?' Biddy wondered as she left the cauldron and drew a stool towards Edela, reaching for her own cup of tea.

Edela frowned, trying to piece together her thoughts. 'Fire again. Tuura was on fire, but it looked very different. It was another time.' She closed her eyes, trying to return to the dream. 'The book!' she exclaimed, her eyes popping open. 'They talked about the girls being in the thrall of the book. As though they did it. Burned Tuura for revenge.'

Biddy looked confused. 'The girls you dreamed about? The beheaded ones?'

'Yes.'

'Which, I suppose, explains why they were beheaded.'

'It does.'

'But not why they burned Tuura in the first place.'

'No, nor what happened to the one who escaped with the book.'

Biddy got up, grabbing a fur from Edela's bed. 'Here, it isn't warm this morning.'

'Thank you,' Edela smiled, lifting her arms so Biddy could tuck her in.

Biddy stirred the cauldron again, then stopped and turned to Edela. 'What if she's the Widow?'

'The girl who escaped?'

'Yes.'

Edela shook her head. 'I don't think so. The Tuura I saw in my dreams is from long ago. Hundreds of years ago, perhaps.'

Biddy crept towards her, her eyes wide with possibilities. 'But no one knows the truth about her, do they? How she could be so old, yet still live? What if the book had a spell that made her live that long? What if she just disappeared with the book? Hid away, became the Widow?'

Edela rested the cup on her knee, thoughtful, listening to the fire and the soft sucking of the simmering porridge. 'That's an entirely plausible idea!' she said at last. 'Perhaps we need to pay a visit to Entorp after breakfast?'

Biddy smiled, quickly reaching for a bowl.

***

Haaron held his tongue as he watched the chests of gold being loaded onto Haegen's ship. It was for the best, he tried to convince himself; a mere drop in the ocean of the real prize he would claim when they conquered Helsabor with the Furycks.

But still, handing his gold to the Islanders made his blood boil.

Bayla stood next to him, smiling. 'You're doing the right thing,' she insisted. 'Putting your family first, our kingdom first. As you should.'

Haaron ignored her and turned to watch Lothar Furyck, further down the pier, giving final instructions to Rexon Boas who was heading to Saala to bring back Jaeger's bride. He smiled to himself. There was at least some pleasure to be found in that arrangement.

Rexon nodded, wishing that Lothar would stop talking so they could get underway. The men were at the oars, shoulders tense, eyes on the Brekkan king who continued to mumble away in Rexon's ear. 'Yes, lord,' he said again.

'Gisila is my queen, *your* queen, so you must make her feel at ease. She will want to see her son, and her daughter, of course, so don't forget to mention that they will both be here waiting for her,' he muttered. 'And don't forget to get the Skalleson girl too!'

Rexon nodded again. 'Of course, my lord.' His eyes wandered towards the helmsman, who looked even more impatient than everyone else. He was sailing with a full crew of Hestians, in one of Haaron's few remaining warships. Rexon was not looking forward to the journey, but at least he was going to be left behind in Saala, which was a relief. He was desperate to get word to his wife.

'I shall let you go, then,' Lothar said, at last, standing back, leaving Rexon to clamber into the ship. 'Do remember to reassure my wife and daughter that all is well. There is nothing to worry about! They will be perfectly safe!'

Rexon turned towards the man on the pier, who unhooked the rope and hurried to jump into the ship before the oarsmen could gain much purchase.

Lothar smiled tightly, watching the ship ease away. He would not feel right until he had Gisila in his bed again, and certainly not safe until Amma belonged to Jaeger Dragos and their families were united in peace. Sighing, he turned towards his host, sweat beading along his upper lip.

It was a warm place, this Hest, but for all that Lothar was enamoured with the size of Haaron's castle and his obvious wealth, he felt uneasy. He wanted to return to Brekka, to his throne in Andala.

He longed to feel like a king again.

***

Axl watched from a first-floor window as Rexon sailed away to get Amma; as Aleksander stood on one of Haegen Dragos' ships waiting to head back to Skorro with the gold. He curled his hands into fists, desperate to scream or punch the brutal stone wall of the chamber they remained imprisoned in.

His shoulders slumped. He was supposed to protect Amma, yet here he was, watching as everyone conspired to marry her to a monster; unable to do anything to stop them.

Osbert lay on the bed opposite the window, his eyes closed, but no doubt that was just for show.

'There's nothing you can do,' Gant murmured, joining Axl at the window. 'If you can accept that, then you can move forward. Act when you need to.' His voice was low, his eyes on Osbert.

'It's not an easy thing to accept.'

'No,' Gant agreed. 'But to help her, you need a clear head and an empty heart.'

They were alone in the locked chamber, just Gant, Axl, and Osbert.

Waiting.

Axl frowned. 'An empty heart?' he mumbled. 'What does that mean?'

'The best kind of decisions are the ones you make up here,' Gant whispered, tapping Axl's head. 'Not here,' he said, pointing to his heart. 'But it is far easier to say than do, of course.'

Axl sighed, turning away.

Osbert rolled over, groaning at the pain in his arms, but happy at the thought of Axl's misery, and Amma's, which was yet to come. And then there was the dream of Helsabor and all that land. He smiled, remembering that Wulf Halvardar was rumoured to have a particularly beautiful granddaughter.

Perhaps his father wasn't such a fool after all?

***

'You need to tell us what you know of her,' Edela demanded. 'I'm dreaming of this for a reason. The Widow is involved in it, somehow, I'm certain now. Certain too, that you know more than you've said. Do you think she has the book?' Edela went on. 'It must be the only way she has lived this long, surely?'

Entorp spluttered under her attack, tipping a cup of fresh milk over his knees. He put his cup on the table, hurrying away to look for a cloth.

'Do you know her?' Edela continued, her eyes following him. 'Have you met her?'

Entorp sighed. He dabbed his trousers with the cloth and returned to the fire, accepting that he was not going to escape Edela's questions, nor evade Biddy's determined eyes.

It was, perhaps, best to face everything head on.

'No, I have not, and no, I do not,' Entorp said quietly. He bit his lip, his head bobbing nervously as he wobbled on his stool. 'What I know of the Widow... is that she is evil. She is pure darkness, absent of any light. Without a soul. Timeless. Ageless. All-seeing. She lives in the shadows, strikes down those who would wish to control or kill her. She is powerful beyond any words.'

Edela's eyes were wide. 'But perhaps not always that way?' she suggested. 'Perhaps the evil of the book corrupted her? If she is, in fact, the girl I saw in my dreams? That girl was lovely and innocent once.'

Entorp looked unconvinced. 'I couldn't say,' he said, jumping at a sudden clap of thunder overhead. He looked up at the smoke hole as rain started falling. 'I'm not familiar with who she was. I only know the stories of who she became.'

'How?' Biddy wondered, pulling her stool closer as the rain grew heavy and loud.

'My wife,' Entorp said, at last, his body aching with the pain of digging up such deeply buried memories. 'She belonged to The Following.'

***

Irenna had finally received word from Silura that her father had survived and she was in a far calmer state as she walked through the hall beside Bayla and Nicolene, her two-year-old daughter, Halla, smiling on her hip.

'We are going to have to work fast,' Bayla was muttering to Nicolene. 'The girl will have nothing suitable to wear. Her father says she is about your size, so you will find one of your dresses for her to wear.'

Irenna tried to suppress a smile as she glanced at Nicolene's indignant face.

'And make it your best dress!' Bayla snapped, quickly cutting across any argument Nicolene had been preparing. 'And you,' she went on, turning to her least annoying daughter-in-law. 'You will see to the flowers and musicians.' Bayla flapped her hands as she walked. 'There are so many flowers around at this time of year. But try to make it as tasteful as possible,' she warned. 'Nothing too bright and hideous.' She stopped, inhaling the scent of warm bread wafting from the kitchen. 'And I shall see to the food and wine. It will not be a large wedding as there is little time to invite anyone from the Fire Lands.' She frowned. 'Come to think of it, I don't imagine your father would be eager to return this way after the disaster he was led into on the Adrano.'

Irenna inhaled sharply, not wanting the reminder.

'But what about Jaeger?' Nicolene wondered coyly. 'He's hardly going to be pleased with the idea of a wedding, is he? Not so soon after Elissa.'

Bayla looked cross. 'Jaeger's father is paying ten thousand pieces of gold to bring him back, after he was responsible for the loss of our fleet and all of those men. I hardly think he's in a position to argue about anything that's been planned, do you?'

Nicolene shrugged herself away from Bayla's harsh blue eyes.

'Besides,' Bayla went on, working hard to convince herself more than her daughter-in-law, 'it will be good for him. He needs sons. Even if they are to be half Furyck. At least this time he will be marrying someone with royal blood.'

Irenna was only half listening as she tickled Halla under her chubby chin. Her mind had wandered to Haegen and what sort of battle he was going to have, trying to convince Jaeger of that.

***

Entorp had their attention, but he was suddenly reluctant to go any further.

'What is The Following?' Biddy wondered, inclining her head.

Entorp stalled, pulling on his wild beard, wondering suddenly where he had last seen his comb. 'It is an old sect. A hidden society that started in Tuura long ago.'

Edela frowned. She had never heard of such a thing. 'And what do they do, this Following?' She shivered as thunder boomed again, closer this time, rattling the door of Entorp's little house.

'They come from the time of Raemus,' Entorp said quietly. 'The First God, he who was made from the Darkness. They were his followers. The ones he entrusted with his magical secrets. The ones he entrusted with his book.' The fire spat angrily, and Entorp picked up his iron poker, nudging the logs. 'I'm sure you know the story of Raemus. Of how he wanted a return to the Darkness, to a time when it was just him and his wife, Daala. But she had brought light and life into the world. She would not return to a place of such bleak emptiness, so she refused. But Raemus would not give up, so he wrote the book as a way of destroying the world, and ending all life as we know it. He enlisted people to help him. Tuurans. Of course, we were all Tuurans once in this land,' he smiled wistfully.

'But I've never understood why those people chose to help him? If it meant that they would ultimately die and just exist in a world of darkness?' Biddy wondered. 'Did they not know what they were doing?'

'I'm certain they did,' Entorp said firmly. 'They believed that he would provide them with a new way of being. That he would set their souls free. Give them freedom from the pain of life. They wanted immortality, to exist as a god, so they took his teaching, and they practised the darkest magic, destroying all around them. Destroying Tuura.'

'But Daala stopped it. She killed Raemus, and the book was lost,' Edela insisted.

'She did, of course,' Entorp said thoughtfully. 'But The Following survived and spread throughout the ages, especially when the Furycks came from Osterhaaven and tore Tuura apart, bringing their own gods, taking our land. They flourished in secret, working in the shadows as they tried to find the book again, to bring back the Darkness that Raemus had so desperately sought. They believed they would find him there, waiting for them.'

'In my dreams, a man gave the book to one of the girls,' Edela said. 'Who do you think that was?'

Entorp shook his head. 'I don't know. Perhaps he was a god? Who else would have possession of it?' He frowned. 'If that book had surfaced again it would explain the destruction you saw in your dreams. The book has a way of claiming souls.'

'And the Widow?' Biddy wondered. 'Was *she* in The Following? Is that how you know of her?'

'No, my wife told me about her. About the things she would do. She was banished from Tuura, hundreds of years ago, but she lived, turning up all over the land, hiding from all but those in dire need of her particular type of services. She would appear, for a price, my wife said. She was not part of The Following, though. They did not claim her as one of their own. They thought she had the book, which is why they were so determined to find her.'

Edela frowned, remembering how Marcus, the Elderman of Tuura, had sent those men after Aleksander because he had visited the Widow; because his mother had, and her mother before her. She shuddered.

'And what about your wife?' Biddy asked delicately. 'Did she believe in Raemus and the book? Did she want a return to the Darkness?'

Entorp shook his head. 'No, never,' he murmured, his heart aching with loss, remembering the woman he had loved so many years ago. 'No, she was not a true believer... which is why they killed her.'

***

Eydis sat on the bench, stroking the cat who had soothed her with his visits; his sleek, warm fur so gentle to touch. The repetitive motion of brushing her hand across that smooth little body had calmed her when she felt ready to cry; when she felt as though there was no hope. But there was, she knew. She had found Jael and Eadmund in her dreams, and they were both still alive.

Amma sat next to her, silent, as she had been since Eydis had revealed her dream. Gisila had tried to encourage her to take a walk along the beach, but Amma had refused, content instead to sit on the bench with Eydis and wait for word.

Any word.

'Someone is coming for us,' Eydis said suddenly, confident in her vision at last. 'They will take us to Jael and Eadmund. We'll all be together again.'

Amma blinked. 'You saw this?'

Eydis nodded, smiling for the first time in days. 'They are waiting for us.'

'And you saw no one else?' Amma asked, grabbing Eydis' arm.

'I saw your father,' Eydis said carefully. 'He was there. And your brother.'

'But not Axl?'

Eydis shook her head. 'That doesn't mean he wasn't there. We were arriving on a ship. There were many people there to greet us.'

'On a ship?' Amma swallowed. 'To where?'

***

'But why?' Edela wondered. 'If she was a member of The Following, why was she killed by them?'

Entorp sighed. 'You are born into The Following,' he explained. 'It is not a choice. They trust no one. They allow no one in but those who marry Followers, and even then, we are all considered very carefully before a marriage is approved.' He stopped. The rain had become so loud that it had started to drown him out.

'My wife, Isobel, was no believer. She was hesitant to involve me in it, but I insisted. I loved her. I wanted to keep her safe.' His eyes burned with tears that had not come for many years. 'She was a dreamer, as many in The Following are. She saw things, heard things that made her uncomfortable.' He swallowed. 'One day, she told me that we were in danger. To this day, I still don't know why. She said that we had to leave immediately, that very night. So I hurried to organise more horses. We had two children, you see. A boy and a girl. We had only one horse, but I wanted four. It took some time. And then there were supplies, weapons, food...' The memories were sharp with pain now. Entorp didn't want to say any more. 'I was gone for much of the day, and when I returned to our house... they were dead,' he said slowly, tears filling his eyes. 'All three of them.'

Biddy and Edela gasped in unison. Biddy reached out, placing a hand on Entorp's shaking arm.

'It was them, The Following,' he croaked, trying to clear his throat. 'Isobel knew something. She must have found something out they didn't want anyone else to know.' He shook his head.

'But you stayed?' Edela asked.

'I was hoping they would kill me too,' Entorp whispered, not meeting her eyes. 'I didn't want to go on after that. I was all alone.'

No one spoke.

The rain dripped continuously down the smoke hole, the flames suffering under its onslaught.

Edela had so many questions, but it was not the time to ask them, she knew.

Not now.

***

Ayla froze as the door creaked open.

She had been half asleep, thinking about Bruno, lost in memories of when they had first met.

'Hello, Ayla,' Ivaar growled, striding towards the bed.

She swallowed, sitting up, backing away into the headboard, fearful. 'I was not expecting you to return,' she lied. 'Not for some time.'

'No?' Ivaar grabbed her thick dark curls, yanking her head towards him. 'No?' he asked again through gritted teeth, his eyes glinting sharply in the hint of fire that was still burning. 'And why is that, Ayla? Perhaps you're no dreamer at all? Perhaps you're of no use to me anymore?'

He reeked of smoke, of ale, of the sea. Ayla shook, fearing what would come next.

'You saw that my father is dead?' he spat, pushing her back onto the pillow. 'Saw that Eadmund and Jael are king and queen now?'

Ayla's eyes widened in terror. She tried to think as he brought his furious face down towards her. 'I did, yes. I saw that it would take some time to defeat them. But that you stood a good chance, with the... with the lords on your side.'

Ivaar yelled, smacking his hand against the carved wooden headboard behind her, Ayla flinching beneath him. 'You think the lords will support me now? *Now*? After the victory that scheming bitch earned them? *Now*?' He glared at her. 'No, Ayla, you're going to have to put your beautiful head to work on a new plan because I'm nowhere near that throne. *Nowhere!*' he screamed. 'And you,' he breathed heavily, leaning over her. 'You are nowhere near having your husband back.'

Ayla turned her head as Ivaar fumbled under his tunic, yanking down his trousers. She gulped, closing her eyes as he bent over her, scowling, his hand under her nightdress. She wanted to cry as he groaned and grunted, pushing himself inside her, hard, painfully, not stopping. She blinked, trying to go back to her dream of Bruno, where she had felt safe.

And free.

CHAPTER THIRTY THREE

'They seem pleased enough,' Eadmund smiled at his wife.

It was not a real smile, Jael thought sadly. Only his lips moved. His eyes remained lifeless. 'Well, it's hard not to be happy with a chest full of gold.'

'Or three,' Thorgils grinned, watching the men load heavy iron chests filled with gold pieces onto the ships as they readied for their departure. 'Though I'm still not convinced I should leave you to go to Hest on your own.'

Eadmund turned away from the shore, wondering what else there was to do before they left. 'You're more use on Oss, and at least this way you won't have to sit through a tedious wedding, listening to Lothar Furyck bleating on again.'

'Thinking about your own wedding, are you?' Thorgils laughed. 'I seem to remember you sleeping through most of it!'

'I found some arrows!' Fyn announced, coming towards them carrying four bushels of arrows in his arms.

'I'll take those!' Jael said happily. Despite what she might have said, she felt uneasy sailing into Hest. Aleksander hadn't seemed worried, but she was a queen now, responsible for more than her own life. It was important to know that Oss was safe, especially with Ivaar disappearing, but at the same time, she couldn't trust Lothar or Haaron. Whatever plans they were making, she knew that they would have little regard for her or Eadmund, especially once Jaeger and Berard were returned. 'Where did you find them?'

'In the kitchen,' Fyn said triumphantly. 'I was looking around for food. They were hidden in a pantry.'

'They do smell a little cheesy,' Thorgils said, sniffing the arrows as Fyn handed them to Jael. 'And did you find any food, perhaps? That would come in handy.'

'Well...' Fyn dodged Thorgils' eager eyes.

Jael laughed. 'It's alright. We're going to a wedding feast. There'll be enough food for us, I'm sure, but poor Thorgils, here, might starve on his journey home!'

'It's true,' Thorgils insisted. 'I do require more food than most, me being an extraordinarily large man.'

'Ha!' Eadmund snorted. 'I think it's just your head that's large. The rest of you looks a little puny to me.'

Thorgils was happy to see Eadmund come to life for a moment. He slapped his friend on the back. 'Envy is not an attractive quality in a king. Just look at all the trouble Lothar Furyck has gotten us into!'

'The gold is loaded now,' Haegen Dragos said impatiently as he walked back to the smiling Osslanders. 'My men are on board, and we're ready to depart for Hest.' He turned his attention to Jael and Eadmund. 'My father will be expecting us to arrive in good time.'

'Well, off you go, then,' Jael smiled. 'Don't let us stop you.'

Haegen bit his teeth together. 'It's best you follow us, so I know my brothers are right behind me. That you're not just going to leave.'

'Well, if you insist,' Jael said airily. 'We just need to secure them onto our ships, and we'll be on our way.'

Haegen frowned, but he nodded and turned to leave, motioning to Aleksander.

Aleksander looked reluctant to follow him.

'You're still my prisoner,' Haegen reminded him. 'Until my brothers are back in Hest, you're with me.'

Aleksander sighed, not wanting to endure another journey in Haegen's dour company. He gave Jael half a smile as he turned to follow him. 'Safe travels.'

'And you,' she said intently, watching him go. For all her light-heartedness, not one part of Jael was taking this lightly. She did not feel safe. 'Lock down the fort when you get home,' she said quietly to Thorgils. 'Put archers on the walls, man the towers at each end of the island. Prepare for an attack. Run drills. Keep everyone alert. Send out warnings to anyone who wants to return to the fort for protection.'

Thorgils nodded. 'I will.'

'And get the ships around to Tatti's Bay,' Eadmund added. 'Don't leave them out for Ivaar to burn if he should try to attack.'

'Make arrows too,' Jael said. 'We need more of those.'

'Alright, alright!' Thorgils laughed, holding up a hand. 'I'll defend the island, you don't need to worry! Just come home safely.'

Jael frowned. She didn't feel so confident.

'You needn't worry,' Thorgils promised again.

'Talk to Edela,' Jael said suddenly. 'She'll see what's coming. She can help you.'

Thorgils nodded patiently, wrapping an arm around Fyn's shoulder, edging him away from his anxious king and queen. 'Now, come and show me where that food is, young Fyn. I've a mind to take a nice little basket with me!' He smiled broadly, disappearing back into the fort, which was eerily quiet now that the Islanders had cleared out.

Haegen was taking most of Skorro's garrison back to Hest. His father would need to send shiploads of men over to repair and restore the fort before it was habitable again.

Morac had waited for his son to leave before approaching Eadmund himself. 'My lord,' he began quietly. 'I think that perhaps I should go back with Thorgils. It will help him to have an experienced head around the place. There will be a lot for him to do. He will need assistance.'

Jael winced at Morac's subservient tone, but she didn't interrupt. They would have to find a way to rule together, and it would not work if the only opinions were hers, no matter how much she disliked the pointy-faced man.

She bit her tongue.

'That sounds sensible,' Eadmund said carefully, avoiding his wife's arched eyebrows. 'But just remember that Thorgils is in charge, so help him, but only at his invitation.'

'Of course, certainly. I wish you a profitable time in Hest, my lord, my lady.' Morac tried not to frown as he nodded to them both and slipped away.

Jael waited for a heartbeat before turning back to the fort. She swallowed all the things she was desperate to say, ignored the growl of her temper as it threatened to burst forth, and instead tapped *Toothpick*, sighing. 'Time we got those prisoners of ours on board, don't you think?' And without looking back, she walked through the gates, ignoring the sick feeling in her stomach that was growing bigger by the day.

***

Gisila was waiting, watching as Rexon jumped out of the ship, into the water. She hurried across the sand, her hands shaking, her heart tied in knots of hope and fear.

Rexon blinked as he waded towards his queen, trying to look more reassuring than he felt. He did not trust Lothar, and the idea that he was to send Gisila, Amma, and Eydis Skalleson back to Hest did not sit well with him at all.

'Rexon,' Gisila breathed, grabbing his forearms as he stopped before her. 'Tell me, how is everyone?' Her rich brown eyes flickered in desperation.

'Fine,' Rexon assured her quickly. 'They're all fine, Gisila.'

'*All* of them?' she asked, swallowing. 'Even Lothar?'

Rexon opened his mouth, closing it quickly as the Hestians

came behind him, pulling the ship onto the beach.

'Where are your men?' Gisila wondered suddenly, noticing the strangers and their strange ship. 'Where's Lothar?'

'He has sent for you,' Rexon began. 'You and the girls. The ship is to take you back to Hest.'

Gisila looked confused. 'Hest? Why?'

Rexon took her hand, slipping it through his arm. 'Come, I could do with a drink and something to eat. A fire wouldn't go amiss either. I will tell you everything on the way.' He felt unsettled as he led her across the windswept sand. He kept thinking of Ranuf.

Ranuf Furyck would never have sent his wife to Hest.

***

Runa was desperate for word of Fyn. Desperate for something to change. She had crept around the house for days, trying to avoid Evaine; going out, just wandering around the fort, trying to avoid Evaine. She had barely slept, her appetite had gone, and despite the fact that her arms had stopped aching, she felt in pain and was barely able to breathe as anxiety exhausted her body and mind.

'Runa!' Edela smiled, stopping in front of the hall steps where Runa stood, looking thoroughly lost. 'Are you alright?'

Runa's tense face creased into a weary smile, and she felt her body loosen its grip on her ever so slightly. 'Yes,' she sighed, 'I am. It's just not easy living with that girl.' She glanced around nervously. 'She's always there, watching me, saying things, threatening me somehow, without ever really saying anything at all.'

Edela frowned. 'I'm sorry to hear that. I wish I knew how to make it easier for you but I don't think that leaving would help, would it?'

Runa shook her head. She had, of course, considered it. 'I wouldn't want to leave the baby in her care, nor poor Tanja, who is more terrified than me.'

'Jael and Eadmund will return soon,' Edela promised. She shook her head, momentarily surprised by the certainty of that feeling; catching herself before she said anything more, especially about Eirik Skalleson. She didn't want that getting back to Evaine.

'And Fyn?' Runa asked urgently. 'My son?'

'I don't know,' Edela admitted, stepping to one side as a band of red-faced children came hurtling past, chasing each other with sticks. 'I'm sorry, but hopefully, you'll hear something soon. And when your son is back, it will be easier, perhaps?'

Runa's face fell. 'Of course, as you say,' she said mutely.

Edela squeezed her hand. 'I'll see what I can do,' she smiled. 'I will keep working on my dreams, don't you worry. Something will turn up. That girl will not win. That is why I've come, Runa.' Edela shook with determination, feeling a surge of strength straighten her stooping frame. 'She will not win!'

***

They had tied Jaeger to the catapult, which seemed the best place for him. No one wanted to be near him. He was quiet, though, as he sat there, slumped, sulking, simmering. Jael watched him as they sped along on a fresh wind, the men talking quietly to each other as they hunched against the gunwales; some rolling dice, others combing their beards, telling jokes, comparing their wounds. But it was all subdued. They were ready to go home.

No one was looking forward to Hest.

Especially not Jaeger.

He thought of Elissa as he sat there. He had loved her, and she had died, and the pain was still sharp in his chest when he tried to picture her face. Three months had passed now, and he couldn't. Jaeger could picture his father's face, though, and that made him grimace. Haaron was going to be furious, and rightly so. He had been in charge of a defeat so catastrophic, so expensive, so embarrassing for their whole kingdom. He had humiliated him. There was nothing Jaeger could say, no way he could argue against this marriage, as much as he wanted to.

But a Furyck?

He shook his head, trying to ignore the ache in his ankles. It was a fair enough punishment and perhaps an opportunity too. In time, once he had mastered the book and his father was ash, floating on the wind, there would be time for revenge. Time to claim that which belonged to him; to destroy those who stood in the way of his destiny.

Jaeger glared at Jael Furyck as she walked down to check on him, her nose in the air. So righteous. Queen of the Slave Islands. The most nothing sort of queen there could be, he thought bitterly.

Jael ignored Jaeger and his eyes that were attempting to bore holes into her skull. She didn't blame him for his fury towards her, but she was worried about how he would treat Amma. Berard, for all that he had tried to defend his brother, had hardly been effusive in reassuring her that he was not the monster she feared he was.

Jael glanced towards *Ice Breaker* as she streamed alongside *Sea Bear*, smiling at Eadmund who was staring at her. He smiled back before lifting a water bag to his lips and turning away.

Sitting down on her sea chest, Jael rested back against the stern and closed her eyes. She needed to think. But in which order?

Evaine? Haaron? Eadmund? Amma?

She was a queen now, and she could feel both her father's pride and shame in that. She thought of Eirik and was suddenly overwhelmed with responsibility. He had entrusted her with his islands; trusted her to save Eadmund. And they both thought she had.

Until Aleksander and Edela had arrived and everything had fallen apart.

Eadmund stood in the stern, weary, and worn. He dropped the water bag down to his feet, and rummaged inside his pouch, pulling out the leather strap attached to Sigmund's blonde lock. He smiled, stroking it gently, trying to remember his son's face, but it would not come. He just had to get through the ridiculous ceremony of another wedding, and then he would be home again, with him.

Eadmund tucked the lock back into his pouch, pulling out the stone Morac had given him, frowning, running his fingers over the strange symbol inscribed upon it.

He looked back towards Jael, but she had slipped down into the stern, and all he could see was her dark hair, blowing in the wind. He imagined that she would be cold, that he would put his arm around her, trying to warm her through. And she would likely push him away and frown, but ultimately find a way to give in and let him touch her. And he would have. Once. Without hesitation. Because she was his. Or so he had thought.

But now?

Eadmund looked down at the stone, lost in the symbol, mesmerised; its twisting shape almost calling to him. He frowned, thinking of Evaine.

***

It had not taken long to pack their chests, which were now being loaded into the Hestian ship as it jerked about in the frothing waves. Despite an overwhelming reluctance to leave Brekka and sail away to Hest with a shipload of large, sullen warriors, all three women and their servants were eager to depart.

'I hope you'll have word about Demaeya soon,' Gisila smiled.

'And your child.'

Rexon's eyes crinkled at the sound of his wife's name. 'So do I. And I hope...' He sighed, doubting any words could ease Gisila's discomfort at being reunited with Lothar. 'I hope that we'll see you again. But perhaps for better reasons next time?'

Gisila nodded, her heart heavy with dread at the thought of a reunion with Lothar. She was choosing to ignore that part of what was coming, choosing instead to focus on seeing Axl again and Jael, Aleksander and Gant. The relief that they were all safe was overwhelming. She didn't want Lothar or his vile snake of a son to intrude upon that joy.

Not yet.

'Let us go,' Gisila said to Amma and Eydis. 'Before those men start to get cross.'

'They will not hurt you,' Rexon assured her, sensing her anxiety. 'You are to be Haaron's guests for the feast, to celebrate his alliance with Lothar. They'll keep you safe and keep their hands to themselves.'

Amma didn't look reassured as she wrapped her arm around Eydis' shoulder, but she was relieved, at least, to hear that Axl was safe. Relieved, but desperate to see for herself. Eydis' dream still haunted her. The idea of her suffering so badly troubled her, and she knew that she would not have a moment's peace until they were all back in Andala.

Rexon walked them down to the water, helping Amma up into the ship, then Eydis.

Gisila turned to him as he gripped her waist, preparing to lift her. 'It's odd, don't you think,' she murmured, so quietly that only he could hear, 'that Lothar and Haaron would so readily make an alliance? Strange how quickly sworn enemies can become friends.'

'It is, I agree. And I fear what it means for Brekka, but what can we do?' Rexon ducked his head, realising that he shouldn't say any more. 'Stay safe, Gisila, and don't give up. Ranuf wouldn't want you to.'

Gisila took a deep breath as Rexon boosted her up and over the side of the ship, his words ringing in her ears.

***

Edela knocked loudly on Entorp's door. She felt a burst of energy, smiling at Biddy, who stood alongside her, not smiling, desperate to get out of the rain as it slid down her legs, into her boots.

Entorp finally opened the door, half asleep and thoroughly confused. 'Oh, come in, come in,' he mumbled, blinking himself awake as Edela and Biddy bustled past him. 'I'm so sorry. I appear to have drifted off in my chair. I didn't hear you over all this rain.'

The women shook themselves by the door as Entorp reached out for their cloaks. 'Here, let me dry these by the fire.' He glanced at the fire, which had gone out. 'Well, once I light it again,' he blushed, further embarrassed.

'Let me do that,' Biddy insisted, already hunting for his tinderbox, which she quickly spotted on a leaning shelf. 'You need to listen to Edela.'

Entorp showed Edela to a chair by the cold fire pit. He had not slept well for the past few nights, haunted by old nightmares, and he hadn't realised how tired he had become. 'Sit down, please,' he murmured, stifling a yawn. 'And tell me what has happened.'

Edela remained standing, smiling, her blue eyes sparkling brightly in the dull room. 'I saw the symbol!' she said excitedly. 'I had a dream about that Tuuran book. I saw the symbol that will break the binding spell. I can draw it!'

Entorp's eyes widened, and he hurried to his table, Edela right behind him. He found another scrap of vellum, covered with various scrawls and symbols he'd been practising, but there was enough space for one more. 'Here,' he said, uncorking his pot of ink and grabbing one of the many quills that littered the messy table.

Edela took the quill, dipped it into the ink and started drawing. When she'd finished, she stepped back, cocking her head to one side. 'Yes, that's it! That's the symbol that can break the spell Evaine has put on Eadmund!'

Entorp frowned. He didn't recognise the symbol at all, but its characteristics did not look unfamiliar. He picked up the vellum, carrying it to the lamp he'd left burning on a small stool next to his bed. 'This looks promising,' he surmised. 'But we must decide where to put it.'

'We need to get into Runa's house,' Edela said carefully. 'It must be carved in there. That's where Evaine is casting that spell every morning.'

'It does,' Entorp agreed. 'Ideally right near where she is doing it. But somewhere she won't see. She needs to keep chanting away to herself without realising that nothing is happening.'

'Runa will have to get her out of the house,' Biddy added, sitting back as flames burst into life around the half-burned wood. 'And keep her out while you work. That won't be easy.'

'No,' Edela agreed. 'We must think of something to help her. Something that will convince Evaine to leave the house willingly.'

***

Evaine was growing more irritable by the day. She paced the main room, Sigmund gurgling over her shoulder, dribbling onto the cloth she had placed over her dress. Tanja's mother was ill, and she had been absent for the last few days. Even Runa was hardly around, always filled with the need to visit the market, or to call in to check on a friend who was ill.

A lot of people were suddenly ill.

But more than that, more than Evaine's irritation with the

constant, nagging demands of her son, and the absence of any real help, was her worry over Eadmund. She was growing frustrated, barely sleeping, waking early, lighting her candle, reciting her spell.

But for what?

How did she know if it was still having an effect? He was with *her*, alone, every day, with his wife.

Evaine sighed, frowning so hard her head hurt. She would have to start doing the ritual three times a day, when no one was home. She could not let Eadmund slip away from her again.

CHAPTER THIRTY FOUR

Eadmund fingered the pommel of his sword as his men hurried around *Ice Breaker*, bringing down the sail and yard, handing out the oars. They were entering Hest's harbour, following Haegen's ship. His eyes drifted to the rock-like castle, chiselled into the cliffs as it loomed before them. Mighty and vast though it appeared, he felt wistful for his small fort on Oss. As a man, and now a king, he had no appetite for such opulence; no desire to take what other men had. Not land nor power.

Eadmund wanted to be a king who kept his people safe and prosperous, but ultimately happy. What part wealth would play in that, for now, he didn't know, nor care. He just wanted to get home and begin.

He hadn't been able to stop thinking about Ivaar on their journey; about how he would kill him and avenge his father. He felt annoyed that he hadn't done it in Saala, or on Skorro. Then it would have been done. But, Eadmund conceded reluctantly, Jael was probably right: they would have struggled for support. Now though, the lords appeared on their side. There was more of a chance they would back his actions against Ivaar, he was sure.

Especially if he could find proof.

***

Varna held her breath as she stood behind Haaron. Meena shuffled around beside her, bobbing up and down, desperate for a glimpse of Jaeger, eager to know that he was unharmed. Varna just wanted to know what had happened to the book. She coughed, listening to the familiar rattle echo in her chest. The book... to think that it had finally surfaced. In her lifetime. She shook her head, smiling, then peered at Meena and frowned. 'Stop all that jiggling about, girl!' she hissed, pinching Meena's arm.

Bayla turned and glared at them both, furious that Haaron had allowed them to be there; certain that Varna was up to something with that odd girl. She inhaled sharply, her nostrils flaring in distaste, and turned back around. 'Why are *they* here?' she grumbled at Haaron.

'Varna has been with me my whole life,' Haaron muttered coldly. 'All of Berard's, all of Jaeger's. She is part of the family, wouldn't you say?'

The horrified look on Bayla's face told him that, no, she wouldn't. She continued to watch from the pier as the ships were steadily rowed towards their moorings. 'If they have hurt my sons...' she began.

'If they have hurt *our* sons, it will be nothing more than they deserve,' Haaron growled, his voice rolling over hers. 'For losing my fleet? All those men? My island fort? My Tower? My gold!' He swallowed quickly, trying to control his temper as it burst into flames. 'Jaeger and Berard should consider themselves fortunate that their father is a man wealthy enough to pay for their freedom. But it is they who will pay for their mistakes, eventually.'

'What does *that* mean?' Bayla asked sharply. 'What are you talking about?'

Haaron fixed his eyes straight ahead, ignoring her.

Bayla bit her lip, nodding irritably at Lothar Furyck who kept smiling at her.

Lothar was so hungry he could barely see straight. He was desperate for his hall and his throne and his wife, but most of all, he was desperate for his cooks. Never before had a king been treated so poorly, he decided. His trousers were hanging off him, and he was too weak to even think properly. But, he tried to console himself, this suffering was going to be worth it in the end, when Brekka's borders reached all the way to the Valgeir Sea. And once Helsabor was his, he would set his sights on Iskavall. He was looking forward to that, especially after what had happened there.

Lothar tidied his beard, ignoring his hunger pains, and smiled as the first of the ships gently nudged the pier, oars in the air.

Gant stood silently next to him, frowning. Only two ships. What had Jael done with the rest of her fleet? He felt Axl straining his neck as he stood, waiting impatiently behind him, desperate to see his sister; no doubt eager to talk to her about rescuing Amma.

If only he could see that there was no hope.

Jael sighed as she jumped down onto the pier, waiting for Eadmund to join her, watching the gathered crowd watch her. She saw Axl with Gant and felt a lift. Relieved. There was no Gisila or Amma, though.

Axl nodded at Jael.

He looked ready to cry, Jael thought, as Lothar hurried to make a fool of himself, embracing her as she stood there, arms by her sides, frowning impatiently, irritated by his ridiculous show of false affection.

'You have made the right decision,' Lothar whispered in her ear. 'Now, beware your tongue. Don't let it get us all in trouble.' Standing back, Lothar reached out a hand for Eadmund. 'My lord!' he said loudly. 'My nephew! My son-in-law even, Jael being my daughter now!'

Eadmund smiled briefly, ignoring his wife's face, which he was certain had twisted into an intense scowl. 'Lothar.'

'Come, come!' Lothar said cheerfully. 'Let me introduce you to our new partner. Our alliance will now grow stronger, our reach even greater as we claim all of Osterland for ourselves!'

Jael fought the urge to open her mouth. Lothar was full of hot breath and farts and little else. She reluctantly followed him towards the Dragos family who were in the midst of welcoming back Jaeger and Berard.

Jaeger stilled, his eyes on Jael.

Haaron gripped his arm, his voice blade sharp in his ear. 'You will not even think of it,' he hissed, releasing Jaeger and stepping away to greet his guests.

'The King and Queen of Oss!' Lothar announced grandly, feeling more confident now that he was no longer a prisoner.

'My lord, lady,' Haaron nodded, working hard at a smile that did not reach his eyes. 'I'm sorry to hear that your father is now with Vidar, although that is a fate many of us would welcome at this stage in our lives,' he muttered, trying not to scowl.

'What did you do to my son?' Bayla snarled at Jael. 'He can't even stand on his own!'

Jael attempted to look surprised. 'Which one?' she asked. 'I can't keep up with how many of your sons I've injured now.'

Bayla clamped her teeth together, her eyes bulging in fury as Haaron quickly grabbed her hand.

'It was a battle, my dear,' he said tightly. 'Be thankful that a few cuts are all they have. It could have been far worse, I'm sure.'

Berard and Karsten came forward then, Haegen helping Jaeger to limp along. Karsten's one eye didn't leave Jael's face. He curled his lips in disgust. He wanted to reach out and stab her in the heart. The bitch. The one who had taken his eye.

'Hello, Karsten,' Jael smiled. 'I like your eye patch.'

Karsten reached down for his sword, gripping the hilt, his knuckles white.

Eadmund ignored him and turned to Haaron. 'If I could see to our men, my lord. Find where they are to sleep?'

'Of course. Karsten will show you.' Karsten frowned, less than thrilled with that task. 'And you will release the Brekkans while you're there. Now that we have made our exchange, there are to be no more prisoners here. Only allies.' It was hard to say, but this alliance would bring greater reward than Haaron had ever anticipated.

If only he could stop his sons from trying to kill Jael Furyck.

***

'I can't.' Runa shook at the mere thought of it. 'I can't, Edela! I can't!'

'Runa,' Edela soothed, smiling encouragingly as she patted her shaking hand. 'If we are to stop Evaine, we need to end her control over Eadmund. If she controls Eadmund, then everything around here will change. For the worse.'

Runa could see that, even as she shuddered at the thought of what Edela and Biddy were planning with Entorp. 'But she won't believe me. She'll wonder why I'm trying to take her out of the house all of a sudden. Why I would choose to spend time with her.'

'Not if you dangle a tasty carrot in front of her,' Biddy suggested, kneeling in front of the fire as she rubbed the freshly washed Ido with an old blanket. 'And the idea of going to the tailors will surely appeal, especially if you tell her that Edela has seen Eadmund on his way back to Oss.'

Runa was shaking so much that she almost spilled the cup of small ale she had been resting on her knee. 'Of course. It would spur her on, the thought of Eadmund returning,' she sighed, finally taking a sip from her cup. 'If only I can convince her that my intentions are genuine.'

'It will be easy enough,' Edela smiled, 'if you think of Sigmund. You have real affection for the boy, so that will come through, I'm sure.'

Runa blinked nervously.

'And Fyn,' Biddy added. 'Think of Fyn. You can do this for him too.'

Runa sighed, closing her eyes.

Fyn.

***

'Stay close,' Jael murmured as Fyn's eyes roamed the castle's high stone walls. 'Don't get lost or one of those Dragos' might eat you!' she smiled as she walked behind Haaron.

Eadmund nudged her, his finger to his lips.

Jael ignored him. She didn't want to be here, pretending to be a queen. Perhaps her father had been right to choose Axl? Diplomacy was not something that came naturally to her, if at all.

Fyn resisted the urge to stop and stare, but just the entranceway of Haaron's castle was longer than any building they had on Oss and four times as tall. He hurried to keep up with Jael, listening to the soft thud of his boots as he walked across the cool flagstones. His mouth hung open as they turned into the hall. Great, round, iron frames filled with candles hung down from the rafters. Torches burned from sconces along each wall. The long, cavernous room was filled with tables set in the shape of a horseshoe; laden with cups and jugs, and plates of food that looked hot and smelled delicious. Fyn was suddenly aware that it was well past any time he would normally have hoped to eat. He thought of his mother then, hoping that she was not suffering too much with Evaine and her crying baby for company, and soon, his father as well. Blinking, he looked at Axl, whose face was bereft as he trudged along, oblivious to everything except the pain in his heart.

Jaeger limped ahead of them. He watched the slaves milling around with jugs of wine, saw more trays of food being delivered to the tables, but he had no appetite. His stomach lurched nauseously, as though he was still at sea. He could feel his father's eyes, scornful and disappointed as they sought his. His mother would not leave him alone, fussing over him constantly. Haegen on his other side, grimaced with the strain of holding him up, trying to assure Bayla that he would recover in time.

Haaron stopped, turning to his guests. 'Please, take a seat.

After being stuck on Skorro, I imagine you will appreciate some real food.' He grimaced through the pleasantries, his attitude more like Jaeger's and Karsten's than he wanted to admit. But he was an old king, with not much life ahead of him now. And, as Lothar Furyck had ultimately proved, it was better to be clever than dead.

Jael wanted to talk to anyone but Haaron, so she quickly chose a seat at the very end of the high table. Lothar frowned at his niece, but he couldn't catch her eye as he took a seat near the middle, wanting to keep as close to Haaron as possible.

Axl sat next to Jael, and Eadmund next to him.

Haegen deposited Jaeger next to Haaron, who looked less than pleased with the company, and Bayla quickly assumed her place next to her favourite child. The rest of the Dragos and Furyck families took their seats, their faces tense, apart from Lothar, who chatted happily to Haaron, his eyes focused entirely on his goblet, which was being filled with wine.

'We need to talk,' Axl whispered to his sister.

'We will, of course,' Jael whispered back. 'Not here, though. Not now.' She reached for her own goblet and gave it a sniff, wondering if Haaron had, in fact, lured them into a trap.

It smelled like wine, though, and only wine.

Taking a long drink, Jael's attention was quickly drawn to a strange red-headed woman with big eyes. She stood against the opposite wall, amongst the expressionless, shaven-headed slaves, her eyes fixed on Jaeger as she tapped her head.

Jael blinked herself away from the woman, smiling at the slave who delivered her plate, smiling even wider as she inhaled the plentiful meal, which glistened and steamed under the soft candlelight.

A definite improvement on dried pork and salt fish.

But still, they were in Hest.

***

Runa eyed Tanja, who sat opposite her, feeding Sigmund. It had been a surprisingly mild day, but Runa had not stopped shivering since her talk with Edela.

She had a dark-blue tunic draped over her knees. It was going to be a surprise for Fyn. She had been adding details to the sleeves, but it was getting dark now, and her eyes no longer responded to candlelight as they once had. Her fingers had not stopped jiggling either. Runa sighed and admitted defeat, putting down her needle and thread. 'Evaine has been gone some time now,' she muttered, folding up the tunic. 'I do not think we should wait any longer. Once he's finished feeding, put him to bed and we'll eat our supper.'

Tanja looked less than thrilled by that idea. 'Perhaps I should go to my mother's house?' she suggested nervously, her eyes wandering to the door. 'Stay there tonight?'

Runa froze. She didn't blame Tanja for wanting to run away, but her company was comforting. Being left alone with Evaine was not.

'But if you stay there, who will feed Sigmund in the night?' Evaine asked sharply as she pushed open the door. 'You know very well that I can't anymore.'

Both women jumped.

'And surely you've spent enough of your day there?' Evaine went on as she handed Respa her cloak. 'I bumped into your sister while I was out. She said that your mother was much better now. That she'd hardly been ill at all.' She glared at Tanja, who looked quickly away, adjusting the position of Sigmund's head on her breast.

Evaine glanced at the meal waiting for them on the table. 'Again?' she grumbled. 'Fish and eggs again?'

'We have an abundance of eggs at the moment,' Runa said quietly, walking to the table, reaching quickly for a cup of mead as she sat down. 'And while the fish is still fresh we must use it up.'

Tanja sat Sigmund up. He had drifted off to sleep, but she needed to get some wind out of him if they were going to have a peaceful night; Evaine was always much more even-tempered when she slept well.

Evaine joined Runa at the table, interested in nothing but a piece of bread which she distractedly broke into small pieces. Her mind was lost on Eadmund, her body rigid and anxious as she perched on the edge of her chair.

'I spoke with Edela today,' Runa began, her voice faltering. She coughed and tried again, ignoring Evaine's frown. 'She said she saw the ships returning soon.'

Evaine's eyes brightened. 'She did?'

'Yes,' Runa went on. 'In a day or so, she said.'

Evaine could barely contain the joy that blossomed inside her chest. 'And Eadmund? Did she mention Eadmund at all?'

Runa shook her head. 'She didn't mention anyone, just that the ships were returning. But, of course, I'm sure that Eadmund will be on one of them.' She swallowed a soggy piece of carrot and put her knife down, taking a deep breath. 'Perhaps you need to organise a new outfit for his return? Something special for you and Sigmund?'

Evaine frowned, surprised by the suggestion, but it was an idea that quickly sparked to life. She was having a new cloak made, but that was for summer, and as for the baby? He had vomited over every outfit he had.

'Sigynn showed me some new wool and linen today,' Runa went on nervously. 'She even has some white furs from Alekka. I was thinking of getting a cloak made for next winter. Although, it is in high demand, as you can imagine.'

Evaine nibbled on a morsel of bread. 'Well, perhaps it's worth a visit tomorrow, then, before it's all gone? I would at least like to look it over.'

'Good,' Runa smiled quickly. 'Shall we go together, then? I

will help you with Sigmund. It will give Tanja a chance to visit with her mother.'

Evaine was too excited by the thought of seeing Eadmund again to give much attention to the nagging question of why Runa was being so helpful.

Her mind was already racing towards which colour she thought Eadmund would prefer to see her in: blue or green?

***

Jael Furyck looked far more like a woman than Bayla had imagined she would. In fact, with a bit of scrubbing and brushing, she was certain there would be an attractive, presentable queen underneath all those filthy male clothes. But her face was hard, and her eyes were sharp, and there was no danger of her being anything like Irenna or Nicolene at all. Perhaps that was to her credit, she considered, thinking of the ridiculously silly girls her sons had married.

She sighed, looking away to where Haaron had cornered Jaeger, who stood, propped up against a mediating Haegen, working hard to defend himself.

'There was nothing to be done against such odds,' Jaeger insisted again, cringing at the sharp pains in his ankles; the right one, in particular, was not healing at all and he could not stand without help.

'*Nothing?*' Haaron sneered, watching the Furycks with their heads together out of the corner of one eye. 'Have you heard of retreat?'

'We are Hestians!' Jaeger insisted, horrified that his father would suggest such a thing.

'We are Hestians with no fleet!' Haaron grumbled. 'And we did not become Hestians by putting inexperienced idiots in charge. My mistake entirely.'

'Father,' Haegen tried. 'There was little chance to escape such a fire, even if they had retreated. We've never encountered anything like it.'

'Well, your father-in-law managed to escape,' Haaron countered. 'He's not sucking shit at the bottom of the sea with all of my drowned men!' He wanted to scream and rage at his son, but here, in the hall, in front of his guests, it was not the right time or place. Now, he admitted, in frustration, was the time for pretence and fakery and preparation, for soon there would be a wedding. 'You need to see Sitha about your wounds,' he grumbled. 'If you are to have any hope of standing at your wedding, you're going to need her help, I'm sure.'

Jaeger flinched but didn't say a word. He knew that he would have to suffer the humiliation of marrying Lothar Furyck's daughter without argument.

'Do you not *know* his reputation?' Jael whispered hoarsely, trying to ignore Osbert's smirking face as he wobbled nearby, leaning on a stick.

Lothar waved Jael's concern away with a pudgy hand. He was full of food and giddy with drink, and he'd not felt this relaxed in some time. 'He is a Dragos,' he muttered. 'You cannot expect him to behave like a Furyck. They are different down here. More... coarse, I have found.'

'*Coarse*?' Jael fumed, trying to keep her voice low, her eyes darting to where Haaron and Jaeger stood.

'Karsten Dragos said he punched his first wife in the stomach while she was pregnant,' Gant interjected, much to Lothar's annoyance. 'Perhaps that's a little more than coarse, my lord, considering that both she and the child then died.'

Lothar's eyes widened at that unpleasant news. 'If he was telling the truth.'

Axl had already revealed as much to Jael, which made her even more determined to do something to prevent the wedding. But she knew Lothar from her own wedding misery. He was not a man about to be moved by anyone; not even his own daughter. Not when there was the much more attractive proposition of Helsabor dangling before his greedy eyes now.

'Amma will be in danger here. He is violent and cruel,' Jael tried, her eyes meeting that strange girl's again. She was still there, following an old woman about; an old woman who looked ready to crumble into dust. A dreamer, she realised, as those ancient eyes snapped to her. A shiver shot up Jael's spine, and she shuddered, suddenly cold all over.

She was here, Varna realised. Within reach. She could stop her now, couldn't she? There were ways, of course there were. It would not take much, just an item of clothing, some hair, some small thing, and they could weave a spell, trap her...

Destroy the one who stood in their way, and then it would be done.

And the prophecy would burn.

***

'Do you believe in dragons, Edela?'

Edela felt her heart stop, all breath leaving her body in a terrified rush.

'Your saviour has just stepped into the mouth of a dragon,' the voice crowed. 'Into the hungry mouth of a fire-breathing dragon!'

Jael.

Edela could see the flames now, bursting up from the darkness as she lay there, trapped on a table, tied down, her arms straining against harsh ropes, the voice booming all around her.

She had to break the bonds. She had to escape.

'You can't, you can't, you can't!' the voice taunted her. 'It's too late now. Your precious Jael is there, and she is too arrogant to think that she can come to any harm. Too busy thinking of her lost husband, or her lost love. Too busy planning how to save the girl. Too blind to see what is right there in front of her!'

Gleeful echoes vibrated around Edela, bouncing off the walls of the cave.

It was a cave.

She could smell the damp; hear the slow drip of moisture from somewhere.

But she couldn't move as she lay there. And she needed to.

Quickly.

She had to save Jael.

CHAPTER THIRTY FIVE

They watched them leave.

Runa, carrying the baby, kept glancing nervously behind herself. Edela shook her head, wishing she would stop. It wouldn't help for Evaine to get suspicious.

Biddy peered at Entorp. 'Are you ready? Do you have everything?'

He nodded, impatient to begin.

Runa's servant, Respa, popped her head around the door of the house, then looking around to check that it was clear, she motioned Entorp over.

Entorp took a deep breath.

'I'll follow them,' Biddy assured him, trying to mask her own anxiety with a firm voice. 'And Edela will wait at that table on the corner over there. We'll stop Evaine before she gets back to the house, I promise.'

Entorp tucked his leather wrap under his arm. 'I must go,' he muttered, hurrying away, not wanting to waste a moment.

Edela touched Biddy's arm. 'You'd better go too,' she urged. 'I don't want them to come back around because they forgot something.'

Biddy nodded and scurried away, leaving Edela to walk to the table.

She walked slowly, her body aching and weary. Her dreams had been a blur and she'd woken up remembering nothing.

Sometimes it could be that way, she knew.

But something was stirring. Edela could feel it.

***

'Meena will find something, won't you, girl?' Varna croaked, nibbling a piece of bread from the loaf Meena had brought up from the kitchen. It was still warm, but neither Varna nor Morana noticed as they sat around the fire with glistening eyes, salivating over the opportunity the gods had presented them.

Jael Furyck.

In Hest.

If only they could agree on how best to harm her.

'If we can bind her –' Varna began.

'We need to *kill* her!' Morana insisted. 'Why bind her? If she's dead, the prophecy is no more!'

'She is powerful,' Varna tried again. 'We could use her for our own needs.'

'And what are *they*?' Morana snorted, ripping off another piece of bread and reaching for a slice of cheese.

'We need to remove the Bear,' Varna smiled.

Meena trembled as she sat on her bed, eating her small share of the meal. Jaeger had not even glanced at her since his return. He had hobbled about, fawned over by his awful mother and glared at by his hateful father. She felt sorry for him. They were a horrible family; though, she admitted with a sigh, far better than her own.

'Not until we have that book,' Morana reminded her.

'True, but once we know where it is, he'll need to be killed quickly,' Varna muttered, curling her fingers in the air. 'Meena, you need to go to Jaeger. Tell him that you've found more ways to understand the book. That you've been going through my spells.

He is certain to show it to you. He will want you to look at it.'

Meena froze. It was everything she wanted, and yet, she felt hesitant.

Because they wanted to trap him.

They wanted to kill him.

***

Respa had shown Entorp up to the mezzanine and left him to it. He shook with nerves, trying to remind himself that Evaine was just a girl. But he knew very well that she was far more dangerous than any girl he knew of.

He kept Edela's sketch next to him as he tapped his chisel across the floorboards, first lightly, then more heavily, scuffing out the wood in circular motions, working as fast as his fingers would allow, jumping at every sound.

It was a detailed symbol. He needed to get it right.

***

Evaine looked unimpressed as she ran her hands through Sigynn's selection of fabrics. 'There's nothing new here,' she said crisply 'It all looks the same to me.'

Runa panicked. 'But what about Sigmund? He must have something for when his father returns, don't you think?'

Evaine frowned. 'Why do *you* care all of a sudden?'

Runa swallowed, certain that she was sweating, there being so many lamps burning in Sigynn's cramped cottage. 'I, I,' she stumbled, shaking her head and thinking of Fyn. 'I've grown quite attached to him,' she said, jiggling the baby in her arms. 'And he is Eadmund's son. You don't want him thinking that you're not taking care of Sigmund, do you? Don't want to present him to his father covered in stains?' She noticed some bright blue wool poking up from beneath a pile of grey cloth. 'That would be perfect. Such a nice colour for a little boy, don't you think? He would look so handsome in that,' she tried. 'Especially if you had something made in a lighter blue for yourself. The two of you together would be very pleasing to the eye.'

'But would there be time?' Evaine wondered, fingering the fabric Runa had spotted. 'It would suit him well, with his light hair, I think,' she murmured, lifting the soft wool up to Sigmund's face.

'And perhaps some little booties?' Runa went on, feeling her heart pound. 'Fur-trimmed ones? With a bonnet?'

'Perhaps,' Evaine said slowly. 'How long would that take?' She turned to Sigynn.

The tailor opened her mouth to answer when Sigmund suddenly burst into tears, wailing as though in terrible pain.

***

'I'm sorry,' Jael said, her eyes full of sympathy as she looked out over the harbour, the sky still covered in a smoky haze. 'I don't see how we can stop it. Not yet.'

Axl felt a spark of frustration as he stood alongside his sister at the end of the pier, watching the gentle rise and fall of the Osslanders' ships as they bumped against their moorings. 'Why won't you ever *do* anything, Jael?' he cried, turning to her. He was desperate to get through to his sister, wanting her to think of a plan. He needed her. 'You don't ever *do* anything!'

Jael sighed, rubbing her eyes. She felt like vomiting, her body swaying as though she were still at sea. 'We're not in any position to attack Haaron and then defend ourselves. Not here, like this. They took all of your weapons.'

'We could find some!'

Jael shook her head. 'This is their kingdom. They would chase us back to Andala or Oss. How many Brekkans or Islanders would die? How could you be certain that Amma or Mother wouldn't die?'

Axl's shoulders sagged. 'But we can't leave her here with him! Married to him! He will hurt her... you know he will!'

The guilt of that thought sat heavily on Jael's shoulders, but she was responsible for more than her brother's happiness or Amma's safety. 'Well, all I can do is keep thinking. The way everything is now... it can change. Given time, we can turn things around.'

Axl barely heard her. 'If only you'd killed Jaeger when you had the chance.'

'Ahhh yes, if only... if only you hadn't made a noise under the bed that night,' Jael said harshly, regretting her words as guilt flooded his already troubled eyes. She caught sight of Aleksander walking towards them. 'We all have choices to make, but we don't always make the best ones.'

Axl turned to her, wondering what that meant.

'Looking for an escape?' Aleksander smiled, trying to brighten the miserable faces before him.

'Trying to think of how to help Amma,' Jael said. 'I just don't see what we can do.'

'Not a lot is the truth,' Aleksander said frankly, 'which I've already told you, Axl. We're weaponless, and we're in their kingdom. And we'd have to fight Lothar as well and defeat him. There's no way around it. Not yet. You'll have to be patient.'

Axl looked even more miserable as he stared out to sea, listening to the birds call to each other; screeching, angry birds, warning of dark things to come.

***

'Take him back home!' Evaine ordered. 'He needs milk. You'll have to find Tanja.'

Runa was doing her very best to soothe Sigmund, patting his back, cooing soothing words in his ear, kissing his bright red cheeks.

It wasn't working.

Evaine was getting irritated, embarrassed by the ear-piercing noises coming out of her son. 'You should leave,' she said impatiently through tight lips, pushing Runa towards the door. 'I'll follow shortly.'

Runa looked helpless. 'Some fresh air might help him,' she suggested quickly. 'Take your time. I'll wait outside. If he doesn't settle, we can always go and find Tanja at her mother's.' She hurried through the door, clasping a screaming Sigmund to her chest.

She had to stop him crying.

***

Egil opened the door, surprised to see the quivering figure of Meena Gallas standing there. He frowned. 'What do you want?' She was an odd, ugly girl, and he had no idea why his master thought she could be of any use to him.

Meena shook her head, twitching her nose. As eager as she was to see Jaeger, she was just as desperate to run away from actually having to face him at all. Her confusing feelings, she decided, were far better contained in a dream.

'Who is it, Egil?' came the tired, throaty voice from inside.

Meena stood up straighter then, shivering.

'That girl,' Egil said distastefully, turning his head back into the room. 'Meena Gallas.'

'Well, bring her in!'

Meena looked at the flagstones as she scrambled past Egil and into the warm chamber, tapping her head with increasing urgency.

***

Biddy was surprised to see Runa rush out of the cottage, but one look at the red-faced baby and she could see the problem. 'Here,' she offered, her arms outstretched. 'Give him to me.'

'I don't know what's wrong with him,' Runa panicked, almost as red-faced as Sigmund. 'He was fed before we left.'

Biddy patted Sigmund's back. 'There, there,' she soothed. 'I think you've just got some wind trapped in your belly.'

Runa paced around, her eyes never leaving the tailor's door.

Sigmund suddenly burped loudly. He got such a fright that his crying ceased immediately.

Runa sighed in relief, and Biddy smiled, handing him back to her.

'What are you doing?' Evaine growled, hurrying out of Sigynn's cottage. 'What are you doing with my baby?'

Biddy and Runa froze.

'I was...'

'Biddy was just passing,' Runa said quickly 'She offered to help. And she did. He is much better now, see?' She held a calm but exhausted Sigmund up to his mother.

Evaine frowned. 'Well, I shall take him home anyway. You need to go and find Tanja for me. He needs to be fed.'

'But what about the new outfit for Sigmund?' Runa asked. 'Don't you need to go back inside?'

'No, we are done,' Evaine said impatiently, holding out her

arms for her son. 'Sigynn knows what I want. I said I would bring him back tomorrow to be measured.' She grabbed the baby, lifting him to her shoulder. 'Now just go and get Tanja, so he can have some milk.' And without another word, she headed off towards the house.

Biddy swallowed, watching her go.

As soon as Evaine was out of sight, she turned, hitched up her dress and ran in the other direction.

***

'Does Varna suspect anything?' Jaeger wondered, trying to read any lies in Meena's eyes as she fidgeted on the bed next to him. 'About the book?'

Meena stared at him. He had lost weight, she thought. His cheekbones appeared sharper. His eyes looked bruised, more intense. Angrier. She couldn't look away. 'No,' she lied, trying not to blink. 'But I have seen more of that writing,' she mumbled into her chest.

'You have?' Jaeger grimaced as he sat up, edging closer to her. 'Where?'

'She, she has a... visitor,' Meena blurted out suddenly.

'Who?'

'Her daughter.'

'She has a daughter?' Jaeger's eyes bulged. '*Varna?*' He scratched his head. Varna had been a steady presence in his life since he could remember. Where had this daughter been all these years? 'And she's here? Where? Who is she?'

Meena started tapping her right foot on the fur rug.

Egil frowned at her as he brought his master a cup of ale.

'Her name is Morana. She's in Varna's chamber. Hiding there.'

'Hiding? Why?'

'I don't know,' Meena said, surprised by that herself.

'Is she a dreamer?'

Meena hesitated.

Jaeger placed his hand on her leg to stop it jerking about. He moved even closer until she could feel the warmth of his arm against hers.

'Yes.'

Jaeger frowned as he stared into Meena's fluttering eyes.

Varna knew about the book.

***

Biddy came stumbling around the corner, her breath completely gone. She had not run since she was a child, and even then, barely. 'Edela!' she panted, waving her arms madly, leaning over, pains in her sides. 'Quick!'

Edela was facing the opposite direction, but her hearing worked well enough for her to spin around and catch the panic in Biddy's eyes. She hurried up from the table and made her way quickly to the house, eyes darting up and down the street. After knocking on the door once, she paused, then knocked again, scurrying away before anyone saw her.

Entorp was still in there. She would need to try and cut Evaine off before she arrived.

***

Lothar inhaled the seductive scent of white jasmine flowers curling around the stone arches of the first-floor balcony. The late afternoon was warm, the sky a hazy blue. It was an impressive location, and an equally impressive castle, he admitted to himself, his eyes lingering on the horizon, wondering if he spied a hint of the Fire Lands in the distance. Those rich, exotic countries overflowed with golden palaces and wealth greater than any kingdom in Osterland possessed.

Lothar's lips were moist with possibilities. He would take Gisila there, to Silura and Kalmera; dress her in the finest silks, drape her in the biggest jewels.

He sighed, missing his wife and the feel of her soft, milky body.

'My lord?' Gant asked cautiously, stepping out onto the balcony.

'Gant,' Lothar smiled, blinking himself away from fantasies of Gisila. 'Have you seen to everything?'

'Yes, lord,' Gant nodded, stopping beside his king. 'Haaron has agreed to move you all to more suitable chambers.'

Lothar sighed with relief. He had grown tired of being marginalised by his host, and he'd no intention of allowing his queen to sleep in such shabby accommodation when she arrived. 'And where are these new chambers? I should like to see them right away,' he smiled cheerfully.

'On the ground floor, my lord. To the rear of the castle. There is an entire wing, with many chambers. Rooms for everyone.'

'Excellent!' Lothar beamed, following Gant back into the room. 'I would like to give Amma some privacy and comfort before she has to marry that man.' He shuddered, surprised by a surge of guilt.

Gant saw it in his eyes, and he stopped. 'It will be very hard on Amma,' he said plainly. 'The things his brother said Jaeger has done...'

Lothar's face turned crimson in a flash. He poked a finger at Gant's chest. 'I will thank you not to lecture me on the choice of husband I make for *my* daughter,' he growled, his voice low and threatening. 'She is not your family, any more than Gisila or her children are. You are my man, Gant, and nothing more. And you will remember that, do you understand me?'

Gant's jaw worked away, clamping down on anything he might have wanted to throw at his king at that moment. There was no point. It would only make things worse. If he lost his place by Lothar's side, he wouldn't be able to help anyone.

***

'Ahhh, just the person I was hoping to see!' Edela called breathlessly, rushing out in front of Evaine.

Evaine froze as she was about to turn the corner towards the house. 'What do you want?' she asked suspiciously, her eyebrows knitting together as she peered at the panting old woman.

'I've had a dream,' Edela gasped. 'About you. I thought you would like to know. Well, I suppose it's not actually about you, but it does concern your son... or at least his father.'

Evaine's eyes narrowed. She did not wish to discuss such personal things in public view. 'Well then, perhaps you need to come to the house? Surely it is something we should speak of in private?'

'Oh no, nothing as secret as that,' Edela assured her. 'I just thought it best to warn you before they came home... Jael and Eadmund.'

Evaine was growing more and more unsettled. 'Well, what is it, then?' she snapped. 'I have to get my baby fed, so I don't have time to stand around here waiting for you to catch your breath.'

'I had a dream that Jael was pregnant,' Edela said quickly. 'It seems that Eadmund is about to become a father again, so your little boy there will soon have a brother or sister.'

Evaine's mouth gaped open. She felt as though someone had just punched all the air out of her.

***

Jael didn't know where to go, but she certainly didn't want to go into the hall and face another meal knee to knee with the Dragos family. It was getting late though; stripes of warm red clouds stretched above her head, and Jael knew that she had to return to the castle before everyone wondered where she was.

'Where have you been all afternoon?' Eadmund smiled as he walked down the pier.

Jael frowned, squinting. It was growing dark, and she doubted herself entirely for a moment, but the closer Eadmund got, the more she was convinced that something had changed. 'Are you alright?' she asked as he stopped and reached for her hands.

Eadmund bent his head and kissed her, slowly and deeply. 'I've missed you,' he said to her lips. 'And no, I'm not alright, but I am better. More myself again, I think.'

And looking into his eyes, Jael believed him.

CHAPTER THIRTY SIX

'Your new bride will arrive tomorrow,' Haaron announced, sniffing at the meat on the end of his knife. It was coated in so much rich sauce that he was having a hard time tasting what it actually was.

'So I hear,' Jaeger muttered, trying not to frown. Lothar Furyck sat next to him eagerly stuffing a large egg into his tiny mouth. It made no sense to make his situation worse, not yet. In time his father would be dead, and he would stab a spear through Lothar's heart before claiming the Brekkan throne for himself.

As impatient as Jaeger was by nature, there was no point in rushing. Not when the book was yet to reveal its secrets. He smiled, enjoying the absence of pain in his ankles for a moment, soothed by his third goblet of excellent wine.

There was no Varna tonight, he noticed, glancing around the hall.

No Meena either.

He wondered what that meant.

***

'Go on,' Varna hissed, jabbing Meena in the back with her sharpest fingernail. 'Go in!'

Meena shook with fear. Of all the people whose chamber she did not wish to break into, Jael Furyck was at the top of her list. 'And what should I take?' she whispered loudly.

'Ssshhh!' Varna groaned, putting that sharp fingernail to her hairy lips. 'Lower your voice, girl! Take something small, something she won't notice, like a comb or a sock. Anything she won't miss. If you find some of her hair, grab that!'

Meena swallowed, allowing herself to be shoved into the chamber like a reluctant dog.

Varna watched her go, then closed the door and spun around, eager to ensure that there was no one about. The passageway was empty, though. Down here, in the western wing of the castle, where Haaron had placed the Furycks, there were not many people.

Varna smiled, pleased that the king had listened to her suggestion.

***

'And did she believe you?' Biddy wondered.

'Who knows?' Edela chuckled, ladling another spoon of hot soup into her mouth, her body relaxing more with every helping. It had been a tense afternoon, but they had finally gathered in front of the fire at the house, sharing a collective sense of relief at a job well done.

'But is it true?' Entorp wondered, dipping a piece of bread into his soup. 'Is she actually carrying Eadmund's child?'

Edela smiled. 'I couldn't say,' she said cheerfully. 'But I certainly didn't dream it. It was all I could think of at the time!'

'I can imagine Evaine's face when you told her,' Biddy laughed. 'How can such a pretty thing have such an ugly heart?

How could Eadmund not see through her in the first place?'

'Well, men can be rather dumb,' Edela said sweetly, winking at Entorp. 'Especially around a pretty girl.'

Entorp nodded, smiling. 'I can't deny that.'

'I hope she doesn't move her rugs around and find the symbol,' Biddy mumbled, suddenly anxious again. 'Imagine what she'd do then?'

'Oh, I think Evaine will have more things on her mind than rugs,' Edela chortled. 'Don't you?'

***

'You're not eating?' Eadmund wondered, looking worried. 'That's not like you.'

'I feel like I'm still at sea,' Jael muttered, distracted, her eyes on Axl and Fyn, who had their heads together, talking with Aleksander. 'I'm sure I'll feel better tomorrow.' She pushed her plate away, ignoring her wine. She felt unsettled, knowing that Amma's arrival would make things worse. If only Lothar had told Rexon about the wedding, perhaps he would have sent Amma far away. But then there was Eydis, and Jael was eager to see Eydis.

'You dislike your meal, Cousin?' Osbert wondered from her right.

Jael sighed, turning to him. He looked terrible and deserved to. From what Axl had told her, it appeared that Osbert had been the one to suggest Amma's marriage to Lothar. She still hadn't gotten over him grabbing her when she was running to save Eirik that night. It had barely been any time at all, but after everything that had happened, it felt like a lifetime ago. 'No, just your company,' she said tartly.

'Well, perhaps it's best to avoid eating in strange places,' Osbert warned. 'You wouldn't want to end up like Eirik Skalleson.'

Eadmund glared at Osbert and Jael could feel his body tighten as he leaned behind her to jab Osbert in the arm. 'Being that you're *not* a king, I'd think it best you keep your mouth shut when talking to a queen, especially one who knows how to use a sword as well as my wife,' he snapped. 'Besides, your father doesn't appear especially loyal to his children, so I wouldn't consider yourself safe.' He sat back down, pushing his own plate away, thoughts of his father removing his appetite entirely.

'Well, we're not going to be invited back, are we?' Jael said lightly.

Eadmund leaned towards her. 'That would make me very happy indeed,' he whispered. 'I want to go home more than anything.'

'Mmmm,' she whispered back, her body relaxing at the warmth in his voice and the familiar look in his eye. He had come back to her. Sad and broken, yes, but hers again. Jael didn't want to stop to think about why or how. Not yet. 'Well, as soon as we have Eydis and can get through this wedding, we'll be able to leave. Hopefully, Thorgils can keep everything under control in the meantime.' Her mind drifted back to Oss, and to Evaine, who was waiting there for them. She shook her head, not wanting that girl in it anymore.

Perhaps Edela could come up with something to help them get rid of her?

Maybe she already had, Jael thought to herself as Eadmund nudged his knee into hers and smiled.

***

Evaine hadn't spoken a word since Runa had returned with Tanja.

Sigmund had been asleep and not needing milk at all, but Tanja had stayed, at Runa's insistence, taking Sigmund away from Evaine, who had sat and stared at the fire as its flames ebbed and flowed and the day turned to night.

'Are you sure you wouldn't like something to eat?' Runa asked again as Respa cleared the table.

Evaine didn't reply.

Something was wrong. Edela was gleeful. Because of the pregnancy, of course, but there was something more, and Evaine couldn't see what it was. She felt a powerful sense of loss; the loss of Eadmund. It felt as though he had slipped from her grasp, but how could that be when she was reciting the spell even more than before?

What had happened?

***

'How can you tell me not to give up hope? What hope do you have with Jael anymore? Nothing's the same for you,' Axl insisted, following Aleksander's eyes towards Jael. She hadn't noticed anyone but Eadmund all evening.

Aleksander cleared any emotion from his face as he turned back to Axl. 'No, it's not, but I hardly think Amma is going to fall in love with Jaeger Dragos, is she?'

Axl shrugged. 'He's handsome, powerful...'

'And evil,' Gant put in. 'Eadmund was a drunk, that's different. You can stop drinking, but you can't change your heart if it's as black as that monster's.'

Aleksander looked at Axl's anxious face. 'I'm not sure that's helping,' he suggested bluntly.

Gant tipped back the last of his ale. 'All I'm saying is that you don't need to worry about Amma. The best thing you can do for her is to stay calm.' He leaned in closely, his voice a rough whisper. 'Think of what your father would do. Ranuf was a passionate man, but he was always in control. It gave him time to think.'

Axl knew they were both right, but he had very little confidence in his ability to control himself. Not when Amma arrived. Not when she found out what her father had planned for her.

***

It was quiet now.

Quiet and calm. They were not moving with much speed, but the sail was mostly full, and the men were able to lie around, curled into the sides of the ship, snoring.

Amma couldn't sleep, though, as she watched the moon, fascinated by its brightness as it stared back down at her. Gisila was snuffling lightly next to her, Eydis sleeping on her other side. Amma hoped that she was dreaming, looking for answers, clues as to what those dark dreams had meant.

She wasn't sure if she wanted to know.

***

The sky Ayla walked towards was bleak.

Eydis could feel her emptiness as she strode along the beach. She saw the pain filling her heart, overwhelming her spirit.

She had lost hope.

Eydis wanted to run after her, to help her, hold her hand, make her realise that something was going to change. She could feel it.

Ayla turned, walking back towards her. 'Why have you come, Eydis?' she said without smiling. 'You do not need to dream of me.'

Eydis didn't know what to say; her tongue tangled inside her mouth. 'I.. I... wanted to know if Ivaar killed my father,' she said, at last, her voice almost lost in the wind.

Ayla's face changed then, softening as she walked closer.

'You showed me what would happen,' Eydis continued, trying not to cry. 'You must have seen him do it?'

Ayla stopped, smiling sadly. 'I wish I had, Eydis, but no, I didn't see who did it.'

Eydis could hear the gentle rush of waves as they crashed onto the beach, the steady beat of her heart. 'But he must have. He must have. He wanted to be king!'

'But he isn't,' Ayla murmured. 'Is he?'

'No,' Eydis sighed.

'So, perhaps Ivaar did not do it at all?' Ayla said, shaking her head. 'All I know for certain is that he will not stop until he gets what he wants,' she warned. 'He will not rest until he is the King of Oss. Until Eadmund and Jael are dead, and he wears your father's crown.'

'And will you help him?' Eydis asked breathlessly. 'Will you help him take the crown?'

Ayla's eyes widened then closed, and everything went dark.

***

Morana could barely contain herself.

Eadmund was there.

Jael was there.

Downstairs, within reach. They didn't have time to be arguing like this.

'It is *enough*,' Varna rasped insistently. 'More than enough! I don't know why you must be so particular. We can bind her with this.' She lifted up the filthy grey tunic Meena had stuffed up her dress and secreted out of Jael and Eadmund's chamber.

'If that is all you wish to do,' Morana sneered, ignoring Meena's wide eyes flicking back and forth as she tapped her head. 'If you think it would work?'

'You think it won't? That she is protected somehow because she is Furia's daughter?' Varna asked, frowning.

'I think she has the sword, but she has no knowledge of what she's meant to do with it. But we can stop her from *ever* using it.'

'You still want to kill her?' Varna asked carefully, jumping as the fire popped.

Morana just smiled.

'I have considered it, of course, but it is a bad idea,' Varna sighed, rolling her eyes. 'You have lived far too long on that island by yourself, Daughter,' she grumbled. 'It has rotted your mind so that you only see in dark and light, but there are many shadows we must weave our way through if we are to be victorious.'

Morana looked at her mother as though she had gone mad.

'If you kill Jael Furyck while she is here, in Hest, in Haaron's castle, it will cause chaos in all of Osterland,' Varna said slowly. 'To kill a queen? A Furyck? Especially that one. Everyone will assume that Haaron did it. It would unite the other kingdoms against him.'

'So?'

'So, we do not need to weaken Hest and put ourselves in unnecessary danger before we have even touched the book,' Varna explained. 'Hest is where all our power lies. We cannot destroy what has been so carefully constructed here, especially now that the book has been found.'

Morana glanced at Meena. 'He still has the book? You did, at least, find that out?'

Meena nodded. 'He talked about it.'

'But not its location?' Morana wondered sharply.

'No...' Meena started, then swallowed as Morana glared at her. 'But he will. I told him I would be able to read some of it. He wants my h-h-h-help.'

Varna smiled, ripping the tunic into pieces. 'Well, that is good to hear.' She picked up a small pewter bowl, shoving it at Meena's stomach. 'Now go and kill something. We need some blood.'

***

'Stop thinking,' Eadmund grumbled softly. 'I can hear it.' He kissed the top of his wife's head, which, despite a thorough wash, still stunk of evil sea-fire smoke.

'I'm not thinking,' Jael murmured as she lay there, in a place she had missed: her head just under his chin, her hand teasing the soft golden hair on his chest.

'There's no way to help Amma,' Eadmund yawned. 'Not yet. Not while we're here, weakened, with only two ships and sixty men. While Lothar is king and he's Haaron's ally. While we're Haaron's ally.'

'I don't know what you're talking about,' Jael whispered. 'I wasn't thinking.'

Eadmund smiled. He felt a welcome sense of peace as he held her. His mind, though weary, was clear, and he could see a straight line between this moment and the next, and even the one after that. He thought of his father and felt an overwhelming rush of loss. 'I owe Eirik a lot,' he said haltingly. 'Forcing us together as he did. Neither of us wanted it, did we? If he hadn't listened to Eydis, swallowed his pride and made that alliance with Lothar, we wouldn't be here.'

Jael thought about that, her mind wandering to Aleksander. She tried to ignore the guilt that always accompanied thoughts of him. She loved Aleksander, there was no doubt of that, and it would never change, but her feelings for Eadmund were different somehow.

He was just hers.

'Well, I think your father would have been happy you thought that,' Jael said sadly. 'And perhaps...'

'Perhaps?'

'Perhaps even... me too.'

Eadmund propped himself up in shock, staring into her eyes. 'You too?' He blinked. 'Are you trying to tell me you love me?'

'No, not that,' Jael said quickly, squirming away from his wide-eyed gaze. 'I'm just happy to think that you're happy. It's good that... you're finally happy.'

'Ha!' Eadmund laughed, lying back down again in frustration. 'You'll never say it, will you?'

'Not likely.'

'Impossible woman.'

'Always.' Jael sat up, leaning over him, her eyes soft, her face kind, her lips almost touching his. 'Always.'

***

Aleksander listened to Axl tossing and turning. He wasn't asleep, he knew. He knew everything Axl was feeling: the sense of helplessness, fear, and frustration; the desperate need to do something to stop them taking away the woman he loved.

But it was no use.

And now he had to tell Axl that, as everyone had told him. Yet he was still there, in that place where pain and hope fought each other and pain always emerged the victor.

What comfort could he truly offer? What hope could he provide?

It didn't matter, Aleksander sighed. Not in the end, because

Amma Furyck was about to be sacrificed by her father so that he might become an even richer, more powerful king.

Jael was right. There was no justice for the many against the power-hungry kings of Osterland.

Not unless they could find a way to turn the tide.

***

Jaeger couldn't sleep. His right ankle was festering, making him irritable. Egil kept coming to check on him, worried that he was turning feverish. Jaeger was determined to hit him if he felt his forehead one more time.

He groaned, wondering how he was going to stand at his wedding. He thought of Elissa and felt the loss of her, the regret of her death. He'd never meant to hurt her, but his temper... it had become difficult to control lately. His bursts of rage had started to overwhelm him, drowning him in fury. He couldn't find a way to stop them, or himself, once in the grip of them.

And now, being forced into a marriage so quickly... to a Furyck? It was his father's idea of revenge, he knew, and after his embarrassing defeat, Haaron was perfectly entitled to exact it.

But soon it would be his turn, for his own revenge upon his father was many years overdue.

'Egil!' he groaned, sitting up.

'My lord?' Egil had just fallen asleep in his bed at the other end of the chamber. He hurried up, stumbling down towards Jaeger. 'Are you unwell, lord?' he asked groggily. 'Is it the fever you feel?'

Jaeger batted away Egil's eager hand as it approached his forehead. 'No! There is no fever. I'm fine. I just want you to leave for Skorro,' he grimaced, pain shooting through his ankle again. 'I need you to bring back the book before someone finds it.'

'Of course, lord. I will leave at first light.'

'No!' Jaeger growled. 'You must go now. If someone sees my servant leaving on a ship, there will be questions asked. Go now. Find someone to take you and pay them well to be discreet. You must not raise any suspicions,' Jaeger insisted. 'If my father were to find out about the book, he would take it and destroy us both.'

Egil nodded, trying to wake himself up. 'And Varna Gallas?' he wondered. 'What will you do now that she knows about the book?'

'Varna?' Jaeger smiled. 'I am yet to determine if I need Varna, because if I don't... well then, we can't have anyone else knowing about the book, can we Egil?'

***

'Oh, my poor Axl,' Edela murmured, tears in her eyes as she rolled over in the darkness. 'Poor, sweet Amma.'

She had felt his pain, seen her tears. Broken hearts, both of them.

She had known, of course, that with Lothar, theirs was a love that was always going to hit a wall of his making. He would not give his daughter to Axl. Never.

Not Ranuf's son, the one who would take his throne.

For she had seen it in her dreams.

That is why Edela had been the one to convince Ranuf not to make Jael his heir. The Brekkan throne, she knew, would one day belong to Axl Furyck.

CHAPTER THIRTY SEVEN

'You look cleaner!' Jael smiled, walking up to Fyn. He was shuffling about on the cobblestones next to Aleksander and Gant, who, ignoring him entirely, were muttering about Axl.

'I had a swim,' Fyn said, looking incredibly awkward. 'The water is not as cold as on Oss.'

'But not as warm as in Eskild's Cave,' Jael said wistfully, nodding at Gant and Aleksander. 'Or in Eirik's pool.'

'Eirik's pool?' Fyn frowned, confused.

Jael bit her tongue. 'Never mind,' she mumbled. 'Where's Axl?'

'That's what we were just discussing,' Gant said quietly. 'I haven't seen him this morning. No one has.'

'Oh.'

A small crowd was gathering at the entrance to the piers, waiting for the ship from Saala to pull in. Jael saw Karsten coming towards her with Berard. She frowned. No Jaeger, thankfully, but no Axl either, and that was a problem.

'Someone needs to find him,' Aleksander insisted. 'In case he decides to go and kill Jaeger Dragos. That would be one way to stop the wedding.'

Fyn, shuffling his feet, looked anywhere but at Jael.

'Fyn can do it!' Jael suggested cheerfully. 'And when you find him, bring him to us. We'll have to watch him over the next few days. He's not going to take any of this well.'

'And who can blame him?' Gant sighed. Axl was growing up, he knew, but that temper of his was still raw, reckless, and certainly not under control.

'Ahhh, my new family!' Karsten mocked, his arms open wide. 'How I have missed you since last night.'

Berard looked away, embarrassed.

'How are you, Berard?' Jael smiled, ignoring his one-eyed oaf of a brother. 'You seem happy to be home.'

Berard's eyes brightened. He found it hard not to like Jael Furyck, which was difficult, as no one else in his family did. But she noticed him and was nice to him. It was rare and surprisingly pleasant. 'Well, after what happened on Skorro... yes, it is good to be back.'

'And how is your brother?' Jael wondered, her eyes serious now. 'Will he be well enough for the wedding?'

'I hardly think that's any of your concern, considering that *you're* the one who crippled him!' Karsten sneered, cutting across his brother whose mouth hung open, words waiting on his tongue. 'You worry about your cousin. We'll take care of our brother.'

Jael didn't even blink as she turned to her husband, who had somehow been trapped by Bayla, and was now being dragged towards them on her arm.

Bayla's smile quickly vanished at the sight of Jael, and she released Eadmund, walking towards her sons. 'Well, come along, then. We can hardly greet the girl properly from all the way over here,' she grumbled, and with a swish of her elegant gold dress, she stalked past them all.

Axl watched from the balcony, wondering at the wisdom of joining the welcoming party. He wanted Amma to know that he was there, but at the same time, he wasn't sure he trusted himself. Not yet.

Not until they told her.

***

Thorgils had grown so sick of the company on board *Fire Serpent* that he was almost looking forward to seeing Odda again.

Otto had been like a fly, buzzing around him, complaining about everything and everyone. And stupidly enough, he'd let Morac travel with them as well, and his company had been even worse. A constant stream of airy turds blew out of his mouth all day long.

As the ships navigated their way into Oss' harbour, Thorgils' body slumped with relief at the sight of those sharp, angry cliffs, half-submerged beneath low, misty clouds. Seabirds perching on invisible ledges called to the returning Osslanders before dipping down towards the black stones.

Thorgils smiled.

It was good to be home.

***

Gisila had a bad feeling as soon as she saw Lothar's face. He was glowing like an ember, ready to burst with happiness. She doubted it was just for her.

'My dear! My love!' he cried, holding out a hand to assist her over the edge of the ship. 'You look well!' He pulled her towards him as soon as her boots touched the pier, dragging her into his arms, inhaling her salty hair as he nuzzled her neck. Kissing her quickly on the lips, he smiled. Relieved.

'I am pleased to see you,' Gisila lied mutely. She forced herself to smile while he looked her over, his eyes devouring her in a way she had not missed.

'And Amma!' Lothar smiled as his daughter turned to watch

Eydis being helped over the side of the ship. He stepped towards her, gripping her hand, bringing it to his lips. 'Are you alright?' he frowned, ignoring Eydis. 'You don't look alright.'

'I did not enjoy the journey,' Amma admitted weakly as she wobbled around on the pier. 'My stomach is ill.'

'Oh,' Lothar shrugged dismissively. 'Now, come along, come along, and I will introduce you to our hosts, and then we can discuss everything that has happened since we last saw each other!'

***

'You're not going down?' Fyn asked gingerly as he approached Axl, who had stayed, watching from the first-floor balcony.

Axl shrugged. 'There's no point, is there?'

Fyn looked uncertain. 'I suppose not. But perhaps Amma would like to see you?'

Axl felt embarrassed, realising that he was right. If he loved Amma, and he did, then he would have to stop thinking about himself.

For she was the one about to be fed to the angry bear.

***

It had taken Jaeger a while to hobble from his bedchamber down to the piers.

Haegen had been patient, helping him, taking his weight for the entire arduous journey, but Jaeger was too big, even for him. 'We need to have someone make you a crutch,' he groaned, struggling to a stop. 'I'm sure there's a tree trunk large enough somewhere!'

Jaeger frowned irritably, having barely slept at all. His mind had been too full of Meena and Varna and the book to relax, and his ankle had not stopped throbbing.

He hoped that Egil would find where he'd hidden the book.

Haegen smiled appreciatively as Amma walked towards them. 'At least she's worth looking at. That's a start.'

Jaeger hopped on his less injured ankle, trying to stand up taller, peering at the pretty brown-haired girl who stood there nervously in a damp cloak. She looked tired, he thought. And scared. He tried to picture Elissa again, remembering the first time he'd met her.

She had looked scared too. Of him.

How right she had been.

***

The men hurried to drag the ships onto the beach, desperate for the arms of their women and children, their mothers and sisters. Thorgils smiled as he jumped down into the freezing water, not noticing as it seeped into his boots. He scanned the beach, looking for his own mother, but she wasn't there.

No one was there for him.

He glanced back at his ship, making sure they didn't need another pair of hands but his men had it under control, so he waded through the water, onto the stones.

'I imagine you're feeling rather hungry?' Biddy said as she came towards him, her eyes scouring every ship.

'Well, I imagine you'd be right!'

'Where are Jael and Eadmund? Where's Eydis?' she asked anxiously, her attention suddenly diverted to the women who were sobbing, being told that their sons or husbands had died.

That their king was dead.

'Hest,' Thorgils said quickly, his shoulders heavy. 'They're all in Hest. It's a long story, but I'll happily tell it to you over a bowl of stew!' He gave Biddy a cheerful wink, seizing her arm as she went sliding on the stones.

Biddy frowned, worried, but at least Thorgils was home, and he would surely know what had happened. 'So it's true, then?' she asked quietly. 'Eirik is dead?'

Thorgils nodded, his lips tight. 'Did Edela dream it?'

'She did,' Biddy nodded. 'We didn't tell anyone, though, not without knowing the circumstances, or who had done it. Not for certain.'

'That would be Ivaar, of course,' Thorgils growled. 'Eadmund has plans for him when he returns, but in the meantime, we need to get the gold inside and prepare the fort.'

'Gold? Prepare the fort? For what?'

'For whatever Ivaar may have in mind,' Thorgils warned. 'Now that Jael and Eadmund are the King and Queen of Oss, Ivaar is not very happy at all.'

They walked past Runa, who stood on the stones, running her eyes over the ships again. There was still no sign of Fyn. 'Morac!' she called urgently, hurrying towards her husband, panic throbbing inside her chest. 'Morac!'

He grasped her hands, smiling wearily, happy to see her.

'Where's Fyn?' she asked desperately.

Morac frowned. 'Fyn? Fyn is in Hest with the new king and queen.'

Runa froze, relieved and then confused. 'What do you mean, the new king and queen?'

'Eirik is dead. He was murdered in Saala.'

Runa covered her mouth in horror.

***

'Eydis!' Eadmund pushed his way through the crowd towards his sister who stood, holding Gisila's hand, her head spinning as she tried to get her bearings.

Gisila released her and Eydis fell into Eadmund's arms, sobbing with relief.

Jael was there too. 'Eydis!' she smiled, squeezing her tightly. 'It's alright, it's alright.'

Eydis couldn't stop crying, though, as she held onto Eadmund and Jael, never wanting to let them go.

Gisila sighed, hurrying to join Lothar who was gesturing impatiently at her. Everything about him was ridiculous. She had not missed him at all. Her eyes wandered around the crowd, spying Aleksander and Gant, neither of whom seemed happy.

But no Axl.

'My wife, Gisila,' Lothar said regally, pushing Gisila forward. 'And my daughter, Amma. This is King Haaron and Queen Bayla.'

Haaron barely looked at Gisila, Ranuf's wife, now Lothar's wife. He smiled at the thought of that. As for the shaking little girl before him, barely a woman... he didn't care that she was pretty. The last one had been pretty, and she had ended up dead. Pretty wasn't important. Land was important. And alliances to get land were important. What Jaeger thought or didn't think of Lothar's daughter meant little to him. 'My dear,' he rasped, his lips barely moving as he clasped Amma's hands. 'Welcome to Hest. We hope you'll be happy here.'

Bayla smiled at the girl, whose eyes were big and terrified, retreating beneath thick, worried eyebrows. She was not plain at all, which would please Jaeger, but she was a Furyck. Her presence here would be difficult. For her.

Amma flinched, confused.

Gisila frowned, disturbed by the way the king and queen were inspecting Amma. In fact, as she looked around, everyone's eyes were on Amma. She turned to the large man who was limping awkwardly towards them, her stomach suddenly clenching.

'And this is my son,' Haaron barked. 'Jaeger. He is to be your husband.'

Amma's mouth fell open and stayed there.

***

'Father!' Evaine was beside herself as she rushed into his arms. She had not wanted to remain in the house, but Runa had suggested that it would be unfair on Eadmund to present herself to him as soon as he returned, in front of his wife.

Surprisingly, Evaine had seen Runa's point. She didn't know if the binding spell was still working, so she decided that it was better to wait until she could see Eadmund alone. But knowing that everyone was down on the beach without her had been torturous.

Morac wrapped his arms around Evaine, pleased for any form of affection after such an arduous journey home. The sea had been choppy, and his body, older and less able to deal with discomfort, was eager to settle and not attempt such a young man's folly again. 'How is the boy?' he asked, releasing her and closing the door behind them. 'And you? You look well again. Such pink cheeks!'

Evaine ignored his questions. 'Eadmund, Father,' she grumbled, panicking. 'Where is Eadmund?'

Morac sighed, admitting defeat. There was obviously no affection on offer from any of his family today. 'Eadmund,' he began, watching the fever build in Evaine's eyes, 'is in Hest, with his wife.'

Evaine's perfectly formed upper lip twitched.

***

Gisila stared at Lothar, her face frozen in horror.

He ignored her.

Amma didn't know where to look. She caught sight of Axl out of the corner of her eye as he walked towards her and quickly turned to him... Jaeger Dragos.

'Isn't that good news, Daughter?' Lothar beamed, trying to cover over the awkwardness of Amma's continued silence.

'Perhaps Amma needs something to drink?' Jael suggested, embracing her cousin. 'Don't worry,' she whispered in her ear, before standing back and smiling at her.

Amma blinked, looking worried.

'Of course,' Bayla sighed impatiently. 'Let us go into the hall.' She looked down her narrow nose at Eydis. 'What is wrong with her?' she wondered.

'*Her*?' Eadmund snapped.

Jael took a deep breath, stepping in front of him. 'Eydis is blind,' she said shortly, biting down on her own anger.

Bayla looked momentarily embarrassed, ushering everyone away from the piers, pointing them towards the castle, ignoring both Jael and Eydis entirely.

Gisila placed a hand on Lothar's arm, urging him to remain behind. Lothar smiled at her, turning for a kiss, but she stepped back and glared at him instead, too furious to be careful. 'What were you thinking?' she whispered hoarsely. 'You cannot marry a Furyck to a Dragos!'

Lothar's lips pursed in annoyance. He stepped closer to his wife, watching everyone depart. Grabbing her arm, he yanked her towards him. 'You do not understand the situation,' he hissed. 'For if you did, you would see that I had little choice in the matter. I needed to negotiate a way out of here for all of us.'

Gisila grimaced. Lothar's grip was hard, and his eyes were cruel, but she did not back down. 'But Amma? You're going to leave her here? With *them*?' She shook her head in disbelief.

'It has nothing to do with you, my queen,' Lothar growled. 'And you would do well to remember your place. For no decisions are yours, and your opinion about mine matters nothing to me!' And pulling Gisila off her feet, he hurried her away after their hosts.

***

They sat around the table in silence.

Morac was devouring his second bowl of fish soup, occasionally sighing with pleasure. He had missed Respa's cooking and the comfortable warmth and silence of his own home.

Runa didn't want to even look at him, wishing he'd never come back; wishing that Fyn sat there instead.

Evaine didn't notice anything at all. She felt disturbed, wondering what was happening with Eadmund. 'And you don't know when they will return?' she asked again.

Morac shook his head, his mouth full. He swallowed, taking a quick drink of ale. 'They have to see to a wedding, which will be a few days at least. But I hardly think anyone will want to stay in Hest for long.'

'Wedding?' Evaine leaned forward.

'Lothar Furyck's daughter to Haaron's youngest son,' Morac muttered, sticking his spoon back into the soup. 'Making another alliance.'

Runa looked surprised and worried. 'Brekka and Hest have made an alliance with each other?'

'And us,' Morac said. 'As we have an alliance with Brekka, we're included too. We will have to go to war again to support Lothar's claim for more land.'

Neither Runa nor Evaine looked pleased by that thought.

'And what of Eirik?' Runa asked sadly, still in shock. 'Who killed him?'

'Eadmund seems to think it was Ivaar.'

Runa frowned. 'Ivaar?' She shook her head. 'Well, I suppose that's no surprise, is it?'

'No,' Morac agreed. 'Not to anyone. I'm sure Eadmund will avenge his father's death when he returns.' He glanced at Evaine, whose eyes lit up at the sound of Eadmund's name.

She was desperate to see him.

***

Eadmund was getting sick of the sight of Haaron's hall.

He stood in a cluster of equally irritated men, watching as Lothar preened himself in front of Haaron; as Osbert hobbled about gleefully next to his father, enjoying the shock on his sister's face and the anger on Axl's.

Axl turned away, worried that he wouldn't be able to stop himself from doing something stupid.

'Here.' Aleksander offered him a cup of wine. 'Have a drink.'

'Do you think that's wise?' Eadmund asked distractedly, noticing the wild look in Axl's eye.

'Do you think it's anything to do with you?' Aleksander retorted crossly.

Eadmund frowned, scratching his beard. As irritated as that made him, he was far more concerned with his wife and sister. Jael had taken Eydis away to find her some milk and somewhere quiet to sit down. He couldn't see where they had gone. 'I think that, more than anyone, I know what trouble drink can get you into. And no, it's nothing to do with me, other than the fact that I'm married to his sister, which makes him my brother.' And with a sigh, Eadmund walked away, deciding that searching for Eydis and Jael would get him into less trouble than having to make conversation with a man who looked ready for a fight.

'Are you alright there?' Gant wondered with a frown.

Aleksander shook his head, cross with himself. He nodded, grabbing a drink from a passing servant. 'It's not always easy.'

'No,' Gant murmured, watching Gisila as she stood next to Bayla and her daughters-in-law, looking as though she would rather be anywhere else. 'No, it's not. But right now, we just need to get through this. There'll be time for thinking when we're home.'

Axl sighed, turning to Fyn. 'I need some air.'

Fyn blinked in surprise as Axl headed out of the hall. Aleksander nodded at him to follow.

'Don't let him out of your sight!' Gant growled, his eyes sharp as Fyn gulped, hurrying away.

***

Thorgils shook his head as he stroked Ido, who had fought his sister for the pleasure of his giant-sized lap. 'You two have been busy, indeed,' he smiled, content to sit and let his body come back to earth. He still felt as though he was rolling on the waves and after two large bowls of stew, he was ready for a long sleep.

'Not quite as much as you, however,' Edela said, relieved to hear that everyone was safe; disturbed though, by the thought of poor Amma and what she was about to endure. 'I'm glad to hear the sea-fire helped.'

'Helped?' Thorgils' eyes bulged. 'You saved us and destroyed them! It was the greatest thing I've ever seen! And we need more of it!'

Edela squirmed in her chair as Biddy finished tidying up the kitchen and came to join them. 'Well, I'm not sure about that. But

I can certainly show you my recipe. Whether you have all the ingredients here on Oss, I don't know.'

'Whatever we have to do,' Thorgils insisted. 'We must have more of it!'

Biddy frowned, wanting to talk about more than battles and fire. 'But how was poor Eydis?'

'She took to Jael's mother and her cousin very quickly,' Thorgils said, trying to reassure her. 'They were taking good care of her. She was looking forward to coming back home, though.'

'Well, if only Lothar hadn't made such a stupid bargain with poor Amma,' Edela grumbled. 'As though she meant nothing to him! Which, obviously, she doesn't.'

Thorgils looked away. 'Yes, Jaeger Dragos is...'

'Is what?' Edela and Biddy glared at him.

'Nobody you would wish to know. Certainly nobody you would wish to marry your daughter to,' he went on awkwardly. 'I'm not sure you'd even want your worst enemy married to that beast.'

***

Amma hadn't heard a thing since Haaron had introduced her to his son. Her face was a serene mask as she looked around the hall, trying to avoid all the inquisitive new faces as they peered at her, but inside she was screaming for help.

'Nicolene has a dress for you to wear,' Irenna said kindly. She remembered what it had felt like when her father had made his alliance with Haaron Dragos, handing her over as part of their agreement. But Haegen had made her happy. She'd been lucky. Luckier than Nicolene, who'd been stuck with Karsten.

Amma nodded, her eyes brimming with tears that would not fall. 'Thank you,' she mumbled.

Nicolene arched a critical eyebrow in Amma's direction. 'Although, you are much wider than me, so perhaps it will not fit?'

Irenna frowned. 'She is hardly any wider than you, that I can see.'

Gisila glared coldly at Nicolene. 'Amma has a chest of dresses with her. I'm sure one of those will be more than suitable. As the daughter of a king, her clothes are of the finest quality.'

Amma wasn't listening. She was trying to avoid Jaeger's eyes. He was there, she could see. So large and terrifying. Taller than Axl and so broad and... she shivered, still in shock, wondering what had happened to Axl. Wondering what Jael had meant by, 'don't worry'.

She was worrying, very, very much.

'Perhaps there is somewhere we could go and wash? And change out of these clothes?' Gisila asked Bayla.

Bayla looked irritated by the question. 'Of course,' she said slowly, her eyes running the length of Amma. 'I will find a slave to show you to your chambers.'

Lothar's smile was cat-like as he turned it on Gisila. 'Don't be long,' he purred.

Gisila shuddered as she turned away, dreading what the night would bring.

Bayla motioned for them to follow the slave she had found, and Amma and Gisila hurried away, desperate for a moment to inhale the shock of what they had just sailed into. Amma gripped Gisila's hand, feeling everyone's eyes on her, ready to run away from them all.

Meena leaned against the wall, trying to make herself invisible amongst the slaves who were waiting to be called upon, watching as Jaeger's bride-to-be scurried away. She felt a burst of unexpected rage coursing through her body, sparking in her fingers and toes. Every sinew, every vein pulsed with a passion that was so unfamiliar to her.

Jaeger was getting married.

She swallowed repeatedly, desperately searching the room for him. And when she found him, she could see that his eyes were fixed on Amma Furyck, following her as she disappeared from view.

CHAPTER THIRTY EIGHT

Thorgils could barely look at Eirik's empty chair. The thought of that night, of his dying face... the pyre. It was so fresh in his mind that he could still smell the ash. Or perhaps that was just the stink of being stuck on Skorro in that burned-out shell.

Sevrin sat opposite him, still shaking his head in shock. 'You really think Ivaar will come?'

Thorgils knocked back the last drop of ale in his cup. He wiped a hand over his beard, tired. 'I think the lords seemed to be on his side for a time, especially Hassi and Frits. But after the battle?' He smiled. 'After that, not so much.'

Sevrin leaned forward, lowering his voice. He was nearly as old as Morac, as old as Otto, who sat quietly in a corner with a group of men, drinking to their king. 'But it would not take much for them to change their minds again.'

Thorgils nodded. Eirik had trusted Sevrin with the fort, and there was a reason for that. Sevrin had a clear head. Whereas Otto panicked and made poor decisions, and Morac was given to being slimy and manipulative, Sevrin saw what needed to be done and got on with it. 'We'll need to work on our defenses. Put new ones in place, all around the island. More lookouts. More arrows.'

'Agreed. And perhaps when Jael and Eadmund return, it would be wise to discuss removing some of those Ivaar friendly lords?'

Thorgils grinned. 'Well, once there's no Ivaar, I don't see that we'll have a problem.'

***

Ivaar sat alone by the fire, his chair as close to the flames as he could place it without turning it to ash. He had not been able to get warm since his return from Skorro. It would hardly reinforce his pleas of innocence that he'd hurried his men away in the dead of night.

He watched the flames, enjoying the silence, remembering his father's death, angry that it had not resulted in his ascension to the throne; furious that Jael's interference had put an end to his plans. He frowned, unable to get Ayla's words out of his head. She had seen him as the King of Oss, so why wasn't he? And as much as he wanted to blame her, he knew that Eydis had seen the same thing. It was not her dreams that were flawed, then, but perhaps the path did not begin where she imagined it would.

There had to be another way into Oss. Onto that throne.

His throne. His crown.

His brother would die by his hand.

Ayla had seen that too.

***

Amma sat on the bed, staring at the floor as Gisila hurried out of her damp clothes. Despite all that was going on, she was desperate to change into something that made her feel more like a queen. 'Jael and Aleksander will think of something,' she assured Amma in a low voice as she rummaged through her chest, frowning at every crumpled dress. 'You can be certain of it. And Gant. Axl too. We will not let your father get away with this.'

At the sound of Axl's name, Amma lifted her head, suddenly worried. This was Osbert's doing, and she couldn't let Axl play into her brother's hands. 'I love Axl,' she said quickly.

Gisila blinked. 'What did you say?' she wondered, turning around.

Tears ran down Amma's cheeks. 'I love Axl, Gisila. And he loves me. I don't want him to do something, to risk anything for me. Osbert is hoping he will get himself killed. I know he is!'

Gisila abandoned her hunt for a dress and came to sit beside Amma. 'I knew you had become very close, but I didn't realise...'

Amma clasped Gisila's ice-cold hands in hers. 'You must keep Axl safe. Get him back to Andala. I don't want him to get hurt. I can stand it here, stand whatever that man will do to me, but I cannot stand to think that something will happen to Axl.'

Gisila nodded. 'Yes, I promise, I promise you that. I want the same thing. But, Amma,' she paused, staring into those big brown eyes which were so full of fear, 'you must not give up hope.' Her shoulders slumped as she thought of Lothar and his hot breath and roaming hands. 'There is a way to survive, a place you can go within yourself where you can be safe, where you can watch as it happens and not be so hurt by it. If you can stay in that place, and lock yourself away, then you can survive. Somehow, all of this will be different,' she said softly. 'One day.'

Amma stared into Gisila's eyes, seeing her strength. She desperately wanted to believe what she was saying, but then she remembered Eydis' dream and any hope slid away into the darkness.

***

Lothar had been looking for a way to broach the subject for a while now, but he couldn't think of anything that wasn't abrupt. Haaron's brooding, sharp-edged face kept him anxious, but Lothar tiptoed towards it anyway. 'My lord, now that we are allies, at last, I will need my sword back,' Lothar started with a nervous cough. 'We all will, of course, but my sword, in particular... it has great value to me, to my family.'

Haaron glared at him, irked by the request. He rolled his tongue around his mouth. 'Well, as you say, we are allies now,' he said, albeit reluctantly. 'And yes, you shall have your sword returned. And those of your close counsel. But the rest of your men?' he frowned, jutting out his chin. 'It makes no sense for me to have a horde of armed Brekkans roaming my kingdom. Not yet. Not while we are still such *new* allies.'

Lothar heard little past the fact that his own sword would be returned. 'That sounds fair,' he smiled, relieved.

'I shall have the rest of your weapons returned to Andala once you have departed,' Haaron went on. 'Your men will need them when we attack Helsabor.'

Lothar's moist lips curled happily. 'I look forward to it. That old man has been so busy keeping everyone out for so long. I can't wait to tear down his walls!'

'Or perhaps burn them down?' Haaron suggested, sharing Lothar's smile as he considered just how beneficial this alliance of theirs might actually be. As distasteful as he found Lothar Furyck, becoming friends with him might end up being one of the best decisions he'd ever made.

***

'I'm not hungry,' Eydis insisted weakly, pushing away the food Jael had brought her. 'I would rather sleep.'

'I doubt you'll sleep much in this strange place, with that gurgling stomach,' Jael frowned. 'Eat something, even if it's small, then we'll take you to bed.'

Eydis sighed, her body rolling, unsettling her. 'I don't feel safe here. This is the place I saw in my dreams,' she whispered. 'Where Amma was crying.'

Jael and Eadmund exchanged a worried look.

'She can't take care of herself like you, Jael,' Eydis said, gripping Jael's arm. 'You must help her.'

'We will, of course we will,' Jael said softly. 'But first, we must look after you.' Her eyes were drawn away to Gisila and Amma who had returned to the hall, both looking fresher in dry dresses. Jael smiled at Eydis. 'Here, Amma and Gisila are back. Let's go and sit with them.'

Eadmund nodded. 'You go, I'd better sit near Lothar and Haaron. If they're going to talk about alliances we're involved in, one of us should be there.'

'Have fun,' Jael muttered, rolling her eyes, happy to avoid making polite chatter with anyone.

Jael led Eydis to the high table, but just before they arrived, Haegen helped Jaeger into the seat beside Amma, and Osbert limped into the seat next to Gisila. Jael stopped, her eyes roaming the length of the table, but Eadmund had taken the last seat, beside Lothar. She happily turned to the next table, where Axl and Fyn were talking with Gant and Aleksander, hoping no one would notice if she disappeared to sit there. With a sympathetic look at Amma, Jael helped Eydis onto the bench beside Fyn.

Amma forced her eyes away from that table, away from Axl, who she knew was sitting there. She could feel Osbert watching her every move, hoping she was as miserable as she looked, as he was certain this wedding was going to make her. She would not give him the satisfaction.

She smelled like the sea, salty, but with a hint of lavender, Jaeger noticed as he eased himself towards his bride-to-be. He was wistful for the familiarity of Elissa but also relieved that his new wife would be equally pleasing to look at. She was a Furyck, of course, which made her inherently grotesque in any true Hestians' eyes, but in the darkness of his chamber, as she lay naked in his bed, it would be him who would have to touch her.

So far, at least, he was intrigued.

'Your sister is a queen?' Jaeger asked, watching as Amma considered her plate of food with a frown.

Amma shuddered, reluctantly turning to him. 'Yes.' She saw Osbert's eyes shining with curiosity over the large leg of pork he was gnawing on.

'And do you have similar ambitions?' Jaeger wondered quietly, his sharp eyes resting on her full lips. 'Do you wish to be a queen?'

Amma blinked, uncertain whether to be more disturbed by his words or his eyes which were so invasive they terrified her. 'No. I have no wish to be a queen,' she said, her voice cracking. She reached quickly for her goblet, sipping the sweet wine, grimacing as it burned her throat.

Jaeger licked his lips, disappointed. She was a child, he thought. She dressed like a child, spoke like a child. But her body... his eyes were drawn towards the swell of her ample breasts... her body might tempt him to ignore all of that.

'Stop looking,' Jael growled under her breath.

Axl shook his head. 'I know. I will.' He dropped his eyes to his plate.

The food was plentiful, but none of them had much of an appetite. Thorgils wouldn't have let anything stop him, Jael was certain. She smiled, hoping he had made it to Oss.

Hoping that Oss was safe from Ivaar for now.

***

They had gone to bed early, too early for Evaine, and she couldn't sleep as she lay there, trying to ignore the twitching in her legs and the racing of her mind.

The news her father had brought home had set her fears alight.

Eadmund had not rushed back to be with her and Sigmund. He had stayed with his wife.

His pregnant wife.

Did he know?

Her father had not mentioned anything, so perhaps not, but still, why had he stayed? Why didn't he feel the pull towards her that Morana had insisted he would; the irresistible desire to be only with her. The clouding of his mind to all other thoughts but her and their son.

Why? What had gone wrong?

She shook her head, cold all over, listening as Sigmund started to stir and whimper next to Tanja.

Evaine thought about her candle, about her stones, and the spell. What had stopped it all working? And what could she do to make it right?

She wished she could speak to Morana. She would know what to do.

***

'It takes time,' Varna insisted, sneezing and snorting as she pulled off her boots.

'You know very well that it doesn't take time!' Morana spat, not at all ready for bed. 'You should be down there, watching her, seeing what is going on.'

'Jael Furyck is bound by my spell,' Varna said firmly. 'And tomorrow, we shall put it to the test. Merely watching her is no test. Besides,' she sighed as she creaked to her feet and padded towards her bed, 'Meena is down there. She can tell us what she has seen in the morning.'

Morana watched as her mother pulled back the furs and groaned into her small bed. Her face flared in the flames. She was unable to sit still. 'Well, you sleep then, Mother, and perhaps I'll tell you what *I* have seen in the morning.' And with that, she stood up, rushing out of the chamber before Varna had even managed to prop herself up in an effort to stop her.

Varna fell back onto the pillow, wondering just what damage Morana was about to cause and whether she had the strength left to do anything about it.

***

Biddy stood at the door, calling for the puppies. She sighed irritably, not wanting to put on her cloak and boots and hunt them down, but not wanting anything to happen to them either. Since Evaine had been plainly marked as an enemy who meant them harm, she was determined to protect everything that belonged to Jael.

And Jael loved those puppies.

'Goodnight,' Edela called from her bed, blowing out the lamp beside her.

Biddy turned, surprised. 'Are you alright?' she wondered, pulling the door to, and coming back into the room.

'Yes, fine,' Edela mumbled, shuffling around on the mattress, wriggling her numb toes. 'I have a lot of work to do if I'm to find out what is happening. It feels as though it's getting murkier by the day,' she yawned. 'And now that they're all in Hest, I need to see if there's any danger there.'

'Well, surely some,' Biddy shuddered. 'Haaron and his sons are no friends of Brekkans or Islanders, are they?'

'No,' Edela agreed, 'which poor Amma is about to find out. I must find some way to help her. There must be a way out of this mess that Lothar has made.'

Biddy jumped as the puppies, damp from the cool night,

came rushing into the house, sniffing the floor, licking their lips. She frowned; they had obviously been up to no good. 'Well, I wish you luck with your dreams, Edela.' She shook her head, heading to close the door. 'I know I'll not feel at ease until they're back. Until we know everything, how can we truly keep Jael safe?'

Edela's eyes were already closed, and Biddy's words disappeared into the darkness. She breathed deeply, shutting out everything but the clouds of her mind as they appeared before her.

Jael, she thought.

I need to see Jael.

***

Jael's eyes were drawn to the red-headed woman. She remembered her from the other day. The hairs on Jael's neck stood on end as she picked at her food, pushing around some pork, ignoring the apparently tasty dumplings, lifting her head regularly to see those large, bulbous eyes staring at her.

Frowning, Jael stood up. 'I'll be back soon, Eydis,' she said quietly. 'Fyn is here if you need anything.' She nodded at Fyn, who looked surprised, and slipped away, avoiding everyone's eyes as she walked slowly around the edge of the hall.

Just as she was about to cross the room, another woman walked in, with even wilder hair, stopping next to the wide-eyed spy; both sets of eyes now trained on her.

Jael shuddered as she walked towards them.

Jaeger stared at Meena as she curled herself against the wall, wondering what she was doing in the hall. As he drew his eyes back to his empty goblet, he caught sight of Axl Furyck who looked ready to kill him; and not for the first time since he'd arrived back from Skorro to find the place overrun with Furycks.

'Your cousin seems very angry with me,' Jaeger noted to Amma who bit her lip in surprise.

Amma's eyes rushed towards Axl, who quickly looked away. 'He is... protective of me,' she tried to explain. 'Like a brother. Our parents are married now.'

'Oh,' Jaeger smiled, not caring. 'I see.' He reached out his goblet as a slave girl approached with a jug of wine. 'You're obviously a very close family,' he murmured. 'So much closer than mine. I'm not sure any of us have much affection for each other at all.'

Amma stilled, gripping her fingers under the table. How could this be happening? She looked at Eydis, wishing she could see her, wanting to reach into her dreams and find a way out. She sighed, knowing that the only things Eydis saw for her were pain and despair. Amma watched as Jael walked across the hall towards two strange-looking women. Perhaps her cousin could offer some hope? She was a queen now. There must be something she could do.

Meena froze as Jael approached, her eyes darting towards Morana.

Morana glanced at the high table, recognising Eadmund, then disappeared, hurrying out of the hall.

Jael followed her. 'Do I know you?' she called as she entered the great entranceway that flowed from the hall to the stairs. The black-and-white haired woman appeared to be heading straight for those stairs.

Morana was certain her heart had stopped as she spun around. She was barely breathing as she stood there within a fingertip of touching the woman who could stop them all. And her sword. Her eyes flitted quickly to that sword, then back up to Jael's cold face. 'Know me?' Morana rasped harshly, her eyes challenging, then running away from Jael's. 'No, you don't.'

Jael felt an overwhelming surge of nausea. This woman was familiar, but why? Who was she? 'Why did you run away?'

Morana didn't blink. 'I am not supposed to be in the hall,'

she said quickly, dropping her head to her chest, hiding her face beneath masses of unbound hair. 'I did not wish to get in trouble.'

Jael cocked her head to one side, considering this strange creature. 'You know who I am?' she asked. 'What I can do?'

Morana shuddered. Angry. 'I know.'

'Perhaps not all,' Jael said slowly. 'Perhaps you don't know that I'm a dreamer, like you. I see things, like you. And if anything happens to my cousin, to anyone I care about, I'll know that it was you.' She stood back, surprised by the words which had suddenly burst forth on their own. She didn't know who was more taken aback: her or the wild-haired dreamer.

Morana shivered all over, desperate to accept the challenge, to throw down her own. She stepped forward, her fingers twitching.

'Daughter!' came the hackled call.

Jael's eyes snapped to the curling stone staircase as an ancient crone crept towards them, slithering across the flagstones. Another strange woman. Another dreamer.

Another threat.

Why? Jael frowned. Why did she suddenly know these things?

Morana didn't turn, but her shoulders tightened, as did the smile on her lips.

'We must be going,' Varna croaked, approaching Morana, snatching her arm between two long, misshapen fingers. 'You are not supposed to be here,' she muttered.

Jael eyed the new arrival suspiciously. 'Perhaps you would like to come into the hall?' she suggested. 'I'm sure King Haaron would be interested to know what you're doing here, when, as you say, you are not allowed to be. Or perhaps he would tell me *why* you're not allowed to be here? I'm suddenly very curious.'

Varna's eyebrows shot up, her eyes bursting with fire. Jael Furyck was not bound in the slightest; she could see that very clearly. 'We must be going,' she growled, pulling Morana around. 'If you wish to speak to the king, then please, do as you wish. My daughter has been punished for being slovenly, so she was confined to her chamber. If you wish to make her troubles worse, there is nothing we can do about that.'

Jael said nothing, watching them scurry away.

'Jael?'

Eadmund.

Varna gulped, tugging Morana more urgently now, and Morana quickly followed her up the stairs.

'Are you alright?' Eadmund asked, his attention on Jael, barely noticing the two women hurrying away. 'Who were they?'

Jael said nothing as she stood there, her body throbbing in shock.

What had just happened?

CHAPTER THIRTY NINE

It had taken Eydis a long time to fall asleep in the small cot in the corner of Jael and Eadmund's bedchamber. It was larger than their own on Oss and furnished in a far more elaborate way. There was a double-sized bed and two finely carved chairs which sat before a stone fireplace. Enormous skins covered the flagstones, and its walls were draped with tapestries, but there was no window. And despite the presence of the fire, it felt cold and smelled of disuse.

Eydis had fretted all evening, overwrought and anxious. Everything about Hest had unsettled her. Jael could tell, and she wished Edela were here, or Biddy. They always had a bundle of herbs on hand to steep in hot water; a cure for every ailment. Although, in truth, there was no cure for the loss of a father, Jael knew.

Eydis was breathing steadily now, quiet at last, and Jael was able to let herself think about what had happened in the hall. She sighed, sinking back into the pillow. Who were those women? Three of them and each one strange.

Dreamers. Haaron had three dreamers. Why?

She shook her head. Well, why not, she supposed? It was his prerogative to have as many dreamers as he liked.

They wanted to hurt her. Her certainty in that feeling was a powerful sensation. Jael sat up, touching her shoulder.

'What's wrong?' Eadmund wondered, watching her move about in the shadows. 'Are you hurt?'

Jael had thought him asleep. 'No,' she mumbled. 'I was just thinking about my tattoos.'

'Why?' Eadmund moved towards her, concerned. 'What's happened?'

Jael didn't know what to say. He had come back to her, and she didn't want him to disappear again. 'Those women I saw tonight are dreamers,' she said quietly. 'I feel unsafe.'

Eadmund frowned, sitting up. '*You* feel unsafe? That sounds bad.'

'Mmmm, it does,' Jael agreed. 'But I can't explain why. I don't know what to tell you. This is not a place any of us wants to be.'

'No. But it's only a few days more, and then we'll leave for Oss.'

Jael wasn't listening. She was remembering the look on the black-and-white haired woman's face; the hate in her eyes, as though she wanted to kill her. And if she was a dreamer, there was much she could do to make that happen.

Jael knew that if they were going to get out of Hest and come up with a way to rescue Amma, she had to stay safe.

She had to protect herself from those women.

***

'She's a *dreamer*?' Morana cried incredulously. 'How is that possible?'

Varna was too surprised to answer. She sat in her chair by the blackened embers of the fire, staring at Meena who shuffled about, preparing for bed.

'She's not a dreamer! She's a warrior!' Morana insisted, pacing the room. 'She's a warrior. Our enemy because she's a warrior! Because she has the sword. Because of what she's meant to *do* with that sword!'

'Her grandmother is a dreamer,' Varna sighed. 'Perhaps that's it? It must be.'

'So why is she not bound to us?' Morana grumbled, sitting down at last. 'Does she see what we're doing? Has she warded herself against us?'

Varna shook her head. 'I do not know. The prophecy tells of Furia's daughter as a warrior queen. But perhaps she is more than anyone knew.'

'Well, we have to do something! If we cannot bind her, if we cannot put any spell on her, then we must try something else,' Morana said forcefully. 'We cannot let her leave Hest alive!'

Varna wasn't listening, though, she was too busy wading through the ancient reaches of her memory, trying to find a clue as to what Jael Furyck might actually be.

***

It was Andala.

Edela smiled at the familiar paths and houses; at the hall, the square, the piers. Everything looked newer and cleaner, though. She looked around as people ambled about in the sunshine, seeing to their tasks. No one appeared in a hurry. There was a comfortable peace about the place that put her at ease. Edela's eyes wandered to the training ground, where a dark-haired little girl sat frowning on a white pony.

Edela almost cried. She knew that little girl.

Jael.

Edela hurried towards her, stopping suddenly as she reached the railings. Fianna was there. Fianna Lehr, Aleksander's mother. She was walking beside Jael, her hand near her back, worried that she might topple over but not wanting to fuss. Jael never liked to be fussed over, even as a child.

Perhaps she was only four.

Fianna was smiling as she spoke. 'There is no need to be scared, my sweet girl,' she cooed. 'You are Furia's daughter, and she will always watch over you.' Fianna glanced around, but there was no one near. 'You are the one they say will save us, and Furia will protect you. And your father will protect you, and I promise you, I will protect you with my life. I will never let anything happen to you, Jael.' She reached down, kissing the top of that little head.

Edela was puzzled, watching as Jael smiled, gripping the reins with her chubby little hands; so much determination on her young face.

'You are more special than you know,' Fianna whispered to her. 'More special than almost anyone knows.'

***

Axl was relieved that Osbert wasn't there. They had happily left him in the hall, drunk and pawing at an exotic looking woman who had obviously been far too drunk herself to see what a pathetic piece of useless shit he was.

'You should sleep,' Gant grunted from his bed. 'It won't help Amma if you're out of your mind. Not the way that bastard was looking at you.'

Aleksander nodded as he pulled back his fur. 'It's easier to say than do, but your father always taught me that your mind is your strongest weapon.'

Axl ignored them both from his stool in front of the shrinking flames of the fire. He sipped the last of his ale, staring at Fyn. No one understood, well perhaps Aleksander did, but he hadn't fought for Jael. He'd let her go, and now Jael loved someone else, everyone could see that. He wasn't about to let that happen with

Amma.

But while Lothar lived, and while Lothar tied them to Haaron, they were all trapped. And his kingdom wasn't his. And Amma wasn't his.

And he was powerless.

***

'What do you think it means?' Biddy wondered as they browsed through the market which was suddenly busy now that most of the men had returned.

Thorgils had everyone rushing around, preparing the fort for an imminent attack, which was worrying. But not quite as worrying as Edela's dreams, which Biddy was having a hard time keeping up with.

'Well, it's confusing,' Edela frowned, picking up a fig and sniffing it. She smiled, popping three into her basket. 'But heartening too.'

'Of course,' Biddy murmured. 'I could never imagine Fianna hurting Jael. Ever.'

Edela had told Biddy about her dream over breakfast. The thought that Fianna had led those men to Tuura that night was now muddled with the idea that she had, in fact, sworn to protect Jael. It didn't make sense, but it was a far more comforting thought to have about Fianna and something she couldn't wait to share with Aleksander.

'Edela!' Thorgils looked anxious as he squeezed through the crowd towards her. Another ship had arrived from Alekka that morning, and the Osslanders who were not under Thorgils' thumb had hurried to browse the new wares on offer. 'I've been looking for you all morning.'

'You have?' Edela looked surprised. 'I didn't know I was so

hard to find!'

Thorgils' smile didn't reach his eyes. 'It's my mother. She's ill.'

'Oh.'

'I thought she seemed odd when I returned, not even coming down to the beach,' he said. 'She doesn't want a fuss, and she refused to let me go and get you last night, but she looks even worse this morning. She can't get out of bed.'

Edela patted his arm. 'We shall come right away.' She handed over a coin to pay for the figs and turned to follow Thorgils, smiling at Runa who walked past them with a miserable looking Evaine.

Evaine frowned after Edela as she scurried away with Thorgils and Biddy, not appreciating the cheerful look on her face. 'Why do you spend so much time with those annoying old women?' she asked sharply.

Runa swallowed. 'They are healers, you know. They have helped me greatly.'

'With what?' Evaine stopped before they entered the market crowd and glared at Runa. 'What have they helped you with?'

Runa didn't know what to say. 'I am getting old, Evaine,' she said quickly. 'And as a woman, you'll find out one day that childbirth can take a terrible toll on your body.'

Evaine cringed, turning her head away. She had barely slept, and despite getting up early to perform her ritual, she felt no sense of peace at all. But what could she do? Her father had assured her that Eadmund had the stone, that he still had Sigmund's hair.

So why was she so unsettled?

***

'I keep thinking that my father wouldn't like this,' Eadmund said as he crossed the square with Jael, some way behind Amma and Eydis. They had all been desperate to escape the castle; eager to enjoy some fresh air and freedom from the strangers who peered at them incessantly.

Especially Amma.

'What do you mean?' Jael wondered. 'Hest?'

'Mmmm,' Eadmund murmured, lowering his voice, despite the fact that there was no one following them as they left the square and wandered along the road towards Hest's marketplace. 'The idea of this alliance bothers me. If there are three partners and you're the weakest, the smallest, you're surely in danger of being swallowed whole by the other two once your usefulness is over. It was different when it was just Lothar to deal with, but Lothar and Haaron together?'

Jael's eyes roamed the cliffs to her right, home to hundreds of tiny stone cottages, jumbled on top of one another; great rows of them dug into walls of rock that seemed to reach up into the hazy morning clouds. 'We've no choice but to go along until we're safely away from here. Then we can decide what to do.'

'There'll be little stopping them if they have a mind to conquer us,' Eadmund frowned.

'I agree,' Jael said thoughtfully. 'But it will take some time for Haaron to rebuild his fleet.' Her eyes wandered towards the expansive harbour. Its six long piers were filled with merchant ships, but only a handful of Haaron's fleet remained. 'He has some, but not enough to defeat us. And don't forget, he lost a lot of men as well. And I hardly think the Silurans will be so eager to come to his aid next time. Not after what happened.'

'Well, that's true,' Eadmund smiled. 'And hopefully, Edela can help us make more sea-fire. That should keep everyone at bay!' He grabbed Jael's hand.

'What?' She turned to him, puzzled.

'What do you mean, what?' Eadmund wondered. 'It's called affection, remember?'

'Oh,' she said distractedly. 'Well, I suppose you can have

some of that, for a moment or two.'

'Very generous of you,' Eadmund laughed, surprised that he felt so happy. His heart was heavy, but he was slowly becoming used to the idea that he was a king now, and his wife, who he loved desperately, was his queen. Soon they would go home to start their new life together.

He would have to think about what to do with Evaine and Sigmund, though.

They couldn't remain on Oss.

***

Odda was grumbling loudly, which Thorgils took as an encouraging sign. He stepped back and peered at Edela, who stared up at Biddy, who blinked.

'Perhaps a tonic of willow bark, yarrow, some garlic and meadowsweet...' Edela frowned, thinking. 'Cowslip too. Do we have any honey left? That will help with the taste.'

Biddy nodded. 'I have all of those,' she smiled. 'I'll go and make it up right away. It needs to steep for a while, though, so I'll bring back some ginger and honey tea to soothe that cough.'

Edela nodded. 'That sounds like a good idea.'

Thorgils was barely listening as he opened the door for Biddy. As much as his mother had tormented and nagged him, she had also raised him, and he was certain that she must have loved him and him, her.

Odda coughed, and it was deep and liquid, making Thorgils cringe. He knew he had to make sure everyone was following his instructions to prepare the fort, but it was hard to just leave her like this, wrapped up in her small bed, alone. She looked so fragile and old.

'I'll stay,' Edela said gently, touching his large forearm. 'You can go and see to the fort.' She glanced around the cold cottage. 'But perhaps bring in a few more logs. We want to keep your mother nice and warm to help bring on a sweat.'

Thorgils nodded mutely. He ducked out of the door after Biddy, leaving Edela to remove her cloak and find herself a stool.

***

Haegen and Karsten watched as their wives dutifully followed Bayla around the hall, enduring her sharp tongue as she hurried to prepare everything in time for tomorrow's ceremony.

'They're certainly rushing it through,' Karsten grumbled.

'Makes sense,' Haegen said, picking an apple from the top of a carefully constructed tower of fruit, and polishing it on his black tunic. 'They're all here. Why wait?'

Karsten turned to his brother, his eye sparking with irritation. 'Why do it at all?'

'You mean marry a Furyck?' Haegen wondered, crunching into the apple.

'Of course,' Karsten grumbled. 'We should be killing them, not fucking them!'

Haegen laughed loudly, incurring the wrath of his mother, who glared at them both before turning back around to issue more instructions to Irenna. 'If you were king, you'd just kill everyone, would you?'

'Of course,' Karsten growled happily. 'Wouldn't you?'

Haegen shook his head. 'Maybe once, but I'm old enough now to see the sense in what Father is doing. Being able to take Helsabor is something we can only achieve with help. Getting all that land?' He sighed. 'We wouldn't have to rely so heavily on trade, on the merchants who come to fleece us every day.'

Karsten shook his head, unconvinced.

'There's always a time for revenge,' Haegen smiled, lowering his voice. 'Especially the revenge you seek so desperately, Brother. But there's also a time for alliances. If we get what we want from the Brekkans and the Islanders, we'll grow even more powerful. Then, if it suited us, we could break the alliance and take everything for ourselves.'

Karsten stared at his brother, pleasantly surprised.

'So be patient, and keep your hand away from your sword,' Haegen whispered hoarsely as their father approached with Lothar and his miserable-looking wife. 'There'll be time for what you seek, don't worry.'

'My sons!' Haaron said eagerly, desperate for company that wasn't Brekkan. 'Are you hiding from your mother over here?'

Haegen threw his apple core onto the table. 'Trying to, but I don't think it's working. She keeps looking this way.'

'Well, I imagine she wants everything to be perfect, which is hard at such short notice.'

'Perhaps it would be better to delay the wedding then, my lord?' Gisila suggested boldly. 'It would give us all a chance to prepare properly.'

Haaron's eyes snapped to Gisila's face. She was an exceptionally beautiful woman. He had heard that, of course, and was pleased to find that it was true, although she was far too scrawny to make a good bed companion; sharp edges suited no one, particularly a woman of her age. 'I have complete confidence in Bayla,' he smiled coolly. 'There is no need to fear, my lady.'

Lothar frowned at Gisila, irritated that she was so intent on delaying the wedding. She had been muttering away about it all morning. Her attitude was quickly ruining any joy he felt in their reunion. 'Perhaps you could go and offer your assistance, my love?' Lothar suggested firmly. 'After all, you have experience of organising weddings at short notice, don't you?'

Gisila looked around helplessly but not one of the men, almost all of them strangers, appeared interested in coming to her aid. 'Of course,' she said mutely. 'I would be delighted to.'

***

Hest's marketplace was a sprawling maze of tightly packed stalls and shouting merchants; bursting with bright colours, fragrant spices, furs, beads, exotic scents; so many things that they had never seen or smelled before. Even Amma, in her morose state, couldn't help but be enthralled.

'Well, this is different,' Jael said, shaking her head as a Siluran merchant rushed up to her brandishing a necklace of colourful glass beads.

'For your wife, lord! For your wife!' he called to Eadmund, who ignored him and kept walking. He had Eydis' hand now, and he pulled her closer as the paths between the stalls narrowed, and the merchants became more aggressive.

'They're all a bit pushy,' Eadmund grumbled irritably, elbowing one of those pushy merchants out of the way as he lunged for Eydis.

'They seem to think you must buy me jewels!' Jael laughed as another man tried to offer Eadmund a turquoise brooch.

'Well, they don't know you, do they?' Eadmund smiled, forging a path for them all to follow. 'Amma, watch out!' he cried as a man jumped in front of them with a plate of cakes.

'It smells good, though,' Eydis said enthusiastically, much recovered after a long and deep sleep.

'I have a few coins if you'd like something to eat?' Eadmund offered, reaching into his pouch with one hand and handing Eydis off to Jael with the other. He gave the cake holder a small silver coin and took two cakes, dripping with honey. 'Here,' he said to Amma. 'Would you like one?'

Amma shook her head. 'No, thank you,' she said quietly, ready to cry. As upset as she was, though, as desperate as she felt, the tears would not come.

'Fyn will take it!' Aleksander smiled, emerging from a pathway to the left with Axl and Fyn. 'He slept through breakfast, and his stomach's been growling all morning!'

Eadmund passed the cake to Fyn, who looked embarrassed, glancing at Eydis and looking even more embarrassed. Not embarrassed enough to stop himself from popping the tiny cake into his mouth, though.

'Nice?' Jael asked, watching as Eydis devoured her own cake, happy to see that her appetite had returned.

'Mmmm,' Eydis mumbled. 'It's so sweet!'

Amma didn't say a word as her eyes sought Axl's. He looked even more miserable than her.

'Perhaps you two could walk ahead?' Jael suggested to them. 'In here, no one will see you. Everyone's too busy in the castle. And you're hardly likely to run into Jaeger.'

Amma shuddered at the sound of that name, but she nodded and smiled at Axl. He smiled back, and they hurried away together.

'Are you sure that's such a good idea?' Eadmund wondered.

'No,' Jael supposed. 'But they need to say their goodbyes somewhere.' She watched them go, sensing Aleksander's eyes on her, remembering their own goodbye not so long ago.

CHAPTER FORTY

'Where is your step-daughter?' Bayla asked sharply. She did not want Gisila's company any more than Gisila wanted hers. 'It would be useful if she were here. We need to ensure Nicolene's dress fits. There is no time for anything else.'

'Of course,' Gisila muttered. 'I will go and find her. I imagine she's eager to explore her new home.' Her emotionless eyes rested on the harsh face of the Queen of Hest; a woman unhappy with her life, Gisila decided. Despite the largess of her kingdom, Bayla Dragos' face told the tale of one who had spent her years angry, bitter, and miserable.

Gisila wondered if her own face told a similar story.

Bayla smirked. 'I'm sure she is. I'll send Nicolene with you. She can show you around and then take you and the girl to try on the dress.'

Gisila tried not to frown as she glanced at the tall, blonde-haired young woman cradling an equally blonde-haired little boy.

Nicolene handed her one-year-old son, Kai, to his grandmother, and lifted up the hem of her new dress, which she had no intention of getting dirty outside. 'I imagine she's gone to the markets,' Nicolene said with a bored sigh. And ignoring her mother-in-law's less than impressed face, she strode out of the hall, not bothering to wait, as Gisila hurried to catch up with her.

***

Hest was a place that had grown out of its landscape. Over the centuries, each king had chipped further and further into the mountains that surrounded its rock-faced cliffs, digging in paths that wound their way out of the castle and into the hillside. The paths were private and cool, hidden beneath canopies of trees; places to disappear into when the summer heat became too much, or the topic of conversation too risky.

Varna used to love escaping into the winding gardens to think and plot and let her mind wander, but her legs were weak now, and so they had simply stopped at the first bench they could find. Morana peered around, but she couldn't see anyone coming as she took a seat next to her mother.

'We cannot kill her,' Varna began breathlessly, holding her withered hand up to silence any protestations. 'All blame will go to Haaron. And that cannot happen. Not now.'

'Why?' Morana spat. 'Why do you care so much about this stone kingdom and your failed king?'

Varna inhaled the fresh, pine scent of the trees, enjoying the warmth of the air. 'Hest has always been my home, and I have been with Haaron since he was a boy,' she said slowly. 'But I could care less about either of them. I care about why Hest needs to remain whole. Why Haaron needs to stay king.'

Morana frowned, confused.

Varna sighed impatiently. 'The book cannot be taken by someone like Jaeger Dragos. It cannot be claimed by a man who is stupid and reckless, who cares nothing for its purpose. He will use it solely for his own benefit.' She shuddered, imagining his giant hands on the precious book. 'All he wants is power and revenge. He is a small-minded boy in a bear's body,' she grumbled. 'He has no concept of what that book is meant for, or why The Following has sought its return all these centuries.'

'And Haaron does?'

'Haaron has respect for The Following,' Varna hissed. 'He has respect for me. He has never turned from me, even if what I suggested was distasteful to him. He will do what he must when I ask. But his sons?' She shook her head. 'They are not so eager to follow the advice of an old woman. If we kill Jael Furyck, Hest will disintegrate. Haaron will not be able to survive, and we need a Dragos if that book's true power is to be realised.' Morana looked ready to protest, but Varna ignored her entirely. 'You know as well as I that she needs more than the sword to fulfill the prophecy.' She smiled, her eyes glistening in a ray of sunlight that had forced its way through the thick brush of trees. 'She needs Eadmund Skalleson. And you have worked hard to take care of that, haven't you?'

Morana nodded. 'Evaine has him bound to her now. There is nothing he wouldn't do to please her, to keep her with him, her and their son. He will turn away from Jael, I have seen that,' she said, feeling a hesitation that troubled her. Eadmund had certainly appeared more attentive to his wife than she would have expected.

'I hope you are right,' Varna wheezed, standing up. 'We need her gone, and quickly. Back to the islands. Alive. And we need that book. That is our purpose. That is what we must focus on. You must ignore the temptation to hurt Jael Furyck. Now that we know she cannot be bound to us, you will let it go. To do anything now would cause great problems, especially if she is a dreamer as she says. If she were to find out about the book...' Varna shook her head. 'We need her gone.'

Morana slouched on the bench, seething, eyeing her mother through the mess of hair that fanned out wildly from her face.

Let Jael Furyck go?

The one who could destroy everything they wanted so badly? She smiled. 'Of course, Mother.'

***

Axl pulled Amma into the crowds, away from anyone who would know or hear them. And when he felt safe enough, he stopped and wrapped his arms around her.

'But someone will see us!' Amma protested into his shoulder.

Axl stood back and smiled. 'They won't,' he promised, glancing around before leaning in to kiss her protesting lips, sighing with pleasure as he held her close. 'They won't find us in here.'

There were merchants and customers, arguing and bartering everywhere they looked. It was almost impossible to hear or see anything in the gaggle of imploring, waving hands and raised voices.

Amma looked up into Axl's eyes. 'I'm so glad you're safe,' she sighed, touching his face. 'So glad you survived the battle.'

He pulled her to him. 'So am I.'

'I don't want to marry him!' she sobbed suddenly.

'I know. I don't want you to either,' Axl insisted, his jaw clenching.

'But there's no choice, is there?' Amma cried. 'I have to do it?'

Axl shuddered, closing his eyes. 'Yes,' he whispered reluctantly.

She'd barely heard him, but she didn't need to; they both knew the truth. 'We shouldn't stay here. Someone will come.' Amma stepped back, wiping away her tears.

'We will find a way to rescue you,' Axl insisted, trying not to cry himself as he kissed her cheeks. 'Jael will help us. She's a queen now, so she has the power to make things happen, Amma. We'll all think of what to do. You won't have to stay here long, I promise. We'll be together soon.'

But Amma could hear the hopelessness in his words and see the doubt in his eyes, and her shoulders slumped.

Axl lifted her chin with his finger, bending towards her,

his eyes full of worry. 'You are strong, Amma. You're a Furyck. Never forget that. It's not only Jael who is a daughter of Furia, is it?' He kissed her quickly and held her hand, not wanting to go, but worried that they had been too long. He didn't want to get her in trouble.

'Oh, there you are!' Nicolene Dragos smiled smartly as Axl quickly dropped Amma's hand and stepped away from her.

Amma jumped in shock as Gisila pushed her way through the crowd, her eyes darting back and forth between their two guilty looking faces.

'I was trying to find my way back to the castle, and Axl found me,' Amma insisted, blinking rapidly.

'That was lucky for you, wasn't it?' Nicolene purred, frowning as she was jostled by two merchants fighting over the same customer. 'Well, it doesn't appear that you got very far, but I can show you how to get out of here.' She grabbed Amma's hand, smiled knowingly at Axl, and pushed herself back into the noisy throng.

Gisila swallowed, looking at the broken-hearted face of her son and squeezed his hand, pulling him along after the quickly disappearing women.

***

Thorgils stood at the gates, watching as the ships left the harbour. He was sending all but two of them around the island to Tatti's Bay. Every Islander knew about the hidden bay, but the ships would not be so exposed there, and they could be stored in the enormous sheds Eirik had built to protect them from Oss' harsh winters. There were sleeping huts there too, and some men would stay to watch over them, to light a signal fire at the first sign of trouble.

It was a difficult place to attack without anyone noticing.

'Perhaps you should come and see your mother now,' Edela smiled, stopping beside him. 'She is already much improved.'

Thorgils sighed as the wind blew through his mess of red hair. He turned to Edela, lifting her into the air. 'Thank you!' he cried happily, surprising them both.

He thought of Isaura and felt an impatience to be with her, to make a family together after all these years apart. Ivaar had taken enough from them both. He had taken the woman meant for him.

And Thorgils was ready to take her back.

***

Isaura watched Ivaar from afar as he walked down the beach, alone.

He had barely spoken to her since his return and he'd thankfully not invited her company much at all; at least not during the day. She shuddered, wishing he hadn't returned to her bed; she missed the sweet solitude she had enjoyed during his absence.

Her children played around her, throwing crumbs to the swooping seabirds, who screeched angrily at them, demanding more.

Ivaar's children. But for how long?

She saw a light of hope now, shining on the horizon.

Ivaar had killed Eirik, she was certain of it. And Eadmund would come for him. Now that he was the king and free to do whatever he chose, he would choose to come for Ivaar. And Thorgils would come with him.

Thorgils would come for them all.

He had to.

***

'What are you doing?' Morac wondered sleepily from his chair. The warmth of the house and the silence since Tanja had managed to get Sigmund to sleep had rendered him almost unconscious.

Evaine was sitting at the table, searching through a book Morana had left for her before she'd disappeared. Help, she'd called it. Help, for if anything went wrong.

And something had gone terribly wrong. Evaine could feel it. 'Nothing,' she mumbled, annoyed by the intrusion into her thoughts, which she wanted to keep to herself. She didn't want to admit that she had done something wrong, or failed to implement Morana's instructions; not when they were all relying on her.

Morac didn't hear her as his eyelids drooped closed and his head dropped towards his slowly rising chest.

***

Amma bit her lip as she stared down at the dress. She had wanted to wear one of her own, but there had been nothing really suitable in her chest, so it had to be Nicolene's dress.

It did not suit her at all.

Nicolene was reed-thin and tall, with barely any hips or breasts to speak of. Her dress, although beautiful and well-made, clung to Amma's body in a way that was far too fitting to make her feel comfortable.

Nicolene stared at her without smiling. 'It's not ideal.'

Gisila looked at Amma's blotchy face, her eyes swollen from crying. 'It doesn't look so bad, though,' she smiled encouragingly. 'Unless you would rather wear one of your own?'

They stood in Nicolene and Karsten's bedchamber, on the

top floor of the castle. Light flooded in from two large windows. Despite the warmth of the afternoon sun, Amma shivered, trying to remember what Axl had said. She blinked at Gisila, who was suffering just as much as she was but trying to be so kind. 'I think it will be fine,' Amma smiled bravely. 'I thank you for lending it to me.'

Nicolene was surprised, glancing at Irenna who had joined them, desperate to escape Bayla.

'You'll not need to wear it for long,' Irenna insisted. 'Once the ceremony is over, you could change into something more comfortable. Something of yours.'

'Yes,' Nicolene agreed. 'And that way you wouldn't get any food on my dress.'

Gisila glared at the viper-tongued girl who looked barely older than Amma but carried herself as though she had ambitions to become the next Queen of Hest. She was thoroughly unlikeable. Irenna, though, was softer, quieter, and thankfully, kinder. 'Why don't you change now, Amma, and we can go down to the hall? I know the queen wishes to speak to you about the ceremony.'

Amma looked terrified. She nodded, though, squeezing out of the delicate silk dress, handing it to Nicolene as she hurried back into her more comfortable, blue woollen dress. Fumbling with nervous fingers, she pinned the straps onto the front apron, trying not to cry; trying not to imagine Jaeger Dragos and his bed, and what he would do to her.

Tomorrow.

***

Despite the constant tapping and the odd look in her bulging eyes, Jaeger was quite pleased for the company. He had grown bored and irritable confined to his bed, waiting for Egil to return.

'Did you wish to show me the book, my lord?' Meena

wondered shyly, wanting to look at him but afraid that he would see into her eyes and discover more than she wanted him to know. 'I can help you read it, I'm sure.'

Jaeger frowned, noting her eagerness; wondering how to react to it. Varna certainly knew about the book. Meena was weak, and Varna was not. Varna would have used every trick she had to peel away any pretence Meena had attempted. It would not have been hard.

He couldn't trust her.

'The book?' he asked casually, grimacing as he pushed himself up, sitting higher in the bed, reaching out a hand. 'Come closer,' he urged. 'You are too far away.'

Meena blinked rapidly, unable to move. Her mouth opened and closed, and she shook her head. 'I, I,' she swallowed. 'I, I –'

'You are not *afraid* of me, are you, Meena?' Jaeger murmured. 'Are you?'

She turned to him then, the sound of his voice so low and smooth; irresistible and frightening all at the same time. 'N-n-no,' she stuttered, wishing her tongue would work properly. It was trapped inside her mouth, and there were loud voices in her head, calling out warnings. She was in danger, they cried urgently. Danger!

Jaeger laughed. 'You sound afraid,' he smiled. 'And you needn't be. We want the same thing, you and I.'

Meena frowned, confused as she edged her way towards him, within reach of those large hands of his, which he ran over his short blonde hair.

'We want freedom! Freedom from those who have made our lives miserable since the day we were born. The ones who have tortured us, made us feel like nothing. Worthless pieces of nothing!' he snarled, his lips curling back angrily as he stared into her eyes. 'They have ordered us about, put us down, controlled us, given us no hope for the future.' He grabbed Meena's hand, pulling it down, away from her head. 'But now it's our turn to take control. To choose our own destiny. And that is where the book comes in.' He leaned forward until his nose was almost touching Meena's.

She flinched but didn't move away, frozen in utter terror. He had her hand. He had her complete attention. 'But Meena,' Jaeger whispered, his eyes never leaving hers, 'how will you ever be free? How will *I* ever be free, if you tell all of our secrets to your bitch of a grandmother?'

***

Jaeger wasn't in the hall, but Amma was, and she looked thoroughly miserable.

Jael felt the guilt of not having come up with a plan yet; not one that involved them all living, at least. She sighed as she walked towards Eadmund, who was smiling sadly at her. 'Are you alright?' she wondered.

He nodded, slipping his arm around her waist, pleased to see that she didn't jump away from him. 'Just wishing we were home. I can't take many more nights like this. This castle feels like a prison.'

Jael nodded, searching the hall for the strange women. The dreamers. She had not seen them all day, but they had not been far from her mind. She hadn't eaten or drunk a mouthful of anything since last night, and she felt irritable and tired because of it.

Jael noticed that Lothar and Haaron had their heads together again, talking with Osbert. 'We should be over there,' she suggested, not wanting to be over there at all. 'Or, at least, you should. Perhaps I'll go and talk to Axl? Make sure he's not planning on getting himself into trouble.'

Eadmund's face contorted as he stared at the conspiring kings. 'I...'

'Well, good then, we can meet up later,' Jael said quickly, slipping away to find her brother.

Eadmund stared after her, frowning, then sighed and headed for the high table.

'Eadmund!' Lothar smiled as he approached. 'We were just talking about you, weren't we, my lord?' He nodded at Haaron, who looked thoroughly unenthused, his face barely moving as he considered the new arrival. 'About how many ships we might be able to put together between us to attack Wulf Halvardar.'

'Well, hardly as many as we might have before you set fire to all of mine,' Haaron said bluntly. He picked up his goblet, desperate for the tedious conversation to be over. His eyes wandered to his sons, who were entertaining the two queens. He couldn't imagine their conversation was any better, but at least their company would have been preferable. Lothar Furyck had had a piece of kale stuck in his teeth all evening, and Haaron was growing tired of looking at it.

'In war, we do what we must to further our own cause, but as allies... we will do all we can to support each other and more,' Lothar said, glancing at Osbert, but his son had turned away, mesmerised by the same woman he had bedded the night before. Lothar frowned and turned to Eadmund instead. 'A drink, my lord?' he asked, nodding towards the jug.

Eadmund shook his head. 'No, I think I'll keep a clear head for tomorrow.'

'Well, I suppose with a niece like mine, it's always better to keep your wits about you!' Lothar chortled, inclining his head towards Haaron, who sat back immediately. 'Your son won't have the same problems, of course,' he smiled, showing off his teeth again. 'Amma is a compliant sort of girl, as she should be.' He glanced towards Amma, who looked morose and lifeless sitting next to Eydis. 'Where is your son, by the way? My daughter appears quite lonely down there.'

Haaron turned to his right, annoyed to have Lothar point out his son's absence. 'Well, he cannot walk on his own, but I imagine he'll be down shortly.' He glared at Lothar's teeth, irritated beyond measure.

***

Jaeger gave up and threw his boot across the room, hitting the wall with a dull thud.

Meena jumped and turned around, fumbling desperately with her dress strap.

'You'll need to help me downstairs,' Jaeger muttered, his impatience with his swollen, festering ankle boiling over. He curled his knuckles into balls, smashing them onto the bed, furious with Jael Furyck and her knife.

'Yes, my lord,' Meena mumbled incoherently into her dress, pushing her hair out of her eyes. 'I will.'

Jaeger stared at her then; his wide-eyed ugly duckling. He wondered if he had done enough to capture her loyalty. He frowned, uncertain; she wouldn't even look at him. 'Meena,' he called softly, raising an eyebrow in her direction. 'Come here. Come and sit next to me.'

Meena shuddered as she shuffled slowly towards him, overwhelmed by an odd mix of discomfort and desire. She was too shocked by the things he had done to her to even speak as she sat down next to him, tapping her foot.

'You won't tell Varna what we did, will you?' he wondered coyly. 'I'm sure she would stop you coming here again if she knew. She'd try to keep you away from me. She doesn't want to see you happy, does she?' He brushed her hair away from her terrified eyes. 'All she wants is the book. And she doesn't care how she gets it, or who she hurts. She wants to help my father. And herself. And if we let her get the book, then we can never be together. They will continue to control us both. Decide who we can see, and when. Who we marry...' Jaeger blinked, suddenly aware that he was supposed to be down in the hall entertaining his bride-to-be.

Amma Furyck.

A smile curled his lips.

He was looking forward to tomorrow night.

CHAPTER FORTY ONE

'Let's go,' Eadmund whispered.

Jael turned around, surprised. She saw the twinkle in his eye she knew so well. 'What about Eydis?' she whispered back.

'I've asked Fyn to watch her,' Eadmund smiled, grabbing his wife's hand.

Jael was caught between guilt and desire. She had missed Eadmund desperately, and there he was, himself again. 'I'll be back shortly,' she muttered to Axl and Gant, avoiding their eyes as she followed Eadmund out of the hall.

Axl watched them go, the way they were with each other, trying to be discreet, but he could see. He knew what it felt like to be in love, to be co-conspirators. His eyes drifted towards Amma who sat next to Jaeger with a look of terror on her face. 'What if that happens to Amma?' he asked Gant. 'Jael loved Aleksander. She didn't want to marry Eadmund. But look at them now. And look at Aleksander.'

They both turned to where Aleksander sat, drinking with some of his men.

Drinking too much again. Utterly miserable.

'Jaeger's not like Eadmund,' Gant smiled encouragingly. 'You've nothing to worry about. Just stay calm, and we'll find a way to give you everything you desire.'

Axl blinked, staring at Gant whose eyes were so unreadable that he wasn't sure what he was saying. 'I want the crown,' Axl whispered. 'It's mine. If I'm the king, then I can make choices instead of being a victim. Instead of the people I love being victims.'

Gant's eyes darted around. The hall was overcrowded, brimming with loud, drunken men and less than impressed women, all mingling together in pre-wedding revelry. Lothar was within view, as was Osbert, and he didn't see another pair of ears nearby. 'I know,' he said calmly. 'Your father wanted it too. Perhaps he saw what Jael would become without Brekka, but he definitely chose you, Axl.' Gant turned to him. 'When we return home, we'll find a way out of this mess.' His eyes wandered to Gisila, who looked ready to cry as she sat wedged between Lothar and Bayla. 'For all of you.'

***

Runa was becoming increasingly concerned by Evaine's state of mind. She had sat at the table, pouring over that book all day long, ignoring everyone; not even touching her meals or looking at Sigmund.

And even now, as the candles flooded and the fire turned to embers, she hunched over the delicate vellum pages, her eyes frantically searching for... what?

Runa glared at Morac, raising her eyebrows towards Evaine.

Morac was almost nodding off and far less inclined to approach Evaine than he was his bed, but he could see Runa's point, and, sighing, he eased himself out of the chair and walked towards her. 'Perhaps it's time we all made our way to bed?' he suggested sleepily, stifling a yawn. 'You've had a busy day, my dear. I imagine your eyes need some rest now.'

Evaine was mumbling to herself, squinting, going over each indecipherable scrawl, desperate for clues as to why she felt that

Eadmund had gone. 'But don't you see, Father?' she croaked, her eyes never leaving the page. 'I must find an answer before it's too late. Before everything is lost. Before *he* is lost!'

Runa's eyes widened. She would have to go and visit Edela and Biddy in the morning. Evaine must know that her spell had broken. But what if she managed to find out why? She swallowed, wondering if Morac would protect her if Evaine discovered her part in everything. Despite her lack of feelings for her husband, she needed a protector, and Morac would have to be it. 'Leave her be,' she called to him. 'Evaine is a mother now. She can make her own decision about when to go to bed. But as for you,' she said with forced warmth. 'You look ready to fall down.' Swallowing, Runa reached out a hand. 'Time for us to go to bed.'

Morac blinked, surprised but happy as he left Evaine and walked hastily towards Runa and this unexpected offer. She had slept in Fyn's bed, outside their bedchamber, since his return. He had missed her.

Evaine didn't even notice them go as she turned another page, her shoulders so tense they felt like wood. But she would not move, would not sleep, would not eat until she'd discovered what had gone wrong.

Until she discovered how she had lost Eadmund.

***

Eadmund kissed her and Jael forgot all about her cold toes.

She ran her hands across the bristles of his beard, so familiar and smoky. His lips were warm and urgent as he bent his head towards her neck, kissing her skin – her chilled, shivering skin – all the way down to her breasts.

'Stop,' she murmured.

Eadmund lifted his head, surprised. 'What is it?'

Jael wriggled away from him, feeling a sense of urgency, worried about those dreamers. 'We have to go back. I don't want to leave Eydis alone out there.'

'Fyn won't let anything happen to her. You know that.' Eadmund touched her face, running a finger over her scar. 'What's wrong?'

Jael shook her head. It was dark in the chamber. No fire had been set, and she was cold, but more than anything, she was suddenly overcome with fear; the fear of loving someone and not being able to keep them safe; the fear that Eadmund would disappear again and not come back. That she would lose him.

She didn't want to lose him.

Jael swallowed. 'Nothing,' she sighed, shutting it all away. 'Nothing. But we should be quick.'

'Quick?' he laughed. 'Is that your way of saying you want to get on top?'

Jael smiled, relaxing again. 'Well, you do tend to take forever.'

'And that's a bad thing, is it?' Eadmund laughed, flipping her over.

Jael looked into his eyes, adjusting her legs, rocking from side to side, getting comfortable. 'Stop talking,' she murmured, leaning forward, her hands on his shoulders as she bent towards his lips. 'We don't have long.'

***

'You look as though you've been sucking a lemon all night, my love,' Lothar grumbled as Bayla left them to talk to Haaron and Haegen. 'It does not suit you to purse your lips so.'

Gisila looked embarrassed, ducking her head.

'Perhaps you need your bed?' Lothar wondered, reaching under the table to run his hand over Gisila's thigh.

Gisila almost bit her tongue. 'Perhaps,' she smiled quickly. 'It was a difficult time to be in Saala, worrying about you. We were all very anxious, especially after what happened to Eirik Skalleson. How he was murdered like that.'

Lothar's body sagged with happiness. There she was again, his perfectly agreeable wife. He patted her leg, edging closer. 'Let us go, then, and quickly,' he shuddered excitedly. 'I've had quite enough of Haaron's company tonight.' Glancing around guiltily, Lothar was relieved to see that Haaron was not within earshot. He grabbed Gisila's hand and hurried her to her feet, farting with utter pleasure at the thought of what awaited him.

'He is a disgusting buffoon of a man,' Bayla sneered as Lothar and Gisila passed on their way out of the hall. 'Somehow, I expected better from a Furyck.'

'I agree,' Haegen laughed. 'They appeared fiercesome from a distance, not foolish!'

'You will be the one who appears foolish if you do not see that Lothar Furyck is hardly typical of their line. I would place a chest of gold on his parentage having been misrepresented to his father,' Haaron said snidely. 'He's not even worthy of being Ranuf Furyck's fool, let alone his brother and usurper of the Brekkan throne!'

'Then why become allies with such a man?' Bayla asked, sniffing the cup of mead Haegen handed her. 'Surely, he will take us down with him?'

'We have legs, my wife,' Haaron smiled knowingly. 'We will leave when the time is right, do not fear. Hest will look after its own.'

'And the girl?' Bayla murmured, her eyes sharp on the simple, little thing that was Amma Furyck, who sat at the high table, shrinking under Jaeger's attention.

'She is perfectly formed, and perfectly timed,' Haaron said quietly. 'Exactly what we need to keep our limping bear busy. He seems quite taken with her, wouldn't you say?'

Haegen nodded, slightly concerned by just how quickly Jaeger had taken to Amma Furyck. He had seen the same predatory look in his brother's eyes when he first met Elissa.

***

Neither woman could sleep.

Biddy's legs kept twitching as she lay there listening to the wind shriek around the house, thinking about everyone who wasn't safe at home on Oss. She would not feel at ease until they had all returned.

Edela was growing irritable. She had set herself the clear purpose of dreaming about Jael, but her thoughts were too muddled to even begin. She could not find the sense of clarity and calm she needed to fall asleep. Sitting up, she gasped at a sharp pain in that annoying hip of hers.

'What is it?' Biddy wondered, propping herself up. 'Are you alright?'

'Mmmm,' Edela mumbled in the darkness. 'Well, not really. I want to dream, but there are so many things that are confusing me. I have too many thoughts in my head!'

'Can I help?' Biddy wondered eagerly.

Edela yawned. 'Well, perhaps if I tell you everything I remember, it will be gone, and my head will become clearer. It is such a noisy mess in there now. I need some peace!'

Biddy laughed, lying back down. 'As long as you don't give me nightmares!'

'Oh, I can't promise you that,' Edela smiled, delving back into her memory, to where it all began, to the first time she had seen Evaine's face. 'I certainly can't promise you that. But don't worry, Biddy Halvor, I'll protect you!'

***

'We should go back,' Eadmund sighed, stretching sleepily.

Jael shivered, hopping out of bed, rushing around the chamber looking for her clothes. 'We should.' She shrugged on her sooty tunic and grabbed her swordbelt. 'Come on, then.'

Eadmund sat up, staring at her.

'What?' Jael asked impatiently. 'What is it?'

'I can't stop thinking about my father,' he started, shaking his head. 'That he's gone. That we're here. It doesn't feel real, as though it was all just a nightmare or something that happened so long ago...' He stopped and looked at his wife. 'And then there's Aleksander.'

Jael sat down beside him, suddenly uncomfortable. 'What do you mean?'

'When he arrived on Oss,' Eadmund murmured, 'it's as though you came alive. You were worried about Edela, I know, but around him... I'd never seen you like that.'

Jael felt her stomach tighten. She didn't know what to say without digging herself a great hole. 'I've known him my whole life, just like you and Thorgils.'

Eadmund laughed. 'I don't think it's like me and Thorgils!'

'Well, not quite,' Jael smiled. 'But, he's my family, and it was hard to say goodbye to him. We were happy.' Her eyes skirted Eadmund's. 'But I don't want to go back to Brekka and be with Aleksander. Not anymore. I want to go back to Oss and be with you.' She swallowed, feeling guilty, knowing that she was being disloyal to Aleksander, but at the same time, Jael knew very clearly what she wanted.

She wanted her husband.

Eadmund reached out and held her hand, sighing in relief. 'Well, that will make things easier, won't it? Being king and queen as we are.' He smiled, not letting go of her hand. 'Let's go back to Eydis, then, and get this whole thing over with. I just want to go home.'

***

Morana's laugh was like a bird screeching as it echoed around Varna's chamber. 'Did you enjoy it, girl?' she wondered slyly. 'What he did to you? When he ran his hands over you? Tried to make you his?' she crowed, circling Meena as she sat shaking in a chair in front of the fire.

Meena hadn't said a thing when she'd returned. She'd been horrified to find that her grandmother wasn't there. Only Morana. And Morana had pounced on her instantly, taunting and poking at her with her barbed insults, trying to get a reaction. Meena had never wanted to see Varna so much in her life.

'But did he tell you anything about the book?' Morana continued, licking her lips. 'Promise it to you? Show it to you? Or was he too busy fucking you to even mention it?'

Meena shuddered, gasping for breath as Morana bent her sadistic face towards her. 'You're worthless to us if you can't get that book from him. Do you understand that, girl? We'll have no need for you soon. Not unless you bring me that book!'

Meena blocked her out, tapping her head, trying to think of Jaeger and the strangely exciting things he had done to her. It had felt so uncomfortable, so invasive, terrifying even. But she was consumed with a throbbing desire to go back so he could do it all over again.

***

Amma had avoided Axl all evening, desperate not to be seen looking at him by the sharp-eyed Nicolene. As she turned to leave the hall, she scanned the room quickly, hoping to catch just one glimpse of him before she disappeared. But instead, she saw

Jaeger hobbling towards her on Karsten's arm, Nicolene peering at her from his other side.

'I'm looking forward to tomorrow,' Jaeger smiled, seizing Amma's hand, pressing it to his lips as Amma forced herself not to squirm. 'Sleep well.'

Nicolene's sharp eyes were fixed on Axl who was coming towards them with Gant, Fyn, and Aleksander. She smiled at Amma, following her husband and brother-in-law out of the hall, her hand on Jaeger's back.

Axl waited for them to leave before turning to Amma who was blinking back tears. He shook his head, wishing he could do something. He wanted to keep her safe. 'Shall I take you to your chamber?'

'I think it's probably best if I do that,' Gant said quickly. 'Axl, you grab hold of Aleksander.'

Axl didn't think that that was the way it should go, but Gant gave him no choice as he unloaded his side of Aleksander's slumped frame onto him.

'It's better this way, I promise,' Gant insisted.

Amma nodded sadly. Gant was not wrong, she knew.

Axl scowled. Gant was completely wrong, he was sure.

Fyn grunted and glared at Axl who was too distracted to notice that Aleksander was tipping over.

Amma blinked quickly at Axl, then turned as Gant led her away, barely noticing that her feet were moving but very aware that her heart was breaking into tiny pieces.

***

Biddy rolled over. 'Do you think the Widow is the one who wants to stop Jael?'

Edela yawned, listening to the soft rumbling snores of Vella who lay wedged into her side; a nice, warming lump. 'I don't know, but she is someone we must consider. She seems to have evil intentions. Although...' she muttered, puzzled, 'it makes me wonder why Fianna and her mother visited her and then sent Aleksander there as well.'

Biddy sighed, suddenly hungry, but far too cold and tired to get out of bed and shuffle into the kitchen for food. 'It's very confusing, knowing Fianna as we did.'

'Indeed,' Edela started, then frowned. 'When I saw Fianna with Jael in my dream, when she was just a wee thing and Fianna was helping her, I could feel how much she loved Jael. There was no one around. It wasn't a pretence. Her love was true and deep. It was as though Jael was her own child, which, looking back, is how I always thought it was. I can't imagine that Fianna ever willingly conspired to hurt her.'

'Which is good news for poor Aleksander.'

'Yes, although we still don't know why she sent that note that led those men to Tuura,' Edela sighed. 'And as for the Widow... I'm certain she's the key to so much we have yet to uncover. If only we could find the prophecy. Perhaps that is what I must dream on?' She closed her eyes, stroking Vella's warm fur, thinking of her granddaughter who she missed with a deep longing. Afraid for her. Desperate to do anything she could to protect her. To help her.

There was so much she didn't know...

***

Eadmund was sound asleep. So was Eydis.

Jael was grateful for the silence. She needed to think. She felt strange all over and had barely found a moment to even breathe since they left Oss.

Since Aleksander had arrived with Edela.

She hoped her grandmother was still well. Thorgils should be there by now, keeping them all safe. Keeping Ivaar at bay. Jael sighed, adjusting her arm, which had been aching all evening, not wanting to think about the problem of Evaine and her son.

Not yet.

Jael needed to think about Amma, and how to get her away from Jaeger Dragos. But the problem and the solution were both so equally huge that she couldn't see how it could be achieved – not without death on a grand scale. One kingdom did not steal a member of another kingdom's royal family; not without severe consequences. And Oss was not big enough to fight off both Brekka and Hest, especially if they were about to be unsettled by Ivaar and the lords.

And then there were those strange women...

Jael knew that they wanted to kill her.

Edela had come to Oss to save her. The Tuuran dreamers had seen that she needed saving. But what if she needed saving from something Edela couldn't see?

Jael was a dreamer; her grandmother had always told her so. But she had closed a firm door on embracing her gift as a child. She had no interest in seeing or feeling anything that she couldn't touch with her own two hands.

She preferred to hold a sword in them instead.

So why now?

Why had she felt compelled to get up and confront those women? Why could she read their thoughts and see their poisoned black hearts throbbing inside their chests?

Shivering, she edged towards Eadmund, resting her frozen feet on his, tired, but not wanting to go to sleep at all.

***

'Varna is wrong about Jael Furyck,' came the voice. A crackling, sharp-edged voice; malevolent and desperate. 'She cares more about saving Hest than stopping the prophecy. Her loyalty is misplaced, though. We have her here. Now. We must kill her! Any way we can. She cannot be allowed to leave Hest!'

The younger woman looked horrified as she tried to back away into the dark corner of the room, glancing anxiously at the door. Edela could hear the galloping thud of her terrified heart as she looked on.

'Get me the book, and I will find a way to kill her. She will not be able to keep *me* out, I promise,' the black-and-white haired woman growled. 'The spells in that book were written by the God of Magic. Spells that no dreamer can ward against! Dreamer?' she laughed wildly. 'How is *she* a dreamer?' She reached out, grabbing a handful of the young woman's dress. 'You will get me the book, do you understand?'

'But I...'

'What?' the older woman snapped. 'He has the book, and now he has you. It will not be hard for you to get the book for me, Meena Gallas.' She leaned forward, her eyes flaming with dark fire. 'Because I know how to read it. And if you want your precious Jaeger to live, you will need me to read it. Because the prophecy says that Jael Furyck is going to kill him!'

***

Edela gasped, reaching her hand up to her throat, gurgling, straining to breathe, lost in the darkness, her eyes blinking uselessly.

'Edela!' Biddy cried sleepily, stumbling out of bed and feeling her way across the room. 'What has happened?' She crouched by her side, peering at the old woman as she tried to sit up.

Edela turned to her, shivering uncontrollably. 'I, I...' She swallowed, the visions retreating quickly. 'I had a dream. Jael is in danger!' She shook her head. It was too much to take in. 'Morana Gallas is in Hest!'

'How do you know?' Biddy asked breathlessly. 'Did you see her?'

Edela nodded, trying to keep a firm grip on the threads of her dream. 'She is trying to kill Jael. Jael is there. She wants to stop her from leaving. She said that Jael is a dreamer, that she needs to try and find another way to kill her. As though she has tried, but it didn't work.'

'You mean because of her tattoos?'

'Yes, and the symbol stone I gave her,' Edela mumbled, her head aching with the strain of holding the dream. She looked up suddenly. 'The book is in Hest! Someone in Hest has the book... Jaeger...'

'Jaeger Dragos?' Biddy looked shocked as her eyes met Edela's. '*He* has the book? How?'

Edela shivered. 'I don't know.'

'If Morana gets the book, can she kill Jael?' Biddy asked, not wanting an answer.

'Yes.'

'But what can we do?'

'We need a fire and some light. I must dig into my chest.'

CHAPTER FORTY TWO

'Evaine,' Morac murmured softly, brushing her tangled blonde hair away from her face as she lay there, sleeping soundly, her head on the book. Sigmund was crying upstairs, and Runa had gone to see if Tanja needed any help. 'Why don't you go up to your bed?' he encouraged gently.

Evaine jerked awake suddenly, groaning from the ache in her neck as she lifted it up from the book and turned it to the side. She blinked angrily at her father, then frowned at the terrible wailing coming from upstairs. Pushing herself away from the table, she stood up.

'You need to get some sleep,' Morac said with trepidation, looking at her crumpled, irritable face.

Evaine didn't argue as she headed for the stairs, too weary to peel back her eyelids. He was right, she knew. There was no answer in that book; not that she could see. She needed Morana to help her. To tell her what had gone wrong.

Runa walked carefully down the stairs cradling a tear-stained Sigmund in her arms, Tanja just behind her. Evaine didn't even notice them. She kept walking, desperate to lie down.

As Evaine approached her bed, she saw the chest and sighed, annoyed that she had missed her morning ritual. She was concentrating so hard on the chest that she didn't notice the wooden rattle lying on the rug. Tripping over it, she fell to the floor, landing on her forearms with a thump.

'Evaine!' Morac called, racing up the stairs towards her.

'I'm fine,' she grumbled, batting him away as he bent down to help her up. 'I'm fine!'

Morac helped her up anyway and led her to the bed. 'We'll take Sigmund out after breakfast so you can have some peace,' he promised, and mumbling away to himself, he headed back downstairs towards his crying grandson.

Evaine sat on the bed, cringing at the pain in her arms, staring at the rattle.

And then the floor.

She cocked her head to one side. The rug had moved when she'd fallen, revealing something strange on the floorboards.

***

'Amma?' Gisila smiled encouragingly, trying to prise Amma out of bed. 'We need to think of what to do with all that hair. Irenna says her servant is an expert at braiding, but she will need some time, so let's get you up and then we can see what would look nice.'

Amma sighed. Her eyes felt so swollen and sore that she wasn't sure she would be able to keep them open for long. She sat up, yawning, trying to avoid Irenna's smile and Nicolene's sneer.

'That's better,' Gisila said, her face taut with worry for Amma and Axl, both. 'Gunni is bringing something up for us to eat, so we can all stay in here and prepare for the ceremony.'

Amma nodded mutely.

Nicolene frowned. 'You're making a very good match, you know,' she said crisply. 'It's not as though you're being forced to marry some commoner. Jaeger is the son of a noble king. The greatest in this land!'

Gisila glared at her, not wanting her here any more than

Amma did. 'Well, that's your opinion. And right now, opinions don't matter. We must focus on getting Amma ready.'

'When I came here from Silura,' Irenna said kindly, taking Amma's hand, 'I was very nervous. I didn't want to leave my home or marry Haegen. And I know that Nicolene certainly didn't want to marry Karsten, but we are both happy now, I would say.' She looked at Nicolene for support and received a barely discernible shrug in return. 'Jaeger is very... handsome,' Irenna went on. 'Every woman in Hest would fight you for the honour of being his bride, I'm sure.' She looked away, worried that her eyes would betray her true feelings and that would hardly help Amma prepare for what lay ahead.

There was so much that Amma wanted to say in return, but Irenna was trying to be kind, so she kept her mouth shut and stood up instead. Closing her eyes, she took a deep breath, shutting away all thoughts of Axl. 'I'm ready,' she said at last.

***

Edela pulled the book from her chest and handed it to Biddy. 'This is where we'll find everything we need for dream walking.'

Biddy eyed the musty, old Tuuran book. 'Do you think you have the strength to do it again?'

'Of course!' Edela said with confidence. 'I need to warn her. If Morana gets hold of that book, if anyone does...' she shook her head. 'Jael needs to know.'

'Well, then,' Biddy sighed, 'show me which page it's on, and I'll gather what we need after breakfast.'

'Good,' Edela nodded, trying to quell the panic fluttering in her chest. 'Hopefully, you'll find everything, for I must do it tonight. I feel such a sense of urgency, a growing darkness. Something terrible is about to happen!'

***

Evaine pulled back the rug, peering at the strange symbol. Tuuran certainly, and fresh too. She ran her fingers over it. The marks in the wood were raw and clean. But what did it mean and who had put it there?

Someone who was trying to stop her.
Someone who was trying to break the binding spell.
Edela.
She hurried down the stairs, looking for a knife.

***

'At least I didn't have to watch you get married,' Aleksander grumbled, shielding his eyes from the intense glare of the morning sun as they walked down the pier with Fyn. 'I'm not sure how Axl will cope. I couldn't have.'

Jael sighed, feeling guilty. 'Best that we convince Lothar to leave quickly, then,' she said quietly, turning to see Karsten and Berard talking in the distance. 'Jaeger seems like the sort of idiot who takes pleasure in making others miserable.'

Aleksander nodded, groaning at the sharp pains in his head that were a constant reminder of his lack of self-control. He felt foolish. Being a drunk wasn't a future he wanted for himself, but it was the only way he'd discovered to dull the pain.

'Are you alright?' Jael wondered with a grin. 'Too much of Haaron's wine, was it?'

'Well, it's one way to cope, isn't it?' Aleksander muttered, not looking at her.

Jael was glad that Fyn was there. She didn't know what she could say to make him feel any better. 'Let's check the ships,' she said instead. 'I want to make sure that nothing will stop us from leaving in the morning.'

'I wish I could come with you, but I'm going to be stuck with Lothar, Osbert, and a long march.'

'I think Haaron is lending Lothar one of his ships,' Jael smiled, jumping into *Sea Bear*, happy to be away from the Dragos' and their dreamers. 'So you should be free of him at least. No doubt he'll lump Osbert on you, though!'

'If Osbert will tear himself away from that woman he's been humping every night,' Aleksander laughed. 'Poor woman. I think he must be paying her!'

Jael looked around the ship; at the hole-riddled house; at the catapult in the bow. The scars of battle were visible, and she felt a sense of pride that she'd kept her men safe from the worst of it. So far. 'Right, what weapons do we have?' she asked Fyn. 'Let's lay them all out on deck. We don't know what we're going to be sailing back into. Ivaar might have decided to cause trouble already. And if we're not prepared, we won't be able to respond quickly.'

Eager to be of use, Fyn ducked into the house and started rummaging through the piles of weapons they had taken from Skorro, and the ones remaining from their own stores.

Jael reached out suddenly, gripping Aleksander's forearm. 'I'm sorry,' she whispered quickly, her eyes meeting his.

He smiled sadly at her, understanding everything and nothing all at the same time. 'I know.'

***

Berard and Karsten had escaped early, desperate to avoid the ear-piercing screeches of their mother who was trapped in a burst of pre-ceremony madness as she raced around the castle, yelling at everyone. They'd had a bench brought out onto the square, and they sat there, drinking ale, watching the sun rise over the calm harbour; watching too, as Jael Furyck and two of her men busied themselves on their ships.

'What do you think they're doing?' Haegen wondered with a sigh as he stopped beside them, Jaeger leaning heavily against him.

'Preparing to attack us?' Karsten laughed.

'I think they're getting ready to leave as soon as the wedding is done,' Berard suggested, standing up so Jaeger could sit down. 'I don't imagine they want to stay here.'

'They're worried that Ivaar Skalleson may be busy taking their kingdom, from what I hear,' Jaeger said, sitting down with a grimace. 'He disappeared while we were on Skorro. In the night. Took all his men.'

Haegen's eyebrows went up at that. 'Brothers... you just can't trust them, can you?' he smiled, only half-joking. 'I imagine that when Father dies, you'll all be trying to kill me?'

Berard looked horrified. Karsten laughed.

Jaeger said nothing.

***

Evaine smiled contentedly as she wandered towards Ketil's fire pit with her father. He was mumbling away to himself, something about going to speak to Thorgils. She wasn't listening. Her attention had suddenly snapped to Edela and Biddy as they stopped to warm themselves by Ketil's fire, examining the contents of a basket, their faces tense. Evaine watched the flames billow in the gusting wind, her father still muttering beside her. She looked intently at the two scheming women, remembering the symbol. The symbol they had carved into her floorboards.

She was certain it was them.

But she had taken a knife to that symbol, and now Eadmund would be hers again. She was not prepared to let anyone stand in the way of what she had worked so hard to achieve; what she had dreamed of since she could remember.

Eadmund belonged to her.

***

Meena stood by the castle doors, watching as all four Dragos brothers laughed and joked their way through another jug of ale, her eyes fixed on Jaeger.

'What are you *doing*?' Varna hissed, hooking her longest fingernail around Meena's apron strap, yanking her away. 'Hoping to get yourself a whipping?'

Meena gasped, surprised, then terrified, turning her eyes towards the floor, tapping her head. 'I, I wasn't doing anything,' she tried unconvincingly, blushing, worried that her grandmother could read her mind.

'Hmmm,' Varna grumbled. 'Well, that's not what I hear. And I hear many things. Much more than my daughter, who appears to think that she will move me to one side and have that book for herself.'

Meena's eyes widened, her hands shaking as Varna leaned in closer.

'And will you help her, girl? Will you give the book to her?'

Meena shook her head, hiding her eyes from Varna as she interrogated her. 'No, no, no, Grandmother!' she insisted, wondering if she meant it.

Varna laughed, and it sounded ominous, rolling over Meena until she shivered. 'Well, here is your chance to prove it, for my dreams tell me that the book is here. Now. In his chamber.

Returned to him at last. So hurry away, little mouse, and get me that book. Prove your loyalty. Save your life, for once I have that book, I will be able to protect you from Morana and anyone else who tries to hurt you.'

Meena's eyes went immediately to Jaeger, just as his turned towards the castle doors. She felt trapped, torn, remembering how it had felt to be in his bed.

Shivering all over, she turned around, but Varna had gone.

***

Eydis frowned; Eadmund wasn't listening.

Bayla was rushing around the hall, yelling at the slaves who were moving tables to make room for the wedding archway, which had been so hastily erected that it was starting to fall apart as it was carried into place. Her orders were growing more urgent, shrieking, echoing around the large stone room, all the way down Eydis' spine.

'Eadmund?' Eydis tried again. 'Could we go outside? It's too noisy in here.'

Eadmund turned to Eydis, at last, almost surprised to see her. He hadn't been sure what to do with his sister while Gisila was helping Amma prepare for the ceremony. Jael and Fyn had disappeared before breakfast, and he didn't know where to put himself that was not in the way. He shook his head, which suddenly felt as though a fog had descended upon it. 'What did you say?'

'Eadmund?' Eydis reached out for him. 'Has something happened? You sound strange.'

Eadmund squeezed her little hand, smiling distractedly. 'No, I'm fine. Just tired. Why don't we go for a walk outside? We might find Jael and Fyn.'

He sounded very distant, Eydis thought, letting herself be led out of the hall.

***

Jael supposed that it was nearly time for the ceremony as they trudged reluctantly back to the castle. Looking down at her tunic, she realised that she needed to change into something more... queenly... although she struggled to think what that might be. But it was most certainly not a dress.

Now that she was a queen, she never had to wear a dress again.

Fyn was talking to Aleksander beside her, marvelling at how they'd uncovered a jar of sea-fire on *Ice Breaker* that must have rolled loose in the battle. It was still intact, and Jael was relieved about that. It was the greatest weapon she could ever imagine possessing, and she was determined to get Edela's help to make more of it as soon as they were back on Oss.

Jael saw Eadmund and Eydis walking towards them, and she smiled, then stopped, frowning, her body lurching in horror.

'What's wrong?' Aleksander asked, turning to her.

Jael couldn't speak as she waited for Eadmund to get closer, hoping she was wrong, but when he stopped and turned his eyes towards her, she knew.

He had gone.

***

Ivaar stood on the shore, watching as his men finished loading their weapons.

Isaura waited behind him, trying to shoo the children away from their father, who was too busy ordering everyone about to pay any attention to them.

Ivaar turned to her, finally, his face clear of any emotion. 'I will send for you when things are settled.'

Isaura wasn't sure what that meant, but she didn't want to ask. She just nodded.

Ivaar looked to the end of the beach where Ayla stood. He sighed, wanting to bring her along, but it was better not to spook his men. They did not take well to women on board, let alone a dreamer, and he would need them on his side for what he planned to do. 'Bernher is in charge,' he said firmly. 'Of the fort, of the island... of you. Do you understand me?' His eyes hardened.

Again, Isaura nodded, watching as he bent to kiss each child in turn. They clamoured for his rare show of affection.

Quickly uncomfortable with their tears, Ivaar straightened up, nodding at Isaura to deal with the wailing children as he turned and made his way towards his ship, desperate to be gone.

***

The well-dressed guests were milling around the hall now as the ceremony grew closer. Each table had been painstakingly prepared and decorated with towering candelabra, silver knives and spoons, pewter goblets and bowls. Trays of fruit and nuts and colourful sweetmeats formed centrepieces, with yellow and white flowers threaded around the displays, cascading over the sides of every table. The wedding archway at the very head of the hall was enormous, taller than any Gisila had seen, if not a bit lopsided. She shook her head as she squeezed through the guests, wondering how they could grow anything at all in this barren bowl of dust.

Gisila had left Amma in Irenna's capable hands, overcome with an urgent need to check on Axl. There was no sign of him anywhere, though, which worried but didn't surprise her. She did find Gant, however, who had managed to escape Lothar for the first time all morning. 'Where's Axl?' she wondered anxiously, her eyes everywhere but on Gant.

'With Aleksander,' he assured her with a smile. 'Don't worry. He won't let Axl out of his sight.'

'You don't think he'll do something foolish, do you?' Gisila whispered.

Gant shook his head. 'No, I don't. Axl can see that he can't help Amma that way.'

Gisila placed her hand on his arm, staring desperately into his eyes. 'I hope you're right,' she sighed. 'I can't have anything happen to him. I want us all to get out of this place alive.'

Gant nodded, moving his arm quickly away from her hand as Lothar announced his arrival with a loud cough.

'My dear,' Lothar muttered tightly, ignoring Gant. 'You'll need to show me to Amma's chamber. If I'm to escort her, I had better know where she is!'

Gisila swallowed. 'Of course,' she said, flushing, sensing his displeasure. 'I will take you.' And slipping her arm through Lothar's, she led him away.

Bayla watched them go before turning around, her eyes frantic as they raced around the hall. The guests were drinking and talking far too loudly for her to think. She reached out her empty goblet to a passing slave, and it was quickly filled with honey-scented liquid.

'Where have you *been*?' she barked at Haaron as he walked towards her.

Haaron blinked at his wife, surprised. 'Me? Why?'

'We are about to begin!' Bayla snapped in his ear. 'And you are the king! I would expect you to be here!'

Haaron smiled, enjoying her chaos, sensing her need for him, rare as it was. 'Well, I'm here now, so what would you have me do?' he asked calmly, sipping slowly from his goblet as he had been doing for most of the morning. As much as he wished that Jaeger was resting at the bottom of the Adrano with his ships and their crews, he had come around to the idea of his alliance with Lothar. The possibilities for Hest seemed suddenly limitless. So much so that he'd even found himself tolerating the idea of having Jaeger around. Whatever threat Varna imagined he posed would surely be outweighed by the benefits to the kingdom. And he was confident that, together, they would eventually find another way to get rid of the ambitious bastard.

***

Lothar was pleased with what he saw. Amma was a very attractive girl when she made an effort, he could see that now. And an effort had certainly been made. He thought of Rinda, his first wife, and what a fright she had looked in her wedding dress. He felt a sense of pride that his daughter would not embarrass him in front of their hosts.

Amma's long brown hair draped softly over her shoulders, nearly reaching her waist. Braids had been delicately threaded through the sides of her hair into an elaborate topknot, upon which sat a perfectly tiny, silver wedding crown. It matched the round silver brooches pinned to her dress and joined to each other by a cascading trio of chains. Nicolene's cream dress fit snuggly around her waist, straining across her breasts. She looked as though she couldn't breathe.

'We will leave you now,' Irenna smiled, glancing at Nicolene, who appeared thoroughly bored. 'Unless you need something else?'

'No,' Amma said blankly. 'Thank you.' Her ears were buzzing, and she was barely aware of anything except the overwhelming urge to throw herself into the sea.

Irenna nodded, hurrying Nicolene away.

Lothar clasped Amma's shaking hands in his sweaty ones. 'Are you ready, then, my daughter?' he smiled.

She wanted to recoil from his touch, and his eyes, which were cold and unsympathetic and did not match his smiling face at all. 'Yes,' she said faintly.

'Good, then let's get you married! I'm sure your husband is eager to get you into the marriage bed!' He put his arm around her waist, his face suddenly serious. 'Now, heed my words, Amma. For your own safety, you must ensure you do everything to keep your husband happy. You're there for his pleasure and his pleasure alone. Remember that, and you will have a long and productive marriage!'

Amma shivered as her father ushered her through the door.

***

Jael turned as Amma walked into the hall on Lothar's arm. She looked beautifully sad, but Eadmund didn't appear to notice. He stood beside Jael, his face completely blank as he stared straight ahead.

Bayla glared at the small cluster of musicians who were plucking away on lyre and harp. They were playing a sad, haunting melody that did little to enliven the dour mood in the hall. It was as though everyone could feel Amma's sadness growing with every step she took towards Jaeger.

Perhaps they knew what would happen to her, Jael frowned, uncomfortable with the ceremony and the pretence. She thought of *Sea Bear*, and her desire to be free again was palpable; to go home to Oss and see Thorgils, Edela, and Biddy... Tig and the puppies.

She felt a burst of worry that Ivaar might already be there, destroying them all.

***

Thorgils waved at Biddy and Entorp as he hurried into the gatehouse. It was a clear day, and he needed to be up on the ramparts, scanning the horizon. He'd been out on Leada as soon as the sun was up, riding the cliffs, checking the new lookouts he was having built. Men were constructing large towers of sticks and logs that could be quickly set alight in warning, all the way down to the headland, past where Fyn's hut in the hill sat. He had ridden to every side of the island, looking for any sign of Ivaar and his ships; any sign that they were under attack.

But he saw nothing.

Biddy smiled at him as she rushed past. She had gathered nearly everything Edela needed, but she didn't have mugwort. Entorp was taking her to a place where they might find a small supply.

'I will help if you like,' Entorp said, hurrying along beside her. 'Tonight. Edela is weak. As much strength as she thinks she has, her illness has lessened her power.'

Biddy looked worried, but she knew that he was right. Edela had not recovered her colour yet. She was still too pale; still tired too easily. 'Do you have a drum?' Biddy wondered. 'I'm supposed to look for that as well.'

'Yes, of course,' Entorp smiled wistfully. 'I helped Eydis' mother, Rada, dream walk sometimes. And perform other rituals. I suppose I was her assistant in many ways.'

Biddy felt relieved to think that he was going to be there.

It needed to work.

She couldn't have anything happen to Jael.

***

Meena stood outside the door, chewing her barely-there fingernails.

They were all at the wedding, she knew, as she shuffled about, crouching before the handle, reaching her hand up, then pulling it away, her eyes darting up and down the corridor. But it wasn't fear stopping her.

It was uncertainty.

There were three choices. Three people. Each one of them seeking her loyalty. Demanding it, threatening her for it.

But ultimately, Meena knew, there was only one person she could ever be truly loyal to.

So, taking a deep breath, she turned the handle and creaked open the door.

PART SIX

Darkness

CHAPTER FORTY THREE

Jaeger supposed that a wife wouldn't be such a bad addition to his bed, especially one as mesmerising as Amma Furyck. He took her hand, his eyes full of interest, watching as she stood, shivering before him in Nicolene's dress, which, he noted, fitted her perfectly.

The volka, Dragmall, the wisest man in Hest, wrapped a slippery white ribbon around their clasped hands and began his wailing cry to the gods, calling on them to bless this royal union.

Jaeger watched Amma's eyes fill with tears as they tried so desperately to avoid his. She reminded him of Elissa: so fearful and timid. He smiled; like Meena too. Was he truly so frightening? He thought of Meena, and his body stirred unexpectedly. She was no beauty. Neither her filthy body nor her odd face excited him, but he was intrigued by what they could achieve together.

With the book.

Power. That was exciting. To both of them, he thought. The idea that they could destroy the ones who had sought to control them. If only he could be certain of her loyalty. He needed her, but did she need him?

Jaeger turned impatiently to Dragmall, who looked even more ancient than Varna as he creaked and rasped before them, reaching the end of his crying plea. '... to bless this marriage between the noble Prince Jaeger, son of Haaron, he who was born of the mighty Valder Dragos, and the virtuous Princess Amma, daughter of Lothar Furyck, she who was born of Furia, Goddess of War...'

Amma wanted her hand back. She hated the suffocating feel of Jaeger's. It gripped hers with such force, as though he was trying to crush her; impose his will upon her. His mark.

His ownership.

The dress was so tight that she could barely breathe and she kept having visions of Axl throwing himself onto Jaeger, stabbing his sword through his heart. Amma blinked, unsure where to look. She could feel everyone's eyes on her. She could imagine Osbert's gleeful little face as he watched his revenge play out just as he'd planned. But she couldn't give him the satisfaction.

She wouldn't.

Amma swallowed, looked up into Jaeger's eyes, and smiled.

***

Edela had put herself to bed as soon as Biddy hurried away with Entorp. She knew that sleep would increase her strength, and she was desperate to find any further clues about what was happening with Jael.

Overcome with panic, it had taken her some time to find a sense of peace; a way into the clouds to search for her granddaughter.

But when she got there, she saw fire.

***

Axl stood between Gant and Aleksander, watching Amma from a place far removed from himself. She was shaking, he could tell, but he would not let himself react because he could do nothing; nothing except get himself killed. And he couldn't save Amma if he was dead. He held onto that one undeniable fact; the only thing tethering him to reason.

Axl thought of his father, trying to focus on Ranuf's hard, emotionless face. It had been nearly three years since his death now, and he struggled to remember much of him at all apart from that look on his face. It had always stayed the same. He had laughed with his men, smiled at his wife, but around his children, Ranuf's face had remained serious, stern, never warm. Jael insisted it was because he had been determined to teach them how to survive, how to be Furycks, to lead their people, protect their family, honour their name. Axl had wanted more than lessons, though. He had wanted an arm around his shoulder and a joke and some fun. But now, when he looked back to that face, as his father rode off to battle with his sister, he saw what it had truly meant. It had been a wall around his father's heart. Nothing had been more important to Ranuf than protecting his family. His life hadn't been about what he wanted or his own desires. As a father, a husband and a king, it had been his job to keep the people he loved safe.

Axl clenched his fists at his sides, his jaw pulsing, his eyes focusing on Amma.

She was his family, and she was in danger. He had to save her.

Somehow.

***

Evaine couldn't have been happier as she hurried home. She had bought herself a beautiful amber necklace with Morac's silver. She smiled, feeling a peace that had been missing for some time.

She felt confident that the spell was working again; that Eadmund would come home to her and Sigmund.

Soon.

And without Eirik, he would have the power to let them stay. No one would be able to remove her now, not when Eadmund was the king and Eadmund loved her.

She stopped suddenly, frowning, watching as Biddy and Entorp scurried towards Eadmund's house, their heads together, carrying a full basket and a drum. Evaine felt a sense of unease tighten her shoulders. Did they know they'd been discovered? Were they trying to stop her again? To find another way to break her spell?

Had Edela seen something in her dreams?

Evaine hurried on, desperate to get back to the house and find Morana's book. There had to be a spell in there that would take care of their interference once and for all.

***

Lothar clapped Osbert on the back, congratulating them both on such a well-executed plan. Somehow, between them, they had managed to avoid death, strike a powerful alliance, and gain Amma a royal husband, all within a few days. He felt elated.

Osbert appeared less impressed as he turned to his father, offering him a cup of mead. 'My sister must change her face if she wants to please her husband,' he said quietly. 'No man wishes to marry a wailing child.'

'Oh, and that's *your* advice, is it?' Lothar laughed. 'Advice from a man who has no wife at all!' Osbert was right, of course, but he didn't care. Amma was married now, and it was her husband's place to discipline her. 'Gisila!' he cried, spying his wife crossing the hall with Axl. 'Gisila!'

Gisila turned with a heavy sigh, fixing a smile on her face as she approached them, Axl following miserably in her wake.

'I was very impressed with how well Amma looked, very impressed indeed, my love. Her husband seemed pleased too,' Lothar murmured, leaning forward to kiss his wife's cheek.

Axl bit his tongue.

'And you, my step-son,' he growled. 'We'll need to find you a wife next. You and Osbert, both. It is time we had Furyck heirs, wouldn't you say? Although,' Lothar smiled, glancing around, 'I think Osbert already has his eye on someone, isn't that right?' He nudged a clearly irritated Osbert, who had not been aware that his interest in Keyta, the daughter of a Kalmeran lord, had garnered so much attention.

'I hardly think so, Father,' Osbert insisted dismissively. 'There is simply little else to do while we wait to leave.'

'But she is a rare beauty,' Lothar noted. 'And her father is extremely wealthy, from what Haaron tells me. Let us at least go and meet the man.' He nodded to Osbert, who looked completely reluctant to move his feet at all. 'Gisila?'

'Perhaps it is better left to you, my love,' she said sweetly. 'I think I must go and find Queen Bayla, to congratulate her on the ceremony.'

'Of course, of course,' Lothar muttered. 'A good idea. But then again, you are a very experienced queen, aren't you?' And smiling to himself, he led Osbert away.

'How are you?' Gisila whispered to Axl as soon as they were out of earshot. 'You haven't said a word all day.' She recognised the stern look on his face. She remembered it well. It was Ranuf's.

'I'm just ready to go home, Mother,' Axl said quietly. He leaned forward to kiss her cheek, then whispered in her ear. 'We can't plan our next move until we're away from here, can we?' He stepped back, grabbing a goblet from the tray of a passing slave.

Gisila watched his eyes roaming the room, desperately seeking Amma, she knew. She reached down and squeezed his hand, giving him a sympathetic smile. 'Well, go and disappear for a while, then. There is time before the feast is served, I'm sure.'

Axl caught Fyn's eye; he looked desperate to escape too. 'I think that sounds like a good idea.' And smiling at his mother, he walked over to Fyn, almost knocking into Nicolene as he tried to squeeze past her and Karsten.

Karsten glared at Axl, who completely ignored him and carried on walking. 'I'll be glad to see the back of those fucking Furycks,' he muttered to his wife, whose eyes were on Jaeger as he pressed himself against his new bride. Karsten looked around the hall, watching as Haegen and Berard chatted happily with Jael Furyck. His brothers were too eager to play nice with the bitch.

If he had his way, she'd be ash.

Jael could feel Karsten's eye piercing through the crowd, aiming for her. She didn't acknowledge him, though, happy to keep him in a constant state of irritation. She frowned instead, trying to ignore her own building irritation.

Eadmund.

He stood next to her, smiling as he spoke with Berard and Haegen, but everything about him had changed. He didn't look towards her, and his body stayed well apart from hers, frozen and removed. He was entirely disinterested in her again.

'I imagine you can't wait to leave,' Berard said quietly to Jael as Haegen and Eadmund shared a joke.

'Well,' Jael began, then paused, watching as Amma cringed away from Jaeger's attempts at intimacy. 'I suppose so.'

Berard followed her eyes, noting her concern. 'Your cousin will get used to us, I'm sure,' he insisted. 'Irenna is very nice. She'll make her feel part of the family.'

Jael wasn't convinced that was something to be happy about. 'If only she could have married you instead,' she whispered to him. 'It would have felt easier to leave.'

Berard blushed from the compliment, smiling awkwardly. 'Oh, well... I'm the last one to have a wife, it seems,' he said shyly. 'But I suppose I must, soon.'

'Do your father's dreamers see that?' Jael wondered slyly.

'That you will marry soon?'

Berard looked confused. 'Dreamers? My father only has the one.'

'Oh.' Jael shook her head. 'I'm certain I've met more than one. A strange girl with wild red hair and another woman, maybe her mother, with black-and-white hair? They all look much the same.'

Berard was puzzled. 'Well, perhaps you met Meena? She's Varna's granddaughter. But she is no dreamer that I know of.' He smiled to himself. Despite her curiosities, Berard had always been fascinated by Meena Gallas. She had noticed him, and would often smile at him, or at least she had until Jaeger started paying attention to her. He frowned. 'But the woman with... black-and-white hair? I don't know of anyone like that.'

Jael was puzzled. She hadn't eaten in far too long, and she felt sick because of it. She needed to eat, though, or she wouldn't be able to think. If the dreamers wanted to hurt her, they would find a way. But she wasn't about to keep starving herself while she waited to find out. 'Berard,' she murmured in his ear. 'Can you show me to your kitchen?'

***

'What will you tell her?' Biddy wondered, ladling cabbage soup into Edela's bowl. 'What can she do?'

Edela felt terrible and not hungry at all. Her stomach lurched as she remembered her dreams, which had been fraught with darkness and fire. She could feel a threat weaving its way around them, and it terrified her. 'Jael will know what to do,' she said confidently. 'If she can leave, she will leave. If she can kill her, she will kill her.'

'If you get through to her,' Biddy mumbled morosely, handing Edela her bowl.

'I will,' Edela said firmly, glancing towards the fire where they had laid out their preparations. 'But we must wait and hope that Morana does nothing before I can reach her.'

***

Jael was ravenous as she looked around the enormous kitchen.

Two fires burned under expansive stone chimneys, a wild boar turning over one, a goat on the other, and a pig over the open fire in the middle of the room. It smelled of so many good things that Jael's senses were utterly overwhelmed.

Berard watched as her eyes widened. 'There will be food served in the hall,' he reminded her diplomatically.

'I know,' she smiled. 'But I can't wait.' Jael was tempted to tell Berard about her fears, but she didn't know him. Despite his kind face and awkward gait, he was a Dragos, loyal to Haaron, to Hest, and perhaps, loyal to Jaeger most of all.

'Well, then,' Berard smiled shyly. 'You should help yourself. Being a queen, I think it would be entirely appropriate.'

Jael wasn't listening, though. She was already hurrying towards the long table stacked with platters of roasted vegetables and legs of glistening meat; her lips wet with anticipation.

***

Amma turned to her goblet. Perhaps wine was the only escape possible? She reached for it, sipping the cool liquid. It burned her throat with its sharp intensity; so strong that she grimaced.

'Is it not to your taste?' Jaeger asked, amused.

Amma blinked. 'It is, not... what I'm used to,' she said quietly, not wishing to offend the queen, who sat on her other side.

'Well, I'm sure you'll get used to it, over time,' Jaeger grinned, raising his own goblet to his lips. 'All the Dragos wives are very fond of the wine in Hest. Though, perhaps that says more about their husbands than the quality of my father's grapes?'

Amma didn't smile at his joke. She was barely listening as she took another gulp, her arms and legs tingling now, and happily so. She wanted to drift away so that she didn't have to feel a thing, for she knew how it would be when he took her to his bed.

***

Jael laughed, draining her cup of wine. She was enjoying herself.

They had made room for themselves at a table near the pantry, mostly out of the way, deciding that there was little point in returning to the hall when they could eat here in peace, without the need for forced conversations with complete strangers.

'Tell me, Berard,' Jael began, pushing her plate away, finally full. She pulled her stool closer to his, aware that the cooks were still rushing around, sending trays into the hall. 'What does your brother want? Surely he's not content to remain Haaron's fourth son? Not a man like him.' Her eyes were sharp, but Berard's were bleary, having quickly drained two jugs of wine since he'd sat down. 'He must have his own ambitions for the throne?'

Berard's eyes rolled around the room, pointedly avoiding hers. 'Haegen will be king here when our father dies,' he said weakly, reaching for his cup, suddenly awkward in her company.

'Well, of course,' Jael said easily, wanting him to relax again. 'He's a good choice too. He seems very much like your father. Very certain. In control.'

Berard frowned. 'Yes, but –' He closed his mouth suddenly,

focusing on his cup as he refilled it.

'But?'

Berard shook his head. 'No, it's nothing.'

Jael tried again. 'Our families are now joined together, united in this alliance. We'll succeed or fail together. It would be better to succeed, don't you think? Taking Helsabor between us? That land will make such a difference to your kingdom, I'm sure.'

Berard nodded enthusiastically. 'We've always longed for some arable land. We have little ourselves. We'll be able to truly farm.'

'Well, then, I hope we can all move forward together,' Jael said quietly. 'I think that's what Haegen wants, isn't it? But Karsten and Jaeger? I'm not so sure they have the best interests of Hest at heart...' She had her hook out, baited, waiting for Berard to bite. She needed to know exactly what Jaeger was planning. She was certain that he was not a man prepared to remain in his place.

But how dangerous was he? Really?

Berard readied a strong defense of his brothers, but it fell apart on his thick tongue. 'Perhaps,' he began, then faltered. 'Perhaps they're thinking about other things? I'm not sure they see the alliance as... necessary.'

'And you?' Jael wondered lightly.

Berard thought on that. There was the book. The book would render all alliances pointless. With it, Jaeger would claim power over the whole land. Osterland would belong to Hest in its entirety; that is what Jaeger had promised. And once Berard had been eager to support his brother in that quest. But now? Now when he thought of land, and the future, he wasn't certain he saw the same things anymore. 'I think my father is wiser than all of us put together.' He picked up a chicken leg and took a bite. 'I think the wisest king sees what is best for his kingdom, not himself.'

That surprised both of them.

Jael leaned towards him, her voice low. 'You're a good man, Berard. Unexpectedly so... for a Dragos,' she said, narrowing her eyes. 'And I need your help.'

***

Biddy closed the door, locking it. 'I'm worried about Thorgils,' she frowned. 'I'm not sure he's even taking the time to eat between caring for Odda and rushing around the island looking after everything else.'

'Mmmm,' Edela murmured distractedly. 'Perhaps you should ask him to come and eat with us tomorrow? He could take some food back to his mother.'

'Good idea,' Biddy smiled, hanging her cloak on a peg by the door. A storm was brewing, and she'd been checking that the animals were secure. Askel had his own house and family to care for, and he wouldn't be back until morning. 'He likes my chicken and ale stew.'

'Well, let's go and see him tomorrow, and we can check on Odda,' Edela suggested. 'If I'm still standing after the dream walk!'

Biddy saw the real fear lurking in Edela's eyes, the lack of confidence in her own strength. She quickly sought to reassure her. 'Of course you'll still be standing!' she smiled kindly, placing a log on the fire. 'You're the second strongest woman, I know!'

Edela smiled, thinking about the first strongest woman. Strong, yes, but so vulnerable right now and completely unaware of the danger she was in.

***

Berard hesitated, his cup touching his lips, his eyes hooded and evasive. 'Help you?'

'I've heard the rumours about your brother,' Jael murmured. 'About what happened to his first wife and son.'

Berard sat up, his body rigid. 'Well, he.... it was an...'

Jael didn't say anything. Berard gave up the argument on his own, dropping his eyes to the table.

'I need you to protect Amma.'

Berard glanced towards the door. 'But she's Jaeger's wife now.'

'Yes, and I want her to stay that way. I don't want her to become Jaeger's late wife. I need her to stay safe,' Jael insisted quietly. 'She's a kind girl. An innocent girl. And she doesn't deserve to be mistreated in any way. You've met her, so I'm sure you agree?'

'But what would you have me do?' Berard asked, leaning forward.

'Watch her, talk to her, become her friend,' Jael suggested. 'She'll need one. Someone who will be honest with her, kind to her. Someone she can come to if she feels scared, or threatened. I want you to protect her. For me.'

Berard squirmed before those insistent green eyes. They were hard to argue against. And so were her words, for, although he was loyal to Jaeger, he had been horrified by what had happened to Elissa. Berard knew that Jaeger hadn't meant to hurt his wife, but at the same time, he was becoming increasingly worried that the book was changing his brother somehow. He appeared to have less and less control over his rage.

And that could become a very real problem indeed.

***

'You appear to have lost your wife,' Haaron noted as Eadmund scanned the hall again. Jael had disappeared with Berard some time ago, and he had no idea why they hadn't returned. The plates were being removed now, and hers had remained untouched, next to his.

'She's not especially fond of weddings,' Eadmund said lightly, ignoring Lothar's jiggling belly as he laughed out loud.

'That is true!' Lothar smiled. 'But she seems content enough with you. Perhaps one day she'll even thank me for gifting her to you as I did?'

Eadmund doubted that. 'Perhaps,' he mumbled into his cup. He felt oddly displaced and couldn't stop thinking about Oss. He missed Sigmund desperately. The idea of returning to his son was all he could think about. That and Evaine. He blinked, confused, feeling guilty as Jael returned to the hall at last.

'Well, mystery solved,' Haaron said. 'Perhaps she was checking on your ships again? She seems eager to leave.'

'We both are,' Eadmund admitted. 'My father's death means an unsettled time for our people. It's best that we're there, ensuring no problems arise.'

'You mean with your brother?' Haaron wondered.

Eadmund was surprised but tried not to show it. 'My brother killed my father, so yes, he's a problem I must take care of. I'm sure you can understand my eagerness to depart in the morning?'

'I can, of course,' Haaron agreed, feeling Lothar's breath on his neck as he leaned into their conversation again. 'Your father ruled for a long time, so it's important to reassure your people quickly before their heads are turned towards... other possibilities.'

Eadmund wasn't sure what he meant by that but Jael sat down in between them, and he didn't have a chance to ask anything further. 'Where have you been?' he wondered sharply.

Jael looked at the curious faces of the men around her. 'Just exploring,' she smiled. 'Since we're leaving early, I wanted one last chance to look around. Your castle is very impressive, my lord.'

Haaron was surprised. 'Thank you.'

'We have plans to rebuild the fort on Oss,' Jael offered by way of a fuller explanation. 'It's a stone fortress, but very small and not impressive at all. We wish to expand it, so your castle has given me many ideas.'

Eadmund's eyes did not betray the surprise of that news.

Haaron's shoulders relaxed as the sense of her explanation sunk in.

'I hope you don't mind me peering into your kitchens and your corridors?' Jael laughed, nodding at the slave who reached out to take her plate away.

'No,' Haaron mumbled. 'I'm glad my son could be of assistance. It is good to know that he's useful for something.'

'Oh, yes,' Jael murmured. 'He was very helpful, indeed.'

***

Entorp tapped away on his drum, distracted. Biddy frowned at him, noticing how sleepy Edela looked as she perched on a stool before the flames. The wind was rattling the door now, rain pelting down the smoke hole. The thunder and lightning had spooked the puppies so much that they wouldn't get off Biddy's feet as she sat there, wishing the night would hurry along.

'I think, perhaps, we ought to begin,' Edela breathed. And pushing herself out of her chair, she took a deep breath. 'I'm ready.'

CHAPTER FORTY FOUR

'You're not leaving?'

Gisila looked anxious as she stopped Gant by the entrance to the hall, her hand on his arm.

'I'm going to check on my men,' he yawned. 'And then find my bed. It's been a long day.'

Gisila glanced back into the hall where she knew Axl was drinking too much.

Gant followed her gaze. 'He'll be fine. I've asked Aleksander to watch him. He'll get Axl to bed soon.'

Gisila didn't look convinced.

'He's doing well,' Gant assured her. 'Many a man would have made things worse today, but Axl has kept himself under control. Don't worry.'

Gisila sighed, quickly removing her hand as Lothar approached.

'Is everything alright?' Lothar asked sharply. 'You seem upset, my love.' He glared at Gant, furious that he'd once again caught him alone with his wife.

'Yes, my lord,' Gant nodded. 'I was just saying goodnight to the queen.' He ducked his head, disappearing around the corner before Lothar could utter another word.

Lothar gripped Gisila's upper arm between his fingers. She winced. 'I think we need to have a talk, you and I,' he hissed in her ear. 'A very serious talk indeed.'

***

'A new fort?' Eadmund yawned as they lay there, listening to Eydis muttering away to herself in her sleep. 'You're really thinking about that?'

'After seeing Haaron's castle? Of course,' Jael whispered, honestly enough. 'Why not? It makes sense to improve it. We need to make Oss as impenetrable as possible. There's a lot we can do.'

'If we're not too late,' Eadmund murmured, rolling over, moving away to the edge of the bed. 'If Ivaar hasn't destroyed it all.'

Jael suddenly felt cold as he disappeared, taking all his warmth with him. 'Don't say that,' she said sadly, rolling to the other side. 'I'm sure we have time.'

Eadmund didn't say anything.

Jael closed her eyes and sighed, wishing she was back on Oss, desperately wanting to speak to Edela.

She needed her help.

***

'I hope he's not going to tear your dress off her!' Karsten slurred, laughing as he stumbled along next to his less-than-impressed wife. 'You do like that dress.'

'I hardly think he'll get so excited that he needs to tear anything,' Nicolene sneered. 'She's a plain girl.'

'Plain?' Karsten snorted loudly. 'If you consider *her* plain, I'd hate to know what you think of Irenna!'

Nicolene glared at her husband, jabbing him in the ribs. 'Lower your voice,' she hissed. 'That's Jaeger's chamber.' She nodded to the door they were passing, dragging her drunken husband away. 'I can't believe you have such low standards,' she muttered as they turned the corner towards their own chamber. 'I don't even want to know what you think of Jael Furyck!'

That put an end to Karsten's fun. He frowned at his wife, blinking her into focus. 'I'd slit that bitch's throat if I could. It doesn't matter what she looks like to me!'

Nicolene was confused as she stared at her wobbling husband. 'What does *that* mean?'

***

Jaeger barely heard the disturbance in the corridor as he sat on the bed, filling his wife's goblet with wine. She seemed more relaxed than earlier, he thought, but her eyes were still nervous when she glanced his way.

His wife. It didn't feel right, not yet. He hadn't imagined marrying again so quickly. He still thought that Elissa would walk through the door, carrying their son in her arms.

Amma swallowed as Jaeger handed her the goblet. He had sent his servant away for the night, and now there was just the two of them, entirely alone for the first time. She felt too warm, uncomfortable. Her head was fuzzy. She thought of Axl and hoped he was alright, wishing he was here to save her from what she knew was coming; from what she feared most of all.

Jaeger leaned towards her, and Amma jumped. He laughed. 'You don't need to be scared of me, although, of course, I understand why you are.' He ran the back of his hand over her cheek, down her neck, around the base of her throat. She visibly shuddered, her eyes fleeing his. 'Drink your wine,' he smiled. 'It will make it easier for you, I promise.'

He had patience.

Well, he had some patience.

He would let her have a moment, and then he would get that dress on the floor.

***

'Perhaps it's time for bed?' Aleksander suggested, nodding at Axl who looked intent on reaching for the jug of wine again. 'We've probably drunk the castle dry by now.' He watched as their men slowly stumbled out of the hall. Most had been stuffed into the empty ship sheds, some were bedding down with Haaron's horses, and the unluckiest ones had the goats and pigs for company. He didn't doubt that they were all as eager to be gone from this place as he was.

Fyn, bleary-eyed, and slightly disoriented, agreed. He yawned, peering at Axl, who appeared to have no intention of moving as he sipped from his cup, glaring at Osbert, who sat at the next table.

'He did this, you know,' Axl grumbled morosely. 'Told Lothar about Amma and me. I'm sure of it. He's like that, always trying to hurt someone. Pathetic bastard that he is.'

Aleksander took the cup from Axl's unsteady hand. 'He is. That's agreed. But let it go tonight. You're not thinking clearly.'

But Axl was thinking clearly enough to get his legs working as he lurched up suddenly from the bench, heading towards Osbert before Aleksander and Fyn could grab him.

Osbert had been drawn to his mysterious Kalmeran woman, Keyta, again. She had exquisitely fine, straight black hair, ebony skin and sultry blue eyes. Despite any protestations to the contrary, he was going to find it hard to say goodbye to her.

'Who is that?' Keyta wondered, her hand in Osbert's lap, her eyes on the tall young man charging towards them.

Osbert looked up as Axl approached, his face red, his eyes bulging. 'That would be my cousin, or even my stepbrother,' he slurred sleepily, distracted by Keyta's roaming hand. 'What bad timing he has.'

Aleksander and Fyn caught Axl just before he reached Osbert, grabbing an arm each.

'Hello, Axl,' Osbert murmured. 'Is there something I can help you with? Or did you just want to start a fight to take your mind off the fact that Jaeger Dragos is upstairs fucking your poor sweet Amma raw?'

Aleksander glared at Osbert, tempted to let Axl go.

Keyta smiled, amused, running one finger over her full lower lip.

Axl felt sick. Bursting with rage. He tried to shake his arms free, but Aleksander and Fyn held on tightly.

'What do you think you're going to do, Axl?' Osbert sneered. 'Try to hurt me? In Haaron's hall?' He looked around calmly. There was barely anyone left now. The slaves had finished clearing up, and most of them had left for their beds. It was late, and Osbert's mind was far more inclined to consider what to do about the tantalising hand in his lap than any problem Axl was about to cause. He turned to Aleksander with disdain. 'Get him away from me before he does something he'll live to regret.'

Aleksander was finding it hard to hold himself back. Osbert had been asking for a severe thrashing ever since he'd strolled into Andala with his father and stolen the throne, destroying all their lives in the process. And he was just as ready to give it to him as Axl.

Fyn coughed, trying to get someone's attention. 'We should go,' he mumbled, pulling on Axl's arm. 'Your mother...'

'Oh yes, that's right, his mother will be busy getting fucked too!' Osbert laughed to Keyta. 'All the women he cares about, getting royally fucked. And poor Axl there, powerless to stop any of it!'

Aleksander had had enough. It was all a game and Osbert

was playing it to titillate his guest, to show her what a tough son of a king he was. 'Come on, Axl,' he growled, helping Fyn pull him away. 'Leave Osbert to his bitter tongue and his tiny cock.'

Osbert clamped his teeth together, lunging at them as they left, dragging Axl between them.

Keyta sat there, enjoying the show. 'I wouldn't say it was *that* tiny,' she smiled as Osbert sat back down.

***

'You had a dream, didn't you?' Edela asked in a hushed voice.

Jael frowned, not wanting to look at her. 'No.'

Edela laughed softly. 'No? Well, I can read minds, you know.'

'No, you can't,' eight-year-old Jael insisted.

'Well, so you say,' Edela smiled. 'But I can read feelings, and I can feel that you are scared.'

'No, I'm not!' Jael shook her long braids, fingering the wooden sword that lay across her lap. She had woken up determined to go and find her father, to ask him to train her again. 'I'm never scared.'

'Oh, yes you are, my sweetest girl,' Edela said, taking her hand. 'I know you better than you think, and you are a dreamer, just like me.'

'No,' Jael insisted again. 'I don't want to be!'

'But you see things, don't you? In your dreams?'

Jael hesitated, the crease between her big green eyes deepening. 'No. I'm not a dreamer, Grandmother. That's not what I'm meant to be. I'm meant to be a warrior. That's what they say.'

Edela held her breath. 'Who? Who says that?'

'The gods,' Jael whispered. 'They tell me that I'll be a great warrior. That I'll save everyone. They come to me... in my dreams.' She looked around guiltily.

'Ahhh, so you have dreams, then?' Edela chortled.
'Everyone has dreams, Grandmother.'
'Not everyone, my darling...'

***

Tears filled Amma's eyes as she turned her head to the side, desperate not to see him, to see what he was doing to her; to catch the look of pleasure on his face that she knew was there. She wanted to disappear into the darkness, to imagine herself so far away, away from him; away from the pain she could feel as he pushed himself deeper inside her.

It hurt.

Jaeger didn't notice as he moaned, bending down to kiss her, turning her face back towards him. She was such a pretty little thing, he thought, admiring his new wife; such a delicate, soft, pretty thing. A lady. A princess. And one day, a queen. Lovely and certainly desirable; her curvaceous body was an endless delight of pleasing sights. He closed his eyes, increasing his rhythm, seeing Meena's face as she gasped and groaned beneath him.

He opened his eyes in surprise, panting, confused.

Excited.

***

Gisila cried out as Lothar slapped her, hard across the face. He was drunk, which made him mean, she knew, but never violent.

Not like this.

Lothar was furious, seething with jealousy, remembering

every look, every touch she had ever given Gant; every time he had caught them together.

He had seen it all.

'Tell me about Gant, *Wife*!' he snapped. 'Tell me what you've been up to behind my back!'

Gisila held her aching face, glancing at the door. She felt unsafe, desperate to leave. 'Nothing,' she swallowed. 'He was Ranuf's man, loyal to our family. They were close friends, like brothers. He cares for Axl. That's all.'

'Cares for Axl?' Lothar spat. 'Why? Why should he care for that pathetic boy? Why, Gisila?' he growled. 'Something you failed to tell Ranuf? Is *he* Axl's father?' He grabbed her arm, yanking her towards him so that her face, already swelling where he'd slapped her, was nearly touching his. 'Tell me!' he yelled.

Gisila shook her head. 'No! No, of course not!' she cried. 'How could you think such a thing?'

Lothar pinched her arm harder. 'Ranuf never liked the boy, did he? Not like Jael. He barely even noticed him from what I heard, so maybe there was a reason. Maybe he knew the truth all along? That you were just a whore!' He pushed her backwards, onto the bed, and lunged at her.

***

Edela hurried to find Jael. She had a sense that there wasn't much time.

It was different than her last dream walk. She felt weak, unable to hold onto the trance tightly enough; to be truly in the dream. But as she rushed along, she saw her granddaughter standing in a vast, empty square filled with endless cobblestones; a huge castle towering behind her under a full moon.

'Jael!' Edela called, rushing towards her.

Jael didn't turn around.

Edela followed her gaze towards Eadmund, who stood in a ship, drifting slowly away from the piers, turning from her without any warmth in his eyes. Jael watched him go, not moving. 'Jael!' Edela tried again, reaching her, grabbing her hand.

'Grandmother!' Jael pulled her close, embracing her. 'Is everything alright? Has something happened?'

Edela was breathless, feeling weaker by the moment. 'I, I,' she tried, stumbling as Jael caught her. 'I came to warn you. You are in terrible danger here! You must leave right away!'

***

Axl had not calmed down at all on the walk back to their chamber. It was deathly quiet. Barely anyone was around now, and he could feel his heart pounding in his chest, Osbert's words ringing in his ears. He felt enraged, ready to vomit, fighting the overwhelming urge to rush upstairs and rescue Amma.

'Let it go,' Aleksander grumbled again, pushing him firmly in the direction of their chamber. 'He's not worth risking Amma's life for, is he? You do something foolish, and *she's* the one who'll suffer. You won't be able to save her if you get yourself killed,' he whispered hoarsely.

Fyn wished he hadn't drunk so much as he staggered along next to them, his head foggy and his legs unsteady as he tried to help Aleksander shepherd Axl in the right direction.

There was a slap, and a scream and all three heads snapped to the left.

Aleksander let go of Axl's arm, and they raced for the door.

Axl threw open the door, his eyes bulging in horror as he took in the scene.

Gisila on the bed, naked, face down, bloody.

Lothar, belt in hand, standing over her.

Axl couldn't move.

Aleksander raced past him, grabbing Lothar's belt out of his hand, shoving him away from Gisila.

Fyn hurried into the room and quickly shut the door behind them all. He wondered if he should get Jael.

Aleksander grabbed Gisila, pulling her off the bed as Lothar lunged for them both.

'Get away from my wife!' he cried in a blind rage.

'You will not touch her!' Aleksander growled violently, clasping Gisila to his chest. She was shaking, too terrified to speak. 'I am taking her. You will not fucking touch her! Axl!' he called, not taking his eyes off Lothar. 'We need to go! The king needs to calm himself down. Fyn, find something for Gisila to put on. We need to go!'

'Axl!' Fyn cried. 'No!'

Lothar turned to Axl, who swung back his sword, and, gritting his teeth until he felt they would break, he brought the sharp blade scything towards the man who had taken everything from his family.

And with it, he took off his head.

Gisila screamed. Aleksander clamped his hand over her mouth.

Fyn was too shocked to speak.

Lothar's headless body folded on top of itself, flopping onto the floor with a thunderous slap. His head rolled under the bed, a thick trail of blood smearing across the flagstones after it.

Axl stood, holding the bloody blade, his arm shaking.

Aleksander blinked himself back into the room, his heart racing, his mind steadying itself quickly. 'Axl, sheath your sword. We need to go.' He looked around the room. 'Fyn, go and get Gant and Jael. Tell them we need to leave. Quietly. Axl, help me hide Lothar.' Aleksander took Gisila to the bed. 'Gisila, you must get dressed. Hurry now. We have to leave. Put on a dress. A cloak. Your boots. Quickly. Jael will come.'

Gisila sat on the bed, too numb to move.

CHAPTER FORTY FIVE

'You mean the dreamers?' Jael asked. 'I've seen them here. Three of them, or maybe two. They want me dead. I know that. Are they working to control Eadmund?'

'Eadmund?' Edela looked puzzled. 'What has happened to Eadmund?'

'He was free, set free from whatever Evaine had done to him,' Jael sighed. 'But it all changed today. He's gone again.'

That was a surprise.

Edela frowned. 'I'll make it right, don't worry about that. We will free Eadmund again. But right now, it's you we must be worried about. You must leave Hest. Morana Gallas is there, trying to kill you!'

Jael looked confused, then realisation dawned as she thought of the black-and-white haired woman. She gripped Edela's hands tightly. 'Yes, she is.'

Edela felt strange, as though she was slipping away. 'Jael! Please, you must listen... there is more. It's about the book...'

'Jael! Jael!'

Jael blinked, disoriented. Fyn?

She turned away from Edela, looking for him, but he wasn't there, and when she turned back around, her grandmother had gone.

'Jael!'

Fyn was there, and she was sitting up with her knife in her

hand, and Eadmund was beside her and Eydis was hurrying out of her bed.

'You must come! We have to leave. Now! Axl has killed your uncle. Aleksander sent me. He said we have to leave!'

***

'Edela?'

Biddy and Entorp hurried to help her onto the bed. She was shuddering, murmuring, weak and limp. Entorp lifted her under the furs as Biddy rushed to open the door to free the house from the suffocating smoke. She poured a cup of water and brought it back to the bed, stumbling slightly, her head thoroughly muddled. 'Edela? Would you like a drink?'

Edela's eyes fluttered open.

'Did you see Jael?' Biddy wondered urgently. 'Is she alright?'

Edela coughed, struggling to speak. 'I...' She sunk deeper into the pillow. 'Jael disappeared. Something happened. Something is wrong. Something's terribly wrong!'

***

Gant was there when they arrived, ashen-faced but wide awake, calm, and fully dressed.

Jael glanced down at the blood on the floor. 'Fyn, cover that with a fur,' she ordered, glancing at the headless body.

At the head.

Both of which had been stuffed under the bed. 'We need to go.'

They all looked at her.

Jael had dressed in her mail, filling her belt with every weapon she had to hand, as had Eadmund. They were both wearing their cloaks. Her head was clear, but her body was unusually warm. Too warm. 'Fyn, go with Eadmund.' She stared at Eadmund. 'You need to find the men. Get them onto the ships. Get the oars in.' Her mind ran through what was on their ships, what weapons they had, which piers Haaron's remaining ships were moored to. 'We'll need a fire. We have to burn their ships so they can't follow us. Grab a torch.'

Eadmund nodded at Jael. 'Good luck. We'll be waiting.' He tightened his swordbelt, his fingers fumbling as he stared at her. 'Don't be long.'

Jael pushed Eydis towards Gisila. 'Mother, your only job is to hold onto Eydis. She needs you. And I need you to keep her safe. Do you understand me?' she asked, staring at her mother who was in total and complete shock, one eye completely swollen shut, the other not focusing at all as she shivered beneath her cloak. 'Eydis, don't make a sound. Just follow Gisila. Hold her hand and don't let go.'

Eydis nodded.

'What about Amma?' Axl asked. 'We can't leave her.'

'Yes, we can,' Gant said firmly. 'You'll die trying to get up there and back again with her. We can't risk it. We need to leave.' He scanned the room as Aleksander poked his head around the door, nodding to them. 'We're going, Axl, and you're going to listen to your sister now. And that is all, do you understand me?'

Axl appeared ready to argue, but he nodded mutely, fighting every sinew in his body that was urging him to run upstairs and kill Jaeger Dragos.

Jael reached down, picking up Lothar's swordbelt, her father's sword tucked into its scabbard. She wrapped it around her waist, buckling it above her own belt. Shifting the scabbard over to the left, and with one hand on each sword, she nodded to Aleksander. 'Let's go.'

***

Eadmund and Fyn walked down the long straight corridor towards the entrance. Moonlight shone at the very end of the darkened passageway, so they knew that the castle doors were still open. It had been a long day of feasting, and drunken guests had been wandering in and out as they liked. Eadmund couldn't remember seeing a lot of guards on duty. But they would be there, he was certain.

They walked towards the wide foyer that bridged the entrance to the hall and the beginning of the stairs. It was completely empty.

Almost.

Eadmund grabbed Fyn's arm as Osbert and his woman sauntered into view, stumbling towards them, drunkenly tangled around each other. He flattened Fyn back against the stone wall, trying to calm his breathing.

Osbert was about to walk straight into everybody.

Taking a deep breath, Eadmund pushed Fyn out into the foyer, swaying, leaning on his shoulder. 'Ahhh, there's Osbert, little Osbert!' he slurred. 'Looking for a bed, are you? Well, maybe we could offer you Axl's? He's feeling very lonely tonight. Come on, Fyn,' he grumbled, turning Fyn around and heading back the way they had come. 'I need to find my wife! Have you seen my wife?' he asked loudly, his head lolling around towards Osbert.

Osbert cringed, his face contorting in disgust at his cousin's mess of a husband. He turned to Keyta. 'I think there are other places we could go,' he whispered in her ear. 'Your chamber, perhaps?'

She smiled, nodding dreamily, and grabbing Osbert's hand, she led him towards the stairs, neither one looking back.

***

'Wait!' Jael hissed as they followed her to the door. She could hear Eadmund. 'Wait....' The voices drifted away. 'Mother, put your head out.'

Gisila hurried to the door, slowly creaking it open. She looked down the corridor, but there was no one there apart from Fyn and Eadmund, disappearing into the distance. 'They've gone,' she whispered, ducking back inside. 'I can't see anyone else.'

Jael took a deep breath. 'We can't run,' she said to them. 'We need to look as though we're just going to find... something to eat. Slowly,' she insisted. 'I'll take Mother and Eydis.' She turned to Aleksander, Axl, and Gant. 'Give us a chance to get out of the castle and then follow. Head for the piers, but avoid the square. Stay out of sight wherever you can.'

Axl nodded mutely.

'And get your knives out. Kill anyone you have to. Quietly. We can't be discovered.'

***

Fyn followed Eadmund as they slipped down the steps and across the front of the castle. He held his breath, too afraid to even blink. Clouds were rushing across the moon, but he wished they'd submerge it entirely, worried they'd be seen.

Eadmund held up his hand as a man stepped out of the shadows. A guard. He glanced around. Only one, but he was standing right in their path.

There was no way around him.

Turning to Fyn, he put a finger to his lips, sliding his knife from its scabbard. He crouched along the thick stone wall of the castle, keeping as close to it as possible, his boots silent on the cobblestones.

Eadmund turned again, instructing Fyn to stay, then crept up behind the man as he stood there, swaying slightly under an unwelcome burst of moonlight. He was pissing, Eadmund realised, hearing a sudden stream of fluid splash against the cobblestones.

He threw one hand over the guard's mouth and rushed his knife across his throat, dropping his jerking body to the ground, kicking him into the shadows. Motioning for Fyn to follow him, they hurried to the shed where he knew the Osslanders were sleeping.

***

Varna groaned, crying out as she tried to move, but her right side was locked in place, and she couldn't shift herself. 'Meena!' she called urgently.

Morana sighed, furious to have been woken. 'Be quiet,' she grumbled, rolling over, away from the noise. 'Go back to sleep, Mother!'

But Varna was not going back to sleep. 'Meena!' she called again. 'Help me up! Quick, girl! I must see the king!'

***

Jael and Gisila walked slowly down the middle of the corridor, approaching the entrance to the hall, Eydis between them.

Jael could feel Eydis shaking as she held onto her, staring

straight ahead, listening for every sound. There were still people in the hall; she could hear the low rumble of drunken voices to her left.

'Jael!'

They all froze, Gisila uttering a small, pained cry.

It was Berard, teetering towards them. He was so drunk that he appeared ready to topple over. He stared at Jael, confused. 'Is it morning already?' he slurred, his eyes drifting towards her companions. 'Where are you going?' He blinked at Gisila, concerned. 'What happened to your face?'

Jael let go of Eydis' hand, motioning for Gisila to take her and carry on. She wrapped an arm around Berard's hunched shoulders. 'Berard,' she smiled warmly. 'Do you need some help, my friend? You look ready to fall down.' She ushered him quickly towards the stairs. 'Are you sure you can make it up those stairs on your own?'

Berard's head swivelled around, looking after Gisila, then back at Jael. 'But what's wrong with your mother? Where are you going?' He caught a glimpse of her mail, shimmering beneath her cloak. 'And why are you dressed for battle?'

'Oh, Eydis can't sleep, not since her father was murdered,' Jael explained softly, quickly. 'And her cries woke my mother, so now she can't sleep either. We're taking her for some air. It might help calm her down, the poor, poor girl. She's blind, you know.'

Berard nodded along sympathetically, utterly confused. 'You go, then, you go,' he smiled sleepily. 'I'll see you when the sun comes up, or perhaps not... for I may need a very, very long sleep...'

Berard turned and waved to Jael as she let him go, conscious of the fact that Aleksander, Gant, and Axl were now approaching.

'Hurry up, Berard!' she whispered, wishing him up the stairs, hoping that he wouldn't fall straight back down them.

Turning around to the three men, she swallowed, following them to the doors, not one of them glancing at the hall as they passed, holding their breaths.

***

Perhaps there were Brekkans in the shed too; Eadmund wasn't sure. There was a torch just inside the door, burning in a sconce, but the bodies were helter-skelter, sleeping wherever they'd managed to find a mound of hay. It was hard to say who was who.

He motioned for Fyn to start waking everyone up as he looked for Beorn. It was easy enough to follow his snoring it turned out.

Clamping his hand over Beorn's mouth, Eadmund whispered in his ear. 'We're leaving, old friend. I need both ships ready to go now. Without a sound.' He took his hand away from Beorn's mouth and put his finger to his lips, backing away to crouch around the rest of the men, desperate to find Villas, *Ice Breaker's* helmsman.

The men started to crawl around, gathering their belts in silence, their sleepy faces quickly tense with anxiety.

Then one man, a Brekkan, yelled out. 'Hey!'

Fyn turned around, throwing the man to the ground before he could make another noise, clamping his hand over his mouth. He drew his knife without hesitation, sliding it across his throat, gasping at the horror in the man's eyes as his life ran away from him. Shaking, and pushing himself off the dying man, Fyn turned towards the torch that Eadmund was now holding.

Their men were all standing, struggling to wake themselves up; fully aware, though, that they were now fighting for their lives.

'When we get to the ships,' Eadmund whispered hoarsely, 'grab an oar and slot it in. Quietly. Fyn and I will fire Haaron's ships. Jael and the rest of them will meet us there.'

Beorn nodded, tying up his swordbelt, blinking into the flaming torch, his heart racing, his mind running over everything he needed to do to get them away as quickly as possible.

***

Haaron was furious to have been woken when he was sure he'd only just closed his eyes.

Varna, the girl said. Varna needed to see him. He hurried to sit up, feeling his wine-soaked head lurch painfully. 'Where is she?' he rasped, his throat so dry that his tongue stuck to the roof of his mouth. He looked around, but there was no Bayla; she barely slept in their bed anymore. 'Varna?' he coughed. 'Where is she?'

The strange girl, Meena, stood there in her threadbare nightdress, holding a lamp, shivering with embarrassment and fear. 'She is coming, my lord,' she mumbled into her chest. 'She is... slow.'

Haaron could barely keep either of his eyes open as he stumbled towards the door, pushing Meena out of the way.

'Lord!' came the screeching cry as soon as Varna saw him. 'I have seen terrible things, my lord! The Islanders, they are escaping!'

Haaron blinked, confused. 'Escaping? From what? Why?' He peered at her face as it glowed menacingly above the lamp she was holding. He was too confused to understand what she was saying, but there didn't appear any time to wait. 'Where?'

Then he heard the shout from down below.

***

'Did you hear that?' Karsten muttered, pushing Nicolene off him.

She grumbled as he fell out of bed, groaning as his hip hit the flagstones.

'What was that?' he frowned, standing up, pulling on his

trousers.

And then another shout and the clashing of blades.

Karsten hurried now, snatching his swordbelt, stumbling out of the room, leaving his naked wife frowning on their bed.

***

'Axl! Take Mother and Eydis!' Jael screamed. 'Go!'

Axl blinked, ready to refuse, but he saw his terrified mother's swollen face as she clutched Eydis to her. Sheathing his sword, he picked Eydis up in his arms, grabbed his mother's hand, and ran.

Gant stuck his sword through the belly of one of Haaron's guards, turning to Jael as more men came running out of the castle towards them. Jael glanced at Aleksander, then turned to see how far Axl was from the ships.

He was approaching the entrance to the piers, she could see. The Osslanders were pouring onto the ships ahead of him. And if they could just hold the Hestians off, they would all be able to escape.

Eadmund had run to *Ice Breaker* with his torch, and dragging a brazier out onto the deck, he set fire to it. He threw the torch into the harbour, his eyes up at the first clash of swords, watching as Haaron's men swarmed into the square in front of the castle. 'Fyn!' he called. 'Get the arrows! The fire ones too! Quick!'

Fyn hurried into the wooden house to grab the weapons. He raced back to Eadmund, dropping the arrows onto the deck, handing him a bow.

'Fire the ships! We have to stop them following us!' Eadmund ordered.

'But what about Jael?' Fyn cried anxiously, grabbing his own bow.

Eadmund's heart was thudding as he nocked an arrow, dipping it into the flames. He drew back the bow, aimed at the neighbouring piers, where Haaron's remaining ships were moored, and released the arrow. He quickly picked up another, watching as Axl ran down the long pier towards *Ice Breaker,* Eydis over his shoulder, Gisila by his side.

Eadmund's eyes went up to where Jael was fighting alongside Aleksander and Gant, keeping the Hestians back, trying to give Axl enough time to get on board. Trying to give him enough time to destroy Haaron's ships.

He had to hurry.

***

Haaron, racing down the stairs, his nightshirt flapping angrily behind him, nearly fell over Karsten, his head fuzzy, his feet unsteady as he stumbled ahead of his father. 'We need to kill *them*!' Haaron yelled furiously as he ran past his son. 'Not each other!'

***

'Go!' Gant called to Jael. 'I'll hold them off!'

'Ha!' Jael laughed, lunging at an axe-wielding Hestian. Spinning around, she kicked out with her foot, slashing *Toothpick* across his stomach, ducking another man's sword blow, stabbing him in the neck. 'I'm not leaving you!'

She saw fire blooming out of the corner of her eye.

'My ships!' Haaron screamed, racing out of the castle, Haegen and Karsten, swords out, running behind him. 'Stop them! Stop them burning my ships!'

Jael turned as some of Haaron's men peeled away, heading

towards the piers after Axl.

'Keep firing their ships!' Eadmund bellowed at Fyn. Changing his own arrows for iron-tipped ones now, he turned, aiming at the men who were racing down the pier.

Axl hoisted Eydis into the ship, helping his mother in after her. He drew his sword, hurrying back to his sister.

'Axl! No!' Gisila screamed, watching him disappear.

'Ten men! Swords and shields!' Eadmund cried. 'Go with him! Get up there and bring back your queen!' He squinted into the night as the moon dipped behind the clouds again. They were completely outnumbered now. And it would only get worse. He turned to his left, watching as Haaron's ships caught fire, flames gusting from deck to deck, from pier to pier. 'Villas! We need to go! Lud!' he called to the man sitting nearest the catapult. 'Untie the ship! Quick! All hands to oars, now! Not you, Fyn, you're with me! We need to get out into the harbour!' Eadmund drew back his bow, shooting over Jael, Aleksander, and Gant as they fought off Haaron's men, listening for a thud that never came, lost amongst the chaos. 'Watch your aim, Fyn! Do not hit your queen!'

Fyn pulled back his bow, drawing the soft fletching past his ear, releasing the arrow, watching it arc high over Jael's head, hitting a man square in the face. He gulped, hurrying for another.

Ice Breaker was pulling away from the pier now, Eadmund's men straining at the oars, not fully crewed. *Sea Bear*, with all hands on board, was still tied to its post.

Beorn stood in the stern, waiting anxiously, his hand clenched around the tiller. His men sat at the oars, wanting to get out and help. 'You hold those oars!' Beorn muttered loudly to the jiggling oarsmen, one eye on the fighting Osslanders. 'You're no good to me with only one arm!'

'Load the sea-fire!' Eadmund screamed above the noise as *Ice Breaker's* oars slapped the water, and his men pulled with every bit of strength they possessed. 'I want it ready to launch!' he cried. 'Turn, Villas! Turn! We need to turn around!'

***

Jaeger looked through the window, horrified by what he was seeing. 'Help me!' he growled at Amma who lay in their bed, exposed, defeated, unable to stop shaking. 'Get dressed, and help me downstairs!' he ordered, limping back to the bed, searching for his trousers. 'It looks like your fucking family is trying to escape!'

Amma sat up immediately.

Axl.

***

Jael dropped her shoulders and stepped back, quickly considering the situation.

Karsten Dragos, shirtless and one-eyed, was charging towards them, at least fifteen men on either side of him. The rest of the Hestians were surging towards the piers with Haegen, trying to save their burning ships.

Aleksander, Gant, and Jael backed into one another, gripping their swords.

'I remember how this goes,' Gant growled, flicking his tongue over his teeth. 'What were you, fifteen, sixteen, when we used to play this game?'

'A long time ago now,' Aleksander said, tightening his grip, his eyes on the men closing in around them.

'There's a lot more of them than I remember,' Jael mused, watching Karsten as he rushed at her, spitting, his sword glinting above his head. 'But then again, we're not fifteen anymore, are we?' She gritted her teeth, swinging *Toothpick* up to meet Karsten's blow.

'You're not going anywhere, bitch!' Karsten screamed, his eye bulging as he slashed at Jael, who caught every furious stroke on the edge of *Toothpick's* blade.

Axl hurried up behind them with a handful of Osslanders. 'Everyone's on board! We can leave!' he called, torn, not wanting to go without Amma.

Jael nodded. 'Well, we can try!' she grunted, and lunging to her left, she stabbed *Toothpick* into Karsten's shoulder, kicking him in the chest, dropping to the ground and sweeping her leg across his ankles, knocking him down. 'Shield! Wall!' she yelled to her men, scrambling to her feet.

They raced up past her, in front of her, locking their shields into place in a clatter of iron rims, forming a protective wall in front of their queen and her men.

'Now, let's get out of here!'

***

Osbert had been far too busy enjoying himself to stop and discover what all the noise was about, but the screaming and clanging of swords had finally driven him out of Keyta's delicious arms and onto her balcony.

He looked down in confusion and horror, watching the scene unfold, before running to find his clothes and swordbelt, hurrying out of the room.

***

'Hold!' Eadmund yelled to the catapult crew.

He watched as Haaron's ships burned; fire spreading rapidly on a blustery wind. Haegen and his men rushed to scoop buckets of water onto the flames in a futile attempt to save the remainder of their fleet.

Eadmund's eyes snapped to Jael and the Osslanders as they backed down the pier. But slowly. And more and more of Haaron's men, and now Brekkans were rushing into the square.

Fyn was still firing arrows, but they would run out soon.

Jael needed to get her men into *Sea Bear* and quickly.

***

'Father?' Osbert knocked on the door again, but there was no answer. Worried now, he turned the handle, stepping inside. 'Father?' he called into the dark chamber.

Something reeked like an overflowing latrine. He crept inside. 'Gisila? There's a commotion outside. I think it's Jael.'

He reached the bed and sat down, feeling around, but there was no one there.

They must be outside too, he thought to himself, his head spinning, mead-thick and confused. He got up to leave, stumbling, his boots slipping on something wet and sticky. Reaching down, he stuck his finger into the liquid, bringing it up to his nose.

Blood?

***

There were too many of them. Jael could see that from behind their small shield wall. Too many in front of them now, too many swarming from the castle, from the sheds and stables. The Brekkans were hesitant, though. They could see Jael, Axl,

Aleksander, and Gant.

They did not attack.

Jael looked to see how far they were from the ships, surprised to see *Ice Breaker* out in the harbour, turning.

Turning?

She smiled.

The Hestians scattered all over the square as Haaron bellowed orders from the back, sending men towards the Osslanders' ships and yet more men to untie his own ships to stop the fire from spreading.

'My Father!' Osbert screamed, racing down the steps with his sword drawn. 'They killed my father!' He turned to the Brekkans who had gathered on the left of the square; uncertain, confused. 'Stop them! Kill them!' he roared, urging his men to fight.

They didn't move.

Jael gritted her teeth, wishing for the hundredth time that there was no Osbert. She stabbed through the shield wall, taking one man in the neck, another in the thigh. Flinching, she jerked back as a sword bit into her leg. 'We're going to run for *Sea Bear*!' she cried over the chaos. 'On me! Wait for my call!'

Jael backed away as the Hestians pounded on their shields.

Karsten Dragos slammed his sword onto the shield in front of Jael, chopping into the wood in a wild-eyed frenzy. 'Break their wall! Break their fucking wall!'

Jael didn't blink. 'Axl,' she said, keeping her voice steady as her heart hammered. 'You're going first. Untie the rope when we get to the ship. Gant, you cover him. Now!' she yelled. 'Run!'

'Axl!'

Axl's head snapped around, and he froze as their men rushed past him, shields over their shoulders, chased down the pier by Karsten and his screaming Hestians.

He knew that voice.

Amma.

Axl gripped his sword and ran the other way.

CHAPTER FORTY SIX

Caught between going after Jael Furyck or her brother, Karsten screamed and turned for Axl.

Because Axl was running towards Jaeger.

Jael spun after Axl. 'Get to the ship!' she called to Aleksander and Gant, drawing her father's sword from its scabbard.

She knew this sword.

Screaming to Furia, she gritted her teeth and ran after Karsten Dragos.

Gant blinked at Aleksander, and together, they hurried after her.

Eadmund watched from *Ice Breaker*, cursing his wife as she turned and raced back into the very melee he was about to send the sea-fire into. 'Hold!' he cried again to the catapult crew, hurrying to the bow, trying to see what was happening more clearly.

His oarsmen were keeping the ship steady, but there was nothing they could do to help Jael if she didn't get out of there. Eadmund lowered his bow, holding his breath, watching as the rest of the Osslanders hurtled towards *Sea Bear*, the bulk of Haaron's men now after them. 'Three men, slip your oars! Grab your bows! Protect those men!' he ordered, hoping there were some arrows left. 'Keep firing, Fyn!'

'Untie the ship!' Beorn bellowed, his hand on *Sea Bear's* tiller. He was well aware that he was missing some very important members of his crew.

He hoped they could swim.

Jaeger had abandoned Amma as soon as he'd found a warrior to help get him into the fight. Sword drawn, he'd limped his way into the crush of bodies, towards Jael and her men as they backed away behind their shields. But now, as they broke, as the man holding him went down with an arrow through his throat, and Jaeger tumbled to the ground after him, he could only watch on helplessly as his wife ran screaming past him.

Towards Axl Furyck.

'Karsten!' he yelled. 'Stop her!'

Axl rushed up to Amma, pulling her to him. 'Ssshhh,' he soothed desperately, his eyes everywhere. 'I won't leave you!' He saw Karsten coming and Jael behind him.

Karsten growled, slashing at Axl with his sword.

Axl jumped back, protecting Amma, his eyes darting to *Sea Bear*, now moving away from the pier.

'Axl, take her!' Jael called, her head spinning. She saw Gant and Aleksander. 'Get her onto the ship! Gant! Help him!' She brought both swords around to Karsten, cutting off his path to Axl.

'I'm going to gut you, bitch, but first I'm going to take out your eyes!' Karsten roared in her face as he swung his sword towards her. Jael dropped her shoulder, sliced *Toothpick* across his knee, spun and slammed her boot into the side of his head. Karsten fell to the cobblestones, screaming as she stuck her father's sword into his side. There was no time for talking. They needed to get out of here.

Jael turned to Aleksander, busy fighting off Haegen who had finally abandoned his father's burning ships. 'We have to go!'

'Karsten!' Jaeger yelled, dragging himself across the cobblestones.

'Archers!' Haaron was screaming from beside his flaming ships. 'Where are my fucking archers? Stop them getting away!'

Aleksander kicked Haegen to the ground, stabbing him in the thigh.

Jael heard arrows.

'Duck!' she called to Aleksander as the arrows screeched over their heads. She wasn't sure whose arrows they were, but there was no time to find out. They had to leave. 'Go! Go!'

Aleksander turned, catching an arrow in the shoulder. Grunting in pain, he stumbled. Jael was at his side, helping him as they ran, arrows whistling in both directions now.

There were no ships left on the pier.

Gant turned around, slashing his blade into a Hestian's neck. The man shrieked, pitching forward into the dark water. 'Jump!' Gant yelled to Axl and Amma, pushing them off the pier as the enemy descended upon them. He couldn't see Jael and Aleksander. 'Swim! We have to swim!' He jumped in after them.

Beorn was watching. 'Archers!' he called. 'Cover them! Tykir! Get the ropes over the side! Rowers, let's stay steady now! Hold water! Wait for them to get on board. Three ropes! Move! Move!'

Eadmund had his heart in his mouth, Fyn by his side, as they watched Jael and Aleksander stumble down the pier. Both of them were out of arrows now, all but two pitch-soaked ones.

They were saving those.

Eadmund lifted his eyes. He could see Haaron's warriors charging; Osbert's reluctant army gathering around him. He glanced back to Jael and Aleksander, certain they were far enough away now. 'Jael! *Run!*' he cried, racing back to the brazier with his bow and arrow.

Jael heard the whip of the catapult as an arrow took her in the leg. She cried out, her right leg buckling as the sea-fire jar shattered across the square at the entrance to the piers. Aleksander seized her arm, keeping her on her feet, his face twisted in agony. Leaning against each other, they limped to the side of the pier.

Jael gritted her teeth at both the pain in her leg and the thought of the cold water. Looking up, she saw Eadmund with his bow, the flame bursting from his arrow. She turned to see the Hestians behind them, swords glinting in the fiery carnage of Haaron's ships.

'Jump!' came Eadmund's scream.

'Quick!' Jael yelled to Aleksander. 'Jump!' And they pulled each other over the side of the pier, blood coursing down her leg and his shoulder as they hit the freezing water with a stumbling crash.

Eadmund drew back his bow, holding his breath, trying to see through the flames flickering at the tip of his arrow. He released it, watching as it flew, up and over the water, dropping with a clatter onto the thick, black sea-fire seeping across the cobblestones.

Suddenly the entire pier exploded; angry, sparking flames shooting up into the night sky. Jaeger and Haegen could only watch from the ground as fire cloaked everything before them in an impenetrable wall.

'What is happening?' Bayla screamed, hurrying down the castle steps with Nicolene and Irenna. 'Jaeger!' she sobbed, seeing three of her sons bleeding on the stones before her.

Haaron was there, his face purple with rage. He'd desperately tried to save his last remaining ships but to no avail. The wind had fanned the flames, and now only carcasses were burning in his harbour.

'Why aren't you *doing* something?' Bayla spat at him as she bent over her youngest son. 'Why are you just letting them get away?'

'Stop them!' Jaeger screamed hoarsely as his mother helped him to his feet. 'Stop them! They have my wife!'

Haaron could only stand and watch. He knew those flames weren't going away in a hurry. 'Archers!' he cried out hopelessly. 'Shoot over the fire!' Some of his men were on the other side of the flames, he knew, but he didn't imagine that any of them could have survived.

***

'Throw down the ropes!' Beorn called as Amma joined Axl and Gant in a wet heap on the deck, all three of them shivering uncontrollably, teeth chattering, but alive.

Jael and Aleksander swam desperately for *Sea Bear*, the arrows in her leg and his shoulder making it slow-going.

Gant popped his head over the gunwale, squinting into the black abyss. 'Come on!' he urged. 'Swim!'

Jael gritted her teeth, digging into the freezing water, trying to get her legs moving. She turned to Aleksander who was slipping back. 'Come on!'

A volley of arrows stabbed into the water all around them.

Reaching back, Jael grabbed Aleksander's hand, dragging him towards the ship. He screamed, lunging for a rope as it swung along the hull, his shoulder completely numb, his ears ringing.

'Hang on!' Gant bellowed, leaning over to pull him up, ducking as another wave of arrows flew in.

Jael grabbed the other rope, banging against the hull as Axl hauled her up and over the gunwale.

'Pull away, Villas!' Eadmund yelled, hurrying to grab a spare oar, nodding at Fyn to do the same. 'We need to turn back around!'

'Pull!' Villas called to his crew. 'Pull!'

Ice Breaker's men heaved, their oars squeaking and groaning with every stroke as the arrows shot over the flames towards them.

***

Morana, Varna, and Meena watched from Haaron's balcony, shaking their wild hair in disbelief.

As horrified as Meena was by the scene unfolding before her, a part of her couldn't help but rejoice as she watched Jaeger's bride sailing away behind the wall of fire.

'What was the fool doing?' Morana snorted. 'He can't even walk!'

Varna grunted. What a bad day Jaeger was having.

First, he lost the book.

Then he lost his wife.

She turned to Meena and smiled.

***

The shields on both ships sat high along the gunwales, creating cover for the oarsmen as they dug in, the wind gusting around them. They would fly, if only they could get out of reach intact.

Gisila sat in *Ice Breaker's* wooden house, her arm wrapped around Eydis, peering through the arrow holes in the walls as *Sea Bear* came alongside, both sets of men grunting with the strain of such speed; an occasional burst of arrows whipping overhead.

Then suddenly, they stopped. The terrifying wail ceased and the Osslanders, arrow-threatened and exhausted, let out sighs of relief as they slipped out of the harbour and into the darkness.

***

Haaron stood next to his sons, screaming helplessly into the night. Turning to Osbert, he glared at him. 'What happened to Lothar?' he growled. 'Who killed him? How?'

'They took his head,' Osbert said blankly, his body still vibrating in shock. 'Jael,' he muttered, blinking, his head so fog-heavy he could barely see. 'It must have been Jael. She murdered my father!'

'What have you done?' Bayla raged at her husband as she bent over Karsten's still body. Nicolene was sobbing next to him. He had already lost a lot of blood. 'What have you *done*?'

Haaron sighed, not ready to be blamed for everything just yet; not while his harbour was a giant-sized, burning mess. 'He'll live,' he grumbled, turning to Haegen, who was up and limping, Irenna fussing over his wounds. 'Get your brother inside!' he spat. 'He's no use to anyone. Again!' He turned, stalking away. 'And where the fuck is Berard?'

***

Jael closed her eyes, gripping the sea chest.

'This will hurt.'

Gant dug into Jael's leg with his knife as she bit down hard on a broken arrow, her ears ringing, her eyes watering as stars danced before them.

'Axl, a bit closer,' he muttered, squinting in the flickering light of the torch Axl was holding, relieved to see that the arrow had gone through the side of her leg rather than burying itself down into the flesh. It wasn't deep.

Aleksander's was though. That was next.

'How many men have we lost? Aarrghh!' Jael yelled as Gant yanked out the arrowhead, nodding at Amma to press a torn piece of tunic onto the gushing wound.

'Here, turn around, hold it on there,' Gant ordered, throwing the arrowhead onto the deck and grabbing a long strip of cloth to tie around her leg. 'One or two, I think.'

Jael let go of the cloth as he tightened the strip.

'Stay still for a while,' he suggested. 'Not that you will.'

'No, not that I will,' Jael said faintly. 'Help me up. I want to go out and see the men.'

The sky was dark, and the wind was still fresh as they skipped over the waves. It was a peaceful respite from the chaos of the night. Jael held her breath as she peered around the deck, catching sight of the bodies of the two men they had lost, at the injured men gripping their wounds, bleeding, in pain.

And all because Axl had killed Lothar.

***

As soon as the sail went up, Eadmund had hurried into the house to check on Eydis, wrapping her up in his arms, sighing at the overwhelming relief that she was safe. She sobbed as he held her, overcome with emotion.

Gisila was in agony as she sat there, her back bloody with cuts from Lothar's belt, her body cold and stiff, too shocked to move. She couldn't stop seeing the moment when Axl had lunged for Lothar; the sheer surprise on both their faces as Lothar's head came off. It didn't feel real at all.

She closed her eyes, wanting to see her mother.

'Are they alright?' Fyn wondered sleepily, popping his head in through the end of the house.

'They seem to be. You?' Eadmund wondered.

Fyn nodded, sighing heavily, his shoulders releasing themselves at last. 'What are we going to do now?'

***

Egil helped Jaeger back to his chamber, his father's curses and his wife's screams echoing in his ears. His eyes drifted to the bed, stripped of all furs. The bed where his wife had been not so long ago. Where he had claimed her, broken her, made her his. He shook his head, too wild to even speak. Limping his way into a chair by the table, he reached for a goblet, his lips twisting in pain, his jaw clenched in fury.

Egil hurried for the wine jug, filling up the goblet. 'My lord,' he muttered nervously. 'What can I do for you?'

Jaeger didn't hear him over the screams inside his head. The memories of the catastrophe were loud and overwhelming. Why had he thought to take Amma out there? It had been like fucking a limp doll, but still, she was his. Why hadn't he left her in the safety of his chamber? He shook his head, tired of making mistakes.

They had stolen his wife. He had to get her back.

'Bring me the book, Egil,' he grumbled, tipping the wine into his mouth, desperate to numb the bitter, angry, pointless rage that boiled inside him.

'Of course, my lord.' Egil bowed his head, scurrying away to the far corner of the chamber. He reached under his bed and pulled out the iron chest he had brought the book safely back from Skorro in.

Opening the chest, he looked inside to find that it was gone.

***

Amma was too shocked to speak, too tired to say a word as she sat next to Axl, cocooned inside his arms. She wanted to sleep. Her eyes hurt, but she was too scared to close them; scared that she'd remember Jaeger and all the things he had done to her.

'Here,' Jael said, limping into the house. 'I've got some spare tunics and trousers.' She handed them around, smiling at Aleksander who lay on his side, grimacing as Gant finished wrapping his shoulder in long strips of cloth.

Amma blushed, suddenly aware that she was wearing her nightdress, wet and clinging to her as it was. Embarrassed, she glanced at Jael.

'We'll make them all turn around,' Jael said wearily. 'Don't worry.' Amma looked traumatised, she thought, amazed that they'd managed to rescue her.

That Axl had.

But at what cost? The whole of Brekka and Hest would unite against them now. 'We need to get to Rexon,' Jael muttered to Gant as he stood and removed his wet tunic, ignoring the bleeding cuts across his chest and arms. 'Get some supplies, tell him what happened.'

Gant nodded.

'But first, we need to go to Skorro. We have to destroy their ships. Perhaps take a couple back to Oss?' Jael pulled off her wet trousers which were stuck to her legs.

She couldn't stop shivering.

***

Edela had finally fallen asleep.

Entorp was curled up in Eadmund's chair by the fire and Biddy could hear him snoring. But she couldn't sleep. She sat on Edela's bed, holding her hand, still tasting the bitter char of smoke on her tongue, the stink of it in her nostrils.

Ido and Vella lay on either side of Edela, looking for comfort from the storm as it continued to hammer Oss. Edela had been so scared by what she had felt, certain that it meant death, convinced that someone would die. Biddy felt sick, wondering who it was, praying that Edela had been wrong.

She sighed, squeezing Edela's hand, hoping that she would

be alright in the morning.

***

There was silence.

Cold darkness and silence.

Edela walked down the steps onto an enormous square. It was wide and flat, cobblestoned and dark. It was the place she had found Jael in her dream. But there was no one here now.

No one at all.

She couldn't hear her boots as she padded forward, uncertain, shivering.

'You think that you've *won*, Edela?' boomed the angry voice as a wall of flames exploded before her. 'Oh, Edela, but you have no idea what I have planned. No idea at all...'

CHAPTER FORTY SEVEN

Jaeger had remained in his chamber for an entire day, ignoring everyone, even Berard, who had banged on his door, begging to be let in, guilt-stricken and embarrassed that he'd slept through the whole catastrophe.

He'd slept through the book being stolen, through Jaeger's wife being ripped away from him.

Through Karsten's and Haegen's injuries.

Through the flaming of the square, the destruction of their entire fleet.

And through their father's screaming curses.

Not even Egil would open the door to him. Eventually, Berard had given up and gone away.

Jaeger stretched out his leg as he stood, holding onto the table, pushing his weight down onto his foot. The pain shot up his leg but he gritted his teeth, ignoring it, sending the sharp agony to another part of him; the part of him that felt nothing.

That part was growing bigger by the day.

He pressed his bare foot onto the flagstones, enjoying the coolness against his burning heel. Letting go of the table, Jaeger felt the pressure of all his weight as his leg started to buckle. His eyes watered, his breath puffing from his nose as he stepped forward slowly, one foot after the other, grunting at the sheer torture of it, but doing it nonetheless.

Jaeger walked all the way to the bed and back to the table,

his head throbbing from all the pain his body was absorbing, his hands gripping the table, shaking in desperation. But he had done it.

He was strong enough.

He was ready.

***

It never felt good to fire a ship and Jael could sense Beorn squirming beside her, but he'd picked the two best Hestian ships to take back to Oss. The rest were aflame on the beach in front of Skorro's fort. Jael knew that they would probably have to send men to Andala and do the same.

'Are you ready?' Eadmund wondered wearily as he nodded towards the last of the men clambering into *Sea Bear*. 'We need to get through the Widow's Peak before nightfall.'

Beorn nodded eagerly beside him. The wind was strong today, and he was not looking forward to navigating those towering stone spires in such white-capped waves.

'Do we have everything?' Jael asked Fyn as he hurried past.

'Mmmm,' he mumbled, chewing on a tough piece of salt fish. 'All the weapons are loaded onto the ships.'

'Well, then, yes,' Jael sighed, deciding that they could do no more. 'Let's head for Saala, and then we can go home.'

Fyn looked relieved as he loped after Beorn.

'Eadmund!' Jael grabbed his arm, hoping to see something familiar in his eyes, but when he turned to her, they were lifeless. Still.

His eyebrows rose questioningly as he stared at her. Through her.

He was there, but not there at all.

Jael shook her head sadly. 'Thank you,' she smiled. 'You

saved my life again.'

He shrugged, turning away. 'I'll see you in Saala.'

She watched him go, walking towards his ship, his head forward, never once turning around.

***

'I'm fine,' Edela insisted as Biddy reached for the door handle. 'You go. I shall probably just stay in this chair and be drooled on by the puppies until you return.'

Biddy's face told her what she thought of the likelihood of that happening. 'Well, stay warm. You need more rest. I mean it, Edela, you couldn't even get out of bed yesterday! Don't expect to suddenly be able to hop around the island.'

'I'm not sure I've ever hopped anywhere in my life!' Edela laughed as Biddy turned to leave. 'See if you can find me some of those figs again!' she called. 'They were so wonderfully sweet.'

Biddy nodded, smiling as she shut the door behind her.

Edela listened as Biddy chatted to Askel, waiting for her footsteps to disappear. She eased herself out of the chair, hurrying to put on her cloak, her body aching with every movement. A day spent in bed might have helped restore her strength after the dream walk, but every single part of her felt as though she'd been in a battle. Well, perhaps Jael would disagree with that, she smiled to herself.

Jael.

Jael was coming. She could feel it.

***

'Where is it?' Jaeger snarled, his large hand pinning Varna to the dripping stone wall of her chamber. Her sagging throat pulsed beneath his fingers but he didn't release the pressure as she gagged and spat before him, desperately trying to breathe, her yellowed eyes bulging at the look in his own. 'Where is my book?'

They were alone.

He had waited for Meena to leave, not wanting her interference; certain that she would wail and cause a horrific, head-tapping fuss.

Jaeger's nostrils flared as Varna refused to answer. She stunk. Her whole chamber stunk. He slammed her head back against the wall.

'Aarrghh,' Varna gargled. 'I... you... the book is not meant for you!'

'What?' Jaeger sneered. 'The book is *mine*! *I* found it. *I* am a Dragos. Why shouldn't it belong to *me*?' He released his fingers, allowing her to speak.

Varna's head was ringing as she sucked in a welcome breath. 'Dangerous,' she gasped. 'Too dangerous.'

Jaeger shook his head crossly, his hand tightening around her throat again. 'Give it to me, Varna!' he demanded through bared teeth. 'Give me my book, or I'll slit your throat!'

'You, you... need me,' she rasped. 'To... read it.'

Jaeger frowned. It was true, of course. 'You? You think I need you? You who knew what would happen on Skorro? Who had my father send me there anyway? Why do I need *you*? You want me dead!' he growled. 'I've always known that!' He pressed his fingers deeper into her neck, feeling her thick veins, watching her eyeballs pop.

'I... read... book...' Varna spluttered.

He wanted her to be wrong, but she wasn't. 'Tell me where the book is, then, and I'll let you live,' he promised. 'Just tell me! *Now!*'

'She's not the only one who can read the book,' said a voice behind him.

***

Edela couldn't stop thinking about Eadmund as she hurried towards Entorp's house. She had felt it herself; he was definitely under Evaine's control again. She hoped that Entorp would be able to help her find another way to stop that evil girl.

'Edela!' Thorgils smiled as he wandered down the alley towards her. He squinted as he got closer. 'You look terrible! Is something wrong?' Reaching out, he grabbed her arm. 'Shall I help you back to the house?'

Edela laughed, shaking her head. 'I can't look that bad, can I? Not if I can still walk about on my own!' She was pale, wobbling slightly as she said that, but determined. There was fire in her eyes.

Thorgils grinned. 'No, not that bad, but perhaps I'll walk with you?'

Edela shooed him away. 'I'm sure you have far more important things to do. But why not come to the house and check on me later?' she suggested slyly. 'I think Biddy is cooking up a nice chicken and ale stew today.'

Thorgils' eyebrows sharpened at the sound of that. 'I think you've twisted my arm, there,' he said, letting her go. 'But promise me you'll head back to the house soon, or Biddy will no doubt tweak my ear!'

'If she could reach it, I'm sure she would!' Edela smiled, shuffling past him.

Thorgils turned to watch her go, his stomach rumbling.

***

Jaeger spun around. He didn't know that voice.

A strange-looking woman crept into the chamber, her body twisted, crouching oddly, wild hair fanning out from her head. Much like Varna.

Much like Meena.

Varna's eyes bulged, her body sagging in relief against Jaeger's hand. He loosened his fingers, staring at the stranger.

'You don't need *her* to read the book,' Morana sneered, ignoring her mother. 'I know where it is, and I can read it. She wants you dead, her and your father. But they are weak and foolish and do not see what I do. How you will rise. How you will be the one to bring the Darkness. You, Jaeger Dragos. You are the one who will set her free.'

Jaeger shivered under the intense glare of those menacing eyes. He licked his lips as Varna kicked and wriggled, desperate to escape the threat of his hand.

Hurt, pain, and anger flooded Varna's body; a wasted life, she thought to herself. What a heavy price she would pay for her loyalty. Varna closed her eyes, praying for Raemus to come back from the Dolma to save her.

To set her free.

Jaeger turned back to her, his eyes glazed over as he squeezed her throat, watching the terror grow in hers. Varna's legs thrashed helplessly against him as he squeezed, not even stopping as her bladder released and she sagged lifelessly onto his hand, her dying body pinned to the wall as he pressed harder and harder, his hand bruising her skin.

Killing her.

He thought of Haaron, and Haegen, Jael Furyck, and her brother. All of them.

He would kill every last one of them.

Releasing his hand, at last, he let Varna's body drop to the floor as he turned and walked towards the strange woman. 'Show me where it is.'

***

Evaine smiled as she hurried down the alley, desperate to get back to the house.

She had been excited to find a spell to protect herself against any attempts Edela might make to thwart her again. Her eyes burned with rage as she thought of that symbol under the rug, certain that Runa had been a willing accomplice to what they had done. But with Morac sharing a bedchamber with his wife again, there was little she could do to harm her.

But Edela? Biddy? Entorp?

She had plans for them.

Evaine rummaged in her basket, pleased to see that she had everything she needed now. She was going to make another candle. Morana had shown her how to do it. And that candle would be for Edela. By the time Eadmund returned, he would be hers, and there would be no one who could stop her. She'd promised Morana that she would keep Eadmund away from Jael and now she knew that nothing could stand in her way.

Morac smiled at Evaine as he passed on his way to the hall, pleased to see her looking so happy. He stopped and kissed her on the cheek. 'Tanja was looking for you before.'

'Was she?' Evaine wondered, barely listening. 'I'm on my way back to the house now.'

'Well, perhaps you should hurry, then,' he called over his shoulder as he continued on his way. 'She said she had to go and see her mother!'

Evaine rolled her eyes, turning around, almost thinking about not going back to the house at all. She was fed up with Tanja and her disappearances, and she didn't plan on being lumbered with a crying baby all afternoon.

She froze.

'What do *you* want?' Evaine growled at the old woman who stood there.

Edela was in shock. She couldn't swallow, couldn't find her voice. She shook her head, gripping the handle of her basket. It was dim in the alley as they stood there, watching each other.

There was no one around.

It was cold.

'Your father killed Eirik Skalleson,' Edela said at last. '*He* is the man I saw in my dream.'

Evaine rushed towards Edela, scanning the alley, ensuring that no one was within earshot. 'You don't know what you're talking about, old woman!' she hissed. 'You'd better keep those ideas to yourself when Eadmund returns. He won't listen to you!'

Edela stepped forward, her legs shaking, her eyes sharp. 'Why? Do you think you can control him? Kill his father? Take this kingdom? Is that what you're trying to do?'

Evaine's eyes narrowed. 'I think that's exactly what we'll do,' she whispered threateningly. 'And you will not stop us. And when your granddaughter returns, she'll be gone too. I'll see to that. Eadmund will not want her here. Not when he loves me.'

Edela's laugh was faint; it did not sound like her at all. She was numb, shaking, fearful, and shrinking. The threat of Evaine towered over her as the sun hurried away. She felt cold all over, and at the back of her mind, she was certain she heard the voice.

Laughing.

'No, you won't,' Edela said boldly. 'You don't know Jael. She will not let you... *I* will not let you!' she cried. 'You will not succeed. I will save Jael!'

'No, you won't.' Evaine bared her teeth and slid her eating knife out of its scabbard, sticking it into Edela's soft stomach, pushing it through her dress until Edela stumbled and fell, gasping in horror as the true realisation of what had just happened hit her.

Evaine reached down and pulled out her bloody knife, slipping it into her basket as she turned and walked quickly down the alley.

Edela lay in the dirt, her legs twisted beneath her crumpled body. She couldn't move, couldn't feel a thing as she watched the darkness creep slowly towards her, clawing its way over her body, eager to claim her.

'Didn't I tell you, Edela?' the voice laughed. 'You should never trust a Tuuran.'

THE END

EPILOGUE

'Is it done?' he asked.

'Yes.'

'And you have the book?'

'I do.'

'You have done well, Morana,' Yorik smiled as he came forward and took her face in his hands, staring at those dark eyes, long-seen, but so familiar. 'And the girl? Our daughter?'

'Evaine knows what she must do. I have faith in her to carry out our wishes. Her and Morac, both.' Morana closed her eyes, enjoying his touch; her body stirring in a way it hadn't for many years.

'Good. I will call a meeting of The Following, then. It is time for us to begin.'

WHAT TO READ NEXT

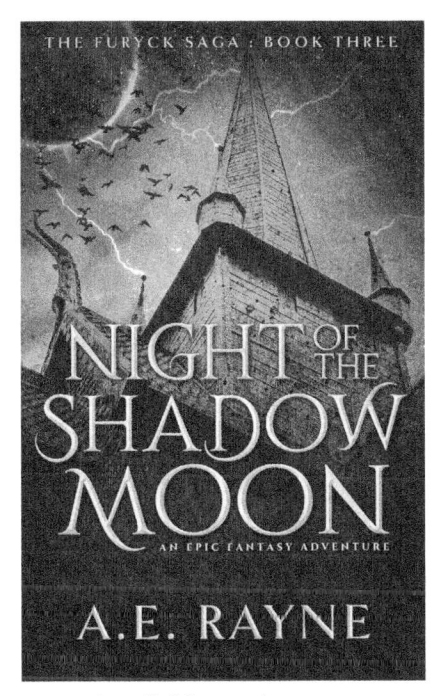

Available on Amazon

THE FURYCK SAGA

THE FURYCK SAGA

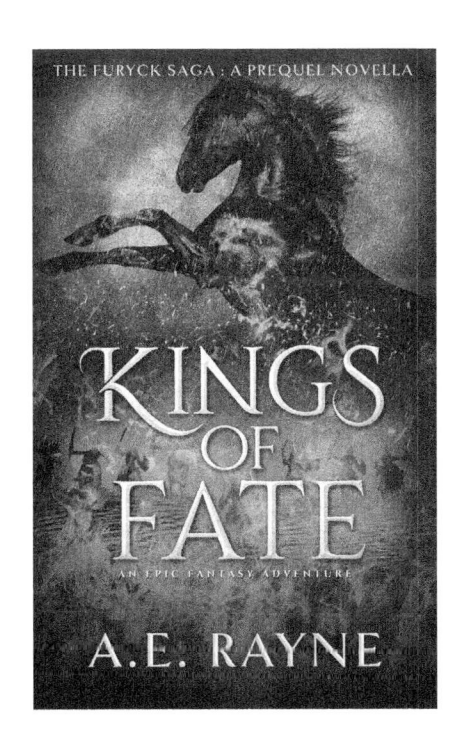

THE FURYCK SAGA

The Furyck Saga: Books 1-3

THE LORDS OF ALEKKA

THE LORDS OF ALEKKA

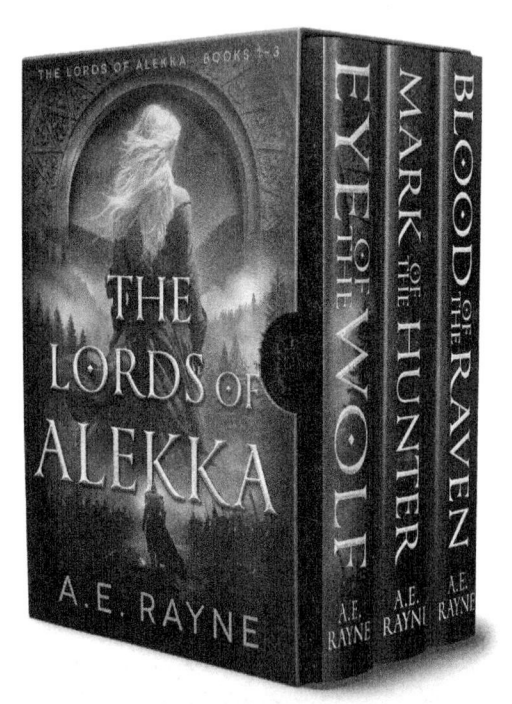

The Lords of Alekka: Books 1-3

FATE OF THE FURYCKS

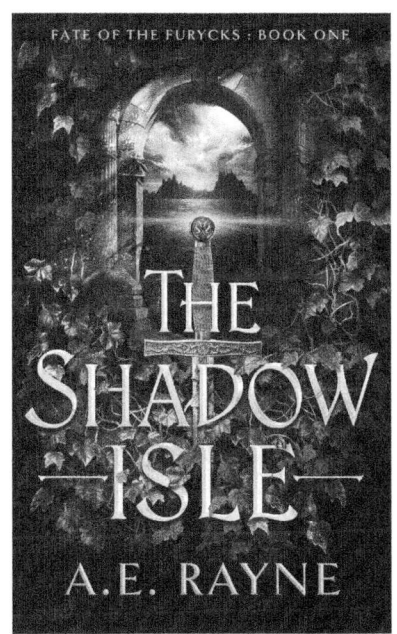

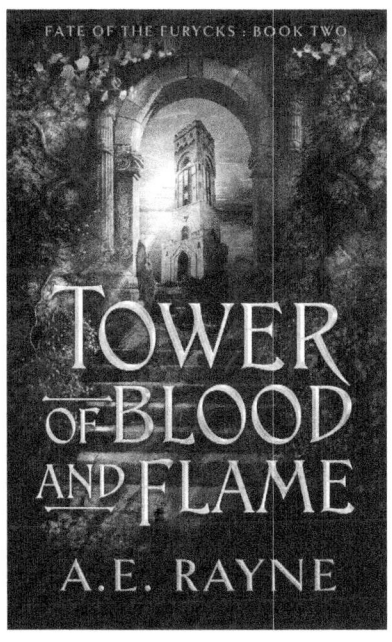

AUDIOBOOKS

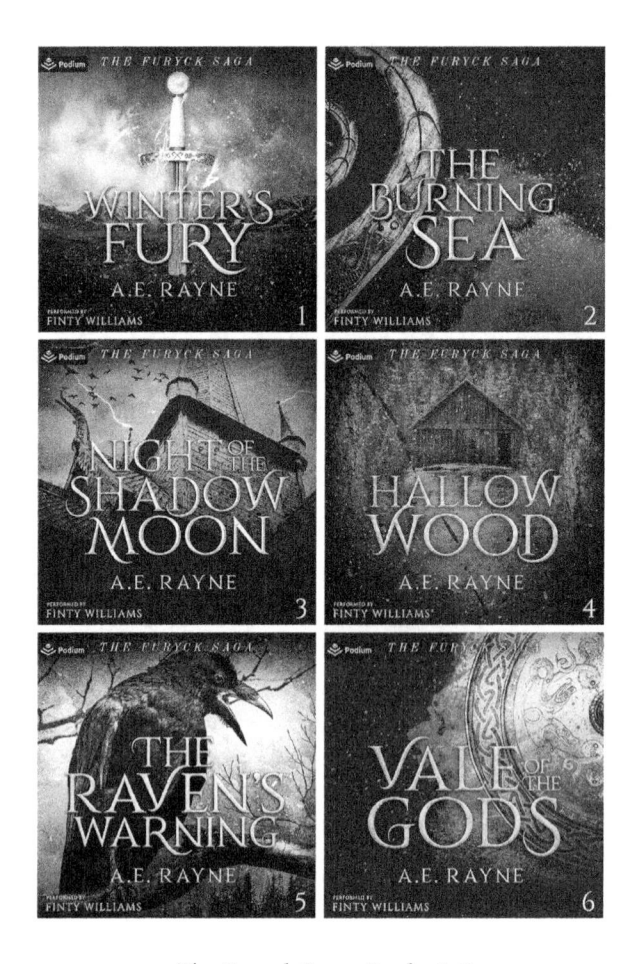

The Furyck Saga: Books 1-6

AUDIOBOOKS

The Lords of Alekka: Books 1-6

ABOUT A.E. RAYNE

I survive on a happy diet of historical and fantasy fiction and I particularly love a good Viking tale. My favourite authors are Bernard Cornwell, Giles Kristian, Robert Low, C.J. Sansom, and Patrick O'Brian. I live in Auckland, New Zealand, with my husband, three children and three dogs.

I promise you characters that will quickly feel like friends and villains that will make you wild, with plots that twist and turn to leave you wondering what's coming around the corner. And, like me, hopefully, you'll always end up a little surprised by how I weave everything together in the end!

Sign up to my newsletter for pre-sale and new release updates
www.aerayne.com/sign-up

Contact me:
a.e.rayne@aerayne.com
www.aerayne.com/contact

***

Copyright © A.E. Rayne 2017
All artwork © A.E. Rayne 2017

A.E. Rayne asserts the moral right to be identified as the author of this work.

This novel is entirely a work of fiction. The names, characters, and places described in it are the work of the author's imagination.

All rights reserved. No part of this publication may be reproduced, distributed, or transmitted in any form or by any means, including photocopying, recording, or other electronic or mechanical methods, without the prior written permission of the publisher (A.E. Rayne), except in the case of brief quotations embodied in critical reviews and certain other noncommercial uses permitted by copyright law.

AMAZON ISBN: 9781973215646

Printed in Great Britain
by Amazon